Harry Thompson made his name as a television producer. He also wrote a number of highly acclaimed non-fiction books. *This Thing of Darkness* is his first and only novel. After a brave fight against illness, Harry Thompson died in November 2005.

'*This Thing of Darkness* is completely brilliant. It's not just quite good – it's stunning. It utilises all Harry's gifts for travel writing and observation. As a single legacy, it would be pretty impressive, but look what else he accomplished as well. You look at his age and you see 45 and you can't believe how much he achieved' Ian Hislop

'Thompson proves a master storyteller, whose vigorous command of character, period detail, weather conditions and fleeting emotions lifts the reader straight from his chair into the middle of a sudden storm, an intense argument, a mood of exhilaration or despair, a squalid street in New Zealand or a desolate landscape in Tierra del Fuego. What sensible reader wants a novel as engrossing as this one to stop?' John Spurling, *The Sunday Times*

'This is a fascinating read' *The Times*

'As a devotee of that master of the sea story Patrick O'Brian, I can say this is definitely in the same league' David Shukman, *Daily Mail*

'Harry Thompson catches the atmosphere, and the language, of Victorian Britain with ⬚⬚⬚⬚⬚⬚⬚⬚⬚⬚⬚⬚ ⬚⬚⬚re of the grim existence aboa⬚⬚⬚

'The meticulous researc⬚⬚⬚⬚⬚⬚⬚⬚⬚⬚⬚⬚⬚⬚ ⬚nday Telegraph

'The spirit of Patrick O'Brian is not far away . . . a superior adventure story' *Independent*

Also by Harry Thompson

Peter Cook: A Biography

THIS THING OF DARKNESS

Harry Thompson

headline
review

First published in 2005 by HEADLINE REVIEW
An imprint of HEADLINE BOOK PUBLISHING

First published in paperback in 2006 by HEADLINE REVIEW

A HEADLINE REVIEW paperback

2

THIS THING OF DARKNESS is a work of fiction based on
(and inspired by) the extraordinary lives of the historical figures in
this publication.

ISBN 0 7553 3155 9 (A Format)

Typeset in Caslon by Palimpsest Book Production Limited, Polmont,
Stirlingshire

Printed and bound in Great Britain by
Mackays of Chatham plc, Chatham, Kent

Headline Book Publishing
a division of Hodder Headline
338 Euston Road
London NW1 3BH

www.reviewbooks.co.uk
www.hodderheadline.com

TO MY FATHER

without whose help this

book could never have been written

'This thing of darkness I acknowledge mine'
The Tempest,
Act V, Scene 1

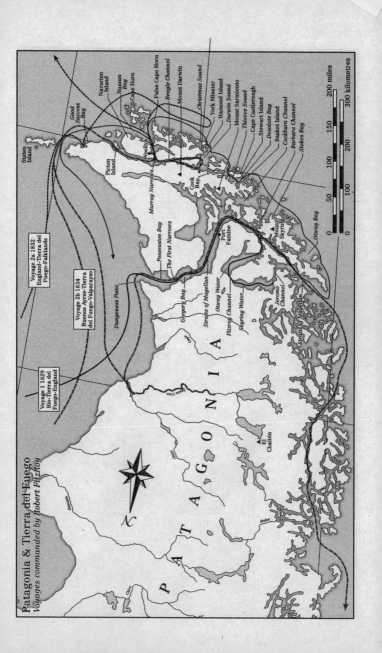

Patagonia & Tierra del Fuego
Voyages commanded by Robert Fitzroy

Voyage 1 1829
Rio-Tierra del
Fuego-England

Voyage 2a 1832
England-Tierra del
Fuego-Falklands

Voyage 2b 1834
Bueos Ayres-Tierra
del Fuego-Valparaiso

Staten
Island

Good
Success
Bay

Navarino
Island

Nassau
Bay

Cape Horn

False Cape Horn

Beagle Channel

Mount Darwin

York Minster

Hamond Island

Mount Sarmiento

Thieves Sound

Cape Castlereagh

Stewart Island

Basket Island

Cockburn Channel

Barbara Channel

Stokes Bay

Darwin Sound

Christmas Sound

Desolate Bay

Picton
Island

Woolly

Murray Narrows

Cook
Bay

Possession Bay

The First Narrows

Dungeness Point

Gregory Bay

Straits of Magellan

Otway Water

Fitzroy Channel

Skyring Water

Port
Famine

Mount
Skyring

Jerome
Channel

Straits of Magellan

Otway Bay

El Chaltén

Santa Cruz

Chico

P A T A G O N I A

N

Deseado

Chico

Boker

0   50   100   150   200 miles
0   100   200   300 kilometres

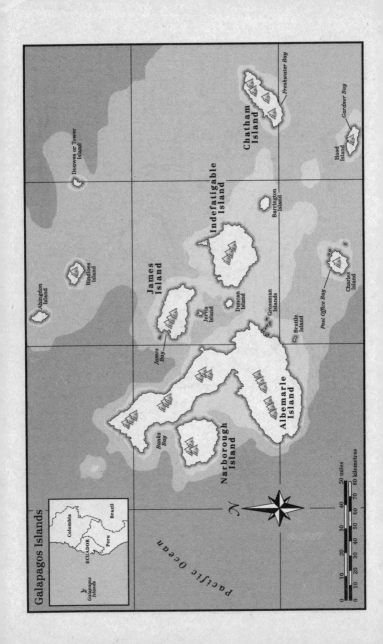

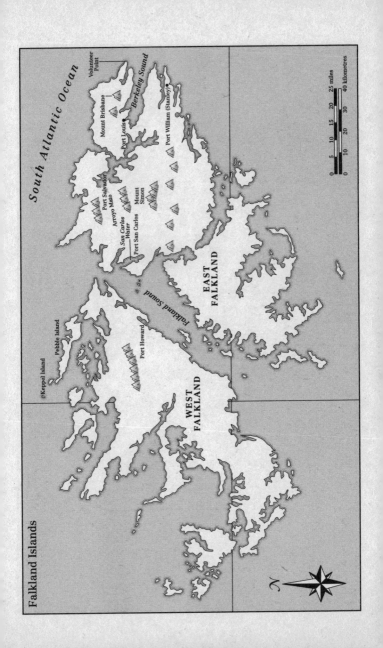

Falkland Islands

South Atlantic Ocean

Volunteer Point
Mount Brisbane
Port Louise
Berkeley Sound
Port William (Stanley)
Port Salvador
Arroyo Mato
San Carlos Water
Port San Carlos
Mount Simon

EAST FALKLAND

Falkland Sound

Pebble Island
Keppel Island
Port Howard

WEST FALKLAND

N

0   5   10   15   20   25 miles
0   10   20   30   40 kilometres

Preface

Port Famine, Patagonia, 1 August 1828

———————

An icy wind shouldered its way into the Straits of Magellan from the west, pummelling the cliff walls and scouring the rocks as it passed. Its thirteen-thousand-mile journey across open ocean completed, it sought out the ancient glaciers of its birth in anger. As a grimy late-morning light ahead signalled the dawning of the brief southern day, it funnelled at speed through the narrows at York Road, before sweeping left into the bay of Port Famine. Darting and jinking as it hunted for a target, it picked out the solitary figure of Captain Pringle Stokes where he knelt. It buffeted him and tore at his clothes. It tugged at his thinning forelock in mock deference. It cut through the sodden wool of his coat, turning his skin to gooseflesh and congealing the blood in his veins.

Stokes shivered. *I am so emaciated*, he thought bitterly, *I can feel my shoulder-blades almost touching each other*. He shifted his weight as another furious gust did its best to hurl him to the ground. His knees jostled together in the cold gravel. His ceremonial scabbard, the badge of his rank, scratched uselessly at the smooth stones. He plastered the damp strands of hair back into place – a tiny, futile act of vanity – but the wind merely caught them again and flung them aside dismissively. *This place*, he thought. *This place constitutes the sum total of my achievement. This place is all that I amount to. This place is all that I am.*

Further down the beach, Bennet and his ratings, all drenched from the waist down, were still struggling to pull the cutter ashore; ants, going about their irrelevant business in the service of an unheeding monarch half a world away. A curse on His Majesty, thought Stokes, and a curse on His Majesty's government, in whose service they found themselves marooned in this wretched place. As he inspected them, the bent, sullen figures seemed to be winning their little war. They were probably wondering where he'd gone. Curiosity, he had learned, is one of the few feelings that boredom cannot kill. As soon as Bennet had the boat secured, they would follow him up the shingle. He did not have much time.

He had conceived his plan weeks ago, but today he would put it into practice. Why today? Nothing marked out this shoreline as different from any other. It was as wretched as the rest. Which was precisely why today was so apt. He had realized it, suddenly, when he had stepped out of the boat. *Today was the day.*

Stokes lifted his head heavenwards, as if seeking reassurance. As always, an obdurate black wall of rock met his gaze, shrouded in lifeless grey. Somewhere above him, hidden from view, was the snow-capped spur of Point St Ann, christened by one of his predecessors – Carteret, or Byron perhaps – in an attempt to imbue this place with spiritual familiarity, a sense of the proximity of God. Yet if ever God had abandoned a place, this was it. The ragged beech forest above the shoreline lay silent. There were no animals to start before a sudden footstep, no birds to soar and swoop, no insects even. Here was a scene of profound desolation. He and the men under his command were alone.

The only man with whom naval etiquette would allow him to converse, that damned fool Captain King, was a couple of miles away at least, another stupid speck in the wilderness. King had spent the winter beating up and down the east coast in the *Adventure*. At least the sun sometimes shone upon the east coast. This was truly a place where 'the soul of a man dies in him'. For if the sharp point of St Ann herself was unable to tear a hole in the suffocating blanket of cloud, then what chance did human beings have of living and breathing in such confines? A curse on King, and a curse on that fat buffoon Otway as well.

The time had come. His frail, icy fingers, lean from long months of low rations, reached down and grasped one of two pistols that hung from his belt. They were pre-loaded on board, of course, prior to any shore excursion, as per Admiralty orders. He couldn't even shit without following Admiralty orders. Would the lords care, he wondered, would they be secretly impressed by his gesture, or would they take offence? Or had he already been forgotten, he and his men, their futile labours destined to be mislaid for ever in the ledger of some consumptive little Admiralty clerk?

The pistol weighed heavy in his hand, and for the first time that day he felt nervous. For one tremulous instant he sought a friendly reflection in the gunmetal, but its dull gleam refused him even that consolation. Instead it offered only a reflection in time, of a sunlit September afternoon eight thousand miles ago, of himself in the doorway of Forsyth's gunshop at number eight Leicester Street. A day when the piece in his hand had shone handsomely, speaking to him of foreign travel, of exciting times ahead, before his life's path had narrowed and hemmed him in. The assistant had stepped out into the street to demonstrate the revolutionary copper-cap percussion system. Mock-aiming the weapon with (he had to admit) a dash of theatricality, the smartly attired young captain had attracted admiring glances from passers-by, or at least he had imagined so. What price those attentions now? It was half as reliable again as a flintlock, the assistant had said. Well, he would be needing that reliability today.

With a deep intake of breath, Stokes rested the barrel carefully against his front teeth, and curled a tapering finger round the trigger. His lips, suddenly dry, closed painfully around the freezing metal. A warm gush of fear welled in his bowels. Another gust plucked mockingly at his hair, daring him to go ahead. He had to do it, really, if he was any sort of man. To pull back now would be the ultimate, the crowning failure. So do it then. *Do it now.* His hand shook. Three. Two. One. *Now.*

Whether it was a last-second change of mind that caused his hand to jerk sideways, or a surge of fear, Stokes never knew. At the exact moment that the powder flashed and the iron ball smashed upward through the roof of his mouth, his hand dragged the barrel round to one side.

And suddenly, the wind was stilled. The crash of water on stone ceased. The clouds receded, and all the brutal discord of the Patagonian winter was gone, replaced by the purest, blinding agony. And then a tiny thought within made itself known: that if he could go through pain of such dazzling clarity and be conscious of it, he must still be alive.

Part One

Chapter One

Rio de Janeiro, 13 November 1828

———

'It took Stokes twelve days to die.'

Captain King's voice carried the faintest hint of accusation. He sat forward, his eyes fixed upon the admiral.

'The powder explosion blew away half of his brain. Never have I seen a man suffer so much. Such great agonies . . . and yet he bore his fate with fortitude. He had' – King paused, remembering the pitiful, mutilated creature brought squealing and snuffling back to the *Beagle* – 'He had no eyes. He made little sense; he merely cried out. He became lucid again on the fifth and sixth days, even philosophical as regards his fate, in spite of the pain. Thereafter he lapsed into incoherence once more. He died on the morning of the twelfth.'

Admiral Otway exhaled at last. 'Poor Pringle,' he murmured to himself, and sat back heavily. The manner of Stokes's death disturbed him, rather than the fact of it.

Sensing an advantage, King persisted. 'It had become clear to me, from reports in the days preceding his death, that the balance of his mind had become disturbed. For instance, he stopped for four days to survey the gulf of Estevan, when the

Beagle's supplies were very nearly exhausted, a survey that I had most emphatically not commissioned.'

'The south has the strangest effect on a man,' offered Otway apologetically.

King held his ground. 'I do not honestly believe, sir, that any of us had ever previously experienced such conditions. The weather was atrocious. The crew were incessantly employed. At Cape Upright, for instance, the *Beagle* was under way all night for four nights. Most of the crew were sick with rheumatic complaints. Four men drowned. Three died of scurvy. Conditions were little better aboard the *Adventure*.'

The accusatory tone of his remarks, King knew, served no purpose other than to provoke Admiral Otway to mild discomfiture. It was mere sport on his part, his meagre reward for months of back-breaking toil. He had no reason to fear Otway, no need to seek the admiral's influence: this was his last commission, indivisible, unalterable, fashioned in Whitehall. His future was already out of Otway's hands. Both men were aware, too, that King had given Stokes the tougher task, ordering him west into the teeth of the gales that howled up the Straits of Magellan. The sad fact was that Stokes had been a bad appointment, a mediocre captain crushed by the pressure of his responsibilities. Goading his superior now, King realized, helped only to ease his own frustrations.

The close tropical atmosphere bore down stickily on both men, as Otway pondered how to put into words what he was going to say next.

King monitored a bead of sweat as it made its way down the admiral's neck, then dissipated suddenly into the stiff, high-necked woollen collar of his frock-coat. The contrast between Otway's immaculate, starched uniform and his own, battered and salt-bleached, struck him briefly as absurd. Instinctively he raised his fingers to the thick, grey-streaked beard that had kept him warm in the south. He had not shaved now for over six months.

Otway closed the book on King's accusations with an expansive gesture, as if to sweep aside the accumulated disasters of the preceding six months. His action prompted King to refocus, to widen his angle of vision. Rio de Janeiro harbour spread itself gloriously behind the admiral, filling the sternlights of the *Ganges*: white sails dotted everywhere like a field of cotton in the sun, cormorants skimming home sleek with their day's catch, the bright terracotta roofs of the new merchants' mansions climbing the steep hillsides alongside their crumbling, mildewed predecessors. Otway had the air of a circus impresario, thought King, installed before this magnificent panorama in his shiny coat, looking for all the world as if he was about to produce a dove from a handkerchief. Abruptly, he realized that this was no idle simile. Otway was indeed on the verge of making a big announcement. The admiral's fingertips met.

'Clearly the *Beagle* requires a commander of considerable qualities. Someone whose powers of leadership are, er, commensurate with your own.'

Don't bother flattering me, thought King. *We both know I'm going back because I have to.*

'She needs someone who can inspire the men to hitherto unsurpassed levels of courage, fortitude and determination. Were the Service blessed with two Phillip Parker Kings' – Otway squeezed out as much counterfeit sincerity as he dared – 'I should have no dilemma. You have taken so much upon your shoulders, with so little support, that my gratitude to you knows no bounds.'

King realized, uncomfortably, where the conversation was headed and decided to interject, although he knew as he did so that it would be futile. 'Lieutenant Skyring has commanded the *Beagle* these last four months, sir. Considering the morale of the men and the state of the ship when Captain Stokes met his end, the transformation that Skyring has wrought is little short of remarkable. I can think of no one better suited to this commission than Lieutenant Skyring.' *Who should have had the job in the first place*, he added to himself.

'Indeed, indeed.' Otway grimaced. 'I have no doubt that Skyring is an extremely capable officer, and I am delighted to hear that he has made such splendid headway. However, the candidate I have in mind is a man of considerable capabilities. He's my flag lieutenant here in the *Ganges*. Only twenty-three, but the most—'

'Twenty-three?' King blurted out. 'Forgive my interrupting, sir, but Lieutenant Skyring is one of my most experienced officers. He has knowledge of the area and the complete confidence of the men. I simply cannot recommend—'

A little wave of the hand from Otway silenced the captain. 'I have already made the appointment,' he stated flatly, picking up a handbell and ringing it to attract his steward's attention. The man entered. 'Would you kindly request Flag Lieutenant FitzRoy to present himself forthwith?'

The steward gave a slight nod and vanished.

'A ship's captain, at twenty-three?' queried King, in more measured tones than before. 'He must be a highly impressive young man.'

'I shall only make him commander, of course,' replied Otway. 'He shall be acting captain of the *Beagle*.'

'FitzRoy.' King let the name drip from his tongue. 'Commander FitzRoy would not, I wonder, be a relative of Admiral FitzRoy, or of the Duke of Grafton?'

Otway smiled, sensing that King was now in retreat. 'Let us simply confirm that Commander FitzRoy will have ample means to fit himself out. In answer to your question, Robert FitzRoy is in fact the son of General FitzRoy, the nephew of both Admiral FitzRoy and the Duke of Grafton, also of Castlereagh. He is a direct descendant of Charles the Second. But much, much more importantly, he is also the most successful graduate ever to pass out from the Royal Naval College in Portsmouth. Not only did he complete a three-year course in eighteen months, and take the first medal, he subsequently passed his lieutenant's exam with full numbers. *Full numbers*. The first man in the history of the Service to do so. And before you enquire about his practical experience, for I can see the question taking shape on your lips, he has been at sea for nine years, lately in the *Thetis*. Bingham had nothing but praise. His record is nothing short of exemplary. I commend him to you, Captain King.'

There was a sharp rap at the door. Even his timing is exemplary, thought King.

Otway bade the young man enter. A slender figure appeared in the doorway, moved silently across the threshold, and seemed to glide into place opposite the admiral, where he dispatched the appropriate courtesies speedily but respectfully. There was nothing foppish about his elegance; King could detect physical resilience beneath his graceful manner, allied to a firmness of purpose. The young man's features were fine-boned, his nose was sharp and his ears were too large, but the overall effect was a handsome one. His countenance was open and friendly, his long-lashed eyes dark and expressive.

'Do you know Captain Phillip Parker King?' Otway asked the new arrival.

'I have not had the pleasure of Captain King's acquaintance, sir,' replied FitzRoy, meeting King's gaze squarely with what seemed to be a genuine smile of admiration, 'but few in the service could fail to be aware of his extraordinary achievements in mapping the western and northern coasts of Australia. Achievements for which' – he addressed King directly – 'I believe you have recently been awarded a fellowship of the Royal Society, sir. I am most honoured to make your acquaintance.' FitzRoy gave a little bow, and King knew instinctively that the tribute had been sincere.

'I have been discussing with Captain King your promotion to commander of the *Beagle*,' boomed Otway, no longer able to conceal the showman's grin plastered across his features, 'and I am pleased to make you his second-in-command.'

'You have obliged me very much by your kindness, sir,' replied FitzRoy, with a knowing nod to King. He's a bright boy, thought King. He's assessed the situation perfectly. Still, that's no reason to give him an easy ride.

'Admiral Otway informs me that you were a college volunteer. Sadly, the benefits of such a formal education were denied to me as a young man. So what precisely do they teach you in the classroom at Portsmouth?'

'A great many subjects, sir. The full list is an extensive one—'

King cut him off. 'I am eager to add to the stock of my own learning. Pray enlighten me.'

FitzRoy took a deep breath. 'I recollect, sir, that we studied fortifications, the doctrine of projectiles and its application to gunnery, hydrostatics, naval history and nautical discoveries—'.

King raised a hand. 'Naval history,' he said. 'I'm interested in naval history. Tell me what you know of the history of your new command.'

'The previous *Beagle* was an eighteen-gun carrier,' began FitzRoy, cautiously, 'which won battle honours at San Sebastian and the Basque roads. Her replacement is a ten-gun brig, Cherokee class, two hundred and thirty-five tons burthen, three-masted. So she's strictly speaking a barque, but commonly known as a coffin brig.'

'Indeed she is,' cut in King warmly. 'And tell me, Commander, why the ten-gun brig is known throughout the service as a coffin brig.' All three knew the answer, that more ten-gun brigs were lost every year than any other class of ship, just as they knew that King was looking for more than that. This was a technical test.

'The ten-gun brig, sir, is a deep-waisted vessel – dangerously so, if I might venture to say so. The top of the rail, I apprehend, is just six feet out of the water, less when fully loaded. Without a forecastle to turn away a large bow wave, she's liable to ship water . . . large amounts of water, sir, which are then unable to escape on account of the high bulwarks. So she's prone to wallow, or turn broadside on to the weather. In which circumstances a second wave, shipped before the first has had time to clear, might well finish her off.'

'Absolutely, Commander,' agreed King with grim satisfaction. 'It's like trying to sail a spoon. So tell me, Commander FitzRoy, how you would modify the *Beagle* to address such limitations?'

'I'd build a poop cabin and a forecastle, sir, to deflect the heaviest seas.'

'An excellent answer, Commander. Indeed, the work has already been carried out by your predecessor. Captain Stokes added a poop deck and a forecastle deck level with the rail. Altogether I'd say he added a good sixty inches to the height of the ship. Then again, Commander, in the Southern Ocean it's not uncommon to encounter sixty-foot waves, whereupon the poop and the forecastle make damn-all difference.'

'Indeed sir.'

'Put bluntly, Commander, the greatest achievement of the late lamented Captain Stokes may well have been that the *Beagle* returned safely to Rio minus only one officer.'

'Yes sir.'

'Do you feel you are up to the task of leading a crew of exhausted, half-starved and demoralized men through such conditions?'

'I am determined, sir, that the men under my command will receive my full attention as regards to their physical and mental welfare,' said FitzRoy, calmly.

'The *Beagle* was also your predecessor's first command. The pressures of that command thrust Captain Stokes into such a profound despondency that he shot himself.'

'So I heard, sir. An awful incident.'

'And you are sure you will remain immune to such pressures?'

FitzRoy hesitated, and for the first time, King detected a note of uncertainty in his confident manner. To his irritation, Admiral Otway chose that moment to blunder to the young man's rescue.

'The south is a place "where the soul of a man dies in him".'

That was the last entry in Stokes's log. He was quoting Alexander Pope, I think – eh, FitzRoy?'

'Indeed sir.'

'But then poor Stokes was a melancholy sort. Not like yourself. Hardly suited for such a lonely post. I blame myself,' he added, in a manner that implied he did no such thing.

'The men are convinced that Captain Stokes's ghost still haunts the ship,' King informed FitzRoy. 'You have an interesting task on your hands, Commander.'

'I'm beginning to see that, sir.'

'A familiar face or two wouldn't go amiss,' offered Otway, 'if you have any requests.'

'I'd like to take Midshipman Sulivan from the *Thetis*, sir, if that's possible. We were together in the *Glendower* as well. He's a capital fellow, and has the best eyesight of any seaman I've ever known.'

'I see no reason why not – provided Bingham has no objections.'

'You'll need a new master as well,' put in King.

'May I take Murray, sir? He's a fine navigator, and ready for his chance.'

'Of course, of course,' replied Otway generously. 'You may take Mr Murray with you. Murray and Sulivan it is.' The admiral produced a sealed package from his desk drawer. 'I have your orders here. You are to complete the survey of the South American coast from Cape St Antonio around to Chiloé in the west, as directed by Captain King. You are to take particular note of all safe harbours, and all suitable refuelling and watering places. You are to observe weather patterns, tides and currents, the nature of the country inland and the people therein, remembering at all times that you are the official representative of His Majesty's government. You and your officers are to avail yourselves of every opportunity of collecting and preserving specimens of natural history, such as may be new, rare or interesting.' Otway slid the package across the table. 'You can read the details at your leisure, Commander, but I would draw your attention to one significant instruction: the naming of topographical features. Grateful as I am to find myself honoured in perpetuity by the title "Port Otway", there has been a tendency of late to ascribe names of a more frivolous nature. I'm thinking in particular of "Soapsuds Cove", where you presumably did your washing. And "Curious Peak". What the devil was curious about it?'

'I have no idea,' replied King drily. 'You'd have to ask Stokes.'

'Admiralty orders are quite specific on this point. The maps you are updating were compiled by Byron, Wallis and Carteret back in the 1760s, since when it has been something of an embarrassment that English charts contain such trivial identifications as "Point Shut-up". The site of some unseemly squabble, no doubt. Try to confine yourself to practical descriptions, or if you must commemorate someone, I would recommend members of the government or the Royal Family. Of course you can commemorate yourselves, but I would suggest a limit for ship's officers of one or two place names each. Understood?'

FitzRoy nodded.

Otway's brisk tone softened. 'The *Beagle* is on her way up from Monte Video. When she arrives, she will be hove down and repaired. Before then I would pay her a visit. Unannounced. That is to say, I think you should make your presence felt.' He grinned conspiratorially, and gestured to indicate that the interview was over.

Formalities completed, FitzRoy and King took their leave of the admiral's cabin, stooping with the instinct of years to avoid cracking their heads as they crossed the threshold. Outside, King paused at the top of the companionway. 'So tell me, Mr FitzRoy. Of all the captains under whom you have served, whom did you admire the most?'

'Sir John Phillimore, sir,' replied FitzRoy without hesitation. The ensuing pause made it clear that King meant him to go on.

'We were escorting Lord Ponsonby to Rio as ambassador, sir. One of the younger midshipmen suffered a terrible injury to his arm, and was in danger of losing it. Sir John gave the

Ponsonbys' cabin to the boy, and himself slept in a cot outside the cabin door, giving instructions that he should be wakened immediately if anything were to befall the lad. We were all much impressed. It was Sir John who reduced the men's daily rum ration from half a pint to a quarter. Which, I must confess, improved the efficiency of the ship considerably.'

King raised both eyebrows. 'Good luck with the rum ration.'

FitzRoy smiled back, and King could not help but like his new second-in-command.

'Skyring's disappointment will be bitter, I confess. But he is not the sort to pay this off on you. He is a generous type. I will give him our supply schooner, the *Adelaide*, which should help soften the blow.'

'I hope so, sir.'

'One more thing, Mr FitzRoy. That quotation in Stokes's log – "the soul of a man dies in him". Who really wrote it?'

'Thomson, sir. It's from *The Seasons*.'

'You'll go far, Mr FitzRoy. I think you'll go very far indeed.'

Chapter Two

Rio de Janeiro, 15 December 1828

With a brisk, matter-of-fact breeze behind her, the little cutter slid easily through the choppy blue of Rio bay, a curious petrel or two in pursuit. Enlivened by the sunshine, the crew put their backs into it. Occasional flecks of foam from the oars flung themselves gaily into Robert FitzRoy's face as he sat in the stern, but on such a day as this, the odd splash was hardly an imposition. It was a glorious morning to be alive; and, as it was certain to be one of the last such days he would see for a year or more, he should really have been able to enjoy it to the full. King's challenge, though, continued to perturb him.

They raced past a fisherman's skiff, its silvery catch glinting in the sun. A large, muscly black stood balanced in the prow, holding aloft the pick of his fish as enticingly as he could, while the cutter skimmed by unregarding. FitzRoy felt a flash of pity for the man, who could never know the world and all it offered, who had not the opportunities provided by modern civilization to make whatever he wanted of his own life.

Dropping behind them, resplendent, the *Ganges* lay at anchor, the pride of the South American station, her jet-black pitch contrasting smartly with her blinding white sails, the

Union flag fluttering from her jackstaff, the blue ensign rippling square from her mainmast. Ahead in the distance, dwarfed by the rounded symmetry of the Sugarloaf mountain, the squat shape of the *Beagle* could just be made out, low in the water like a lost barrel. His first commission. It was hard to keep the butterflies subdued. Make your presence felt, Otway had said.

By his side in the cutter's stern, Midshipman Bartholomew Sulivan, just turned eighteen years of age, chattered away about home, about matters naval, about the task ahead of them, about anything. He really did take the palm for talk sometimes, but a cheerier, more optimistic companion was not to be found anywhere. Guiltily, FitzRoy realized that he had not been paying attention for some minutes.

'. . . and do you remember that Danish fellow, Pritz, who pressed three of our men for the Brazilian navy? And old Bingham telling him' – here he adopted Bingham's fruity tones – '"I hear my boat's oars. You had better give me back my men." And the look on the Dane's face when we climbed over the rail and he realized he must knock under! And do you recall him all crimson, shouting at us as we rowed off? "Remember Copenhagen! Remember Copenhagen!"' Sulivan's face flushed with excitement at the memory.

'We raced each other over the rail, as I recall,' admonished FitzRoy, 'and you were first over, even though you were supposed to be in the sick list that day.'

'It was the devil of a spree!' said Sulivan, and the ratings at the nearest oars grinned discreetly at the youngster's high spirits.

FitzRoy's mind, though, could not settle. *I am now responsible for this young man's life. His life and the lives of more than sixty others. Every decision I take affects their survival. Any misjudgement I make could kill us all.*

Had the commission been his four months earlier, this golden morning would have found FitzRoy his usual confident self, speeding across the waves towards his future. The depression that had overwhelmed Stokes would have seemed as distant a prospect as the wild channel where the poor fellow had surrendered himself to it. Four months earlier, however, there had occurred a . . . disturbance: that was the only word for it. An isolated incident, which had filled FitzRoy with disquiet, and which now refused to be forgotten.

It had been just such a day as this, the air at its sweetest, the sunshine clean and clear, and he had felt a sudden surge of elation as he prepared to order the signal to Wait for Dispatches. A kind of giddy excitement had seized him, a wild happiness, which led him in a whirling, mischievous dance. Glowing with joy, he had been struck by a tremendous idea. Why not run up all the flags in the locker in a splendid array? What a fine sight it would make! How in keeping with everyone's mood on such a blessing of a day! Then, why not add all the night signals, the white lights, guns, horns, bells and flares, in a magnificent celebration?

The midshipmen had laughed when he had described his plan, taking their cue from his own merry countenance, but their smiles had slackened and disappeared at the realization that he was not joking. He had tried to persuade them, pumping their hands, invoking their Christian names, urging them excitably to join in the entertainment. They had failed to understand, had assumed him to be drunk. There had been a scuffle – a vulgar push-and-pull, his uniform ripped – which had culminated in them locking him in his cabin, still flushed with fatuous excitement. The incident had been hushed up – Bingham had been told he was sick – and quickly forgotten by the others, but what the devil had he been thinking of? What malign spirit had taken control of his mind?

The next morning had been even more inexplicable. He had woken in a state of what could only be called fear. A black despondency had suffocated him, squeezing all other thoughts from his mind, isolating him from the world outside his cabin. He had lain alone in his cot, shivering and frightened. In this state of overwhelming helplessness, there had seemed no point to his life, no point to his work, no point even to existence itself.

Gradually, the darkness had seemed to take shape in his mind. As he was still in the sick list, his friends had presumed him to be battling the dog of a hangover, but this was a much fiercer beast. It slavered at him, mocked him. *You are completely in my power,* it seemed to say, *should I ever deign to visit you again.*

Within a few hours, however, the creature had stirred itself and padded away. He had emerged from his cabin shaken, cowed and deeply embarrassed. Since that day, everything had been as it should, but the incident continued to loom large in his consciousness. Had the creature really departed? Or was it merely biding its time, toying with him, waiting to return at a moment when men's lives depended on his skill and judgement?

He had thrown himself at phrenology, had turned himself into an expert on the subject, staying up late to study Gall and Spurzheim, had spent hours in front of the mirror feeling the bumps and hollows on the surface of his skull, but to no avail. He thought of his uncle: a formidable intellect, one of the foremost statesmen of his age. Castlereagh had taken his own life. He thought, too, of Stokes. Had he, Robert FitzRoy, come face to face with whatever those men had encountered in their final moments?

Profoundly troubled, he realized that Sulivan had stopped chattering, and was looking at him with an expression of concern. 'I say, FitzRoy, is everything all right?'

'Of course. My dear Sulivan, you must forgive my inattention. It is not every day one is given a vessel of one's own to fret about.'

'And three cheers to that!'

'Even so, my rudeness is quite inexcusable.'

'Not a bit of it, old fellow, not a bit of it.'

FitzRoy sat up in the boat. Loath as he was to dampen the young man's enthusiasm, he felt obliged to make a little speech. 'Look here, Sulivan . . . now they've sewn a couple of stripes on my sleeve, we shall still be the best of friends, of course – the very best of friends – but you do understand that it would not be fair on the other officers, the other midshipmen especially, if I were to show any sign of special friendship towards you? A ship's captain eats alone, reads alone, even thinks alone. I have to be fair and just. I'm determined to do the right thing, Sulivan, the right thing by everyone, even if I end up the loneliest old man on the ocean. I hope you understand.'

'Oh absolutely, old chap, absolutely. I mean, it couldn't be any other way. It will be a privilege to serve with you, sir.' Sulivan looked up at his new commander, and could only see everything that he wanted to be.

By now, they were close enough to the *Beagle* to hear the water's slap against her sides, and to see the welcoming party gathering at the rail. Whatever Otway's recommendations of surprise, King was not the sort to leave Skyring and his men caught unawares by the visit. FitzRoy could make out Skyring by his uniform now, taller than the others, perhaps thirty years of age, his face dominated by a Wellingtonian nose and topped by a shock of dark hair. As the cutter pulled alongside, the lieutenant's leaning gait seemed to suggest that the fierce southern winds had left him bent permanently at an alarming angle.

FitzRoy climbed gracefully up the battens, waving away offers of help, and shook hands enthusiastically with Skyring. His predecessor's rueful smile indicated that no more needed to be said by either man, and that FitzRoy could consider the matter of his leapfrog promotion closed.

'How do, Lieutenant?' said FitzRoy, warmly.

'Your servant, sir,' replied Skyring. 'May I introduce to you Lieutenant Kempe?'

Kempe, a cadaverous, unsmiling man, whose teeth seemed to be fighting to escape his mouth, stepped forward and offered a calloused hand. On closer inspection the crew, like the ship, had a weatherbeaten aspect. Skyring had obviously done a good job during his brief tenure: the *Beagle* was freshly caulked, her decks white, her sails free of the tropical mildew that could take hold seemingly in hours – but there was no disguising the beating she had taken. Everywhere there was evidence of running repairs, in her rebuilt masts, repaired rigging and the fragile patchwork of her sails.

'This is Mr Bynoe, our surgeon.' A dark-haired, clean-shaven young man with a friendly countenance stepped forward and pumped FitzRoy's hand rather more encouragingly. 'At least, he has been acting as surgeon. He'll be resuming his duties as assistant surgeon when Mr Wilson arrives,' added Skyring, in wry acknowledgement of the parallel. A broad grin from Bynoe, to whom FitzRoy instinctively warmed.

'This is Midshipman King,' went on Skyring. 'Midshipman Phillip King.'

FitzRoy had no need of the warning, although he was grateful for Skyring's gesture. The boy before him, no more than a child, was a scaled-down replica of Phillip Parker King. 'I take it that you are related to the captain of the *Adventure*?'

'He's my father, sir.'

'Your father is a great man and a fine captain, Mr King.'

'Yes sir. He is, sir.'

The younger King seemed harmless enough at first encounter, but this was an unexpected handicap all the same.

'And this is Midshipman John Lort Stokes.' Skyring indicated a robust-looking youth with a military air and a correspondingly firm handshake.

FitzRoy raised a quizzical eyebrow.

'No relation to the late captain, sir,' explained Stokes, briskly.

'Mr Stokes hails from Yorkshire,' said Skyring, as if that clarified the situation.

FitzRoy breathed an inward sigh of relief.

Further introductions were made between the two midshipmen and Sulivan, Stokes being deputized to show the new man the ropes, before Skyring moved on to the warrant officers.

'Bos'n Sorrell, sir.'

Sorrell, a square-framed man with thinning hair, who looked as if he had been fat in a former life, was clearly eager to talk. 'The late captain was a fine man, if I may say so, sir, a fine man. He saved my life, sir, and many others.' He bobbed uncomfortably before FitzRoy, as if in need of an urgent visit to the heads.

'Mr Sorrell was formerly in the *Saxe-Cobourg*, a whaler that was wrecked in Fury Harbour,' explained Skyring.

'The captain, sir, he sent two boats to row eighty miles down the Barbara Channel to look for survivors, sir,' said Sorrell, sweating with gratitude. 'If it hadn't have been for him, I wouldn't be alive today. A fine man he was, sir.'

'Well, Mr Sorrell, I hope I will be able to live up to Captain Stokes's many achievements,' said FitzRoy. *All except the last one.*

Coxswain Bennet, a ruddy-faced, flaxen-haired young man, was the final member of the welcoming party. He had preferred to keep his counsel throughout the previous exchange, and his blank expression, FitzRoy guessed, betokened an instinctive sense of diplomacy rather than any intellectual shortcomings. Skyring's introduction of Bennet had been almost an afterthought.

The formalities over, Skyring came straight to the point. 'I'm afraid the damage below is far worse than anyone thought. The forefoot and the false keel have been torn clean off. A little run-in we had with the rocks at Cape Tamar. It'll take at least two weeks to put right.'

'Two weeks? My orders are to turn her straight round and head south again. The *Adventure* and the *Adelaide* are to leave in four days' time, and we are to sail with them.' A collective groan escaped the assembled officers. 'Mr Skyring here is to command the *Adelaide*.'

'Then it would appear I shall be leaving you behind. The copper bottom is absolutely shot to pieces and will need replacing. It appears you will be enjoying Christmas in Rio.'

The officers' expressions brightened a little. FitzRoy did his best to join in with the smiles, but levity did not come easily at this point. His first order as captain, and he would be unable to fulfil it promptly.

'Shall we take the grand tour?' offered Skyring, and motioned the others towards the rear of the tiny main deck. With the ship at anchor, the deck watch were mostly idle: sailors slouched here and there playing cards, or lay curled up asleep in coils of rope. They were a ragged lot, dressed in a battered mixture of slops and ducks, threadbare blue pea-jackets and patched-up canvas blouses. There was no singing, no laughter, no animation. These were hollow-eyed, exhausted, sullen men, observed FitzRoy, malnourished in body and soul. They observed him too, suspiciously and with barely concealed contempt. FitzRoy thought he heard the derisive whisper as he passed, 'College boy.' *That's all I am to them,* he thought, *a boy just out of school. Nine tough years in the* Glendower, *the* Thetis *and the* Ganges *mean nothing to them. I must prove myself from scratch. Perhaps they are right. Perhaps that is how it should be. I have experienced nothing like the ordeal they have been through. It is my duty to win them over.*

Sorrell blustered ineffectually, lashing out left and right with his rattan. 'Look lively, lads! Jump up now! Make way for Captain FitzRoy!'

The men shifted, but their movements were lifeless and perfunctory. After a few short steps the party arrived at Stokes's new raised poop deck, in the centre of which stood a solitary door.

'This is the poop cabin,' said Skyring. 'Captain Stokes preferred it to the captain's cabin so he used it as his own. He built it himself, which may account.'

FitzRoy lowered his head gravely, and stepped into the room where Stokes had died. It was cramped, extremely so, which was not unusual for a coffin brig: the distance from floor to ceiling could not have been more than four foot six. This cabin, though, appeared to be more uncomfortable than was strictly necessary. Not only did the mizzen-mast run straight through the middle of the room, but the steering gear was stashed under the chart table, taking up all the available legroom. A tell-tale noise from the other side of the wall informed FitzRoy that the officers' water closet was right next door. A sparse selection of water-damaged volumes occupied the shelves that lined the back wall, for the cabin had also doubled as Stokes's library. His cot still hung from the ceiling in memoriam, directly above the table and immediately beneath the skylight, as if spreading itself to absorb every ray of sunshine that filtered through the greasy glass. *That was why he wanted this cabin*, FitzRoy realized instinctively. *He was reaching towards the light.*

'Sometimes there are only two or three hours of it,' said Skyring, who had followed his gaze. 'Daylight. Down south. In winter.'

His eyes met FitzRoy's. 'Will you be wishing to keep this cabin? The men suppose it to be haunted.'

'I presume the captain's cabin is still below decks?'

Skyring nodded.

'Then I shall take the captain's cabin as normal. Irrespective of any ghosts.'

With Stokes's spectre thus dismissed, they stepped back into the warm Brazilian sunshine, where the other officers stood waiting, then all proceeded down the dark hole of the after companionway to the lower deck. A familiar reek assaulted FitzRoy's nostrils there: the concentrated smell of men who have not washed themselves in several months, mixed in a treacly stew with the wet scent produced by holystones, sand, water and wood, as the below-decks watch scrubbed half-heartedly on their hands and knees. Sorrell again tried to whip up some enthusiasm with his rattan, and one of the men, a grinning, red-haired Cornishman, wished FitzRoy a polite good morning that could have been either friendly or mocking, he could not tell which.

The captain's cabin, at the bottom of the companionway, proved marginally roomier than Stokes's berth in the poop, but no taller and a good deal more gloomy. Despite the presence of a small skylight, it was impossible to see into the corners. On the wall in the half-light, like religious artefacts, hung Stokes's three chronometers: scientific icons, without which measurements of longitude could not be taken, without which there could be no expedition, without which the world could not be captured on paper, tamed and subjugated in the name of God and King George. They were obviously government-issue chronometers, their glass foggy, their metal housing battered, and one of the dials disfigured by a deep, vertical crack, but they did at least appear to function. FitzRoy made a mental note to dismantle them, clean, oil and reassemble them before the ship headed south once more. *This tiny cabin*, he thought, *will be your home for the next two years*; and for a brief moment he allowed himself the indulgent realization that the flag lieutenant's quarters on the *Ganges* had been utterly luxurious by comparison.

Having acquired a lantern, which seemed to make no difference whatsoever to the gloom, the party inspected the gunroom and the midshipmen's berth, and peered into the chain locker. FitzRoy could hear Sulivan chattering away behind him, befriending his fellow midshipmen with characteristic ease and rapidity, even though they could barely see each other. As they moved past a line of neatly spaced hammock hooks, however, FitzRoy was brought up short by the sight of two unstowed hammocks and their contents, a pair of ample Brazilian whores sleeping off their night's exertions. For the first time in their tour of inspection, Skyring began to struggle. 'The men have been away since the end of 1826. They haven't seen a woman in two years – with the exception of a brief leave period last December. I thought . . . well, you know, Admiralty regulations do permit women on board in port.'

'Married women.'

Skyring grimaced and indicated a cheap wedding ring, which adorned the fat hand spilling out of the nearest hammock. 'It doesn't actually state whom they should be married to,' he offered.

'Mr Bennet,' said FitzRoy, 'perhaps you would be kind enough to wake the two . . . ladies, and arrange for them to be escorted back ashore in the jolly-boat.'

'It'll be a pleasure, sir.'

Skyring attempted to look at the ceiling, but was already forced to stoop so low by the lack of headroom that he found himself staring instead at the back of Bennet's head.

FitzRoy said no more, and the party finally emerged, blinking, through the fore hatchway. As they arrived on deck and straightened their backs for the first time in a quarter-hour, FitzRoy turned, to be greeted by another unexpected sight. 'What in heaven,' he enquired, 'has happened to your yawl?'

Where the largest of the surveying boats should have been, bridging the gap between the foremast and the mainmast, was a crude, white-painted vessel cut from twisted timber. Inside it, where a smaller cutter should have resided, lay only a few tools.

'Our original yawl was dashed to pieces by waves in the Gulf of Estevan,' explained Skyring. 'The one you see here was constructed by May, the carpenter, from driftwood. The cutter was stolen.'

'Driftwood? Stolen by whom?'

'The Indians. They'd steal the *Beagle* herself if you turned your back for an instant. The Fuegian Indians are the most degraded creatures on God's earth – little better than animals.' There was a murmur of assent from the company. 'And if the Indians don't take the boats then the elements will. Between the three ships we've lost eleven boats, all told. I'd say that of all the men on board –' Skyring leaned further over than usual, and confided in FitzRoy '– May is the one indispensable man on the manifest. Lose May and you might as well set sail for home.'

'I should very much like to meet him.'

May was duly summoned, and proved to be a short Bristolian whose hair had apparently been cut by a blind man.

His cheeks were permanently flushed and reddened by scores of tiny broken veins.

'I must compliment you on your ingenuity, May.'

'Sir.'

'This boat of yours is a remarkable achievement.'

Silence from May, who appeared taciturn to the point of mulishness.

'Don't worry about him,' said Skyring, when May had returned to his duties. 'He rarely obliges any of us with conversation.'

FitzRoy shifted his attention to the nearby rigging, which enmeshed the foremast in a thick tracery of blackened rope. He gave it a spirited tug. First impressions were encouraging, but then he took a closer look at what appeared to be a repair and picked at the tar covering with a fingernail. Something caught his eye. 'Would you come here a moment, Mr Sorrell?'

The boatswain bobbed forward uncertainly.

'Take a look at this, please.' Sorrell peered at the exposed fibres. 'Now tell me what you see.'

'It – it's not hemp, is it, sir?'

'No, Mr Sorrell, it's not. It's sisal.'

'Yes sir. Most definitely sisal. God's my life, sir, I have no idea how this happened.'

Skyring and Kempe exchanged glances.

'Who carried out this repair?' asked FitzRoy.

'Able Seaman Gilly, sir.'

'Fetch him here.'

Within a few seconds Sorrell had scurried back with a reluctant Gilly, who proved to be an oldster, as grimy and wiry as any of the crewmen FitzRoy had seen so far. Gilly eyed his new commander suspiciously.

'Did you carry out this repair, Gilly?'

'Aye aye sir.'

'How long have you been in the Service?'

'Nine year or thereabouts.'

'And how many years an able seaman?'

'Six.'

'And have all those years not taught you that sisal is insufficiently strong for rigging?'

'Couldn't find no hemp, could I?'

FitzRoy's voice was iron. 'I cannot look over this, Gilly. You have endangered your fellow crewmen's lives. Once my commission has been read, you will be flogged at the gangway at six bells of the forenoon watch.'

Gilly said nothing, but gave FitzRoy a look of contempt.

'You may return to your duties.'

The man turned on his heel without a word and walked away.

'Shall I make it a batty, sir?' Sorrell, relieved to have escaped a tongue-lashing, was now attempting to distance himself further from the crime by recommending a severe punishment.

'Mr Sorrell, you know as well as I do that more than a dozen lashes are expressly forbidden, and have been for as long as you or I have been in the Service.'

'I know, sir, but Captain Stokes always—'

'Captain Stokes, God rest his soul, is no longer with us. You will carry out a sentence of a half-dozen lashes at six bells. Furthermore, Mr Sorrell, when the *Beagle* is hove down, you will personally inspect every rope, every inch of her rigging and every link in her chains. Is that clear?'

'Aye aye sir. I'll do it most zealous, sir,' said Sorrell, shifting his weight from one foot to the other and back again.

'Tell me, Mr Sorrell, how many minutes does it take the *Beagle* to make all sail?'

'In good conditions, sir? From reefed? I'd say about a quarter-hour, sir.'

'Well, Mr Sorrell, let's see if you and I can get that down below twelve minutes, shall we?'

Sorrell, who had not dared breathe for the past minute or so, emptied his lungs at the prospect.

'And now, if you will oblige me by mustering the ship's company aft, with Lieutenant Skyring's permission I should like to address them.'

The order was piped and men began to emerge, from the lower deck, from the hold, from the magazine, from coalholes, lockers, storerooms and even – limping – from the sick bay, until it seemed impossible that the narrow deck would hold them all. They formed themselves into a ragged square, the red-coated ship's marines to the left, while Skyring read FitzRoy's commission.

FitzRoy himself stood on the poop, flanked by his officers in their peaked caps, dark coats and white trousers, until Skyring had finished. Then he stepped forward. He placed his hands on either side of the compass housing as if it were a lectern and spoke in a clear, firm voice. 'My name is Robert FitzRoy. I am directed by my lords commissioners of the Admiralty to take charge of this vessel. My orders are to complete the survey of the South American coast begun by Captain Stokes, from Cape St Antonio in the east to Chiloé Island in the west, under the direction of Captain King in the *Adventure*. Lieutenant Skyring is to accompany us in the *Adelaide*. We shall make sail in approximately two weeks, after the ship has been hove down and repaired. Most of you, I know, will not relish so hasty a return to the south, but we may consider ourselves fortunate in some respects. The service is decreasing in size every day, as the war becomes no more than a memory. Ships are being broken up, commissions are not being renewed. The ports and taverns of England are packed with men who clamour for a berth. I know – I have been home recently. We are the lucky ones. And we have an opportunity not just to sail one of His Majesty's ships, but to do so for the benefit of future generations. To survey unexplored territory, to map it and to name it, is to contribute to history. This is the chance offered us today.

'I have learned from Captain King and Lieutenant Skyring of the hardships borne on your first voyage, of the inclement conditions, the sickness and the lack of food. The weather that we encounter will, of course, be a matter for our maker. But I give you my word, as God is my witness, that the health of every man on board, and the sufficiency of victuals and provisions, shall be my prime concern.

'There shall – as a consequence – be new regulations. For the avoidance of ship fever, every man is to wash himself thoroughly a minimum of once a week. All clothing is to be boiled every two weeks. All decks are to be scrubbed with vinegar every two weeks.

'For the avoidance of scurvy, there will be an antiscorbutic diet, which will be compulsory for all those on board. No man is to go more than three days without fresh food caught locally. Hard tack, salt meat and canisters of preserved food are not sufficient. Every man is to take a daily dose of lemon juice. Lime juice is not sufficient. I shall also be asking Mr Bynoe to supply extra rations of pickles, dried fruit, vinegar and wintersbark. The daily wine ration is to remain at one pint, while supplies can be maintained. But for the avoidance of drunkenness, the daily rum ration is to be reduced from half a pint to a quarter of a pint.'

FitzRoy paused to let this sink in. The shocked gasp at the prospect of weakened grog was audible across the deck.

'No man under the age of sixteen is to receive a rum ration.'

Another pause, punctuated this time by a smaller, higher-pitched gasp.

'There will be no gambling. There will be no women in port. Before divine service on Sundays, all officers and men who can read and write, and I include myself in this, will be expected to contribute to the education of those who cannot. This will be a modern ship, run along modern lines. But the punishment for anyone who disobeys any of the new regulations, or any order for that matter, will be of the most old-fashioned sort. In particular, anyone who by his laxity endangers the ship, or the life of anyone aboard, will be flogged, as Able Seaman Gilly has discovered.

'The refit will make the next two weeks a busy time for all of us. Nonetheless I shall ensure that every man is granted a period of shore leave. I trust that you will enjoy yourselves ashore. I trust also that you are all familiar with the penalty for desertion.

'When you return to the ship, your work will begin in earnest. I intend to make the *Beagle* the best-drilled, best-handled vessel on the ocean. My object is that every one of her people shall be proud of her. That is my task, and yours too. Thank you for your time. You may go about your business.'

The crew milled about for a few seconds, murmuring among themselves, then disappeared back into the myriad hatchways and crevices of the ship. FitzRoy released his grip on the compass housing.

'Well done sir,' breathed Sulivan.

'At least they didn't come charging up the quarter-deck waving cutlasses and crying, "Liberty",' said Skyring. 'Now, if you will permit me, Commander, I'll go and gather my effects. The very best of luck to you. They're not the best crew that ever sailed the ocean, but they're not the worst either. There is potential in them. I am sure you will unlock it.'

'You oblige me with your kindness,' smiled FitzRoy politely, and the two men shook hands once more.

There remained only the matter of Able Seaman Gilly. As was normal custom, the ship's company reassembled before the gangway at six bells to witness the flogging. Gilly was stripped of his rough canvas jacket and tied down. It was clear from the scars that laced his back that he had aroused the ire of Captain Stokes – and, no doubt, various predecessors – on numerous occasions. Sorrell, eager to impress, laid it on thick from the first blow, but Gilly clamped his teeth fast together, determined not to make a sound.

As the second blow fell, FitzRoy's gaze shifted from the errant sailor towards the shore. In the distance, proceeding slowly away from the ship as it lifted and fell on a freshening breeze, he could just make out the jolly-boat, and in it, Bennet's distinctive flaxen mop, almost hidden behind the wide backs of the two plump Brazilian women seated side by side. He turned back to observe the deck again, and the sea of watching faces under his command; only to become aware, uncomfortably, that every man jack of them was staring not at the flogging, but directly at him.

Chapter Three

Maldonado Bay, Uruguay,
30 January 1829

It was a glorious evening. A damp tropical breeze behind the *Beagle* nudged her softly towards the south-west. She slid silently into the mighty estuary of the river Plate, where the fifty-mile-wide sweep of warm brown river water gushes into the dark, welcoming depths of the Atlantic. A sliver of black-and-white on a shining sea, she navigated the divide between river and ocean, milky tea to her right side, port wine to her left. Giant columns of cloud marched across the landward horizon, golden shafts of sunlight angling between them, as if someone had lit a fire in the temple of heaven.

Robert FitzRoy stood by the wheel, Lieutenant Kempe a mute presence at his shoulder, and allowed his senses to bathe in the grandeur of the scene. In the distance ahead he could see the sharply curved promontory of Maldonado Island, the only interruption in the otherwise level plane of the horizon, jabbing up like a thorn from the flat stem of a rose; and in the shelter of Maldonado Bay beyond, he could just make out the spars of the *Adventure* at anchor. The glimpse of stitched canvas and carved wood promised friendly faces and welcome reunions for the *Beagle*'s crew after a month alone at sea. FitzRoy's orders were to rendezvous with King in the *Adventure*, Skyring in the *Adelaide* and Admiral Otway in the *Ganges* at Maldonado before the day was out. The *Beagle* was only just on schedule, but she had been handling increasingly well for such an ungainly little vessel, and would arrive before dusk. He could take justifiable pride in the changes he had wrought during the preceding weeks.

They had hove her down off Botafogo beach, to the south of Rio de Janeiro, the crew camped along the shore in tents. Naturally enough it was Sulivan who had volunteered to inspect the damage to her false keel, who had dived again and again into the shimmering water. Finally he had been hauled back aboard exhausted, the skin on his back lacerated by the jagged copper below. FitzRoy had been forced to take over the task himself, to prevent his shattered subordinate flinging himself back into the sea. The youngster had paid for his exertions, though, with a bout of dysentery, and now lay weak in a sick-bay cot with a high fever and a chamber pot for company.

They had hauled the *Beagle* out of the water using ropes, her fat belly ripped and encrusted with barnacles, gasping and glistening like a landed whale as the seawater streamed off her in a hundred cascades. They had laid her down by hand on a platform constructed from four large market-boats. They had re-payed the cracked pitch in her seams and sealed it with hot irons; they had cleaned out her bilges, oiled her blocks, blacked her meagre armaments and painted the gun-carriages; they had polished her brightwork to a mirror finish with brick dust. And then she had been lowered snugly into the water again, to be welcomed back by the warm waves lapping around her hull.

Between Rio de Janeiro and the river Plate he had drilled the men relentlessly: reefing and furling sail in all weathers, sending down sails and yards for imaginary repairs, or waking the crew in the middle of the night to fix non-existent leaks. They had performed gun drill at all hours, summoned to action stations without warning by the drums pounding out the rhythm of 'Heart of Oak'. Piped orders were practised again and again. Orders that had needed to be yelled through the speaking trumpet at first were now kept to a minimum. The boatswain had only to bark, 'Make sail!' and the bare trees of the *Beagle*'s masts would bloom white within minutes. She would always be an ungainly little brig, her decks awash even in the lightest seas; she would never dance adroitly to the tune of her captain like one of the elegant ships-of-the-line. But she was at last assuming a sturdy reliability that did her company credit. FitzRoy was beginning to feel proud of his sailing-spoon.

'It begins to look very dirty to leeward, sir.' Lieutenant Kempe was one of those perverse customers whose smile – half grin, half grimace – carried a hint of satisfaction at unfortunate developments. But he was unquestionably correct. The giant pillars of cloud on the western horizon were filling and darkening, and appeared to be increasing in size – which did not make sense, as the warm, gentle breeze that half filled the *Beagle*'s sails was blowing from the north-east.

'Barometer reading?'

'Steady sir, 30.20. That's up from 30.10 half an hour ago.'

Everything was as it should be. The barometer said so. But tiny alarm bells rang in FitzRoy's mind. Most of the crew didn't hold with barometers – he'd had a hard job, in fact, persuading his officers that such gadgets had any part to play in modern seamanship – preferring their captain to handle the ship by instinct. A good captain, of course, was capable of marrying science and nature in his deliberations. The barometer may indeed have been adamant that nothing was wrong, and the nor'-easterly behind them may have contained barely enough vigour to ruffle the milky sheen of the estuary, but this, he was keenly aware, was no ordinary estuary. More than twice as wide as the English Channel at Dover, the river Plate was notorious for its sudden *pampero* storms. None of the crew had ever seen one, but they had heard the stories. Their instincts tensed like violin strings.

A long dark roll of cloud had curled into being on the horizon, filling the spaces between the vapour columns and blotting out the setting sun. Should they cut and run for the shore, he wondered? Or should they drive ahead to the sanctuary of Maldonado Bay? The former would involve disobeying orders. The latter risked being caught in the open, if this was indeed a *pampero*.

'Barometer reading?'

'Steady sir, 30.20.'

This simply didn't make sense. If a storm was indeed in the offing, the barometer should have been sharing his alarm. He resolved to stay on course for Maldonado.

'No, wait a minute, sir. The quicksilver is dipping. 30.10 sir . . . it's dipping fast sir. It's dipping really fast sir. 30 dead sir. It's dipping really fast sir.'

Even as the master relayed the bad news, the nor'-easterly wind behind them dropped away to nothing. The sails fell slack against the masts. Only the creaking of the rigging betrayed the *Beagle*'s presence in a world of silence. There was a moment of hush on deck, as officers and crew stood in awe and watched the cloud columns grow, thousands of feet high now, grotesque black billows at the core of each pillar like the smoke from a cannonade.

FitzRoy's ribcage constricted. *It's so easy to know what action to take when you are only the subordinate. I have to take charge. Now.*

'Barometer reading 29.90 sir. The temperature's dropping too sir.'

'Take her into the shore, Mr Murray. Any shelter you can find.'

Murray made a quick calculation. 'Lobos Island is only a few miles off the coast, sir, but there's no breeze.'

'I believe we shall have a sufficiency of wind before very long, Mr Murray.'

'Aye aye sir.'

The master relayed the instructions to the helmsman. 'Larboard – I mean, port – a hundred and thirty-five degrees.'

The cadaverous half-smile continued to divide Lieutenant Kempe's bony features. The crew were still learning to use the word 'port' instead of 'larboard', at FitzRoy's insistence: 'larboard' could sound uncommonly like 'starboard' in the middle of a storm.

The helmsman swung the wheel down smoothly with his right hand, and the ship inched slowly to starboard, reluctantly answering the call of her rudder.

'Double-reefed topsails, Mr Sorrell, and double-reefed foresail. Batten the hatches and put the galley fires out.'

The boatswain piped the orders to the crew, and within seconds the rigging swarmed with figures: younger, lighter hands in the tops and out on the yard-arms, burlier sailors in the centre, wrestling with the heavier, more uncooperative shrouds of canvas.

A few seconds, and the adjustments were made. Now all they could do was wait like sitting ducks, and hope that the storm, when it came, would fill their reduced sails sufficiently to drive them towards the darkening shore.

'Barometer reading 29 dead sir.'

'That's impossible,' breathed FitzRoy. He had never known the quicksilver fall so far so fast. Swiftly, he crossed the deck to check for himself. There was no mistake. You could actually see it falling with the naked eye.

'Hold on to your hats,' murmured little King, somewhat unnecessarily. They were clearly in for the blow of their lives. Hands closed silently around ropes, rails and brass fittings – anything that looked securely screwed down.

'Look sir,' said Bennet, ruddy-faced under his flaxen mop. He'd come up on deck as the ship had changed course, and was now leaning over the port rail and squinting upriver to the west. All eyes followed the direction of his gaze. Before the rolling black cloud lay a lower bank of what appeared to be white dust, skimming across the silken brown waters towards them at incredible speed.

'What is it? A sandstorm?'

FitzRoy reached for his spyglass. Even at closer quarters, the white band across the horizon was difficult to make out. 'Great heavens . . . I think it may be . . . *insects*.'

As he breathed the last word, the vanguard was upon them. Butterflies, moths, dragonflies and beetles arrived by the thousands, a charging, panic-stricken battalion, driven helplessly by the surging winds at their back. They flew into blinking eyes and spluttering mouths, snagging in hair and ears, taking refuge up nostrils and down necks. They clung to the rigging and turned the masts white. The sails disappeared beneath a seething mass of tiny legs and wings.

Even as the crew fought to clear their faces of these unwanted guests, the sea did it for them. Thick spume arrived in a volley, borne on a wall of wind that smacked into the port side of the *Beagle* with a shudder. Suddenly the sails filled to bursting, the wind squealed through the rigging, and the little brig darted forward as if released from a trap, keeling violently to starboard as she did so. The spume thickened into dense white streaks of flying water, the ocean itself shredded and torn as the elements launched their frenzied attack, raking the ship's side like grapeshot. The sound of the wind raised itself into an indignant shriek, and then, beneath it, came something FitzRoy had never heard before: a low moan like a cathedral organ. *How appropriate*, he thought – for this was indeed shaping up to be a storm of Old Testament proportions.

Straining under the press of sail, and foaming in her course, the little brig drove crazily forward, her masts bent like coach whips.

'Another hand to the wheel!' shouted FitzRoy. No one heard him, but no one needed to: already two or three men were moving forward to assist the helmsman, who grappled with the wheel as it bucked first to port and then to starboard in his grasp. Like a burst of artillery fire, the fore staysail, the thick white triangle of sturdy English canvas that led the ship's charge, flayed itself to ribbons as if it had been a mere pocket handkerchief.

'Storm trysails, close-reefed!' FitzRoy screamed from an inch away into Sorrell's ear. Again, the crew barely needed the boatswain's frantic attempts to relay the instruction. Figures swarmed back up the masts like monkeys, into the rigging and out on to the violently swaying yards. Even though they were close-reefed, the sails flapped madly, fighting like wild animals to cast aside their handlers, but gradually, steadily, they were brought under control. The storm trysails were FitzRoy's only remaining option. Too much sail and the wind would rip the canvas to pieces. Too little and the ship would lose steerage, leaving the elements free to batter her to destruction.

The sea was heavy now, the ship rolling, the decks swept every few seconds by several feet of thick, foamy water. The sky had turned black, but incessant lightning flashes were now illuminating the scene, both from above and below. *It's like an immense metal foundry*, thought FitzRoy. *God's machine room. If just one of these lightning bolts strikes a mast, we're all dead men.* A flash illuminated Kempe's skeletal face to his left, and he could read the fear written there. The lieutenant's smile was frozen mirthlessly on his face. *I must not give in to my own fear. If I do they will smell it. They will know.*

Hanging grimly to the taffrail behind them, Midshipman King stood open-mouthed in wonder. *Even during two years in the south, he's never seen a storm like this*, FitzRoy marvelled. Then he followed King's gaze. Then he saw the wave. And then all of them saw it, illuminated in a white sheet of electricity. A wall of water as big as a house – forty feet high? Fifty? Sixty? – towering above the port beam, a sheer brown cliff frozen in the lightning's flash.

'All hands down from aloft!' he tried to shout, but the words died in his throat as he realized there wasn't time. Every man on deck slid his arms and legs deep into the rigging, each desperately trying to sew himself into the very fabric of the ship, muttering prayers that the ropes would hold fast. FitzRoy looked up and saw the topmen scrambling in from the yards to the crosstrees on the mast. Another lightning flash, and his eyes locked with the terrified gaze of the Cornishman who had greeted him on his first day aboard. The man was clutching for dear life to the main-topmast cap.

A moment later, and the wave took the weather quarter-boat, effortlessly crumpling the little cutter to matchwood. Four brisk rifle shots snapping across the wind indicated that the windward gunports had blown in. Then the wave slammed across the deck, illuminated stroboscopically by the lightning, bulldozing into the men tangled in the rigging, pulverizing everything in its path. It felt like being hit by an oxcart. The *Beagle* tipped at an alarming angle, the whaleboat on the lee side dipped momentarily under the surface, instantly filled to the brim with water and was gone. *She's going over on her beam-ends. Dear Lord, we're going down.*

As the wave passed, FitzRoy looked back up for the Cornishman, but the entire main-topmast was gone, the main-topsail and the crewman with it. The fore-topmast was gone too, and the jib-boom, while the maindeck bow gun, which had been lashed abreast of the mainmast, had jack-knifed in its lashings, carriage upwards. Most of the remaining sails were flying free of their stays, flapping insanely. The lee side of the deck was still under water. The ship sagged helplessly, seemingly uncertain as to whether to right herself or give up the ghost and slide silently into the depths. FitzRoy could see the drenched figure of Midshipman Stokes, up to his waist at the lee rail, hurling the life-buoy into the surging waves. Beyond him two figures in the surf struck out powerfully for the *Beagle*'s side, only to be swallowed by the darkness. When the lightning flared again, there was no sign of either man.

Even as Stokes performed his vain rescue act, FitzRoy screamed and gestured to Murray, who had lashed himself to the wheel, to bring the stern round into the wind; but it was clear from the helpless look in the master's eyes that the *Beagle* would no longer answer her helm. And yet agonizingly, unwillingly, the natural buoyancy of the little ship began to assert itself over the weight of water that had flooded her below decks. Like a cask she rose, and slowly regained her trim. As she climbed gradually towards safety, a second big wave cascaded across the decks. Stokes, caught in the open, slipped to the floor and was slammed against the lee rail, a mass of broken spars and tangled ropes piling after him, but somehow the water pouring through the sluices pinned him there, bruised and bloodied. Again the *Beagle* fought to right herself.

This is my ship. I must do something, before the next wave destroys us. FitzRoy slithered across the incline of the deck, grabbed a hatchet and hacked through the stern anchor-rope. Kempe, frozen to the compass-housing, looked on in horrified confusion, clearly thinking his captain had gone mad – but one or two of the seamen cottoned on, and stumbled across to help him. Between them, they grabbed the biggest fallen spar, lashed it to the rope-end, and hurled it overboard. Then FitzRoy hauled the dazed and bleeding Stokes back up the planking by his collar, just as the third wave made its pulverizing way across the deck. The waves were coming every thirty to forty seconds now, the crest of each peak level with the centre of the *Beagle*'s mainyard as she floundered her way through the troughs.

Curled in a dysentery-racked ball of pain in his cot below decks, Bartholomew Sulivan was shaken by the sight of the sickbay door slamming open, forced off its catch by a waist-high tide of green water, even as the ship lurched and threatened to pitch him into it. Outside the door he could see crewmen, those who would normally have been resting between watches, bailing furiously for their lives. There was no time to feel for his uniform in the guttering flame from the oil-lamp, so he plunged through the cabin door in nightshirt and bare feet, and waded towards the companionway leading to the upper deck.

Gradually, the *Beagle* began to slew round. The anchor cable had run right out to the clink, and the lashed-on spar, acting as a huge rudder, was pulling her stern round into the wind. Sulivan took in the scene at a glance, his white nightshirt flapping madly in the wind. One or two crewmen froze in astonishment. Was this the ghost of their former captain, come to claim their souls?

FitzRoy froze too, but for different reasons. *I'm not running a damned kindergarten here, you young idiot! Get back inside!* He gestured angrily for Sulivan to retreat, but the youngster was not to be deterred. He had the best eyesight of any on the ship, and a lookout was needed. Barefooted, adrenalin dulling the vicious pain in the pit of his stomach, he sprang into the mizzen-mast rigging, and clambered up into the wildly swaying tops. Shorter and stouter than the other two masts, the mizzen-mast was the only intact vertical remaining on the *Beagle*'s deck. With the ship's stern into the wind, it would now be taking the brunt of the waves. In the circumstances, it was an almost suicidal place in which to locate oneself.

Sulivan did not have long to wait. The first really big sea to approach from the stern thundered up underneath the rudder, like a horse trying to unseat its rider. As the little brig's stern climbed towards the crest, her bow wallowed drunkenly in the trough. Broken spars and torn canvas shrouds cascaded down towards the bowsprit, some fifteen feet below the wheel. Then, with a smack, the wave broke over them from behind, punching the air from the sailors' lungs and flooding the main-deck to waist height. Such was the weight of water that the *Beagle* slewed off course, her stern drifting to starboard; and FitzRoy, Bennet and Murray fought the wheel, every sinew straining, to prevent her broaching. FitzRoy barely dared look up at the mizzen-mast, but look he did, and there, sheened by lightning, was the wild, drenched figure of Sulivan, his face flushed with excitement, punching the air by way of a return greeting.

Another mighty sea came billowing over the stern, and another, and it became clear to the exhausted men at the wheel that they must soon lose their battle to keep the ship in line with the wind and the waves. All but one of the storm trysails were gone now, ripped into convulsing shreds by the banshee winds. With insufficient sail to guide her, it was only a matter of time before the *Beagle* slewed beam-on to the weather again.

FitzRoy fought to clear his mind. *If the steering chains or the rudder quadrant snap we're finished anyway.* He gripped the wheel ever more tightly with cold, shaking fingers. *We'll have to bring her head round into the wind. It's our only way out of this. I'll have to take a gamble with our lives.*

There must, he calculated, be about thirty-five seconds on average between waves. To bring the *Beagle*'s head right round would take longer than that. If she was caught beam-to between waves in her battered state, she would certainly be rolled over. But if she stayed where she was, with big seas breaking repeatedly over her stern, the end would only be a matter of time. FitzRoy took a decision. Prising his fingers from the wheel, he grasped the hatchet once more, fell upon the anchor rope, and severed the rudimentary rudder that was keeping her in position. Then he seized the wheel from the bewildered Murray and waited for the next wave. Lieutenant Kempe, long past understanding, stood like a statue, clinging bedraggled to one of the uprights of the poop rail. Little King, open-mouthed, sea-battered and frozen in shock, no longer a naval officer but a stunned child, seemed barely to know where he was.

Another big breaker reared up behind them. FitzRoy could not see it, but he felt his knees give way as the deck surged up beneath his feet. As it did so he swung the wheel down violently to his right. The ship yawed to starboard, surfing down the rising face of the wave as the wind caught the tattered remnants of her canvas.

Of course, thought Murray, who suddenly understood. FitzRoy had used the force of the wave to accelerate the *Beagle*'s about turn to gain her a few vital extra seconds. It was an extraordinary gamble, for as she swung round, she rolled exaggeratedly to port, almost on her beam-ends once more. The lee bulwark dipped three feet under water, all the way from

the cat-head to the stern davit. Foaming eddies of water
barrelled across the deck, thumping into the chests of the crew,
grabbing at their clothing, inviting them down into the depths.
The skipper's mistimed it. She's going down. The main-topsail
yard blew right up to what remained of the masthead, like a
crossbow fired by a drunkard who'd forgotten to insert a bolt.
Incredibly, tiny figures still hung from each yard-arm, tossed
about like rag dolls but somehow still clinging to braces and
shrouds. Up on the mizzen-mast, like a gesticulating lunatic
on the roof of Bedlam, Sulivan swung far out above the boiling
sea, the mast dipping so low over the water it seemed as if he
would be pulled under by the next wave.

But somehow, slowly, ever so slowly, the *Beagle* rose again,
her prow swinging, inch by inch, round into the gale. Water
sluiced through her ports as her decks emerged once more
from the angry foam. A flash of lightning illuminated the next
monstrous peak. It was some way off, but it was coming in
fast. The little ship seemed to be taking an age to manoeuvre
herself into the wind. FitzRoy could only pray now. *Come
round faster. For God's sake, come round faster.* It was as if the
little brig herself was rooted to the spot in fear. Imperceptibly,
she felt her way by degrees to port, painstakingly precise in
her movements, a frail, unwilling challenger turning to face a
champion prizefighter.

The lower slopes of the wave slid under her bow, feeling
her weakness, hungrily seeking the leverage to roll her over.
The *Beagle* began to climb, but she began to roll too. Higher
and higher she climbed; further and further she rolled to port.
And then the peak of the wave furled over the prow, to deliver
the final, killer punch. The *Beagle*'s bowsprit pierced the wave's
face at an insane, impossible angle; then she took the full
impact three-quarters on, a foaming maelstrom powering
unstoppably across her decks.

FitzRoy could see nothing. Surging white water filled his
eyes and mouth. He no longer knew whether he was facing
upwards or downwards. He merely fought for life, the breath

sucked from his lungs by the thundering impact of the wave. Was this it? Was this to be his death, here, off the South American coast, at the age of twenty-three? Then, suddenly, there was air, and with a wild surge of elation he knew that she was through, that the *Beagle* had gone through the wave, that she had come round into the wind.

And then he saw Sulivan, like an extra sail tangled in the mizzen-tops, screaming soundlessly and pointing to the stern. He followed the line of Sulivan's jabbing finger but there was nothing there, only blackness. Another big sea furled over the prow. The *Beagle* shuddered and backed off, but she had ridden the wave sufficiently to hold her course. By now Sulivan was positively frantic. FitzRoy's eyes tried to follow his wild signalling once again, and there, framed by an encompassing sheet of lightning, he saw what Sulivan had been trying to warn them of: the sheer rock face of Lobos Island, not eighty yards off the stern. Gesticulating for all hands to follow him, he lunged across the deck and fell upon the larger of the two remaining bower anchors, still attached to the ship by thick iron cables. Other crewmen fought with the second anchor, and with a clanking rush that in ordinary circumstances would have been deafening, but could barely be heard above the crash of the storm, several hundred pounds of cast iron disappeared over the side and into the water. The anchors bit immediately. Just how shallow the water was became apparent as another wave slammed into the prow, and the *Beagle* juddered back again, her hull actually scraping across the smaller of the two anchors as she did so. The chains began to pay out, and they could all now see the face of the island rearing behind them, maddened white surf thrashing about the rocks at its base. It was a matter of yards now. The *Beagle* shipped another towering sea, which forced them to give yet more ground, towards the solid wall at their backs. To have come this far, to have fought against such odds, only to be dashed to pieces against the shore!

Then, a shuddering sensation, which ran the length of the deck, announced that the cable had run to the end of its scope. Now it was up to the anchors to hold them. FitzRoy thanked God he had ordered the boatswain to inspect every link of her chains, and hoped to Christ that Sorrell had done his job properly. Another wave thumped into the prow, and all of them felt the rudder scrape against shingle; but the *Beagle* gave no more ground. As long as the cables did not part, they might yet be safe from destruction. FitzRoy stared back up into the mizzen-tops once more, hoping to acknowledge Sulivan's presence, hoping to let him know that he had saved them all, but there was no sign of life from the young midshipman.

Exhausted, every drop of energy spent, Sulivan clung, barely conscious, to the swaying rigging, a shapeless white bundle of rags flapping against the night sky.

'By the looks of it you were knocked about like peas in a rattle.'

Admiral Otway chuckled to himself, while FitzRoy wished he had moored somewhere else. Once more, he found himself standing to attention in the admiral's cabin, this time with the *Beagle* clearly visible through the sternlights. She did, he had to admit, look a sorry sight: not only was she battered almost beyond recognition, but what remained of her rigging was festooned with drying clothes and hammocks. Ragged wet sails hung limp from her booms.

'The locals say it was the worst storm for twenty years. You must have enjoyed a pretty half-hour.'

Half an hour? FitzRoy's mind reeled. It had felt like eternity.

'If you ask me, it's your own deuced fault, Mr FitzRoy, for cutting matters so fine.'

'Yes sir.'

'So, what damage to report?'

'Both topmasts were carried away, with the jib-boom and all the small spars. I didn't even hear them break. We lost the jib and all the topsails, even though they were in the gaskets. Two boats were blown to atoms – just shivered to pieces – and . . . and two men were drowned. Another two were crushed by a falling yard, and another badly cut by a snapped bowline.'

'A couple of matlows are neither here nor there. You can have some of mine. But the damage to the ship is more serious. You'll have to put into Monte Video for new boats and running repairs.'

Otway's tone mellowed, as he sensed FitzRoy's distress. 'Would you care for a glass of madeira? It's a devilish fine wine.'

FitzRoy demurred.

'Don't censure yourself unduly, FitzRoy. The *Adventure* was laid right over on her side and lost her jolly-boat, and she was safe in harbour. The *Adelaide* didn't go undamaged either. Sailors die all the time.'

'I don't understand it though, sir. The barometer gave no indication there was going to be such a blow.'

Otway grunted. 'Still taking the advice of the little gentleman and lady in the weather-box? That machine of yours is little more than a novelty, and the sooner you appreciate it the better.

"When rain comes before the wind,
Halyard, sheets and braces mind,
But if wind comes before rain,
Set and trim your sails again."

That's the only wisdom I've ever needed in thirty years.'

FitzRoy remained silent.

'Now. One other matter. This Midshipman Sulivan of yours. What sort of fellow is he?'

'He's a trump, sir. I never saw his equal for pluck and daring. He can be eager and hasty, it's true, and he is, well, not the neatest of draughtsmen. But I'd say there's not a finer fellow in the service, sir.'

'Excellent, excellent.'

'He's a Cornishman, from Tregew, near Falmouth. He has the most extraordinary powers of eyesight. He can see the satellites of Jupiter with the naked eye. He's also an exceptionally devout officer, sir.'

'What sort of "devout"?'

'Midshipman Sulivan is a sabbatarian, sir.'

A harrumph from Otway. 'Can't say I hold with evangelicals myself. The Church of England should be good enough for any civilized man. Still, he sounds just the fellow. A vacancy has arisen for an officer of the South American station to study for a lieutenant's examination back in Portsmouth. He can join the *Ganges* for a week or two, then transfer to the *North Star* under Arabin. She'll give him passage home. It's a splendid opportunity for the boy.'

FitzRoy bit his lip. 'Yes sir. Yes it is.' As weary and exhausted as he felt, the spirit drained from FitzRoy more profoundly than it had at any point during the previous evening's ordeal. They were taking away his only friend.

Sulivan found FitzRoy seated at the table of his tiny, sopping cabin, adrift on a sea of home-made charts and diagrams scribbled across salt-damp paper. The young man ducked his head to enter and rested his hand on the washstand; his body was still weak from the effects of dysentery.

FitzRoy gestured for him to sit. 'You are supposed to be in the sick list, Mr Sulivan. I'm surprised the surgeon has allowed you up and about.'

'He . . . I didn't really feel it necessary to tell him, sir. I'm really very much better.'

'You don't look it. But, as it happens, it was necessary for me to pay you a visit. The entire vessel owes you a vote of thanks for your bravery. Your foolhardy bravery, I should attest.'

Sulivan coloured. 'Not a bit of it, sir. That's why I came to see you . . . I felt you should know that the crew are saying you saved their lives. The officers and the men. Nobody else could have navigated us through that maelstrom.'

'I didn't save anybody's life. I cost two sailors theirs by my own incompetence.'

'That's not true!' Sulivan blurted out.

'At the first sign of those unusual cloud formations, I should have stood in to the shore, reefed the sails, struck the yards on deck and sat tight. I made a serious mistake.'

'You had orders to follow!'

'Orders set out a month previous, with no foreknowledge of the weather that was to befall us. I should have had the courage to act by my own initiative.'

'Orders must be obeyed. You know that – sir. You did the only thing you could do.'

'Did I? I misread all the meteorological signs. The state of the air foretold the coming weather, but I did not have the experience to diagnose it.'

'Nobody can foretell the weather, sir. It's impossible.'

'Come, come, Midshipman Sulivan. Every shepherd knows the value of a red sky at night.'

'Those are old wives' tales, surely.'

'I grant you they have little obvious basis in natural philosophy. But they are valid observations all the same. Look at this.' FitzRoy indicated a pencil sketch of what looked like a small white cheese wedged beneath a large black one. 'Remember the conditions before the storm hit us? Warm air blowing from the north-east, barometric pressure high, temperature high. Then the conditions when the tempest began – cold air from the south-west, the temperature right down, pressure collapsing. This white wedge is the warm tropical air from the north. The black wedge is the cold polar air from the south. The cold air was moving so fast it dragged against the surface of the land, so the forward edge of it actually flowed *over* the warm air and trapped it underneath. Hence all those giant clouds. And it trapped us underneath with it.'

Sulivan's mind raced to keep up.

FitzRoy's eyes were alight with enthusiasm. He flung out a question. 'What causes storms?'

'High winds.'

'No. High winds are the *result* of storms, not the cause of them. That storm was caused by warm air colliding with cold air. Where are the stormiest locations on earth?'

'The Roaring Forties. The South Atlantic. The North Atlantic . . .'

FitzRoy let Sulivan arrive at his own conclusion.

'. . . The latitudes where the cold air from the poles meets the warm air from the tropics?'

'Exactly. The barometer didn't get it wrong yesterday. I did. The barometer stayed high because we were at the front of the heated air flow just before it was overwhelmed by the colder air above.' Excited now, FitzRoy warmed to his theme. 'What if *every* storm is caused in the same way? What if every storm is an eddy, a whirl, but on an immense scale, either horizontal or vertical, between a current of warm air and another of cold air?'

'I don't know . . . What if?'

'Then it could theoretically be possible to predict the weather – by locating the air currents before they collide.'

'But, FitzRoy – sir, there must be a myriad uncountable breezes . . . The Lord does not make the winds blow to order.'

'Every experienced captain knows where to find a fair wind or a favourable current. Do you think the winds blow at random? Those two poor souls who died yesterday – was that God's punishment or the result of my blunder?'

'I know it was God's will.'

'Mr Sulivan, if God created this world to a purpose, would He have left the winds and currents to chance? What if the weather is actually a gigantic machine created by God? What if the whole of creation is ordered and comprehensible? What if we could analyse how His machine works and fore-tell its every move? No one need ever die in a storm again.'

'It is too fantastical an idea.'

'What if the elements could be tamed by natural philosophy? What if the weather is really no more than a huge panopticon? It's not a new idea. The ancients believed there was a discernible pattern to the weather. Aristotle called meteorology the "sublime science".'

Sulivan looked amiably sceptical at the notion that pre-Christian thinkers might have had anything valid to say about the Lord's work. 'But even if you could predict these . . . these air currents, how could you communicate with the vessels in their path?'

'What is the prevailing direction of storms?'

'From the west.'

'Why?'

'I don't know.'

'Neither do I. Perhaps it is something to do with the rotation of the globe. But if the winds and currents in one place could be logged and analysed, and the results sent hundreds of miles to the east . . . Think about it. The Admiralty can get a message from Whitehall to Portsmouth in thirty minutes by semaphore telegraph. Surely it might be possible to get a message to every fishing fleet in Britain in advance of any impending storm. Think of the lives that could be saved!'

'From the middle of the Atlantic? How?'

The runaway carriage of FitzRoy's enthusiasm came to a juddering halt. He laughed, and released his grip on the pencil that he had been waving about like a magic wand. 'I don't know.'

Sulivan grinned too, and despite his objections FitzRoy could see the excitement in the boy's eyes, dark and shining in his pale, drawn face. Not the excitement of discovery, but the excitement of friendship.

And then he remembered what he had to say to him. 'Mr Sulivan, I've been across to the *Ganges* to see Admiral Otway.'

The youngster grinned conspiratorially. It was as if their old friendship had been revived, refreshed, allowed to resurrect itself here in the private confines of FitzRoy's cabin. 'What did the old goose want?'

'The "old goose" wants to send you to England, to make of you a lieutenant.'

Silence. Sulivan froze in his seat as if a dagger had been plunged into his back. Eventually, he spoke. 'How did you respond?'

'I coincided with him. It is an opportunity you cannot afford to turn down.'

Sulivan's eyes filled with tears. 'No, you cannot. Hang me if I shall go—'

FitzRoy interrupted softly: 'Sulivan, I don't set up to disappoint you – I am as wounded as you are. But this is the best step for you, as we are both well aware. I would not have acceded to his request without it were so.'

'I will not go.'

'Orders must be obeyed. You know that.'

Sulivan's face was sheened with wet. He dragged back his chair, raised himself to his feet and fled, the door slamming shut behind him.

With a heavy heart, FitzRoy returned to his meteorological calculations. The clouds that had advanced so menacingly on the *Beagle* had been hard-edged, like Indian-ink rubbed on an oily plate ... Hard-edged clouds always seemed to presage wind ... It was no use. He could not concentrate. He thought of putting down his pencil, and going in search of Sulivan. He need not have bothered, however, because a moment later a gentle knock announced that Sulivan had returned. 'Commander FitzRoy, sir. I wondered ...' Sulivan hesitated. 'When I first went to sea, sir, my mother made me promise to read from the psalms daily, and to pray the collect. I have never omitted that duty. She also gave me this. I have read from it every day.' He pushed a battered red copy of the scriptures across the captain's table. 'I'd like you to have it.'

'I cannot accept. Your mother meant for you to have it.'

'I'd like you to have it, sir. It would mean a deal to me.'

'My dear fellow, every lonely old captain on the seas turns to God or the bottle. It is considerate of you to drive me away from the latter prospect but ...' FitzRoy tailed off.

Sulivan summoned up all his resolve, more than he had required to climb the mizzen-mast during the previous night's storm, and addressed his captain. '"Be strong and of good courage; be not afraid, neither be thou dismayed: for the Lord thy God is with thee whithersoever thou goest." Joshua one, verse nine.'

And with that, tears stinging his eyes, he turned and left FitzRoy's cabin for the last time.

Chapter Four

Dungeness Point, Patagonia, 1 April 1829

The three motionless figures stood sentinel on the shore, drawn up on horseback in line abreast. Some twenty feet up the beach, a lone horse stood to attention, riderless, without a saddle, but perfectly still.

'They're Horse Indians. Patagonians.'

FitzRoy took the spyglass from Lieutenant Kempe. It was difficult to make out many details of the distant trio and their solitary companion, but it was clear from their attitude that they were an advance guard, posted to greet the ships.

'Whoever named this place Dungeness was spot on,' piped up Midshipman King. 'I've been to the real Dungeness with my father. This is the living spit.'

It was indeed. A deep indigo sea smeared against a beach of rounded shingle, backed by a low, thorny scrub. The sky was a pale cornflower blue. It could easily have been a beautiful, breezy autumn day on the Kentish coast, except for two crucial differences. First, the beach was dotted with penguins: fat, fluffy ones moulting in the sunshine, downy feathers floating off them like dandelion seeds puffed in the wind; and sleek, more confident black-and-white birds, slithering down to the sea on their bellies and launching themselves into the surf. The shallows were thick with bobbing penguin heads. The three statuesque sentries and the riderless horse, who provided the second aberrant note, now came into focus.

'Either their horses are very small, or the Indians are extremely big,' observed FitzRoy, squinting through the lens. 'The giants of Patagonia, perhaps?' he murmured.

'I beg your pardon, sir?' enquired Kempe.

'I've been reading about the Patagonians in one of Captain Stokes's books. A Jesuit missionary called Faulkner met one chief who was seven and a half feet high. Admiral Byron apparently met a man so tall he couldn't reach the top of the fellow's head. And Magellan reported giants here too. When he saw their footprints in the sand he exclaimed, *"Que patagones!"* What big feet. Hence the name of the place.'

'I can't say we ever encountered any that big, sir, but they certainly average more than six feet. You should converse with Mr Bynoe, sir. He's interested in the savages.' Kempe's tone made it clear that he found Bynoe's interest a trifle eccentric.

Midshipman Stokes attracted FitzRoy's attention. 'The *Adventure* is signalling, sir.'

All hands looked across to King's vessel, a hundred yards away across a field of white horses, where a line of little flags was in the process of being hoisted. King was back in charge now, with the admiral gone to do His Majesty's business at Monte Video, and would remain so for the rest of the expedition.

'Captain King wants you to lead a shore party, sir.'

'Very well. Mr Bennet, if you'd care to prepare the whale-boat and select six men. We'll need firearms and ammunition. And ask Mr Bynoe if he would be good enough to join us.'

'I'll go below and get the medals ready, sir,' offered Kempe. 'Medals?'

'Presents for the savages. They have a moulding of Britannia on one side, and His Majesty on the other. Savages love shiny things, sir.'

'I am told you are something of an anthropologist.'

Bynoe's earnest young face flushed slightly. They were bouncing towards the shore in the *Beagle*'s whaleboat, pulled along by six pairs of wiry arms. 'I wouldn't say that, sir. That is, I'm interested in all areas of natural philosophy but I have no great learning. Stratigraphy is what really interests me, sir, but I know so little.'

'Well, you've had ample opportunity to study the coast of Patagonia as it hasn't changed one whit these last thousand miles. How would you diagnose it?'

Bynoe stared across at the featureless plain that stretched hundreds of miles into the interior, which found its end here at the southern tip of Dungeness Point. There were no hills to break the monotony, no trees, not even a solitary thicket. There had been only salt flats, low, spiny bushes and tufts of wiry, parched grass since the last white settlement at the Rio Negro; and no sign of life either, other than a few grazing herds of guanaco and the occasional disturbed, flapping ibis. 'It's not very interesting, is it, sir? Well, not to the other officers. They don't reckon it much of a hobby to have the steam up about a lot of rocks.'

'Is it not part of the officers' duties to take a keen interest in the surrounding landscape?'

'Well, yes, I suppose so, sir, but that rather became pushed to one side when we reached Tierra del Fuego. Conditions are so tough there. It's just me interested now, sir – and Mr Bennet, of course, sometimes.' Bynoe hastily added the last part, having noticed a cloud of panic pass over the coxswain's normally sunny countenance.

'And your stratigraphic diagnosis?'

'I'd say there were three layers to the coastline, sir. Gravel on top, then some sort of white stone – maybe a pumice, I don't know – then a layer of shells in the ground. I've had a look on a shore expedition. I couldn't identify the white stone but I'll tell you a curious thing about the shells. They're mostly oyster shells, but there are no oysters hereabouts. So it looks as if the oysters have become extinct since the shell beds were laid down.'

'That's very good, Mr Bynoe, very good indeed. Has it occurred to you that the central white layer might also consist of shells, but shells that have been crushed to a powder and compressed into stone?'

'Crushed by what, sir? There's only a thin covering of gravel above.'

'By the action of the water, perhaps. Why is the land hereabouts covered in salt flats? I would hazard a guess that this country was once submerged under a great many feet of seawater. A sudden inundation, perhaps, that deprived the oysters of the oxygen needed to sustain their life.'

'By Jove, sir, I do believe you've got it!'

'I wouldn't go that far, Mr Bynoe. I am only hazarding a guess, but tell me what you know of our friends on the shore there.'

'They'll be from the settlement at Gregory Bay, sir. We stopped there in 'twenty-seven. They're led by a woman called Maria, who speaks a little Spanish. The Horse Indians have been trading with the sealing-ships for hundreds of years, so they're well used to Europeans. I doubt we'll be needing those.' He indicated the Sea Service pistols, the bag of shot, the wad cutters, rammers and the box of flints in the bottom of the boat.

'A few hundred years ago they were hostile, and armed with bows and arrows. Sarmiento built two settlements, called San Felipe and Jesus. I believe there were three hundred settlers at Jesus, but the Indians left no survivors. Then in San Felipe there were about two hundred settlers, who starved to death for the most part. There were only fifteen left when Thomas Cavendish sailed by. They being Spaniards, he . . . well, he put the rest to death. He renamed the bay Port Famine. You can still find a few ruined walls in the beech forest. It's where Captain Stokes took his life, God rest his soul.'

'We must thank God that we live in civilized times.'

'Absolutely, sir.'

FitzRoy sat back. Inquisitive penguin heads surrounded the boat now, craning to look over the side as it passed, then darting forward to the prow to get another look. On the beach, the three sentries were close enough to examine in more detail. There were two men and a woman, tall, muscular and broad-shouldered, each over six foot in height, with long, luxuriant black hair divided into two streams by metal fillets at the neck. What was visible of their skin was dark copper, but their faces were daubed with red pigment and divided in four by white crosses, like the flag of St George reversed. Their flesh was further ornamented by cuts and perforations. Their noses were aquiline, their foreheads broad and low beneath rough black fringes. The woman's eyebrows were plucked bald. About their shoulders they wore rough guanaco-skin mantles, the fur turned inwards. They were armed with bolas and long, tapering lances pointed with iron. They carried an air of lean strength and wary pride. Their horses, by contrast, were small, woe-begone, shaggy creatures, controlled by single reins attached to driftwood bits. Rough saddles and spurs cut from lumps of wood completed the rudimentary trappings. For FitzRoy, the comparison with Don Quixote was irresistible.

As the whaleboat scrunched into the shingle, scattering penguins, he stepped lightly ashore. One of the horsemen broke ranks, trotted forward and gravely handed him a stained piece of paper. He unfolded it with what he hoped was comparable gravity and read:

'To any shipmaster:
From Mr Low, master of the *Unicorn* sealer.
I write hereunder to emphasize to him the friendly
disposition of the Indians, and to impress him
with the necessity of treating them well, and not
deceiving them; for they have good memories,
and would seriously resent it.

I beg to remain Sir
Wm. Low
Master, the *Unicorn*
6 February 1826

FitzRoy refolded the paper and returned it with a nod that indicated he had understood. The horseman spoke in a low, guttural language – rather as if his mouth was full of hot pudding, thought FitzRoy – and produced a spare guanaco skin from under his saddle. Leaning forward, he proffered it to the Englishman. FitzRoy could smell him at close quarters, a deep, pungent animal smell.

'*¿Agua ardiente?*' the man asked, in Spanish. FitzRoy shrugged his shoulders to indicate that he had none. '*Bueno es boracho.*'

'*¿Habla español?*' FitzRoy asked.

'*Bueno es boracho,*' the man repeated. *It's good to get drunk.* With that he turned and galloped away with his two companions. The lone, riderless horse further up the beach remained, as before, utterly motionless. Only then did FitzRoy and Bynoe notice that the animal was quite dead. And, furthermore, that it had been stuffed.

'They've gone without their medals,' murmured Bynoe.

Dungeness was drawing round to the *Beagle*'s quarter when the ship caught the first gust of the howling gale that blows perpetually through the Straits of Magellan. Funnelling through the narrows, where the rocky banks are so close that it seems as if a passing vessel cannot but scrape her spars against one side or the other, the winds exploded from their constricting bottleneck and swept at high speed across the shoals and sandbanks of Possession Bay. Windbound, with topmasts struck, the *Beagle*, the *Adventure* and the *Adelaide* approached the narrows in tight formation, jinking delicately between the underwater obstacles: not just sand and rock, but huge tangled gardens of giant kelp, whose strands can grow to twenty fathoms long in just fifty feet of water.

'Apart from the westerlies, there's an opposing tidal stream of eight knots,' explained Kempe. 'The tide here is above seven fathoms. Last time out it took us more than a week to get through the first narrows.'

FitzRoy was painfully aware that, as the lead vessel of the formation, the *Beagle* must be first to attempt the narrows. She was already making ever shorter tacks in an attempt to zigzag against the headwind and the current. It was hard to see how she could possibly manoeuvre through the pinched opening ahead in the face of such a gale. At least the crew were putting their backs into the process of tacking. The lower sails were clewed up and the lee braces slackened, while the weather braces became the lee braces and vice versa, and the whole process began again. It was back-breaking and repetitive work, and for every ten yards they gained against the wind, nine were lost to the current. The sailors sang as they hauled.

'When beating off Magellan Straits, the wind blew
        strong and hard,
While short'ning sail two gallant tars fell from the
        topsail yard;
By angry seas the lines we threw from their weak hands
        was torn,
We had to leave them to the sharks that prowl around
        Cape Horn.'

'I do wish they wouldn't sing that particular shanty,' FitzRoy murmured.

'They have a song for every occasion,' said Lieutenant Kempe, with his death's head smile.

'Would it please you if I started off a different one, sir?' offered Boatswain Sorrell.

'No, thank you, Mr Bos'n. I do believe I should be well advised not to interfere in such a matter.' FitzRoy made a mental vow. *I will not let the elements dictate to me this time around. I will make my own luck.*

As the afternoon wore on the *Beagle* made repeated attempts to tack through the narrows, but a breakthrough proved impossible, and eventually the weary afternoon watch had to admit defeat. During the dog-watches of the early evening the *Beagle* stood off the narrows instead, making short tacks merely to stand still, the wind too strong for her to heave to and drift. As the sun settled, the breeze finally fell away, and the dusk was dotted like starlight by the fires of the Indians along the northern shore. The curious shrill neighs of the guanaco herds sounded from far off in the darkness. Where the deck had earlier been a scene of frantic, sweaty activity, now the dim light from the binnacle illuminated only the men at the wheel. The night lookouts took up their positions at the four corners of the ship. FitzRoy, frustrated, stalked the starboard side of the poop deck. 'We could have made it through the narrows in this light breeze.'

'It's too dark now sir,' said Bennet, self-evidently, eager to please. It was his turn at the wheel.

'If there's a seven-fathom tide flowing eastward through the narrows during the afternoon,' pondered FitzRoy, 'then presumably it flows back west during the night.'

'I suppose so sir.'

'And this dip in the wind speed. Does it occur every night or is it an aberration? Last time you were here, trying to fight your way through for a week, did the wind speed drop every evening?'

'I can't rightly remember, sir.'

'Mr King, fetch me Captain Stokes's weather book, if you please.'

The youngster scurried off importantly, and returned with the volume. The late captain's weather book did not really do justice to its title. It was supposed to contain all the readings of the day and the hour – wind direction and force, sympiesometer and barometer values, air and water temperatures, latitude and longitude readings – but the details recorded were sporadic at best. On this occasion, however, fate had been kind. There, in the entry for December 1826, with early-voyage enthusiasm, Captain Stokes had recorded calm evening after calm evening at the blustery exit of the First Narrows.

'Pass the word for the bos'n,' ordered FitzRoy. Duly summoned, Sorrell scurried on deck. 'Mr Sorrell, bare poles, if you please.'

'B-bare poles?' Sorrell could hardly believe his ears.

'You heard me, Mr Sorrell. Furl all the sails. We are going to ware through the narrows under bare poles. There's eight knots of tidal stream that will take us through.'

'But it's pitch-black, sir.'

'The current can see where it's going, Mr Sorrell.'

'But we could hit a shoal, sir, or – or—'

'Surely you are not questioning Mr Bennet's skill at the wheel?' A grin from Bennet found an answering smile. 'Those who never run any risk, who sail only when the wind is fair, are doubtless extremely prudent officers, Mr Sorrell, but their names will be forgotten. I do not intend the name of the *Beagle* to be forgotten.'

'Lord preserve us. Aye aye sir.'

Sorrell piped the order to a disbelieving crew. There was activity, too, on the *Adventure*, where King and his officers came to the side with nightglasses to try to make out what was afoot on board the *Beagle*. Across the water came the characteristic creaks of the capstan turning, as the soaking anchor cable began its journey up the maindeck and back into the cable tier, the ship's nippers darting here and there to straighten its passage as royal pages would shepherd home a sozzled master. Almost silently by comparison, the great dark sheets of the sails were furled up into the yards, revealing a mass of glittering stars through the *Beagle*'s rigging. And then, slowly, she began to drift on the tide, gliding between the shoals, riding the stream towards the dark gate ahead.

Nobody made a sound on the *Beagle*'s decks as she slid through the chasm, the coxswain at the helm applying the deftest touch here and there to keep her aligned with the current. The rocks to either side appeared as misshapen silhouettes, black spaces where the starlight had been sucked away into nothingness. All ears were strained for the sound of tearing copper or splintering wood that would presage disaster. It never came. The *Beagle* ghosted through the narrows with some elegance, as if guided by an invisible pilot.

After perhaps twenty minutes the hemming rocks on either side took a step back, conceding defeat, and the channel widened out into the flat bowl of Gregory Bay. As the narrows gradually fell astern, it seemed that nobody would dare be the first to speak. Finally, Bennet broke the silence. 'Well *done* sir,' he breathed.

'What *will* my father say?' wondered King.

Out on the gloom of the maindeck, some unknown voice raised a hurrah.

'Three cheers for Captain FitzRoy!' And the crew gave a rousing hip-hip hurrah that brought a broad smile of relief to FitzRoy's face, and set the dogs barking out by the campfires on the northern shore.

A week later, the *Adventure* and the *Adelaide*, their crews no doubt flogged with exhaustion, were still battling miserably to break the wind's stranglehold on the narrows. From the maindeck of the *Beagle* it was possible to catch occasional glimpses of them tacking back and forth at the entrance, desperate to force a passage but unwilling to emulate FitzRoy's risky experiment. The delay was becoming a matter for concern, as only two days' supply of fresh water was left on the *Beagle*, the rest being sealed and stored in the *Adelaide*'s barrels. There would be plenty of fresh water further south, amid the glacial streams of Tierra del Fuego, but here there was precious little: water was the one commodity that the Horse Indians were reluctant to trade. There was no shortage of food, however, and the crew had dined on fresh guanaco meat, mussels and limpets, and an unfortunate pig brought from Monte Video, which had been killed and roasted. The cook had even proudly announced the preparation of a special feast for the captain, of baked shell-pig, in honour of his navigational daring: FitzRoy had eaten the entire baby armadillo upside-down in its carapace. To ward off scurvy, the men had been sent to gather cranberries and wild celery, much to the mystification of the Indians, who seemed to subsist entirely on a diet of lukewarm guanaco meat without suffering the slightest ill effects.

FitzRoy had also dispatched the officers to record their surroundings, dividing them rather arbitrarily by subject on the basis of any slight inclination or aptitude he had been able to discern. Bynoe had been appointed ship's stratigrapher; Midshipman Stokes, who was revealed to have been a keen huntsman in his native Yorkshire, became the *Beagle*'s naturalist; the new surgeon, Wilson, rather reluctantly took on the role of collecting and recording sea life; Kempe was put in charge of all meteorological observations; FitzRoy himself concentrated on the anthropology of the native peoples. Midshipman King, desperate to become involved, was appointed general assistant to everybody. No animal, fish or shellfish could be eaten until it had been logged, examined and recorded on paper, preferably in colour. FitzRoy's cabin was already disappearing under piles of King's badly illustrated fish. Stokes had made the startling conjecture that the two types of penguin they had seen, distinguished as Patagonian and Magellanic penguins under the 'Aptenodytes' section of the ship's natural encyclopedia, were actually adult and young forms of the same bird. The Indians of the Gregory Bay settlement were becoming used to the sight of FitzRoy and his officers poking about their tents and asking questions using sign language: strange, inquisitive white men, quite unlike the seal-catchers, who only wanted to trade, or purchase women. The investigators from the *Beagle* had also solved the riddle of the stuffed horse: the animal marked the grave of a *cacique*, or chief. All great men, it was discovered, were buried sitting up in the sand, with their favourite horse stuffed and mounted facing the spot, to watch over them.

'Mr Kempe says that the savages are a different species from us. On account of their dark skin.'

'Does he, indeed.'

FitzRoy had taken Bynoe, who seemed to be the most intelligent and eager of the officers, on another tour of the Indian camp.

'Whereas Mr Wilson says they are the same as us. They are only brown because of the smoke and ochre particles incorporated into their skin.'

'With all due respect to the surgeon, I feel that the absence of a qualified natural philosopher on board leaves us all somewhat in the dark.' Really, this was too much. Even King's fish paintings put such nonsense to shame. But the racial origins of the Patagonian tribes presented a conundrum: why were the Horse Indians such wiry giants, while a few miles to the south, across the water in Tierra del Fuego – the *Beagle*'s eventual destination – the Canoe Indians were by all accounts sleek, fat midgets? Every day posed new questions that FitzRoy was desperate to answer.

The Gregory Bay encampment smelt like a penguin colony. Groups of Indians sat amid their tents, spindly affairs constructed from brushwood stakes and guanaco skin, which shuddered in the strong breeze that gusted off the bay yet somehow managed to stay upright. One circle of men passed round a clay pipe; another group played cards with painted squares of guanaco skin; a woman, naked but for decorative smears of clay, grease and animal blood, breast-fed an eight-year-old child. All ignored the two white men. FitzRoy selected an isolated group of three, whom he found sitting in a huddle, combing each other's hair and munching any lice they found. He reached into his pocket and drew out three of the fruits of European technology: a whistle, a small music-box and his pocket watch. The whistle produced delight; the music-box, curiously, was of little interest; the ticking of the watch, however, left the Indians both fascinated and thunderstruck.

Good relations established, Bynoe produced a notebook and pen from his satchel.

'*¿Habla español?*' asked FitzRoy.

The men looked blank. The sailors had found few people at the camp who spoke any Spanish. The celebrated Maria appeared to be absent.

FitzRoy resorted once again to sign language. 'Englishmen.' He pointed to himself and Bynoe. One of the Indians heaved himself on to his haunches. His face was dramatically daubed with animal blood and charcoal streaks, an apparently martial design offset by the laconic manner with which its owner now produced a fist-sized block of salt and helped himself to a large bite. Eventually he spoke. '*Cubba.*'

'*Cubba?*'

Another bite of salt.

'*Cubba.*' White men.

They had the first entry for FitzRoy's dictionary. 'Indians.' He gestured to the trio.

'*Yacana.*'

Bynoe made another entry. The Indians were incurious about this: they appeared to know no system of writing or hieroglyphics. FitzRoy pointed at the tents. These were '*cau*'. A dog was a '*wachin*'. A fur mantle was a '*chorillio*'. And so on, until Bynoe had some fifty everyday words listed.

Now FitzRoy changed tack, and pointed across the bay to the southern horizon where a heaving swirl of grey cloud masked the rain-soaked mountains of Tierra del Fuego.

'*Oscherri.*'

With a flat hand, he gestured to indicate a short man from '*Oscherri*'. A Canoe Indian. The men laughed derisively. '*Sapallios.*'

One spat into the dust. Others of the tribe had gathered round to watch now, and FitzRoy noticed that one individual wore a tiny crucifix on a chain round his neck, presumably a gift or trade from the sealers. He pointed it out, and gestured at the sky. It was time to widen his linguistic horizons.

'God,' he said, adding a quick mime of thunder and lightning for good measure.

The man nodded that he understood.

'*Setebos.*'
FitzRoy gripped Bynoe's arm in excitement.

*"His art is of such power
It would control my dam's God Setebos."*

'Mr Bynoe – that's Caliban, from *The Tempest*! If Shakespeare employed such a word in 1611, it must have been furnished by a matlow from Drake's expedition – perhaps even by Drake himself!'

The Indian with the crucifix began to speak, jabbing a finger at FitzRoy, then indicating the heavens to the west. Bynoe offered a diagnosis. 'I think he's asking if we've been sent by God. Or if we know God.'

FitzRoy shook his head at the man, but it seemed to make no difference. The Indian beckoned for the two Englishmen to follow him, and the crowd parted to show them a way through.

'Let us follow this Caliban, and see where he takes us,' suggested FitzRoy.

And so, obligingly, they allowed themselves to be led across to a nearby tent. The flap was pulled aside, releasing a thick plume of smoke, and they crawled in. A brushwood fire occupied one corner, which poured smoke into the interior of the tent, although there appeared to be no means for it to escape. Through red eyes they made out a frightened, naked woman crouched over the prone figure of a sweating baby, which was daubed with clay. On the other side of the sick child, a priest or medicine man was waving a rattle in the air, and muttering prayers or incantations over a neat pile of dried bird sinews. He looked at the new arrivals with resentment.

'They want us to cure the child,' breathed Bynoe.

'Then by good fortune they have invited the appropriate person into their tent. What can you do?'

Bynoe placed his palm across the child's forehead.

'It seems to be a simple fever, sir. Normally I'd recommend a calomel purgative. Failing that, a draught of hot port wine and a wintersbark tonic. I have tonic and wine with me – the port is cold, but it could be heated easily enough over the fire.'

The young assistant surgeon decanted a measure of port into a small glass vessel, which he laid briefly in the embers, before administering it to the shivering patient. Then he slid the draught of wintersbark down the child's throat. It was accepted with a hiccuping cough. Coughing himself at the thickness of the woodsmoke, and wiping his streaming eyes on his sleeve, FitzRoy gave quiet thanks for the efficacy of modern medicine. The two phials were passed round the crowd of Indians which had assembled at the tent flap, most of whom took an exploratory sniff. A faint murmur of scepticism seemed to pass among them. Finally, the owner of the crucifix – the father, perhaps? – indicated that he would like to borrow the captain's pocket watch. FitzRoy obliged. The man took the watch reverentially, and passed it back and forth across the child's face. The loud ticking filled the tent, seeming to still the buffeting breeze outside, and a whisper of approval passed between the Indians. *If only they knew how useless that is*, thought FitzRoy.

A steady, sleeting rain had set in by afternoon, persisting into the evening, and blotchy watercolour clouds obscured the fires on the shore. As usual the breeze died with the passing of daylight, enabling the *Beagle* to let go its anchors; the hustle and bustle of the afternoon was replaced by the ceaseless, soothing rattle of the chain cable as it passed back and forth over the rocks below. The officers had spent the afternoon teaching the alphabet to the illiterate men. Then FitzRoy had ordered painted canvas awnings to be set up to keep the decks dry, for the official 'song and skylark' period during the last dog-watch. Conducted by the ship's fiddler, this was a compulsory session of hornpipes and sarabands for the entire company, by order of the Admiralty. As Bynoe earnestly explained, the increased blood-flow generated by dancing helped to combat scurvy.

A perfunctory divine service had rounded off the afternoon's activities. FitzRoy's prayer was a standard fair-weather

imprecation, but the theme of the Noachian flood had served
to bring together the concerns that occupied his mind:

> 'O Almighty Lord God, who for the sin of man didst
> once drown all the world, except eight persons, and after-
> ward of thy great mercy didst promise never to destroy
> it so again: we humbly beseech thee that, although we
> for our iniquities have worthily deserved a plague of rain
> and waters, yet upon our true repentance thou wilt send
> us such weather as that we may receive the fruits of the
> earth in due season; and learn both by thy punishment
> to amend our lives, and for thy clemency to give thee
> praise and glory; through Jesus Christ our Lord. Amen.'

Now FitzRoy paced the damp decks, a solitary figure, trying
to thread together the Patagonians, the beds of extinct shells
and the events of the Old Testament into a coherent whole.
Who for the sin of man didst once drown all the world. Was this
the deluge that had crushed a million shells to white powder
on the Patagonian shore?

The night watches had been colder of late, as the freezing
Falklands current brought the sea temperatures plunging, and
he pulled his oilskin about him. Below decks, everything had
been battened down to keep the warm tobacco fug trapped
inside. Through the streaming skylights, smoky oil-lamps
swung invitingly on their gimbals. In the fetid, sweaty atmosphere, the men talked about life and drowning and money and
women. FitzRoy paused as he paced by the messroom skylight
where the sound of Master Murray telling a joke issued forth
clearly into the night.

'So Smith, who stutters, is on the tops'lyard. And he shouts
to the mate below, "Me w-w-whatnots are j-j-jammed in the
block of the reefing tackle." "Yer what?" shouts the mate. "I
said me w-w-whatnots are j-j-jammed in the block of the
reefing tackle." So the mate shouts, "If yer can't speak it, me
bucko, sing it." So Smith sings out, clear as you like,

'"Slack away yer reefy tackle, reefy tackle, reefy tackle,
Slack away yer reefy tackle, me whatnots are jammed!"'

A pent-up explosion of masculine laughter greeted the final
lines, and FitzRoy was overcome with a desire to join in, to bathe
in the atmosphere of camaraderie and warmth. He descended
the after companionway and opened the messroom door; but
the instant he did so, the atmosphere died as if asphyxiated.

'Good evening, sir,' said Murray politely.

'Evening, sir,' from Bynoe.

Drinks were hastily put down, and pipes and snuff were
laid on the table. Stokes was there too, and Wilson and Kempe.

FitzRoy did his best to muster an urbane smile. 'Good
evening, men.'

'Anything we can do for you, sir?'

'No, thank you, Mr Stokes. I am much obliged. I merely
came by to thank you most kindly for all your efforts today,
and to bid you all goodnight.'

'Thank you, sir. Goodnight, sir.'

'Goodnight.'

And with that FitzRoy withdrew, outwardly unruffled, but
inwardly smarting that he could make such a fool of himself.
On the *Thetis* or the *Ganges*, of course, he would have been
part of such an evening's entertainment; not by any means the
most gregarious part but an integral part nonetheless. Now he
was excluded by his rank. That was the way of the world, and
he must accept it. Never again must he entertain such absurd
emotional disarray. *I may guide them and shepherd them through
difficulty and help them learn, but I cannot engage with them. I
am not allowed to be their friend.* He shut the messroom door,
crossed the planks, and made his way into his own cramped
cabin. There he sat at his table, lit a lantern and drew the salt-
stained volume of Admiral Byron's voyages from the shelf.

Byron had been shipwrecked in Tierra del Fuego on the
Wager half a century before, one of four to make it home to
England from a ship's company of some two hundred men.

Something FitzRoy had read in Byron's account stirred in his memory now, and he leafed restlessly through the pages to find it. There it was:

> 'What we thought strange, upon the summits of the highest hills were found beds of shells, a foot or two thick.'

Beds of shells. On the summits of hills. Higher than those on the Patagonian shoreline. Higher than the salt crystals of the inshore salinas. Shell beds actually on the summits of hills. He took down the copy of the scriptures that Sulivan had presented him, and turned to Genesis 6: 7:

> 'And the Lord said, I will destroy man whom I have created from the face of the earth; both man, and beast, and the creeping thing, and the fowls of the air; for it repenteth me that I have made them.'

Was this not proof, then, of Genesis? How else did shell beds come to be on mountaintops, unless the mountains themselves had been inundated by floodwaters? There had been just eight survivors, according to the weather prayer. Had eight survivors really repopulated the entire planet? His eyes were drawn across the page, as if invisibly guided, to Genesis 6: 4:

> 'There were giants in the earth in those days . . . mighty men which were of old, men of renown.'

Giants in the earth in those days. The giants of Patagonia? Eagerly, he began to devour the verses that followed, dealing with the repopulation of the earth by Noah's sons Shem, Ham and Japheth: how Shem begat the Semitic people, how Ham begat the Egyptians and Libyans and Cushites – the blacks – and how Japheth begat the Greeks, Parthians, Persians, Medes and Romans. How, a generation or two later, Esau married a daughter of Ishmael and begat the copper-coloured men. The red men of Patagonia and Tierra del Fuego.

Why, then, the disparity in height between the seven-foot Patagonians and the tiny fat Fuegians they so despised? The Fuegians apparently resembled the Esquimaux and Laplanders of the north. Perhaps the exposure to cold, wet and wind, the long winters cocooned in their tents, had shortened the legs of the Fuegians and increased their body fat. Perhaps the Patagonians, like the Swahili tribesmen of Africa, had grown tall and wiry because of the fine climate, the flat terrain and the enormous distances they had to cover in following the herds. Was it really possible that humans, originally cut from the same divine template, had adapted into a score of different varieties at the behest of the climate and of their surroundings? He had so much to discuss, and no one to discuss it with. He would have given so much, at that moment, to engage in conversation with a skilled anthropologist, mineralogist, or even a priest. Did Noah, he wondered, have anyone to converse with? How unimaginably great would have been the pressures of a divine command!

A commotion outside woke him from his reverie, and there was a knock at the cabin door. It was Boatswain Sorrell, perspiring slightly. 'If you please, sir, I think you may care to come up on deck.'

FitzRoy ducked out of his cabin and leaped up the companionway to the maindeck. It took his eyes a moment or two to adjust to the darkness, but he could already guess what had transpired from the sounds of cheering about him. Across the bay to the east, two small dark shapes had emerged from the gloom and the drizzle of the first narrows. After a week of fruitless, back-breaking toil, the *Adventure* and the *Adelaide* had taken a leaf out of FitzRoy's book, and had slithered through the rocky gates – thankfully unscathed – on the tidal current.

Chapter Five

Desolate Bay, Tierra del Fuego,
4 February 1830

'Are there any news, Mr Kempe?'

'None, sir. The search parties have found no traces.'

FitzRoy clamped his teeth in exasperation. Murray was now more than a week overdue. He had taken a party in one of the two whaleboats to survey Cape Desolation and the south-western side of the bay. Their provisions would have run out four days ago. It was a wild, surf-pounded coast, exposed to all the moods and frustrations of the Pacific Ocean, which made it all the more dangerous for men in a small open boat.

Up to this point, everything had gone as smoothly as FitzRoy could have hoped. The ships had sailed south from Gregory Bay towards Tierra del Fuego, the scenery changing dramatically as they did so. Ahead of them stood a battalion of sombre mountains, their sides plunging sheer into the sea, their summits white-capped, shrouded by mists and swirling storms. Gloomy beech forests, some of the trunks a good twelve or thirteen feet across at the base, clung in a tangled, yellow-green mass to the leeward shores. Wherever one looked, the mountain wall was riven with inlets; islands dotted its feet, mere crumbs of stone, as if the cliffs had been hewn by a giant with an axe. Here and there, in isolated coves, slender crescents of shingle provided the only flat land. Low clouds raced and tore themselves into strips against the bare rock. Once, just once, through a ripped coverlet of grey, a glittering, frosty peak had revealed itself, towering above its fellows. This was the awesome 'Volcan Nevado' recorded by Pedro Sarmiento in the sixteenth century. Captain King had seen it too, in the early days of the expedition, and had renamed it Mount Sarmiento. Nowhere in all this forbidding vista was there any sign of life. If the inhabitants of Tierra del Fuego were observing the ships, they gave no indication as yet of their presence. Instead, the dark channels that sliced through the mountains appeared to lead beyond the confines of the world of men, to the far ends of the earth.

King had split the three ships up. He had turned east in the *Adventure*. Skyring in the *Adelaide* had been sent into the labyrinth ahead, to explore and map the Cockburn channel as it wound between sheer rock walls to the south coast. FitzRoy in the *Beagle* had been ordered to follow the Straits of Magellan, turning west at Point Shut-up, then beating north-west towards the Pacific. There were inlets and channels leading off the north side of the straits, recorded a half-century before by Byron, Wallis and Carteret, that still had not been explored, surveyed or named; or, as in the case of Point Shut-up, renamed. They would keep the mountain wall of Tierra del Fuego to their port side, tacking up into the westerlies, while they explored the flatter, barren tundra of southern Patagonia to starboard. FitzRoy was looking forward to the task with enthusiasm; the only sour note was that King had transferred Bynoe to the *Adelaide*, where Skyring was in want of a surgeon, leaving FitzRoy to the conversational mercies of Mr Wilson in his place. Once again he had been denied the company of a potential kindred spirit.

He had sought solace in the solid efficiency of Midshipman Stokes. Crop-haired, compact and muscular, the Yorkshireman

belied his eighteen years with a performance of almost metronomic reliability. Once an order had been given to Stokes, it
could be safely forgotten. Swiftly, he became FitzRoy's most
trusted surveyor. Although taciturn by nature – he was not one
for a messroom chat about the finer aspects of stratigraphy or
anthropology – he was unfailingly even-tempered, and stuck
by his captain through thick and thin.

As autumn had turned to winter, FitzRoy and Stokes – the
former commanding the whaleboat, the latter towed behind
in the yawl – had set out with a month's supplies to investigate the Jerome Channel, a narrow opening on the north side
of the strait. They were well prepared: every man in their party
carried a painted canvas cloak and a south-wester hat like a
coal-heaver's cap. In the absence of fresh food they packed the
boats with tin canisters of Donkin's preserved meats, which
made an agreeable mess when mixed with the occasional wild-
fowl – any bird unlucky enough to have delayed its winter
migration found Stokes an unerring marksman. But despite
all FitzRoy's precautions the weather tested their powers of
endurance to the limit. Sometimes icy rain would set in for
days; in the mornings their cloaks would be frozen hard about
them. The winds whipped up short, awkward seas, which
frequently threatened to capsize them, and made it impossible
to land in the high-breaking surf; on occasions they had to
row all night just to keep the two boats aligned with the waves.

Then there was the time-consuming, exhaustive work of
the survey itself. This was modern, scientific map-making, not
the broad guesswork of old. Soundings had to be made in every
bay using the yawl's leadline, while the whaleboat foraged in
the shallows rudder up, making transects with the lead line at
various angles. At every land station, heavy theodolites had to
be manhandled up hills, small portable observatories had to be
set up, and the ship's chronometers had to be rated. It was a
thankless task, but the men set to it with vigour.

And what discoveries they made. To their astonishment, the
Jerome Channel widened out into a vast inland sea some sixty

miles wide, hitherto unsuspected, which FitzRoy named Otway Water. A side-channel was named Sulivan Sound in honour of his departed friend; the celebrated Mr Donkin's preserved meats were commemorated at Donkin Cove, while bays were named after Lieutenant Wickham of the *Adventure* and FitzRoy's sister Fanny. At the far end of Otway Water, a narrow, twisting passage opened in the hills, which led, astonishingly, to another vast inland sea sixty miles long by twenty miles across. Frozen blue Niagaras of ice marked its western terminus, riven by serrated channels, where improbably shaped icebergs barged and jostled each other with silent grace. FitzRoy named this second reach Skyring Water, in honour of that gentleman's steadfast good humour in accepting his situation. Their provisions ran low before they could ascertain whether or not there was any exit from Skyring Water to the sea; so they made their way back to the *Beagle*, their thick winter beards streaked with ice. FitzRoy himself had lost two toes through frostbite; but no man had uttered a word of complaint, and their commander burned inside with a fierce pride. He would turn the *Beagle* into the best, the most efficient survey packet the Royal Navy had ever sent forth.

The rest of the winter had been taken up with following the straits to their conclusion, searching for channels in the cold rain and sparse daylight. Sulivan had been remembered again at Cape Bartholomew; King had been commemorated thrice in one vista at Cape Philip, Cape Parker and King Island. They had seen seals teaching their pups to swim, supporting them with one flipper, then gently pushing them away into deep water to fend for themselves. At a dark reach lined by black cliffs, now for ever entered into posterity as Whale Sound, Boatswain Sorrell had screamed 'Hard a-port! There are rocks under the bows!' which had revealed themselves instead to be a passing school of humpback whales. The beasts had accompanied the ship for some miles before peeling off to the south, at which juncture one had performed a graceful leap of farewell across the *Beagle*'s stern.

The human inhabitants of the straits had revealed them-selves rather more cautiously at first. Not that they could hope to hide themselves from the strangers – far from it. The contin-uous fires – the most precious possessions of each Fuegian family, which were never allowed to go out – signalled their presence on the hillsides in the dark of night, like ascending banks of church candles. Theirs was a world revealed by dark-ness, when their dogs barked and their drums spoke. In the daytime the Indians fell silent, and followed at a careful distance in their boats. These canoes were curious, collapsible little vessels, sewn together from tree bark and invariably split into three sections: women, children and dogs in the rear, the women paddling; men at the front, armed with sticks, stones, wooden spears or daggers, the points beaten from shipwrecked iron; and taking pride of place in the centre, the divine, unceasing fire on its bed of clay. Alongside the fire, invariably, green leaves would be piled high for making smoke signals, so that the *Beagle*'s progress was tracked and monitored by all as she passed slowly up the straits. Occasionally, naked men would come to the shore in brave little clusters, shouting the single word '*Yammerschooner!*' and waving ragged pieces of skin at the strangers; but whenever FitzRoy put down boats to establish contact, the Indians would flee into the trees long before the shore party made the beach.

These men were nothing like the 'noble savages' of Patagonia. They were short, round, oily creatures, four feet fully grown, who seemed to spend as much time in the icy water – which could not have been more than a degree or two above freezing – as they did on land. They could hold their breath for several minutes at a time, before emerging from the cold black depths with the mussels and sea-eggs that seemed to comprise the bulk of their diet. It was hard to connect them with any other tribe on earth. Indeed, they seemed more like porpoises than men. They were, thought FitzRoy, like a satire on humanity.

At Mount de la Cruz, in that part of the western straits

that Cook had christened 'The Land of Desolation', they made contact. A group of men appeared furtively on the shore, waving skins and shouting, '*Yammerschooner!*' as ever. One was painted white all over, another blue, another bright red. The rest were daubed with white streaks. FitzRoy gave orders for the ship to pull in to shore. It had been sleeting heavily for days, her yards and rigging were icebound, and the men's fingers were blue with cold. The *Beagle* pirouetted slowly round, like a fat ballerina. Despite the temperature, the natives on the shore were quite naked, except for the occasional tattered fox pelt thrown about their shoulders.

Bennet squinted through a spyglass as the Indians began to jabber and gesticulate excitedly.

'My eye! That crimson fellow reminds me of the sign of the Red Lion on Holborn Hill.'

'Red, white and blue,' pointed out Kempe. 'They've run up the Union flag to greet us.'

'It looks a regular crush on that beach, my boys,' laughed Murray. 'Do you reckon that shore is Terra del's equivalent of a fashionable saloon?'

'And what would you know of fashionable saloons, Mr Murray, hailing from Glasgow?'

A chuckle ran around the poop deck.

'Do you think I could hit him from here?' pondered King, raising his gun to the port rail. 'That would light a fire under the red savage's tail!'

'Put that down!' snapped FitzRoy. He strode across the deck, eyes blazing, and grabbed the weapon. 'What the deuce do you think you're about?'

'I'm sorry, sir.' King was smarting, bewildered. 'I was only going to fire over his head, sir. You should see the savages scoot, sir, like ducks. It's funny, sir. Captain Stokes always permitted gun amusements, sir. I wasn't really going to shoot him, sir.'

'So I should think not. They are not animals, put on God's earth for our sport! I'm ashamed of you, Mr King.'

'But – but they ain't human, sir.'

'They most certainly are men, just as you or I. Unfortunate men, maybe, forced by accident of circumstance to inhabit this Godforsaken spot, but they are our brothers nonetheless. They do not look like us because their physiognomy has adapted itself to the cold and rain. Were I to cast you ashore, Mr King, and were the good Lord to take pity on your soul and spare your life, then within a generation or two your progeny would very likely be short, plump and jabbering away like the lowliest Fuegian.'

'But it doesn't mean anything – does it, sir? Those noises they make?'

'How do you know? To the best of my knowledge, no Dr Johnson has ever taken the trouble to compile a dictionary of their language. An omission I intend to remedy personally. Instead of waving a loaded gun about the maindeck, Mr King, you would be better advised to improve your intelligence of such matters. I suggest you consult the scriptures, commencing with the Book of Genesis.'

With that, FitzRoy turned on his heel and stalked away, leaving a silence both uneasy and amused in his wake.

'They say the bottle is a strict master,' murmured Lieutenant Kempe, 'but the good Lord is far stricter, and no easier to turn aside from.'

They put the boats down, but by the time they reached the shingle, the natives had fled. In a clearing amid the first few trees of the wood, they found abandoned wigwams: not the spindly, elegant constructions of the Patagonians, but clumsy, squat affairs made from branches, leaves, dung and rotten seal-skins piled into rounds. Carefully, FitzRoy positioned two empty preserved meat canisters at the entrance to one of the tents, then withdrew.

The next few hours, all that remained of the short southern day, were spent climbing to the frost-shattered summit of Mount de la Cruz to survey the land around. Even though the peak was only two thousand feet above the shore, it was a hard slog. All of Tierra del Fuego's lowlands seemed to be covered by a deep bed of swampy peat: even in the forest, the ground was a thick, putrefying bog, overlaid with spongy moss and fallen trees, into which the party frequently sank up to their knees. Finally, they reached the sleet-scoured rock above the treeline, took their round of angles, and left a soldered canister – containing a crew list and a handful of British coins – beneath a cairn for posterity.

When they clambered back down to the beach, there was still no sign of the Fuegians, but the canisters were gone. FitzRoy took another two, placed them in the same location, and retreated to the edge of the clearing. Then, with the exception of Midshipman King, he sent the sailors back to the boats. With precautionary pistols loaded, he and King sat on their haunches, their breath condensing in the evening gloom, and waited silently for night to fall.

After a long, cold half-hour, the dark rectangles between the tree trunks were brought into focus by smoky torches. There was a whispering in the forest, a strange, guttural confection of clicks and throat-clearings. King, nervous, edged closer to FitzRoy. Finally, the red-painted man appeared at the far edge of the clearing, tentative, wary. They could see him better now. He had the eyes of a Chinee, black, slanted at an oblique angle to his nose, which was narrow at the bridge but flattened at the point, where his nostrils flared against his face. Beneath these two black holes his face was split in two by an exceptionally wide, full-lipped mouth. His teeth, bared in his nervousness, were flat and rotten, like those of a badly tended horse; no sharp canine points disturbed their even brown line. His chin was weak and small, and retreated into the thick muscular trunk of his neck. His shoulders were square, his upper body tremendously powerful under its broad coating of fat, weighing down on the short bow legs beneath it; his feet were turned inward, his toes levelled off in a perfect rectangle. As the Indian paused, considering flight, FitzRoy could see that the backs of his thighs were wrinkled like an old man's; presumably from a lifetime of squatting on his haunches. He was like no other creature, man or beast, that FitzRoy had ever seen.

The Fuegian advanced slowly and cautiously towards the two canisters, keeping his eyes on FitzRoy and King throughout, inching forward until his fingers closed on his prize. His fellows watched from behind tree trunks and flaming brands, poised for a general evacuation. But just as he was about to dart for the safety of the woods clutching his reward, FitzRoy spoke in a calm, clear voice: '*Yammerschooner.*'

The man bared his horse-teeth again, not from nerves, this time, but in a smile. Then he seized the two canisters and darted back a pace or two, but stayed poised there, half lit on the edge of the clearing.

Slowly FitzRoy extracted a box of Promethean matches from his pocket, with a small glass bottle containing the ignition mixture of asbestos and sulphuric acid. He unscrewed the lid and dipped the match head into the liquid. It ignited instantly, and a gasp ran round the clearing to see fire flare so mysteriously from one end of a tiny wooden stick. FitzRoy held the flaming Promethean aloft.

'*Yammerschooner*,' he repeated.

Curiosity overcame the red-painted man's fear, and he edged forward.

'Mr King,' whispered FitzRoy, 'do you have any tobacco about your person?'

'Yes sir.'

'Slowly now.'

Gingerly, King removed his tobacco pouch from his pocket, extracted a pinch and held it forward.

'*Tabac, tabac*,' said FitzRoy. It was a word the Patagonians had learned. Perhaps it had filtered this far south as well. Certainly the sight of the dried leaves seemed to interest the Fuegian. A few clicks with his tongue and he beckoned the white-painted man and his blue colleague into the clearing.

'He's got something in a sack, sir.'

The white-daubed Indian was indeed holding a sack sewn from animal skin, which appeared to be wriggling in his grasp. The man edged forward, gestured eagerly at King's full tobacco pouch, then opened the sack to reveal the wet eyes and bemused face of a month-old puppy. From the Indian's gestures it was clear that he wanted to trade.

'Shall I give him the tobacco, sir?'

'Well, we might benefit from a ship's dog. Why not?'

King poured the tobacco into the proffered sack, keeping the leather pouch back for himself, and took the puppy from the Fuegian by the scruff of its neck. There were friendly grins all round.

King, however, wrinkled his nose in disgust. 'The stench is frightful, sir.'

It was indeed. On close inspection, it became clear that the Indians, as well as decorating themselves in outlandishly bright colours, had smeared their naked bodies from head to toe with an insulating coat of rancid seal fat. King had to restrain the puppy from licking its former owners.

'Keep smiling, if you can bear to,' said FitzRoy, through a fixed grin.

The white-painted man gestured for the pair to enter the wigwam. King looked enquiringly at FitzRoy, who nodded, and they crawled beneath the tent-flap, into a close, dark world, which reeked of stale smoke and rotting sealskin. The men followed, extinguishing their flaming brands, and more men after them, then women and children, until the tent was heaving with Indians, and curious faces filled the triangle left at the open flap. Brushwood was brought, and before long the wigwam was filled with leaping flames and eye-watering clouds of smoke. Again, FitzRoy mounted a match-lighting demonstration to the amazed crowd, before making a present of box and bottle to the red-painted man.

'Prometheans,' he said.

'Prometheans,' repeated the Fuegian, remarkably accurately. FitzRoy placed a finger to his own chest.

'I am Captain FitzRoy.'

The red man pointed to his own chest and repeated gravely: 'I am Captain FitzRoy.' The watching crowd in turn indicated themselves and murmured that they, too, were Captain FitzRoy.

FitzRoy smiled, genuinely this time, and gestured to indicate King and himself. 'Englishmen,' he announced, and then, pointing to the red man, he added: 'Indian.'

'Englishmen,' repeated most of the Fuegians, each indicating his or her fellow, before pointing out FitzRoy and announcing, 'Indian.'

'Did you fetch the notebook?' FitzRoy asked King, whereupon a chorus of Fuegians also enquired whether King had fetched the notebook.

'They're first-rate mimics, sir. It's why nobody has ever learned their language,' King explained, handing the book across.

'Why nobody has ever learned their language,' added a small boy.

'They're first-rate mimics, sir. It's,' said a fat lady helpfully.

'Look,' said King, shoving a finger up one nostril and crossing his eyes.

'Look,' repeated the Fuegians, and every Indian in the tent pulled the same face.

'This is getting us nowhere,' sighed FitzRoy.

'This is getting us nowhere,' sighed the blue man.

So FitzRoy took the pen, and started to sketch a nearby woman instead. Eagerly, the Indians gathered round to look. A reverential silence settled upon the tent. Emboldened, FitzRoy produced his handkerchief and wiped the white streaks from the woman's face. She did not object, but adopted the air of a dignified hospital patient. When the sketch was finished, to general approbation, FitzRoy was rewarded by his model, who ornamented his face with white streaks in turn. There were murmurs of approval all round.

Food was brought: mussels, sea-eggs, yellow tree-fungus

and a huge slab of putrid elephant seal blubber two and a half inches thick. This last item reeked more fiercely – if such a thing were possible – than any of the inhabitants of the tent. The Fuegians took it in turns to heat the blubber on the fire until it crackled and bubbled, before drawing it through their teeth and squeezing out the rancid oil. Then the slab was passed on so that the next person might repeat the process, all of them expressing exaggerated delight at the richness of this delicacy. Finally, the blubber was offered to King.

'I would refrain from trying that if I were you, unless you wish to spend the next fortnight clutching your stomach in the heads,' remarked FitzRoy, to a chorus of imitations.

Both men politely declined the offer, which seemed to cause not the slightest offence. The blubber slab was passed instead to a small child, whose mother tried ineffectively to hack off a piece with a sharpened mussel shell. FitzRoy drew his knife and came to her assistance, an action that drew gasps of admiration – not for his gallantry but for the razor-sharp blade he had produced. Making beseeching noises, the white-painted Fuegian who had traded the dog for King's tobacco now indicated that he wished to have the knife as a gift. FitzRoy demurred: it would not do, he reasoned, to start arming the natives.

A general consultation followed, and with great reverence a wicker basket was produced for FitzRoy's benefit. He opened it. Inside was a sailor's old mitten, and a fragment of Guernsey frock.

'These are regular museum pieces,' breathed FitzRoy. 'They must be all of a century old.'

'I wouldn't give a farthing for them,' snorted King under his breath.

Encouraged by the apparent show of interest, the white-painted Indian patted his stomach enthusiastically, then patted FitzRoy's stomach and chest in a show of friendship, but to no avail. Still the Englishman would not trade. Rebuffed, the Indian left the tent in some dudgeon, whereupon the nocturnal silence outside was interrupted by curious thrashing and beating sounds, as if the would-be trader was laying about the nearby vegetation with a switch. After a minute or two he returned, flushed but evidently pleased with whatever he had done. FitzRoy and King were on the point of dismissing the episode as just one more of the evening's inexplicable curiosities, when the man suddenly lunged forward, grasped the knife from its sheath on FitzRoy's belt, and hurled himself at one wall of the tent. The skins on that side gave way immediately, and the white-painted man was gone, away into the night air by means of the passage he had just created. *Of course. How could I have been so foolish?* FitzRoy admonished himself. *He has built himself an escape route while we sat here like two idiots.*

The other Fuegians in the tent now flinched in fear, as if afraid that the Europeans might lash out and strike them, as a punishment for the misdeeds of their fellow. But so nonsensical was the whole episode that FitzRoy burst out laughing instead, as much at his own stupidity as at the antics of the thief.

'I think we can overlook the loss of one case-knife in the circumstances,' he conceded, and King concurred gratefully.

The evening had not delivered its last surprise, however. Within a quarter-hour the man had returned, painted black this time, his hair fluffed up wildly, and without a grass pleat that had previously functioned as a headband. FitzRoy, astonished, jutted out a hand to demand the return of his knife. Assuming an expression of aggrieved innocence, and with much headshaking and shoulder-shrugging, the Indian endeavoured to indicate that he had no idea what the Englishman was talking about.

'Extraordinary,' murmured FitzRoy to King. 'He thinks that this disguise – for such we must presume it – has fooled us thoroughly.'

'Extraordinary,' agreed a nearby woman.

'Fooled us thoroughly,' added the blue-painted man.

'They're like a crowd of little kids,' scoffed King.

The newly blackened Indian went on the attack now,

shouting angrily at King, pointing at the puppy and demanding its return. He was sweating profusely in the fire-heat, FitzRoy noticed, as were all the Indians, even though they were naked and the outside temperature had dropped below freezing.

'I feel it would be best if you returned the dog,' he whispered to King.

'But the savage has got all my tobacco, sir.'

'On this occasion, the better part of valour is discretion. Let us take our leave.'

So they bade farewell to the assembled throng, and made their way down to the boats by moonlight, expertly parroted quotations from *Henry VI Part 2* ringing in their ears.

As winter had given way imperceptibly to spring, the *Beagle* had finally battled its way up to the Pacific, where the three boats had made a rendezvous once more. This time King had ordered the *Adelaide* north, to explore the galaxy of tiny islands which constituted the coast of Araucania, while the *Beagle* had been sent south, down the storm-beaten west coast of Tierra del Fuego, a maze of islets, rocks, cliffs and fierce breakers. Ceaselessly they probed for channels, close-working against the wind and tide amid howling blizzards; it was, as FitzRoy wrote in his log, 'like trying to do a jig-saw through a keyhole'. He had become as bearded, wiry and weatherbeaten as his crew, but he prided himself that their morale had stayed high, and that not one man had been lost to disease or sickness.

After the disaster of the Maldonado storm, the barometer and sympiesometer had proved reliable watchdogs, warning them to find sheltered anchorage ahead of the worst gales, and no further crew members had been lost to the elements. It was not the same, he knew, on board the other ships. Mr Alexander Millar of the *Adelaide* had died of inflammation of the bowels, and both vessels had as many as a quarter of their people in the sick lists. The *Beagle*'s only casualty had been Mr Murray, who had slipped on a wet deck and dislocated his shoulder, in a bay that had subsequently been named Dislocation Harbour; the master had since made a complete recovery.

Slowly the map of the west coast had taken shape. They had discovered Otway Bay, Stokes Bay, Lort Island, Kempe Island and Murray Passage, and had successfully climbed Mount Skyring, a peak discovered by the *Adelaide* in the Barbara Channel the previous winter. The rocks on the summit had been so magnetic as to render FitzRoy's compass useless; he had reason once more to regret the absence of a stratigrapher on board. What if there was mineral wealth waiting to be discovered in the mountains of Tierra del Fuego? There had been shell beds, too, on Mount Skyring. Was this further proof of the Biblical flood? As he dined in his cabin on soup and duff, the rain lashing against the skylight, he wrestled alone with these great questions.

January – high summer, although it was hard to discern any difference from the southern winter – had found the *Beagle* warping in and out of Desolate Bay; a risky process, with the ever-present danger of losing an anchor, but nonetheless safer than trying to close-manoeuvre a square-rigger in such a confined space. She had anchored at last in a narrow road, and boats had been sent out to survey the barren granite hills of Cape Desolation. FitzRoy and Stokes, their work done, had made it safely back to the ship. Now Murray and his men were missing. The search parties had found no sign of a sail. Had Murray struck a rock and drowned? To lose so many men . . . It simply did not bear thinking about. FitzRoy shivered, turned up his collar against the rain, shut his eyes momentarily against the stress, and steadied himself instinctively against the pitching of the deck. He headed for the companionway and the sanctuary of his cabin.

He was awakened just after six bells of the middle watch by his steward pounding on the door. 'By your leave, you'd better come quickly, sir. There's a sail.'

FitzRoy fumbled for his watch. Ten past three in the morning. He grabbed his uniform, struggled into it and made his way up on deck. On the port side of the ship, lookouts with lanterns were straining their eyes towards a tiny, indistinct shape in the water. It most certainly wasn't the whaleboat. It wasn't a native canoe either.

Boatswain Sorrell, who had charge of the middle watch, was directing operations with more agitation than ever; he seized upon the advent of FitzRoy's authority with conspicuous relief.

'I called, "What ship?" sir, but the wind was too loud for them to hear – leastways, they never replied.'

'Send up a night signal, Mr Sorrell. A flare.'

'Aye aye sir. Which signal, sir?'

'*Any* signal, Mr Sorrell. Something we can see them by,' said FitzRoy, exasperated.

A moment later, the flare went up.

'Bless my soul,' exclaimed FitzRoy.

There, fifty yards off the port bow in a choppy sea, was some kind of . . . basket, roughly assembled from branches, canvas and mud, half full of filthy water. Inside, drenched, emaciated and shaking with cold, were three white-clad figures. The man at the paddle FitzRoy recognized from his hair as Coxswain Bennet. The other men, bailing furiously with their south-westers, were two of the sailors – Morgan and Rix, by the look of it. They were clad only in their flimsy cotton undershirts. How the ramshackle vessel had ever made it on to water at all, let alone half a mile out into the bay, was a complete mystery.

'Hoist out the cutter at once!'

'Aye aye sir!'

A burst of frenzied activity followed, and within five minutes FitzRoy was lifting the sodden, exhausted men aboard personally. Blankets were furled round them, and hot soup forced between chattering teeth. Concerned as he was, it was clear that FitzRoy could not afford to waste a second.

'What happened, Mr Bennet? Where is Mr Murray?'

'We were attacked, sir, by the savages. They stole the whale-boat in the night, with its masts, sails and all our provisions and weapons. Their vicinity was not at all suspected.'

'Were not lookouts posted, as I ordered?'

'I repeat, sir, that their vicinity was not at all suspected. Cape Desolation is a most remote location. They showed a most dexterous cunning, sir.'

'And this – this basket?'

'Morgan is from Wales, sir. They sail such baskets on the rivers there.'

'We call it a coracle, sir,' chipped in Morgan.

'Morgan constructed it from a canvas tent and some branches and mud. We volunteered to paddle it back to the *Beagle*, sir, but we were attacked by more savages – maybe the same ones, I don't know. They were armed with spears, and took our clothes. We have been two days and nights on our passage, sir, with only one biscuit each.'

'Good God, you poor wretches. But where are Mr Murray and the rest of the men?'

'Still at Cape Desolation, sir.'

'Then they must be rescued at once. Morgan, you have my congratulations and my heartiest thanks. And now we must get the three of you to the surgeon forthwith.'

Within a quarter-hour, the cutter had been fitted out with a fortnight's provisions, two tents, six armed marines and five hand-picked sailors: Robinson, Borsworthwick, Elsmore, White and Gilly, who had become the stoutest of loyalists since his first-day flogging. They pushed off at once, just as a few early grey streaks pointed up the horizon, into a dreary maze of splintered islets and black, surf-battered headlands. The wind being against them, they did not even try running up a sail: instead, seven hours' hard pull found them off the Cape, where the stranded survey party was easily spotted, huddled together on a cheerless beach. An almighty roar went up from the rescued men at the familiar sight of the cutter, and within a few minutes they, too, were being treated to soup and blankets.

The marines, meanwhile, fanned out and searched the island for the stolen whaleboat. They found deserted wigwams, a smouldering fire and half of the whaleboat's mast, which appeared to have been chopped apart with the boat's own axe. Perhaps inevitably, they found no other trace of the thieves or their prize.

'I'll order the surveying equipment stowed on board the cutter, shall I, sir?' enquired Murray cautiously, still unsure whether or not any blame was to be apportioned.

'That won't be necessary. The second whaleboat will be here soon, to furnish your passage back to the *Beagle*.'

'But what about the cutter, sir?'

'The cutter and its full complement, Mr Murray, is to go in search of the whaleboat that you have mislaid.'

Sarcasm aside, FitzRoy had decided not to pursue Murray's failure to post sentries. The missing whaleboat, however, was not a matter he could easily overlook.

'But it could be anywhere, sir. You may never find it in such a labyrinth. It may well have been scuttled until we've gone, or chopped up for firewood.'

'It is our duty to try. That boat is the property of His Majesty, which has been entrusted to our safe-keeping. Without it our surveying capacity is cut by one-third. Furthermore, it is our duty as emissaries of a civilized nation to teach these people the difference between right and wrong. We cannot simply sail away and let them keep it.'

'But there must be upwards of a hundred islands hereabouts, sir. We haven't even named most of them.'

'Then we shall remedy that omission on our passage. Have you christened this island yet?'

'No, sir.'

'Then we shall call it "Basket Island", in honour of Morgan's ingenuity.'

'Right sir. If you please sir — may I have your permission to accompany the search party?'

Murray was clearly exhausted, but if he wanted to atone for losing the whaleboat, fair enough.

'Permission granted, Mr Murray.'

Late afternoon found FitzRoy's party heading north-east across Desolate Bay, in the direction taken by Bennet's attackers. They made good progress, the sail filled out by a blustery breeze chasing in from the sea behind them. Ahead in the distance, the bay narrowed into a sound, a line of islands marking its north-western boundary. Behind these to the north rose ranks of snow-capped peaks, smothered for the most part by cloud; hidden somewhere among them was the mighty southern face of Mount Sarmiento. The cutter headed for the northern shore. The thieves were unlikely to hide on one of the outlying islands, FitzRoy reasoned, because their retreat might be cut off. More likely, they would have taken refuge in some cove or inlet. Murray and some of the others might have been sceptical of his plan, but with the cold spray biting his face, FitzRoy felt seized with optimism. The anxiety that the survey party might be dead had given way to a burst of exhilaration. This was, after all, why he had joined the Service as a child. Mapmaking was all very well, but he was twenty-four years old and – if one did not count the boarding of a rotting Brazilian gunship – he had never seen action. This might be his chance. His fingers closed instinctively around the pistol handle at his belt.

'There's a canoe up ahead, sir. They're making a run for it.'

The small black shape of a native canoe was visible against the grey hummocks of the islands off the port side. It was paddling for the safety of the shore with all haste; but the cutter's full sail and six enthusiastic oarsmen made for an unequal contest. The fact that the canoe was fleeing suggested to the pursuers that they had struck lucky right away. Within twenty minutes they had run her down, guns and swords arrayed in a powerful display, and had made the flimsy bark vessel fast to their own. Inside the canoe sat a Fuegian family, sullen, unmoving, staring at the European sailors. One of the women in the rear section was breastfeeding. It had begun to snow, thick white crystals whipping in on the breeze and melting against the sailors' faces. FitzRoy noticed that the snow did not dissolve on the Fuegians' skins: mother and child sat in a mute tableau, a white mantle slowly forming on the woman's breasts and the child's face.

'Search the vessel, Serjeant Baxter.'

Baxter and two of his marines stepped into the canoe, sending it wildly rocking, and poked with their rifles into mounds of mussel shells, brushwood and rotten seal meat. One sent the fireside pile of green leaves flying.

Silently intimidated, the Indians did not move. Hidden in the base of the leaf-pile was a curled section of the whale-boat's leadline.

'Well, well, well,' said FitzRoy.

'Well, well, well,' said one of the Fuegians helpfully, the first time that any of them had spoken. FitzRoy ignored him.

'We will take a hostage, Serjeant Baxter. It is what Captain Cook did when his cutter was stolen in the Pacific, and the boat was returned. Take one of the young men, who has no dependent wife or children.' He pointed out the youth on the near side of the canoe. 'Let him be given to understand that he must lead us to the whaleboat, if he values his liberty.'

With various gestures, mainly of the cut-throat variety, and much waving of the severed end of the leadline, the young man was given to understand that he had better co-operate. With a disarming eagerness, he climbed aboard and waved his captors north, between the row of islands, to a narrower, more confined sound that ran parallel to the first.

As they sailed into the unknown, a rough map began to assemble itself in their wake, its legends bearing hasty and literal witness to their passage: Whaleboat Sound, Cape Long Chase, Leadline Island, Thieves Sound. Finally, in the gloom of the mid-evening, spurred on by their eager hostage guide, they rounded a promontory and found themselves in full view

of a small Indian village: a cluster of wigwams, men warming
seal blubber around a circle of glowing embers, a woman
carrying water in a bark bucket, another sewing together two
sealskins, children playing naked in the icy shallows. The cutter
was upon the unwitting villagers almost before they had realized it. The men round the fire were first to react, jumping
to their feet and fleeing into the beech forest. A small child
ran terrified towards its mother, who seemed torn between
flight and the pull of maternity. As the boat slid rapidly
through the shallows, the red-jacketed marines were already
over the side and splashing through the low breakers in pursuit.
The woman fled. The child began to scream, incessantly,
standing forlornly in six inches of cold water.

'Are they not going in too heavy-handed, sir?' said Murray,
who looked worried. 'We don't even know if these people had
anything to do with the theft.'

There was a warning glint in FitzRoy's eye. 'Justice is not
always pretty, Mr Murray. One of the reasons these people live
in such a degraded state is that they seem to have no laws. Not
even the law of God – any sort of god. If we do not teach them
the difference between right and wrong, then who will do so?'

Murray remained silent. There was something odd about
the captain – something not quite right.

After five minutes, the marines had secured the beach, their
final tally of prisoners totted up at six women, three children
– including the screaming infant – and a man apprehended
sleeping in his tent. They had also discovered part of the whaleboat's sail, the boat's axe and tool-bag, an oar – already refash-
ioned into a short paddle – and the loom, roughly carved now
into a seal club. FitzRoy indicated the lone male, who was
squatting on his haunches, cowed and unsure.

'We appear to have apprehended one of the miscreants, and
six of their wives. Take that man hostage. He is to be our
second guide. We shall embark immediately.'

'Don't you think we should pitch camp ourselves, sir? It is
practically dark.'

'You would do well to keep your counsel, Mr Murray.'

Again Murray saw the strange light in FitzRoy's eye, and did as he was bidden.

Led now by two mysteriously enthusiastic guides instead of one, both grinning and gesticulating to the sailors to continue rowing north-east, the exhausted party reached the head of Thieves Sound just after nightfall. They had been battling the elements now for almost eighteen hours. Two tents were wearily improvised using the boat's sails, oars and a boat hook. The two hostages were invited to sleep on the shingle, under a tarpaulin that Murray had given them. FitzRoy, though, could not sleep: he felt alert and alive and suffused with excitement. Odd sensations stirred through his muscles and across his skin, as if his body was no longer his own. He paced the beach until dawn broke, listening to the waves lapping loud against the stones, turning over possible courses of action in his mind. At five o'clock, as the western hills took on the faintest rosy halo, he ordered the marine sentries to wake the sleeping sailors and the two hostages.

A moment or two later, as he stood staring fixedly out into the sound, there was an embarrassed cough behind him. It was one of the marine sentries. 'Sir. The prisoners have escaped, sir.'

'What?'

'The prisoners. They've escaped, sir.'

'I heard you the first time.'

FitzRoy strode angrily up the beach and threw back the tarpaulin. Two roughly human-sized mounds of stones were positioned where the two Fuegians had lain the previous night. Murray and Serjeant Baxter emerged blearily from the tent, just in time to inspect the damage.

'Serjeant Baxter, I thought I gave orders for night sentries to be posted.'

'I posted them, sir.'

'Then why were two Indians able to get up and walk away under their very noses, after first constructing these – these simulacrums?'

'I don't know, sir.'

Baxter looked daggers at the two sentries.

'And as for your confounded tarpaulin, Mr Murray, it became a cloak for all evils.'

'Were you not awake yourself, sir? Did you see nothing during the night?'

'You are insolent, Mr Murray!' snapped FitzRoy, eyeball to eyeball with the master. 'Hold your tongue or I shall have you flogged like a common sailor!'

There was a shocked silence. The wind tugged mischievously at the corner of the tarpaulin. The captain, it seemed, was a changed man.

'Pack and stow the tents. We shall embark in ten minutes. We shall return to the village forthwith.'

After four hours' hard rowing, the hungry sailors found themselves back at the Indian settlement, but it was deserted. FitzRoy himself felt no hunger, no exhaustion. He felt guided by instinct now, or by some unseen force, as if the world itself was leading him. It was as if he could see himself from the air, moving forward decisively, with conviction. Optimism roared within him. *It is my duty to do the right thing. My sacred duty. I must not fail. I simply must not fail in my duty.*

Three canoes lay drawn up on the beach.

'Burn their canoes. Then spread out and search the vicinity. We must find them.'

Silently, the odd exchanged glance their only sign of apprehension, the sailors and marines fanned out through the ragged beech forest.

After twenty minutes' walk, the trees thinned and gave way to a slope of rain-soaked bare rock criss-crossed with crevices and gullies. By signals and gestures, one of the marines indicated that he had seen something ahead. About eighty yards in front, a thin plume of smoke was drifting from a fissure in the rock. FitzRoy felt all his senses tensed, intensified, accelerated. *Others will one day see the path we have taken. They will chart the angles and shapes our footsteps have made, as surely as we chart the bays and islands. They will see that we have followed the only path.*

He called the search party together. 'They have taken refuge in that cave. We will attack them immediately. Robinson, Borsworthwick and Gilly, make your way to the right of the cave. Elsmore, White and Murray to the left. When you are in position, you will lay down an enfilade, whereupon the marines will launch a frontal assault. Make all haste.'

With pistols and cutlasses drawn, the sailors moved forward in their two groups, keeping to the concealment of the forest edge as closely as possible. About fifty yards on, however, a ferocious barking announced that they had been spotted, by the Fuegians' dogs if not by the Fuegians themselves. Some of the sailors shot questioning glances across to FitzRoy, who beckoned them urgently to proceed. Still there was no sign of life from the mouth of the cave. Fifty yards further, and the left-hand party found their progress blocked by a rushing stream some ten feet across, edged with muddy banks. FitzRoy beckoned them to cross. Seaman Elsmore, who was the foremost of the party, took a running jump in an effort to clear the stream at one bound, but lost his footing on the far bank and slithered back into the water. As he tried to claw himself back up the slope, his fingers dug helplessly into the slippery mud. Suddenly two squat figures appeared from behind nearby rocks, then another, and another. Clutching large, sharp stones as weapons, they fell upon Elsmore, raining blows upon his head. As he fought to free himself, a huge stone was brought down two-handed into his eye-socket, which disappeared in a welter of blood. Insensible, his body was held under water by two of the Indians. The others continued to batter him, crimson bubbles marking the last of the air leaving his lungs.

At the moment that Elsmore had been attacked, FitzRoy had raised his loaded pistol and fired. *God has brought us here. This is our destiny. We must not fail Him.* But the weapon had missed fire: the powder, soaked through on the journey, had failed to burn. The Fuegian with the large rock raised it above his head again, ready to administer the fatal blow. Then, there was a deafening powder explosion and the man staggered back, a look of complete astonishment on his face. Murray had shot him clean through the heart. But he did not drop his rock. Somehow, with speed, precision and a strength that appeared positively superhuman to his European adversaries, he hurled the stone straight at Murray. The blow knocked the master off his feet, and shattered the powder-horn that hung from his neck. It was the Fuegian's last act: abruptly, he pitched forward into the stream, dead before he hit the water. White was the first to arrive on the scene, pulling Elsmore back up the bank, cushioning his shattered face in his lap. Murray, only seconds behind, lifted the head of the dead Fuegian from the water by his hair. It was the second of the two hostages to whom he had given the tarpaulin the previous evening.

By now the other Indians were streaming out of the cave in fear, having witnessed the inexplicable and sudden death of one of their number. FitzRoy urged the marines forward, their weapons no longer necessary. Instead they fought to subdue the terrified Fuegians, who struggled with extraordinary strength. FitzRoy and Serjeant Baxter grappled with one slippery, brawny, barrel-bodied specimen, who – upon finally being manhandled to the ground, face flushed, eyes blazing – turned out to be a young woman of some seventeen years. Within a few minutes the contest was over, the majority of the Fuegians fleeing unhindered into the beech forest. There were eleven prisoners: two men, three women, and six children. The trophy count was far less impressive than before: merely a piece of the whaleboat's tarpaulin, vandalized into small squares to no discernible purpose.

Breathing hard, his uniform ripped, FitzRoy ordered the prisoners to be frogmarched down to the cutter.

'We will take the women and children on board the *Beagle* as hostages. Then the men will guide us to our missing whaleboat. The custody of their families will act as a security far stronger than rope or iron.'

The next morning the *Beagle* headed back south, out through the jaws of Desolate Bay, and round to Cape Castlereagh on the wave-lashed tip of Stewart Island. Fat, placid and apparently unperturbed in the sleeting rain, a gaggle of Fuegian women and children sat on the maindeck, gorging themselves on fatty pork and shellfish, swaddled in woollen blankets. They seemed profoundly undisturbed by the change in their surroundings, be it the staring Europeans or the waves that occasionally swirled among them, soaking their legs and haunches. At the prow the two male 'guides', as eager as their predecessors, urged the ship on with enthusiastic gestures and hand signals, apparently oblivious of the glorious mass of billowing sails above their heads. Crew members stood around bemused, unsure how to react to the invasion. Surveying operations, which had been carried out by Stokes in FitzRoy's absence, had now been suspended. Both the cutter and the remaining whaleboat were provisioned for a week, and ready to embark at a moment's notice. Lieutenant Kempe, who had charge of the forenoon watch, had assumed control of the *Beagle*'s steerage. FitzRoy, isolated, seemingly unable to communicate with anyone, paced the poop deck, a lonely figure grappling with his thoughts. *I must do the right thing by God. He has brought me to this place to do His will. I am not of Him, but He has created me. It is my duty to administer justice. To distinguish between right and wrong.*

They put the cutter and the whaleboat into the water in bitter drizzle at Cape Castlereagh, FitzRoy and Bennet in the former, Murray commanding the latter. Led by their two willing guides they came upon a scattering of deserted wigwams just before nightfall, the native fires still smouldering, and were rewarded with a small prize in the shape of the remaining half of the leadline. They erected their makeshift tents on the shore once more, their Indian guides wrapped in blankets on the beach beneath the open sky. This time FitzRoy did not pace the shoreline, but lay awake in one of the makeshift tents, wrestling with his disembodied thoughts. *I am doing the right thing. I am the only one who realizes this.*

At three o'clock he rose and left the tent, knowing that the Indians would be gone. Sure enough, two mounds of round stones lay under the blankets on the beach. He stood there, staring at the piles of stones and the thrown-back blankets, his senses crackling like sheet-lightning, every nerve-end tingling. The end of his journey to salvation was near now. He could sense it. Gradually, he became aware of a presence behind him. It was Murray.

'Mr Murray. Did I not order a watch to be posted over the prisoners?'

'No . . . you did not, sir.'

Neither man said a word. Finally, after a long interval, FitzRoy spoke: 'We must return to the *Beagle*.'

'Aye aye sir.'

Murray was looking at him oddly, FitzRoy could see that. Did the man not understand? Could he not see God's holy truth, staring him in the face?

The journey back passed in silence. The men at the oars were going through the motions now, rowing blindly and mechanically. Visibility was poor, and rain drove horizontally and ceaselessly into their backs and down their necks. It was a tired, sad and confused party that sighted the *Beagle* late on in the forenoon watch, a day after they had left it. Boatswain Sorrell came to the side, a look of woe on his face.

'Mr Bos'n. What news of your prisoners?'

'They are gone, sir. All except one, sir.'

'Gone? Gone where? We are in the middle of the ocean!'

'Gone over the side, sir. All three women and five of the children. Gone over the side like porpoises in the night, sir.'

FitzRoy grasped a manrope in each hand, and scaled the wooden battens on the *Beagle*'s heaving flank with uncommon agility. He hauled himself on to the deck and stood face to face with the quivering boatswain.

Lieutenant Kempe came across to intervene. 'There was nothing anyone could do to stop them, sir.'

FitzRoy looked at Kempe, and realized that his eyesight had become crystal clear. He could see the skin on Kempe's cheek, and the tiny lines on its surface in all their minute detail. All around him, the colours of the world were now so rich and deep that they seemed to resonate inside him.

'Don't you understand?' said FitzRoy.

Don't you understand? God has brought us here and announced to me my destiny. He has re-created me, an ordinary man, in His image. He has re-created me after His likeness. Can you not see that, Mr Kempe? Can you not see that?

The inside of the cabin was dark and silent. A faint rattling and creaking indicated that the ship was still at anchor. FitzRoy stirred. The worst of the night's terror had drained away now. Fear and dread had come in the dark, had choked him and mocked him, tugging his emotions this way and that, playing with him like a bird of prey with a mouse. But now they were gone, and shame and embarrassment flooded his mind, together with a terrible, crushing disappointment that the tiny glimpse he had been given, of something infinitely strange and wonderful, was now snatched away from him for ever. He opened half an eye, and the grimy skylight blurred into focus. He realized that a blanket had been laid over the outside, to keep his cabin dark. How long had he been lying there? How long had his madness lasted? The events of the previous days came flooding back now in all their hideous detail. *Dear Lord, what sickness possessed me? Please, God, what damage have I done?*

There was a knock at the door, and Stokes came in with a bowl of soup. FitzRoy shifted in the fusty darkness, uncoiling his stiff limbs within the frame of his tiny cot. After a moment or two he tried to speak. 'I have not been well.'

'No, you haven't.'

FitzRoy was glad that Stokes had abandoned the due military formalities for the moment.

'How came I here?'

'The coxswain and I fetched you. You was not right in yourself.'

'How long have I been here?'

'About thirty hours.'

'Is everything under control?'

'Everything is under control.'

'What news of Seaman Elsmore?'

'He will lose the sight of one eye, but he will not drop off the hooks. He is recovering of his wounds.'

'And the whaleboat?'

'We shall never see it again.'

What madness to think otherwise, FitzRoy realized.

'Am I better now?'

'I can fetch the surgeon if you so wish, but I would reason from your questioning that, yes, you are better now.'

'To whom do I owe apologies?'

'You are the captain. You do not *owe* apologies to anyone. If you so prefer it, you might have conciliatory words with Mr Murray, Mr Kempe, the bos'n . . .'

'Thank you.'

FitzRoy swung his feet gingerly to the floor. Every muscle in his body ached as if it had been pummelled repeatedly. Stokes raised a hand in mild protest. 'Do you not think it would be better to rest further? This kind of delusional fit . . . the surgeon seemed to think you might need a considerable period of rest.'

'No . . . no thank you, Mr Stokes. I feel that the madness is now behind me. But thank you most humbly for your kindness.'

Feeling grubby and sticky-eyed, FitzRoy pushed past Stokes and opened his cabin door. A marine sentry stood to attention, his expressionless face speaking volumes. FitzRoy inched unsteadily up the companionway and out on to the maindeck. A hushed silence greeted his appearance. Crewmen seemed to give ground imperceptibly as he made his way forward to the cluster of officers gathered at the wheel. Kempe was there, and King, and Murray, and Boatswain Sorrell.

'Mr Bos'n. It seems I owe you an apology.'

Sorrell bobbed unhappily. 'Not a bit of it, sir, not a bit of it. You was just unwell, that's all.'

'Mr Murray.'

'No trouble sir. As the bos'n said, sir. The south is tough on a man, sir.'

'Mr Kempe.'

'Please don't mention it, sir.' Kempe smiled his half-smile.

'I understand, Mr Kempe, that you have been in control of the *Beagle* during my absence. I am much obliged. I owe you a vote of thanks.'

'My privilege sir.'

'She has handled well?'

'She has handled well, sir.' Kempe paused. Whether he was enjoying the moment or was disturbed by it, FitzRoy could not tell. But there was evidently something more. 'Just one small matter to be resolved, sir.'

'Yes, Mr Kempe?'

'What are we to do with *her*, sir?'

Kempe gestured towards the binnacle box. There, playing happily with a makeshift rag doll, a wide, appealing smile on her face, sat the rotund figure of an eleven-year-old Indian girl.

Chapter Six

York Minster, Tierra del Fuego, 3 March 1830

'How are you feeling?' Surgeon Wilson leaned forward, narrowing the gap between them, shepherding as much sympathy and confidentiality as he could into the intervening space.

FitzRoy thought hard about the question. 'This morning . . . not very bad.'

Not very bad? Not very bad, when I must consider making an invalid of myself and resigning my command? Not very bad, when I have taken leave of my senses, when I have endangered my ship and risked the lives of its crew? Not very bad?

'Well, physically, Commander, I would say you are in extremely good keep.'

Indeed he was. FitzRoy's physical strength had never been in doubt. But it was no sort of weapon against whatever had assailed him, first a year and a half ago in the Brazilian sunshine and now here in the Stygian south. The original attack, back in his flag officer days, had been allowed to slip unlamented into the past, dismissed as an isolated incident, a mere oddity. But the wheels of time had now crunched suddenly to a halt, as if paralysed by fear: not just the constricting, terrifying panic that had served as the climax to each of the two attacks, but a groundswell of dread in the pit of his stomach that he knew would remain with him as long as he lived. Something primeval lurked inside him, something that frightened him because he did not know if he could ever exert authority over it. He had travelled to Tierra del Fuego to chart the wilderness, to list it and catalogue it, that it might be tamed and civilized; to bring the primordial darkness under control. But what of the darkness inside him, which waxed and waned and flexed its strength seemingly at will? Was that to be tamed? And what of the good Lord? Would God be his beacon against the darkness? Or was God punishing him for his presumption? Was this perhaps some sort of test, an examination of his faith? Had the darkness indeed been created by the light? He wondered if this was how Captain Stokes had felt, alone and afraid at the *Beagle*'s helm, rendered small and puny in the face of the mute, prehistoric wilderness all around, the deep-tangled forest that threatened to envelop him and pull him down into its consuming maw. *Please help me. Please help me, God. If not for me then for the sake of my men.*

'And you say you had no warning of the attack?'

'None. It took me quite by the lee.'

Wilson pursed his lips in a suitably diagnostic manner. A column of smoke from his pipe spiralled aristocratically towards the low ceiling of FitzRoy's cabin. But despite the surgeon's stiff-backed manner and the prematurely greying hair that lent an air of dignity to his prognostications, his rumpled and frayed uniform gave away the fact that he was anything but a medical expert at the top of his profession. This was a career naval surgeon going through the motions. FitzRoy did not hold out much hope of a cure. He felt, nonetheless, that he should ask the question that mattered most. 'I wonder if my illness will not unfit me for my command.'

'My goodness, no. This kind of morbid depression of the spirits is not unheard-of here in the south. Why, only last week one of the crew thought he had seen the devil. It turned out to be a horned owl. I have been a surgeon since ten years, and if I had a guinea for every time a man found himself in the dismals I'd be a rich man. No, Commander, we'll soon have you right as a trivet.' Wilson held his pipe at what he hoped was a reassuring angle to his teeth.

He hasn't got a clue how to deal with this, any more than I have. 'Well, Mr Wilson, I've dipped into my phrenology manual and tried a little self-examination in the mirror, but it's an infernally difficult and delicate business.'

The surgeon digested this information with a condescending smile. 'Ah, yes. They do say craniology is all the rage in London. I've never been a bumpologist myself. Bone up on this or that, and before one knows it, some other technique is in fashion. You know, I prefer to rely on more tried and tested prescriptions. My recommendation, Commander, is that you drink a glass of hot wine well qualified with brandy and spice twice a day, once upon waking and once before sleeping. Then I'd like you to take a Seidlitz powder with calomel after every meal. In due course, I think you'll find the purgative effect will rid you of all the impurities that have accumulated in your blood vessels during the course of the voyage.'

Seidlitz powders. Calomel. The basic, unthinking cure-alls in the top drawer of every journeyman apothecary.

'Will that be all, sir?'

'Yes, thank you, Mr Wilson. You oblige me with your kindness. I am most grateful to enjoy the benefits of your medical wisdom.'

Wilson ushered himself out. FitzRoy stood for a moment by the skylight, pensively. Then, in a moment of decision, he took the purgative powders and the companion phial of liquid that Wilson had left behind and emptied them into the icy shallows of the wash-hand basin.

The immense perpendicular tower of rock, named York Minster by Captain Cook for its uncanny resemblance to the celebrated cathedral, loomed threateningly over the port bow. Eight hundred feet high, jet black and guarded by lesser spires, it reared out of the sea, devouring all the dismal daylight it could and reflecting nothing back by return. FitzRoy took care to stand the *Beagle* well out to sea, despite the invitingly calm look of the waters at the base of the tower. Experience had taught him to avoid 'williwaws', the sudden hurricane squalls that could rush over the edge of a precipice, carrying with them a dense flurry of spray, leaves and dirt. Before one had time to react, a ship could be over on her beam ends, in the middle of a previously placid harbour. In fact they had lost their best bower anchor in yet another gale in Adventure Passage, the ship pitching bows under; but this storm had been accurately foretold by the barometer, so they had shortened sail by degrees in the face of its advance. The topmasts and yards had been struck well before the worst of the weather had hit, and there had been no further damage. The quietly ingenious carpenter, May, had even moulded a replacement anchor, in a home-made forge below decks. Subsequently, upon finding a large shipwreck spar thrown up on the shoreline, the carpenter had demanded to be left on a beach in Christmas Sound with a party of sailors, where he intended to construct a replacement whaleboat too – the local beechwood apparently leaving much to be desired as a boat-building material. FitzRoy could only marvel at the man's craftsmanship and utility.

Standing now on the raised poop, the captain scrutinized the torn, choppy sea in their path. About a hundred yards dead ahead, there sat a solitary Indian canoe, seemingly impervious to the waves that tossed it up and down, to all intents and purposes waiting calmly for the *Beagle* to run it down. He could just make out the occupants as they rose and fell, by turns visible and invisible behind the grey ridges of seawater. Was this to be a sequel to the episode of the stolen whaleboat? Or had the eighty miles of close-worked sailing they had put in since Desolate Bay taken them into another part of the Fuegian nation, where news of their running battles with the Indians had yet to percolate?

Any sense of relief that FitzRoy might have entertained at the prospect of putting that episode behind him were promptly punctured by the sound of a childish giggle at his feet. There, smiling coyly up at him, was the little round Fuegian girl, an ever-present reminder of his aberration. Her face was freshly scrubbed, her hair had been cleaned and tied in two neat bunches, and she wore a rather fetching patchwork dress, which had been fashioned by one of the seamen from rags found at the bottom of the slops basket.

'Shall I carry her below, sir? Is she getting in your way?' Boatswain Sorrell reached a hand down affectionately to the little girl.

'No, no, thank you, she's fine where she is. It is no trouble.'

'She's become a regular pet on the lower deck, sir. The men call her Fuegia Basket, sir, on account of Morgan's sailing basket.'

'Yes, I had heard that. It rather suits her. Has she picked up any English yet?'

'Not so as I could say, sir, but she can repeat anything you like straight back at you. She knows her lines as regular as a prayer-and-response.'

'Make sure everybody keeps trying. Then I'm sure she will soon get in the way of it.'

'Very good sir. She's a sweet little thing, sir, seeing as how them's little more than animals.'

'Quite so, Mr Bos'n.'

FitzRoy decided to let the comment pass. He had in fact been sidetracked by a sudden blinding realization: that in all his dealings with the Fuegian race, stretching back the better part of a year now, he had not seen a single old man or woman. Every Fuegian they had encountered was young, strong and fit. Where were all the elderly people? Where were all the cripples, the invalids, the mental defectives? Were they simply unable to survive the harsh southern winters? Or was the answer more sinister than that? He glanced down at the gurgling, happy little girl at his feet once more, as if to read her mind, but she just beamed sweetly back at him.

By now the lone canoe was no more than ten yards ahead of the *Beagle*'s prow. With a few deft paddle-strokes the natives within brought her alongside, hauling on the *Beagle*'s manropes to make her fast. The sturdiest and tallest of the Fuegians, a relative giant at some five feet tall, climbed out of the canoe, scaled the battens on the ship's side and stepped on to the deck. At once his fellows detached their grip on the ropes, and their canoe sheered off to starboard. The man stood stock still, the cynosure of all eyes, a primitive, feral visitation in the centre of the maindeck. Powerful, brooding and quite naked, with arms and legs like tree trunks, he stared around him through narrowed eyes. He exuded physical confidence. FitzRoy felt the hairs at the nape of his neck rise instinctively. *Who is the animal now?* he thought.

'Do we take paying passengers, then?' asked King, coolly.

'Place is turning into a regular menagerie,' mumbled the boatswain to himself, disapprovingly.

Fuegia Basket was the first person to move. Clutching up her skirts, she skittered across the maindeck and presented herself to the visitor. Giggling with delight she spoke, the first time she had done so in her own language, with the now-familiar concoction of guttural clicks and throaty noises. Poised motionless, holding himself rigid with a solemn muscular reserve, the stranger replied: a slow, low, brutal voice, the words obviously selected with caution and delivered with exactitude. Fuegia Basket's eyes widened in response, and there was a second's pause. Then, suddenly, she threw back her head and erupted in a peal of laughter, turning delightedly to share her merriment with the watching crew.

FitzRoy kept his eyes on the new arrival. The man's expression remained as unmoving as stone.

On a height above Christmas Sound, reading angles, FitzRoy was able to take in the sheer impossibility of his task: a hundred peaks, a thousand caves, a million tiny shards of rock flung into the sea. The subtle undulations of the land were obscured by thick beech forest, no riot of vegetation but a slow, dull march, close-ranked and impenetrable. Metronomically accurate now in his map-making observations, not so much immune to the cold as habituated to it, he allowed his thoughts to drift to the *Beagle*'s two new acquisitions. The male Indian, named York Minster by the crew after the location where he had boarded the ship, could not have been more different from little Fuegia. Sullen and taciturn, he continued to say nothing, but FitzRoy could tell that he was watchful. His eyes were as restless as his posture was immobile. In particular he watched after the girl, his narrow gaze never once leaving her as she skipped about the decks. She would dance merrily with the crew in the evenings, or play with her makeshift dolls, a whole family now sewn together from rags by some kind soul. All the while his eyes would bore into her back from his squatting position up by the foremast chimney grating, where he stored his uneaten food like some big cat back from the prowl. It seemed to FitzRoy that York's was an intelligent gaze; whether this was conventional intelligence of the European kind, or merely low animal cunning, it was hard to tell. Certainly, dressed as he was now in the slops and ducks of the common sailor, York Minster could have passed at first glance for an unusually short and stout member of the crew. His immense physical strength, though, marked him out from the others. Challenged to arm-wrestling matches, he was – once he understood what was required of him – easily a match for any two of the sailors put together.

FitzRoy could tell from York and Fuegia's chatter, from the way that new sensations stimulated them to communicate with each other in their strange clicking language, that some kind of shared reasoning power united these two disparate characters. He felt enormously frustrated by the limits to his understanding. *There is less difference between most nations or tribes than exists between these two individuals. If I could help to prove that all men are of one blood, what a difference it would make.*

He had consulted Captain Stokes's copy of the *Dictionnaire Classique*, which divided men into thirteen distinct races, but to no purpose. The book marked Tierra del Fuego down, quite erroneously, as a Negroid area. Nobody, it seemed, had ever deigned to study the curious inhabitants of South America's southern tip. Cracking the code of language, FitzRoy knew, would be the key. Unfortunately, York would not talk to any of the sailors. Fuegia would only parrot English with a wide, beaming smile. But they did speak to each other: already he had identified a noise like the clucking of a hen as 'no'.

So long as we are ignorant of the Fuegian language, and so long as the natives are equally ignorant of ours, we will never know about them, or their society, or their culture. Without such an understanding, there is not the slightest chance of their being raised one step above the low place which they currently hold in our imaginations.

And then, on that wild, lonely peak above Christmas Sound, FitzRoy was struck by a big, beautiful idea.

If I carry a party of Fuegians to England, if I acquaint them with our language, and our habits and customs, if I procure for them a suitable education, and equip them with a stock of articles useful to them, if I return them safely to their own country; then they and their fellows will surely be raised from the brute condition in which they find themselves. They can spread their knowledge among their countrymen – the use of tools, clothes, the wheel! It could even be the start of a friendly Fuegian nation. They could facilitate the supply of fresh provisions and wood and water to ships rounding from one ocean to another. And if I could go further, and form them in the ways of polite society, then it would prove to the world that all men are created equal in the eyes of God.

The idea whirled in his brain, simple but fabulous. He would need Admiralty permission, of course, and both King and Otway would have to give their blessing, but if the Fuegians were educated at his own expense, then the Admiralty could hardly complain. The next survey ship could return the party to Tierra del Fuego. What could possibly go wrong?

A crack of gunfire from the beach below jolted him from his reverie. May's boat-building party, hard at work on the replacement whaleboat, were under attack. Most of the sailors, armed only with tools, were rushing to take cover behind one end of the half-built boat. One of the crew, who must have been caught out in the open, lay face down in a pool of blood on the shingle, apparently dead. Two Fuegian women, who had apparently attacked him with sharpened rocks, were retreating from his body towards the far end of the beach, where a further ten or so of their number now gathered, chanting. They wore the white-feathered grass bands about their heads that, FitzRoy had come to learn, denoted hostility. Alone in the middle of this panorama, walking calmly up the beach towards them, firing into the air, reloading, walking a little further and then firing once more, moved the figure of Surgeon Wilson, a most unlikely hero. Perhaps Wilson's apparent lack of imagination really betokened a serene inner strength after all, wondered FitzRoy. He ran forward down the hillside, Stokes at his heels, both men already drawing their pistols.

By the time they reached the beach it was all over. Wilson, normally one of the more invisible officers, had been fêted as a hero, and was now engaged in trying to save the life of the injured man, whose skull was fractured. The Indians had taken to their canoes, but had been swiftly overhauled by a party of sailors in the cutter. All but one of the pursued Fuegians had dived over the side to escape capture, the exception being a frightened, slender youth, who now stood bewildered and shivering in the rough grasp of Davis, one of the crew. Beside him on the shingle was a length of the leadline (identifiable by its white five-fathom marker), a few tools and several empty beer bottles from the missing whaleboat. Shaking with rage, Davis pressed the muzzle of a loaded pistol to the boy's temple. 'Shall I shoot him now, sir?'

'No! Put your gun down. This man is drunk.'

'They've buzzed all the beer from the whaleboat sir. Every last drop sir.'

'Let go of his arm.'

The boy fell slack on his back, looking up at FitzRoy, his unfocused eyes white with fear, his feathered headband limp with seawater.

Mortal fear is the only manner in which these people can be kept peaceable. It is a state of affairs I have to change, if I can. I must do everything in my power to bring about a mutual understanding between our two races.

'Shall I just let him go then, sir?' asked Davis, confused.

'No. Bring him on board. Let him join his fellows on the *Beagle*.'

The newcomer was quickly christened 'Boat Memory' by the crew, as their last potential link to the vanished whaleboat. He seemed eager to help out around the ship, as if to atone for his part in the murderous attack at the beach, but for that very reason he found it difficult to gain acceptance. Furthermore his slender physique, most unusual for a Fuegian Indian, made him unsuited to physical tasks that – had he been similarly amenable – York Minster could have carried out without breaking sweat. York treated the new arrival with the utmost contempt, perhaps on account of his status as a defeated warrior, refusing to speak to him or even acknowledge him. They took to squatting at opposite ends of the ship, staring at each other through the thickets of rigging, the one baleful and contemptuous, the other cowed and frightened. It was left to Fuegia, inevitably, to act as go-between: unaware of any such nuances, she treated Boat Memory to the same winning display of affection that she served up to everybody else. FitzRoy felt the boy's sense of isolation keenly, and realized that this might provide him with the opening he needed. He found Boat Memory sitting forlornly by the poop cabin skylight, playing with a length of rope. FitzRoy stood ten yards away from him, and spoke in a loud, clear voice: *'Yammerschooner.'*

Without a word, obediently, Boat got to his feet, walked forward and presented himself humbly to the captain, holding out the length of rope.

FitzRoy could hardly contain himself. 'It means "Give to me,"' he breathed excitedly. '"*Yammerschooner*" means "Give to me."'

'By Jove sir, you've got it!' squeaked King over his shoulder, a delighted grin plastered across his puppyish face.

FitzRoy wiped any trace of levity from his own features. He stared directly and unwaveringly at the Indian, and pointed a finger at his own eyes. 'Eyes,' he announced.

'*Telkh*,' replied Boat Memory, without hesitation.

'Fetch your notebook, Mr King,' murmured FitzRoy, relief mingled with pleasure. The other officers began to gather round, interested despite themselves.

'Forehead,' tried FitzRoy, moving his finger upward.

'*Tel'che.*'

'Eyebrows.'

'*Teth'liu.*'

'Nose.'

'*Nol.*'

King scurried back breathless, notebook and pen in hand. FitzRoy ignored him and kept going.

'Mouth.'

'*Uf'fe'are.*'

'Teeth.'

'*Cau'wash.*'

'Tongue.'

'*Luc'kin.*'

'Chin.'

'*Uf'ca.*'

'Neck.'

'*Chah'likha.*'

King scribbled away, desperately trying to transliterate Boat Memory's words and make sense of all the tongue-clicks. FitzRoy kept it slow, his eyes trained on his subject.

'Shoulder.'

'*Cho'uks.*'

'Arm.'

'*To'quim'be.*'

'Elbow.'

'*Yoc'ke.*'

'Wrist.'

'*Acc'al'la'ba.*'

'Hand.'

'*Yuc'ca'ba.*'

'Fingers.'

'*Skul'la.*'

'Have you got them all, Mr King? Tell me you have translated them all so far?'

'I think so sir, except for a couple when I was getting the book.'

FitzRoy took the notebook from his midshipman and read out the first entry as best he could. Pointing to his own eyes once more, he tried out: '*Telkh.*'

Without averting his gaze, the young man pointed to the same spot on his own face and said, clear as day: 'Eyes.'

Then pointing to each body part accurately in turn, he continued without hesitation: 'Forehead. Eyebrows. Nose. Mouth. Teeth. Tongue. Chin. Neck. Shoulder. Arm. Elbow. Wrist. Hand. Fingers.'

There was a complete silence for at least ten seconds on the upper deck. Quite simply, nobody dared breathe. Finally, FitzRoy spoke.

'My God,' he exclaimed.

May's new boat was finished on the twenty-third. Kempe, meanwhile, had supervised the watering of the ship, and the stitching of new topmast rigging. As soon as the work was over, the *Beagle* weighed anchor, warped to windward and made sail out of Christmas Sound, steering small amid the profusion of rocks and islets. She made her way south-east along the coast to False Cape Horn, that cunning natural replica that lies some fifty miles up the coast from the real thing. There she turned north into Nassau Bay, her binnacle lamp a lonely pinpoint of light in the darkening winter evenings. The sick list was lengthening now, an untidy catalogue of colds, pulmonic complaints, catarrhal and rheumatic afflictions, not to mention two badly injured men. The fresh food of summer – the seabird meals of redbill, shag and bittern – had become a rarity. Anything they could catch or shoot now was offered first to the sick, and then to the Indians, on FitzRoy's orders. Nassau Bay, long known but long unexplored, was to be their final 'boat service' of the trip, for which the captain was duly grateful. Surgeon Wilson had impressed upon him that the crew's health was in dire need of recruiting. FitzRoy was all too painfully aware that this decline had begun following the episode with the whaleboat. Even though there had been no sign of any relapse on his part, it was as if the crew took its communal health – silently, invisibly – from him, as if damage to the head was reflected in the spirits of the body corporate.

The education of Boat Memory was now coming on so fast that FitzRoy could hardly bear to break off to recommence surveying operations. Fuegia, too, amazed to find that FitzRoy could suddenly communicate with her in her own tongue, had started to learn English with an astounding rapidity. Only York Minster, a brooding, intimidating presence to all but Fuegia, stayed silent. He sat in his berth up by the chimney grating in all weathers, surrounded by his secreted piles of food, oblivious of the cold and rain. Some among the crew thought he brought bad luck, or wished storms upon them, but none dared to confront him. To approach York felt like walking towards the entrance of a bear cave.

'I'm afraid the water in the wash-hand basin is a mask of ice, sir.'

FitzRoy's steward had arrived to waken him, bearing a bowl of steaming skillygalee porridge, but he had already been roused to half-sleep by the rattle of the anchor chain below.

It was just before six o'clock, halfway through the morning watch, and it would not become light for a good couple of hours yet. Snow lay dark and thick on the skylight above. In terms of personal discomfort this was no more than FitzRoy was used to, but it did mean that much of the day would be taken up with the tiresome business of de-icing the rigging. He wolfed his breakfast, struggling into his uniform as he did so, and left his cabin, unwashed, as the sentry rang four bells. It was too cold to clean the decks, so the ship's company were already busy lashing up and stowing their hammocks. A tired-looking Murray, who was on duty at the wheel, seemed relieved to see a friendly face. 'I think it's going to be a fine day, sir. The stars are out and we have a good anchorage – one of the few on this coast fit for a squadron of line-of-battle ships.'

'Excellent.'

Murray paused. 'I'm afraid we lost the small bower anchor in the night, sir. The seaward cable parted through frost. It froze right through, sir. I had the remainder of the small bower cable shackled to the best bower, and rode with two-thirds of a cable on the sheet, and a cable and a half on the bower. I've had the men keep the cables constantly streaming wet at the hawse-holes with seawater all night, sir, to prevent any more icing up.'

'Well, it's a pity about the small bower, but you've done well, Mr Murray. I am grateful to you for your quick thinking.'

'Thank you sir.'

As FitzRoy's eyes became accustomed to the gloom, he became aware of a dim column of warm breath beyond the foremast, which signalled the solitary presence of York Minster, shrouded in a blanket in his accustomed spot. Boat and Fuegia had been persuaded to sleep below decks, but York chose to keep guard out in the open.

'He's been there all night, sir. As usual.'

The *Beagle* had anchored in darkness, but the emerging moon now illuminated steep wooded hillsides, hemming in the ship on three sides. Towards the northern end of the bay these slopes converged in a mess of islands. Here, as so often,

FitzRoy, Stokes and Murray would have to hunt for channels, short-cuts and hidden routes into the interior of Tierra del Fuego.

A sudden commotion arose at the far end of the deck. York had sprung to his feet, all his senses alert like a hunted animal's. His eyes scanned the darkness intently, and then he began to shout. The head of Boat Memory soon appeared at the companionway, and behind him Fuegia Basket scampered on deck. All three began to run about agitatedly, dashing up to the rail where they would scream derisively and pull faces into the darkness, before shuttling back again, as if afraid to show themselves for too long.

'What the deuce are they shouting at?' wondered FitzRoy.

Neither he nor any of the lookouts could see anything, even with a nightglass. But then, conducted like electricity through the clear black air, came faint answering shouts and catcalls. At first they came by the score, and then, as they came closer, by the century. Screwing up his eyes and squinting into the gloom, FitzRoy could see tiny silhouettes, black shapes cut in the moonlit sheen of the distant channels. Canoes, a good hundred of them. Boat Memory ran past waving his arms and shouting, '*Yamana! Yamana!*' Even the normally solemn York was running about in agitated circles. Fuegia, FitzRoy noticed, was in tears.

'What is it, Boat? Who are they?'

Boat was too panicked to answer. FitzRoy grabbed his arm roughly as he hurtled past and spun him round. 'Boat. Who are these men?'

'Bad men. Yamana! Kill Boat Memory!' He gestured to two scars on his arm as proof of the strangers' murderous intentions.

'Yamana?'

'Yamana! Bad men. Kill Alik'hoo'lip.'

'You are Alikhoolip? You and York and Fuegia?'

'Yes. Yamana kill Alik'hoo'lip! Bad men!'

'Nobody will kill you here. Understand? Nobody will kill you here.'

But Boat was already charging to the starboard rail to deliver another volley of insults into the darkness.

FitzRoy gave the order to beat to quarters, and the *Beagle*'s drums thundered out into the blackness of the sound. Locks were produced for the guns, along with trigger lines, priming wires and powder, handspikes and rammers. The decks around the guns were wetted and liberally sanded. After a minute of frantic activity the men were standing by, waiting for the order to load.

'Are you going to give the order to open fire, sir?' asked Murray.

'I hope to God it will not be necessary. The recoil could play merry hell with the chronometers.'

A great flotilla of canoes was converging on the *Beagle* now, from more than one direction. Silhouetted figures stood in the little boats, waving otterskin mantles the size of large pocket handkerchiefs, or holding what appeared to be substantial wooden clubs in their fists. The shouts of the men in the canoes jostled and competed with each other to cross the gap between them and the ship. Now that they were closer, the jeers of Boat and York, and the wails of Fuegia, seemed suddenly pathetic by comparison. Steadily, the Yamana canoes converged into a tight ring around the *Beagle*, but still no attack was launched. The sailors stood tense and nervous by the guns; FitzRoy, pistol drawn, held himself in readiness to give the order to fire.

'Sir! Sir!' It was Coxswain Bennet who had shouted. 'They're not clubs, sir, they're fish!'

'I beg your pardon, Mr Bennet?'

The coxswain wore a huge grin of relief. 'Those aren't clubs they're holding, sir, they're fish. They've come to sell us fresh fish!'

At first light, leaving Kempe in charge of the *Beagle*, FitzRoy sent Murray east to map the open end of Nassau Bay, and Stokes west to explore the side-channels there. He, Bennet and King, fortified with plenty of fresh-cooked fish, headed north, where the walls of the bay narrowed. Strange, bright green conical structures lined the shore, which proved on closer inspection to be huge mounds of discarded sea shells, turned emerald by mould, and a profusion of wild celery shoots twisting through and around them. Despite the cold, this was the most heavily populated area they had visited: it was dotted with ramshackle, cone-shaped, brush wigwams, which looked like badly tended haycocks. The people seemed even poorer, muddier and more degraded than those to the west, having no sealskins, but their manner – in spite of Boat, York and Fuegia's terror – was unquestionably friendlier and more tractable. As soon as they saw the cutter they would rush to their canoes to trade fish and shellfish, waving their tiny ragged otterskins to attract attention. They would shout for a '*cuchilla*', the Spanish for 'knife': evidently, at some point in history, a party of Spaniards had passed this way. Miles of stubbly shingle beach fringed this end of the bay, guanaco hoofprints showing in the muddy banks of streams; after a year in the storm-battered depths of Tierra del Fuego, even the knowledge that a herd of guanaco was nearby felt like a friendly harbinger of civilization.

They sailed the cutter up into the northern arm of the bay, where it narrowed to a twisting channel barely wide enough for two ships to pass. Here, they came across an obstacle: three native canoes in line abreast, blocking their way.

'They don't wish us to go any further,' said King.

'They're trying to protect something,' said Bennet, realizing.

'Proceed slowly.'

The cutter pushed forward and, without a sound, the three native canoes parted to let it pass. The morning sun shone brilliantly for the first time in months; the water was glass. The sailors' breath rose and condensed frostily in their overgrown hair. At a quarter speed, the cutter drifted inch by inch along the final hundred yards of the narrows, to the place where the rock walls opened out once more. There it stopped; some of the men stared to the west, and some stared to the east, but in whichever direction they chose to look, the sight before them took their breath away.

'Well hang me,' murmured King.

'Great heavens,' said FitzRoy.

They were sitting in a channel between the mountains, except that the word 'channel' hardly sufficed. This was a ravine, a chasm, an axe-cut running through the heart of the continent, straight as an arrow, for perhaps sixty miles in either direction. It was about a mile or two in width, with snow-capped mountains three or four thousand feet in height ranged on either side, their sunny summits apparently suspended vertically over the deep blue water. Beneath the mantle of white, countless magnificent azure glaciers gushed cascading meltwater from side valleys balanced hundreds of feet in the air. Every arm of the sea in view was also terminated by a tremendous glacier; occasionally a steepling tower of ice would crumble from one of these cliffs into a distant corner of the sound. The far-off crash would reverberate through the lonely channels like the broadside of a man-of-war, or the distant rumble of a volcano. Hundred-foot ice blocks would bob gently through the water, like polar icebergs in miniature, and when the ripples reached the cutter, dazzling light flung itself out from their surface and broke into stars. Along the entire length of the ravine, the tree line ran absolutely level, as if drawn by a child with a ruler. The beech leaves clinging to the cliffs glowed an autumnal red at the base, merging into the customary yellow-green further up, where the cold had retarded the action of the seasons. Not for the first time, FitzRoy wished that an official ship's artist had been retained aboard the *Beagle*.

'This is unbelievable, sir. It's incredible. We have found a channel to rival the Straits of Magellan.'

'Indeed we have, Mr Bennet. If its two ends can be located and are joined to the sea, as they surely must be, then we have found a navigable channel that escapes the necessity of rounding the Horn.'

'What should we call it?'

'The narrows that brought us here will be named after Mr Murray. This channel is too important to be named after any one man. I think we should call it the Beagle Channel.'

'Are we to survey it ourselves, sir?' asked King.

'It would take a month at least. We are in want of provisions – we have only a few weeks' aliment left – and we are ordered to reach the Brazils by June. No, this is a task for some future expedition.'

They sat in silent awe for some twenty minutes further before finally setting to work. They surveyed the immediate locality of the channel and the Murray Narrows, climbed a nearby summit (which they named Mount King) by following the guanaco trails, collected greenstone samples for stratigraphic analysis, and gathered specimens of local barnacles and other shellfish. They camped that night on a narrow shelf of shingle, close-packed and shivering in their makeshift tent.

On their return through the narrows the next morning, the three silent canoes, each containing its own family, lay strung across the channel exactly as before, like guards of honour to an invisible potentate. A gentle breeze had sprung up, presaging the end of the precious clear spell, so the crew of the cutter tacked back down the narrows, a judicious oar here and there helping to keep them on course.

'Pull alongside that canoe.'

'Sir?'

'We have three of the western tribe aboard the *Beagle* – the Alikhoolip. We do not have any of the Yamana.'

'We are to take them with us? As specimens?'

'Not as specimens, Mr Bennet. As fellow men, to share in our civilization, that we may form them in the ways of our society. Besides, the die is now cast. We have not the provisions to return to the west, but if we release our three Indian guests here I suspect they will be torn limb from limb. So, yes, we are to take them with us.'

As bidden, the cutter slid alongside the middle canoe, over which a man in his mid-thirties appeared to preside. His face was crossed laterally by two painted stripes: a red one, running from ear to ear across his upper lip, and a white one that ran above and parallel, linking the eyelids. FitzRoy stood up and gestured to the man, suggesting that he, or one of his family, might like to join him in the cutter. The man grunted suspiciously, but a short, round youth alongside him, plucked by curiosity, stood up and peered at the strangers. A low, clicking conversation ensued, and the boy finally clambered into the cutter alongside the waiting FitzRoy. The older man, who was presumably the boy's father, held his hands outstretched and essayed a beseeching look, to indicate that he ought to be given something for his trouble. It was an awkward dilemma. FitzRoy had wanted a volunteer; he had not wanted to purchase another human being. But this was not a transaction, he told himself, merely a consideration paid out of respect to an elder of the tribe. He was here to help these people, not exploit them. He rummaged in his pocket and found a solitary mother-of-pearl button, which he tossed, not entirely convinced by his own argument, to the Indian in the canoe.

The rotund boy alongside him seemed placidly unperturbed by the exchange, but the older Indian gasped as if he had been showered with gold doubloons. He held up the shining button to the sunlight in wonderment and then, gesturing to the rest of his family, indicated to FitzRoy that for another button he might take whomever he wanted. His wife? His daughter?

'All hands to the oars. Let us make for the *Beagle*.'

And so the cutter set off back down the channel, tacking to port and then to starboard against the breeze. The Indian's canoe, presumably mistaking the zigzagging of the cutter for evasive action, clung gently in its wake, striving to follow its movements. The putative salesman stood in the bow throughout, now grinning and gesticulating enthusiastically to indicate that his entire family was for sale, if only the Europeans could provide another shiny object; the family in question, meanwhile, paddled calmly but energetically in pursuit of their reluctant purchaser.

'I can't say I care for this fellow overmuch,' observed FitzRoy, casting another embarrassed glance over his shoulder.

The boy alongside him grinned delightedly at the chase, urging the sailors via sign language to redouble their efforts, but it was to be a good hour before they shook off the enthusiastic salesman. In the meantime, FitzRoy endeavoured to distract his new charge's attention by producing a looking-glass, as much for his own interest as for the boy's entertainment. The young Indian took it in astonishment, gazing first at his reflection, then over and over again behind the looking-glass in search of his imaginary twin, then even behind himself in confusion. Finally he arrived at the stage of pulling faces, testing his reflection, pushing the *Doppelgänger* in the glass to extremes in the hope that it could be provoked into nonconformity. Relieved to have so captured the boy's interest, FitzRoy indicated to him that he could keep the looking-glass for himself.

In the early afternoon, as the crisp autumnal light began to fail, they arrived back at the *Beagle* to find a scene of pandemonium. The ship was still at the centre of a flotilla of canoes, packed with Indians eagerly trying to trade fresh fish, shellfish and ragged otterskins. York, Boat and Fuegia appeared to have taken charge of the trading, and were hurtling about the deck collecting worthless scraps – strips of cloth, rusty nails, glass beads and so forth – which they were exchanging for food. They appeared to have overcome their fears of the previous morning, and had adopted the swagger of stallholders at a country fair.

FitzRoy was first out of the cutter. 'What is going on here, Mr Kempe?'

'Your savages, sir' – Kempe was careful to put the stress on the *your* – 'are trading with the other savages. Your only orders were that they were not to leave the *Beagle*. As they are not part of the chain of command, sir, I confined myself to implementing precisely those orders I received from yourself.'

Boat Memory ran past at this moment, laughing all over his face. 'Capp'en! Capp'en! Yamana, *foolish* man! Yamana, *foolish* man! Boat give Yamana button! Yamana give Boat fish! *Foolish* man! *Foolish* man!' And he ran off excitedly to find another button, having used up all those on his own jacket. How excited would Boat have been just a few weeks ago, FitzRoy pondered, to exchange a fish for a button? At least they were learning.

A moment later, Coxswain Bennet escorted the Yamana boy over the rail. The effect was instantaneous. Seized with shock, York, Boat and Fuegia froze to the spot.

The youth, overcome with fear, began to cry. York strode forward, jabbed a finger at him, and shouted, 'Yamana! Yamana!'

The boy quailed in terror, and began to shake with sobs. FitzRoy stepped between them. Boat ran up and jeered at the new arrival over FitzRoy's shoulder. 'Yamana! No clothes! No clothes! Yamana *foolish* man!'

'No clothes! No clothes!' yelled Fuegia excitedly.

Unable to understand, the frightened youth blurted a few words back, through his tears.

'What does he say, Boat? What does he say?'

'Boat no understand. Boat no talk Yamana talk.'

My God. Of course. They do not have one language. Theirs is not one nation. These two do not understand a single word the other says.

Fuegia ran up and spat in the boy's face. 'No clothes! No clothes!' she screamed.

Chapter Seven

Rio de Janeiro, 1 August 1830

———

The sun stole down behind the dark, high mountains that threw a protective arm over the city to the west. The sea was quite smooth, but a freshening breeze on the *Beagle*'s quarter carried her on, at an exhilarating thirteen knots, towards the harbour entrance. Behind, her foaming wake glowed with a pale, sparkling light, and before her bows, two milky billows of liquid phosphorus parted to let her through. Sheet lightning played incessantly on the northern horizon, and sometimes the whole surface of the sea was illuminated. As the daylight faded, the *Beagle* hauled her wind and stood in the offing for the night. Her sails were clewed up and stored, the anchors were let go, and a light was hoisted to the fore yard-arm, shining like a lone star against the setting sun.

'It's a beautiful evening, isn't it, Jemmy?' said FitzRoy.

Jemmy Button, as some wag had christened the Yamana boy, glanced up from the looking-glass that had become his constant companion.

'It's a beautiful evening, isn't it, Capp'en Fitz'oy? God make stars, God make sun, God make sea. God make Jemmy,' he grinned.

Humour and vanity were combined in Jemmy in equal measure. Sporting an ever-present smile, he would pick his way across the deck with a delicacy that belied his pot-bellied proportions, never taking his eyes off his own reflection, but never once tripping over a block or coil of rope. He looked after his new clothes with a fastidiousness bordering on obsession. The months since he had joined the ship had seen his relations with Boat Memory and Fuegia Basket cautiously advance towards the cordial; as for York Minster, Jemmy had established the same warily mute relationship with which everyone but Fuegia had to content themselves. The language barrier separating Jemmy, Boat and Fuegia had forced them to converse in English, which had lent unexpected impetus to their education. Jemmy's ready tongue and constant grin had made him even more popular with the crew than the little girl was, and FitzRoy sensed that the sailors had become proud of their human cargo. They were making a difference, they felt, helping to bring light to the darkness. The next survey ship that returned the four Indians would be like an arrow fired into the heart of the savage nation, an arrow tipped with the elixir of Christian civilization, which would spread through that country's bloodstream until all Tierra del Fuego was suffused with the word of God.

'Look, Jemmy! The sun is drowning!'

The passing sailor who offered this cheery greeting was none other than Elias Davis, who had been so ready to blow Boat Memory's brains out on the beach not a few months before.

'Gammon!' replied Jemmy, who relished English slang words. 'Sun no *drowning*. Tomorrow morning get up again. Sun go round earth, come again tomorrow. Earth is round.'

'Your people know this, Jemmy?' enquired FitzRoy. 'That the earth is round?'

'My people know this, Capp'en Fitz'oy. Climb mountain, you see far. Earth not flat. Earth round.'

These people are very, very far indeed from deserving to be called savages, thought FitzRoy.

'Do your people have a God, Jemmy?'

'All people have God, Capp'en Fitz'oy. God love everybody.'

'No, Jemmy. I mean, do your people have their *own* God?'

'No, no. My people not know God. My people *foolish* people.'

'Do your people think somebody made them? Who made you, Jemmy?'

'Jemmy's mother and father make Jemmy.'

FitzRoy laughed. 'Who made the mountains, Jemmy? Who makes the weather? Who makes it rain?'

'A big black man in the woods.'

The voice was not Jemmy's. Boat Memory had materialized at FitzRoy's shoulder, slender and earnest, his fine-boned features caught in the glare of the distant lightning sheets. As ever, his expression held a serious aspect, in contrast to the beaming cherub at FitzRoy's left.

'A big black man in the woods?'

'Yes. My people believe such man makes the rain and the snow. If food is wasted, he becomes angry and makes the storm.'

Boat Memory's English had advanced by incredible leaps and bounds since he had come aboard, but FitzRoy continued to be taken unawares by the sheer agility of the Indian's intelligence. He feared that his own contributions to their conversations were all too frequently mundane and unimaginative by comparison.

'There are no black men in the woods, Boat. You will see black men in London. You will see black men in Rio. Many black men.'

Boat looked longingly at FitzRoy, his eyes two inkwells. 'I dream to see London, Capp'en Fitz'oy. See St Paul's. See Wes'minster Abbey. See Temple Bar.'

Jemmy chipped in: 'My people say white man from the moon. White man white like moon. When white man take off clothes, wash in river, body white like moon.'

'I'm not from the moon, Jemmy,' smiled FitzRoy, 'I'm from England.'

'Englan' not on the *moon*. Foolish Indians think Englan' on the *moon*. This is bosh.'

'My people thought Mr King was English woman,' revealed Boat Memory. 'They don't know he is boy because he has no hair on his face.'

'Because he has no beard,' said FitzRoy, highly amused.

'Because he has no *beard*,' said Boat, savouring the new word, rolling it around his tongue and storing it away for future use.

'Beard look like tree on face,' giggled Jemmy. 'Jemmy no like beard.' And he glanced admiringly into the looking-glass once more.

FitzRoy caught sight of his own beard momentarily in Jemmy's glass. He would be shaving it off the next morning before he reported to Admiral Otway. It sat oddly here, a wild intruder on his face, in some ways more redolent of the savage south than the two Fuegian tribesmen leaning against the rail to either side.

He had written to the Admiralty back in early May, requesting permission to bring the four Fuegians home with him, hoping to secure the guarantee that His Majesty's Navy would return them to their own country the following year. The *Beagle* had spoke the packet *Caroline* off Good Success Bay, bound from Valparayso to Falmouth, and had consigned the letter to her. It was now August, so with luck the Admiralty's reply would be waiting for him at Rio; although what he was supposed to do if the answer was in the negative was beyond him. There were, in fact, five Fuegians on board, as Wilson had preserved the body of the attacker shot down by Murray in ice below decks; he intended to present it to the Royal College of Surgeons for scientific study. Wilson's own post mortem had discovered a thick fatty layer of insulation below the skin, closer to that of a seal than a human being. Both Wilson and FitzRoy thought that this subcutaneous layer, and the distinctively top-heavy body structure of the Fuegians, were adaptations, created by the harsh climate and the Indians' peculiar mode of life; it would be interesting to see whether or not the experts of the Royal College concurred.

None of the other Fuegians seemed remotely concerned by the presence of their fellow countryman's corpse. His death apparently failed to concern them at all. Indeed, the only disturbance of an otherwise uneventful return journey had been Jemmy's white-eyed terror on catching sight of some distant horsemen on the Patagonian shore. These, he explained, were the 'Oens-men', who would cross the mountains when the leaf was red, to kill or enslave the Yamana and steal their food. The three Alikhoolip, who had neither encountered nor even heard of the Patagonians, ignored Jemmy's wild, quivering fear with a calmness and equanimity verging on the perverse. Jemmy, meanwhile, took an enormous amount of soothing and convincing that he was safe from the mounted Oens-men, even half a mile out at sea; he was so terrified that he soiled his precious breeches. But the episode did not appear to linger in his mind. The next day, he was back to his old, prancing, chuckling self.

Empty of all her supplies now, the *Beagle* was hard to handle; she was too easily pushed around by the wind, and worked badly. But she had been making good time, until she became becalmed in a patch of constantly shifting light air just south of Monte Video. The endless hauling on the braces wearied the crew, and it was only the knowledge that they were nearing journey's end that kept the men focused on the task in hand. FitzRoy was determined that their mental discipline should not slacken. He did not want their arrival in port to be the equivalent of slumping wearily into an armchair after a long march. So the *Beagle* was given a new coat of black and white paint, the masts were scraped and repainted, as were the boats, the serving on the rigging, and the tips of the booms. The deck was scrubbed until it was spotless. Even the anchor cables were hove up on deck, to be chipped and checked.

They had finally arrived at Monte Video two weeks late,

only to be informed by Captain Talbot of the *Algerie* that both the *Adventure* and the *Adelaide* had been and gone, and that they were now to rendezvous at Rio instead. Again, it was a moment when the crew's instincts would have been to slacken their efforts, but again FitzRoy refused to let this happen. And now, some nineteen months after their departure, the *Beagle* prepared to enter Rio harbour, in a palpably better condition than that in which she had left. Admiral Otway, FitzRoy knew, would be watching.

The following morning dawned dead calm, the ship marooned in banks of fog, which the sun drew upwards and slowly dispersed as the day wore on. At noon the midshipmen had trouble measuring the position of the sun, so harsh was its image as reflected by their quadrants. Soon after midday the Port Health Officer came aboard, to issue the 'Pratique' certificate of health. Black, curling ripples were already stealing across the glossy surface of the water as the *Beagle* weighed anchor and steered proudly for the harbour entrance.

'Away, bullies, away! Away for Rio!' exulted the crew, as they made sail.

Blue through the haze to port rose the mighty ridge that curled round the city, punctuated by the sharp spurs of the Corcovado and the Tijuca, and the flat-topped Gavia. To starboard the Organ Mountains stabbed upwards with their curious needle-points, and there, within the harbour itself, slumped the familiar hummock of the Sugar Loaf. Beyond that, a dazzling world of white sails awaited, clustered together at the feet of the great metropolis. Even among this wonderful constellation of ships there was no mistaking the *Ganges*, and just behind her, the *Samarang*, crossing the harbour in full sail, two of His Majesty's ships-of-the-line, imperious and haughty, towering over the little *Beagle* as she skated slowly towards them. A squabbling, barging rabble of masked boobies plunged for fish in the *Beagle*'s wake, as if to emphasize her inferior social status. FitzRoy ran up the numbered signal to identify himself.

'Keep a sharp eye open for any returning signals, Mr King.'

'Aye aye sir.'

King did not have long to wait. Grasping the signal book so tightly with excitement that his fingers practically turned white, he was rewarded by a line of signal flags fluttering into position in the lofty heights of the *Ganges*. 'The admiral's ordering us to moor alongside the *Samarang*, sir,' he gasped.

'That's unusually specific, isn't it?' queried Lieutenant Kempe.

FitzRoy grinned. 'Why, the old devil . . . It's a contest! He wishes us to compete with the *Samarang* in furling sail. He wishes to see how close we can run her. Well, we shall see about that! Mr Bos'n, make it known to the crew, would you?'

Sorrell marched down the deck, bawling at the top of his voice. 'All right, boys! Seems the admiral wants a set-to between us and the *Samarang*! Wants to see us put in our place at furling sail! Well? Are we going to be made fools of by a crowd of jumped-up fancies? What do you say, boys?'

A huge answering roar came back in the negative.

There were only a couple of hundred yards before the two ships would be abeam of each other. A state of high excitement obtained aboard the *Beagle*.

'I want every man in position, Mr Bos'n, but nobody is to move until I give the order.'

'Aye aye sir.'

The gap halved. There were just a hundred yards to go. And now fifty. Thirty. Twenty. Ten. *Now.*

Both ships began to turn into the wind at the same time. Figures swarmed simultaneously on to the yards of both the *Beagle* and the *Samarang*, hauling frantically on the clew lines, pulling the corners of the sails upwards into the masts. At breakneck speed, the courses, topsails and topgallants lost their billowing contours. The foretopsail, meanwhile, pressed against the mast, acting as a brake, slowing the *Beagle* to just a few knots. FitzRoy gave the order and the main bower anchor thundered into the water, sparks flying as the chain rattled deafeningly through the hawse. Almost at the same time, the foretopsail – its job done – began to curl up into the yards as well. FitzRoy stood tense on the poop deck, his pocket watch apparently ticking faster than normal.

'Ten minutes . . . ten minutes fifteen seconds . . .'

'Has a sounding ship ever beaten a man-of-war?' murmured Kempe.

'Not to my knowledge,' replied FitzRoy calmly. The *Beagle* was winning. It would be a close-run thing, but even across a hundred yards of water he could feel a creeping sense of panic enveloping the *Samarang*.

'Eleven minutes twenty seconds . . . eleven minutes thirty seconds.'

And then it was done. There was no doubt about it. The last inch of the *Beagle*'s sail was taken in. Across on the *Samarang* there were still corners flapping, edges of sail here and there still being drawn diagonally upwards by the topmen. An almighty cheer went up from one end of the *Beagle* to the other, which was immediately answered by another huge cheer from the crew of the *Ganges*, delighted to see their rivals on the *Samarang* humiliated in this way. Not just humiliated, but humiliated by a surveying brig!

'I wouldn't care to be on the *Samarang* tonight!' squealed King, dancing around the binnacle box for joy.

'They say old Paget is a real tartar,' said Bennet. 'Heads will roll!'

'Mr Bos'n, that was immaculate – quite immaculate,' said FitzRoy, with profound gratitude.

Sorrell, stilled at last, hung his head and blushed scarlet.

'And now, Mr Bos'n, when every last sail is taken in aboard the *Samarang*, I'd like every inch of canvas on the *Beagle* set.'

'You want me to *set* sail, sir?'

'Well, we wouldn't wish our colleagues on board the *Samarang* to think that was just a flash in the pan, would we?'

'Right you are, sir!'

Sorrell was grinning like a small boy on Christmas morning

as he beetled off. The order to set sail again took the *Samarang* by surprise, but only for a few seconds. Paget's exhausted crew were back in the rigging only a moment later, but they were already beaten men. The momentum was with the *Beagle*'s crew now; heads had dropped, fatally, aboard the man-of-war. Midshipman King was leaping about the poop deck so delightedly that he was practically bouncing off the rails, but nobody was in the mood to rein him in. 'We're rubbing their noses in it! We're rubbing their deuced noses in it!' he declared.

Another massive cheer, echoing across the harbour, announced that the *Beagle* had defeated the *Samarang* not once but twice. Unchristian though it was to show off, FitzRoy simply could not resist this moment of triumph. 'Mr Bos'n, give the order to furl sail once more.'

'Aye aye *sir*,' purred Sorrell.

And so, for a third time, the crew poured into the rigging and out on to the yards, all their tiredness long since evaporated, their movements smooth and well drilled, confidence and exhilaration written on every face. The *Samarang*'s second attempt at furling sail, by contrast, was ragged and lacklustre. The contest, what remained of it, was a foregone conclusion. Suddenly, a crash of cannon echoed across the harbour. The men on the *Beagle* were taken by surprise, but only for a moment.

'They're saluting us, sir! The *Ganges* is saluting us!'

Indeed they were. The admiral's flagship was saluting a surveying vessel. All her crew stood in the rigging, waving their hats and cheering for all they were worth.

'My God, this must be a first in the history of the Service,' said Murray. 'Well *done*, sir.'

'Well done sir,' echoed Kempe, cautiously. 'And may I say it's been a pleasure serving with you, sir. A real pleasure.'

'Why thank you, Mr Kempe. Thank you very much indeed.'

'Marvellous! Simply marvellous! Commander FitzRoy, you have my congratulations.'

Admiral Otway, thumbs hooked into his waistcoat pockets, leaned back in his chair with ill-concealed delight. 'I had Paget across for supper last night, otherwise I'd have seen you sooner. He didn't say one word all evening. Beaten by a surveying brig! Priceless!' Otway roared with laughter at the memory.

It was the following morning. King and FitzRoy were reporting to the admiral's staterooms on the *Ganges*, just as they had nearly two years previously. This time, FitzRoy too wore the grizzled, salt-bleached aspect that had characterized King on the previous occasion.

'I have with me Captain King's official report as to your conduct, Commander. Would you care to hear the conclusion?'

FitzRoy glanced at King. 'I'd be delighted, sir.'

Otway paused briefly for effect, then began his performance. '"Commander FitzRoy, not only from the important service he has rendered, but from the zealous and perfect manner in which he has effected it, merits their lordships' distinction and patronage; most particularly in the discovery of the Otway and Skyring waters, and of the Beagle Channel, made by Commander FitzRoy himself, in the depths of the severe winter of that climate; and I beg leave, as his senior officer, to recommend him in the strongest manner to their favourable consideration. The difficulties under which this service was performed, from the tempestuous and exposed nature of the coast, the fatigues and privations endured by the officers and crew, as well as the meritorious and cheerful conduct of every individual, which is mainly attributable to the excellent example and unflinching activity of the commander, can only be mentioned by me in terms of the highest approbation." Pretty damned good, eh, Mr FitzRoy?'

'You oblige me with your kindness, sir,' said FitzRoy warmly to King.

'I wrote that, Commander, before I had an opportunity to speak to my son. He paid a visit to the *Adventure* last evening, and was most forthcoming about your voyage.'

'Indeed, sir?'

A cold hand reached round FitzRoy's heart and held it still for a moment. Had Midshipman King confided to his father the episode of the stolen whaleboat, and all that had followed? There was an awful pause, as Captain King's eyes seemed to bore into those of his subordinate. 'According to my son, Commander, it would appear that you are the finest commanding officer in the history of the service. A position, I should add, that I formerly held myself. It seems I have been utterly supplanted in the young man's affections – an achievement for which I suppose I should congratulate you.'

'Midshipman King is most unaccountably generous, sir.' Relief streamed from FitzRoy like water pouring from the *Beagle*'s prow in a heavy sea. King caught his gaze for a moment longer. Was there something else in it, something unspoken? He could not tell.

'Now, Commander, these savages of yours,' boomed Otway.

'Yes, sir.'

'Personally I can't imagine what you were thinking of, cluttering up the maindeck with those benighted creatures, but it seems the Admiralty sees things differently. I have a reply to your letter from Barrow in the Admiralty office:

"Having laid before my lords commissioners of the Admiralty the letter from Commander FitzRoy of the *Beagle*, relative to the four Indians whom he has brought from Tierra del Fuego under the circumstances therein stated, I am commanded to acquaint you that their lordships will not interfere with Commander FitzRoy's personal superintendence of, or benevolent intentions towards these four people, but they will afford him any facilities towards maintaining and educating them in England, and will give him a passage home again."

And so on, and so on.'

'That's wonderful, sir.'

Otway harrumphed. 'Well, I can't see any good coming of it myself, but each to his own.'

'I have the four Fuegians present, sir, on the *Ganges*. If you please, I thought perhaps you might care for them to be presented to you.'

'They are here on the *Ganges*? Good Lord! Well, I can't say I've ever met a Fuegian. Very well, bring the brutes in.'

Boat Memory, Jemmy Button, York Minster and Fuegia Basket were ushered in and introduced to the admiral. Boat and Jemmy bowed, as they had been trained to do, and Fuegia lifted her skirts and performed a perfect curtsy.

'Most impressive, FitzRoy, most impressive. Their manners would do credit to many a matlow.'

'Thank you, Capp'en Admiral, sir. It is a great pleasure to make your acquaintance.' The speaker was Boat Memory.

Otway practically jumped out of his skin. 'Good grief, FitzRoy. It speaks English.'

'You have very beautiful cabin,' chipped in Jemmy. 'One day Jemmy have very beautiful cabin like you have.'

'Three of them speak excellent English, sir. We are making slower progress with York Minster here, whose real name is Elleparu. Jemmy here was born Orundellico. Fuegia's name is Yokushin. And Boat here—'

Boat Memory cut in: 'Please. My name is Boat Memory. I wish to have proper English name.'

'Well, quite. Absolutely. Who wouldn't?' said Otway, almost at a loss.

Fuegia broke ranks and charged up to the admiral, beaming from ear to ear. 'My name is Fuegia Basket. I have a pretty dress.'

Otway was on the point of shooing her away when, overcoming his prejudices, he found himself seized with a sudden impulse of generosity. 'Come here, my little creature, and sit on Admiral Otway's lap. Do not be afraid.' And he reached out a beckoning hand.

As Fuegia skipped forward, Otway felt sure he heard a low

animal growl in the stateroom, but there were no animals to be seen, and no one present appeared to have made a sound. Perhaps he had imagined it. But − there was no denying it − the hairs on the back of his neck were standing on end. Looking about him he could see no rational reason for this, but some primitive instinct told him to beware the big, silent one, the muscular Indian who had yet to speak. Somehow, innately, Otway knew that York Minster was the source of the tangible sense of threat that now assailed him.

FitzRoy and King observed a curious expression steal across the admiral's face, rather as if a fly had settled on the tip of his nose. He halted Fuegia, just as she was about to clamber aboard his lap.

'Yes . . . well . . . quite . . . Anyway, FitzRoy . . . I'm sure you have plenty to be occupying yourself, what with refitting and such.'

'By your leave, sir, the *Beagle* has no need for refitting. She is in a first-class state of repair.'

'Really? Good heavens. Well, I'm sure, nonetheless, you have much to do.'

'Yes sir.'

Otway turned Fuegia about and propelled her gently towards the others. The big Indian was still staring intently at him, but the brute was saying nothing. As Fuegia toddled back across the stateroom carpet, Otway felt the hairs on his neck lose their charge and fall slack. He was still unsure what had happened, but as FitzRoy and his Indians disappeared through the door, his body gave a little shiver, and a feeling of relief washed through him.

Riding back to the *Beagle* with the mail sack, FitzRoy resisted the temptation to investigate its contents. All the crew, he knew, would be hanging by the rail, as eager as hungry dogs for the slightest titbit. He did, however, allow himself a glance at the latest newspapers, which were full of talk of reform, the successful trials of the Rocket and the Lancashire Witch, and the forthcoming opening of the Bolton and Leigh goods railway. What, he wondered, would the Fuegians make of a railway, or a steam ferry, or all the other appurtenances of the modern world? What, for that matter, would they make of the bustle of Rio de Janeiro? He would find out on the morrow.

Back at the *Beagle* he found himself surrounded by a pushing, shoving crowd of seamen, naval discipline hanging by the merest thread. Boatswain Sorrell fought gamely to restore order. FitzRoy had the letters distributed in the order that they came out of the sack, regardless of rank. *As cold waters to a thirsty soul, so is good news from a far country.* Of course, some poor souls would always go without mail, even after four years at sea: orphans, perhaps, or once-pressed men whose families had no idea of their whereabouts, or those whose wives had simply abandoned them. He, at least, would be sure to have received a letter from his elder sister Fanny, who had yet to let him down. And sure enough, there, towards the bottom of the sack, was a letter addressed in her hand, affording him a familiar glow of love and nostalgia. Only when he turned it over did he see the black seal, as did everyone else present, and a hush fell over the deck. The nearest crewmen moved almost imperceptibly backwards and away from him.

FitzRoy was quiet. 'Mr Kempe, would you complete the distribution of the mail, please?'

'Aye aye sir.'

He took the letter from Fanny into his cabin, and leaned back against the bookshelves, his heart pounding against his chest wall, and he broke the black seal, and read what she had written.

His father was dead.

In a rush, all the air was forced out of his lungs, as if he had been kicked in the gut. His head swam. A wave of nausea rose in his throat, and he thought he would be sick there and then. Everything he had become, everything he had achieved, he had done with the purpose of his father's approval at the back of his mind. Why? He had barely seen his father since he had been sent away to school at six, and only twice since he had joined the Service at twelve. His father never wrote to him. His memories of his mother, who had died when he was five, were richer and more tangible than even his most recent recollections of his father. It was not as if he could ever have confided in his father, or opened his heart to him. And yet . . . *and yet I looked to his approbation as the true reward of any hard times I might pass. I have been influenced throughout everything by the thought that I might give him satisfaction. I always valued his slightest word.*

He wanted to confide in somebody now, to sit one of the officers down and tell them all about his father. The way his father spoke, the way he smiled, the way he sat on his favourite horse, the way he had once held his little boy. But it was out of the question. Even if naval etiquette had not forbidden it, he knew that any potential listener would be paralysed by rank, any sympathy they had to offer lost in the abyss between the two pillars of their respective status. A captain simply did not invite his subordinates to explore his personal grief.

FitzRoy looked up as the door of his cabin creaked open slowly. He was about to upbraid his visitor for failing to knock, and the marine sentry for failing to see that such formalities were observed, when he saw the reason for it. The visitor was Fuegia Basket, who peered wide-eyed past the door jamb. She wore a bright yellow home-made dress, like a single flower against the dark wood of the little cabin.

'Capp'en Fitz'oy,' she said. She crossed the floor and climbed into FitzRoy's lap. 'Fuegia love Capp'en Fitz'oy,' she said. And he put his arm round her, and he held her as tightly as he possibly could.

They made the *Beagle* fast to the quay with the anchor cable, which was unshackled and heaved around a quayside bollard, then lashed to the bitts. FitzRoy went ashore with Bennet and the four Fuegians, who were dressed as inconspicuously as possible, their hats pulled down over their eyes. He need not have worried. In their European clothes they passed easily for local Indians, and did not merit even a passing glance.

The reactions of the four Fuegians themselves were not so incurious, however; as the party made slow progress through the sweating crowds thronging the mole, and across the *praça* before the palace and the cathedral, lines of half-naked blacks carrying huge bundles atop their heads passed glistening in the other direction. Boat, Jemmy and Fuegia quailed visibly, the little girl clinging to York's breeches for protection, no doubt mindful of the black man in the woods who controlled the weather. Even York himself, FitzRoy thought, appeared less assured than normal: an air of tension pervaded his usually rock-like calm. Then, the sight of an ox-cart before the cathedral pulled them up in their tracks. All the sculpted baroque wonders above their heads were of scant interest compared to this fascinating horned beast, which set the three Alikhoolip chattering eagerly among themselves. FitzRoy had to pull them away before a crowd could gather to see what was so riveting.

He decided they should take the Rua do Ouvidor, where ox-cart traffic had been banned, to avoid any further zoological confrontations. It was, as Bennet remarked, 'precious warm', and even without the usual farmyard-deep carpet of ox dung, the stench in the city centre almost made the officers gag after two years at sea. A babbling brown brook of human effluent ran down the cobbled gutter in the middle of the street, naked children paddling and splashing therein with happy abandon. Crooked, maimed blacks stared at the little group, leaning pitifully on their sticks, the offensively poor, unemployable detritus of the slave trade. Others peered through rusty wrought-iron balconies that seemed to imprison them behind pastel walls of mildewed, peeling stucco. FitzRoy felt faintly ashamed that the modern civilization to which he had brought the Fuegians appeared even more desperate than their own.

A padre with a long coat and a square hat bade them good

day, and a handsome West African woman sailed by in muslin turban and long shawl, dripping with amulets and bracelets. At the mighty door of the Church of São Francisco de Paula they headed south, past the magnificent arched aqueduct that fetched the city's water down from the mountains, climbing now towards the more respectable suburbs of Santa Tereza and Laranjeiras. Imported trees grew everywhere here, plum and banana and breadfruit trees by the roadside, and long stands of bamboo transplanted from the East Indies. The houses were bigger, with tumbling vines and verandahs, each one a barrack square for a platoon of potted poinsettias. There were glimpses of olive-skinned children playing in back gardens, under the care of black nurses. FitzRoy took the piece of paper with the address from his pocket to check it once more. They ascended two more narrow cobbled streets, the roads here too steep and twisting for carriages, the Fuegians sweating copiously now in the heat, until eventually a sign in Portuguese indicated that they had arrived at their destination: the premises of Dr Carson Figueira, physician.

FitzRoy pulled the bell, and a silent black serving-girl came to the gate. She showed them through a terracotta-coloured patio lined with potted palms, into a dark, cool, empty room containing only a wall cabinet and a scratched mahogany desk, where she left them to themselves. A few minutes later Dr Figueira himself, a man as colourless as his office walls, appeared in the doorway.

'You must be Captain FitzRoy. I am pleased to make your acquaintance. I am Dr Figueira.'

The physician's accent was novel to say the least: it was flat and buttery like that of a New Englander, but it had also been dipped in the dark honeypot of Brazilian Portuguese. It was hard to equate such a rich, dominating voice with its undistinguished-looking, world-weary owner. 'My mother was American,' added Dr Figueira, in response to FitzRoy's unspoken question.

FitzRoy introduced himself, the coxswain and the four

Fuegians, and wondered privately about the bareness of Figueira's consulting room.

'So these are the Indians your message spoke about?'

Figueira opened York's mouth and began to inspect his teeth as if he were a horse. York's eyes bored into the physician's, but otherwise he reacted with diffidence to being manhandled.

'My name is Boat Memory, sir. This is my friend Mr York Minster, whose teeth you are making inspection of.'

'*Nossa Senhora*. You've been teaching them English, Captain.'

Dr Figueira ignored Boat Memory's greeting, and it occurred to FitzRoy that he did not entirely take to the Brazilian physician.

'It is my belief, Dr Figueira, that the Fuegian nation shows a considerable potential to be elevated above its savage state. That is why I am bringing them to Europe. It is why I have brought them here.'

'You'll need to make uncommon haste, then. The Buenos Ayreans are heading further south every day. When they reach Tierra del Fuego, the Indians will go the way of the blacks, and be fit only for slaves.'

'Do you believe that blacks are fit only for slaves, sir? This very afternoon we have encountered most handsomely dressed black gentlewomen, habited in turbans and shawls, who had nothing whatsoever of the slave about them.'

'Those will be Mina Negroes from West Africa. Handsome they may be, but they're quite unfit for domestic service. They're too wild, too independent. But they are less than slaves, Commander. Lusheys, for the most part.'

Figueira had completed his cursory examination.

'The inoculation for smallpox is an expensive business, Commander. If you wish me to inoculate four savages I will, as long as your money is as good as the bank.'

'I shall have no trouble meeting your settlement here and now,' said FitzRoy coldly.

Figueira produced a metal tray, upon which lay a lancet, a

cloth, a jar of vinegar and a glass phial containing a clear liquid. Dipping the cloth in the vinegar he cleaned a spot on Boat Memory's upper left arm, and prepared to make a small incision with the lancet. Boat's eyes widened. 'It's just a variolation,' explained the surgeon. 'A series of small cuts with a lancet dipped in the cowpox vaccine.'

'It's all right, Boat,' said Bennet softly. 'We've all had the same treatment.'

'It's medicine, Boat,' FitzRoy added. 'It will keep you safe from illness in England. You must have it done now, because it takes some weeks to work. If you like, I will take it first.'

'No, Capp'en Fitz'oy. I believe you.'

And he shut his eyes and submitted to Dr Figueira's ministrations.

Jemmy, who was quaking like a jelly, came next. He winced and gasped in fear as Figueira cut into both arms, then promptly smiled again the moment it was all over. Fuegia Basket, who was third, had seemed unconcernedly braver than the other two until the physician had her in his grasp, whereupon she began to whimper loudly. Both FitzRoy and Bennet started forward instinctively to comfort her, but Figueira was there first, placing his hands squarely on her shoulders. 'Do not fret, little miss. I will not hurt you, I promise.'

And with that he cut into her arm. Fuegia squealed and burst into tears. Before anybody could move, York was across the room, and had slammed Figueira up against the wall by the throat. FitzRoy and Bennet tried to pull him off, but York's arm was as rigid as gunmetal. Now it was Figueira's turn to widen his eyes in fear. York's fingers squeezed gently into the physician's neck; and then, to everyone's surprise, he spoke, in a low, harsh voice that came up from the depths of his throat: 'Hurt her, I will kill you.'

FitzRoy and Bennet slackened their futile grasp in sheer astonishment. Figueira, whose windpipe was too constricted to speak, shook his head as best as he could to indicate that nothing could be further from his mind.

'York . . . you can speak English!' gasped Bennet redundantly.

'He! He! He!' Jemmy, in the corner, was laughing. 'Mr York, he learn English all time! Fool Capp'en Fitz'oy, fool everybody. He! He! He!'

The packet *Ariadne* sailed into Rio de Janeiro harbour the next morning with the news that George IV was dead. The King had passed away at Windsor six weeks previously, on 26 June. It took some time for the news to percolate through the South American fleet, as there was no actual signal to indicate the King's death – it having been decided by Sir Home Popham some time previously that it would demoralize the men to include such a communication in the signal vocabulary. In fact, most of those on the *Beagle* were secretly delighted at the news: the new king, William IV, was a Navy man, who had served as Lord High Admiral in Rio. He had been known as a drinking man, a no-nonsense officer and a good sport. There was a general consensus among the crew that – as a former matlow – King Billy would see the Service all right.

An official period of mourning was declared throughout the fleet, as per regulations, and FitzRoy sat down to prepare the divine service that must be held in memory of His Majesty. His mind, though, was still reeling with its own grief, too consumed by its own misery to care about the death, six thousand miles away, of the man he had served so assiduously for two years. He had to force himself to concentrate. *I must throw myself fully into my employment. Only through forced occupation will I get through the days. I must not allow myself to be unemployed and alone, or the demons will come again.*

He remained stunned, too, by the revelation of the afternoon before. He had been obliged to part with a handsome sum to placate the aggrieved Dr Carson Figueira, but not before both Fuegia Basket and York Minster had consented to be inoculated; this after a nice speech in their own language by Boat Memory, who had – he later explained – urged them to put their trust in Capp'en Fitz'oy. The capp'en had given them his word, he said, that the white man's medicine would protect them against ill health in the future, and the capp'en's word was his bond. The momentarily loquacious York Minster had not uttered a single word since.

FitzRoy opened the battered copy of the scriptures that Sulivan had given him, and leafed through it. Whether he found the text of chapter fourteen of the Book of Job by accident, or whether he had read so much of the Old Testament by now that the chapter lay buried in his subconscious, he did not know. *As the waters fail from the sea, and the flood decayeth and drieth up; so man lieth down, and riseth not.*

He felt suddenly weary in himself, and at that moment he saw life as a struggle to placate an uncompromising Old Testament God; a God who could wipe out most of the earth's population in an instant with a mighty deluge, or take the life of one defenceless man, however good, however powerful, as was His wont.

The waters wear the stones: thou washest away the things which grow out of the dust of the earth; and thou destroyest the hope of man. Thou prevailest for ever against him, and he passeth: thou changest his countenance, and sendest him away. His sons come to honour, and he knoweth it not; and they are brought low, but he perceiveth it not of them.

It was not the most immaculately turned-out group of men that had ever bidden farewell to a monarch. The crew had been drawn up in two rectangles on either side of the upside-down whaleboat, which bisected the maindeck on its skids, its keel slicing the air like a half-submerged shark. They were as smartly dressed as they could manage, but the innumerable repairs and patchings-up that quilted their motley garments testified to the constant needlework required on a long voyage south. The file of red-jacketed marines to the left, their drummer boy at the far end, did lend the occasion an air of formality, although their uniforms would hardly have borne close inspection either. The officers at least presented a dignified prospect, a row of peaked caps behind their commander on the raised poop, their formal black frock-coats and white stockings cleaned and crisply pressed by their servants.

'Caps off!' commanded Lieutenant Kempe.

For a moment there was silence on board the *Beagle*, broken only by the creaking of the rigging as she rode, windlessly, at anchor. FitzRoy stepped forward to the azimuth compass, which had come to serve as his lectern whenever he needed to address the men. The creaking of the ship seemed more insistent now; almost rhythmic. He fought hard to keep thoughts of his own father from overwhelming his mind. 'We are gathered to give thanks for the life of His Gracious Majesty King George the Fourth.'

The rhythmic creaking was coming faster now, not loudly but insistently, from somewhere close by. King and Stokes exchanged questioning glances. Kempe glared inquisitively at Sorrell, who shrugged his shoulders in mystification.

'I shall read from the Book of Job, chapter fourteen. "Man that is born of a woman is of few days, and full of trouble. He cometh forth like a flower, and is cut down: he fleeth also as a shadow and continueth not."'

Even FitzRoy was forced to take note now. The creaking, accompanied by a gentle knocking noise, insinuated itself relentlessly into his concentration. He paused, and murmured to Sorrell, 'Mr Bos'n, is every member of the crew present?'

'Yes sir, excepting those in the sick list, sir.'

The sound was coming from one of the tiny cabins under the poop deck companionways, the one to the starboard side, which was occupied by Midshipman Stokes. Now it was Stokes's turn to shrug his shoulders with bemused innocence.

FitzRoy cleared his throat and began to read: '"And dost thou open thine eyes upon such an one, and bringest me into judgement with thee?"' He broke off. There seemed to be a jaunty, almost enthusiastic quality to the creaking and knocking now.

He strode briskly down the companionway, turned sharply

at the bottom and flung open the door to Stokes's cabin. Stokes's hammock, the source of the creaking, was up on its hooks, stretched from one wall to the other. In it, his face a mask of furious concentration, his breeches about his ankles, lay York Minster. Bouncing astride York, her skirts gathered about her waist, her head bent against the ceiling, sat Fuegia Basket. Still bouncing, she turned delightedly and favoured FitzRoy with her most beaming smile. 'Fuegia love Capp'en Fitz'oy,' she said.

Chapter Eight

Plymouth Sound, 13 October 1830

———————

'They must be married at the earliest convenience.'

'Married? How can she be married, sir? She is not yet thirteen.'

'I mean, they must be betrothed. At the very least, we must have the banns published in Plymouth, or I shall obtain a marriage licence from Doctors' Commons when we reach London.'

The issue of York and Fuegia continued to vex FitzRoy. As her legal guardian – for such he surely was, ever since the Admiralty's acknowledgement of his letter – he was responsible for the child's welfare. To allow her relationship with York Minster to continue unchallenged was out of the question. But to separate the Fuegians from each other would surely go against the purpose of his scheme, as well as being an interesting physical proposition, given York's frankly superhuman strength. The only answer FitzRoy could find was to legitimize their union. How he wished for spiritual guidance on the matter, but as there was no chaplain aboard such a small ship, he himself was the sole source of spiritual authority on the *Beagle*. Instead he had turned for solace to the wholly inadequate figure of Wilson, the surgeon, whose reaction to FitzRoy's concerns was predictably dismissive.

'Sir, these people, if they are indeed such, are of the lowest rung on God's ladder. Such behaviour is hardly unexpected at the basest levels of society. Take a carriage ride up the Haymarket and you will see girls of the lowest class, girls as young as eight or nine, offering themselves to the highest bidder. When the famines bit in Kent and Sussex and Hampshire, poor farmers sold their daughters at market, some, I have heard tell, in a halter like a cow. These savages are lower still, barely a step above the brute creation. To behave in this manner is in their nature.'

'Mr Wilson, I have given my word that these people will be raised from their base condition, and given every advantage of polite society. That is the purpose of their sojourn in England. If the girl finds herself with child when she is in my care, I will have failed in my duty before their visit has even begun.'

'But if they are betrothed, sir, how will they even know it? One is no more than a child, the other keeps his counsel like a simpleton.'

'You would do well not to underestimate their intelligence, Mr Wilson. York Minster may be a displeasing specimen of humanity in many respects, but stupidity is not one of his vices. Fuegia, too, is sharp of mind. I shall put the proposition to him, and to her, over dinner.'

'Over *dinner*, sir?'

'Over dinner, Mr Wilson. I intend to invite them to dinner, if the four of them can squeeze into my cabin. It will not be the noblest repast, as we are down to hard biscuit, salt pig and salt horse, but I have asked the cook to keep back the last few canisters of Donkin's soup and preserved vegetables. Even if a formal betrothal does not result, we may at least educate them in the way of a few table manners.'

The Fuegians filed into FitzRoy's cabin just after midday, their naturally crouching gait a useful attribute in view of the low ceiling. Suspicion was etched across all their faces at the sight of the captain's formal linen and glassware, even more so than when faced with Dr Figueira's tray of medical instruments. They had become accustomed to meals below decks, where food was eaten by hand or with a single knife, and drink was slurped from an open bowl; here, a veritable obstacle course was arrayed on the tablecloth. Coxswain Bennet – whom FitzRoy had also invited, as he had somehow drifted into the role of unofficial nursemaid to the Fuegians – entered with them, his burly form bent practically double in the tiny cabin, cheerily ushering his charges to their seats. FitzRoy's steward became the seventh person to try to insinuate himself into the tiny space, in a desperate attempt to pour water into the guests' glasses, but as a lesson in etiquette this got the afternoon off to a bad start: he was compelled by the lack of standing room to hover in the doorway and reach over the heads of those nearest to him.

Barely had York Minster's crystal goblet been filled with water than he grabbed it, and threw the contents down his throat in one swift move.

'York,' said FitzRoy gently, 'today I wish to teach you how to behave at dinner in England. It is thought polite to wait until everybody has their food or their drink before starting.'

York said nothing, but leaned towards the unlit candelabra in the centre of the table and sniffed at the candles.

'These are "candles". They give light from a little flame. At a polite dinner in England they would be made from beeswax. At a simpler meal, or here on a naval vessel, they are made from beef tallow.'

Once more York sniffed at the candles, which sat plumply in their twisted silver cradles, then abruptly grabbed and ate all three, cramming them into a capacious mouth. FitzRoy sighed. It was shaping up to be a long afternoon.

Jemmy, meanwhile, was holding each item of silver cutlery to the skylight in turn, an expression of wonderment on his face. 'Beautiful. Many beautiful knifes.'

Bennet, who was about to enlighten him, checked himself. He had only dined with a senior officer once before in his young life, when Admiral Bartlett had invited all his junior officers to dinner in groups aboard the *Persephone*. It had been, he remembered, a terrifying and painfully silent affair: officers were strictly forbidden to broach any topic of conversation until it had first been raised by their commander. Fortunately FitzRoy spotted his hesitation and gave him the nod.

'The spoon on the outside is for the soup course, Jemmy. Then the fork and knife on the inside are for the second course. With each course, you move in to the next two pieces of cutlery. Finally, your pudding cutlery is at the top of your place setting.'

'When Jemmy is rich man in Englan' he will have many courses, many cutleries.' Jemmy's eyes swam delightedly at this suggestion, and he bared his teeth with pleasure. 'Many beautiful knifes.'

'When a man and a woman are married in England, Jemmy, they are given presents for their home. This is how most people obtain their cutlery, and linen, and crockery.' FitzRoy indicated the three items in turn.

'Please, Capp'en Fitz'oy, what is married?' asked Boat.

'"Married" is when a man and a woman come together in the sight of God.' FitzRoy cut to the chase. 'When we reach England I believe York and Fuegia must be married.'

'Please, Capp'en Fitz'oy, York and Fuegia are already come together.'

'I believe York and Fuegia must be married!' squeaked Fuegia.

'They are together, yes, Boat, but their union has yet to be blessed by God.'

'God is late,' protested Jemmy. 'York and Fuegia come together many months ago.'

The servant began distributing ladlefuls of Donkin's soup, a thin, evil, green liquid, among the dinner guests. York lowered his head into the steam and sniffed warily.

'Remember, the outside spoon,' said Bennet helpfully.

York gave him a scornful sidelong look, lowered his face into the scalding fluid and began to slurp loudly. Jemmy, meanwhile, held a spoonful of bright green liquid to his lips, his grasp awkward but his technique surprisingly dainty. 'York is rough fellow. Very rough fellow,' he observed, down the length of his nose. York's green face rose bubbling from the steam, and silenced him with a glare.

'Do you not have marriage in your country, Boat?' enquired FitzRoy hastily. 'When the two families come together and celebrate?'

'Oh yes, Capp'en Fitz'oy. When a man is old enough to hunt and a woman is old enough to bear childs. The family of girl will sell her to family of young man. But my people do not understand God's mercy. This is not a proper English married.'

'I believe York and Fuegia must be married!' squealed Fuegia, once more.

'We have a big celebrate, Capp'en Fitz'oy. It goes on for many days. We kill seal. Everybody come from many miles. Everybody celebrate – young people, old people.'

FitzRoy's memory was jogged. 'There is something I have been meaning to ask you, Boat. You speak of old people. But I saw no old people in Tierra del Fuego. No grey-haired men or women.'

'There are old people in my country, Capp'en sir.' Boat looked unhappy.

'But not many. I saw none in a year and a half.'

'You did not look for them well, Capp'en Fitz'oy.'

There was something wrong now, FitzRoy could tell. Boat Memory was staring fixedly into the emerald depths of his soup bowl.

Jemmy, immune to the gathering crisis, chattered on obliviously. 'Sometimes my people very hungry, in winter. No food!' He gesticulated eagerly, rubbing his pot belly to indicate the unimaginable awfulness of not being able to fill it. 'Then we eat old people. Put head in smoke, they die quick. Women eat arms, men eat legs. Leave rest. Sometimes old people run away. Sometimes we catch, bring back. Sometimes no find, die in woods.'

Fuegia giggled.

FitzRoy became aware that Bennet had dropped his spoon, his ruddy countenance frozen in horror. A single virulent green rivulet was making its way purposefully down the starched white of his napkin. FitzRoy felt his gut seize and tighten at the revelation he had unleashed, but he ploughed on with grim anthropological fascination: 'But Jemmy, you have dogs. If your people are starving – hungry – do you not eat the dogs first?'

'Oh no, Capp'en Fitz'oy!' laughed Jemmy. 'Doggies catch otters! Old women no!'

Boat Memory continued to stare red-faced at the table-cloth. Fuegia Basket suppressed another giggle. A strange snorting guffaw bubbled up through the shallows of York Minster's soup plate. It was the first time, FitzRoy realized, that he had ever heard York Minster laugh.

It was a very English dawn that broke over the Royal Dockyard at Devonport as the *Beagle* and the *Adventure* made their final approach: grey, featureless and nondescript, and therefore all the more welcome to the men, who had dreamed of such an English morning for the last four years. Here was the familiar heartland of His Majesty's Navy. Even the statuesque ships of Rio de Janeiro harbour would have paled alongside the mighty men-of-war that towered above the Devonport quays and, indeed, over the town itself. But there was no hammering or banging to be heard as one would expect in a naval dockyard, no vibrancy, few signs of life, even. The men-of-war lay deserted, painted bright yellow against the elements, their yard-arms, masts and rigging stripped. The war was long since finished. The titans that had defeated Napoleon and wrested control of all Europe from the dictator lay chained up, silent but proud, reduced to this sorry state by clinical economic necessity. HMS *Bellerophon*, heroine of Trafalgar and the Nile, wallowed rotting and unpainted, the cramped and sweating quarters below her decks packed with convicts due for transportation to Australia.

The *Beagle* and the *Adventure* trod a silent path between these fallen giants, the men lining the rail navigating their own path between pride, regret and the simple thrill of homecoming. Alone on the grey wharf, a small crowd had gathered to meet the ships, for news of their arrival had travelled rapidly up the coast from Falmouth.

The four Fuegians crowded alongside the sailors, eager for a glimpse of the land about which they had heard so much.

'This is Englan', Capp'en Fitz'oy?' asked Boat Memory, for the third time, as if unable to believe the evidence of his eyes.

'This is England, Boat.'

'By the deuce, it may not look up to much, but this is old England all right,' enthused King, who had not seen England since he was ten.

Indeed, it did not look up to much. The flat grey-green landscape; the uninteresting little town, wreathed in wisps of smoke, that stumbled down the eastern bank of the river; the broad, deserted avenue paved with marble chips that ran white and lifeless from the dockyard gates; none of these could be compared with the sights and sounds that the *Beagle*'s crew had encountered over the previous four years. But this was home, and the gaggle of wellwishers crowding the quayside was made up of friends and family.

'I have dreamed of this day,' breathed Boat Memory, and he looked at FitzRoy, his eyes a wet slick.

'Jemmy too have dreamed of this day,' said Jemmy, as convincingly as he could, although – in all truth – this was not the shiny golden England of his imagination.

And then the hush was broken, suddenly, by a monstrous, clanking, belching sound, which took everybody on board by surprise. The Fuegians reacted first, their self-preserving instincts honed, Boat, Jemmy and Fuegia diving for cover, the little girl whimpering in terror as she curled herself into a ball inside a coil of rope. York, undecided between flight and furious resistance, bent down to the deck and shouldered a massive spar that two crewmen would have been hard put to lift. Brandishing it like a colossal spear he stood, nostrils flaring, cheeks flushed, legs braced apart, ready to confront his adversary.

'Good God,' said Kempe in amazement at this physical feat.

'He's a ruddy marvel,' said Stokes.

'It's a steam-ship, York,' said FitzRoy, soothingly. 'It's just a steam-ship. A ship powered by steam.'

York, unsure whether to trust FitzRoy, stood rigid and transfixed, a perfect physical specimen poised to face down his enemy in mortal combat. But the steamer waddled past unconcernedly in the opposite direction, its big side paddle-wheels clunking ineffectually at the water, coal smoke belching filthily from its two chimneys.

'They've witnessed the future and they don't like it,' scoffed King.

'Have you ever seen a railway train, Midshipman King?'

'No sir,' said King, addressing his own feet.

'Fuming like a grist mill and clanking like a blacksmith's shop? When you have seen one such run smoking past you, then I venture you may understand what it is to see your first steam-ship.'

'Yes sir,' muttered King, suitably chastened.

It was not difficult to spot Sulivan in the reunion crowd, mainly because he towered over most of them. FitzRoy had to pinch himself to equate this giant with the slender eighteen-year-old midshipman who had bidden him such a tearful farewell two years previously. And then, of course, there was the conspicuous white stripe on his sleeve, which indicated that this was now Lieutenant Sulivan. The two men navigated through the throng and pumped each other's hands so delightedly and so vigorously it seemed they must do themselves an injury.

'My dear Sulivan – my dear *Lieutenant* Sulivan.'

'It's wonderful to see you safe and sound, sir – and not a scratch on the *Beagle*! Oh, but I am being remiss in my manners. Miss Young, may I have the honour of presenting to your acquaintance Commander FitzRoy of HMS *Beagle*.

Commander, this is Miss Young of Barton End, and her companion Miss Tregarron.'

FitzRoy became aware of two young ladies, waiting patiently arm in arm at Sulivan's elbow, and immediately swept off his cap. 'The pleasure is entirely mine, ladies.'

'Will you accompany us, Commander?'

'I would be delighted, Miss Young. And might I be so forward as to enquire of your Christian names?'

'Of course – I am Sophia. Miss Tregarron's Christian name is Arabella.'

'Do not Miss Young and her companion look well this morning?' beamed Sulivan, although the rapt way he pronounced the words 'Miss Young' left no room for doubt as to where the compliment was aimed.

'After four years at sea, my homecoming has been doubly blessed that I should find myself in the presence of such delightful company.'

The two women blushed prettily.

Like matching peacocks, they were arrayed in identical dresses of bright turquoise silk trimmed with broderie anglaise, their waists fashionably constricted, the outlines of their hips and legs concealed by a demure gathering of petticoats. Miss Tregarron, the chaperone, dipped the brim of her bonnet faintly and took a discreet step back into the crowd. Miss Young, round-faced and fresh with the beauty of youth, continued to gaze up adoringly at Sulivan. FitzRoy, too, stared up at his former midshipman, who had grown by at least three inches.

'When I last saw Mr Sulivan he was but a middie, and very much a boy. Now he has grown into a fine figure of a man.'

'He is five foot and eleven inches tall,' glowed Miss Young, so close now to her beau that they were almost touching. 'But I fear, Commander, that Mr Sulivan is demonstrating undue modesty this morning. Will you not tell the commander of your remarkable accomplishment in the lieutenant's examination?'

Sulivan's face suffused with scarlet. 'I passed for lieutenant with full numbers,' he confessed.

'Only the second person in the history of the Service to do so!' said Miss Young, so overwhelmed with affection it seemed she must burst. 'Following yourself, of course, Commander FitzRoy.'

'These are the most marvellous news!' FitzRoy would have thrown his arms around Sulivan and hugged him then and there, except it did not do for naval commanders to hug lieutenants in the middle of the Royal Dockyard.

'But it is you, sir, who must take all the credit. Everything I have learned about handling a ship, Miss Young, and I mean everything, I have learned from Commander FitzRoy here. Many is the hour that the commander gave of his free time in the *Thetis* to pass on his exhaustive knowledge of seamanship, from box-hauling to flatting in, from French shroud knots to selvagees—'

'Mr Sulivan talks about you continuously, Commander, in the most glowing terms.'

'Mr Sulivan talks continuously, Miss Young, but not always accurately. All that he has achieved, he has achieved by his own hard work and intelligence – I will not accept one iota of credit. Do you have a ship yet, Lieutenant Sulivan?'

'Not yet.'

'Then we shall exert all our influence to rectify the omission. At least with full numbers you will not go to the back of the mates' list.'

'Thank goodness for that! Of course I do not have a handle to my name, and they say that some who are without must wait ten years for a berth—' FitzRoy smiled, and Sulivan coloured at the realization of what he had just said. It would be hard to find a more useful 'handle' than 'FitzRoy'. Sulivan stumbled on, 'That is, my father has a large family, therefore it was a great object to him to achieve so good an education for me free of cost—'

'Pray excuse me.' This time it was Miss Young who had interrupted, her widening eyes fixed on the *Beagle*. 'But is that . . . a *little girl* I see on the deck of your ship?'

FitzRoy turned, just in time to see Fuegia dart behind the mizzen-mast with a cheeky grin. She was playing hide-and-seek with him.

'It is, indeed.' He laughed. 'That is Fuegia Basket. Come aboard and I will introduce her to you.' He proceeded to relate the story of the four Fuegians. 'It is my intention,' he concluded, as Sulivan helped Miss Young up the accommodation ladder, 'to secure for them a Christian education in this country before returning them to their own, so that they might draw benefit as a nation from the advanced condition of our society.'

'How wonderful, Commander – and how provident that the Lord has delivered you into our hands today! For I am acquainted with the Reverend Mr Harris, the vicar of Plymstock – he is the most prodigious friend of my father. He is also the local representative of the Church Missionary Society, whose very purpose is the provision of religious instruction to savages.'

'Then we must effect an introduction this very afternoon – that is, if you are amenable to the suggestion, sir.'

'Capital, my dear Sulivan – that would be capital!'

Fuegia ran up and hurled herself into Sophia Young's turquoise skirts.

'Pretty dress! Fuegia want pretty dress like this one! Fuegia be pretty lady too!'

'Why, Commander FitzRoy, she is delightful,' smiled Miss Young, stroking Fuegia's wild tresses, 'and it is to her great good fortune, I am sure, that the Lord has appointed you guardian angel to these poor unfortunate creatures. You have the power to give them life – eternal life – where once there was only misery and suffering.'

I hope so, thought FitzRoy. *I only hope so.*

The savages have been removed to Castle Farm outside Plymouth, in order to enjoy more freedom and fresh air, where they are said to be satisfied with their present situation. As soon as they are sufficiently acquainted with the language, and familiarized with the manners of this country, they will begin a course of education adapted to their future residence in their native country.

FitzRoy put down the *Hampshire Telegraph and Sussex Chronicle* in irritation. How the deuce had the journalist tracked them down to Castle Farm? And how did he presume to comment on the Fuegians' satisfaction or otherwise, when he had yet to make their acquaintance? The *Morning Post* was even worse.

The *Beagle* has brought to England four natives of Tierra del Fuego, taken prisoner during the time that the ship was employed on the south-west coast of that country. Captain FitzRoy hopes that by their assistance the condition of the savages habituating the Fuegian Archipelago may be in some measure improved, and that they may be rendered less hostile to strangers. At present they are the lowest of mankind, and, without a doubt, cannibals.

FitzRoy tossed down the paper in disgust. '"Taken prisoner"? What do they mean, "taken prisoner"?'

Bennet felt it wiser to keep his counsel. Morrish, the phrenologist, looked up from under beetling brows but said nothing, and continued to unpack his Gladstone bag.

'Please, what is "taken prisoner"?' asked Boat Memory nervously.

'It means you do not wish to be here.'

'This is not true. This is a bad man who does not speak the truth. Boat Memory is happy to be here in Englan'. One day Englan' and my country will be frien's. Good frien's, like Boat Memory and Capp'en Fitz'oy.'

'That's right, Boat. One day our two countries will be friends.'

But how had the journalists discovered so much? FitzRoy was inclined to suspect the Reverend J. C. Harris, vicar of Plymstock, a fat, fussy, fluttering cleric, whose appeal to the

Church Missionary Society had more or less come to naught: the clergyman had returned after a fortnight's absence wearing a woebegone face and bearing bad news, a letter which declared brusquely that 'The Committee do not conceive it to be in the province of this Society to take charge of these individuals.' They had, at least, referred FitzRoy to the National Society for Providing the Education of the Poor in the Principles of the Established Church; an appointment had been fixed with the secretary, the Reverend Joseph Wigram, who was assistant preacher at St James's, Westminster, when the *Beagle* reached journey's end in London. She was due to set sail from Devonport on the day after the morrow. In the meantime, he had taken a vacant cottage in Castle Farm as a billet for the Fuegians, in an effort to protect them from prying eyes and from the international assortment of diseases for which Plymouth, as the hub of the country's naval activity, was justly famous. He had also written to the First Secretary of the Admiralty, Sir John Croker, requesting special leave for Murray and Bennet to accompany the Fuegians onshore. It would be no great travail to navigate his way up the Channel to the Port of London without a master and a coxswain.

The three officers and the four Fuegians were now arranged in the front parlour of Castle Farm cottage, watching the drizzle fleck the panes of the little windows embedded in the thick walls. The officers, especially, were not used to inactivity. FitzRoy had hired the phrenologist — which he had been meaning to do for some while — from the extremely limited selection available in the Plymouth area, in order to kill time. Boat Memory, who was to be the object of study, remained wary. 'Will it hurt, Capp'en Fitz'oy? Like Dr Figueira and his medicine?'

York Minster wore a contemptuous expression.

'No, Boat, it won't hurt. Dr Morrish is a phrenologist. He surveys the human head, just as I survey the seabed and the coast. He will feel your head, and make a map of it. It will be quite painless.'

'I do not feel well, Capp'en Fitz'oy. Boat Memory feels too sick for his head to be maked into a map.'

'I told you, Boat, you will feel nothing, and it will all be finished in a minute or two. Just a minute or two. That's all.'

Reluctantly the Fuegian signalled his acquiescence, as Morrish produced a variety of sinister-looking measuring devices in metal and polished wood, and proceeded to calculate the size of Boat's head from every conceivable angle. Then he set to work with his fingers, probing smoothly and expertly through the dark thickets of Boat's hair.

'The head is uncommonly small at the top and at the back. There are fewer bumps for the craniologist than one would find in the skull of a civilized man – but that in itself is significant. The forehead is ill-shaped. The propensities are large and full. The sentiments, however, are small, with the exception of cautiousness and firmness. The intellectual organs are small, as one would find with the coloured races or, of course, with the French and the Irish.'

Morrish paused as Boat leaned forward to scratch his ankle. 'Please, Capp'en Fitz'oy, I do not understand.'

'Phrenology is the science of the brain, Boat. The shape of the skull – the bone – corresponds with the shape of the brain. Experts have identified thirty-five areas of the brain, each of which can be read from the outside.' FitzRoy aspired to his most reassuring tone, but privately he was irritated at these medical men who continued to examine the Fuegians as if they were deaf and dumb animals.

'There is cunning here, and indolence, and passive fortitude. A want of energy and a deficient intellect.'

'That is if the physiology can be trusted, Dr Morrish,' said FitzRoy, feeling himself bound to disagree.

'Oh, the physiognomy of man will always reveal its secrets to the trained hand, Commander. You are not to worry: this is anything but an unexpected diagnosis. Savages are entirely different from civilized men, both in outward feature and in mind. They are incapable of progress.'

'But surely, Dr Morrish, all men are equal before God.'

'The presence of the organ of veneration in all men, Commander, is direct proof of the existence of God. But if all men were equal, then all men's skulls would be equally configured. A savage cannot progress into a civilized man.'

Boat scratched his ankle again. 'Am I a savage, Capp'en Fitz'oy?'

FitzRoy did not know what to say.

'Am I a savage, Capp'en Fitz'oy?' parroted Fuegia.

'No, Boat, you are not a savage.'

'Then one day, Capp'en Fitz'oy, I too will be a phrenologist.'

Morrish raised his eyebrows but said nothing. Jemmy, bored, fixed his gaze on his looking-glass, and pushed his nose up to see what it looked like reflected.

'Please, Capp'en Fitz'oy, Boat feels sick.'

'It is almost over now, Boat. The doctor will finish examining your head in a moment.'

'Boat's head does not feel sick. Boat feels sick. Boat's ankles hurt.'

'Your ankles, Boat? What is wrong with your ankles?'

Obligingly Boat leaned forward once more and hitched up his left trouser leg. There was a bump as Morrish dropped his measuring-tool in shock, his chair and its occupant clattering back into the table. FitzRoy stood rooted to the spot, and thought for sure that his heart had stopped. The red rash about Boat's ankle was unmistakable. The first spots were already beginning their transition into the clear pustules, which – within a week or two – would signify the onset of full-blown smallpox.

If he dies, I will have robbed him of his life as surely as if I had allowed Davis to pull the trigger. Yet if he lives I will have robbed him of his handsome features, and of his innocence.

FitzRoy paced his side of the quarterdeck bitterly, left alone by the crew, who knew better than to trouble him. The fresh grey air of the Channel ballooned the *Beagle*'s sails and flung FitzRoy's hair hither and thither till it stung his cheeks, but could not shift the weight of putrefying fear that sat heavy in his stomach.

Why had Boat not properly imbibed the vaccine? Was the whole batch bad? Or had that damned fool Figueira botched the inoculation – had he drawn too much blood with his lancet? Would the others catch the disease? Please, God, do not let the others catch the disease.

He had called in the Admiralty's offer of assistance – *how* he had called it in – by arranging for the Fuegians to be admitted to the Royal Naval Hospital at Plymouth, quarantined in a whole ward of their own, under the care of the eminent specialist Dr David Dickson. He had ordered Bennet and Murray to remain at Castle Farm to monitor Boat's progress. FitzRoy thought keenly of the Fuegians now, bewildered and alone in their empty ward, watching the disease take hold, watching Boat's open, friendly features becoming increasingly and hideously disfigured before their eyes. The cavernous Royal Naval Hospital, so packed with the wounded in wartime, boasted few patients now: just the odd pneumonia case, and one or two sailors driven out of their senses by syphilis. The corridors echoed only to the clacking footsteps of the doctors and orderlies. Or would they be echoing now to the screams of Boat Memory? FitzRoy shuddered and pulled his coat about him.

The *Beagle* swung to westward at the Isle of Thanet, beating up the Thames estuary against the previously friendly breeze. The river traffic thickened as the banks came in sight of each other: elegant frigates with uniformed crews, dark barges swarming with silhouetted figures in coal-dirty smocks, tiny skiffs scurrying to avoid being run down, all went about their business oblivious to the little brig that had travelled to the far end of the world and had returned with such an unusual cargo. There were East Indiamen loaded with cotton and pepper, West Indiamen bearing coffee, rum and sugar, and tobacco ships from the United States, awaiting clearance to enter the mighty fortress gates of the new dockyards. This was the throbbing, filthy hub of the greatest modern commercial city in the world: the newly constructed tobacco warehouse at Wapping, it was said, was the largest building to be constructed since the Egyptian pyramids. The *Beagle* picked its way through a converging winter forest of bare masts, sidestepping shoal after shoal of struggling oars, the water by turns stained purple with wine and white with flour. A clangorous noise, half-familiar but its sheer intensity forgotten, assaulted the eardrums of the crew; the unflinching stench of stale herrings and weak beer insinuated itself into their nostrils.

They berthed their vessel at the Naval Dockyard at Woolwich, there to be paid off, stripped and cleared out, her pendant hauled down, her company dispersed, never – in all probability – to meet again. *All of us who have passed so many rough hours together, scattered like chaff on the wind.* They were expected at Woolwich, their berth already prepared, the Admiralty as always aware of the exact movements of each and every one of its ships; the precision with which their lordships gathered each vessel in at the end of its voyage matched only by the careless abandon with which each and every crewman was tossed aside. It should have been a proud, emotional time, of farewells and handclaspings and promises to meet again, when old shipmates' virtues loomed large and their vices were generously set aside, to be diminished for ever by the sentimental glow of memory. But FitzRoy could think of nothing except the young man who lay fighting for his life in the Royal Naval Hospital, beset by a strange disease in a strange land, a young man who had put his trust in him, a young man to whom he had given his word that he would become an English gentleman. Oh, there were handclaspings all right, for Kempe and King and Stokes and Wilson and Boatswain Sorrell and all the others, but these were uncommonly muted farewells on both sides. Eventually, his duty of care towards the *Beagle* finally discharged, FitzRoy said his own silent farewell to her, and stepped on to the wharf. He adjusted his watch by twenty minutes, from Plymouth time to London time, signalled to the waiting coachman, carefully supervised the loading of his trunk, climbed aboard his carriage and set off for London.

*   *   *

'I may – ah – I may be able to be of assistance to you.'

The Reverend Joseph Wigram, a young man prone to slight, mannered hesitations, tapped out his pipe and lit it anew. The smoke curled upward, searching for an escape route from the study, but the heavy moreen curtains that stood guard against the daylight forced it to circle restlessly above his head. Really, Wigram was too young even for a post of such uncertain status as the secretaryship of the National Society for Providing the Education of the Poor in the Principles of the Established Church. Without doubt, it was an appointment that owed much to the good offices of his father, Sir Robert Wigram of Walthamstow House. But the younger Wigram's earnest countenance and his obvious eagerness to be of assistance betokened well. The clergyman smoothed his hair down for the third or fourth time: the presence of such a distinguished visitor as Commander FitzRoy of HMS *Beagle* had obviously unnerved him. He maintained the air of a man who had arrived late for an important appointment.

'I have the – ah – the honour to be the governor of Walthamstow School. I share the honour with the rector of Walthamstow, William Wilson. Are you familiar with Walthamstow? It is – ah – a small village to the north-east of London. Most agreeable. I am sure it would be possible to enter the – ah – the four savages as boarders and pupils. They can start as soon as they are ready.'

'I am most indebted to you, sir, for your kindness. You are more than generous.'

'Not a bit of it, sir, not a bit of it. We are all as one before God. But I must own that ours is only a small and ill-funded institution, ill-equipped for all but the most basic instruction. As I am sure you are aware, sir, these are straitened times.'

'The most basic instruction, Mr Wigram, is all that could be wished for in the present circumstances. I would desire the Fuegians to become fluent in English and the plainer truths of Christianity, as the first object, and in the use of common tools, a slight acquaintance with husbandry, gardening and mechanism as the second, all areas of instruction which you have convinced me are well within your capabilities.'

'Absolutely – absolutely. And may I enquire as to their – ah – their present whereabouts?'

'They are currently residing at Plymouth.'

FitzRoy paused. Should he convey the full, awful circumstances to Mr Wigram, that one of the Fuegians – and perhaps before long all of them – was engaged in a desperate struggle for life? His hesitation was brief. He had no right to withhold the truth from anyone, particularly not a man of the cloth who had so generously answered his prayers.

'They are at the Royal Naval Hospital. Tragically, one of them has contracted smallpox. I had them inoculated, but it was not properly imbibed. I am, however, confident that he will make a full recovery.'

'Indeed – indeed. So I have read in the *Morning Post*.'

FitzRoy was exceedingly glad that he had not sought to dissemble. The young man's question, it seemed, had been disingenuous.

'We must hope, Commander FitzRoy, that the good Lord in His infinite mercy will spare them the ultimate punishment for their formerly base lives. Might I enquire the – ah – ages of the four savages?'

'York Minster, the oldest' – the Reverend Wigram raised one eyebrow at York's unusual name – 'appears to be about twenty-six. Boat Memory, the, ah, patient' – FitzRoy discovered Wigram's verbal tic to be infectious – 'is of some twenty summers. The boy Jemmy Button is perhaps sixteen or seventeen, while the little girl Fuegia Basket is, I would guess, eleven or twelve.'

'Excellent, excellent. I am sure that the – ah – age gap will not present a problem. It is, after all, a uniform level of ability that determines the homogeneous composition of any classroom.'

'The age gap, Mr Wigram?'

'Did I not say, Commander FitzRoy? Walthamstow is an

infants' school. The average age of our pupils is between four and seven.'

FitzRoy emerged into broken sunshine, walked down the rectory steps and turned through the wrought-iron gateway. He hired a hackney coach at the stand on Piccadilly, tipping the waterman a penny. Judging by the faded coat of arms, the deep, comfortable seats and the exhausted suspension, the vehicle had once belonged to a nobleman. He felt like an infant, swaddled and jiggled helplessly by its nurse, as the coach shuddered its way through the London traffic. He paid off the driver outside the Admiralty, where he was to begin the task of supervising the final drafting of several hundred charts and plans.

A familiar figure was waiting for him on the Admiralty steps, but the extreme unfamiliarity of the context led him to hesitate for a moment, trying to place the apparition. It was a figure he was better used to seeing at the wheel of the *Beagle* as she bucked into a head-on gale.

'Mr Murray?'

Murray said nothing, and FitzRoy ran the whole gamut of emotions in an instant, from fearing the worst to believing that events must have come to a satisfactory conclusion. The Scotsman simply handed him a letter, his face a blank canvas on which FitzRoy had painted a thousand imaginary expressions before he had even broken the wafer and unfolded the wrapper.

The letter was signed by Dr Dickson, of the Royal Naval Hospital.

Sir

I am sorry to inform you that Boat Memory died this afternoon in the eruptive stage of smallpox. He was perfectly covered with the eruption; but the pustules did not advance to maturation as they should have done, and as the breathing was much impeded, I had little or no expectation of his recovery. He has been saved much suffering – and those about him from attending a loathsome Disease. In the boy Button the appearance of the vaccine bacilli is satisfactory – and as the others have been revaccinated, I am in hope they will be saved from the fate of their countryman.

I beg to remain

Sir

Yours faithfully

D.H. Dickson

FitzRoy looked up from the letter, and realized that the expression on Murray's face had not been a vacant one; it was the look of a man whose heart has been scoured out from the inside.

Part Two

Chapter Nine

The Mount, Shrewsbury, 29 August 1831

The mail coach from Oswestry disgorged Charles Darwin and three other passengers into the crowded inn-yard of the Lion, where he stretched his cramped legs and waited for his pack to be unloaded from the roof. Post-boys in smart red jackets and pedlars in smock frocks swarmed around to see to the horses and passengers respectively, most persistent of all being an urchin claiming to possess a trained bullfinch that would whistle 'The White Cockade' for a penny. Although the afternoon was grey and faintly sticky, Darwin decided to make his way to the Mount on foot. The trip from North Wales on macadamized roads had hardly taxed his muscles; the milestones had ticked rapidly by, although the relentless quickset hedges that arrowed into the distance had quickly become monotonous. Both his limbs and his senses were in need of exercise. Piqued as his curiosity was by the prospect of a singing bullfinch, he was keen to be home and marched off up Wyle Cop at a good pace. His long legs covered the ground with rapid strides, leaving the disappointed little boy – who thought he had sensed a business deal – to give up the chase some thirty yards beyond the inn gates.

Before long the streets and houses had given way to stands of acacia and copper beech, which in turn receded to reveal the great red-brick mansion that his father had built. It was an impassive rectangle boasting of solid provincial prosperity, its clean lines broken only by the classical portico at its base, put there to remind the visitor of the culture and learning that had literally elevated the Darwin family to this comfortable spot. Charles could see the servants going about their business on the lawn, and a tall, willowy shape – his sister Caroline, to judge from the brown mass of curls escaping from under the bonnet – compiling a bouquet of flowers. Before long, one of the housemaids spotted the dusty figure striding vigorously through the gates and sounded the alert. Maids scurried to check that Master Charles's room was properly prepared, while the waterman rushed to fill a bucket with hot water. By the time he had reached the sitting room, the whole house was aware that its youngest son had returned.

'Charley!'

His sister Susan put down her embroidery, pitter-pattered across the room and threw her arms round him. 'You look uncommon well.'

'Hello, Susan. Hello, Catty.'

His younger sister Catherine also rose to embrace him, but not before she had finished her paragraph in the *Weekly Magazine of the Society for the Diffusion of Useful Knowledge*.

'Charley dear. We thought you were never coming back.'

'If you thought I would forgo the start of the partridge season, then you do not know your beloved brother.'

'Have you had any sport in Wales?'

'After a fashion – I have been hunting old red sandstone, which is the next best thing. Professor Sedgwick and I walked all the way from Llangollen to Great Orme's Head, looking for a band of sandstone that is on Greenough's map. Well, it is there on the map right enough, but by the Lord Harry there is none in the ground. Old Greenough's map is pure fiction!'

His face flushed with exhilaration at the memory of his and Sedgwick's discovery.

'How exciting,' said Susan brightly.

'How I should love to go geologizing,' said Catherine, quietly.

'Oh, you wouldn't like it, Catty, really you wouldn't. It's the most fearful slog, all that tramping and hiking through rocks and mud and gorse – it's really no hobby for a gentlewoman. It's all frightfully boring – just measuring and collecting samples. Although I was able to make use of the clinometer that Professor Henslow gave me.'

'What's a clinometer?'

'It measures the inclination of rock beds. It really is the most splendid instrument, in brass and wood. I must write to thank Henslow once more. Oh, but this is all I, I, I! I see your sister has begun another embroidery.'

'It is to be "Fame Scattering Flowers on Shakespeare's Tomb",' explained Susan. 'Why, you may have it when it is finished, if you approve.' She gave him another kiss.

Caroline, the eldest of the three sisters, now made an entrance from the garden, having demurely exchanged her bonnet for an indoor cap.

'The wanderer returns,' she beamed, hugging her brother and joining in the fuss. 'Have you told him about the letter yet?'

'The letter, of course,' cried Susan with excitement, and went to fetch it from the hallway, too flustered to call for a servant.

'A most urgent letter,' Caroline explained conspiratorially. 'Express delivery, at treble the cost. There were two shillings and fourpence to pay. We had to send Edward to the inn twice, as he had insufficient coin with him the first time.'

'Papa had to tip up for it, so of course he grumbled for a good half-hour,' confided Catherine. 'He said you could hire a man to ride to Cambridge and back for less.'

'It's from Cambridge? Where is Papa?' A hint of trepidation crept into Darwin's voice.

'In his study, with window-curtains drawn as usual. Papa has not been able to get about much these last few weeks – even less so than usual.'

'I am sorry to hear it.'

Susan returned bearing the letter, and the three women formed a tall white palisade about their brother. Each was eager for news, hungry for anything out of the ordinary.

'Talk of the very devil – it's from Professor Henslow himself,' said Darwin, glancing at the superscription. He broke open the wafer and unwrapped the brown paper.

'Well?'

'What does it say?'

'It is about a certain Captain FitzRoy.'

'Read it out.'

'"Captain FitzRoy is undertaking a second voyage to survey the coast of Tierra del Fuego, and afterwards to visit many of the South Sea Islands, to return by the Indian Archipelago. The vessel is fitted out expressly for scientific purposes, combined with the survey; it will furnish, therefore, a rare opportunity for a Naturalist. An offer has been made to me by the Hydrographer's office, to recommend a proper person to go out with this expedition; he will be treated with every consideration. The Captain is a young man of very pleasing manners, of great zeal in his profession, and who is very highly spoken of. I have stated that I consider you the best qualified person I know of who is likely to undertake such a situation. I state this not on the supposition of your being a finished Naturalist, but as amply qualified for collecting, observing and noting anything worthy to be noted on Natural History."'

Darwin broke off. 'A voyage around the world,' he breathed. 'What would I forfeit to go on such a journey? Imagine it!'

'Oh, Charles,' squeaked Susan. 'I can't.'

'I can,' said Catherine.

'He admits I am not the first candidate – the Reverend Mr Jenyns has turned it down, and Henslow has too – "Mrs Henslow looked so miserable that I at once settled the point." And he writes a word or two as to the cost . . . it will be thirty guineas per annum to mess, plus some six hundred guineas in the way of equipment. Well, there, I think, will be the stumbling block. It is a pretty sum.' His mind turned once more to the forbidding prospect of his father, awaiting him in the darkened study.

'If he grumbled about two shillings and fourpence, think what he will say to six hundred guineas,' murmured Caroline, whose thoughts had strayed in the same direction.

'*Do* go on,' said Catherine, impatiently.

'"Captain FitzRoy wants a man (I understand) more as a companion than a mere collector, and would not take anyone, however good a Naturalist, who was not recommended to him likewise as a gentleman. Don't put on any modest doubts or fears about your disqualifications, for I assure you I think you are the very man they are in search of.

So conceive yourself to be tapped on the shoulder by your affectionate friend, Professor John Henslow."'

Susan exhaled, and Caroline looked faintly anxious.

'Well,' breathed Catherine finally, 'it sounds to me like a pretty desperate way of avoiding having to pay your tailor.'

The first thing Charles saw upon entering the study was the shape of an inverted crescent moon, where the daylight, split into shafts by the heavy drapes, illuminated the bald rim of his father's head. As his eyes struggled against the twilight his father's colossal silhouette took form, all six foot two and twenty-three stone of it. Dr Darwin was wedged into his favourite stiff-backed armchair or, rather, he seemed to grow from it, as if man and chair were hewn from the same enormous slab of rock. Charles could barely make out his father's features, but memory filled the void: the heavy black brows angled severely in to the bridge of the nose, contrasting with the neatly trimmed white tufts over each ear; the defiant bulldog jowls; the pursed, unsmiling mouth, the lower lip curled contemptuously against the world as a matter of routine. Any resolve he had felt upon entering his father's study evaporated in an instant.

'You have returned, Charles.'

'Yes, sir.'

'Your trip was satisfactory?'

'Most satisfactory, sir.'

'I have received an account, Charles, from Christ's College, Cambridge. An account for two hundred and three guineas, seven shillings and sixpence in unpaid battels. An account which I have settled.'

Charles's heart sank. He had quietly prayed for that particular chicken to refrain from coming home to roost just yet.

'Thank you, sir.'

'Do you have anything to say for yourself, Charles?'

'I'm sorry, sir.'

'You have an allowance, Charles. A most generous allowance. And yet you have exceeded it importunately. Have I not been generous, Charles?'

'You have been most generous, sir.'

'I have also had to part with the sum of two shillings and fourpence for an express letter from Cambridge. Does it contain another account in need of settlement?'

'No sir. It contains an offer from Professor Henslow, the professor of botany at the university. He has recommended me for the post of supernumerary naturalist, sir, on a Royal Naval expedition travelling around the world.'

Charles awaited the expected explosion, but it did not come. Yet. Instead, the doctor's eyes remained hooded in the darkness; his head lifted from his shoulders like a cobra's, his already broad neck seeming to thicken as it did so.

'And is it your intention to accept this offer, Charles?'

Charles took a deep breath, and stuck out his own neck. 'I do consider it to be an invaluable opportunity, sir, for one of my lowly standing in the scientific community.'

'Indeed. I was not aware that you were a member of the *scientific community*. I was under the impression that you were taking instruction in theology as a preliminary to entering the curacy. Is it now the business of a priest to encircle the globe? Does the route to heaven go via Cape Horn?'

'Professor Henslow is a priest, sir. As is Professor Sedgwick, with whom I have been studying geology in North Wales.'

'Then why does not *the Reverend* Professor Henslow apply for this exalted position himself?'

'He is . . . indisposed, sir, on account of his family. And the Reverend Mr Jenyns, sir, who was offered the position before me, would have travelled but for his duty to his parishioners at Bottisham.'

'It is to be wondered, then, that the parishes of England are not wholly vacant. And how, pray, do you intend to maintain yourself on this voyage of – forgive me, for I omitted to enquire of its duration.'

'Two years, sir. Possibly three.'

'Two years, possibly three. How, then, do you intend to maintain yourself during this considerable length of time?'

'I had very much hoped, sir, to lay claim to your generosity in this matter.'

'You had hoped to lay claim to my generosity in this matter.'

'You have been generous enough, sir, to defray the cost of my brother Erasmus's year in Switzerland and Germany.'

'Your brother Erasmus has completed his medical studies at Edinburgh University, and now furthers them on the continent. Your brother Erasmus did not leave off his studies after spending two years riding to hounds and collecting rocks when he should have been studying medicine. Your brother Erasmus did not exceed *his* most generous allowance.'

'I should be deuced clever to spend more than my allowance while cooped on board a naval vessel, sir,' chuckled Charles, in an unwise attempt at levity.

'But they all tell me you are very clever, Charles, not, I must confess, that I can discern any trace of it in this instant. So, to the crux. What, pray, is the expected cost of this adventure?'

The young man swallowed. 'Approximately . . . approximately seven hundred guineas all told, sir.'

There was silence. Charles had hoped that his eyesight would have better accustomed itself to the gloom, but his father's study seemed darker than ever. He could barely make out Dr Darwin's face, but instinct, coupled with a gradual change in the doctor's breathing, told him that it had turned a shade of purple he knew all too well. And then the explosion came.

'You care for nothing, do you hear me? You care for nothing but shooting, dogs and rat-catching, and you will be a disgrace to yourself and all your family! You dare to suggest that I pay for you to alter your profession for the third time in six years! And not, indeed, for the sake of any respectable position but for the sake of a wild scheme – a thoroughly useless undertaking – that would be entirely disreputable to your character as a clergyman hereafter! How should you ever settle down to a steady, respectable existence after such a – a jaunt? Clearly, nobody else can be found who will take on this utterly discreditable enterprise; many others have obviously turned down this – this *escapade* before you. From its not being previously accepted, one can only surmise that there is some serious objection to this vessel or expedition. Sailing ships are like gaols – brutal discipline, filthy conditions, with the additional disadvantage of being drowned!'

Even in the midst of a rage, Dr Darwin was not averse to quoting Johnson.

'What was the name of the vessel that went down with all hands not a few months back? The *Thetis*, was it? I cannot permit you, Charles, to involve yourself in such a foolish and costly undertaking. Whatever would your mother have said?'

Charles's train of thought diverted automatically to the inadequate framework of memories he had constructed to represent his mother. The edge of her work-table, seen from below. The rustle of her black velvet gown. Her white face on her deathbed, on a July afternoon. The smell in the room. Not once since that bewildering and frightening day had his father even mentioned his mother, still less invoked her name. *He's frightened of me dying too*, Charles realized. *Behind all that thunderous rage at unpaid accounts lies genuine fear at the prospect of losing another member of his family*.

'I understand, sir. Thank you, sir.'

'If you find any man of common sense – *any* man – who advises you to go, I shall give my consent. Otherwise, I suggest in the strongest terms that you write to Professor Henslow, declining his offer.'

'Yes sir.'

And with that, Charles left the study and emerged blinking into the hallway, heading for the front door and escape. Hearing his footsteps, Catherine came out of the sitting room, the obvious question framed upon her lips, but as soon as she saw her brother's burning cheeks and corrugated brow she had her answer.

Charles strode around to the back of the house, tactfully left to himself by his sisters, and halted at the edge of the terrace. In the distance, the river Severn curled through a lush, inviting panorama of soft green meadows. Below him the ramshackle dwellings of Frankwell, Shrewsbury's poorest suburb, lapped against the foot of the hill like a dull grey sea. Resentfully, he turned on his heel and headed inside to compose his letter of refusal to John Henslow.

The first day of the partridge season saw Darwin rise early and take the curricle over to Maer to go shooting with his uncle Jos. He had opted for that particular vehicle as it was light and fast, but even in the early morning the road to Stoke-on-Trent seemed unusually littered with obstacles. A sleeping tollman. A gang of navvies macadamizing the road. A flock of sheep on their uncomplaining way to Market Drayton. A ridiculously slow cartload of pulverized stone pulled by a single donkey that looked fit only for cartwheel grease. Waggonloads of bleak-faced agricultural labourers, who had in all probability lost their homes, roaming the countryside in search of late harvest-work threshing oats or barley.

Darwin sat up on the box with the coachman, as if stealing an extra foot or two would get him to Maer sooner. His mood had not improved: the past couple of days at the Mount had been made awkward by the business of Henslow's letter, and he was glad to get away. A labourer seated outside his cottage waved a respectful good morning, his breakfast of bread, onions and donkey milk spread out before him in the sunshine, but Darwin was in no mood to return the greeting. There were endless such cottages bordering the road, the crude, single-roomed lath-and-plaster constructions of the rural poor. Was he expected to salute every single occupant? They passed a crowd of women lining a stream, beating their threadbare laundry with wooden paddles. It seemed incredible that the countryside could support so many people in such squalor. Surely, in this age of mechanization and modernization, somebody could do something for them?

After Market Drayton the traffic thinned out somewhat, but his father's coachman kept a careful course between the whitethorn hedgerows, anxious not to scratch Dr Darwin's paintwork. Six miles south-west of Stoke they turned off on the rough track towards Maer, whereupon Charles's new stock, which he had put on for the benefit of his female cousins, chafed at his neck with every bounce of the curricle. It was with an enormous sense of relief that he finally spied the gates of Maer thrown welcomingly open, and beyond them the warm, ancient stone of Maer Hall itself amid the trees. The thirty-mile journey had taken more than four hours.

As he expected, he found the Wedgwood family on the

garden side, out on their picturesque porch, gathered adoringly around Uncle Jos and Aunt Bessie. A great shout of excitement rose up as he marched round the corner. How friendly, how informal, he thought, how different from the rigid courtesies of life at the Mount. Uncle Jos strode forward and extended all five fingers, rather than the polite double digit, for his favourite nephew to shake. 'Charles. I had a feeling we might see you today.'

Darwin laughed. 'You could not keep me away, sir. Good morning, Aunt Bessie. Good morning, everybody!'

Uncle Jos's eyes shone with pleasure as greetings and embraces were exchanged. An obsessive hunter and shooter, he had suffered the misfortune of siring four sons, not one of whom had ever shown the slightest sporting interest. His nephew, on the other hand, lived for the hunt as he did.

'Oh Charles,' teased Fanny Wedgwood, 'would you not like to come boating with us on the pool? We should *so* love you to come.'

'Oh yes *please*,' echoed Emma, who sat with her arm round her elder sister's waist.

Beyond the flower garden, a steep wooded slope ran down to the sparkling mere that had given the hall its name in the seventeenth century. Fed by clear springs, its marshy end, adjoining the house, had been cleared by Capability Brown and transformed at great expense into a fishtail-shaped landscape feature. Water-birds now paddled in the shallows, or flapped lazily across the surface, scanning the reeds for insects.

'Ladies, that would be a high treat indeed,' affirmed Darwin, his bad mood swiftly evaporating. 'But I fear your father and I have business at hand.'

'Oh Charles,' protested Emma with mock reproach. 'I am sure that you would prefer to go boating if Fanny Owen were present.'

'Ladies, you are making a game of me,' mumbled Darwin, but he knew that he was blushing. It was not merely the mention of the infuriatingly flirtatious and delightful Fanny

Owen that had embarrassed him so, but that he appreciated the quietly competing charms of Emma herself just as keenly.

'Come on, my lad. Out with it. Something disturbs you, I can tell.'

Unlike Etruria, the family's former home, which sat grandly on a ridge above Stoke-on-Trent, overlooking the pottery factories that had yielded the vast wealth of the Wedgwoods, Maer Hall nestled amid woods and wild heathland. Walking its sandy paths in search of partridge, one might never imagine that the hustle and bustle of the nineteenth century lay so close by.

'It is nothing, sir. I have been offered a place as a naturalist on a naval expedition around the world – I was recommended by Henslow, the professor of botany at Cambridge – but my father, I suppose understandably, is reluctant to allow it. He says it is a wild scheme, which will be disreputable to my future character as a clergyman. And it will be costly, too. I think he fears I will end up in the sponging-house.'

Uncle Jos smiled. 'You have felt the rough edge of his tongue, I do not doubt.'

'Yes, sir.'

'Your father cares for your safety, Charles. I saw this with Susannah when she was alive. Although a casual observer might have thought him unduly formal, I could see that he loved your mother very much. But as to this being a wild scheme, and disreputable to a clergyman's character, well, with all due respect to your father, I am bound to disagree. I should think the offer is extremely honourable to you. The pursuit of natural history, though certainly not professional, is very suitable to a clergyman.'

'My father also thought the vessel must be uncomfortable – that there must be some objection to it, as I am not the first to be offered the post.'

'Well, I am no naval expert, but I cannot conceive that the Admiralty would send out a bad vessel on such a service. And if you were appointed by the Admiralty, you would have a claim to be as well accommodated as the vessel would allow. Did your father entertain any other objections?'

'He considered that I was once again changing my profession.'

Uncle Jos laughed. 'Well, you have not been the most steadfast apprentice to the professions that have been selected for you. If you were presently absorbed in professional studies, then I should probably agree that it would be inadvisable to interrupt them, but this is not the case. Admittedly, this journey would be of no use as regards a curacy, but looking upon you as a man of enlarged curiosity, it would afford you such an opportunity of seeing the world as happens to very few.'

'Those are my very own thoughts on the subject – my own thoughts exactly, sir.'

A tiny spark of hope ignited somewhere deep in the young man's heart.

As the last rays of the summer sun flared through the trees, Fanny Wedgwood sat on the porch, working on a rolled-paperwork decoration for a tea canister, while her sister Emma read out passages from the *Ladies' Pocket Magazine*.

'There is a delightful walking-dress pictured, of striped sarcenet, sea-green on a white ground. The border has a double flounce, the sleeves have mancherons of three points bound round with green satin, the hat has a white veil, and it is ornamented in front with three yellow garden poppies. It says here that all the most distinguished ladies in Kensington Gardens are wearing coloured skirts and dresses this year, trimmed with fine lace. "Silk pelisses are generally seen on our matrons", apparently.'

'You have a silk pelisse or two, Fan,' cut in Hensleigh Wedgwood. 'Does that make you a matron? After all, you are twenty-five.'

Fanny threw a handful of rolled-paperwork trimmings at

her brother. 'The canister will be next if you utter another word.'

'Really, Hen. You must learn to be more courteous with your sister,' chided Bessie Wedgwood maternally.

Just then Charles and Jos appeared through the trees bordering the mere, and trudged up between lines of geraniums towards the house. Charles held forth a solitary partridge by its neck, looking curiously pleased with himself for a man with such a paltry bag. 'Just the one,' he called in confirmation.

'A good job we were not expecting partridge pie for supper,' laughed Fanny.

'All the more left over for the poachers,' scoffed Hen.

'And there are certainly enough of those, if the last quarter-sessions are anything to go by,' grumbled Jos.

'Still, even a solitary partridge is one in the eye for the Duke of Wellington!' Charles's comment was deliberately intended to flatter his uncle who, as Whig MP for Shropshire, had helped win the battle to make game licences available outside the squirearchy for the first time.

'Very true,' beamed Jos. 'Mind you, with only one partridge in the bag that's a devilish dear game licence I've shelled out for.'

'Never mind, dear,' said his wife. 'I'm sure you will have better luck on the morrow.'

'On the morrow? Ah, but we shall not be shooting on the morrow.'

'On the second day of the partridge season? Why ever not, dear?'

Jos grinned at Charles conspiratorially. 'Because Charles and I shall go off tomorrow to return Robert Darwin's curricle to its owner.'

The door to Dr Darwin's study was pushed warily open. The silent dust motes, unexpectedly disturbed, whirled about in panic-stricken eddies. Charles moved forward cautiously into the darkened room.

'Charles?'

'Father.'

'I thought you were at Maer, for the partridge.'

'I have just returned from there, sir. Father . . . would you consider Uncle Jos to be a "man of common sense"?'

Dr Darwin could just make out a stiff-backed figure silhouetted in the doorway behind his son, a pair of neatly trimmed grey sideburns illuminated by the daylight from the hallway. 'Your uncle Josiah? . . . But of course. That goes without saying. What an absurd question. Why ever do you ask?'

Josiah Wedgwood stepped forward into the study.

'Good morning, Robert,' he said.

'I am the devil of a fellow at hunting – the best shot in my family, sir. One day I intend to be an admiral. The best way for me to arrive at that position, it seems, will be for me to serve on the *Beagle*. The arrangement will benefit you and it will also benefit me.'

Charles Musters looked FitzRoy squarely in the eye. Coolly, FitzRoy returned his gaze. They were sitting facing each other across a desk in a borrowed Admiralty office, where FitzRoy was recruiting the few remaining officers required for the second surveying voyage of the *Beagle*. At the back of the room, Musters's mother raised her eyes despairingly to heaven. Charles Musters was eleven years old.

'I could have gone to the Royal Naval College in Portsmouth, but my father says it is better to learn seamanship on a ship than in a classroom. My father says that college volunteers are all soft-handed whelps, sir.'

'Your father may well have a point,' conceded FitzRoy gravely, 'but I'm sure he would be the first to stress the importance of practical knowledge as well.' He opened a desk drawer, took out a copy of *The Young Sea Officer's Sheet Anchor* by Darcy Lever, and passed it to the boy. 'Now, Mr Musters. If you can learn the entire contents of this book, by rote, by the time the *Beagle* sails in October – and no slacking, for I shall test you on it – then I may just have a place for you as a volunteer. You will need to bring your own south-wester, two pairs of canvas trousers, two flannel shirts, a blanket, a straw mattress—'

'A donkey's breakfast, sir.'

'A donkey's breakfast indeed. One pair of shoes – without nails – a panikin, a spoon and, most important of all, your own knife.'

'A sailor without a knife is like a woman without a tongue, sir.'

'You certainly know a fair amount about seamanship for one who has never sailed, Mr Musters,' conceded FitzRoy, giving silent thanks that the boy's father had not taught his son the full unexpurgated version of the quip. 'Your salary will be ten shillings a month. I look forward to seeing you at Devonport in October, Mr Musters.'

'The pleasure is all mine, sir.'

The interview over, FitzRoy stood up and formally shook the boy's hand.

'You will take care of him, won't you?' breathed Musters's mother.

'As if he were my own son, madam. There will be another volunteer aboard – my new clerk, Edward Hellyer, who is an altogether . . . quieter boy, who writes a good hand, so Charles will not go short of company his own age. I am sure they will get on famously. Rest assured, madam, I will do everything in my power to ensure your son's safe return.'

FitzRoy ushered Mrs Musters and Charles into the corridor, where he was surprised to find a large, bleary-eyed, unshorn youth in a chair, surrounded by vast piles of luggage, his huge, knitted brows buried deep in a copy of the *Edinburgh Review*. As the Musterses bade him farewell, the youth looked up.

'Captain FitzRoy?'

'Yes?'

'I'm so sorry I am late. I came as soon as I could. I caught the Wonder – the lightning coach from Shrewsbury. It makes the journey up to London overnight, non-stop. It's remarkable – they sound a bugle, and the turnpike opens up, and you thunder straight through like a mail coach.'

'Remarkable,' assented FitzRoy. 'But there is not the least occasion for any apology.'

The youth rose to his feet, revealing the crumpled wreckage of a gentleman's woollen country suit, which contrasted sharply with FitzRoy's own immaculate buckskin tights. The stranger was extremely tall – at least six feet in height, thickset and shambling, with long arms, a pleasant round face and friendly grey eyes. His bulbous unsightly nose was squashed against his face like that of a farmer recently defeated in a tavern brawl. All in all, it struck FitzRoy that there was something vaguely simian about the young man's appearance.

'Please excuse my apparel. I have come directly from the inn by hackney coach. I have not slept at all.'

'I beg you won't mention it,' murmured FitzRoy.

'I hope I am not too late. Did you receive a copy of my letter?'

'It seems not,' advanced FitzRoy, cautiously, now utterly bewildered as to the stranger's identity.

'Thank goodness for that. You must disregard it if you do. Everything has changed. I say, would you mind awfully helping me move my bags into your office?'

FitzRoy, who felt in no position to refuse such an urgent request, complied politely.

'I believe I have brought everything I need. A hand-magnifier, a portable dissecting microscope, equipment for blow-pipe analysis, a contact goniometer for measuring the angles of crystals – that's bound to be useful –'

'Bound to be,' acknowledged FitzRoy.

'– a magnet, beeswax, several jars with cork lids, preserving-papers for specimens, a clinometer, dinner drawers and shirt – do you dress for dinner? – thick worsted stockings, several shirts – I've had them all marked "Darwin" – a cotton nightcap—'

The stranger broke off, for FitzRoy had begun to laugh.

'I'm sorry, is my inventory at fault? I did my best to conceive of everything that might be needed, but what with the shortage of time . . .'

'My dear sir, you must forgive me. My manners are atrocious. But I do believe you have omitted to tell me your name. Although I must thank your shirts for furnishing me with a clue.'

'By the Lord Harry, what a buffoon I am! I am Charles Darwin,' explained the stranger, as if that settled the matter.

'Charles Darwin,' repeated FitzRoy blankly.

'I am the naturalist invited on your voyage by Professor Henslow.'

'Ah!' FitzRoy exhaled, beginning to understand. 'I am delighted to make your acquaintance, Mr Darwin. Please forgive my inexcusable confusion. I did enquire of the hydrographer, Captain Beaufort, some weeks back, as to finding me a naturalist and companion for this voyage, but I had heard nothing by return. In the meantime I have also pursued other avenues. I fear I must own' – here FitzRoy improvised hastily – 'that the position is already taken, by a Mr Chester. Do you know Harry Chester?'

'No,' said Darwin bleakly, his face a picture of misery.

'He is the son of Sir Robert Chester. He works in the Privy Council office.' It was true that FitzRoy had offered the post to Harry Chester, who, fearing for his life, had turned him down flat inside five minutes. But now that he had lied about Chester's acceptance, FitzRoy began to feel like a thorough scoundrel.

'I suppose I had better leave, then.' The young man addressed the remark unhappily to his own oversized knees.

'No, wait. Please tell me about yourself. Who knows? Perhaps Mr Chester will change his mind. You are a botanist? A stratigrapher?'

'I do a little in that way. I am a parson. A parson-to-be, at any rate. That is to say, I am a student. I am doing an ordinary arts degree, preparatory to a career in orders. But I am fascinated by all branches of natural philosophy. I always have been. Even when I was at Mr Case's school, aged eight, I used to fish for newts in the quarry pool. And I collected pebbles – I wanted to know about each and every stone in front of the hall door. My nickname at Shrewsbury School was Gas. My brother Erasmus and I had our own laboratory. It was in an old scullery in the garden. We used to determine the composition of commonplace substances, coins and so forth, by producing calxes – you know, oxides. And we used to buy compounds and purify them into their constituent elements. We naïvely thought we might isolate a new element of our own. We had an argand lamp for heating the chemicals, an industrial thermometer from my uncle Jos, and a goniometer – the same one that's in my bag.' The young man's enthusiasm, which had nostalgically begun to pick up speed, came to an abrupt halt at the thought of all the useless equipment gathered about his feet.

What on earth was Beaufort thinking about? wondered FitzRoy. *Sending me an enthusiastic student – a typical country gentleman in orders, who rides to hounds and fancies himself a philosopher. And not even a finished one at that. And if he reads* the Edinburgh Review, *it's ten to a penny he's a Whig.*

'We used to heat everything over an open flame,' Darwin went on, aimlessly filling the silence in the room. 'More often than not the substances exploded.'

'Is that how you came by the scar on your hand?'

'Oh, no, that was done by my sister Caroline when I was but a few months old. I was on her lap, and she was cutting an orange for me, when a cow ran by the window, which made me jump, and the knife went into my hand. I remember it vividly.'

'If it happened to you as a baby, then surely you have been told what happened since and have visualized the incident in your mind.'

'Oh no, because I clearly remember which way the cow ran, and that would not have been told me subsequently.'

For the first time, FitzRoy sat up and took notice. Something in that one act of analysis told him that here was a mind worthy of further investigation, however unpromising the state of the individual that housed it.

'How are you on stratigraphy, Mr Darwin? For I fear there is not much call for a chemist on a naval survey vessel.'

'Oh, but we must now call it geology, Captain FitzRoy. I am fascinated about it. After hunting, it is my second love. I have recently returned from surveying the Llangollen area with Professor Sedgwick – the professor of geology at Cambridge University. He is a marvellous man, sir – a visionary, in my notion. He says that our knowledge of the structure of the earth is much like what an old hen would know of a hundred-acre field, were she scratching in one corner of it. But he says that were we to expand our knowledge sufficiently, we might arrive at the all-embracing hypothesis that would explain the earth's history – the scientific truths that would finally reveal God's intention.'

'I must say, I find myself in complete agreement with your Professor Sedgwick. Not that I am much in the way of geology. Does he have anything to say about the flood?'

'Absolutely. He believes that the investigations of geology can prove that the deluge left traces in diluvial detritus, spread out over all the strata of the world.'

'Proof of the sacred record, in the strata of the rocks?'

'Exactly.'

'Tell me, have you read Buckland's *Reliquiae Diluvianae*?' FitzRoy's enthusiasm was all fired up now.

'About Kirkdale Cave?'

'The very same – hyena and tiger bones, elephant, rhino, hippo and mastodon remains, all in the same North Yorkshire cave. Proof that such beasts once lived and breathed here in Britain. Beasts that must have drowned in the great Biblical deluge.'

'I have been to Whitby to see the incredible fossils exposed by the alum mining there. Have you read William Smith?

Professor Sedgwick calls him the father of English geology. He was surveying the digging of canals when he realized that red marl was always to be found over coal deposits. As the strata were angled upwards to the east, one only had to find red marl at the surface, then look to the east to find coal. Such a simple observation, but brilliant nonetheless.'

'Mr Darwin, I often feel there is an underlying simplicity to God's plan that continues to elude us all.'

'But our understanding of it changes every day. Those who pause even for a moment are liable to be swept away by the waters of progress.'

'We are making intellectual progress indeed, but is there such a thing as stratigraphic – I mean, geological progress? I have been reading Lyell's *Principles of Geology Volume One*. Lyell himself has asked me to send him a report from South America. He believes that geological changes are not progressive but random.'

'How can that be? Surely all God's works could be said to advance mankind and the world we live in. Hence the development of modern man from his primitive ancestors.'

'Lyell believes that the idea of geological progress plays into the hands of the transmutationists. That to allow for progress in nature allows for the profane possibility that beasts might gradually have been transmuted into men.'

'Ah. Always an awkward subject in my family, Captain FitzRoy.'

'But of course!' replied FitzRoy, thunderstruck at his own slow-wittedness. 'You must be related to Erasmus Darwin, the transmutationist poet.'

'He was my grandfather. A remarkable man, too, in many ways. But rest assured – I have not the least doubt of the strict and literal truth of every word in the scriptures. Otherwise, how could I lead men to heaven in later life?'

'I am glad to hear it, Mr Darwin. Very glad indeed. Here – I shall make you a present of Lyell.'

He handed his copy of Lyell's book across to Darwin, who

leafed through the first few pages. The volume, Darwin observed, had been inscribed by its author. 'But, Captain FitzRoy, I cannot possibly accept this. It is personally dedicated.'

'On the contrary, sir, it is my great privilege to make you a present of it. In due course I beg to make you known to the author himself.'

'You are too kind, sir – too kind.'

'But tell me, Mr Darwin, why a country parsonage for such an enquiring mind?'

'Oh, I was all set to be a physician, sir, like my father. I studied medicine at Edinburgh University but I am afraid I did not come up to the scratch. I was too squeamish. I saw the amputation of a child's leg as part of my studies. It was a very bad operation – the poor thing was screaming fit to burst and lost a sight of blood. So I quitted, and transferred to marine biology under Professor Grant. We collected invertebrates together in Leith harbour. And I read up for natural history under Jameson – zoology, botany, palaeontology, mineralogy and geology. When my father found out he was furious, and withdrew me from the university. Although I have since wondered whether he was not simply worried that I might fall into the clutches of Burke and Hare.'

FitzRoy chuckled.

Darwin went on, in full flow now: 'Jameson was a quite dreadful speaker, but I think you will be in accord with the principles governing his philosophy, as I was. He believes that the very aim of science is to prove God's natural law. To obtain a detailed view of the animal creation, which affords striking proofs and illustrations of the wisdom and power of its author. He believes that nature is governed by laws laid down by God, laws that are difficult to discern or capture in mathematical terms, but to understand which is the highest aim of all natural philosophy.'

'But that is one of the very purposes of my voyage, Mr Darwin, to advance such knowledge as best we are able! But, tell me, what did you do when you left Edinburgh?'

'My father entered me for Christ's College, Cambridge, to train as a priest. But theology is a broad church, Captain FitzRoy! I studied Paley's natural theology. Do you know of William Paley? He believed that the Creator has designed the universe as a watchmaker would fashion a watch. I must say, sir, I found his logic irresistible. The rest of the time I spent hunting, or collecting beetles with my cousin Fox. We discovered several new species in the fields outside Cambridge. They are all in Stephens's *Illustrations of British Insects*. I tell you, sir, no poet ever felt more delight at seeing his first poem published than I did at seeing the magic words "Captured by C. Darwin Esquire". On one day, I found three new species under the same piece of bark. I put one in each hand and popped the third into my mouth. Alas, it ejected some intensely acid fluid that burnt my tongue. So I was forced to spit out the beetle and all three were lost.'

FitzRoy roared with laughter. 'Well, Mr Darwin, I have had one or two unusual meals in my time, but nothing to match that.'

'Oh, we formed a club at Cambridge, the Glutton Club, with the sole intention of consuming strange flesh. We tried hawk, and bittern, and a stringy old brown owl, which tasted quite disgusting. All consumed with claret over a game of *vingt-et-un*. Anything we could shoot, really. I stuffed the skins myself and divided them between my own and Fox's rooms. I was taught to stuff birds in Edinburgh by a blackamoor servant.'

'My dear Mr Darwin, will you excuse me for a minute?'

FitzRoy stepped outside and stood in the corridor, his back against the wall, pondering his dilemma. Really, this was not the sort of person he had envisaged taking around the world. Phrenologically speaking, the man's squashed nose spoke of insufficient energy and determination. But his sheer enthusiasm, his quick mind and his training in natural theology had combined to win over FitzRoy. Furthermore, the young man had made him laugh. He had not been able to laugh, not once, since Boat Memory's death. The news of the loss of the *Thetis*, sunk with all hands off Cabo Frio, had compounded his misery. All those close friends drowned. Hamond, Purkis, de Courcy, even Captain Bingham; indecisive, fussy, well-meaning Captain Bingham, who had once nursed him through a potentially fatal bout of cholera. Only he, Murray and Sulivan had escaped, by virtue of transferring to the *Beagle*. All the others were dead. There but for the grace of God. And now God had sent this ridiculous young man to resurrect his spirits. FitzRoy made up his mind, turned, and went back into the room.

'It seems you are in luck, Mr Darwin. I have just heard from my friend Mr Chester. He has sent a note to say that he is in office, and will not be able to travel.'

'But – but this is wonderful news!' stammered Darwin. 'You – you are sure?'

'Never more so. But I want you to be aware that there are certain conditions attached to your acceptance of my offer. The voyage may take at least two years. I make no guarantee that we will be able to visit every place stipulated on our route. Your accommodations, I must make clear, shall not be numerous. There shall be seventy souls or more aboard the *Beagle*, so the want of room on such a vessel shall be considerable. We must live poorly – as my companion, you will have no wine and the plainest of dinners. And most important of all: shall you bear being told that I want the cabin to myself? If not, probably we should wish each other at the devil.' *I am hoping that you will save me from the devil*, thought FitzRoy. *But if you cannot – if he comes for me once more – then nobody can see me in the midst of that struggle. Not you. Not anybody.*

'I understand completely, Captain FitzRoy. As long as I have the freedom to make whatever shore excursions I require – I have been reading Humboldt on the tropics, you see, and am eager to explore – then everything you describe shall be to my satisfaction. If you can suffer me, then I shall accept with the greatest delight.'

'Excellent. You will be borne on the ship's books for provisions. I have already fixed this matter with the Admiralty.'

'My dear FitzRoy, I insist that I pay a fair share of the expenses of your table. My father is a rich man, having made a considerable fortune from funds and consolidated annuities, and a most generous individual. I assure you that it will not present any problem for me to pay my share.' A terrifying vision of Dr Darwin in his darkened study loomed into his son's thoughts, but he resolved to face this obstacle at a later date.

'My dear Darwin, as long as you are comfortable according to your own terms, we shall co-exist happily. I am sure we shall suit. Tell me, are you a Whig?'

'All my life and proud of it, sir. My uncle is the Whig MP for Shropshire.'

'Well, you are to room with a stalwart Tory, from a family positively riddled with Tory MPs. So I suggest that we give the subject of politics a wide berth.'

'As my friends say, who can touch pitch and not become a Tory?'

FitzRoy laughed. 'Your friends will also tell you that a sea captain is the greatest brute on the face of the Creation. I do not know how to help you in this, except by hoping that you will give me a fair trial.'

Darwin laughed too, and realized in that moment that he was intoxicated with the captain's perfect manners, his understanding nature and his quiet authority.

'By the bye, Mr Darwin, do you believe in phrenology?'

'Of course.'

'Well, then, I must confess that when you first came into this office, I deduced that the shape of your forehead, and of your nose, might make us ill-suited as companions for a long sea voyage. I must now admit, sir, that your nose spoke falsely.'

And the pair leaned back in their chairs and rocked with laughter.

*　　*　　*

'Hang me if I shall give sixty guineas for pistols!'

Darwin could hardly believe his eyes.

FitzRoy, having scheduled no further interviews for the rest of the day, and being in such an enthusiastic state regarding the learned discussions he was to have with his new-found friend that he wished to commence them straight away, had dragged Darwin with him on a spending spree that very afternoon. Normally the West End would have been deserted at this time of year, but the coronation procession of William IV was due in three days' time: the pavements were bedecked with flags, gas illuminations, crowns, anchors and little decorative WRs, and the streets were packed with gigs, phaetons and carriages of every shape and size. FitzRoy's own gig had positively crawled past Regent Street's shiny colonnades, before eventually depositing the pair on the steps of Collier's gunshop at number forty-five the Strand. It was, as FitzRoy pointed out, the most expensive gunshop in London, but indubitably the best.

'Mr Collier may be an American but, by Jove, he knows his stuff,' he exclaimed, raising a Brunswick rifle to the light from the window. 'See? The bullet has a raised band on it. It engages with spiral grooves inside the barrel, which imparts spin.'

'My dear Captain FitzRoy—'

'Call me FitzRoy, please.'

'My dear FitzRoy, these rifles are two hundred guineas apiece.'

'I'm all for economy, Darwin, except on one point. The point where one's life, or the life of a fellow crew member, is jeopardized. Besides, I suspect the silver filigree work does not come cheap.'

Once again, the image of an oversized purple parent swam into Darwin's mind.

'Well, I suppose I might give sixty guineas for the pistols,' he conceded, trying hard to convince himself that this would be regarded as a safety measure back at the Mount. 'They are good strong weapons, double-barrelled with top-spring bayonets. They should keep the natives quiet. I dare say we shall have plenty of fighting with those damned cannibals, what? It would be something to shoot the King of the Cannibal Islands!'

Notwithstanding Darwin's enthusiasm for intellectual enquiry, there was a youthful quality to his manner that reminded FitzRoy irresistibly of Midshipman King. 'Actually, Darwin, I shall introduce to you some cannibal friends of mine. That is to say, they are ex-cannibals, of course. They really are quite charming – at least, two of them are. They are presently staying at Walthamstow, and we shall be returning them to their homeland in Tierra del Fuego. I am sure they will be delighted to make your acquaintance. If you like,' he added mischievously, 'I shall invite them to dine with us. I can assure you that their manners are immaculate. Although you can bring your new pistols if you are worried.'

Three days later, Darwin and FitzRoy bought jellies at Dutton's, gave a guinea each for front-row seats to see the coronation procession, and allowed themselves to be childishly swept away by patriotic fervour. Their places were located right opposite the mansion of the Duke of Northumberland, which lit up as dusk fell like the palace of an eastern potentate.

'I was in London for the illumination to launch the Reform Bill, and this is much grander,' marvelled Darwin.

'A comment, perhaps, on his lordship's successful resistance to reform.'

'Well, he has certainly compensated for it this time. The little gas-jets in the windows are almost painfully brilliant.'

'Were not the Life Guards magnificent this afternoon?' exclaimed FitzRoy. 'And prodigious tall. They do say that each of those fellows is over six feet.'

Darwin grinned. 'Then there is hope for me finding yet another profession! I say, when the crowd spilled into the roadway I thought that the captain on the black horse would kill a score at least. One would suppose men were made of sponge, to see them shrink away so.'

'I have never seen so many human beings in one place. Even now it is like a raceground.'

The crowds gathered for the evening's fireworks were, if anything, thicker than those that had lined the route during the day.

'One wonders what the poor of London must make of so much gilt and show. I mean, I'm none of your radicals, but with all the riots and hangings and transportations of late, I cannot imagine their humour will be much improved by such a display. Even you as a Tory, FitzRoy, must concede the point. To subsist on bread and coffee, and then to have to witness a bejewelled buffoon like that fellow accompanying the King's regalia – who was it again?'

'The Duke of Grafton.'

'The Duke of Grafton. It must put them in mind to pain. Do you not concede the point?' Darwin, a rosy flush seeping across his face, looked every inch the eager student.

'On this occasion, my dear Darwin, I shall concede the point,' replied FitzRoy with extreme gravity. 'But not as a Tory.'

'Indeed, sir? Then how so?'

'I shall concede the point from personal acquaintance. The Duke of Grafton is my uncle.'

Darwin's face, frozen in horror, was a perfect picture. FitzRoy's features, by contrast, showed no expression. The young man endeavoured to stammer an apology.

'M-my dear FitzRoy, I must beg – no, I must crave your forgiveness. I have behaved like an absolute blackguard. My conduct has been inexcusable – quite inexcusable. I offer you my most sincere, heartfelt apologies. I really do not know what—'

FitzRoy could keep a straight face no longer. He threw back his head and roared with helpless laughter, revelling in the sensation of enjoying himself for the first time in months.

Captain Francis Beaufort, the distinguished hydrographer of His Majesty's Navy, hobbled painfully across the turkey-carpet to his chair. His femur had been shattered just below the hip by a musket-ball, fired at him by pirates in the Eastern Mediterranean in 1812; a catastrophic event undoubtedly, but one that had initiated perhaps the most distinguished naval career ever to unfold from behind a desk. Wiry and energetic of mind, if not body, Beaufort gave no hint of his invalidity when seated behind a solid block of mahogany, at the heart of his empire. As a fellow 'scientific' sailor, FitzRoy regarded him with the deepest respect.

'I must extend the most profound thanks to you, sir, for finding me such a suitable companion. Mr Darwin is young, extremely so at times, but any rough edges will be well and truly polished after two years at sea. I am in a thoroughly good cue at the prospect of his company.'

'You may not thank me when you hear what I have to say.' Beaufort's normally gentle Irish tones sounded unexpectedly gruff and awkward.

'If it is the chronometers, sir, then the Admiralty board have already written to me to explain their reasoning in limiting me to five instruments. I shall ensure that the other four are returned to stores immediately. Meanwhile I have taken the liberty, sir, of purchasing a further six chronometers at my own expense, for a total outlay of three hundred pounds. I feel that for absolute accuracy of observation, one cannot have enough—'

Abruptly, Beaufort waved FitzRoy to silence. His tone was unhappy. 'You're not going.'

'I beg your pardon, sir?'

'I said, you're not going. For reasons of economy, their lordships have decided that the previous survey undertaken by yourself and Captain King will be "entirely sufficient in compiling first-rate navigational charts of Tierra del Fuego and the surrounding waters".'

Stunned, FitzRoy fought to clear his head. He felt, suddenly, as if he were drowning. 'With all due respect, sir, that is wholly untrue. Their lordships appear to be unconscious of the fact that the previous survey barely scratched the surface.'

'You have no need of convincing me, FitzRoy. I have already argued your case, without success. Their lordships' decision is final. Their intention is to prosecute no further surveys of the South American coast.'

'But – but there must be other avenues. I have relatives. Lord Londonderry. The Duke of Grafton.'

'That is a dangerous course to pursue, FitzRoy, and I would strongly advise against it. Your journey might indeed go forward on this occasion, but you will make dangerous enemies of those who are overruled. They will bide their time, mark my words. And the Tories are no longer in power.'

'Indeed not, sir. But I have given my word to the three Fuegians that they will be returned to their homeland before long. I cannot go back on that.'

'Your word, FitzRoy? Your standing will hardly be diminished if you are unable to fulfil your obligations to three natives. They can simply remain here – I am sure they will find an existence wholly preferable to their former lives. They can enter domestic service or somesuch – I gather their grasp of English is reasonably advanced.'

'Sir, I have given my word as a gentleman that they shall be educated as gentlemen – and gentlewoman – and returned to the country of their birth.'

'Well, I am sorry, FitzRoy, but short of taking them back at your own expense, that is not a pledge you will be able to fulfil.'

'In that case, sir, I beg your permission to request a year's leave of absence.'

'I beg your pardon, FitzRoy?'

'I request, sir, that I be allowed to take my leave of the Royal Navy.'

Chapter Ten

St Mary's Infants' School, Walthamstow, 17 September 1831

'This is the way we wash our hands
Wash our hands
Wash our hands
This is the way we wash our hands
Early in the morning.'

Jenkins felt his customary warm glow of pride as the children sang, sweetly and harmoniously, making the appropriate hand gestures that accompanied each line. The Indian girl was perhaps the most enthusiastic contributor of all: she wriggled with pleasure on her fat little thighs, a wide beam curving from one ear to the other. As the class moved on to 'This is the way we wash our face', the schoolmaster allowed his gaze to drift benevolently across the heads of his charges, until it came to a rude stop, as it always did, at the hulking form of the big Indian. He alone was not joining in, as he never did. His face wore the same brutal sneer it always wore. He loomed threateningly over the tiny children to either side, as always. What on earth had prompted the Reverend Mr Wilson to invite him here? And who in God's name had thought to christen this remnant of base creation with the title of one of England's finest cathedrals? The Lord did indeed move in a mysterious way that he should test his loyal servant Edward Jenkins so. Jenkins fingered the smallpox scars that had pitted his cheeks since childhood. There had been sterner tests before, and there would be others to come. It was up to him to rise to this challenge.

'Now, children, there are seven things that are an abomination unto the Lord. Can we remember all seven?'

Several hands shot up.

'Alice?' He chose the most tentative.

'A lying tongue, sir.'

Alice, a quiet, undernourished waif who walked in every day from a farm labourer's cottage a few miles south of Walthamstow, had barely spoken a word during her first few months at the school. She ranked as one of Jenkins's proudest achievements.

'Very good, Alice,' he smiled. 'William?'

William, a rake-thin five-year-old lost in a large, ragged smock, let his answer slip out shyly. 'A proud look, sir.'

'Excellent, William.' Such was the Lord's way, he thought: to reproach him gently for his pride, through the mouth of a child.

It was Jenkins's practice to disregard the claims of his more insistent pupils, but the other Indian, the one who was always gazing at his reflection in a looking-glass, had his arm so far in the air it was in danger of popping out of its socket. Like a scarlet balloon tethered to his front row seat, he appeared ready to burst.

'Yes, Jemmy?'

'Hands that shed innocent blood, sir!' exclaimed Jemmy Button, savouring each syllable with undue relish.

'Very good, Jemmy. The Lord abominates hands that shed innocent blood.'

Why couldn't the big one be as keen as this one, as willing

to please? Not for the first time, he decided to tackle York Minster's brooding presence head on. 'York. Can you think of anything that is an abomination unto the Lord?'

The big Indian simply stared at him, a look of surly contempt on his face.

'Do you have an answer for me, York?'

Silence.

Jenkins opted to provoke his adversary.

'Do you all see this little boy?' he asked the class.

An affirmative chorus responded.

'I am very sorry for him for he does not allow the Lord into his heart. Are you not sorry for him, boys and girls?'

'Yes, sir,' chorused the class.

'Let us all try to make him a good boy, for if he is a good boy, we shall all love him, and the Lord shall love him too. Remember, York, "A child is known by his doings" – Proverbs chapter twenty, verse eleven.'

Nothing. The barbarian simply did not react at all, but continued to stare intently in his direction. Jenkins admitted defeat, and moved behind him to the girl, the poor creature who had the misfortune to be betrothed to the brute.

'And you, Fuegia, do you have something to tell the class? Can you think of anything that is an abomination unto the Lord?'

Fuegia smiled her biggest, most appealing smile.

'Feet that be swift,' she replied, in her thickly accented English.

'Feet that be swift . . .' He waited in vain for her to finish the quotation, before supplying the remainder himself: '. . . in running to mischief, Fuegia. Feet that be swift in running to mischief.'

Really, the contrast between this delightful child and the feral savage seated in front of her could not have been greater. He reached out an avuncular hand and stroked Fuegia's hair.

And then, he felt it again – that strangest of feelings. The tiny hairs on the nape of his neck rose as if charged with an electric current. His every instinct told him to run for cover, as if there had been a tiger in the room. He glanced round wildly at York, but all he could see was the back of his square, brutal head. It was as if the animal could *sense* his affectionate gesture towards the girl. He tensed, and withdrew his hand abruptly. A flustered pause ensued. A sea of eager faces was looking expectantly up at him, all except one. Jenkins pulled himself together.

'An heart that deviseth wicked imaginations, York. You could have said, an heart that deviseth wicked imaginations.'

'How utterly delightful is the countryside hereabouts!' exclaimed Mrs Rice-Trevor. 'And so close to the city.'

As the carriage clattered across the new metal bridge spanning the river Lea, the surrounding woodlands parted to reveal a marvellous vista of London beyond the marshes, distant clouds of kites wheeling above the city in the late-summer sunshine.

'Why, all that smog and filth and wretchedness is rendered almost tranquil at such a distance, Mr Wilson. You are fortunate indeed to minister to such a peaceful parish.'

'Sadly, Mrs Rice-Trevor, I rarely see it in the summertime. You see, I have a plural living.' The Reverend William Wilson, who had become utterly entranced by Mrs Rice-Trevor, flushed with the sheer exertion of trying to impress her. 'In winter, I minister to the people of Walthamstow. In summer I minister to the parish of Worton, near Woodstock, itself a place of rare beauty; but not even the considerable beauty of Worton, madam, would stand comparison with your own. We are most honoured that you are able to bless us with your society.'

'Why, Mr Wilson, you are too kind.' Fanny Rice-Trevor blessed the clergyman with a smile that flowed through his bloodstream like a tot of warm whisky, stirring every doubt he had ever nurtured as to his calling. 'I am sure that the three Indians in your charge could not be more fortunate, Mr Wilson. Is that not the case, Bob?'

Suppressing a smile, FitzRoy took the hint and came to his sister's rescue. 'I think there can be no doubt that fortune smiled upon them when the Reverend Mr Wilson consented to admit them to his school. I trust they are advancing well?'

'Oh, there has been considerable progress, Captain FitzRoy, considerable progress. That is, by the boy and the girl. The man is harder to teach, except mechanically. He is interested in carpentry and smithying and animal husbandry, but he is a reluctant gardener — apparently he considers it to be a woman's work.' Wilson smirked in what he hoped was a man-of-the-world fashion at Fanny. 'Jenkins tells me that he quite refuses to learn to read. But in general I must report that they are well disposed, quiet and cleanly people, and not at all fierce and dirty savages. You have done a remarkable job in civilizing them, Captain FitzRoy.'

FitzRoy demurred. 'I am sure that the credit is entirely yours, Mr Wilson.'

'And what about the one who died, Mr Wilson?' Fanny enquired. 'Boat Memory — do they ever mention him?'

'Never, madam, to my knowledge.'

'Bennet tells the same story,' added FitzRoy. 'But he reports that when Boat died, the other three blackened their faces with a mixture of grease and charcoal from the grate.'

'Remarkable,' said Wilson.

'Perhaps not so remarkable, Mr Wilson,' suggested Fanny. 'Do we not mourn the death of a loved one by dressing in black? In their society they have no clothing but animal skins, so they must decorate themselves in black instead. Perhaps they are not so very different from ourselves, after all.'

'Perhaps not,' murmured Wilson, unconvinced.

Coxswain Bennet watched as the carriage rattled into the centre of Walthamstow village. He tapped out his pipe on the old flint wall of St Mary's Church and straightened his posture. He would be glad to see the skipper again. His paid billet in Walthamstow had been a welcome rest to begin with – keeping an eye on the three Fuegians had hardly been an arduous detail – but the inactivity had begun to pall, and he was eager to return to sea once more, to man the *Beagle*'s boats and ride the waves.

A pair of watchmen moved to challenge the carriage – day patrols had been instituted in the light of the reform riots sweeping the countryside – but almost immediately relaxed again as they recognized Wilson's rubicund visage at the window. The vehicle swept to a halt outside the Squires' Almshouses, from where a little path ran up through the graveyard to the church. Bennet made his way between two lines of jumbled headstones. As the coachman jumped down to open the door for Fanny, he sprang forward to assist her. FitzRoy followed and pumped the coxswain's hand.

'It's good to see you, sir.'

'And you, Mr Bennet, and you. Mrs Rice-Trevor, may I introduce to your acquaintance Coxswain Bennet? Mrs Rice-Trevor is my sister.'

'I'm delighted to make your acquaintance, Mr Bennet. My brother tells me that he might not be here today, if it were not for your courage and resolution.'

'It's quite the other way round, ma'am, I'm sure. It's an honour to make your acquaintance, ma'am.'

Bennet's features had reddened under his flaxen mop. Fanny had that effect on people.

'All's well in Walthamstow, Mr Bennet?'

'All's well, sir – no sign of any rioters or revolutionaries. To be honest, sir, it's been a little dull. I've sometimes found myself hoping for a baying mob to come round the corner.'

'I'm not sure I'd fancy your chances, Mr Bennet. The mobs are getting bigger. I read in the *Morning Post* that three thousand people have demolished fifty miles of fencing at the Forest of Dean. And the army have shot and killed several iron-workers at Merthyr Tydfil.'

'The French have a lot to answer for,' grumbled Wilson, coming round from the other side of the carriage where he had been attending to his luggage. 'All of this is their doing. Good afternoon, Bennet.'

'Afternoon, sir.'

'Rest assured, Mrs Rice-Trevor, we'll have none of that sort of thing in Walthamstow. The extra day patrols of watchmen will see to that.'

'How very comforting, Mr Wilson.'

Bennet struggled without success to picture the two portly, middle-aged watchmen in their greatcoats and broad-brimmed hats, beating off a three-thousand-strong mob of starving farm-workers. Wilson, meanwhile, marched the party across to the infants' school.

'St Mary's, Mrs Rice-Trevor, was the country's first Church of England infants' school, constructed and paid for entirely by myself.'

'How very generous of you, Mr Wilson.'

'My father made a considerable fortune, madam, from the manufacture of silk. The school has been established according to the principles of the great educator Mr Samuel Wilderspin. Are you familiar with Mr Wilderspin's teachings, Mrs Rice-Trevor?'

'I admit that I cannot say so.'

'Wilderspin believes that the years between two and seven are a wasted opportunity. That the early period in a child's life is vital for impressing those Christian values and teachings that might otherwise be debased by the beliefs and actions of crudely educated parents. By the time each of our children starts national school they have attained a religious and moral excellence, an understanding of personal cleanliness, as well as a basic standard of reading and arithmetic.'

'How very laudable.'

'Our children learn by singing and clapping. They are encouraged to learn, Mrs Rice-Trevor, and never beaten or punished physically. I can think of no better environment for the education of three members of a primitive race, whose mental development is akin to that of an English child.'

FitzRoy kept his counsel at this.

Bennet's mind swam at the thought of the carnage that would ensue if Schoolmaster Jenkins ever tried to beat York Minster.

The party made its way into the school and through to the schoolroom that occupied the majority of the building.

It really was an impressive construction – light and airy, with arching ecclesiastical windows – quite unlike the gloomy workhouse conditions of the national school across the road. However self-regarding Mr Wilson might be, FitzRoy could only admire the generosity with which he had built and endowed St Mary's.

Jenkins was midway through an arithmetic lesson when the schoolroom door opened. Every member of the class, except York, shot to his or her feet. After a brisk 'Carry on, Jenkins,' from Wilson, he continued to teach in that slightly stilted manner common to all schoolmasters under scrutiny.

'We shall take our rhymes from *Marmaduke Multiply's Merry Method of Making Minor Mathematicians*,' he announced, brandishing the book for all to see. Tiny beads of sweat formed visibly upon his upper lip. The dignitaries were there to see the savages perform, he knew that.

'Four times five are twenty – Fuegia Basket?'

'Jack Tar say – his purse is empty!' beamed the little girl.

'Very good, Fuegia. Seven times ten are seventy – Jemmy?'

'Now we're sailing very pleasantly!' Jemmy grinned across at FitzRoy, seeking approval, and won an answering smile.

'Excellent, Jemmy, well done. Nine times twelve are a hundred and eight . . .'

York's eyes bored into the schoolmaster's. The brute seemed to grow in his seat. Surely there was no chance of a response from that quarter?

'. . . Peter?'

'See what a noble, fine first-rate!' chimed Peter.

I don't blame you, thought FitzRoy.

'Well done, Peter. All our rhymes today have a nautical theme, Captain FitzRoy, in honour of your visit.'

'I am indeed honoured, Mr Jenkins.'

'Thank you, Jenkins, that will do,' interrupted Wilson. 'Now, children, you all know Captain FitzRoy. What do we say?'

'Good afternoon, Captain FitzRoy,' chorused the school.

'And this is the captain's sister, Mrs Rice-Trevor.'

The school said its good-afternoons.

'Mrs Rice-Trevor has an important announcement to make, regarding our three Fuegian friends.'

Fanny swept to the head of the room, graceful and gorgeous in a carriage dress of Indian red satin, with a cloak and bonnet of black velvet; she appeared to the children as a dark, mysterious princess. *What a beauty*, thought Bennet.

'Children, I have an invitation here, from Colonel John Wood, the extra messenger in His Majesty's Household. Our friends Jemmy, Fuegia and York have been invited to London, to St James's Palace, for a private audience with King William and Queen Adelaide. They are to have tea with the King!'

A gasp ran round the room. Jenkins's glance darted instinctively to York Minster. Was that the ghost of a smile passing across the barbarian's features?

'What do you say, Captain FitzRoy? Is it not a pretty scheme?'

The party had adjourned to the Vestry House, adjoining the school, where Mrs Jenkins afforded refreshments, each serving accompanied by a little paean of praise to the all-round charm and sweet nature of that 'good little creature' Fuegia Basket. The Reverend William Wilson, inbetweentimes, continued to hold forth.

'Two missionary volunteers to return to Tierra del Fuego with your Fuegians. That way, the savages may be taught such useful arts as will be suited to their gradual civilization. The Fuegians who have learned God's truth here can provide assistance in establishing a friendly intercourse with the natives, and establishing a missionary settlement among them. I hope you will not think me forward, Captain FitzRoy, but a subscription has already been set on foot. What do you say? Will you take them in the *Beagle*?'

'I will not be returning to the south in the *Beagle* – the Admiralty has other plans for her. The journey is to be a private undertaking. But—'

'Not in the *Beagle*?' interjected Bennet, stunned. Unsure of his manners in such company, he had chosen – despite being invited to take a seat – to hover by the door like a sentry standing easy. And now he had let himself down.

'I shall explain later, Mr Bennet.'

'I'm sorry, sir.'

'I must own, Mr Wilson, that your proposition takes me by surprise. Of course, any such venture would have to receive the blessing of the Admiralty, as they have sponsored the education of the Fuegians. Provided that you can find two brave souls willing to habit that Godforsaken coast, I see no reason why I should not be of assistance, but that is a considerable provision. Tierra del Fuego has claimed many European lives. I would not consign any man to those wild shores without his being fully cognizant of the dangers involved.'

'The modern evangelist is a muscular Christian, Captain FitzRoy. He has tamed the cannibal islands of the South Seas and has made inroads into darkest Africa. We cannot exempt any part of God's earth from receiving the light of His love.'

Any further discussion on the matter was postponed by the return of Mrs Jenkins, with the news that classes were over, and that Jemmy, York and Fuegia were waiting to receive their visitors in their lodgings above the school.

The boarders' rooms in the eaves proved surprisingly attractive and spacious, with exposed beams and simple wooden furniture. As the party climbed the creaking staircase to the upper floor, they were intercepted by a little yellow blur, as Fuegia Basket launched herself like a cannonball into Fanny's skirts. 'Capp'en Sisser! Capp'en Sisser!' she squealed delightedly.

'Why, Bob, she's the *sweetest* little girl,' Fanny exclaimed, giving her a hug.

'Good afternoon, Fuegia. York.'

York Minster, a burly shadow standing sentinel in the corridor ahead, nodded in acknowledgement to FitzRoy.

'Where's Jemmy?'

'I – am – *here*!'

Jemmy stepped smartly out of his room on cue, and struck a dandyish pose in the corridor. The visitors could only gape. He was attired in skintight white buckskins, tucked into knee-length boots that had been polished to a mirror finish, an extravagant neckcloth of Flemish lace, and, topping off the whole ensemble, a long-tailed, double-breasted dress riding coat of the brightest pink, its gathered waist straining gallantly across its owner's pot belly. His hair had been plastered down with pomatum. FitzRoy murmured under his breath to Bennet, 'When I said, "Take him to the tailor's to purchase a suit of clothes," Mr Bennet—'

'He absolutely insisted, sir,' whispered Bennet unhappily. 'You know what he's like. The minute he saw the cloth, wild horses could not have diverted him.'

'I think it looks *marvellous*,' announced Fanny loudly. 'You have the appearance of a real English gentleman, Jemmy.'

Jemmy's face lit up with pleasure.

'You've certainly taken my breath away, Jemmy,' confessed FitzRoy. 'Are you well?'

'Hearty sir, never better!'

'You are pleased with your accommodations?'

'By Jove, indeed I am. We are given many presents! People are very kind.'

'And you, York? I gather you have been your usual quiet self in class.'

A half laugh, half snort from York.

'All those months of divine study, York – is there not one lesson from the scriptures that you have taken to heart?'

York grunted. 'Too much study is weariness of the flesh,' he said pointedly.

*　　*　　*

Early on the Monday afternoon, FitzRoy left Messrs Walker &
Co. of Castle Street in Holborn, where the last of the charts
drawn up by the Hydrographic Office from his surveys had been
committed to copper plate, and called for his carriage. He drove
east, out of the city proper and down the Commercial Road,
thick as it always was with empty waggons heading out to the
docks and loaded ones struggling back in. Where the road divided
he took the southern fork, past the moated fortress of the West
India Dock, down Old Street to the South Dock, the old City
Canal on Limehouse Reach. It was high water, so the river had
flooded the marshes on the Isle of Dogs, and despite the lateness of the season the air was thick with mosquitoes. Only the
Deptford and Greenwich Road on its newly elevated embank-
ment remained above the water, cutting the silver sheen of the
Thames in two as it curved to the ferry landing at the end of
the peninsula. This was one of the poorest parts of the river:
narrow lanes lined with mean slums ran down from the road,
straight into thick Thames mud. Sickly, half-starved children,
their limbs bowed with rickets, foraged in the treacly silt for
driftwood or rotten fruit discarded from passing cargo ships.

The *John* was berthed about half-way along. Its owner, John
Mawman, was waiting for him on the quayside. A taciturn
Stepney merchant, Mawman kept his manners to a minimum.
This suited FitzRoy. In the light of the transaction he was
about to undertake, he was in no mood for pleasantries.

'There she is, sir. That's my brig. John Davey is her master.'

FitzRoy climbed aboard and had a look round. At two
hundred tons she was of roughly the same dimensions as the
Beagle, and the same colour – black, with a white stripe running
round her rail – but there the resemblance ended. Her paintwork was dirtied where the crew had thrown slops over the side,
rather than lowering buckets. Ropes lay untidy and uncoiled
about her deck, like the back of a chandler's shop. Her blocks
were in need of oiling, her pitch was cracked and in need of re-
paying. The bilges stank for lack of pumping. But all this was
not uncommon in the merchant service, where naval discipline

did not apply. She was basically sound and seaworthy, he could see that. Her timbers were solid. She would do.

'You choose an opportune moment to depart the country, sir. If there is not reform soon, I do not doubt we shall all have our throats slit in our beds.'

FitzRoy ignored him. 'There shall be seven passengers, Mr Mawman — myself, Mr Bennet my coxswain, the three Fuegians and two volunteer missionaries.'

'You said five passengers.'

'As our provisions are accounted for separately I take it that this does not amount to a problem.'

'No, it does not. I believe the sum agreed was one thousand pounds?'

'It was.'

'Pilotage fees will also be extra.'

'As we discussed.'

He could have negotiated the sum down a little, FitzRoy knew, but haggling invariably made him feel sordid. He produced his pocket-book and took out the cheque for a thousand pounds, drawn on his London bank. It was a huge amount: enough to buy a sizeable townhouse in the city. The hire of a brig and her crew to voyage into perilous waters for six months was no small undertaking. But he had given his word to the Fuegians. He handed the cheque to the merchant, and signed Mawman's fourteen-page contract.

'You realize, Commander, that if you abandon the trip for any reason you will forfeit the entire sum?'

'I am fully aware of the conditions binding our agreement, Mr Mawman.'

They shook hands on the deal. FitzRoy stepped back into his carriage, and joined the laden cart-stream heading back towards the city.

'I've done the deed, Fan.'

'Oh, Bob, I do hope you know what you're doing. How much has it cost you?'

'One thousand pounds.'

A faint, high-pitched whistle of breath escaped Fanny Rice-Trevor's lips. 'Do you have so much to spare?'

'If I did not, I should have to find it. I cannot go back on my word.'

'Of course not. I understand.'

His sister's tone was soothing, but the candlelight from the chandelier illuminated a wet gleam in her eyes. A hundred tiny flames shimmered in her concerned gaze.

The occasion was a private coronation ball, at the house of Mrs Beauchamp in Park Lane. Of course the ball season normally ended in late July, when the evenings began to draw in, but the coronation had made 1831 an unusual year. At one end of the ballroom, a small orchestra had begun the opening quadrille, and black-and-white-clad dancers whirled past in stately formations. Their hostess wove her way through the chattering crowds at the dancers' edge to where the FitzRoys stood, a quiet island amid all the activity. 'Are you young people enjoying yourselves?'

'Quite so, Mrs Beauchamp. Your hospitality is always generous, but this year you have surpassed yourself.'

'My, you look dashing, Commander FitzRoy. And what a wonderful dress, my dear. I adore the white lace over the blue satin. How very wise of you to wear blue to offset the orange of the candlelight. Now, if either of you finds that your appetites are in need of recruitment, I have placed refreshments in the small room at the far end. There will be a proper supper downstairs, of course, but we can't have you catching a chill passing down that draughty staircase for lemonade and biscuits. Or something stronger if you prefer, Commander.'

'You are as thoughtful as ever, Mrs Beauchamp.'

FitzRoy's imagination could not help but compare the potential draughts on Mrs Beauchamp's staircase with the 'draughts' he could expect on the exposed bridge of the *John*: South Atlantic gales screaming into his face, icing the rigging and raising surging walls of grey water thirty or forty feet high.

Mrs Beauchamp wove away again, her heavy skirts shouldering aside the flimsier creations of the younger ladies.

'She's right, Bob. You do look dashing,' Fanny said, adjusting her brother's already immaculate white tie. 'We must find you a dancing partner. It really would be most unfair to a multitude of ladies if such a fine catch were not to be made available.'

'Really, Fan, there is no need—'

She waved away his protests. 'Come with me. I shall play master of the ceremonies. I shall present you to Miss Mary O'Brien. She is the daughter of Major-General O'Brien, of County Wicklow. I would mark her card for you, except that Miss O'Brien is not the sort to carry a dance-card. She is a rather serious and devout young woman – just the sort for you, if you are to spend six months arm in arm with a brace of missionaries.'

Still protesting feebly, FitzRoy allowed himself to be dragged in the direction of Miss O'Brien; and so it was that, five minutes later, he found himself bowing to her, and she curtsying in reply, as they lined up facing one another for the commencement of the Sir Roger de Coverley. They were the third pair in line, so they had time to exchange a few words before they were called upon to promenade between the two lines of dancers. Their conversation was formal: friendly enough, but stilted. FitzRoy preferred the silence of the dance, which he found not at all awkward but serene. Miss O'Brien wore a plain dress of white satin, slender-waisted and decorated only with three narrow rouleaux at the base. Her hair, unlike that of the other ladies present, was not arranged in clusters of curls about her face, or tied up in a swirling Apollo-knot: rather, it was parted in the centre, swept back and secured simply at the neck by a cameo. It was raven-coloured, and FitzRoy thought that she looked like a Catholic saint from Madrid or Andalucía. There was a beatific quality to her: the overall effect was pure, not severe. She gazed at him intently when they danced.

As they whirled under the giant chandelier that dominated

the centre of the ballroom, a fat drop of hot wax fell from the wrought iron and splattered on to the upper slope of her breast, at the place where it disappeared into the V of her dress. Miss O'Brien did not react; there was no indication that she had even noticed. FitzRoy watched the hot liquid congeal instantly against her cool, white skin, and knew at once it was an image that would never leave him.

FitzRoy's carriage, curtains drawn, made staccato progress up the Strand. Jemmy, once more attired in his alarming pink coat (he had refused point-blank to leave Walthamstow unless permitted to wear it), peered in wide-eyed astonishment through the narrow ruler of light at the street outside. A scene of wonder revealed itself. Two giant boots, all of eight feet tall, were trying to negotiate their way past a seven-foot hat. Three enormous tin canisters with human feet, each marked 'Warren's Blacking – 30 Strand', walked alongside the carriage in single file. A man carrying a vast pair of teeth on a long pole met Jemmy's eye and glared at him. There were men with picture placards advertising single-exhibit museums – a stuffed crocodile here, a civet cat there – dioramas of the Emperor Napoleon's funeral, and paddle-steamer crossings to Rotterdam. There were milkmaids, grape-sellers, cane-chair menders, butchers' and bakers' carts and men offering hunting prints from upturned umbrellas. Towering above the whole seething, shouting, yelling mass was a monstrous four-storey advertisement for Lardner's blacking factory, comprising a number of enormous three-dimensional plaster models of hessian boots, Oriental slippers, and inverted blacking bottles suspended over boot-jacks.

'Goliath's boots! Goliath's hat!' shouted Jemmy excitedly. 'They kill Goliath, bring his boots and hat!'

'No, Jemmy,' laughed FitzRoy. 'It's called "advertising". They want you to buy their hats, or their boots, so they build big ones to attract your attention. The Strand is London's main shopping street. One cannot escape it, these days.'

Jemmy's astonishment gave way, at least partly, to confusion. 'Big teeth! Very big teeth!' he said hopefully.

'Another advertisement,' FitzRoy reassured him.

York and Fuegia were peering between the frame and the curtain now, both wriggling uncomfortably in their Sunday best, a demure pair of pantalettes poking out beneath Fuegia's Christian frock.

'I suppose they have not seen the city before,' said FitzRoy to Bennet.

'Well, no sir. They came up from Plymouth to Walthamstow by inside stage. I was wondering, sir, but should you permit it – might I take them up to London for the day, before they go home?'

'Oh *yes please*, Capp'en Fitz'oy! *Yes please!*' begged Jemmy, his gaze now distracted by the extravagant window displays of a row of clothes shops.

'I don't know, Jemmy. There is jeopardy in travel, these days.'

'There are police in London now, sir. It's safer in town than out in the countryside, and safer than when I was a lad.'

'Of course, Mr Bennet – I had forgotten that you are a Londoner.'

'In my notion it's safer than Tierra del Fuego too, sir.'

'*Yes please*, Capp'en Fitz'oy!'

FitzRoy found himself outvoted. 'Very well, Jemmy. You may all travel up to London with Mr Bennet. On a different day.'

They emerged from the chaos of the Strand into the wide empty space of Trafalgar Square, that eternally unfinished building site so brutally carved out of the teeming city. Then west along Pall Mall to St James's Palace, the home of the Royal Family, a mere stone's throw away from another great building site, the New King's Palace that George IV had ordered to be constructed in Green Park. A phalanx of red-jacketed soldiery had been posted outside St James's to protect His Majesty from any rioting mobs, but their presence was

largely superfluous. King Billy, after all, had celebrated his
accession by throwing a party for the poor of Windsor, all
three thousand of them. Earlier in the summer he had
eschewed the tiresome job of swearing in privy councillors and
had climbed out of a palace window instead, preferring to take
a stroll down Pall Mall alone; he had eventually been rescued
from the attentions of an adoring crowd by the members of
White's, just as a prostitute was about to kiss him on the lips.
This was one monarch who was safe from having his throat
cut in the night.

Coxswain Bennet was left in a palace anteroom, where
Fanny Rice-Trevor had been waiting for them. Today she wore
a satin dress shot with gold and a train of black velvet. Together
they were escorted to the state apartments and into the presence of the King and Queen.

'Your Majesty. Your Royal Highness.'

FitzRoy acknowledged both in turn and introduced his
party, who bowed and curtsied, according to sex. The three
Fuegians having been carefully schooled in the correct
etiquette, even York managed a little bow, sensing perhaps that
it would not do to antagonize the most powerful man in the
world; Jemmy, meanwhile, performed the most extravagant of
scrapes, reaching almost to the ground.

'How do? Come in, come in.'

All signs of protocol absent, King William beckoned them
to a little table, surrounded by Louis XIV chairs, where tea
and fancy biscuits had been laid out. His Majesty proved to
be a plump, florid man in his mid-sixties, his immensely high
forehead surmounted by a ridge of white hair standing neatly
to attention. Although squeezed into a formal crimson dress
uniform, his manner was informal and jocular in the extreme.
Queen Adelaide, a small, round, quiet German with sad eyes,
was already seated. The royal couple, it was said, had little to
do with each other outside their official duties.

'D'ye take tea? A cup of tea for my friends here. That's a
splendid coat, young man.'

Jemmy preened. 'Thank you, Your Majesty.'

'Tell me, how d'ye like London?'

'London is best city in the world! Better than Rio. One day I will build city like London in my own country.'

'Capital, capital! Tell me about your own country.'

'My country is good country. It is called Woollya. Plenty of trees. There is no devil in my land. Plenty of guanaco. My people hunt many guanaco. No guanaco in York's country.'

'Guanaco?'

'It is a type of llama, Your Majesty,' explained FitzRoy.

And so, for the next half-hour, the King continued to question Jemmy Button – rather intelligently, FitzRoy considered. York sat in inscrutable silence while Fuegia beamed enchantingly at Queen Adelaide, who occasionally prompted the little girl with a supplementary question.

'They do you credit, Commander. They do you prodigious credit. They are uncommonly well conducted.'

'Your Majesty is most kind. I have taken the liberty of bringing Your Majesty and Your Royal Highness a chart of Tierra del Fuego, prepared from the survey expedition commanded by Captain King. It is the first one off the Navy's copper press, sir.'

'Capital, Commander, capital!'

FitzRoy unrolled the chart and spread it before the King and Queen, pointing out Woollya, Desolate Bay and York Minster, the homes of the three Fuegians.

'And these blank spaces – I dare say you'll fill them in when you take these three back in the *Beagle*?'

FitzRoy seized his chance. 'No sir. The Admiralty has decided to prosecute no further surveys of the area. Although I understand that the French have sent an expedition to that quarter under the direction of the naturalist Captain du Petit Thouars.'

'The French? The devil take 'em. What are those damned fools in the Admiralty playing at?'

'I understand there are economic limitations, Your Majesty.'

'Economic limitations be hanged. We can't be outdone by

the French. What about all those uncles of yours? Do not the dukes Grafton and Richmond interest themselves about you?'

'Unfortunately, sir, I have had to request a year's leave from the Service to enable me to keep my faith with the natives using my own means. I hope to see our friends here become useful as interpreters, sir, and to be the means of establishing a friendly disposition towards Englishmen on the part of their countrymen.'

'Absolutely. Any fool can see that's a capital idea.'

Fanny looked across at her brother, a worried expression stealing across her face. He was taking an enormous risk, manipulating the conversation like this.

'We can't have good men like you lost to the Service, Commander. You leave their lordships to me. Economic limitations, indeed!'

His Majesty levered his portly frame from his chair, grunting with the exertion involved, indicating that the interview was over. Queen Adelaide, meanwhile, left the room for a moment, then returned with one of her own bonnets, a gold ring and a small purse of coins, which she gave to Fuegia Basket. She tied the bonnet under the little girl's chin and slipped the ring on to her finger. 'The money is for you, my dear, to buy travelling clothes.'

'What must you say, Fuegia?'

'Thank you, Your Royal Highness.'

The ring alone, FitzRoy realized, was valuable enough to keep a working man's family in food for a year.

Bennet rose before dawn, in the little room that discreetly separated Fuegia Basket's quarters from York Minster's, and woke the three Fuegians. Jemmy donned his pink coat and Fuegia her new bonnet, from which she utterly refused to be parted. They assembled in the shivering half-dark of the schoolyard, where they boarded Wilson's carriage, which the clergyman had kindly donated for the day. They took the road for Islington, a cold grey light at their backs. Half-lit brick kilns, orchards, cow-yards, tea-gardens and tenter grounds rattled past, allotments rising as islands from sodden, misty fields. On either side of Hackney village there were bare strawberry allotments, where early-risen women with rough clay pipes in their mouths were potting runners from the summer's exhausted plants.

At first, theirs had been the only carriage on the road, but as they neared Islington the traffic thickened. Milkmaids from the outlying farms took to the road, bowed under the weight of their heavy iron churns. Boys with sticks drove massive herds of cattle and pigs uncomprehendingly forward into the maw of the metropolis, to feed the insatiable appetites of the one and a half million citizens who teemed and sweated in the cramped lattice of streets and alleyways. After Islington, where the new tenements lining the Lower Road disgorged an anthill of clerks, the City Road, St John's Street and the Angel Terrace heading downhill towards Battlebridge became a veritable swarm of commuters, mounting their inexorable morning assault on London. No one, it seemed, had occasion to pause, even for a few seconds: passers-by grabbed buns and biscuits from pastry shops *en route*, tossing their pennies through the open doorway. Floating serenely above the jostling river of humanity in their opulent carriage, Bennet and his three charges felt as if they were being carried shoulder-high into the very heart of the city. They could see London below them now, drifts of yellow smog lining its alleys like mucus, the ever-present kites soaring and wheeling high above.

At Battlebridge came the first of the city's great sights.

'A mountain!' exclaimed Jemmy.

'A mountain of rubbish,' clarified Bennet, inviting them to look again. It was indeed a mighty triangular summit of ordure, cinders and rags, its secondary hillocks of horse-bones swarming with ravenous pigs. Cinder-sifters and scavengers combed the upper slopes, ragged panting children and women with short pipes and muscled forearms, more wretched than their Hackney sisters, with strawboard gaiters and torn bonnet-boxes for pinafores.

'All of London's rubbish, all her waste, is piled up here,' said Bennet, by way of explanation.

'What for do they want rubbish?' asked Jemmy.

'Tin canisters are re-usable as luggage clamps, old shoes go for Prussian blue dye. Everything is re-usable.'

'These are low people,' said Jemmy. 'Not gentlemen.'

'That they are not, Jemmy. All of this is to be flattened, they say, to make way for a great cross, in memory of His Late Majesty King George IV. Take it all in, for you will never see its like again.'

At the top of Tottenham Court Road they had to queue for their second turnpike. 'This area,' explained Bennet, 'belongs to Captain FitzRoy's family. Not to the captain himself, but to his family. It's called Fitzrovia.' Grand terraces and squares rose behind allotments and smallholdings to the west.

'If it belongs to capp'en's family, it belong to capp'en.'

'Not quite, Jemmy. It doesn't really work like that.'

'All family not live together?'

'They don't live here at all.'

Jemmy subsided into his seat, completely baffled.

'I love Capp'en Sisser,' offered Fuegia.

At the bottom of Tottenham Court Road, the rush-hour traffic finally congealed. A hundred stationary horses tossed their heads and blew steam from their nostrils, while the drivers bellowed greetings and friendly obscenities at each other. Bennet invited the Fuegians to step down from the carriage, and arranged to rendezvous with their driver at the same spot that evening. They pressed through the crowds and turned right into Oxford Street.

After his years of exile in the Southern Ocean and the many long, quiet months in Walthamstow, even James Bennet, a Londoner, was momentarily stunned by the sudden assault on his senses that ensued. It was as if they had stepped not into a main thoroughfare but into the middle of Bartholomew Fair.

The street seethed with activity. The rattle of coachwheels competed with the buzz of flies. There were German bands clashing with bagpipes, who clashed in turn with Italian mechanical organs mounted on carts. Dustmen rang their bells. News vendors blew their tin horns and bragged of 'Bloody News!' and 'Horrible Murder!', their headlines screaming loudest of all. One side of the street was plastered with song-sheets, as if some unseen authority were orchestrating the cacophony.

Everyone, it seemed, had something to sell. There were knife-grinders and pot-welders and women selling huge blocks of cocoa. There were toy theatres with hand-drawn characters cut and pasted on to cardboard, their owners peddling seats in the street at a penny a ticket. There were jugglers, conjurors and microscope exhibitors. There were men offering tickets to dogfights, cockfights, even ratfights. There were dancing bears, performing apes, and a model of the battle of Waterloo pulled by a donkey. There were baked-potato men, men offering plum duff 'just up', pudding stalls, egg stalls, shoe-cleaners and beggars by the score. Starving lynch mobs might well have been roaming the fields of southern England demanding reform, but here within its heavily policed boundaries, London pursued its pushing, shoving, shouting commercial life without shame, without hindrance, without distraction.

And then there were the children. Literally hundreds upon hundreds of them, begging, offering themselves up for work holding horses, fetching taxis, opening doors, or simply performing cartwheels for a halfpenny. 'D'you want me, Jack? Want a boy?' came the clamour of shrill voices as every passerby was besieged. There were black, unwashed climbing boys, their brushes standing to attention against their shoulders like rifles. There were silent, diseased children curled in corners, the ones who would not live long, wasting away in pale misery. There were proud, red-jacketed boys chasing after carriages, collecting fresh horse manure as it fell and placing it in roadside bins; bunters, scooping up dog excrement for the tanning trade; and crossing sweepers, clearing paths through the ordure for gentlemen wishing to cross the street. There were nimble children easing silently between the crowds, risking the gallows by picking pockets. There were drunken children, leaning against the long mahogany bars of the myriad gin palaces, slumped beneath serried ranks of green-and-gold casks, fumbling with their pipes, or challenging each other to meaningless, swaying punch-ups. These people are multiplying, thought Bennet. They are multiplying indefinitely.

Surprisingly, it was York who spoke first. 'So many people,' he said simply.

'So many *people*,' echoed Fuegia.

'There are one and a half million people in London. When I was a boy it was just over one million.' *These figures mean nothing to them*, he realized. *I must find another way to express it.* 'There are more people in this street, now, than in the whole of Tierra del Fuego. In this one street. Do you understand me? That is why this is the biggest city in the world.'

The colours of Oxford Street's inhabitants were so vibrant, so dazzlingly, tastelessly lurid: there were scarlet breeches, candy-striped waistcoats, lime green petticoats and lemon yellow riding jackets. The races that sported these extravagant clothes came in all shades as well: there were Africans and Indians and Spaniards and Chinese and Jews and Malays and West Indians. Any fears he might have entertained as to the conspicuousness of his charges, Bennet realized, were groundless; a Fuegian Indian in a pink coat, even though he might stop the traffic in Walthamstow, would not merit a backward glance on Oxford Street.

The palette on which this kaleidoscopic array had been daubed was jet-black. The buildings on either side were thick with soot and grease. Fallen soot had blended with horse manure to create a three-inch layer of soft black mud in the middle of the road, through which the crowds surged heedlessly. The air was thick with a cloying yellow mixture of seacoal dust and water vapour, which insinuated itself into eyes, ears and noses, and worked relentlessly to dampen the garish extremes of colour in its clammy shroud. Jemmy kept to the new raised wooden pavement until it ran out, then hopped carefully from one dry patch to another, in a vain attempt to keep his shining boots unspattered. He dabbed at his increasingly sooty pink sleeves with a crisp white handkerchief, faintly distressed mewling sounds coming from under his breath.

'Don't worry, Jemmy, it will wash off,' Bennet reassured him.

Blackest of all were the narrow alleys that led off Oxford Street, from which no light at all seemed to emanate. There were only glimpses to be had of the subterranean creatures who inhabited these worlds: painted women with swollen features, ragged Irishmen with uncombed, waist-length hair, canine children, wolfish dogs. Round white eyes peered from desperate black faces. Windows were stuffed with rags or paper, the window-frames themselves loose and rotten.

'Is it a cave?' said Fuegia, transfixed.

'Don't go in there,' said Bennet, grabbing her arm to hold her back, a gesture that sensibly went unchallenged by York Minster. 'Those are the rookeries. Where the St Giles blackbirds live. The black men. And the Irish. It's dangerous. You must not go down any of the bye-streets.'

To distract her, he shelled out fourpence for four tickets to see 'The Smallest Man in the World', with his fellow exhibit 'An Enormous Fat Woman'; followed by a further tuppence to look through the viewfinder of a kaleidoscope, a contrivance that sent Jemmy into raptures.

Finally, in the centre of Oxford Street, the narrow overhanging buildings and patchwork windowpanes of the last century opened out into a wide circle of pale, graceful stone.

'This is Oxford Circus. This is modern London,' Bennet explained. 'And that is Regent Street.'

To the south ran two elegant lines of white pillars, so new as to be barely stained by coal dust, in a curving Doric colonnade. The buildings behind them soared skywards in blinding white stucco.

'It is a new construction, built by Mr Nash, running from Regent's Park at the north of London, down to Waterloo Place at the far south. It is lit up by gas at night, like a starry sky. It is said to be the most beautiful street in the world. On the west are the streets of the nobility and the gentry. On the east is Soho, where the mechanics and traders reside. They had to knock down a hundred lanes and alleys, and a thousand shops and homes, to build it. And there will be other grand streets like it. Old London is being torn down, the London I was born in. In its place they are building a new, modern city, a beautiful city of wide roads and circuses and parks. London will become the most beautiful city in the world.'

'The most beautiful city in the world,' breathed Jemmy. York looked blank. Fuegia stared at a crimson dress in a nearby shop window. Jemmy was the only one of the three to have taken Bennet's little speech to heart.

By some unspoken common consent, the crowds promenading up and down Regent Street were of a different class from those who thronged Oxford Street. There was money on display, both in the shop windows and on the customers' backs. Two men whose blue swallow-tail coats and top hats gave them away as policemen no doubt had a part to play in keeping the pickpockets away, but that could not have been the only factor: it was as if old London had been fenced in by the new street, as if all that gaily coloured squalor was slowly being squeezed by the advancing metropolis, with its stern, clean, white lines.

They walked down to Waterloo Place, keeping a block to the west of the Haymarket's prostitutes and litter, then headed east to Charing Cross, where another huge construction site marked the final remains of the old Hungerford Market. A low growl from York indicated that something was amiss. Jemmy and Fuegia looked confused. Bennet turned to see what had agitated his companion so, but he could see nothing. York was frozen in the same pose he had adopted back in Plymouth Sound, to signal his aggressive intent towards the paddle-steamer. One or two passers-by were starting to stare. Finally, Bennet looked up, and located the source of the challenge: a stone lion atop Northumberland House. He placed a gentle hand on York's forearm, just as it dawned upon the Fuegian that the creature had not moved for several seconds. He relaxed.

They went to see the new market at Covent Garden, where classical colonnades had once again marched across acres of ramshackle sheds and flimsy stalls; they saw pineapples that had been brought from overseas by fast ships; they joined the crowds staring at daffodils and roses out of season, and fuchsia plants from the other side of the world. Then they went down to the river to see the new London Bridge, five elegant arches confidently spanning the river, overlooking its shamed predecessor, which sat rotting and disused a hundred feet downriver.

'King William and Queen Adelaide opened this bridge only last month,' explained Bennet, leaning over the parapet. 'There used to be houses on the old bridge. And they used to put bad men's heads on spikes there. They don't do that any more.' His mind leafed back to the day when his father had taken him, as a child, to see the heads of the Cato Street Conspirators. His father was dead now.

'They're building a tunnel under the Thames as well. Do you see over there, to the right?' He indicated the Southwark side of the river. 'Look. New factories. There's a steam flour mill. And there's the Barclay's Brewery – there are giant steam engines in there, and vats of beer, each one as big as a house. And there's a factory where meat and soup are sealed into tin canisters.'

He looked down at the rickety, lopsided warehouses beneath the bridge, the crowded pubs almost spilling into the water, the flocks of ragged mudlarks and the foul-mouthed watermen in their numberless ferry-boats; then across once more at the factories advancing inexorably up the Surrey shore, black smoke trailing eastward in their wake; and he felt a pang of regret for the London of his childhood, mingled with a surge of pride for the new metropolis rising all around him.

'Some people say they shouldn't spend so much money on building the new city. They say it should be given to the poor people instead. But the more money they give to the poor people, the more children the poor people have, and the more poor people there are.'

'London is the most beautiful city in the world, Mister Bennet,' said Jemmy gravely. 'One day I will build some city like London in my country. There will be big streets, and factories making canisters. I will call this city New London.'

'Cities like London don't just spring up overnight, Jemmy,' said Bennet. 'It takes thousands of years of gradual change. The old London that they're knocking down – once that was new London, and it swept away what went before it. Now it is old London, and it is weak and rotten, and it will lose its mortal fight. Perhaps I shouldn't say this, but the people down there in the mud with their rushlights and their sailboats will get weaker, little by little. And the people over there, with their gas lamps and their steam engines, will get stronger, little by little. And slowly, with each succeeding year, the people over there will encroach towards the heart of the city, and the people in the mud will give way, and London herself will end up bigger and stronger as a result. That is how great cities are created.'

'But, Mister Bennet,' said Jemmy, 'I do not want to be in mud. I want to be one of the people with steam engine. You can teach me.'

They ate at a little dining house on the Strand, for discretion's sake in a curtained booth lit by an oil lamp, where Bennet's natural cheeriness reasserted itself over a plate of chops, devils, bread and pickles. The Fuegians wolfed everything they could lay their hands on, as they always did, as if their lives depended on it. After dinner they bought outside shilling seats on the new omnibus to Vauxhall Gardens, where Bennet took them to see the iceberg. This proved to be something of a damp squib, as the three seemed not in the least surprised to find a large iceberg adrift in the middle of a South London park.

'Go ahead and touch it,' said Bennet, prompting.

'Big ice,' said Fuegia.

'Mister Bennet, we have many big ice in my country,' said Jemmy.

'No, but it's not real. It's made of wood. Go and touch it.'

Jemmy walked over and touched the iceberg. It was warm. Jemmy looked confused.

'Sir John Ross has sailed to the Arctic, to find the North West Passage. That's at the other end of the world from Tierra del Fuego, but just as cold. So they have built an iceberg here to give people an idea of what the North Pole looks like.'

Jemmy appeared none the wiser.

It was at this inopportune moment that Black Billy, the celebrated black street violinist who had lost one leg to a French cannonball in his Navy days, approached to offer the party a tune. Pink feathers bobbled from his jester's hat, his good leg was encased in aggressively blue-and-white striped breeches, and a nautical jacket completed the ensemble. Fuegia, taking fright, screamed and grabbed York's leg. The three began to hoot, hiss and make faces. The appearance of a painted clown on stilts behind Black Billy merely added to the Fuegians' trepidation; Bennet thought it best to beat a hasty retreat.

'They were entertainers. Street entertainers,' he grumbled, as they sat on the omnibus clattering back towards Regent Circus. 'They aim for you to enjoy yourself. The Vauxhall Gardens are *pleasure* gardens.'

Jemmy could not rid his mind of the spectre of the black man in the woods. Bennet shook his head in theatrical resignation.

On the way they passed yet further trenches and construction sites, where the innards of the city had been laid open for all to see. Exposed wooden pipes criss-crossed each other in the moist earth, like a decayed forest of fallen trees.

'They are building pipes to bring gas light and washing water into gentlemen's homes.'

'Light and water? In a pipe?'

Jemmy tried hard to take it all in. He tried to remember his own family home back at Woollya, but it all seemed so long ago.

As dusk gathered they found themselves back on Oxford Street, where they ate a supper of fried fish in oily paper, with ginger beer. A gentle drizzle was falling, and Jemmy stared with undisguised envy at the clinking metal pattens under the ladies' shoes, which protected the blacking from the mud and the wet. Carts splashed by, bearing huge advertisements for theatres and shows; women sang maudlin ballads on street corners, collecting tins at their feet. The square gas lamps on their wrought-iron posts had been lit, and every shop window was illuminated by a hundred candles. The ever-present coal-damp mist settled on London for the night, flaring yellow in the lamps' buttery glaze and softening the pinpricks of candle-light. It was a gorgeous effect, as if all the stars in a black velvet sky were overlaid with the golden halo of the setting sun. Fuegia, wide-eyed and entranced, began to dance in the street with slow, intense, happy movements, her arms twirling out and away from her body.

'When it is dark, London not sleeps.'

'No, Jemmy, it never does. The chop-houses and beef-houses and public-houses will stay open half the night. The oyster-rooms by the theatres in the Strand will still be packed at three o'clock in the morning.'

'Not like Walthamstow.'

'No, Jemmy, not like Walthamstow.'

Fuegia had danced away from them now, fifty yards up the street, bathing herself in the candlelight, immersing herself in its glow. And then she stopped by the coal-black entrance to a side alley, like a mouse transfixed by an aperture that it feels compelled to enter. Suddenly, she was gone, sucked by curiosity into the dark hole of the rookeries. Bennet shouted a warning, but it was too late. He began to run, his feet slipping on the cobbles. Something streaked past him and he knew it was York, his immense, muscular frame devouring the intervening distance at an inhuman speed. Somewhere behind them, picking his way delicately between the mounds of horse dung, a little cry indicated that Jemmy was falling behind. They were becoming separated. It was the worst thing that could happen, but Bennet did not have time to think what to do. He reached the entrance to the passage that had consumed Fuegia and York. There was no sign of them. Panic iced through his stomach. He plunged in.

He found himself in a rabbit warren thick with urine and human faeces, the stench strong enough to stop a horse in its tracks. A maze of filthy, ill-constructed courts and alleys led away in all directions. As his eyes became accustomed to the gloom, he became aware of faces staring at him: wan children crouched in filthy staircases, their eyes filled with futility and despair. He chose a passageway randomly, and ran down it: another junction. A rushlight glowing in a glassless window provided the only glimmer. He took the right fork, between crumbling masonry and mildewed fencing, disturbing a prostitute and her client, her ragged, greasy skirts gathered about her waist, a momentary glimpse of pink flesh. Then, down another dark court, a flash of yellow told him that he had found Fuegia. And there was York; thank God, he had found Fuegia as well. But they were not alone. Even as Bennet arrived at the passageway leading to the courtyard, dark shapes detached themselves from the surrounding buildings and uncoiled from the shadows.

'What 'ave we 'ere, boys?' said a voice.

'A werry respectable gen'leman to be aht on a night like this, an' in St Giles an' all,' said another.

'For why's you fetched your doxy down our way, mister gentleman?' said another, Irish-accented this time.

York did not speak.

'My mate arksed you a question. Wot's-a-do, cully, someone put a turd in yer mouth?'

Bennet never even saw the knife as it flashed from its owner's pocket towards York's kidneys. But York did; or, rather, he sensed it. As York spun round, Bennet saw that the

Irishman's wrist was pinioned fast in his vice-like grip. He heard the blade skitter harmlessly away across the cobbles.

Still York did not speak. He simply increased the pressure of his grasp, forcing his attacker on to his knees. Bennet could see the whites of the Irishman's eyes, and the fear ringed therein. The man let out a cry of pain, but it did not sound like a human cry, more the whimper of a terrified animal come face to face with its own death. York took the Irishman's windpipe carefully between the finger and thumb of his right hand; he looked straight through, into his victim's soul, with cruel, hooded eyes. The other assailants were backing away now, their most primitive instincts beseeching them to turn and flee, any bravery they might have summoned up on their friend's behalf long since evaporated. York's finger and thumb began to close on each other like heavy machinery, twin cogwheels engaging with industrial precision. A faint gargle escaped from the Irishman's throat.

'York!' commanded Bennet.

York froze.

'We must leave.'

For a moment, York did not move, and Bennet feared that he might disobey. Eventually, however, the Fuegian released his grasp, and the Irishman slumped to the ground.

'Come.'

Bennet tried to keep the quaver out of his voice. York took Fuegia gently by the hand and led her out of the courtyard, the little girl still beaming as if nothing had happened. As he moved forward, so the dark shapes fell back, deferentially, to let him pass.

Chapter Eleven

Plymouth, 25 October 1831

FitzRoy reached the inn-yard of the Royal Hotel a mere half-hour after the arrival of the Portsmouth stage, to find a familiar, oversized, crumpled figure waiting for him.

'My dear Darwin.'

'My dear FitzRoy, please excuse my tardiness – but what a journey I have had! All London's in a panic – there is a cholera outbreak in the city.'

'My dear fellow, your lateness is of no account. You are safe and sound, that is all that matters.'

'I say, would you mind . . . ?' Darwin patted his pockets. 'I find myself a trifle short of cash at present.'

'Of course, of course.'

FitzRoy distributed a few coins among the upturned palms of the attendant post-boys.

'But what a terrible business! When I got to the Swan With Two Necks in Cheapside, all coaches to the West Country had been suspended. They said that rioters in Bristol had burned the Bishop's Palace and the Mansion House, and a score of merchants' stores, and had thrown open the gates of the prison!'

'It is worse. Lieutenant-Colonel Brereton, the governor, has taken his own life – he shot himself through the heart – to avoid court-martial for failing to arrest the progress of the riot. And his deputy, Captain Warrington, is to be court-martialled for failing to order his troop to kill the rioters.'

'Good God! The country is close to collapse! Luckily I managed to secure an outside seat by the Chaplin's coach to Portsmouth, but I was made to sit up-a-top next to a stone-faced guard with a blunderbuss. Then I have been on this dreadful little rattly chaise for the last two days. Of course there isn't a turnpike road between Portsmouth and Plymouth. In some of the hamlets we went through, we afforded so much excitement, one would think they had never seen a stage coach before. The road was a disgrace, and the wind was in the horses' faces all the way. Between Wool and Wareham I thought my stomach was about to spill its contents. Heavens, it was a damnable place: flat, open heathland with one or two hovels and not a scrap of shelter. God knows how the residents live off such land.'

'It sounds as if you have had the very devil of a time. Now that you are to be a seafaring man, perhaps you will take the steamer in the future.'

They took a hackney to the Royal Dockyard at Devonport, the clip-clop of the horse's hoofs echoing down the regimented lines of deserted barracks, the wheels crunching on the marble chips of the approach road. Eventually three statuesque masts hove in sight. They alighted and FitzRoy paid off the coachman.

'Wait until you see the *Beagle*. She looks magnificent. She has been completely rebuilt, with mahogany and brass fittings. She has an entirely new upper deck, raised by eight inches aft and twelve inches for'ard. It has added materially to the comfort below decks – at last, one no longer has to bend double at all times.'

FitzRoy glowed with pride. The loss of the considerable sum he had laid out on the *John* seemed as nothing, now that he had the *Beagle* back.

'I must say, FitzRoy, I was thrilled to hear that the voyage was reinstated, and doubly thrilled to hear that you had secured such a luxurious refit. Forgive my landsman's ignorance, but surely she is a long way from being ready for sea? Is she normally painted bright yellow?'

FitzRoy burst out laughing.

'My dear Darwin, that is not the *Beagle*. That is the hulk of the *Active*. That is the *Beagle*, moored alongside.'

'*That* is the *Beagle*? I thought it a tender, or a tug-boat.'

'That is the *Beagle*.'

'But she is the length of a cricket pitch!'

'Come, come, my dear fellow, one must not insult a lady. She is a full eight yards longer than a cricket pitch – she is ninety feet long.'

Still taken aback, Darwin allowed himself to be led on board.

'Here, let me show you your quarters. I have put you in the poop cabin, behind the wheel at the rear of the maindeck.'

FitzRoy threw open the door, to reveal a cabin some five foot six inches wide, some five foot six inches deep, and some five foot six inches high. The starboard and stern walls were lined with books from floor to ceiling. Just inside the door was the thick tree trunk of the mizzen-mast. Behind that was a large chart-table, and behind that, in the narrow gap between the table and the bookshelves, stood a thin, balding figure, blinking through a pair of bottle-glass spectacles.

'Ah. Mr Darwin, may I introduce to your acquaintance Stebbing, our librarian? Stebbing is the son of the mathematical instrument-maker at Portsmouth. Mr Darwin is to be our natural philosopher. I should have explained that your cabin doubles as the library.'

Stebbing extended a limp finger for Darwin to shake, but the young man was too stunned to remember his manners.

'See, Darwin – we have Byron, Cook, Milton, Humboldt, Lyell, Euclid's *Geometry*, Paley's *Evidence of Christianity*, all twenty volumes of the '*Cyclopaedia Britannica*, even Lamarck!'

'My dear FitzRoy . . . the want of room . . .'

'My dear fellow, this is one of the largest cabins on board.

Even with the bookshelves, I am sure you will all fit into it most comfortably.'

'All?'

'Did I not say? You are to room with Mr King and Mr Stokes, whom I have promoted to mate and assistant surveyor. Stokes will need to share the chart-table with you. I should have said that your cabin also doubles as the chartroom. And as the locker for the steering-gear, which is under the table. But do not worry – Mr Stokes will dress and sleep outside under the companionway.'

'And where am I to dress?' Darwin managed to gasp.

'Here.'

'And where am I to sleep?'

'Here.'

'But, FitzRoy, I see no bed.'

'You and King are to sleep in hammocks, slung above the table.'

'But I am taller than the room is long.'

'Ah – not so. The wonders of modern naval design – observe.' FitzRoy pulled out the top drawer from a chest built against the forward bulkhead, and indicated a brass hook in the shadows within. 'The foot-clew of your hammock attaches here,' he smiled.

Darwin gaped like a landed sturgeon. Midshipman King chose this exact moment to cross the deck, so FitzRoy hailed him and made the necessary introductions.

'Ah, my cabin-mate,' said King. 'It's good to have you aboard, Mr Philosopher. I'm sure we shall rub along just fine. I shall be happy to show you the ropes, of course, or answer any questions that may arise. You'll pick it up in no time, I'm sure. Now, you must excuse me, for there is work to do.'

'Er, quite,' gurgled Darwin, and King made a businesslike exit.

'FitzRoy,' whispered Darwin under his breath, 'I am sharing my cabin with a small boy.'

'Well, of course you are. Surely you would not rather share

with our burly coxswain? This way you shall have all the more room.'

'All the more room? I have just room to turn round and that is all.'

'My dear fellow, why on earth should you wish to turn round? If you did so, you should be facing the wall. I promise you, I shall take the utmost care to ensure that this corner of the ship is so fitted up that you will be comfortable, and will consider it your home. Besides, you will have the run of my cabin as well. Come, I shall show you.'

They descended the companionway to FitzRoy's cabin, which proved to be no bigger: another work-table, with a narrow cot to starboard doubling as seating and an even narrower sofa to port. A marine sentry stood guard outside.

'This stout fellow protects the magazine hatch and the locker containing the chronometers. There are twenty-two in all, hanging in gimbals and bedded in sawdust. Eleven belong to His Majesty, six I have purchased myself, four were lent by the makers, and one has been lent by Lord Ashburnham.'

He threw open the door to the narrow locker. A thin, balding figure with bottle-glass spectacles had somehow succeeded in squeezing himself inside.

'Stebbing winds them all at nine every morning. Only he and I are allowed to touch them.'

'But how did he . . . ?'

'Oh, there are many routes about a ship. I have no doubt you shall learn them all in due course. Come, let me show you all my improvements. The canals of England have been over-loaded with naval supplies these last few weeks!'

They headed back to the maindeck, Darwin feeling big and clumsy behind the wiry FitzRoy, who sprang exuberantly from one deck to another like a young deer.

'I must confess myself thoroughly delighted that so many of the officers and men chose to return from our first voyage. Almost everybody volunteered for another tour, excepting Wilson, my surgeon, who has retired, and Mr Murray, the master, who sadly accepted another berth when he thought our trip cancelled. I had a positive herd of lieutenants to choose from. In the end I went for my old friend Mr Sulivan, recently qualified, and Mr Wickham, who was first lieutenant on the *Adventure* last time out, under Captain King. A splendid fellow all round – let me introduce you.'

A cheerful, hearty officer with a stentorian voice was directing refitting operations from the centre of the maindeck. Darwin found himself greeted with a warm, friendly smile: Wickham, who looked to be in his early thirties, had an open, round face, surmounted by a mass of short, dark curls.

'So you're the philosopher, eh? Excellent. Well, Mr Darwin, I run a neat and tidy ship here, so if you can keep your messier specimens out of my way, you and I shall be the best of friends. *Entiende?*'

'Of course, of course.'

'Glad to hear it!' said Wickham, pumping Darwin's hand before going on his way.

'Of course, they would not do for St James's,' admitted FitzRoy, discreetly, 'but a more dedicated, intelligent, active and determined set of fellows you will not find anywhere. Wickham's a top-notch botanist, by the way.'

'Who is *that*?' asked Darwin. A harassed-looking individual in shirtsleeves and shapeless woollen breeches was supervising work on a mast.

'That is William Snow Harris, the inventor. He has devised a lightning-conductor. That is, he invented the device some seven years ago, but so far nobody had dared to use it.'

'A lightning-conductor?'

'Lightning is one of the mariner's greatest adversaries. Not only are a ship's masts a hundred feet higher than any other point for miles around but during a storm they are soaked with salt water – an excellent conductor of electricity. Harris has devised a copper strip that is let into the masts and grounded at the keel, which will actually attract the lightning to the ship.'

'But surely that would be suicidal?'

'No, no – think of it! The copper strip is *grounded*. It attracts the lightning *away* from the combustible wood, and tar, and pitch, and disperses it harmlessly into the water. Simple physics, one would think, but apparently I am the first to put my faith in Harris. I am having conductors installed in every mast, in the bowsprit, even in the flying jib-boom.'

'What an ingenious idea,' enthused Darwin, momentarily forgetting his concerns about his own size relative to that of his cabin.

'One of the many on board. I have spared neither expense nor trouble in making our little expedition as complete with respect to material and preparation as my means will allow. We have a new Frazer's closed galley stove, which does not have to be put out in rough weather. All the cannons are of brass, not iron, so as not to have a deleterious effect on the magnetism of the ship's compasses. We have a patent wind-lass instead of the old capstan. The rudder is of a new type. All the boats are new, and have been constructed on the diag-onal principle—'

'Forgive me, FitzRoy. Did you say *your* means?'

'I did.'

'But surely the Admiralty pays for the fitting-out and manning of its own expeditions?'

'Well, the Admiralty and the Navy board between them, but only up to a point. The *Beagle*'s refit has cost seven and a half thousand pounds, and for that they could have had an entirely new brig. I have chosen to supplement the Admiralty's most generous allowance with a contribution from my own funds.'

Darwin's imagination reeled at the scale of the sums involved, but he said no more on the subject.

Meanwhile, FitzRoy's eyes lit up. 'Come, let me show you the scientific instruments. We have a sympiesometer – it is like a barometer only there is gas above the quicksilver to measure radiation – a pluviometer for the rain and an anemometer for the wind. They are all from Worthington and Allan. I ordered the ship's telescope, though, from Fullerscopes in Victoria Street. Do you know them? I think their instruments superior to Dollond's.'

'I have brought my own telescope, FitzRoy. And my own aneroid barometer and microscope – it is a Coddington's folding microscope. I must show you when my luggage arrives – it is most ingenious.'

'My dear fellow, you must indeed.'

And so the pair spent a happy hour discussing scientific instruments, until Darwin, fired with enthusiasm, realized that an all-consuming naval fervour had come over him.

'I tell you, FitzRoy, I shall become a seafarer yet. With my pistols in my belt and my geological hammer in hand, shall I not look like a pirate at the very least?'

'The key to seafaring, my dear fellow, is to think like a seaman, not a landsman.'

'How does one think like a seaman?'

'It is a state of mind. For instance, the east, the west, the north and south – are they places or directions? The moon – is it a flat disc of light in the sky, put there by the good Lord in order to illuminate the trysts of lovers? Or is it a celestial body of such overwhelming power that it can pull thunderous tonnages of water from one side of the world to the other – a body deserving of careful study and immense respect?'

FitzRoy's reference to trysts with the opposite sex had set Darwin thinking of Fanny Owen.

'Ah, I see that I have distracted you. May I ask, is there a particular lady who will lament your absence?'

'I – well – that is . . .' Darwin, flustered, dissolved into incoherence.

'My dear fellow, please excuse my question. It was unforgivable.'

'No, no, not at all. There is one young lady – well, I will tell you, FitzRoy, she is the prettiest, plumpest, most charming personage that Shropshire possesses. The want of her company is certainly something that shall try me sorely. But as to whether she shall lament my absence, I cannot tell.'

He brought to mind her letters, so forward, so flirtatious, referring to him archly as 'Dr Postillion' and herself as 'The Housemaid'. 'You cannot imagine how I have *missed* you already,' she had written to him in London. And yet, and yet – at the Forresters' midsummer ball she had seemed to have eyes only for Robert Biddulph, whose father was an aristocrat and a Member of Parliament. She played him, he knew, like a musical instrument, but to what tune?

FitzRoy could sense the troubled journey of his friend's thoughts, and left the subject there. 'Now, my dear fellow, it is time to go ashore. I have taken a room for you at Weakley's Hotel until such time as the *Beagle* is ready for departure.'

'Ashore? Then I am not to sleep aboard when she is in harbour?'

'Forgive me, Darwin, but I would have imagined that the less time you spend in that ridiculously small cabin, the more comfortable you will be – do you not think?'

FitzRoy grinned at him conspiratorially.

The flotilla of small boats bounced around to Devonport from the steamer dock in line abreast, dancing upon the waves like the participants in a drunken late-night quadrille. Jemmy Button, in the bow of the lead boat, gave a shout of excitement as they rounded Devil's Point and turned a-starboard into the dockyard.

'The *Beagle*! Look, Mister Bennet, the *Beagle*!'

'So it is, Jemmy. But there's something different about her. There are more trysails. The skipper's had the deck raised too, and the rail lowered.'

'The *Beagle*! The *Beagle*!' squealed Fuegia Basket.

By the time they had moored alongside, a small reception party had assembled to meet them, headed by a puzzled FitzRoy. He could see Jemmy, York, Fuegia and the coxswain, but where were the two missionaries they were expecting –

the two 'muscular' Christians? He could see only a pale, wispy youth of about seventeen, sitting alongside Bennet. And what was in all those boats?

'I love Capp'en Fitz'oy!' shouted Fuegia, levering her increasingly spherical frame on to the quayside with surprising agility and hurtling into his arms. Finally, he extracted himself from a series of high-spirited reunions and said his how-dos to Bennet.

'Commander FitzRoy, may I introduce the Reverend Richard Matthews, of the Church Missionary Society?'

'Welcome to Devonport, Mr Matthews.'

'It is an honour to meet you, Commander.'

FitzRoy extended a hand to assist Matthews, who was labouring to clamber out of the boat, and simultaneously flashed Bennet a what-the-hell-is-going-on? look behind the missionary's back. Bennet responded with a grimace that – he hoped – conveyed his powerlessness with regard to any decisions taken at Walthamstow, however ill-judged.

'Forgive me, Mr Matthews, but I was under the impression that you were to be accompanied by a colleague.'

'Unfortunately not. I have with me a letter from Mr Wilson that explains the situation.'

FitzRoy took the letter and unfolded it.

My dear Sir

I write to introduce the Reverend Richard Matthews, who is to be the permanent representative of the Church Missionary Society in Tierra del Fuego. He is possessed of such knowledge and information as seem calculated to promote the present and eternal welfare of the savages of that region. I very much regret that we could not meet with a suitable companion for him. However, we have provided Mr Matthews with all such articles as appear to be necessary for him, and which could most advantageously be supplied from this country. I hope that they will not be found to amount to a quantity to occasion you inconvenience; and I think you will be of the opinion that no part of his outfit could, with propriety, be dispensed with.

Believe me, my dear Sir,

Yours faithfully

The Reverend William Wilson

FitzRoy refolded the letter. *With propriety?* What did he mean, *with propriety?* What were these articles?

Under Wickham's direction, crewmen pulled back the tarpaulins on the boats to reveal a series of enormous packing cases.

'Some kind Christian friends have supplied these most essential articles, Commander. I trust that space will be found for them in your hold.'

FitzRoy found himself transfixed by Matthews's moustache or, rather, the lack of it. A few downy hairs were struggling against all odds to take hold on the slopes of his upper lip.

Lieutenant Wickham cut in: 'Mr Matthews, the hold of the *Beagle* is packed to the gunwales with six thousand canisters of Kilner and Moorsom's preserved meat, vegetables and soup. There is absolutely no chance on God's earth of fitting these crates below decks.'

'We must break them open – it is our only course of action,' ordered FitzRoy. 'Distribute the contents about the ship as best you can, Lieutenant. Anywhere there is space.'

'Sir.'

And so, under Matthews's forlorn gaze, the packing cases were shouldered on to the quay and levered open one by one. Gradually, the contents came to light: an astonishing assortment of wine-glasses, butter-bolts, tea-trays, soup tureens and fine white linen, as if someone had transplanted the entire window display of a fashionable Bond Street store to the Devonport quayside. The sniggers and guffaws of the crew were entirely audible, and FitzRoy could see Wickham trying to suppress a smile. One crewman produced an earthenware chamber pot and cracked a joke under his breath. Laughter rippled through the company.

'I am not entirely sure that I see any occasion for levity,' observed Matthews, coldly.

'Quite so,' said FitzRoy, trying to compose his features as best he could.

'Look!' shouted Jemmy, who had found an elegant silver looking-glass with a delicate tracery of filigree-work on the back.

'That's him happy,' said Bennet.

Fuegia was prancing around the quayside in a beaver hat. York had uncovered a cut-glass decanter set, and was holding each piece skyward to catch the glint of daylight as refracted through the glass. Several complete sets of crockery were beginning to stack up, not to mention an entire mahogany dressing-table and a set of French doilies.

'Mr Matthews, are you entirely cognizant of the conditions prevailing in Tierra del Fuego?' FitzRoy asked gently.

'I have not previously left these shores myself, sir, but my elder brother is a missionary near Kororareka in New Zealand. Like him, I will make it my study and endeavour to do these poor creatures all the good in my power, in every practicable way. I shall promise the glory of God and the good of my fellow creatures, and I shall be strong in the grace that is Jesus Christ.'

'Good heavens, sir, an entire packing case of Bibles,' reported Wickham.

'I intend to make the scriptures the basis of all my teaching, Commander. Let us not forget the great theological principle laid down in the sixth article of the Church of England – that Holy Scripture containeth all things necessary to salvation.'

'Absolutely, Mr Matthews. It is a principle I adhere to faithfully myself.'

'By the deuce!' exclaimed Midshipman King. 'Someone's only been and bought up the whole of Swan and Edgar!'

FitzRoy half turned away. As fiercely as he struggled to keep his facial muscles from creasing and his shoulders from heaving, he was losing the battle. Silent tears of laughter trickled down his cheeks.

The rhythmic clump of heavy footsteps, as lines of men tramped on board carrying table-linen and expensive glass-ware, was counterpointed by high-pitched shrieks of pleasure from above, as Musters and Hellyer chased Fuegia Basket up the rigging and around the crosstrees.

'Really. The *Beagle* is becoming a nursery, with all these deuced kids running about the place,' grumbled King.

FitzRoy had half a mind to let them continue, as it kept Fuegia happy and occupied, but the last thing he needed now was a child with a broken neck. 'Mr Musters! Mr Hellyer! Get down here this instant.'

'Sir!'

The two boys scrambled obediently to the deck.

'Mr Hellyer, I presume by all this foolery that there are no more invoices or pay-tickets to be checked and signed. Have you completed your work?'

'Yes, sir.'

'Have you signed off the inventory from the victualling department?'

'Yes, sir.'

'Good lad. Now, this is Midshipman King. I am going to place you both in his charge.'

King rolled his eyes in despair.

'Over the next few months, I expect you to hang by his every word, after which I hope you will both know everything there is to know about seamanship.'

'I expect I shall know most of it already, sir,' averred Musters, stoutly.

'Quite possibly. But if I hear that you have missed even one nugget of useful information, Mr Musters, you will feel the business end of Mr Sorrell's rattan. Is that clear?'

'Yes, sir.'

'Now go about the business of learning to be a sailor.'

FitzRoy was glad, a moment or two later, that he had put

an end to the two boys' larking, when a well-appointed scarlet carriage with livery servants made its way down the approach road towards the *Beagle*. When it drew to a halt, no less a person than Captain Francis Beaufort, His Majesty's hydrographer, climbed down. *Any more visitors*, thought FitzRoy, *and I shall have to employ a footman to collect calling cards on a salver.* He hissed at Wickham and the sailors present to look lively, but he need not have worried. The carriage was sufficiently distinguished that the entire crew had stood to attention even before it had disgorged its occupant. Beaufort limped up the accommodation-ladder, disregarding offers of assistance, and nodded a greeting.

'FitzRoy.'

'This is a most unexpected honour, sir.'

'No need to flatter yourself unduly, FitzRoy, my presence in Plymouth is on Admiralty business. But while I am here I have good reason to pay you a visit.'

His practised eye took in the new trysails between the masts, the brass cannon, the gleaming whaleboats and the hand-painted figure of Neptune on the ship's wheel, with the motto 'England expects that every man will do his duty' circled elegantly around it.

'My, you have dug deep into your capital,' he observed. 'The rail is lower than in an everyday coffin brig, am I right?'

'You are, sir. The deck is raised but not the bulwarks, so as to make her less deep-waisted. It also means that more air will be trapped inside her hull to resist a capsize if she goes over on her beam-ends.'

'You are a marvel, FitzRoy. Although I fear you will bankrupt yourself at this rate – we don't wish to see your name printed in the *London Gazette*, I'm sure. Shall we speak in your cabin?'

They repaired to the cubby-hole that would be FitzRoy's home for the next couple of years.

'So, it seems you have interest enough to get the *Beagle* sent on whatever track you like.'

'My uncle, Lord Londonderry, was kind enough to be interested about me.' FitzRoy though it best to avoid mentioning His Majesty.

'Well, I for one am glad of it. Let us sincerely hope that you have not made enemies in the process. Now, to business. How many chronometers, ultimately, were you able to withdraw from stores?'

'Eleven. I have procured a further eleven myself.'

'Excellent. So the *Beagle* will be better equipped to calculate longitude than any previous vessel to sail from these shores. I want you, FitzRoy, to run a chronometric line around the world. To fix accurately the known points on the surface of the globe *in relation to each other*. Isolated observations are all very well but no one has ever made a complete chain of measurements around the globe before.'

'That's wonderful, sir, but that is to be in addition to the South American survey?'

'Nothing has changed on that account. Use the southern winters to survey the Patagonian coast between Buenos Ayres and Port Desire. Complete the survey of Tierra del Fuego during the summers. And you will be required to provide a full survey of the Falkland Islands as well.'

'The Falklands as well?'

'It is not strictly necessary for the Admiralty's navigational needs, but Buenos Ayres is making noises about inheriting the Spanish claim to the islands. Your presence may act as a deterrent. All ships in the area have been ordered to make a stop there.'

'All of this is to be completed with the one vessel, sir, in two years?'

'You will be wasting your time, FitzRoy, if you pursue the infinite number of bays, openings and roads of Tierra del Fuego. Yet I cannot stress sufficiently that no good harbour should be omitted.'

Do not enter every bay. But do not miss a good harbour on any account. A contrary instruction if ever there was one.

'There will be no time to waste on elaborate maps, Commander. Plain, distinct roughs with explanatory notes shall suffice. After all, you can hardly fail to improve upon the Spanish charts, which are the product merely of a running view of the shore.'

'And if it is discovered that I have omitted a navigable harbour?'

'Then – not to put too fine a point on it – the blame will attach to you. Remember that you are the one who has pursued this commission. There are those who will not be unhappy to see you fail. I suggest that your best course is not to omit one.'

So I shall be damned if I undertake the task properly, and damned if I do not.

'I also desire you to pursue another enquiry for me, in the Pacific. A modern and very plausible theory has arisen regarding coral: that reefs do not ascend from the sea bed, but are raised from the summits of extinct volcanoes. I want you to exert every means that ingenuity can devise of discovering at what depth the coral formation begins.'

Under normal circumstances, a fascinating enquiry. Under normal circumstances.

'Finally, are you familiar with Alexander Dalrymple's proposed numerical scale for the recording of weather conditions? Well, I have long considered that wind and weather should be logged on some intelligible scale, right across the Service. Terms such as "fresh" and "moderate" are ambiguous. I have devised two scales, based upon Dalrymple's, which I should like you to pilot for me. There is a letter code for meteorological observations, and a numerical code for wind strength. Here.'

Beaufort passed a sheaf of papers across the table.

'It ranges from nought – dead calm – to twelve, that which no canvas could withstand. Hurricane strength. Although I doubt very much that you would be in a position to report anything back to me, were you to encounter force twelve winds. Let us hope, God willing, that the eventuality shall not arise.'

FitzRoy thought back to the storm at Maldonado Bay, which had nearly cost them all their lives. Would that have counted as a twelve on Beaufort's new scale?

'It will not incommode us, sir.'

'Oh, one more thing, FitzRoy. Do you have a surgeon on the *Beagle*?'

'There is Bynoe, sir, the assistant surgeon. He has acted as surgeon before. He is young, sir, but a regular trump.'

'Well, I am afraid he will have to remain assistant surgeon for the duration of the voyage. A surgeon named Robert McCormick shall be joining you. He was in the Arctic with Parry, but was invalided home. I should warn you that he has been invalided home from overseas a further three times.'

FitzRoy's heart sank. 'Invalided home', both men knew, was a euphemism for 'sacked'. McCormick's previous captains had clearly found him intolerable.

'I have met him, and he seems a sound, good fellow at the bottom. Perhaps a trifle brusque – he would have made a fine Army man.'

FitzRoy smiled.

'He studied natural philosophy at Edinburgh, so he is well qualified to carry out the job of ship's naturalist.'

'I already have a naturalist aboard, sir.'

'Ah, yes, young Mr Darwin. Well, I am afraid that Mr McCormick must take precedence – it is his right, as surgeon. But I am sure that they can rub along together. Perhaps they can be encouraged to concentrate on different areas. Natural philosophy is a wide discipline, is it not?'

'It is indeed, sir.'

'I'm sorry, FitzRoy, but it is the price you pay for their lordships' consent to your commission. You are not the only man in the Service with influence in high places.'

'And if Mr McCormick were to be invalided home once again, sir?'

'I should not advise it.'

It was a rueful FitzRoy that followed the hydrographer's

limping progress up the companionway and out into the glare
of the maindeck. As their eyes adjusted to the light, they found
themselves standing behind Midshipman King, who was
crouched mid-instruction with his new charges.

'Remember to show willing by tailing on to any ropes that
are being pulled. Ropes are always coiled out of the way – the
way the sun goes round. Right toe, left toe, out in front of
you – see? Now, if you're sent up to loose the sails, be sure to
take hold of the shrouds and not the ratlines. When the sails
are loosed and set, you will hear the orders given for backing
and filling them. It is to keep control of the ship's course. The
orders will sound like Greek at first, I expect.'

'Not to me they won't,' said Musters.

Beaufort smiled indulgently, and turned to FitzRoy. 'That's
the age at which I started. You, too, I expect.'

'Near enough, sir.'

Hearing the officers' voices behind them, the three boys
jumped to their feet and saluted smartly.

'You two younkers – what are your names?'

'Volunteer First Class Musters, sir!'

'Volunteer First Class Hellyer, sir!'

'How old are you?'

'Eleven, sir!'

'Twelve, sir!'

'Is this to be your first voyage?'

'Yes sir!'

'Excellent, excellent,' chuckled Beaufort. 'Take good care of
these two in the south, Commander, for lads like these are
the future of the service.'

'I intend to, sir.'

'Here – not strictly naval procedure, but I think we might
stretch a point, seeing as this is your first trip.' Beaufort reached
into his pocket and extracted a handful of loose change. 'Hold
out your hands.'

He pressed a shiny half-sovereign into each of the two boys'
palms.

'That's not fair,' grumbled King, as Beaufort hobbled off the ship.

'I had hoped to be posted to a frigate, sir, or some other desirable ship,' said Robert McCormick, his dark moustache bristling. 'I am, frankly, wearied and tired out with all the buffeting about one has to endure in a small craft. Ofttimes I've had to put up with uncomfortable little vessels on unhealthy stations. But I intend to make my name as a naturalist, sir, which is why I have decided to accept the surgeon's commission on the *Beagle*.'

'I am much obliged to you, Mr McCormick,' said FitzRoy, drily.

'Don't mention it, sir,' said McCormick, entirely missing the sarcasm.

There was a woodenness about the man, thought FitzRoy, an immobility to his bovine features, which was entirely offset by his waxed military moustache. McCormick's moustache quivered animatedly when he spoke, and shuddered in time to his every emphatic declaration. It was as if the moustache spoke for him, in some queer disembodied fashion. The contrast with Matthews's sparse growth struck FitzRoy as faintly ludicrous.

'Captain Beaufort tells me you have voyaged to the Arctic with Parry in the *Hecla*.'

'I did, sir, for my sins, and a more damn-fool expedition was never mounted on the surface of God's earth. Parry's plan was to get to the Pole in wheeled boats pulled by trained reindeer. Of course the damned things were too heavy, and the reindeer couldn't shift 'em. Parry was a fool,' he said scornfully.

FitzRoy wondered what terms his new surgeon would find to describe him behind his back.

'The axles were buried under a foot of snow. So there we all stood in raccoon-skin caps, hooded jackets, blue breeches and white canvas gaiters, straining like idiots to shift 'em even an inch. We must have looked like a party of elves!' McCormick suddenly roared with laughter at the memory.

He has a sense of humour at least, thought FitzRoy. 'So, tell me, Mr McCormick, how have you occupied your time more recently?'

'Well, I have been without a ship since ten months. I've been having a monstrous good time in London, though – boxing, rat-hunting, fives and four-in-hand driving. I've been lodging at my father's place – the old man has lots of tin. But all good things must come to an end, what? Oh, I say, sir, what's that?'

The two men were strolling through the lofty white rectangles of the Royal Dockyard, towards quay number two, where the *Beagle* and the *Active* were moored.

'What's what?'

'On your deck, sir. Looks like a gang of Hottentots.'

'They are Fuegians, Mr McCormick. They have been educated in England at Admiralty expense, and are being returned to their home country to establish a mission.'

'Extraordinary. Wish I'd known – there's a feller of my acquaintance runs the Egyptian Hall in Piccadilly. We could have made a pretty penny exhibiting your savages to the general public.'

'In fact, Mr McCormick, they are very far from the savage state. Three better-mannered and more agreeable souls it would be difficult to find.'

'Wonders will never cease.'

They went aboard, McCormick's brisk, stiff military bearing at variance with FitzRoy's lithe informality. Introductions were made to those officers present on deck, before FitzRoy decided to show the new surgeon the library. They found Stebbing within, entering book titles in a catalogue.

'I say, sir, there must be over three hundred volumes here,' enthused McCormick.

'There are in excess of four hundred.'

'I must say, though, sir, I'm surprised to see Lamarck here. Should we really be giving house-room to a transmutationist? Beasts evolving into men? Typical of a Frenchman to espouse the most atrocious revolutionary principles and the most dangerous Godless doctrines.'

'I hold no more with transmutationism than you do, Mr McCormick, but is it not preferable to understand the arguments of one's enemy than to dismiss them out of hand?'

'Well,' snorted McCormick, 'if there is a halfway house between man and beast, then it's your Frenchy, and no mistake. Personally, I'd chuck the whole beastly nonsense overboard. Ah, I see you have a copy of Lyell. Another damned fool.'

'Mr Lyell is one of our foremost geologists. He has expressed an interest in the results of our expedition.'

'Has he, by Jove? Lyell's the fellow who devised all that gammon about the world's geology being the result of internal heat. Well, I studied under Jameson at Edinburgh – a genius, sir – and he has proved conclusively that both granite and basalt are formed by crystallization from a watery soup. The earth's core is an underground sea – that's where the flood came from.'

'Now you are interesting me, Mr McCormick. We must discuss this with Mr Darwin, the – ah – my companion.'

'Your what, sir?'

'I have engaged a gentleman companion for the voyage, a Mr Charles Darwin. He too is interested in natural philosophy, and intends to make a collection.'

'Well, as long as it doesn't interfere with my official work as surgeon and naturalist.'

'I gather that he, too, studied under Jameson at Edinburgh.'

'Did he? Splendid.'

Although I seem to recall that he was not as complimentary in his assessment of the professor.

'He is presently in the Atheneum Gardens assisting Stokes, my assistant surveyor. He is to mark the time and take observations on the dipping needle, while Stokes calibrates the chronometers for their initial readings. We have selected the Atheneum as the starting point for a chain of chronometric measurements around the globe.'

'Is that usual, sir, for a civilian to assist with naval surveying matters?' McCormick looked decidedly piqued to hear of Darwin's involvement in the scientific life of the ship.

'It may not be usual, Mr McCormick, but the arrangement is most satisfactory to all concerned.'

'Of course, sir.' McCormick took the hint. 'I say, you there.' The surgeon indicated Stebbing. 'I'm absolutely gasping for a drink. Fetch me a glass of wine, will you, well qualified with brandy and spice.'

Stebbing looked bewildered.

'There is no alcohol on the *Beagle*, Mr McCormick,' cut in FitzRoy. 'This is to be an alcohol-free voyage. Shall I show you to your cabin?'

'No alcohol! Good Lord. Belay that. And I felt just like swallowing off a glass.' McCormick wore a bleak expression. 'It's going to be a deuced long two years, sir.'

The officers' cabins were forward of FitzRoy's own cabin on the lower deck, leading off the old messroom, which had been converted into a well-appointed gunroom. McCormick flung open his cabin door: a cot, a washstand and a cramped chest of drawers consumed almost all the meagre space available.

'The cabins in these coffin brigs are so damned poky,' he complained. 'Are they all painted white?'

'It affords some reflected light, given the paucity of natural light below decks.'

'I'm not sure I wouldn't prefer French grey. It's more restful. On second thoughts, it is a French colour. Hmm. I shall give the matter due consideration.'

Shall you indeed? thought FitzRoy, who was beginning to wonder how he would last two hours in McCormick's company, let alone two years. McCormick, he realized, had now fallen silent, for the first time that afternoon. The surgeon had pulled open the cabin drawers one by one, and stood open-mouthed before them.

'Excuse me, sir,' he said finally.

'Yes, Mr McCormick?'

'My cabin appears to be full of French lace, sir.'

*   *   *

FitzRoy marched up George Street in a disturbed frame of mind, a silent Darwin trailing a yard behind. The impossibility of completing his commission in the time available bore down heavily upon him; the callow inexperience of Matthews, and the imposition of McCormick upon what had been a close-knit group of colleagues only made matters worse. He felt a vague sense of urgency as a physical need, an itch he could not scratch, a strange discomfort for which there was no relief. Anxiety had made him tired through lack of sleep; a sense of the pointlessness of all his meticulous preparations was creeping over him, even though his mind was too filled with thoughts to be still. The wider panorama of problems that assailed him was for the most part impossible to address; but on a more intimate scale he could, at least, remedy the ludicrous surfeit of crockery aboard the *Beagle*. So it was that he marched through the doorway of Addison's china shop in combative mood, Darwin – bringing up the rear – wondering all the time what had happened to his *beau idéal* of a sea-captain.

'Commander FitzRoy, is it not? May I be of assistance, sir?' The proprietor – presumably Addison himself – glided from behind the counter to greet his distinguished visitor.

'You may indeed. I have recently had occasion to purchase several complete sets of crockery from this very shop.'

'I remember the occasion well, sir.'

'It seems I have over-ordered. I will have to return them.'

'The items in question have provided every satisfaction, I trust?'

'I told you, I have over-ordered.'

'Then forgive me, Commander' – here Addison indicated a sign – 'but goods may not be returned unless they are found to be faulty.'

'I beg your pardon?' said FitzRoy, taking a step forward with sufficient intent that the proprietor was forced to take a step back.

'G-goods may not be returned, Commander, unless they are found to be faulty.'

'Do you see this, sir? And this, and this?' FitzRoy indicated the most expensive items on display. 'I would have purchased these – all of these – had you not been so disobliging. You are a blackguard, sir!'

'Really, Commander, I must—'

'I said, you are a blackguard, sir!' FitzRoy seized the principal teapot from the nearest crockery display, and dashed it to the floor. Darwin stood, stunned. Addison, unable to believe his eyes, remained rooted to the spot, shaking and confused. FitzRoy swept out of the shop.

With only a brief, panic-stricken glance of sympathy at the proprietor, Darwin followed him into the street. 'My dear FitzRoy, what the deuce—'

'You do not believe me? You do not believe that I would have purchased those items?' His nostrils flared; his features were contorted with rage.

It was, thought Darwin, as if a complete personality change had suddenly overwhelmed the captain. 'But the *Beagle* already has a surfeit of crockery,' he pointed out.

'I tell you sir, I – I – I . . .' FitzRoy tailed off, and stood there on the cobbles, outwardly silent; but Darwin could see that a superhuman struggle was taking place inside his friend's mind.

FitzRoy could see Darwin now, a ghostly grey shape embodying calm and reason, superimposed against that other Darwin who had inexplicably driven him to anger just a moment before. It was as if another, different reality was showing through, a palimpsest behind the reality that currently intensified each and every one of his senses, that stretched his every nerve-ending like india-rubber. A surge of panic threatened to overwhelm him, as he felt himself on the edge of an abyss, a terrifying black hole of enveloping hopelessness and despair. But he was also conscious of the fact that, for the first time, an alternative course presented itself, if he could only find the strength to reach for it.

'FitzRoy?'

'Darwin, I – I . . . I'm sorry, but I . . .'

He wanted to complete the sentence, but he realized that he could not recall the start of it. Big tears, huge dollops of salt water, began to roll helplessly down his face. *I'm all right,* he realized. *I'm all right. Whatever it was, it went away.*

He had come back from the brink. But was his sudden salvation anything to do with his friend's presence? Had the very fact of Darwin's companionship driven the demons of loneliness away? Or was his recovery mere coincidence, another unpredictable fluctuation in the electric current that seemed to course unchecked and undirected through his mind?

'FitzRoy? Are you all right?'

'Yes . . . yes, I'm fine. I am most terribly sorry . . . Please, let us leave now.'

And he led his friend back down George Street towards Devonport.

Chapter Twelve

Barnet Pool, Devonport,
24 December 1831

'Deep in wide caverns and their shadowy aisles
Daughter of Earth, the chaste Truffelia smiles;
On silvery beds of soft asbestos wove,
Meets her gnome-husband, and avows her love.'

Darwin giggled when he reached the end of the verse, and
shot FitzRoy an I-told-you-so look.

'And you are seriously informing me,' repeated FitzRoy,
'that these lines were written about two truffles mating underground?'

'I do not jest.'

'Extraordinary.'

'It is not the finest verse ever composed.'

'It is certainly the best entertainment I have had this last
month.'

The *Beagle* had received Admiralty permission to leave in
late November, and had moved to the holding area at Barnet
Pool beneath Mount Edgcumbe, ready for departure. No
sooner had she done so than a persistent gale had set in,

flinging squall after squall up the Channel from the west; there had been no break in the weather for nigh on a month. Bucking and dipping and bouncing where she stood, the little brig strained continually at anchor like an impatient dog trying to break free of its lead. Attempting to tack a square-rigger into such a head-on gale, as FitzRoy explained to Darwin, would be a waste of all their efforts; a point made emphatically on 17 December, when the *Persephone*, a brig that had set out for the Bay of Biscay two days before the storm broke, was driven unceremoniously back into Devonport.

It was Christmas Eve. FitzRoy and Darwin had taken refuge in the library; the other occupants of the cabin, King and Stokes, were part of the last dog-watch from six to eight, and so were hunched in their thick woollen surtouts outside, the elements at their backs. Sleeting winds and rain swept mercilessly across the decks, and inside the library, beat their muffled tattoo against the skylight. The oil lamp swung from side to side in its gimbal, bathing the cabin in its warm yellow glow, and tossing out little parabolas of smoke with every rise and fall of the ship. As the lamp swung back and forth, the two men's shadows alternately grew and shrank against the cabin walls, like pugilists advancing and retreating.

Darwin, who had been feeling queasy for a whole month, was endeavouring to distract himself and entertain FitzRoy by reading aloud from a book of his grandfather Erasmus's scientific verse.

'I say, listen to this. It's about the reproductive process of the *Gloriosa* flower:

"Then breath'd from quivering lips a whisper'd vow,
And bent on heaven his pale repentant brow;
'Thus, thus!' he cried, and plung'd the furious dart,
And life and love gush'd mingled from his heart."'

'By the deuce, that's racy stuff!'
'My grandfather did sire a prodigious number of children.'

As their conversation dissolved into laughter the cabin door banged open, and the outside world roared in. The lantern flame guttered, sending their shadows boxing each other crazily across the walls. Pages of poetry flickered past at high speed, as a gust of wind raced dismissively through their contents. McCormick ducked into the cabin, shook himself like a wet spaniel, and shut the door. 'Deuced filthy night, sir,' he observed.

'Good evening, Mr McCormick,' said FitzRoy, finding manners, as so often, a useful cloak for his feelings.

'Poetry,' remarked McCormick suspiciously, picking up the volume on the chart table and leafing through it.

'"Organic life beneath the shoreless waves
Was born and nurs'd in Ocean's pearly caves
First forms minute, unseen by spheric glass,
Move on the mud, or pierce the watery mass;
These as successive generations bloom,
New powers acquire, and larger limbs assume."

'I say, who wrote this bosh?'

'My grandfather did.'

'Sorry,' grunted McCormick, in a tone more or less devoid of apology.

'It is his volume of "scientific" verse.'

'Forgive me, Darwin, but I don't see that the mystery of creation is within the range of legitimate scientific territory.'

'Do you believe so?' asked FitzRoy. 'Surely the purpose of philosophic enquiry is to illuminate all God's works, and to understand the laws by which He has created the universe?'

'Yes, sir, but to suggest that man is just another creature crawling out of the slime, well, it's a beastly and damnable creed that has no place for honour, or generosity, or beauty of the spirit, or any of the qualities given by God to man alone.'

'I'm inclined to agree with you, Mr McCormick. But, if Darwin will forgive me –'

'Please carry on.'

'– my principal objection to the theories of Erasmus Darwin, and Lamarck, and their fellow transmutationists, would be a scientific one. Their contention that living beings can develop useful characteristics and somehow pass them on to the next generation allows no mechanism for doing so. A farm labourer may develop muscles, but he cannot pass them on to his son through inheritance. How can mere matter generate its own variations? It is a question that they cannot answer. I'm afraid, my dear Darwin, that your grandfather undermines the distinction between mind and matter by endowing matter with inherent vitality.'

'Yes, absolutely, of course, that too, sir,' agreed McCormick, his brows knitted. 'But hang it, sir, life comes from God, not from the mind or from matter, for that matter. That is, I didn't mean . . .' McCormick became momentarily confused. 'I mean, all this nonsense about new species developing. It's been scientifically established that God created every single species of plant and land animal on the same day – Saturday, the thirtieth of October 4004 BC.'

FitzRoy allowed McCormick the debatable contention that Bishop Ussher's dating had been 'scientific'.

'The French Philosophical Anatomists would disagree with you.'

'With all due respect, sir, they *are* French.'

'Not all of them,' said Darwin. 'Professor Grant at Edinburgh was as Scottish as oatcakes.'

'With all due respect, Darwin, Professor Grant is a damned scoundrel.'

'When I was at Cambridge,' persevered Darwin, 'Professor Henslow made a very good case for incorporating philosophical anatomy into the theory of natural theology. He believed that God's laws of creation did allow for new species to occur.'

'Damned scientific Whiggery,' snorted McCormick.

Darwin gave him a supercilious stare. 'I, too, am a Whig, Mr McCormick. As is my father, and as was my grandfather, who – however misguided his scientific principles may have been – believed in liberty, social advancement, industrialization and cultural improvement.'

'So he was a Jacobin, sir, in both his politics and his chemistry,' McCormick shot back.

'If you will forgive me, gentlemen, I have an appointment for supper in the gunroom.' Darwin rose stiffly, taking care not to bang his head on the ceiling, pulled on his benjamin and disappeared through the dark rectangle of the doorway. Once more a flurry of lashing rain and gusting wind disrupted the equilibrium of the cabin, before calm reasserted itself. FitzRoy was left facing McCormick across the chart table.

Finally, the surgeon broke the silence.

'Deuced filthy night, sir,' he said.

'Well, if it isn't the Philosopher!'

'Come in, Philosopher, and make yourself at home!'

'Hello there, Philos!'

The fug of pipe-tobacco in the gunroom was warm, friendly and cosseting. Sulivan stood up, clapped Darwin on the back and offered up his seat.

'Supper won't be long, Philos. We've some rare tackle – a nice bowl of warm soup, boiled duck and onions, with hot duff to follow. How will that suit?'

'Wonderful, thank you.' The idea of filling his stomach with hot food appealed to Darwin, but he was aware that his stomach might take its usual contrary view. He squeezed in between Bynoe and Usborne, the new master's assistant.

'So, Philos, how are you liking your new life on the rolling deep?'

'I dare say I shall like it a deal more, gentlemen, when this fearful storm abates.'

A thunderclap of laughter rolled round the table.

'Fearful storm? This is barely a stiff breeze!'

'Wait 'til Tierra del Fuego, Philosopher, then you'll see a blow or two!'

'It's when the bulkhead's under your feet and the deck's by

your left ear that you should start to fret, old man!'

'So, how is your study of the art of seamanship advancing, Philos?' enquired Wickham. 'Have you mastered all the technical terms yet?'

'I feel I have made some progress. I have learned the names of all the sails, and the masts and the parts of the ship. So while not quite a seafarer yet, I am beginning to hold my own.'

'Capital, capital. These are exactly the areas of knowledge that will save your life, when you are atop the mast in a howling gale in the Southern Ocean.'

'When I— My dear Lieutenant Wickham, I do not propose to climb the mast at any time, still less during a howling gale.'

'But Philos,' said Bynoe, a worried look on his face, 'did you not realize? When the order is given for all hands on deck, that means all hands. Even the civilians.'

'In a gale we all pull together,' confirmed Bennet.

'Did the skipper not mention it?' said Usborne.

'Do not worry yourself unduly, Philos,' said Wickham. 'As a passenger, you will be asked to reeve the halliards through the block at the peak of the driver, or something like that.'

Darwin's face wore a worried look. 'The driver? That's a . . . temporary sail, if I recollect, hoisted up the mizzen-mast?'

'Spot on,' said Bynoe. 'You do know your stuff. I presume you know your halliards also – outer halliards, middle halliards, inner halliards, throat halliards?'

'Well, I . . . throat halliards?'

'Oh, it's perfectly simple,' Wickham reassured him. 'The throat halliards are reeved through a block lashed at the mizzen-mast head. But when the sail is large – and it is important you remember this – the lower block of a luff tackle is hooked to a thimble in the throat cringle or nock, and the upper one is hooked to a strap round the mizzen-mast head. The sheet rope is reeved through a sheave-hole in the boom, and clinched to an iron traveller; in the other end, a thimble is spliced, the outer block of a luff tackle is hooked to it, and the inner one to a bolt on the boom. I say, Philosopher, are you all right?'

Panic-stricken, Darwin scanned the room. A circle of grave, concerned faces met his gaze.

'It's just that I . . .'

There was a worried silence. Sulivan, still standing behind him, ended it by breaking into laughter.

'Enough! Enough, you rotters, you have had your sport.'

The table erupted in hilarity.

'My dear Philosopher, they are having a game with you,' said Sulivan, throwing an arm good-naturedly around Darwin's shoulders. 'If we find ourselves at the mercy of a gale in the Southern Ocean, you will be tucked up like a babe in your hammock, as sure as eggs is eggs!'

The grave faces of a moment before had been replaced by a sea of merriment. Bennet, right before him, was literally weeping with laughter, tears rolling down his rosy cheeks. 'Jimmy' Usborne, to his left, was clutching his ribs as if in pain. Darwin, still stunned, sat in silence for a moment; and then, gradually, a smile stole over his features, and he began to chuckle too. Just a cautious chuckle at first, then a full-throated guffaw, until he was laughing with the best of them.

Two hours later, the dog-watch over, hammocks piped down, all the lights and fires out except for a yellow glow from the gunroom skylight, Darwin stood at the rail. He stared out at the black, choppy surface of Barnet Pool and tried not to frighten himself with the thought of fifty-yard swells, or mighty walls of water that could crush a three-decker to matchwood, waves that might snap the *Beagle* in two like a twig. He had eaten too well, and had taken snuff for the first time, and he felt queasier than ever, for what seemed an inexhaustible variety of reasons.

An hour later still, FitzRoy knocked at his cabin door, and found him attempting forlornly to climb into his hammock.

'It sounded like an enjoyable evening.'

'It was.'

Darwin did not elaborate.

'You are having trouble?'

'I am having the most ludicrous difficulty. Every time I try to climb in, I only succeed in pushing the deuced thing away, without making any progress inserting my own body.'

'Here. Let me show you. The correct method is to sit accurately in the centre of the hammock, then give yourself a dextrous twist, and your head and your feet will come into their respective places. Like so.'

FitzRoy swung easily into the hammock, then hopped down again. Darwin carefully replicated his movements, and succeeded, finally, in wedging himself between the folds of cloth.

'Pray let me tuck you in.'

'Really, FitzRoy, there is no need.'

'My dear fellow. If you will suffer me . . .' And he arranged the blankets tenderly about Darwin, and pulled them up to his chin. 'I am sure you will feel better on the morrow.'

'My dear preserver, I do hope so.'

FitzRoy extinguished the light. 'Happy Christmas, Darwin,' he said.

'Happy Christmas, FitzRoy.'

The officers took their Christmas dinner ashore at Weakley's Hotel. They ate mutton chops washed down with champagne, followed by plum-dough with raisins, and watched the rain lash into the window-panes, the streets of Plymouth rendered as grey watercolour smears by the streams cascading down the glass. FitzRoy, though, was optimistic: whatever the despondency engendered among his men by the weather, the barometer told a different story. It was on the turn, indicating that they would in all likelihood be able to set sail the next day. He had given most of the crew Christmas Day off as a consequence, and had left charge of the *Beagle* to a small party of men notionally commanded by Midshipman King – partly to give the boy a taste of responsibility, and partly to keep him away from the champagne. Sulivan, who had worked like a Trojan during the preceding months, was in a cheery mood, like his captain, despite his exertions, for such was his nature. Theirs was a merry end of the table. Fuegia Basket hurtled about, admiring the ribbons and the candles, teasing Musters and Hellyer, and playing with a model boat that the captain had given her. FitzRoy felt gladdened to be in such happy company.

Darwin found himself in mid-table, seated opposite Augustus Earle, the new ship's artist, who had been employed by the captain in a private capacity to provide a visual record of the trip. He found Earle an odd fish: nearly twice his age, the man sported a stubbly beard, wore a shabby top-coat and a filthy stock.

'I apprehend that you are an American, Mr Earle.'

'I was born there, Mr Darwin, but I am a man of the world. I have not seen the States since 1815. I have lived in Chili, Peru, Brazil, Madras, India, and Tristan da Cunha. Lately I have spent three years in Australia, employed upon the portraits of colonial governors. When the supply of subjects was exhausted, I passed nine months in New Zealand, painting the natives.'

'I am sorry to hear of your disappointment. I imagine the Australian commission was a lucrative one.'

'Oh, there was no disappointment, Mr Darwin. Producing identical portraits of minor officials to hang before their families is no appointment worth speaking of. It merely paid my way. The New Zealander, by contrast, is a challenging subject for any painter. I like to think I captured something of his vitality, his athleticism. But there ain't many as want to buy a portrait of a New Zealander. It's why I moved on.'

'Do forgive me, Mr Earle, but I cannot imagine who would wish to purchase a portrait of a black man.'

'Well, our own Captain FitzRoy is an admirer, sir. He said I had a sympathetic eye, along with a capacity for detailed observation. It is how I have found myself in his employ. I have also written a book about New Zealand, which is to be published in Port Jackson, Australia, next year.'

'Is there no end to your talents, Mr Earle? May I know the substance of your narrative?'

'The substance of my narrative, Mr Darwin, is that the New Zealanders are an intelligent, spirited people whose way of life is threatened with destruction by what we term Christian civilization.'

'But how can Christian civilization be a destructive force? Is that not a contradiction?'

'You are a parson-in-waiting, Mr Darwin. If you had seen Christian civilization from the other side of the fence, as I have, then you would have a different appreciation. I lived with a native woman for nine months, and saw first-hand what Christian civilization is doing to her people.'

Darwin was horror-struck. 'You mean you were *familiar* with a black savage for nine months? Unwed?'

'Yes, sir, I was.'

'Was she . . . well, was she *clean*?'

'Cleaner 'n me, that's for sure.'

Darwin sat back, stunned, unsure what to say. There were some things in this world simply beyond his comprehension. Clearly, the voyage would have a lot to teach him.

'Tell me, FitzRoy . . . tell me about your home.'

'My home? My home is in the *Beagle*.'

FitzRoy and Darwin sat before the fire in the smoking room at Weakley's. The younger man felt emboldened, drawn by the embers' intimate glow into making the kind of personal enquiries that can only be conducted between two gentlemen who are well known to each other.

'I mean, your family home.'

'I was brought up at Wakefield Lodge, which is by the village of Pottersbury in Northamptonshire. But since as long as I can remember I wanted to go to sea. My uncle was an admiral, which put him on a par with Nelson in my eye. I dare say my father was not best pleased. He was a general, and had me down for a career in soldiering, but I badgered him and badgered him until he put me down for the Service.'

Mentally he saluted his father's generosity in giving way to an insistent six-year-old son.

'I was quite the explorer even then. Once, during the servants' dinner hour, I took a laundry tub and slipped out of the house. I was determined to sail the uncharted waters of the large pond, to discover what lay upon the far shore. I could have walked round, I suppose, but that would have been too prosaic a solution. I even took with me a pile of bricks, to act as ballast – I had heard of ballast from my uncle, I think. Sadly I had not thought to anchor my ballast, so when I stood up halfway across to survey the way ahead, all the bricks slid to one side and my little craft capsized. I was saved from a watery grave by one of the gardeners, who dived in and swam out to rescue me. It was an early lesson in nautical mechanics.'

FitzRoy laughed at the memory.

'My word, I'll wager you suffered the most fearful thrashing. What did your mother and father say?'

'I'm afraid my mother died when I was five years old.'

'Just like my own. I'm sorry.'

'My father never found out about my escapade. He was never there. As I'm sure you can imagine, the French were keeping him rather busy in those days. On top of which he was the MP for Bury St Edmunds.'

'Your father is a Member of Parliament? But, my dear FitzRoy, when I told you my uncle was an MP you said nothing.'

'One does not like to boast of such things,' said FitzRoy, abashed. Somehow, he felt reluctant to share his precious memories of his father, so few and far between were they. 'My father is no longer with us either. He died . . . he died some time ago.'

'My friend, I am sorry.'

'I have an older brother, George, who has the house, I suppose, but I hardly know him. He was sent away to school when I was but one. It was my sister Fanny who brought me up. Then I, too, was sent to school at six. First Rottingdean, then Harrow, then the Royal Naval College when I was twelve. Everything you see before you was fashioned there. They do not simply teach seamanship, or the classics like a normal school. I learned everything from foreign languages to fencing and dancing. It is the most advanced of educational establishments. It was also my first ship, if you like – certainly, that was how we were encouraged to see it.'

'I attended Shrewsbury School, down in the town, learning nothing but Latin and Greek. It was cold and brutal, and I abhorred it, but at least I had the consolation of returning home to my sisters each night.'

FitzRoy gave a little nod of accord. How he had once longed to return home to his sister's affection and love of an evening.

'But the sea is my home now, and the officers and men my family. With the exception of Fanny, I do not believe I have a close friend ashore. I keep rooms in Onslow Square, but they feel to me like an hotel. I am never truly at ease on dry land. I think you will catch the feeling during the voyage, when you journey ashore yourself. You will start to think of the *Beagle* as your home.'

Darwin was too appalled by FitzRoy's circumstances to consider the notion. 'My dear friend! There is no one, here in England, awaiting your return? Apart from your sister, I mean – you have no one?'

FitzRoy thought of Mary O'Brien, and the splash of hot wax falling from the chandelier on to her pale skin.

'No . . . there is no one.'

Concern was etched into Darwin's face. FitzRoy was touched, but hurried them through the moment with a sympathetic smile. 'It does not signify. Come, you are to be my guest, in my house, for the next two years or more. Let us make it a voyage to remember.'

'Here's to that! And let us make it a voyage that shall be remembered by others. I have a suggestion, FitzRoy. What say we publish a book, you and I, an account of our voyage together?'

'Well, I must write a journal of the expedition as part of my official duties, and I have Captain King's journal of the first voyage. We could publish them as two volumes, and you could append a third of your geological and natural observations.'

'What a capital idea!'

'We are agreed, then?'

'Most certainly!'

It was drawing late, so the pot-boy came through to dampen the fire with slack and put up the fire-guard. The two would-be authors retired to bed, aglow with excitement about the voyage to come.

Just as the barometer had predicted, Boxing Day dawned calm, the sun glowing red through an early mist. By the time it had lifted the officers had washed and dressed, and had emerged from the hotel to discover a glorious morning in progress. There were mare's tails in the east, and the smoke from the early-morning chimneys was streaming westward into a crisp blue sky, signalling the way ahead. When they reached the quayside at Devonport, however, there was no sign of the cutter, and they had to endure the embarrassment of borrowing another vessel's craft to get across to Barnet Pool. As they rowed themselves nearer to the *Beagle*, it was clear that something was amiss. Even at a distance, her decks were deathly quiet. There was only one sentry on duty, a diminutive sailor lost in a large, shapeless coat, whom FitzRoy did not at first recognize; although there was something familiar, he thought, about the man's bearing. As they made their boat fast to the *Beagle's* flank, the mystery of the sentry's identity became clear. Inside the coat, shaking with cold and fear, his fingers, nose and ears an icy purple, was Midshipman King.

'Mr King? What on earth . . . ?'

'I'm s-sorry, sir. Th-they wouldn't listen to me, sir.'

'Who wouldn't? Where is the sentry?'

King's eyes pricked with tears. 'He said he would no longer

stand on duty, sir. He told me to . . . he told me to go to the devil, sir. There is not a sober man in the ship, sir.'

As FitzRoy hauled himself up the battens and over the rail, the chaos of the maindeck told its own story: the uncoiled and jumbled ropes, the smashed bottles, the wet slick of vomit by the scuttle-butt. 'How long have you been standing sentry, Mr King?'

'Since yesterday afternoon sir. Fourteen hours, sir.'

'I think you had better go below and get some rest, beneath as many warm blankets as you can muster.'

'Am I to be c-court-martialled, sir?'

'No, Mr King, you will not be court-martialled. I must take much of the responsibility for what has happened myself. Now, hurry along. And thank you, Mr King, for your devotion to duty.'

'Aye aye sir.'

'Mr Wickham, I want this deck shipshape and clean as a shirtfront within the hour. Mr Sorrell, Mr Usborne, Mr Chaffers, I want everyone who is below standing to attention on deck in five minutes. Any who are insolent or who are too drunk to stand will be thrown in irons in the hold. Mr Stokes, Mr Bennet, you will search every tavern and gin-palace in Plymouth, and you will find and bring back every single one of our people. And then there will be hell to pay.'

As the officers went about their allotted tasks, the last of the civilian members of the party climbed aboard. Jemmy Button gingerly prodded the very edge of the vomit slick with an immaculately buffed toecap.

'Too much skylark. Far too much skylark,' he observed.

Fuegia poked a finger into the yellow stew, held it up to her face, and wrinkled her nose in disgust. Augustus Earle grinned.

'All of you who are not members of the ship's company have my most sincere apologies,' announced FitzRoy, his quiet anger condensing into white clouds on the morning air. 'To say that these events are unacceptable would be the most prodigious understatement. I give you my word that nothing of this like shall happen again for the duration of the voyage.'

Darwin was not listening, but had wandered up the main-deck towards the prow. Indeed, he had paid little heed to anything that had occurred since their departure from the hotel, when a letter had arrived for him in that morning's post. He had opened it, discreetly, in the boat. It was from his sister, Catherine, announcing Fanny Owen's betrothal to Robert Biddulph. He unfolded it now and scanned the last page for the third time.

> ... I hope it won't be too great a grief to you, dearest
> Charley. You will find her a motherly old married woman
> when you come back. You may be perfectly sure that
> Fanny will always continue as friendly and affectionate
> to you as ever, and as rejoiced to see you again, though
> I fear that will be but poor comfort to you, my dear
> Charles.
> God bless you, Charles,
> Yours most affectionately,
> Catherine Darwin

He did not know whether to cry, or break into bitter laughter. His heart felt fit to break in two. He was torn between a desire to abandon the voyage there and then, take the next stage to Shrewsbury and confront the pair in righteous anger; and a mad urge to dash about the deck, slashing ropes and cutting cables, to free the *Beagle*, to see her dart forward on her way, to see the shores of England recede as quickly as possible. Perhaps he should leave the ship in New Zealand, and take a black savage for a lover, as Earle had done? That would show her – that would show Fanny Owen the disastrous error of her ways. But even as luridly vengeful images of a distraught Fanny flashed into his brain, he knew them for the fantasies they were, and banished them from his imagination. He screwed Catherine's letter into a tight white ball and tossed it over the side, where it sat upon the indigo surface of Barnet Pool, bobbing and mocking.

'Man the windlass!'

Carpenter May knocked the chocks out from beneath the bars, and the men began the back-breaking work of pulling up the main bower anchor.

'Heave, lads! Heave 'n' she must come!' commanded Boatswain Sorrell.

It was the morning of the twenty-seventh, which, fortunately for all, had dawned bright and gusty, not that the blue skies had taken the edge off FitzRoy's temper. He had elected to save all punishments until the *Beagle* was out to sea: fear of what was to follow would galvanize the men, he knew, whereas the aftermath of the mass floggings that must result from such an act of near-mutiny would leave many in no state to get the *Beagle* under way, least of all an exhausted Bos'n Sorrell.

Every man at the windlass was putting in every last drop of effort, desperate to impress, straining to drag the anchor up from its stubborn, slimy resting-place. Slowly, the ship inched towards that part of Barnet Pool where she was hooked, until she lay directly above it; then the chain clanked vertically upwards into the ship, where the anchor was catted and fished, until it was lashed fast to the fo'c'slehead.

'Up jib.'

The *Beagle*'s masts blossomed white and the stiff easterly breeze filled every sail.

'Muster all the officers on the poop deck.'

'Aye aye sir.'

Where the devil was Sulivan? FitzRoy wondered angrily. So hard had his second lieutenant worked, running himself into the ground over the preceding weeks, then combing almost every street in Plymouth the previous day, that he had been given leave to attend a ball with Miss Young on his last night ashore. Sulivan had not been seen since. After the drunken desertions of Boxing Day, it would be just too much if one of his officers had committed the same crime.

Down on the starboard side of the lower deck, in the cramped wooden cot that constituted most of his tiny cabin, a confused Bartholomew Sulivan was woken by the ship's sudden leap forward as the wind caught her sails. He shouted for the officers' steward, who put his head round the door.

'What is the time, if you please, Sutton?'

'Eight o'clock in the morning, sir.'

'What? I have missed the ball? I was only to have a short rest! Why did you not call me to gunroom tea yesterday evening as bidden?'

'I did, sir.'

'Then, when I did not appear at tea, why in heaven's name did you not call me again? I was to go ashore and dress thereafter!'

'You did appear at tea, sir.'

'What?'

Frantically, Sulivan clambered into his uniform. In the passageway outside, still fumbling with his buttons, he ran into Wickham, heading for the captain's muster on the poop deck.

'Wickham, old man. Am I going mad? Did I appear at gunroom tea last evening?'

Wickham laughed heartily. 'You could say that, dear fellow. In fact, "appeared" is quite the word for it. You appeared at half past seven, in your nightshirt and nightcap, with a large duck gun at your shoulder. You placed the gun in the corner, went to your place at table, drank the tea put before you, then rose, shouldered the gun again and marched off to bed. My dear chap, we thought you plainly overwrought, and we did not wish to awaken the somnambulist.'

'But – but – Miss Young!'

FitzRoy, gathering his officers about him on the poop deck, was relieved to see the face of Lieutenant Sulivan appear at the top of the companionway; but less impressed when he realized that his second lieutenant was not only unshaven but that the buttons of his uniform were misaligned; and even less so when the officer in question hared past him to the rail, and began screaming at two distant female figures on the Devonport dock, two tiny specks in distinctive turquoise skirts. Was one of them waving? It was near-impossible to tell.

'Miss Young!' yelled Sulivan, but his words were blown back past him, for'ard of the ship, in the direction in which the *Beagle* was headed. Even had their recipient been standing fifty yards astern, it was doubtful that she would have been able to make them out.

'Mr Sulivan.' FitzRoy's icy tones sliced through the sea breeze like a sabre thrust. 'I suggest that it would be most strongly in your interest to join us forthwith.'

Reluctantly, Sulivan relinquished his place at the rail and said a mental farewell to the tiny turquoise speck.

'Let me make matters clear in the outset of our departure,' emphasized FitzRoy. There was steel in his voice. 'The events of the last twenty-four hours are beyond the pale. We are all of us, officers and men, culpable. There will be no repetition of these events. Furthermore, I put all of you on notice that it is my intention not to lose one crewman, one boat, one mast or even one spar during this voyage. If any man falls overboard – if we even ship a single sea – I shall punish the officer of the watch. Is that clear?'

There were nods all round.

'No one is to go out of sight of the ship except in company with at least two others. Thereby if one man is hurt, one comrade may stay with him while the third goes for assistance. There are to be no exceptions to this rule. Is that clear?'

Once more the officers gave their assent.

'Now. All hands will be mustered aft.'

Within five minutes, Boatswain Sorrell had assembled the men to await the reading of the punishment log.

FitzRoy addressed them in a firm, clear voice. 'Able Seaman William Bruce: disrated to landsman for breaking his leave and drunkenness. Bos'n's mate Thos Henderson: disrated to able seaman for breaking his leave and drunkenness. Captain of the foretop John Wasterham: disrated to able seaman for breaking his leave and drunkenness. Carpenter's mate David Russell: a dozen lashes for breaking his leave, drunkenness and disobedience of orders. Elias Davis: a dozen lashes for breaking his leave, drunkenness and insolence . . .'

And so the list went on, seemingly interminably. A forlorn Darwin made his way to the prow, sickened by the roll of the ship and the catalogue of impending violence. As the *Beagle* nudged past the breakwater and stood out of the harbour, she pitched into short, steep seas, where her roll was quick, deep, and awkward; at least the spray freshened his face and countered his giddiness. After an interval a similarly forlorn Sulivan joined him at the rail, fresh from a severe dressing-down.

'Good day, Philosopher,' said Sulivan, in an attempt to be of good cheer. 'How does it feel to be heading south in one of His Majesty's bathing machines?'

'Does he have to flog so many men?'

'Philosopher, the skipper hates corporal punishment. He abhors it. But the lives of every one of us aboard ship depend upon immediate decisions and instant obedience. If he is decisive now, then with good fortune he will obtain that obedience, and will have no occasion to flog anyone else for the rest of the voyage.'

'But why floggings? Why not this "disrating"?'

'Oh, many a man would prefer the flogging. A disrating involves less pay. But they will get their rates back, and the scars of the floggings will heal. They knew what they were doing, Philos. Drunkenness is the sole and never-failing pleasure to which a sailor always looks forward. They expect to see floggings, and if the skipper does not deliver, why, they will lose all respect for him. They have sown the wind, and they shall reap the whirlwind.'

Darwin was silent.

'There isn't such a fine captain in all the world, Philos. He would not take this course were it not absolutely necessary.'

The *Beagle* swung out into the Channel, and as her crew prepared to bring her nose round to starboard, the men began to sing:

'Scrub the mud off the dead man's face
An' haul or ye'll be damned;
For there blow some cold nor'westers, on
The Banks of Newfoundland.'

Darwin shuddered. *What is this antiquated world of peremptory justice and sadistic medieval vengeance that I have joined of my own will?* he asked himself. *A world where men take floggings with equanimity and are as like as not to end their lives drowned in soft brown mud? I must have taken leave of my senses.*

Sulivan guessed what sentiments lay behind the expression on Darwin's face, and smiled. 'It's only a piece of metal, Philos.'

'What is?'

'The dead man's face. It's a triangular piece of metal with three holes in it, used when the ship is moored for long periods, to connect the two anchor chains and prevent them twisting round each other. Ofttimes, it gets muddy. That's why it needs scrubbing.'

Darwin felt small, and stupid, and pale and giddy and sick. He went to his cabin, and climbed with recently acquired expertise into his hammock. As he lay there, he felt waves of nausea undulate through him, so he shut his eyes and listened as the screams of the first of the flogged men echoed through the ship.

Part Three

Chapter Thirteen

Rio de Janeiro, 3 April 1832

———

They had come for Darwin at dawn. A hand clamped roughly over his mouth had wakened him from sleep, others had pinioned his arms, and a blindfold had been wound round his eyes. He had been led, stumbling and shaking with nerves, up the companionway and out on to the maindeck; there, he was roped roughly to a chair, which was lifted on to a plank and swung out over empty air. Wind blew against his cheek. He could feel the sway of the plank and hear the ripple of water below.

'Is that you, Darwin?' It was FitzRoy's voice.

'Yes.'

'Are you all right?'

'I – I think so. Will they kill us?'

'Will they kill us? What in heaven do you mean?'

A drumbeat commenced off to Darwin's right. His blindfold was whipped off, and a hideous apparition leaped into view: a crewman, semi-naked, daubed entirely in green, brandishing a rough-hewn spear. Other demoniacal beings swarmed about him, stripped to the waist, rings of red and yellow paint radiating out from their bulging eyeballs as they danced high and low.

'Welcome to the Kingdom of the Deep,' intoned the green crewman. 'I am King Neptune!'

'It is a sort of ritual they like to perform whenever we cross the equator,' explained FitzRoy, wearily. 'It is called "Crossing the Line". It affords them the greatest satisfaction.'

Darwin looked down, and saw that the rippling water below was contained in a huge sail held taut by several sailors.

'Shave them!' shouted King Neptune.

An evil-smelling mixture of paint and pitch was brushed about their faces, then scraped off again with a rusty iron hoop.

'Rinse them!'

Two grinning urchins appeared, extravagantly warpainted, who were revealed on closer inspection to be Musters and Hellyer. Gleefully, they emptied buckets of cold salt water over FitzRoy's and Darwin's heads.

'You see?' said Musters to Hellyer. 'I told you they would let us do it. What larks!'

'I assure you, Darwin, it would be a deal worse were you not my travelling companion,' insisted FitzRoy, in his most placatory tone.

'I do believe, FitzRoy, that this "ceremony" is in some way parodic of the sacrament of baptism. I am not sure that I entirely approve.'

'The effects of these mummeries are entirely positive on those who prepare them. They speak of them for a long time afterwards.'

Any further conversation was rendered out of the question as the two planks were dipped forward, and FitzRoy and Darwin tumbled head over heels, still tied to their chairs, into cold salty water.

'What fools these sailors make of themselves,' grumbled Darwin, as they towelled themselves off in FitzRoy's cabin shortly afterwards.

'It is an absurd piece of folly,' said FitzRoy.

'Most disagreeable,' said Darwin.

*   *   *

The rituals of the equator aside, it had been a largely uneventful crossing, punctuated only by the disappointment of not being allowed to put in at Tenerife, where news of London's cholera outbreak had preceded them. They had picked up the north-east trades at the Cape Verde Islands and had made rapid passage thereafter. Darwin had filled his time trawling for jellyfish and microscopic sea-creatures, using a home-made net constructed from bunting and an iron hoop. Lieutenant Wickham had cursed the 'Flycatcher Philosopher' for the specimens that oozed and glistened across his pristine deck, but always with his tongue in his cheek.

'If I were skipper, all your damned mess would be chucked overboard, and you after it!' he had bellowed.

FitzRoy's day was always the same: breakfast at eight, a morning inspection of the ship, a midday check on the chronometers, a one o'clock dinner of rice, peas and bread with Darwin, then the afternoon spent with Hellyer seeing to the ship's logbook and papers. He still found time, however, to teach Darwin how to dry, preserve and log his sea creatures; how to make drawings, notes and measurements; how to attach matching labels to the specimens and their containers, and how to catalogue when and where they had been caught. Darwin, for his part, was mildly surprised that FitzRoy did not spend his days striding about the deck in full dress uniform, like Nelson in the heat of battle.

When the day was over, after their antiscorbutic supper of meat, pickles, dried apple and lemon juice, Darwin would join Wickham or Sulivan for a little conversation at the wheel; unless it was a Sunday, of course, when Sulivan would be excused duty on religious grounds. On windless evenings in the tropics, Darwin sat out on a boom with Midshipman King, watching the waves furl past the prow. These were the evenings he liked best: when the air was still and deliciously warm, the heavens shone clear and high, and the white sails filled with soft air and flapped gently against the masts.

When the wind got up, however, and the *Beagle* bowled

along, the old seasickness returned, and he took to his cabin at the 'lively' end of the ship. If Stokes was working at the chart table, he could not put up his hammock, so the assistant surveyor would allow him to lie curled on the tabletop instead, and would work around the philosopher's recumbent body. 'Old fellow, I must take the horizontal for it,' Darwin would gasp, before prostrating himself across unrolled charts of the Brazilian coast.

Jemmy Button would come by to sympathize. 'Poor, poor fellow,' he would exclaim, but then he would turn away, trying not to smile, for he could not understand how the mere motion of the sea could make anybody ill.

Sometimes, when FitzRoy was immersed in his paperwork, and Usborne or Sulivan was officer of the watch, they would discreetly reduce sail to lessen the philosopher's woes. There never was such a fine body of men, thought Darwin through his queasiness. He even forgave Sulivan for rousing him from sleep one morning, with the excited shout that a grampus bear had been seen swimming off the port bow. Haring up to the maindeck in his nightshirt, he had been greeted by the massed laughter of the morning watch. It was, of course, the first of April.

Two days later they had made Rio harbour, entering proudly under full sail, scattering flocks of yellow-billed boobies left and right. There they had careened to an extravagant stop alongside the *Ganges*, and FitzRoy had ordered every inch of canvas taken in and immediately reset. Every ship in harbour was watching, he knew, but he asked God to forgive him such little acts of vanity. The display was immaculate: no man-of-war of any nation would dare to take on this little sounding ship in a sail-setting competition again. Every skipper in Rio knew of the *Samarang*'s humiliation. Even Darwin volunteered to help with the sail display, so Wickham gave him a main royal sheet to hold in each hand and a topmast studding sail tack to bite between his teeth, and told him to let go the instant he heard the order to 'shorten sail'. Standing there in his top-coat and tails, his double-breasted waistcoat, his stock and his cravat, a rope in each hand and one clamped in his mouth, he made a remarkable sight. It was perhaps a little mischievous of Wickham to have positioned him like that some five minutes earlier than was necessary, but the philosopher was too excited to be part of South America's number one crew to notice his shipmates' amusement.

At midday FitzRoy and Stebbing rated the chronometers, double-checking the position of Rio de Janeiro on the charts, and were able to confirm what they had begun to suspect during the *Beagle*'s approach to the city: something was seriously wrong with the existing map.

'It is unmistakable.' FitzRoy outlined the problem to Darwin over dinner. 'There is a four-mile discrepancy between the positions of Rio and Bahia. Which means that one of them has always been located in quite the wrong place.'

'Who made the charts?'

'They are French, drawn up by Baron Roussin. The Admiralty has never seen the necessity of duplicating his work.'

'McCormick will be pleased.'

'The inconvenience is terrible.'

'Why? How long will it take Stokes to draw a new chart?'

'As long as it takes us to sail back to Bahia.'

'Back to Bahia? But that is eight hundred miles up the coast! Can you spare the time?'

'No. But I have no choice. I cannot complete a chain of meridian distances around the world if there is a flaw at the very commencement of the calculation.'

'How long will it set us back?'

'Two months. But I suggest that you would be best served by passing the time on shore, my dear fellow. You might profitably explore the tropical forest and collect specimens. I shall give Earle shore leave also, to make drawings, and Mr King.'

'Mr King?'

'To be quite frank with you, Mr Stokes will need the chart cabin all to himself. I do not wish the Admiralty's new map of the Brazils to have to incorporate our ship's philosopher's left knee.'

'Just think yourself lucky, my dear FitzRoy, that you do not have to journey back over the equator twice more.'

'Here's to that.'

They clinked their water-glasses.

Darwin removed his Panama hat – he had exchanged his top hat for a Panama as his one concession to informality – and mopped his brow. The thermometer read ninety-six degrees. He looked enviously across at Patrick Lennon, who appeared altogether cooler in an unbuttoned shirt and cotton breeches; but as the natural philosopher of the *Beagle*, Darwin did have certain standards to uphold. Lennon was a young, charming and energetic Irish coffee planter whom he had encountered at a formal dinner aboard HMS *Warspite*, who had offered to escort Darwin upcountry to see his *fazenda*. Their party was seven-strong in all: four Portuguese and a thirteen-year-old mulatto guide made up the numbers. They had started early, mounted on glossy black horses, and had ridden into the hills behind Praia Grande, through rounded plantations of coffee-bushes and rustling sugar cane. As the sun rose, the blue dawn light had faded away to be replaced by all the intense colours of the forest: slender green palms swaying like ship's masts, brilliant turquoise butterflies making random sallies, immense copper-coloured anthills inching methodically skyward, and all of it bedded in a warm, rich, red earth that accumulated stickily upon the fetlocks of the horses. Darwin was enraptured: no engraving, he thought, could ever capture the ruddy glow of this scene. The forest was at its most beautiful at midday, he felt, when the upper branches shone bright emerald, and shafts of sunlight filtered down as if through a transept window. Writhing beneath was a wild, untidy, luxuriant hothouse, criss-crossed by a hundred shady pathways.

They breakfasted on black *feijão* beans and *farinha* flour at Ithacaia, a poor African village twelve miles north of Rio. It was the Brazilian custom to breakfast many hours into a journey, and to rely on thick black coffee to wake the sleeper. Thereafter they pushed on, through veils of mimosa and mazy skeins of hanging tendrils, in the direction of Ingetado. The silence of the forest was astonishing: while the *Beagle*'s passage along the Brazilian coast had been greeted by a shore battery of insect-calls audible a hundred yards out above the surf, here in the vaulted forest no sound could be heard. The only exception was the determined chatter of an ebony battalion of shiny-headed leaf-cutter ants, which stretched as far as the eye could see in either direction. Darwin stopped to place a rock in their path. The ants would not head round it, but instead launched sally after furious sally against their immutable attacker. Was this the species discovered by Linnaeus in 1758? he wondered. Lennon and his companions could provide no help. Every time Darwin asked the given name of a flower, the same answer invariably came back: '*Flores.*' Whenever he enquired the identity of an animal, he was told: '*Bixos.*' Taxonomy, it appeared, was not a local speciality.

They slept in a thicket under the dim moonlight, and beneath the stars the forest came alive. A concert of rhythmic frogs began, lit by winking fireflies, the plaintive cries of snipes providing a contralto melody. Breakfast of *feijão* beans and *farinha* flour was taken at Madre de Dios village amid sheets of rain, birds fluttering madly between the passion flowers. After the deluge had abated, steaming columns of dense white vapour poured upwards from the surrounding woods as the moisture returned to the sky.

At the Rio Macaé, where they had to swim alongside the horses to ford the torrent, they came across a gigantic rock rising from a plain of rhododendrons.

'That is where a gang of runaway slaves hid out, not a year or two back,' related Lennon. 'They were all recaptured, except one old woman, who, sooner than be taken again, dashed herself to pieces from the summit.'

Darwin shuddered. The forest was a cruel environment,

there was no doubt of that. Everywhere one looked, strangulating creepers twisted about each other like tresses of braided hair, each fighting to squeeze the breath from its adversary. Luxuriant parasitical orchids drank the fluid of their victims with dainty care. Lianas crawled over the rotting corpses of fallen trees, the trunks split and gaping open in the fixed attitudes of death. He felt torn between a sublime devotion to the God who could create such marvellous beauty, and awe at the cruelty of Him who would devise such a world, founded as it was upon a pitiless struggle for survival.

They slept the second night at Ingetado, following a hearty meal of *feijão* beans and *farinha* flour. In the morning they rode past a lagoon, many miles from the sea, its shores a mass of broken shells. Was this the proof of the Biblical flood that FitzRoy was so keen to establish? Darwin collected specimens, delving under logs and stones, chasing pale fat worms through clammy leaf litter, and peering into the rainwater traps of bromeliads in search of gaudy spiders. In a pile of decaying wood he found a wriggling heap of gorgeous orange-and-black flatworms, like striped and dandified slugs. But these were sea creatures! What were aquatic *planariae* doing here, so far from the sea? He had discovered a species new to science, he realized, but what was the connection between these land flatworms, their marine cousins and the flood? His brain whirled with possibilities.

They spent the third night in the *venda* at Campos Novos, where the innkeeper had learned a smattering of English and was keen to practise his skills.

'What have you for supper?' Darwin enquired hungrily.

'Anything you choose, sir,' the man replied grandly, his fingers spread upon his belly.

'Thank goodness for that! So, is there any fish you can do us the favour of giving?'

'Oh! No, sir.'

'Any soup?'

'Oh! No, sir.'

'Any bread?'

'Oh! No, sir.'

'Any dried meat? *Carne secca?*'

'Oh! No, sir.'

Lennon laughed like a drain. 'Welcome to the Brazils, Mr Darwin.'

After an interval, it was established by one of the Portuguese members of the party that the innkeeper could offer either *feijão* beans or *farinha* flour, or both.

On the fourth day the forest thickened and the showers closed in, and the little mulatto guide had to hack at the fronds with a sword to clear the path up into the high hills. Finally, towards the end of the morning, they reached Lennon's *fazenda*. A large bell clanged out and a cannon was fired to announce the arrival of the *senhor*, and a crowd of black slaves rushed forth to be blessed by the white men. A neat slave-line formed up in starched white smocks, to sing a Catholic morning hymn of the most sublime harmonic sweetness. Lennon lived like a little god here, Darwin realized, his wealth untold, his power absolute. The Irishman smiled and invited him on up to the house.

The *fazenda* proved to be a white-painted two-storey mansion with rustic blue shutters, a thick reed roof and a wrought-iron balcony, which sat on a gentle rise under a permanent blanket of low, sticky clouds. Even here, nature's myrmidons kept up their ceaseless assault: tree roots slithered across the courtyard, blotchy green mould insinuated itself beneath mirror-glass, while the opposing forces of mildew and whitewash grappled for possession of the walls. Dogs, baby chickens and little black children ran left and right through the ground floor of the house. Piles of banknotes lay aimlessly about the heavy gilded furniture, comprehensively chewed through by grubs.

'Nothing I can do with it,' remarked Lennon, indicating the money. 'Nothing I can do to stop it,' he added, with reference to its gradual consumption. 'I have everything I want

here, without recourse to money. Take some, if you like.'
Darwin declined as politely as he could.

A servant showed him to his room on the first floor. There
were rifles mounted on the walls, a cast-iron cot in the corner,
and no glass in the windows. In the dark, gloomy wardrobe
were two jars of yellow fluid, the pickled grey snakes inside
coiled lifelessly against the glass. He changed, laid out his
sweat-stained clothes to be washed, and descended the stairs
once more. Lennon had been joined by a short, spherical,
olive-skinned Portuguese, and his younger, heavily made-up
female equivalent, who had squeezed herself into a liberally
frilled dress.

'Mr Darwin, I have the honour to present Dom Manuel
Joaquem da Figuireda, my partner in business, and his daughter
Donna Maria. Donna Maria is married to Mr Lumb, a
Scotchman.'

Lumb, who had the lugubrious air of a half-asleep walrus,
moved from the shadows to shake Darwin's fingers, but said
nothing. Darwin sensed that Lumb had seen in Donna Maria
a match to improve his financial situation.

'Do you ride to hounds, Mr Darwin?' asked Dom Manuel,
unable to conceal a grin.

'Of course, Senhor. What well-born Englishman does not?'

'Excellent. Then tomorrow we shall have a hunt.'

'You have hounds, here?'

'We have five hounds,' said Donna Maria, in the clipped
accent of one who has carefully studied a foreign language.
'Trumpeta, Mimosa, Clariena, Dorena and Champaigna.'

'But what do you hunt? Surely there are no foxes!'

'Monkeys, Mr Darwin. We hunt bearded monkeys!' Dom
Manuel cackled and clapped Darwin on the back.

'You see, Mr Darwin, even here in the Mata Atlantica there
is no aspect of civilized society that we cannot replicate,' smiled
Lennon. 'Would you care for coffee?'

Coffee was kept bubbling continuously in a big black skillet
on the iron kitchen range. Presently, a small greasy-fingered

black boy appeared with a full jug and several cups, and handed one to Darwin.

'Pray excuse me,' said Darwin, with a trace of embarrassment. 'Would you mind if I exchanged my cup? There is a fingermark.'

Immediately, Lennon picked up a riding-crop and lashed it across the little boy's head, not once but three times. The child screamed in pain and terror. A red rivulet streamed from his nose, and across his upper lip, before dividing into smaller streams between his teeth; he fled sobbing from the house, a further coffee-cup tumbling with a smash as he ran. Darwin sat frozen with horror. Dom Manuel and his daughter continued to smile as if nothing had happened. Lennon, as charming now as he had been before the attack, offered his apologies: 'I'm sorry for the slave boy. Those people know no better. There are too many damned kids about the place. I think I shall sell some of them at the public auction in Rio.'

'The children will be sent to market ... separately from their mothers and fathers?' Darwin was still stunned, so his words came out slowly.

'Oh, they are well used to it, Mr Darwin. Savages do not enjoy the same emotional closeness as we civilized people.'

They rode out the next morning, past the long, low sheds housing the hundreds of plantation slaves and the little stone chapel adjoining. Black huntsmen in maroon jackets rode ahead, to encircle the forest wildlife and drive it back towards the guns. Then an old Portuguese priest in a wide-brimmed hat blew upon a hunting-horn, and the main party moved forward. Before long they ran into the squawking, whooping mass of monkeys, parrots, toucans and other creatures that had been corralled towards them, all of which were unceremoniously blasted out of the sky. The monkey's prehensile tails tightened as they died, so their corpses hung farcically from the branches while the huntsmen rode around in circles beneath, trying to bring them down. Darwin did not enjoy his sport. The episode with the slave boy had affected him badly, and he was keen to return to the coast.

The next day, he seized the opportunity of accompanying the mulatto guide back to Rio de Janeiro; they took a different route, heading for the only ferry crossing on the Rio Macaé, riding in silence on account of the language barrier, which Darwin felt was the least of the divides separating them. He collected an insect that was disguised as a stick, a moth that was disguised as a scorpion, and a beetle that was disguised as a poisonous fruit, but his heart was no longer in his work.

When they arrived at the riverbank, a powerful black ferryman stood to attention alongside a rudimentary raft, a punt-pole held aloft by his side in the style of a medieval pikeman.

'*Onde você gostaria de ir, Senhor?*' asked the ferryman.

'I should like to cross the river,' explained Darwin.

Both guide and ferryman looked at him, their faces full of incomprehension.

'*Eu não entendo. Onde você gostaria de ir, Senhor?*' the ferryman repeated.

'I should like to cross the river,' explained Darwin for the second time, waving his arms in the direction he wished to take. But as he gesticulated, the big ferryman cowered, his pupils widening in fright; the man dropped his hands, shut his eyes, and dipped his head in supplication. He fell to his knees and began to beg for mercy in Portuguese, pleading with the white man not to strike him. Darwin immediately understood what had happened; and he felt only shame and disgust.

FitzRoy dined alone, his plate of rice and peas strangely devoid of flavour in the absence of his friend. A knock briefly and foolishly raised his spirits, but they fell once again when the door opened to reveal McCormick. Despite his ever-rigid bearing, the surgeon's moustache showed him to be in a state of some agitation. In his left hand, he carried a large wire birdcage, which housed a bright green parrot.

'Excuse me, sir, but I must speak with you.'

'I am at dinner, Mr McCormick. This is most incommoding – can it not wait until we are under way?'

'I am afraid not, sir. It is uncommon urgent.'

'So urgent that you have to bring your parrot with you.'

'I have purchased the parrot this very morning, sir – at a most Jewish price, as it happens – for reasons of scientific investigation. It belonged formerly to an English merchant seaman, from whom it has gleaned a rudimentary grasp of our language. I intend to make a study of animal intelligence, sir, and to investigate the extent to which such creatures appreciate the import of their words, and the extent to which they merely mimic what has been expressed in their presence.'

'I am glad to see that you are taking your responsibilities seriously, Mr McCormick. Pray tell me what English words your parrot has yet grasped.'

'As yet it has but two English expressions, sir. One of them is "Great heavens" –'

'Great heavens!' interjected the parrot.

'– and the other expression, common decency forbids me from repeating, sir.'

'Go to the devil!' shouted the parrot.

'That is the other expression, sir.'

McCormick's face remained blank, but the ends of his moustache twitched violently.

'But I must inform you, sir, that it is not regarding the matter of this parrot that I have come to see you.'

'Indeed.' FitzRoy transferred a forkful of peas elegantly in the direction of his mouth.

'No sir. I have come to see you regarding Mr Darwin, sir.'

'Indeed?' The peas paused in mid-air. 'What about Mr Darwin?'

'I have heard tell, sir, that Mr Darwin's specimens have been sent to England carriage free, aboard His Majesty's packet *Emulous*. Is this true, sir?'

'It is.'

'Great heavens!' observed the parrot.

'Then I must protest, sir.'

'About what, Mr McCormick?'

'Mr Darwin is not responsible for bringing together a natural history collection for the Crown, so it is not proper for the Service to see to the freight of his private specimens. Nor is it proper, sir, for his specimens to litter the deck, or for the ship's carpenters to make packing cases for their transportation.'

'What is proper, Mr McCormick, and what is not proper, are matters for me to decide.'

'I find myself in a false position, sir. Mr Darwin sits at your table, discussing books and whatnot, whereas naval practice dictates that any philosophical debate on board should fall strictly under my jurisdiction as ship's surgeon. Furthermore, sir, I hear that Mr Darwin intends to retain the right to ownership of his specimens upon their reaching England.'

'That is so,' confirmed FitzRoy.

'Great heavens!' added the parrot.

'Have you considered, sir, that Mr Darwin might intend to sell such items of natural history for his own personal profit?'

'Your suggestion is absurd, Mr McCormick.' FitzRoy's voice hardened. 'I suggest that you withdraw your allegation forthwith.'

'It is vulgar, sir, to receive money for one's researches.'

'I will say it once more, Mr McCormick. I suggest that you withdraw your allegation forthwith.'

'Great heavens!'

'I demand, sir, that Mr Darwin be dismissed from the *Beagle* immediately.'

'What?'

'I demand, sir, that Mr Darwin be dismissed from the *Beagle* immediately.'

'Go to the devil!'

'Otherwise, sir, I shall tender my own resignation as ship's surgeon immediately.'

'I accept your resignation, Mr McCormick.'

'What?'

'Great heavens!'

'I said, I accept your resignation as ship's surgeon, Mr McCormick.'

'Great heavens!'

'I think I have your gauge, sir,' said McCormick grimly, through hardened lips, 'and I shall make it known throughout Whitehall when I return. Rest assured of that!'

'You do not frighten me, Mr McCormick. Pack your bags and leave the ship immediately. You shall have ten minutes' warning.'

His face a mask of suppressed fury, McCormick picked up the birdcage and headed for the door.

'Go to the devil! Go to the devil!' shouted the parrot merrily at FitzRoy, as its cage disappeared from view.

With a gentle downward pressure, Darwin sliced the head off the firefly. Its lifeless body continued to glow brightly against the gloom of the verandah steps.

'Yeurch,' said King.

'Look! Look at this!' said Darwin, eager with the excitement of discovery. Augustus Earle put down his fiddle – which in truth was a blessing, as his technique was rudimentary at best – and did as bidden.

'The glow is continuous in death,' explained Darwin, 'which means it is involuntary. So when the firefly winks his light, he is turning it off, not turning it on.'

'I see,' said Earle, returning to his fiddle.

The three had taken a cottage four miles south of the city, between Corcovado and the *lagoa*, on the road out to the botanical gardens. It was, to Darwin's mind, a veritable Elysium, free from seasickness and slavery. There were graceful coconut palms in front, with heavy clusters of fruit and long, plume-like drooping flowers. Passion vines climbed all over the house, dark crimson flowers concealed seductively between the leaves. He had spent a month making an exhaustive study of the insect life of the neighbourhood, with a pruriently thrilled Midshipman King as his sole audience. Together they had documented the gruesome habits of the hymenop wasp, which paralysed its victim before injecting eggs into the living tissue, there to hatch and feed and grow into fat, wriggling larvae. He found it hard to reconcile such suffering with the love of a merciful God, but then had not Job suffered horribly at the hands of the Lord? He did not, of course, share his theological confusions with his collecting partner.

King, in return, told him tales of the south, of icebergs and crimson seas and giant whales that leaped clean out of the water, tales that sounded too tall to be true. 'Come, King,' he would gibe informally, 'do not come your traveller's yarns on me,' and the boy would aver, hotly, that every word was true. He had discovered that he preferred King's company to that of Earle, whom he found rather intimidating. The artist was old now – he was nearly forty – and troubled by the rheumatism that comes with age, so he would sit barefoot on the verandah, painting or screeching away at his fiddle, while Darwin and King gleefully roamed the neighbourhood with their insect-nets. It felt as if they were on holiday from school.

Their supper guests arrived just before eight, brought by a covered cart with big solid chariot wheels, two spherical slabs of wood like Saxon war-shields. A pair of statuesque mulatto women alighted, attired in layer upon layer of brightly coloured shawls, their hair piled high and twisting into extravagant headdresses. Their lips and cheeks were rouged, their eyes rendered dark and mysterious by lashings of makeup. Darwin had no idea where Earle had procured them, but they resembled – he realized uncomfortably – two ladies of the Haymarket.

'Mr Darwin, Mr King, may I introduce to your acquaintance Rita and Rosa?'

This is all wrong, thought Darwin. He has introduced us the wrong way round. The man has no sense of propriety.

The introductions over, they went through to the supper-table. The ladies had no English, but seemed content to giggle among themselves. The only communication between the two halves of the supper-party was via Earle's pidgin Portuguese, a dialect in which the artist proved himself singularly adept at flirting.

The servant brought out bottles of red wine, and plates piled high with *feijão* beans, *carne secca*, bread and a strange, sausage-shaped, creamy-coloured fruit.

'Pray what is this?' asked Darwin.

'Banana,' replied Earle.

'Oh! I have never eaten a banana before.'

'*Ele nunca havia visto bananas antes,*' remarked Earle to the two women, who giggled voluptuously.

'May I know the source of the amusement?' enquired Darwin, reddening.

'I simply informed them of your virginity *vis-à-vis* the banana.'

The two women continued to giggle, one concealing her merriment behind a Chinese fan, and Darwin thought that perhaps there was something attractive about them after all. With a glass of wine under his belt, he was prepared to admit to himself that they did not share the normally disagreeable expression of the mulatto. They were not *ladies*, in the sense that Fanny Owen was a *lady*, but they definitely possessed a certain charm. He glanced across the table at King as if in search of endorsement, but the normally talkative lad had become utterly tongue-tied since their guests' arrival. In fact, he had spent most of the evening trying to steal furtive glances at the women's cleavage, between long periods spent staring fixedly at his plate.

'*Você gosta de bananas?*'

'Rita wishes to know how you like your banana.'

'I find it rather mawkish and sweet, without too much flavour, I am afraid,' replied Darwin stiffly; for some unaccountable reason he had begun to feel embarrassed.

'That is beyond my meagre Portuguese, I fear,' smiled Earle. 'I shall tell her yes.'

'*Você gosta do Brasil?*'

'How do you like the Brazils? Rosa wishes to know.'

'Tell her that hers is a most gloriously attractive nation, but that I most heartily wish it were not disfigured by the curse of slavery.'

Earle attempted a translation, and it was clear from the women's response that they were in agreement. They crossed themselves and spoke in low tones of something called a *matican*.

'The *matican*,' explained Earle, 'is a slave-hunter. He is paid to hunt down slaves who escape and to kill them, be they man, woman or child. And when he has run down his quarry, he slices off the ear as proof of death.'

'I used to do that with rats for my father, when I was a boy,' offered King, pleased at last to be able to contribute something to the conversation.

'Perhaps I will not translate that into Portuguese, Mr King.'

'Will you excuse me for a moment?' said Darwin suddenly, rising from his seat as he spoke, his gaze fixed unwaveringly on the window opposite.

'Is everything all right, Mr Darwin?' asked Earle.

Darwin did not answer, but shot through the doorway and out on to the verandah, reappearing a moment later on the outside of the window, his nose pressed to the glass. There, in front of his face, a tiny copper-coloured frog clung to the smooth surface, its eyes wide and unmoving, its throat palpitating silently to its own inner rhythm. Darwin reappeared in the doorway. 'That frog. It has suckers on its feet, so that it may climb a vertical sheet of glass!'

'Gosh!' said King, excited.

'Many of them do,' said Earle, who had to explain to the confused women that the gentleman was a *filosofia da natureza*.

Darwin resumed his seat, and the supper-party continued as before, Earle complimenting his guests extravagantly in Portuguese, Darwin offering the occasional politeness, and

King unsure where to look. Eventually it grew late, but there was no sign of the two women preparing to leave or of their cart returning. As another burst of merriment erupted from their end of the table, Darwin was seized by an uncomfortable thought.

'I say, Earle,' he whispered awkwardly.

'Yes, Darwin?' Earle leaned back, his collar undone, his face flushed with drink.

'I hope it is not your intention that I . . . *entertain* one of these ladies after supper has finished.'

'Certainly not.'

'Of course not, of course not,' said Darwin hurriedly, his voice suffused with relief. 'I just thought for one moment that . . .' He tailed off.

Earle fixed him with a pointed look. 'Both these two are for me. You want company, Darwin, you go fetch your own.'

The *Beagle* sailed into Rio harbour – now correctly located on the Admiralty chart – in mid-May, ahead of time but low on fresh food and water. They had tried fishing for groupers, but fearless sharks would invariably seize the fish from the lines before they could be reeled in, so seamen Morgan, Jones and Henderson were detailed to take the dinghy (as FitzRoy had decided to rename the jolly-boat) on a snipe-shooting expedition around the islets of the bay. The voyage had left FitzRoy disturbed: they had passed two frigates anchored off Cabo Frio, which had been identified by challenge-and-response as the *Lightning* and the *Algerine*, engaged in salvaging bullion from the wreck of the *Thetis*. How many of his old shipmates had been taken by the sharks, he wondered. Or was such an end preferable to death by drowning, and that terrifying, lung-bursting moment when the victim knows he can hold his breath no longer and must accept his agonizing fate?

A knock at the door interrupted his morbid reverie. It was Seaman Morgan, who had built the coracle, and Volunteer Musters.

'Permission to speak, sir!' Musters stood ramrod straight.

'Yes, what is it, Mr Musters?'

'Able Seaman Henderson has cut his leg, sir, and will be unable to take part in the snipe-shooting detail. As the best snipe-shooter in the ship, sir, I would like to take his place. Furthermore, sir, as the expedition has no officer in charge, I feel it is only right that I should command the expedition, sir.' Musters had managed to cram his entire request into a single breath, and now exhaled with relief.

'Is this true, Morgan?'

'Henderson has cut his leg, sir, and the lad, I mean Mr Musters, well, he's a fine shot for his age, sir.'

FitzRoy smiled. 'Very well, Mr Musters, you may command the snipe-shooting expedition. As long as you remember that you are to do exactly what Seaman Morgan tells you at all times.'

'Yes sir!'

A beaming Musters retreated, Morgan clutching his cap behind.

The cutter collected Darwin, King and Earle late the next morning, together with a score of boxes, crates and specimen jars.

'My dear Philos! I see that you have been busy!' was FitzRoy's warm greeting to his friend.

'Indeed I have, my dear FitzRoy. Professor Grant always stressed the importance of the analytic method, by which one derives one's conclusions from as many observations as possible. I fear it will not please Mr Wickham, nor our Mr McCormick, who prefers to start with a hypothesis and illustrate it with observations; but then, he is a philosopher of rather an ancient type.'

'Mr McCormick is gone. Bynoe has taken his place.'

'Gone? Gone where?'

'He is "invalided home" once more, on HMS *Tyne*.'

'Well, my dear fellow, he is no loss. I must confess that he put me in mind of Mrs Campbell's performance as Lady Macbeth.'

Both men laughed.

'Mr McCormick was an empty-headed coxcomb, but I fear the consequences of his departure. I can ill afford the Admiralty's displeasure on this matter.'

'My dear FitzRoy, we shall not return to England these next two years, by which time I am sure that all will be forgotten. Now, let us to dinner, for I could eat a horse – or a plate of rice and peas, at any rate.'

'Rice and peas be hanged. Today, in honour of the philosopher's return, we shall have fresh snipe!'

The pair squeezed themselves into FitzRoy's cabin and ate royally, while Darwin told of his discoveries, of Earle's disgraceful licentiousness and of the idyllic cottage by the *lagoa*, upon which he had laid out no less than twenty-two shillings a week.

'I fear I shall have to write to my father for a further fifty pounds. In the meantime, you couldn't make it convenient . . . ?'

'Of course. Seek out the purser Mr Rowlett after dinner, and tell him that I have authorized a loan. I fear that by the end of our voyage your poor father will have become a slave to his son's *divertissements*.'

'My dear FitzRoy, slavery is a term I would prefer not to hear used in jest. If you had only seen what I have seen!' And he proceeded to relate the story of his journey to the *fazenda*, the cruelties he had witnessed there, and his conclusions as to the social repercussions of the trade in human beings. 'I fear that slavery has already entailed some of its lamentable consequences upon the Brazilian nation, in demoralizing them by extreme indolence, and its accompaniment, gross sensuality.' As he fulminated, his thoughts strayed momentarily to Earle's two supper companions, hurrying quickly past the ambivalent feelings he himself had entertained that night. 'Slavery is an affront to every civilized nation!' he concluded hotly.

'Indeed it is. We must thank the Lord that ours *is* the only civilized nation. The only nation of any consequence to have abolished slavery, to have made it a capital offence, and to have taken action against the slavers.'

'Abolished slavery? But it is still legal in British dominions overseas!'

'It is only a matter of time before such vested interests are overcome. Already the free people of colour in South Africa have legal equality with the whites.'

'You say that we have taken action against the slavers – but here we are, sitting in a naval gunboat, in a harbour belonging to one of the world's biggest slaving nations. I am unconscious of you taking any "action".'

'I? My dear Darwin, I am the commander of a surveying-brig! Are you suggesting that I unilaterally declare war against a nation that our government considers to be its principal ally in South America?'

'Of course not. But I fail to see the logic of a policy that would see the captain of a Brazilian slaveship hanged were we to intercept him in international waters – yet should we meet him here in Rio, we should doubtless take high tea with him! Surely at the very least we should be blockading the coast against this inhuman cargo?'

'Darwin, do you have any idea for how many miles the coast of the Brazils extends? You would have a ninety-foot brig blockade a nation the size of Europe? My orders are to survey the bays and inlets of Patagonia and Tierra del Fuego. And my remit as commander of this vessel is to follow those orders, not to take issue with the policies of His Majesty's government.'

'You would follow any order you were given, however immoral, however illogical?'

'Now you are being absurd. My orders are not immoral or illogical. But in answer to your question, yes, I would follow any order given to me. Not to do so would constitute an act of mutiny.'

'But FitzRoy, picture to yourself the threat ever hanging over *you*, of *your* wife and *your* little children – those objects that nature urges even the slave to call his own – being torn from you and sold like beasts to the first bidder! And these deeds are done and palliated by men who profess to love their neighbours as themselves, who believe in God and pray that His will be done on earth! It makes one's blood boil to think that we Englishmen and our American descendants, with their boastful cry of liberty, have been and are so guilty.'

'Are you not forgetting the African who sells his brother man to the slavers, the Arab who first turned Africa into a slaving-ground, and every other nation on earth that partakes of this vile trade?'

'Do not try to abjure our national guilt over this matter, FitzRoy. The fact is, you Tories have always had cold hearts about slavery.'

'What gammon. I abhor slavery as much as you do.'

'But consider those innocent children, FitzRoy, plucked from the very bosom of their family! Brought up in a world where freedom is for ever to be denied them!'

'Mr Darwin, you will allow me to observe that I was entered for the Service when I was twelve years old. Mr Musters is eleven. Mr Hellyer is twelve. Mr King has been on this vessel since he was ten. Almost every soul aboard has been afloat since they were young children. Some of the oldsters were once pressed men, torn from their families. It is the lot of each and every one of us to do exactly as we are told. If a sailor disobeys an order, he is flogged. If he disobeys again, he is hanged. If he escapes and is recaptured, he is hanged. If I did as you suggest, my fate would be no different. Do not speak of slavery as if it were somehow unique.'

'If an equivalent misery is caused by the will of our institutions, then great is our sin – but how this bears on slavery, I cannot see.'

'It appears that you cannot see very much. All is relative. Compare the lot of the starving farm-worker in southern

England with the well-fed slave whose master is merciful.'

'At least the farm-worker suffers by his own hearth. Even the best-trained slaves wish to return to their countries.'

'Repatriation would be impossible. Nobody can hope to know which slave came from where. They do not even speak each other's language. I repeat, I am no advocate for slavery, but I have met slaves who knew enough of the world to realize that they were better off where they were.'

'And was their master present when they asserted so?'

'I cannot possibly recall.'

'Even if he was not, the slave must indeed be dull who does not calculate on the chance of his answer reaching his master's ears. It is you who are naïve, not I. I know what I speak of. My family has stood steadfastly against slavery for three generations. Both my grandfathers, Erasmus Darwin and the first Josiah Wedgwood, pledged to fight this scandalous trade. It was Josiah who produced the famous cameo depicting a Negro in chains with the slogan "Am I not a man and a brother?" – a brooch that he sold in the thousands, if not the hundreds of thousands, to concerned gentlefolk across Great Britain.'

'And where did the profits of that most popular trade find their resting-place? Were they donated to the fight against slavery? I very much doubt it.'

'I beg your pardon?'

'I believe that you heard me.'

'My grandfather lived right among his labourers, all fifteen thousand of them, at the Etruria works in Stoke-on-Trent.'

'And your uncle Jos? Does he live at the works? I think not. I think that the proceeds of the cameo to which you refer purchased him a handsome manor house, while his workers continue to live at the mercy of the factory system, a form of penury more iniquitous than which it would be difficult to imagine.'

'My uncle's workforce is free to come and go as they so please. How dare you make a comparison with the slave trade?'

'Free to come and go as they so please? So your uncle's

workers are not tied to his cottages, his insurance societies, his penny-halfpenny wages?'

'Each and every one of the lower orders in my uncle's employ has the potential for advancement.'

'The potential for advancement? Fifteen thousand people are confined to your uncle's slums, amid disease, poverty, grime and filth, and you claim that any one of them has the potential for advancement when their families are daily broken up? When mothers and children are forced to labour twelve hours or more per day because their husbands and fathers earn insufficient for their keep? When babies are brought up by their sisters and fed on laudanum tonic to keep their silence? And a further consequence of the factory system, as we both know, is an entire absence of all regard for moral obligations relating to sex – you know well the manner in which many young women brought up in the shadow of our factories are forced to supplement their income!'

'How dare you, sir? How dare you?' Darwin's voice rose to a shout. 'Do you think that the lower classes of the Tory shires are happier? At least my uncle's workers do not starve, sir.'

'At least the farm-workers of England know what it is to see daylight, sir.'

'I thank my better fortune that living in proximity to you has not made me a renegade to my Whig principles. The devil take you, sir!'

His face drained of blood by fury, FitzRoy called for his steward. 'Tell Lieutenant Wickham to present himself to my quarters immediately.'

'Aye aye sir.'

The two fumed in silence in the few brief seconds before Wickham made himself known.

'Mr Wickham.'

'Sir.'

'Mr Darwin has made himself presumptuously impertinent to me. He will not be taking his meals in this cabin henceforth. Please escort him from my quarters at once.'

Cold with rage, Darwin rose to his feet, his neck bent as ever to avoid a collision with the ceiling, and stalked out. Wickham followed in silence and shut the door. As Darwin placed his first furious tread on the companionway, Wickham lightly touched his arm.

'Philos? It sounded as if you and the skipper had fallen to loggerheads back there.'

'You heard?'

'It could be heard throughout the ship.'

'Pray forgive me the disturbance.'

'Philos? If you would care to mess with us in the gunroom henceforth, I am sure it could be arranged.'

'Thank you most kindly, Mr Wickham. I appreciate your consideration.'

With that, Darwin climbed up to the maindeck and went into his cabin to begin packing. He was perhaps halfway through the task when a knock at the door announced the presence of Lieutenant Sulivan.

'Philos?'

'Yes?'

'Compliments of Captain FitzRoy. The captain extends his humblest apologies – he wishes to say sorry for his unreasonable behaviour – and begs you to continue to live with him.'

'Is this your doing, Sulivan?'

'No, Philos, it is not.'

Darwin considered. 'Please tell Captain FitzRoy that, on the contrary, the fault was entirely mine, and that I should be delighted to continue to live with him.'

Sulivan smiled with relief. 'Thank goodness for that. The skipper has need of you. You must forgive him, Philos. He is a remarkable man, and a brilliant officer. All of us reverence him. But the pressure placed upon one man's shoulders is immense.'

'I will tell you, Sulivan, he is altogether the strongest marked character that I ever fell in with. I never before came across a man whom I could fancy being a Napoleon or a Nelson. If he does not kill himself, he will achieve wonderful things.'

'Let us hope it is the latter, shall we?' replied Sulivan brightly, and headed back in the direction of FitzRoy's cabin.

Two cannon salutes, one each from the *Warspite* and the *Samarang*, rolled across Rio de Janeiro Bay as the wind rippled the *Beagle*'s sails and she made for the harbour entrance. She was a popular little vessel, who had impressed everybody with her smartness and efficiency, and the mighty stalwarts of the South American station were sorry to see her go. They knew, especially, that she was headed – unaccompanied – into unknown and uncharted waters, where a hidden spear of rock could send a little surveying-brig to the bottom at any instant, and they wished her well. The *Beagle*'s crew revelled in their moment of fame, and proudly put their backs into all the heaving and pulling of departure.

'Close-hauled, Mr Chaffers, we should be able to lay south-east comfortably,' FitzRoy remarked to the master.

'Come on, Mr Musters!' barked Midshipman King, at his young charge. 'Tail on to that rope and put some effort in! Damned kid, thinks he's a lieutenant already.'

Musters plunged on to the end of the rope and heaved with all his might. FitzRoy, pacing the deck, saw him totter with the effort.

'Is everything all right, Mr Musters?'

'I don't feel very well, sir,' replied Musters feebly. 'I feel hot and sweaty.'

'It is probably a little fever from your snipe-shooting trip. I am sure it is nothing. Come with me to Mr Bynoe – I have no doubt he will make much of you.'

FitzRoy led Musters below decks to the sickbay. The *Beagle*'s was a fully equipped modern pharmaceutic facility, with ventilation, hanging cots and a full range of medicinal drugs, quite unlike the dark, windowless, unhygienic sickbays of the past. It was with every confidence that FitzRoy flung open Bynoe's door; a feeling of assurance that evaporated immediately when he saw the expression of Seaman Morgan, who was seated on a stool within. Fear was etched around Morgan's eyes, his face a pale, sweaty mask.

'Hello, young 'un,' he breathed. 'You here too?'

No one was in the mood to correct the informality.

'Yes,' said Musters, biting his lip uncertainly, sensing that something was wrong.

'It's just a fever, lad. We'll be set all squares on the morrow,' Morgan reassured him, and all the adults in the room knew him to be lying.

'May I speak with you a moment, sir?' asked Bynoe.

He and FitzRoy stepped outside. Concern tinged the young surgeon's every word. 'I am afraid, sir, there is every certainty that these men have contracted malaria.'

FitzRoy was stunned. 'How? In the islets of the harbour?'

'They followed the snipe flocks into the estuary of the Macacu river.'

FitzRoy clenched his fist into a ball of frustration. 'I categorically ordered them to stay away from dry land.'

'They did, sir. They stayed out in the waters of the estuary at all times.'

'Then how . . . ?'

'Pestilential malaria is caused by a miasma or vapour arising from marshland when it is affected by the heat of the sun. Dr Ferguson has shown that the poison is generated by the drying process, which is why hot climates are the most unhealthy. There were outbreaks in the marshes at Westminster, if you remember, during the hot summer a few years back. But the vapour can be carried out to sea by the winds. Many is the instance, sir, of native populations being decimated by European diseases brought by white explorers, the reason being that the vapours containing the disease are blown along on the same winds as their ships. The miasma is at its most concentrated in the darkness, so by sleeping in the estuary overnight, all three men will have undoubtedly exposed themselves to the windblown vapours.'

'Is there any physic that you can give them?'

'Quinine is known to alleviate the symptoms. The only cure lies with the Lord. Our best recourse is to pray, sir.'

'Thank you, Mr Bynoe.'

The surgeon returned to the sickbay while FitzRoy reeled back against the wall of the passageway in despair. He thought of the promises he had made to Musters's mother, of how he would take all care of little Charles. He struggled to make sense of the medical diagnosis. *If the miasma evaporates from the marshes during the heat of the day, why then is it at its most dangerous in the cool of the night? Is it because of a check to perspiration caused by sheets or blankets? If so, then why is a sleeper outside a tent more vulnerable than one inside?* Something was wrong with the orthodox medical explanation, he could tell – but what?

Overcome with his own intellectual impotence, he felt tears well in his eyes. They were tears of frustration, he knew, as much as tears of sadness.

Five days out of Rio, Bos'n Sorrell and his mates wrapped Mr Musters, Seaman Morgan and Seaman Jones in their hammocks, weighted them with roundshot, and sewed them in. Each was covered with a flag and placed in turn on a hinged plank, the same one that had been used when 'Crossing the Line', from which vantage-point they slid silently into the waters of the Atlantic. FitzRoy read the funeral service. No other sound was heard on deck.

'Poor kid,' whispered Jemmy, when he had finished.

'Poor kid,' echoed Fuegia, and then the deck fell quiet again.

The silence followed FitzRoy into his cabin afterwards, where he sat motionless before a blank page of the ship's logbook for the better part of an hour. Eventually Edward Hellyer, his budget of papers similarly ignored, ventured to speak.

'Sir?'

'Yes, Mr Hellyer?'

'Sir, why did God take Mr Musters? Had he done something bad?'

'No, Mr Hellyer, he had not done anything bad.'

'Then why did God take him, sir?'

I do not know how to answer that question.

'Maybe God loved Mr Musters so much that He wanted him at His right hand. I can think of no other explanation.'

There can be no other explanation. Dear Lord, how can there be any other explanation?

Chapter Fourteen

Punta Alta, Bahia Blanca, 22 September 1832

———

'By God, it's enormous.'

'What the deuce is it?'

'That will probably suffice with the pickaxe, Mr Sulivan. Here comes Philos to the rescue with his box of tools.'

'Thank heaven for that.'

Sulivan stepped back from the earth bank, perspiring. Embedded in the indigo clay before them, surrounded by a starburst of broken shells as if propelled violently through from the other side, a vast head, half exposed, grinned out at them. It measured a good four feet from side to side, each lifeless black eye-socket a whole foot in diameter.

Darwin picked his way up the beach, shivering. A chill breeze blew insistently from the south-east, and snow was visible on the distant Sierra de Ventana. Behind him, the descending tide had exposed a muddy lattice of shallow, silt-choked channels, a treacherous labyrinth into which FitzRoy had not dared steer the *Beagle*. Up and down the coast, as far as the eye could see, low sand hillocks lay in endless serpentine humps, forming a drab backdrop to an equally lifeless shore. One or two of the nearer humps had been garrisoned by mangy vultures, no doubt hoping that the unusual activity portended a much longed-for meal.

'This looks exactly like Barmouth,' he remarked, to nobody in particular. 'Except for the vultures.' Then he observed FitzRoy and his officers, some fifteen feet or so above the high-water mark, clustered about a section of clay bank that had collapsed, exposing its innards. Then he saw what held their attention.

'My God,' he said, arriving. 'What is it?'

'We were hoping you would be able to tell us,' admitted Bynoe, glad to hand over the baton of geological expertise.

'We thought it was a rhinoceros at first,' said FitzRoy, 'but it is far too large. These teeth are many times greater than those of any land animal living today.'

'What's the stratigraphic diagnosis, Philos?' said Sulivan good-humouredly. 'Tell us all.'

Darwin stared, transfixed, into the monstrous eye-sockets.

'I do believe it is a Megatherium,' he offered finally. 'If so, it would be only the second to be discovered. The first was found at Buenos Ayres in 1798, and resides in the King's Collection at Madrid – where, for all purposes of science, it is as much hidden as if still in its primeval rock. This is an incredible discovery!'

'How long has it been buried here, Philos?'

'Well, this earth is a conglomerate of quartz and jasper pebbles, which means it is comparatively new in geological terms. And these broken shells must also be of recent origin – all these creatures are extant today. This creature cannot be more than a few thousand years old.'

He indicated a small section of shoulder-plate that had been exposed by Sulivan's pickaxe, below the jaw-bone.

'Do you see how its bones have been buried in alignment? That suggests its remains were fresh and still united by their ligaments when they were deposited in the silt. This creature appears to have drowned.'

'Yet it is fifteen feet above the high-water mark,' FitzRoy pointed out, his heart thumping at the implication.

'Bless me, Philos,' said Sulivan excitedly, 'these could be the remains of an animal wiped out in the great flood itself. An animal too large to fit into the ark.'

FitzRoy observed that Darwin chose not to reply. Instead, the philosopher began to scratch at the exposed bank, where a number of jet-black plates, septagonal in shape and osseous in nature, protruded like bad teeth between the jumble of white shells.

'What are they, Philos? Are they part of its carapace?'

'I would say these were typical of the plates on an armadillo's back. Except they are enormous. To sport such a coat, an armadillo would have to be the size of a carriage – perhaps eight feet high and ten feet long.'

'A giant armadillo!' Midshipman King conjured up a thrilling mental image of the creature rampaging down Piccadilly.

'"*The end of all flesh is come before me*,"' murmured Sulivan.

'Let us not waste any more time in chatter,' said FitzRoy. 'It will take all afternoon to dig this fellow from his grave.'

So they set to the cliff with a will, the soft conglomerate rock crumbling before their onslaught, and gradually the head of the Megatherium emerged. Each took a turn at making bolder progress with the pickaxe, while Darwin took charge of the more delicate excavations and made notes with his bramah pen. Their task was almost complete when a shout from below alerted them to the presence of two schooners running into the bay. At least, FitzRoy could not find a better description than 'schooner': the two vessels were tiny, no bigger than the *Beagle*'s whaleboats, but each was possessed of twin masts and a covered deck. The lead schooner appeared to be crewed by a single sailor of quite enormous bulk, who clung to the mast shouting and waving, the little craft lurching from side to side so violently beneath him that it seemed he must upset her. The overall effect was that of a hugely overloaded bobbin, its spindle swaying fit to break.

'He's calling to us,' said Sulivan.

Despite its ungainliness, the little schooner and its fellow-craft were being expertly piloted, sidestepping the muddy shoals and darting through the watery channels towards the beach at great speed.

'The Bill is passed!' bawled the man.

'What's that?'

'Are you Englishmen, sir? I said, the Bill is passed!'

A shudder of excitement ran through the little group. The Reform Bill had passed through Parliament at last!

'Mr James Harris, sir, and this is Mr Roberts.' Florid with exertion, the fat sailor squelched into the shallows, crushing a dozen small crabs in the process. His face wore a just-boiled look.

'Commander Robert FitzRoy, captain of His Majesty's surveying-brig *Beagle*,' responded FitzRoy, stepping forward. He threw manners out of the window. 'Does His Majesty still reign or is there a republic?'

'I know not, sir. We spoke to a mail packet bound for San Francisco. All I know, sir, is that every man of property shall have the vote. The Bill is passed!'

Every man stood thrilled, transfixed, but fearful, too, that there might no longer be an England to go back to.

'You are sealers?' FitzRoy's practised eye took in the two vessels at a glance, both of them smeared with a filthy black cocktail of rancid seal and sea-elephant-oil. Harris and Roberts themselves were no less well greased.

'That we are, sir. I constructed them myself.' Harris gestured towards the boats, perspiring proudly. 'The *Paz* displaces fifteen tons, and the *Liebre* nine. I converted her from a frigate's barge.' Roberts's craft was little bigger than a coffin. 'As you will have seen, sir, the channels hereabouts are too shallow to risk a brig at low tide, or a barque. But at high tide an open boat like your own runs the risk of being swamped. The tide races are strong and the seas are uncommon heavy. These vessels present the ideal solution. The decks keep out the waves. If they go aground, one simply steps overboard and heaves them afloat. And one's own bodyweight answers admirably in trimming such craft.'

Yours especially, thought FitzRoy uncharitably. 'There are many such bays further down the coast?' he enquired.

'A hundred miles of them, sir, and each a maze of muddy creeks. But I am tolerably acquainted with them all.'

FitzRoy's mind raced, and a plan began to formulate therein.

The two sealers had come ashore to visit the fort at Argentina, the last permanent military encampment on the coast, in search of supplies. In view of Harris's advice regarding the incoming tide, FitzRoy instructed the shore party to pull the boats on to the shore and bivouac for the night, and went ahead with Harris and Darwin to the lonely outpost. A few miles' brisk walk across a level greensward, cropped short by semi-wild horses and cattle, brought them to La Fortaleza Protectora Argentina, a squat polygonal fortress some three hundred yards across, boasting thick mud walls and a defensive ditch. The walls were pitted and scarred, their wounds a vivid testimony to the number and intensity of recent Indian attacks.

An assemblage of creaking pulleys raised the main gate at their approach, and a reception party issued forth to greet them. At their head was an immensely tall half-caste mounted on a lean horse; dark of visage, his combination of army uniform and Indian dress was as confused as his lineage. Behind him rode several gauchos, wild, unshaven and desperate-looking, each man liberally adorned with knife-cuts; yet they were as gaily dressed as if in the service of an Eastern potentate. Gleaming white leather boots with shiny spurs jutted up from hand-carved wooden stirrups; voluminous scarlet drawers billowed over their boot-tops; and above those, the whole was enveloped by the swirl of their brightly striped ponchos. Bringing up the rear was a far less impressive straggle of uniformed foot-soldiers, sad-eyed white boys taken against their will from the suburbs of Buenos Ayres. The leader of this curious platoon spoke, in slow, deliberate Spanish. '¿*Viernes*

de Buenos Ayres con provisiones?' Do you come from Buenos
Ayres with supplies?

'I am a seal-man,' replied Harris in fluent Spanish. 'I have
come to Argentina to purchase supplies.'

'There are no supplies here. Buenos Ayres has forgotten
us.' The tall horseman spat derisively upon the ground.

'There must be beef,' objected Harris.

'There is always beef. But who are these men? They are
not seal-men.' He indicated FitzRoy and Darwin.

'They have come by ship from England.'

'I am Commander FitzRoy of His Majesty's Ship *Beagle*.'
FitzRoy spoke for himself, equally fluently, while Darwin, who
was still learning the language, struggled to keep up. 'I represent King William of Great Britain.'

'I do not know of such a place. You must report to the
commandant.'

The three allowed themselves to be led through the fortress
gate to the far side of an outer courtyard where raucous children played. A group of naked and frightened Indian prisoners crouched shackled together, gnawing at the carcass of a
roasted horse.

'What will happen to those men?' enquired Darwin of
Harris.

'They will be sent north to be interrogated. Then they will
be shot.'

'They will be shot? In cold blood?'

'You should see what the Indians do to white prisoners.
Shooting is a mercy by comparison.'

The party was escorted to a simple room where pieces of
rough wooden furniture stood upon a floor of beaten earth, and
squares cut into the walls served as windows. There they were
instructed to wait for the commandant. Two enormous pewter
plates of beef were brought, one roasted, the other boiled, and
an earthenware jug was filled from a water-butt in the corner.
No cutlery or drinking-vessels were provided. Presently, the tall
horseman returned, fetched back by his curiosity.

'Your country,' he enquired. 'It is to the north?'

FitzRoy assented.

'Is it warmer or colder than here?'

'Great Britain is colder than here in the summer, but warmer in the winter.'

'I have heard of Mendoza, and the United Provinces, and of Roma where the Holy Father lives. But I have never heard of this country you speak of.'

'*I* have heard tell of Great Britain.'

The voice came from behind them: although weary in tone, its rich texture evoked the wisdom of years. All turned to see the *comandante* framed in the doorway. He was a lean, erect, narrow-shouldered man, somewhat lost in a bleached and frayed major's uniform, his sun-gnarled face divided by a sagging grey moustache. In any other army, in any other part of the world, he would surely have been pensioned off many years previously. Clearly normal rules did not apply out here at the frontier, here in his personal domain.

'Great Britain is a city in the country of London, which is connected by land to the United States of America. Am I right?' The major sat down stiffly opposite FitzRoy, Darwin and Harris.

'That is approximately correct,' answered FitzRoy, diplomatically.

'Please. Eat.' He gestured to the two vast mounds of beef.

'Will you excuse me?' Darwin, whose fingers were still caked with the blue clay of the Punta Alta shore, poured water from the jug on to his hands and rubbed them vigorously. For good measure he splashed some on his cheeks, still flecked with mud from his geological exertions.

'You are a Mahometan?' asked the major.

'No.' Darwin looked puzzled.

'Then why do you wash? I have heard that only Mahometans wash themselves.'

'I am a Christian. In our country it is common for Christians to wash.'

'You are a follower of the one true Catholic faith? You have confessed your sins?'

'No . . . I am not a Catholic, but I am a Christian.'

'If you are not a Catholic, you cannot be a Christian. You must be a Mahometan. It matters not. If you have a God, then you will be safe under my roof. You are sailors?'

'I am a sailor,' clarified FitzRoy. 'My friend Mr Darwin is a naturalist.'

The *comandante* looked puzzled. The term *naturalista* evidently fell outside the scope of his knowledge.

'A naturalist is a man who knows everything,' explained Harris helpfully through a mouthful of beef.

'You know *everything*?' The major raised an eyebrow.

'No, no. I should say I *wish* to learn everything about your country.'

'You are not a spy?' The old man's eyes narrowed.

'I wish only to learn of the animals and birds and plants and rocks. Today we have made a most wonderful discovery – a great head. The head of a mammal – a dead animal – many thousands of years old. It is as wide as a man is tall. On the beach at Punta Alta. It is a great rarity.'

'A big dragon-head.' Realization dawned upon the old major. 'The children like to play games with them. They knock out the teeth with stones. It is a good game.'

Darwin was momentarily nonplussed. The *comandante* gestured to the side door of the room. Darwin half rose from his stool, and craned his neck to see into the courtyard outside. There, grinning toothlessly back at him, was a Megatherium head identical – other than dentally – to the one they had spent all day excavating at the beach.

'I will sell you three for a paper dollar, if you wish,' said the major.

When the constraints of time eventually forced FitzRoy and his officers to abandon excavations at Punta Alta, the exposed cliff had yielded two further Megatherii, a Megalonyx measuring seventy-two feet from snout to tail, an icthyosaurus longer than the *Beagle* herself, an ant-eater the size of a rhinoceros, a twenty-foot armadillo, an extinct variety of horse and an aquatic rodent the size of an elephant. The ship's once-pristine deck was thick with giant bones caked in blue clay.

'Damned seal and whalebones!' Mr Wickham shouted in exasperation. 'Philos, you bring more dirt on board than any ten men!'

FitzRoy decided to run the *Beagle* back to Buenos Ayres to see if the specimens could be dispatched home by an English merchant there. Over a supper of water-hog shot by Bynoe, he and Darwin debated the implications of their haul.

'The approach of a general calamity – the rising waters – would have affected the animals' instinct for self-preservation,' hazarded FitzRoy. 'They would have been *drawn* to the ark. Then, as the creatures approached, might it not have been easy to admit some, perhaps the young and the small, while the old and the large were excluded?'

'I don't know,' said Darwin unhappily. 'The stated dimensions of the ark are but three hundred cubits by fifty cubits. How could all creation be herded into one vessel? Would the beasts not simply have destroyed one another? The story has always vexed me.'

'Master Charles,' admonished FitzRoy gently, 'does not the exclusion of these monstrous creatures answer your question? Where are they now? Drowned, of course, in the deluge.'

'Where, then, are the human fossils? If all humanity was wiped out at the same time, should not there be human bones entombed with those of the Megatherium, or the other great beasts that have been found across the globe? Perhaps these vast creatures walked the earth at a different date, an earlier date.'

'A different date? My dear fellow, I need hardly tell you of all people that the scriptures allow no room for debate on the issue. Genesis two, nineteen: "And out of the ground the Lord God formed every beast of the field, and every fowl of the air, and brought them unto Adam to see what he would call them."'

'Come, come, my dear FitzRoy, you know as well as I that the scriptures are contradictory. In Genesis one, twenty-four, the Lord brings forth all living creatures *before* He maketh man on the sixth day, having already created fish and fowl on the fifth day. What if, as de Luc contends, these "days" were not days as we know them but great ages, epochs lasting many thousands of years? What if man never encountered these monstrous beasts?'

'But, my dear Philos, you heard the *comandante*. A "dragon-head", he called it. What, pray, are dragons, wyverns, griffins and so forth, if not the memory of huge mammals and reptiles handed down by tradition? What were the leviathan and the behemoth if not the megalosaurus and the iguanodon? Human folk-history contains innumerable mentions of such beasts. As to the human fossils, de Luc also contends that, in many places, earth and sea have changed places over the centuries. Perhaps human fossils await discovery at the bottom of our great oceans.'

'But what if early man derived their dragon-tales from the discovery of great skeletons such as we have found? What if, far from actually encountering such beasts, they merely wove them into their myths and stories? Answer me this: if there was indeed an ark, why are the animals of the New World entirely separate from those of the Old? Why are the armadillo and the ant-eater confined entirely to South America, and the elephant and the rhinoceros restricted to the rest of the globe? If all creatures issued from the one ark, would they not follow each other to all corners? But no! All creation is divided into geographical groups. And what fossils do we find in South America? *Giant* armadillos. *Giant* anteaters. The monstrous relatives of the modern animal population. Just as fossil elephants and rhinoceros are only to be found in Africa and Asia.'

'Great heavens, Philos, one would hardly believe you a parson-in-waiting. Let me bring you over. Did not Noah's sons

Shem, Ham and Japheth go forth separately and beget the different races in the different parts of the world? Would it be beyond the good Lord to spread the animals of the ark over the lands newly laid dry *according to their origin*? Would He not logically return the armadillo to the lands whence it came, and the same for the rhinoceros? Besides, your argument is disproved by our friend the horse. The Spaniards introduced the horse to the New World. When they arrived, the horse was unknown to the native population. It has since thrived. Yet what did we discover at Punta Alta? A fossil horse. This is perfect horse-country, yet every horse that once inhabited these lands was wiped out at some point in history. Only a mighty deluge could have done such a thing. Which is why, perhaps' – FitzRoy smiled – 'the good Lord brought the Spanish here, to restock the horse population.'

'Please. My dear FitzRoy, I do not doubt the majesty of God's creation for one instant. But a wooden vessel, stocked with pairs of animals by a six-hundred-year-old man? Noah is said to have been fetched an olive-leaf by a dove when the waters receded. Yet how did a deluge that would flatten and submerge the very mountains themselves fail to uproot or flatten a simple olive tree? It is a most unbelievable tale!'

Irritation began to temper FitzRoy's affection for his friend. 'You doubt the Noachian deluge? Have you not seen the diluvial evidence for yourself? There are water-smoothed stones and shell beds on mountainsides, drowned creatures above the high-water mark, unsorted deposits of clay and gravel and huge boulders scattered across the high hills and valleys – why, the very shape of the hills and valleys themselves shouts out to us of the deluge. And what of the evidence of the heathen peoples? Mesopotamian texts speak of the earth being destroyed by a mighty flood. Even the Hindoos know of the deluge. They speak of one man alone, Manu, being spared by God from the destruction of all humankind. Clearly, it is a garbled account of the Biblical flood. With such compelling evidence before you, can you doubt that the creatures at Punta

Alta were wiped out by a massive catastrophe – the very catastrophe described in such detail in the Book of Genesis?'

'I do not seek to undermine the Book of Genesis, FitzRoy, or the word of God. What do you take me for? But there are contradictions therein, anomalies, passages that could be interpreted figuratively. For instance, the lower one geologizes into the rock, the earlier the strata, the simpler the life-forms one finds: not human beings, but great reptiles, giant armadillos, even. Does this not suggest to you an older earth than one which was created in seven days?'

'You presume that the rock is older because the life-forms are simpler. You presume that the life-forms are simpler because the rock is older. You are dating one by the other. Perhaps the strata are not as simple or as progressively layered as you seem to think. What of the modern-day shells preserved in the clay *below* the Megatherium head? Besides, who is to say that a giant armadillo or ant-eater is any simpler than a small one? One might argue the very opposite. Your arguments begin to sound dangerously like those of your grandfather, or of Lamarck.'

'Perhaps the smaller versions of these creatures were better suited to the sparse vegetation of these parts. Perhaps their bigger cousins did not have enough to eat – who is to say? I am only speculating. Such enormous herbivores would have required a colossal supply of vegetation. Perhaps they were forced to compete for it, and lost that competition.'

'The vegetation of Africa is no less sparse than the vegetation of these parts, and yet it supports vast numbers of elephant and rhinoceros. In the Brazils, however, where the vegetation is lush and abundant, there are no large herbivores. What you suggest does not follow. Besides, we know nothing of the state of the earth before the flood – or the atmosphere surrounding it; we do not know if it moved in the same orbit; or if it turned on its axis in the same manner; or whether it had huge masses of ice near the poles. Have not fossil rhinoceros bones been found near the Arctic?'

'Cuvier believes that there may have been a series of floods.'

FitzRoy seized a book from the shelf behind his head and riffled through it. 'Allow me to quote Buckland, a geological authority without peer, I think you will agree. "The grand fact of a *universal deluge* at no very remote period is proved on grounds *so* decisive and incontrovertible that, had we never heard of such an event from scripture, or any other authority, geology *of itself* must have called in the assistance of some such catastrophe to explain the phenomena of diluvian action *which are universally presented to us.*"' He slammed the book down on the table.

'"Great men are not always wise" – Job thirty-two, nine,' Darwin responded stubbornly.

On the point of raising his voice in frustration, FitzRoy thought better of it. 'Tell me, my dear friend, is it the case that you are no longer inwardly moved by the Holy Spirit?'

'Of course I am,' said Darwin, 'but . . .' He tailed off.

'Do you wish to talk to me about it?'

Spruced up with red ochre, coal-tar and whitewash, and scrubbed free of the fatty coating of a thousand boiled seals, the *Paz* and the *Liebre* had metamorphosed into smart little cock-boats. The crew gathered around admiringly as they bobbed jauntily beside the *Beagle*, while inside his cabin FitzRoy put the final touches to the contract: to Mr James Harris of the Rio Negro, for one year's hire of both boats, plus the services of himself and Mr Roberts as pilots, the sum of £1680.

'And I thought the headroom on the old *Beagle* was barely sufficient,' said Stokes ruefully, lowering himself into the main cabin of the *Paz*, which – although a spacious seven foot square – was an ungenerous thirty inches in height. He would be sharing this cramped space for the next twelve months with Roberts, the sealer, and Midshipman Mellersh.

'Pretty boats!' said Fuegia Basket, and clapped her hands with delight.

'Think yourself lucky you will not be sharing with Harris,' laughed Wickham, who was to have the privilege of wedging himself into an even smaller cabin in the *Liebre*, alongside the boat's owner and Midshipman King.

The prospect of being second-in-command of his very own vessel, on a year's expedition to survey the bays and channels south of Bahia Blanca, had seemed to King the very idea of heaven on earth; until, that is, he too had inspected the principal cabin. Then the reality – that he would be spending the whole of the following year squeezed into a corner by Harris's sweating bulk – had sunk in. He and Darwin stood forlornly at the starboard rail. The philosopher's initial guilty pleasure at getting their whole cabin to himself had dissipated somewhat, as he had come to realize how much he would miss the dependable Stokes, the egregious Wickham and his best pal, the young midshipman by his side. Sulivan, who would become acting first lieutenant of the *Beagle*, looked on with misgivings of his own, for he did not wish to accede to Wickham's position in such a manner. He steeled himself to beard FitzRoy in private.

'Let me go in Wickham's place, sir. It will be a rotten uncomfortable year for them, and Mr Wickham takes such a pride in the *Beagle*.'

'Your suggestion is generous to a fault, Mr Sulivan. However – naval etiquette bids me do otherwise. If the expedition is to divide in two, then my second-in-command must take charge of the second part.'

'Then how about Stokes? He has been with you from the start, sir – he has surely earned his place on the *Beagle*.'

'Mr Stokes is my best surveyor. I doubt that anyone else in the ship could map such a maze. Besides, were you to replace him, then I should find myself *sans* lieutenants.'

'If only the Admiralty had sanctioned the hire of two more luxurious vessels – they are but cockleshells.'

'Only cockleshells, I fear, possess a sufficiently shallow draught for the task. Besides, the Admiralty has not sanctioned the hire of any vessels.'

'But then how—?'

'They are requisitioned on my own responsibility.'

'You are not authorized?' Sulivan's face wore a faintly appalled look.

'I have memorialized Whitehall seeking authorization. I hope to obtain it retrospectively.'

'But if you do not?'

'Then I shall be sixteen hundred and eighty pounds the poorer.'

Sulivan gasped. It was an astonishing sum for one man to bear, even a wealthy man like FitzRoy.

'I believe that their lordships will approve of what I have done. But if I am wrong no inconvenience will result to the public service, since I am alone responsible, and am willing to pay the stipulated sum.'

'No inconvenience to the public service, perhaps, but to yourself? It would be more than mere inconvenience ...' Sulivan's expression clouded over with worry.

I can ill spare the sum, it is true, but he cannot know that.

'I am willing to run the risk. Without it our task cannot – simply cannot – be completed. If the results of these arrangements should turn out well, then I trust I will stand excused for having presumed to act so freely. Besides, I have given my word to Jemmy, to York and to Fuegia that they will be home before the summer. I have given my word, Mr Sulivan, as one gentleman to another.'

The point, Sulivan had to concede, was unanswerable.

The little city of Buenos Ayres lay in flat green meadows along the river Plate's southern shore, hugging the ground, its domes and towers rising cautiously from rough, muddy streets and squares. The brown river washing thickly at its banks appeared richer and creamier than ever, as if it would curdle against the docks and jetties. As the *Beagle* made sticky progress upstream, the river seemed to adhere to her flanks and clog her passage.

The cannon-shot rang out unmistakably across the lapping

water. Most of those on deck turned in time to see a white puff of smoke drift languidly up through the rigging of the city guardship. The three Fuegians, poised, alert, froze midway through a reluctant passage of Bible study with Mr Matthews. FitzRoy, on the poop deck, and Mr Sulivan and the master at the wheel, were held in a split second's limbo of indecision before their training took over. Darwin, confused, spun like a top, attempting to locate the source of the sound. Only the few oldsters on board who had seen action as nippers and powder monkeys in the Great War flung themselves instinctively to the deck. A second later, a faint whistle overhead, accompanied by the ripping of parting ropes, announced that the cannonball had passed harmlessly through the rigging. Only then did the realization dawn, fully, that the *Beagle* was under attack.

'How dare they?' exclaimed FitzRoy. 'How *dare* they? Bring her round, Mr Chaffers, and beat to quarters!'

She was already sailing as close-hauled as she could, some six points off the breeze, which was gusting from the northern shore. It was an easy matter for her to reach across the wind, her sails bellying, and swing into a course that would bring her bearing down alongside the guardship. The drums sounded their intent, and there was a scene of furious activity on deck as the guns were made ready.

'Damn them,' cursed FitzRoy. 'A shot into the works of a steam engine would not do so much damage as a shot too close to our chronometers.'

'But why did they fire at us?' asked a panic-stricken Darwin, who had located a safe place to hide, crouched behind the huge Megatherium head.

'Another revolution, I shouldn't wonder. Revolutions are the fashion in these parts. When they are not fighting the Indians, they fight each other. Whoever controls Buenos Ayres controls the silver route from Upper Peru. So it is just one *caudillo*, one strong man, after another – except that none is strong enough to hold on to power. They say General Rosas is the strongest, but he will not enter the fray until he is sure of victory.'

The *Beagle* was closing rapidly on the guardship now, and Darwin could see the gunners scurrying to their positions on the enemy vessel. The disparity in bulk between the two ships was becoming increasingly apparent as they drew nearer, the *Beagle* giving away a good few hundred tons to her rival. Surely, thought Darwin, we shall not dare to take on a ship twice our size, broadside to broadside? He buried his head as deeply as he could in the Megatherium's eye-socket.

'Mr Sorrell, back the fore-topsail!' ordered FitzRoy. Drilled to perfection a hundred times, the men jumped to their tasks, hauling the fore-topsail yard round in opposition to its fellows, to bring the *Beagle* juddering to a near-stop. The gleaming brass snouts of her new guns bristled aggressively along her starboard side: two six-pounders before the chesstree, a six-pound boat-carronade on the forecastle, and four lone, wicked-looking nine-pounders abaft the mainmast. As they drew alongside the guardship, FitzRoy leaped up on to the rail and, balancing there, shouted across the intervening channel of chocolate-cream water: 'If you dare fire another shot, we shall send our whole broadside into your rotten uncivilized hulk! Is that understood?' And then, for good measure, he repeated the statement in Spanish.

There was silence, and then, across the water, a brief flurry of activity as the Buenos Ayres gunners stood down from their posts. The *Beagle* drifted on past her, into open water, and Darwin drew his head cautiously out from the black depths of the eye-socket.

'You did not fire,' he ventured redundantly.

'I had no intention of doing so. The damage to the chronometers from our own recoil would have been catastrophic. Besides, such a firefight would have been sheer folly. We would have been blown out of the water. He was twice our size, did you not see?'

'But – but how did you know that their captain would not fire?'

'Did you see the state of that ship? The sails were mildewed, the paintwork filthy, and you can smell their bilges from here. You can tell a lot about a man from the state of his ship. My dear Philos, I knew he would not fire.'

By sundown they had swirled down with the current to Monte Video on the river's north-eastern shore, where His Majesty's frigate *Druid* was moored on permanent station. FitzRoy went across in the cutter to pay his respects to Captain Hamilton, and to make his formal report of the insult to the British flag – an incident that would not, of course, go unpunished. As he clambered aboard, he was stopped in his tracks by an apparition: a pale but welcome face he had never expected to see again.

'My God – Hamond!'

'FitzRoy!'

'I thought you drowned – lost with the *Thetis*.'

'N-no, sir,' replied Hamond, who had not outgrown his stammer. 'I was b-back in England, taking my lieutenant's examination – I'm a p-passed mid now. Everybody else d-drowned, sir.'

'But, my God, you're alive!'

And the two men threw their arms around each other in a most un-naval fashion.

By the time the *Druid* had hauled her anchor at sunrise, and had set sail for Buenos Ayres to demand the arrest of the guardship captain, FitzRoy had obtained not just restitution but a new mate: Robert Hamond would chum with Charles Darwin in the library of the *Beagle*.

The celebratory mood was not to last, however. A stack of mail had been waiting for Darwin in the *Druid* – he had excitedly unwrapped the latest volume of Lyell, sent by Professor Henslow – but then, lurking malevolently in wait at the bottom of the pile, he had spotted the black seal. Feverishly, he had torn open the letter, almost ripping it in two in his haste to get at the contents. His cousin, his sweet, mischievous cousin

Fanny Wedgwood, was dead of cholera at the age of twenty-six. His thoughts flashed back to that perfect afternoon the previous summer when he had sat out on the porch with Fanny and Emma and Hen and Uncle Jos and Aunt Bessie, Fanny teasing him, inciting him to go on the voyage, urging him to take care of himself, Emma's arm curled about her sister's waist. Fan had worried for her cousin's safety, *his* safety, and now it was *her* fragile existence that had been crushed by a heartless or careless or loveless deity. He felt simultaneously lucky, and frightened, and angry at the senselessness of it. This was not some meaningless native whose life had been taken, but a beautiful, intelligent young *lady* in the prime of her life. He knew what FitzRoy would say, that it was God's wish, that one should not challenge His will, that there were reasons for everything that could not always be revealed to us. FitzRoy would probably be right, but that did not mean he wished to hear him express the sentiments. Damn it, he would follow the man anywhere – what magnificent pluck he had shown in facing up to the Buenos Ayres guardship – but he was always so *certain* of everything.

Darwin's reverie was interrupted by the crackle of gunfire. At first he thought it must be the *Druid*, laying waste to Buenos Ayres city centre in an orgy of retribution; then he remembered that the river Plate was so ludicrously wide at its mouth that a good hundred miles lay between the two cities on their opposing banks. No, the firing came from the centre of Monte Video itself. Presently a small boat appeared, rowed somewhat inexpertly by four gentlemen in top hats and tailcoats, one of whom stood up and began to wave and gesticulate frantically at the *Beagle*. FitzRoy came to the rail to try to discern what was being shouted, no easy matter as the man's relinquishing of his oar was causing the little boat to go round in circles.

'Where is the *Druid*, sir?' bellowed the slowly revolving figure.

'Gone to Buenos Ayres,' shouted back FitzRoy.

'Then you are our only hope, sir!'

Eventually the little craft was secured alongside, and the portly gentleman and his comrades were helped up into the *Beagle*.

'Richard Bathurst at your service, sir,' gasped the man. 'British consul-general in Monte Video. Allow me the honour of grasping your hand. May I introduce to your acquaintance Señor Dumas, the police chief of Monte Video.'

Señor Dumas made the position clear. 'There is mutiny in the city. President Lavalleja is away in Colonia, and the commander of troops here in Monte Video has seized power in his absence. He has opened the gaol and armed all the prisoners. They have occupied the citadel – the seat of government. It is a military *coup d'état*.'

'What do these soldiers desire to bring about with their *coup d'état*?' asked FitzRoy.

'Some wish for the reinstatement of President Rivera, who was overthrown by President Lavalleja. The Brazilian soldiers want the city returned to Brazil. The soldiers from the United Provinces want the city to become part of the United Provinces. The Uruguayan soldiers want it to remain part of Uruguay, although some of them want the country to revert to its old name of "Banda Oriental". The black soldiers want the slaves to be freed. They want many things. Please, Captain, you must help us. Only you can help us.'

'I feel for your predicament, Señor Dumas, but you must realize that I simply cannot interfere in South American politics. As captain of one of His Majesty's ships, I must maintain a strict neutrality at all times.'

'I don't think you understand, sir,' said Bathurst, who was still panting for breath. 'There are British families in the city whose lives and property are at risk. British women and children, sir, whose honour is at the mercy of these villains.'

'That changes the position. Then, sir, my forces are entirely at your disposal. How many are the mutineers?'

'Approximately six hundred, including the freed prisoners.'

'I can muster some seventy men all told.'

'We are four, sir, plus perhaps the same number in the city.'

'All stout men, sir, all stout men,' volunteered the third member of the party, a brisk elderly gentleman with a fierce military moustache, who had armed himself with a broom handle.

'I say – Colonel Vernon?' Darwin came forward, recognizing the voice.

'Good Lord – it's young Darwin, isn't it?'

'You know each other?'

'Know each other?' barked the colonel. 'More than that, sir! We have ridden to hounds together!'

'Colonel Vernon is the brother-in-law of Miss Gooch,' explained Darwin hurriedly, as if that clarified matters. 'But what are you doing here, sir?'

'I am making a tour of South America. I intend travelling by land to Lima, and so by Mexico back to Europe. May I introduce Mr Martens, who is the son of the Austrian consul to London? He is an artist travelling independently.'

'Delighted to make your acquaintance, gentlemen,' said Martens, a short, fine-boned character with coppery sideburns and a pugnacious expression.

'Gentlemen, please, time is pressing,' said FitzRoy, with a trace of exasperation. 'Where are the British families now?'

'They have taken refuge in the customs house on the mole.'

'Then our first task will be to stow them safely in the *Beagle*. They shall have the officers' cabins. Mr Bennet, prepare the ship's boats for their passage. Mr Chaffers, you will take charge of the *Beagle*. Trice up the boarding netting, load the guns and aim them at the shore. Should anyone approach who is not of our party, you have my permission to blow them to kingdom come. Mr Sulivan, you will organize a platoon of fifty men to be armed with muskets, pistols and cutlasses. Mr Bos'n, open the armoury, if you please. We shall make the best of our way to the fort, and attempt to secure it. I think it constitutes the key to the city. If we can but hold the fort and the harbour, then we shall be impossible to dislodge, and we shall control the approaches to Monte Video by land and sea. The mutineers will have met no resistance as yet, so they will in all probability have relaxed their guard. They may even, if we are fortunate, have begun to celebrate their success somewhat prematurely. At any rate, we shall give them a substantial argument to convince them that they must not plunder British property.'

Darwin's admiration for the man redoubled. There are times when certainty *is* of paramount importance, he concluded, and this is one of them. British women were at risk, British women like Fanny Wedgwood, whose lives he could help FitzRoy to save. He would rather follow FitzRoy with fifty men, he realized, than anybody else with five hundred. And follow him he would, with a musket in one hand, a pistol in the other and a cutlass between his teeth.

'The very best of luck, sir! Give them hell, sir!' said Jemmy Button, warmly, appearing at the edge of the group in his morning-coat and kid gloves.

'I say,' murmured Colonel Vernon, 'is that an *Indian*?'

'A Fuegian Indian, yes,' confirmed Darwin.

'Extraordinary.'

The men of the *Beagle* formed up on the mole between a rickety line of dockside cranes and a collapsing row of wooden sheds opposite. There they began their march into the city, through the long narrow avenues that followed the line of the peninsula. The river was a constant presence, a deeper brown here than at Buenos Ayres, but catching the sun, a dark rectangle glittering to left and right at every intersection. Legions of rats scattered at their progress, darting from their hiding-places in the mounds of vegetables, offal and stale fruit that lay strewn across the cobbles. Although the occasional crack of gunfire could be heard echoing down side-streets, there was no sign of the mutineers, who remained barricaded in the citadel. The city appeared empty, save for the occasional carrion, human and bovine, and the rodents busily gorging themselves upon it. The citizens, who were well used to such episodes, had wisely disappeared into their houses. The sailors could hear the eerie percussion of their own marching footsteps reverberating back from the walls, an intrusion that sounded almost impolite in the quiet, narrow lanes.

Beyond the moated, muddy walls of the city, the bay curved round to the west, where it swept up into the towering headland that gave Monte Video its name. There, atop the peak, sat the Fortaleza del Cerro, a white, elegant beacon risen above the chaos. The rough track to the fort was deserted. It took them a full two hours to march its length, FitzRoy striding grimly at their head. Darwin, who had matched him stride for stride with manly enthusiasm at the outset, began to sweat uncomfortably in his top-coat and thick woollen waistcoat, but he was determined at all costs to keep up. Bathurst, the consul-general, panted by his side, his little legs working like pistons.

Really, if its defenders had been determined, the fort would have been impervious to any sort of attacking force, unless supported by several men-of-war with heavy cannon. Certainly their approach – in fact, their entire progress around the bay – could have been spotted from the battlements without much trouble. But FitzRoy had been correct in his surmise: when they reached the edge of musket range he sent scouts forward, who reported that the fort's gates were flung wide open. The building was guarded by just two men, both of them insensibly drunk by the looks of it and fast asleep. Six stealthy matlows were dispatched, who overwhelmed the guards and placed them under arrest. Within the quarter-hour, the *Beagle* party had taken possession of the fort.

FitzRoy and Sulivan strode out on to the high, flat roof and sized up the situation. A magnificent panorama presented itself. A distant church bell struck three at that moment, and the little white city set on its jutting finger of rock in the sunshine looked for all the world as if it were at peace with itself.

'What do you say, Mr Sulivan? Two miles and a half as the crow flies? Well within the range of these sixty-four pounders?'

'Absolutely, sir,' grinned Sulivan. 'They're sitting ducks.'

The fort's big guns, trained west and south to deter invasion by land and sea, were hauled round to the eastern side to face the citadel. Now the picturesque vista was gated off by the stark black silhouettes of the gun barrels, arrayed in parallel lines along the battlements. Geometric pyramids of cannonballs were hastily assembled at their base, proclaiming a veritable abundance of ammunition.

'Señor Dumas?'

'¿Capitan?'

'I should be very much obliged if you would lead a deputation to the mutineers. Kindly inform them that the Royal Navy has taken possession of the fort and the harbour, and that HMS *Druid* shall return from Buenos Ayres on the morrow. Their position is hopeless. They have until nightfall to return to their barracks, after which no more will be said about the incident. If, however, they fail to comply, I will begin shelling the citadel at first light. And when HMS *Druid* appears, I shall signal to her to do likewise.'

Dumas scurried off to carry out his appointed task. There was nothing left to do but to blockade the main gate, post sentries and wait. A store of juicy beefsteaks was located in the kitchens, which were cooked up in the little courtyard, and washed down with flagons of beer from the cellar.

Munching hungrily on a fat steak, Darwin was swept by a sense of exhilaration at their easy victory, coupled with a faint, muddled tinge of disappointment that FitzRoy had avoided bloodshed once again. Oh, to have *really* tested himself as a sportsman, to have potted a swarthy mutineer or two!

Colonel Vernon strolled over, a massive slab of grilled beef in one hand.

'A very good afternoon to you, Colonel,' said Darwin politely. 'And how are you enjoying your tour?'

'Well, to be quite frank, my dear chap, I hadn't thought

Uruguay up to much before today. But now I realize that the place is capital – simply *capital*!'

The next day passed as if the revolt had never occurred. The mutineers had accepted FitzRoy's offer, sobered up, and returned to barracks. For the citizens of Monte Video, life returned to normal, if indeed there had been anything abnormal about the previous day's events. President Lavalleja returned from Colonia, and announced that FitzRoy would be fêted at a grand restoration ball, to be held at the Teatro Solis. The streets were mysteriously cleared of debris, the shops were opened, and the ladies of Monte Video recommenced their elegant daily promenade through the streets, in their close-fitting gowns and black silk veils. Veils that concealed not just their heads and shoulders but one eye as well, leaving the other to flutter its dark, enticing invitation; or so it seemed to Darwin and Hamond, who sat in the Plaza Independencia with Augustus Earle, admiring the spectacle.

'They are veritable angels,' groaned Darwin, as one lady sashayed by, her skirts clinging to the outline of her hips as she passed. 'And most demure – the veil is a most demure touch. They are gentlewomen, there is no question of that.'

'They d-do not walk, they g-glide,' moaned Hamond.

'It makes one realize how foolish many Englishwomen are, who know neither how to walk nor to dress.'

'How ugly the word "m-miss" sounds after "s-senorita".'

'It would do the whole tribe of Englishwomen a great deal of good to come to South America. The grace of these Spanish ladies is almost . . . well, *spiritual*.'

Augustus Earle said nothing, but did not take his eyes off the view.

Darwin and Hamond had occasion to continue their conversation the following Saturday night at the Teatro Solis, where they sat in a gilded box observing the whirling dance-floor below. The ladies of Monte Video had exchanged their silken veils and slinky gowns for ostentatious hair-combs and the most extravagant peacock gowns, which – from above – unfurled as swirling rosettes with every swing of the wearers' hips. The music was slower than at an English ball, and the dancing more formal, but it was one-on-one: there were no linked arms, no set-tos, no bow-and-curtsies. The dancers seemed to stare into each other's eyes with a studied ardour. There was something unsettling about the cool, intense formality of it all, and Darwin began to feel hot under the collar. He noticed Augustus Earle, who had somehow managed to secure himself a dancing partner, advancing boldly through the fray. It was hard to say which was the more irritating: that Earle knew the steps, that he had bothered to shave and spruce himself up (the first time he had done so in many months), or that he had found a partner with such apparent ease.

'That man,' observed Darwin, who after several months' abstinence had drunk rather too well, 'is unduly forward.'

'He has m-missed his step?' said the equally inebriated Hamond, misunderstanding.

'I mean, I fear that his intentions towards that good lady might not be as ... respectful of her honour as she might wish.'

Earle's dancing partner chose that moment to throw back her head and let out a lascivious laugh, soundless above the blare of the orchestra.

'The way her hair is b-brushed back into a b-bow ... reminds me of a p-painting of the Virgin I once saw. She has the s-same innocence.'

'And yet anybody here might ask her to dance. Anybody! There is no master of the ceremonies. The arrangements of the house are quite unsatisfactory.' Darwin warmed to his theme. 'The event is entirely open – *entirely* open – to the lowest classes of society, and yet nobody seems to have imagined the possibility of disorderly conduct on their parts. How different are the habits of Englishmen, on such jubilee nights!'

'Quite d-different.'

Augustus Earle had succeeded in snaking one arm round his uncomplaining partner's waist.

'One might fear for public decorum at such an event!' Darwin grumbled.

'Perhaps they are happy b-because they are not d-dead. All my friends are d-dead,' said Hamond, balefully, taking another gulp of lemon shrub.

'That's true. They could have been killed in the revolution. *We* could have been killed in the revolution.'

'We could all d-drown in the south.'

'We could indeed.'

This particular thought crystallized, hard, in the mist of Darwin's drunken reasoning. He could have died in the mutiny. Thank heaven FitzRoy had avoided a firefight. He might, as Hamond had so graphically put it, drown in the south. But he wasn't ready for heaven yet.

'If we d-drown, do you think we shall g-go to heaven?' Hamond had read his thoughts.

'Of course we shall.'

But would he? Had he not doubted the scriptures? Had he not questioned the Biblical account of the flood? Would the Lord not damn him in the hereafter on account of his presumption? Should he not atone, now, before it became too late?

'Hamond?'

'Yes?'

'Do you think there must be an English chaplain here, in Monte Video?'

'Of c-course. There is an English chaplain in every m-major city.'

'Do you feel it would be wise to have the sacrament of the Lord's Supper administered to us previous to journeying south?'

'What – right now?'

'When else? We set sail on the morrow. It is an ordinance that many see as a vow to lead a better life – a vow that might stand one in good order with the Lord.'

'I s-see what you mean.'

And so it was, after a few discreet enquiries, that two some-what confused gentlemen – fortified still further, following their earlier conversation – could be seen hammering on the door of a house in the Avenida Bolivar, in the small hours of Sunday.

'He's taking an unconsciably long time. An uncon-sciousonably long time.'

'Perhaps he's s-sleeping.'

'It *is* a Sunday morning.'

Finally, they heard the sound of bolts being scraped back, and the door creaked open. A bushy-eyebrowed gentleman in a nightcap and gown stood before them, peering irascibly through the yellow glow of an oil lamp.

'*¿Qué diablos quieres decir con, golpeando mi puerta a esta hora?*'

'Reverendo Mr Maynard? We are British.'

'I said what the devil do you mean, hammering on my door at this hour?'

'We were h-hoping you might administer the Holy S-Sacrament. In case we d-drown.'

'It wants twenty to two in the morning!'

'We appreciate the lateness of the hour, sir, but it is most – *most* important that you administer the Holy Sacrarament, so that we do not go to hell.'

'To hell? That is precisely where you deserve to go, waking decent gentlemen at all hours of the night! Get out of here at once, before I call the watch, do you hear? Go to hell indeed, sir! Good night, gentlemen – if I may call you that!'

Maynard withdrew and slammed the door loudly in their faces, leaving the pair alone in the darkened street.

'Hamond?'

'Y-yes?'

'I don't think that went particularlarly well.'

The Patagonian shore lay low on the horizon, no more than an ill-defined smudge of blue on the starboard beam. The *Beagle* plunged through the swell, holding her course loosely, sacrificing navigational precision for speed, lest any rudder adjustments slow her progress. FitzRoy was keen to get south, to carry out the task in hand. They had been delayed quite enough by indiscriminate gunfire, by army mutinies and by grand celebrations. The fossils had been successfully dispatched to England and the decks were pristine once more – how Wickham would have approved, had he been present. A repentant Darwin lay curled on the chart table in the throes of sickness, as so often before, except that this time the sea had little to do with his condition. Hamond, who was in a similar state, could enjoy no such luxury, but instead suffered in silence at his station, a pale, dull-headed presence on the maindeck. His only consolation, perhaps, was that his condition did not stand out, for it was the first morning of official winter beard growth. With the breeze getting up, and drizzle flecking their faces, all the crew sported rough coats, greased boots, south-westers and a day's stubble.

There were exceptions to this grimy parade, of course: Jemmy Button could be seen promenading around the deck in a dress-coat of well-brushed scarlet broadcloth, a cravat, a fob watch and his favourite white kid gloves. He had manfully sweated his way through the tropics in this and similar outfits, and now that the weather had cooled down was reaping the reward for his persistence. All knew, however, that the smallest blemish on his boots, the faintest smear of tar or grease, would send him scurrying below, to where Messrs Day and Martin kept the officers' shoe-cleaning materials. Jemmy was also clean-shaven, and York likewise, for the Fuegians concurred with the better elements of British society in regarding facial hair as rather primitive, more a matter for beasts than for men; although these days, of course, the two Fuegians used a razor, rather than plucking out each hair with a sharpened mussel-shell. As for their mentor, the Reverend Mr Matthews, he, too, wore no beard for the simple reason that he had tried and failed to grow one.

The only member of the crew who would naturally have sported any facial growth, Augustus Earle, had suddenly left the ship in Monte Video. Officially, the artist had cited advancing rheumatism, a condition that would not have benefited from the bleak chill of a southern summer, but many suspected that a certain competing attraction in the Uruguayan capital had also influenced his decision. His last-minute replacement, the little Anglo-Austrian Conrad Martens, now sat in the lee of the poop deck, wrapped in a tight Petersham coat, completing a topographical sketch of the coastline. Fuegia Basket, still religiously attired in her increasingly shabby royal bonnet, peered over his shoulder for a moment, then skipped up the companionway to hold York Minster's hand. As she did so, Mr Matthews stepped diplomatically to the other side of the burly Indian. For all his attempts to ingratiate himself with the Fuegians, he had learned the hard way that it was not a good idea to cross the invisible line separating York from his beloved.

'What are you doing?' Fuegia asked Sulivan, who was standing at the rail with a spyglass, jotting down notes with a metallic pencil.

'I'm keeping a geological record of the coastline. I'm writing down all the stones. For the philosopher, who is too sick to do it himself.'

He showed her his pad, upon which he had scribbled: '*Thick white layer. Chalk? Pumiceous? Layer of porphyry pebbles above.*'

'Poor, poor Philos,' said Jemmy. 'He does not like when the boat goes up and down.'

'Absolutely,' said Sulivan, sparing Darwin's blushes as to the real cause of his sickness.

'My confidential friend Mr Bynoe will make him better. He has many good medicines.' Jemmy had taken to calling Bynoe his 'confidential friend' after trying out various of his remedies for stomach upsets and minor ailments. In fact, so impressed had Jemmy been with Bynoe's assortment of jars and bottles that the incidence of his supposed illnesses had escalated dramatically. It was a rare day indeed when he could not be seen marching proudly from the sickbay with a phial of Gregory's powder, calomel or some other such purgative.

Suddenly York seized Sulivan by the arm, his normally implacable features lit up by surprise. 'Look, Mr Sulivan, look! A bird, all same as a horse!'

'Where?' Sulivan spun round.

'There! Running on beach! A bird, all same as a horse!'

'On the beach?' Even Sulivan, with his astonishingly keen vision, could barely make out the beach, let alone any details thereon. 'Do you see anything, Jemmy?'

'Oh yes, Mr Sulivan, a big bird. It is running fast. It is a tip-top goer!'

'Bird all same as a horse!' parroted Fuegia Basket.

'Blessed if I know what they're talking about,' said a peevish Matthews, squinting at the horizon.

Sulivan raised his spyglass to one eye and scanned the distant shore from left to right. Then, as he scanned back again – there! He saw it. A large male rhea, scampering into the shallows, its powerful thigh-muscles flexing and unflexing with every stride.

'It's a rhea, York, an American ostrich. But that you could see it from here! Captain FitzRoy – an incredible thing, sir.'

FitzRoy came over, and was apprised of the astonishing discovery – made a full two and a half years after they had first come aboard – that the Fuegians' powers of eyesight were well beyond those of normal men.

'I have heard tell of such birds, sir,' said Jemmy dismissively. 'In the land of the Oens-men they are common-or-garden.'

York glared at Jemmy, who took a nervous step behind the tall figure of Sulivan.

There is so much that we do not know about them, thought FitzRoy. *I have been so determined to bring them forward into our world that I have neglected to study what makes their own world so different, so special.*

'Does everybody in your country have such powerful eyesight, Jemmy?'

'Of course, Capp'en Fitz'oy. My tribe is a good tribe, see very far. My country is a good country. Plenty of trees. Plenty of seals. When you see Woollya, you will say, "This is a beautiful country, as beautiful as Great Britain."'

Jemmy favoured FitzRoy with a warm, proud smile. FitzRoy smiled back.

He has not seen his country for nigh on three years, he thought. *By the Lord's grace, I hope he shall not be in for a rude shock.*

Chapter Fifteen

Good Success Bay, Tierra del Fuego, 17 December 1832

The *Beagle* nosed cautiously into a thick bank of alabaster fog. Even here, in the safest anchorage on the east coast of Tierra del Fuego, it was as well to be careful. Since its discovery by Captain Cook in the previous century, the bay had yet to be surveyed properly, so the little brig felt her way forward, her decks cool and damp in the waxy air of the early morning, her sails hanging limp. Momentary eddies in the mist revealed only the dark, featureless forest: scores of fallen beech trees lay uncleared amid the ranks of their silent fellows, like a battalion of foot-soldiers cut down by musket fire, frozen for ever at the moment of impact. The vegetation was as thick as in any tropical jungle, yet here it was drained of all colour and movement. In these solitudes death, not life, seemed the predominant spirit.

Their voyage south had taken them through a series of startling natural phenomena, as if nature wished to signal that the boundaries of human civilization had been crossed, that they were entering her domain. Each spectacle had been more extraordinary than the last. Not far south of the river Plate, they had woken one morning to find the *Beagle* turned red. The entire ship was covered from topmast to keel by miniature crimson spiders, millions upon millions of them, each furiously competing to trace out its gossamer web in the calm morning air. The first breath of wind had blown them all out to sea in an agitated red cloud, never to be seen again. Then, off the Bay of San Blas, it had snowed butterflies. A vast white cloud of fluttering wings two hundred yards high, a mile wide and several miles deep had enveloped the ship. Fuegia Basket had stood in the heart of the blizzard, twirling and flapping her arms with delight. They were, calculated Darwin, a variety of *Colias edusa*. But what had caused these huge migrations? The animals were hurtling to their destruction, but to what end? It was hard to see a purpose, divine or otherwise, in this almighty extermination.

Near the entrance to the Straits of Magellan the sea itself had turned crimson: the cause, they soon determined, a monstrous shoal of tiny crustaceans. But more impressive still were the humpback whales that twisted and churned at the centre of the maelstrom, gorging themselves on their infinitesimal prey by the ton. One great beast flung himself almost completely out of the water, landing with a magnificent crash that sent a shudder through the hull of the *Beagle*; and Darwin remembered Midshipman King, and his earnest claims made out on the verandah of the little house at Corcovado, and he wished then that he had not seen fit to doubt his young chum.

This clammy morning in Good Success Bay found a quiet, solitary figure up at the cathead, half enveloped in mist. Bynoe, taking his morning constitutional around the deck – as surgeon he was spared the discomfort of night watches – spotted Jemmy Button there, and sensed at once from the Fuegian's defeated posture that something was wrong.

'Jemmy? Are you all right?'

'My confidential friend.'

The greeting was not delivered in Jemmy's usual effusive

style; rather, it came out in a husky croak, and Bynoe could see that his eyes were rimmed with wet.

'Jemmy? Have you been crying? What is the matter?'

'My father is dead.'

'Your father . . . ? What makes you think that?'

'A man came beside my hammock in the night. He told me.'

'What man? York Minster?' Jemmy and York messed together, forward with the crew. Fuegia, for obvious reasons, slept aft at the officers' end of the ship.

'No, not York Minster. A man.'

'A crewman?'

'Not man from this world, Mr Bynoe. A man from this other world.'

'That's a dream, Jemmy, just a dream.'

Jemmy shook his head. 'No, my confidential friend. Not a dream. A man from this other world. My father is dead. It is very bad.' He reached up and wiped the corner of his eye with his sleeve.

'Jemmy . . . I am sure that when we get back to Woollya you will see that your father is alive and well. Mark my words.'

Jemmy smiled, with pity and affection combined, at Bynoe's lack of understanding; and the surgeon could not think of anything else to say.

Further along the rail, FitzRoy scanned the curtain of white and called for another depth sounding. Forty fathoms, came back the reply, and clean sand as before. Still, the billowing fog would reveal nothing. Darwin came to join him, glad of the chance to be up and about at last.

'My dear FitzRoy, whatever do you look like in that beard? It has become quite patriarchal!'

'Much like yourself, I should imagine.'

'I? I resemble nothing so much as a half-washed chimney-sweeper!' Darwin grasped his own enormous beard, leaving a gingery tuft protruding from his clenched fist. 'What a pair we must make. Tell me, my dear friend, shall I have a chance to explore the beech forest?'

'Of course, when the fog lifts. But be careful. Stick to the guanaco paths. When Cook was here, Mr Banks and Dr Solander mounted an expedition into the forest and became lost. Then night fell, and two of the men died of cold. Solander himself was lucky to escape with his life. I should not wish the same fate to befall our own dear Philosopher.'

'Rest assured, I—'

Darwin's next words were cut off by a blood-curdling cry from the forest. It was a human cry – at least, he thought it was a human cry – but it seemed to him an utterly primeval sound, a harsh, rudimentary cry left over from the dawn of creation. Then, as if on cue, the milky curtain parted to reveal the source of the noise. There, not eighty yards distant, on a wild crag overhanging the sea, perched a small group of naked Fuegians. As they became visible to the *Beagle*'s crew, so they became aware of the ship and sprang up, gesticulating and yelling, their long hair streaming, each of them waving their tattered guanaco-skin cloaks. In answer to their calls, other ragged, yelling creatures emerged from the entangled forest, until the little crag was clustered with frantic, energized figures. One young Fuegian, his face daubed black with a single white band, began to hurl stones, as if to drive the *Beagle* away, but of course the projectiles fell well short of their intended target.

'My God,' breathed Darwin. 'They are naked. Absolutely naked, in this inclement country. I had never, ever imagined anything like this. It is incredible.'

Those who had not journeyed south on the first voyage were transfixed. Hamond stood open-mouthed at the rail. Matthews, although he kept his feelings in check, could not disguise his fascination. Those like FitzRoy, who knew the Fuegians well, watched the watchers, riveted to see again their own initial reactions.

'Look – look at that one on the right!' Darwin pointed out an older man, with circles of white paint round his eyes, his upper lip daubed with red ochre, his tangled hair gathered in a fillet of white feathers. 'He is like a stage devil from *Der Freischutz*! My God, FitzRoy, they are demoniacs! They are like – like the troubled spirits of another world!'

'They are no worse than I supposed them to be,' said Matthews piously.

Hamond shook his head sadly. 'What a p-pity such fine fellows should be left in such a b-barbarous state.'

'Fine fellows?' Darwin raised his eyebrows. 'I would hardly dignify them with the description "fine fellows". They are hideous! Their growth is stunted, their features are literally beastly, their skin is red and filthy, their hair is greasy and tangled, their voices are discordant and their gestures are violent! To think Rousseau believed that savages in a state of nature would lead idyllic lives! Why, if the world was searched, no lower grade of men could be found. They are barbarians, my dear Hamond, utter barbarians!'

'They are ignorant and savage, perhaps,' said FitzRoy softly, 'but not contemptible. Does not the example of our friend Jemmy here indicate what may be done to improve their lot?'

For the first time, the officers at the rail turned to look at Jemmy. His face, they realized, was burning with shame and humiliation.

'Philos is right,' he said, jabbing out each word. 'These men are not men. They are beasts. Fools. My land is quite different. My tribe is quite different. You will see. My friends will be happy to see Capp'en Fitz'oy. My friends will honour Capp'en Fitz'oy, will honour all *Beagle*. These men are *beasts*.'

Four days later, Darwin arrived at dinner clutching a copy of Commodore Byron's *Narrative*; it was an uncannily calm and sunny day off Cape Horn, and Bynoe's skill as a marksman had provided their table with a fat roast steamer duck each.

'So much for the famous Horn,' remarked Darwin breezily. 'A gale of wind is not so bad in a good sea-boat. Have you read this?'

'I suggest you wait until we ship a sea or two before you write off the famous Horn,' replied FitzRoy drily. 'And yes, I have.'

'Not only are these Fuegians of yours cannibals, it would seem they practise incest and bigamy as well. After the shipwreck Byron lived with a native who had two wives, one of whom was his daughter! And he beat them both regularly! Poor Byron was treated as a dog – quite literally. They fed him on scraps.'

'Disagreeable as it is to contemplate a savage, Philos, and unwilling as we may be to consider ourselves even remotely descended from human beings in such a state, remember that Caesar found the Ancient Britons painted and clothed in skins exactly like the Fuegians.'

'Worst of all,' said Darwin, ignoring him, 'is this passage here:

"A little boy of about three years old, watching for his father and mother's return, ran into the surf to meet them; the father handed a basket of sea-eggs to the child, which being too heavy for him to carry, he let it fall; upon which the father jumped out of the canoe, and catching the boy up in his arms, dashed him with the utmost violence against the stones. The poor little creature lay motionless and bleeding, and died soon after. The brute his father shewed little concern about it."

'Was a more horrid deed ever perpetrated? They are the most grotesque race. I feel quite a disgust at the very sound of the voices of these miserable savages!'

'Forgive me, Philos, but I think you are wrong to distinguish them as a race. I think there is more variance between any two individuals than between the different races. Could three more distinct individuals exist than Jemmy, York and Fuegia? Yet are any of them so very different from Englishmen you have met?'

'Well, it is true that I could scarcely have believed how wide was the difference between a savage and a civilized man. It is more strikingly marked than between a wild animal and a domesticated pet! But is that not what you have done with your three savages – tamed them, like dogs? They do not yet appear to boast of human reason or of the arts consequent to that reason. Take these very ducks, here. What was it York Minster said, when Bynoe shot them? "Oh, Mr Bynoe, now much rain, much snow, blow much." It appears the steamer duck is some sort of sacred animal to him! He considers the elements themselves to be avenging angels! Only in a race so little advanced could the elements become personified so. It is absurd.'

'If you will suffer me to object, Philos, you say they are backward, and do not share all our qualities, but what of their own qualities? What of their astonishing gift for mimicry? They can instantly memorize and repeat several lines of an alien tongue!'

'Come now, that is merely a consequence of the more practised habits of perception, and the keener senses, common to all men in a savage state.'

'What of their unique powers of eyesight?'

'They live upon the sea! It is well known that sailors, from long practice, can make out a distant object better than a landsman.'

'What of their powers of intuition?'

'Such powers are more strongly marked in women, as well as being characteristic of the lower races. They are powers characteristic of a past and lower state of civilization. Does not man achieve a higher eminence, in whatever he takes up, than a woman can attain? There is your proof.'

'You continue to speak of the "lower races". There are no such things. Genesis one, twenty-six: "And God said let us make man in our image." There is nothing in the scriptures about lower men. Genesis nine, nineteen: By the three sons of Noah "was the whole earth overspread". Esau begat the copper-coloured race, with the daughter of Ishmael. No doubt the climate, and their diet, and their habit of living have all helped to adapt them, but they are men, Philos, just as you and I.' *Please, my friend, it feels as if I am losing you. Please turn back before it is too late, for this way blasphemy lies.*

'My dear FitzRoy, the races may have been *conceived* in equality, but who would deny that they are now utterly distinct and utterly unequal? The emotional and intellectual faculties of the Fuegian Indian have been diminished. Their language scarcely deserves to be called articulate – it sounds like a man clearing his throat. Even their gestures are unintelligible! If, as you say, they have been rendered hideous by cold, want of food and lack of civilization, then have they not *become* a lower race? What skills they have may now be compared to the instinct of animals, for they do not seem to be improved by experience. Their canoes, for instance, have not changed at all since Byron wrote his book a hundred years ago.'

'The fact that their society has degenerated does not make them a lesser race. They are innocent, that is all – innocent of so much. What of the English, when the Romans left our shores? Were we then a "lesser race"? Progress is a social ideal, not a measure of physical development. History is not by definition a process of improvement.'

'You think not? I tell you, FitzRoy, at some future period, not very distant I imagine, the civilized races of man will almost certainly exterminate and replace the savage races throughout the world. It is already happening. Wherever the European has trod, death pursues the Aboriginal. Varieties of man act upon each other as do species of animal. The strong extirpate the weak. There is nothing we can do about it.'

'Yes, there is. I have tried in my small way to do something about it. I do not compete with the Fuegians. I support and encourage them because I am a Christian and such is God's command.'

'But not all men are as upright, as dedicated to God's truth as you are, my dear friend. Already the Europeans are reaching further south, beyond Punta Alta. The Fuegians cannot survive, just as the Aborigines of Australia cannot survive, or any other of the degraded races of blacks. And when the higher apes, the anthropomorphous apes, are exterminated in turn, then the divide between man and the animal kingdom will be even greater, and civilized man will reign supreme.'

'What do you mean, "the divide between man and the animal kingdom will be even greater"? How can it become greater, or lesser?'

'I mean the gap between the Caucasian and the lower apes – such as the baboon – is greater than the gap between, say, the Negro and the gorilla.'

'What are you saying? I cannot believe you are saying this!'

'Come, FitzRoy. Look at the orang-utan – its affection, its passion, its rage, its sulkiness, its despair. Then look at the savage – naked, artless, roasting its parent. Your Fuegians remind me of nothing so much as an orang-utan taking tea at the zoological gardens. Compare the Fuegian and the orang-utan and *dare* to say that the difference is so great.'

FitzRoy was angry now.

'Oh, I *dare* to say that, Philos, I *dare* indeed. We humans – notice how I use the word *we* – walk on two legs; the apes – be they "higher" or "lower" – walk on four. We humans feel love and affection, and reason, and shame, and embarrassment, and pride. The apes have only a breeding season, a cycle of sexual receptiveness. We have a complex vocal language. They do not. We are, in the main, hairless. They are covered from head to toe in fur. They are *animals*. You can civilize a human, *as I have proved*. You cannot take an orang-utan to enjoy a civilized conversation with His Majesty the King of England.'

'My dear FitzRoy, I can see that I have angered you. I do not set up for one second to deny that man is created by God to reign over the animals, that the two are utterly separate, that there can be no transmutation between one and the other. As I told you, I have no truck with Lamarck. I meant only that the Fuegians have fallen so far as to *adopt* some of the ways of the animal kingdom. They seem to exist, for instance, in a state of equality like a herd of cattle; a way of living that can only retard civilization and prevent improvement. And man here is in a lower state of improvement than in any other part of the world.'

FitzRoy did not know whether to make concessions to Darwin's conciliatory tone or go on the attack; but he was saved from the need to decide by a knock at the door.

It was Sulivan. 'I'm afraid it begins to look pretty filthy to westward, sir. The barometer is falling. I think you had better come on deck.'

FitzRoy rose. 'Well, Philos. It seems you spoke too soon about the famous Horn.'

What had begun as an ominous line of inky clouds on the western horizon was to become a twenty-four-day nightmare for the crew of the *Beagle*, as gale after gale pinned them just to the west of Cape Horn. Pummelling winds and relentless seas battered them day and night, until everyone and everything in the ship was drenched. At the end of each watch the exhausted men, with no dry clothes to change into, turned in 'full standing': bones aching, they retreated to their soaking hammocks still wrapped in their sopping oilskins, and fell asleep in an instant.

The temperature plummeted. Even though it was supposedly the middle of summer, the watch on deck were whipped by sharp snowflakes and stung by driving hail. It was impossible to stand upright below decks, and almost as difficult on deck, where the planking had become a slippery sheet of ice. Masts, spars, rigging, everything was sheathed in a thick icy coat, which had to be continually chipped off at severe risk to life and limb. Even the officers of the watch froze into ghastly attitudes, their oilskins masked with ice, lashed to the wheel under a crazily swinging oil lamp. Great green rollers powered ceaselessly aboard, a good foot of water coursing freely through the gunports, but the momentary relief such waves afforded, being warmer than the air, was soon lost as further layers of ice crusted quickly on the men's clothes.

In the poop cabin behind the wheel, Darwin lay in a permanent pool of vomit, his specimens ruined, his dried-flower collection a sodden mess. Christmas came and went, and New Year too, but nobody noticed. There was no sign of a let-up in the mountainous breaking seas. Finally, on 13 January, through sheets of spray that obscured the horizon, they caught sight of the stark black tower of York Minster, their destination, looming amid driving clouds. They had come just a hundred miles in three and a half weeks.

'There she is, sir – jolly old York Minster!' yelled Bennet cheerily over the howling wind.

'Excellent!' FitzRoy was in a good mood. He had just been to inspect the chronometers with Stebbing. Oilskin thrown off, his head wrapped in a towel to prevent dripping, he had dried the glass top of each machine and scattered flour upon it. Then, through a magnifying glass, he had checked the grains for signs of vibration or slippage from the horizontal. Nothing. Every chronometer and every gimbal was in perfect working order.

'Biblical weather, ain't it, sir?' roared Sulivan.

'Now we know how Noah felt,' added Bennet. 'Do you think we shall have the full forty days and forty nights?'

'"In the morning thou shalt say, would God it were even. And at even thou shalt say, would God it were morning!"' Sulivan laughed out loud. FitzRoy gave silent thanks that the men of the *Beagle* were so indefatigable, so good-natured, whatever the obstacles placed in their way.

An albatross wheeled about the ship, gliding effortlessly against the buffeting wind. On each pass it would sweep gracefully down into the wave-troughs, breaking the occasional crest with an exploratory wingtip, before soaring up the face of the next rising arch, never once needing to flap its wings.

'That bird. How long has it been following us?' FitzRoy asked, disappearing up to his thighs in a surge of green seawater.

'As long as we've been on watch, sir.'

'And has it been flying clockwise about the ship throughout?'

'Yes sir. Leastways, I think they always do fly clockwise, sir.'

'I wonder – is that because of the magnetism of the earth? If one were to release an albatross in the northern hemisphere, would it fly anticlockwise?'

'Shall we try to catch it, sir?'

'No, no. I do not wish to lose an officer to the cause of natural philosophy, however noble the enquiry. But it leads one to ponder the incredible migrations of birds, their astonishing sense of direction – might it be magnetic, do you think?'

Another peak furled across the deck, water blasting violently through the gunports. FitzRoy yelled into Sulivan's ear, 'Mr Sulivan, would you ask Mr May to have the gunports secured? Let us try to reduce the amount of water on deck. It is like trying to stand in a sluice.'

'Pardon me, sir, but do you think that is a good idea? The weather is worsening. If any really big waves get up, and the deck becomes flooded, fixed gunports could trap the water in the ship, sir.'

He indicated the line of cliffs off to the north-east, all of two hundred feet in height, where a vast battering surf was sending spray scattering over the cliff-tops.

'Let us put our faith in the old girl – she is more buoyant than she used to be,' insisted FitzRoy.

'Very well, sir.' And Sulivan rushed off in the gap between waves to locate the carpenter. He found May in the galley, desperately trying to warm himself against the scalding iron of Mr Frazer's patent closed stove.

'Mr May? Captain says you're to secure all the gunports.'

May sighed. Although hardly dry, he had at least steamed a little water out of his saturated clothing over the preceding two hours. Now he was to go back on deck, and give himself another soaking. 'Aye aye sir.'

'And Mr May?'

'Sir?'

Sulivan hesitated. He would never countenance disobeying any superior officer, but this was not exactly disobedience.

'Keep your handspike about you in case they need to be opened in a hurry.'

'Sir.'

On the way back up to the maindeck, Sulivan put his head round the door of FitzRoy's cabin to check on Edward Hellyer. It was the young clerk's first real storm.

'You all right, young man?'

'Yes sir, thank you, sir.' Hellyer, pale and scared, did not look at all convinced.

Sulivan glanced over the boy's shoulder at the ship's log. 'Hard at hand, I see,' he said approvingly, and scanned the boy's work. 'Well done, Mr Hellyer. That's first-rate. When we look back and argue about this here blow, your log is the place we'll come for all our answers. You're doing a splendid job.' He clapped Hellyer on the back and the lad seemed to brighten up, for the moment at least.

By the time half an hour had elapsed, it was clear that an already desperate situation was getting worse. FitzRoy's concern was for the masts, which for all their girth were straining like saplings. 'We must take the topgallant sails off her. She is careening to her bearings.'

Bos'n Sorrell resorted to the speaking-trumpet: 'Very well, my lads, very well indeed! Topgallants clewed up and furled!' In an instant the icy rigging was alive with dark shapes, carrying out the order with well-drilled precision.

'I fear, sir, we cannot carry the topsails much longer,' said Sulivan. He knew that FitzRoy liked to keep a main topsail and five reefs as a minimum, even in the worst weather, to ensure steerage way. But such a rig would be impossible to maintain any further: the wind was screaming through the rigging now, and increasingly mountainous seas were rising ominously beneath the ship. The boundary between sky and sea was becoming blurred: seething white froth filled the air, and breakers were hurling themselves continuously across the deck. FitzRoy gave orders to take her down to storm trysails, close-reefed. He was now barely in charge of the *Beagle*: the storm had all but wrested control of her.

The men were still in the rigging when they saw coming towards them, head-on, a vast, implacable cliff of grey water advancing at speed. *Dear God*, thought FitzRoy, *that wave is almost as tall as the boat is long. A monster.* The equation was simple. Any taller, and they would go down. Any less, and they might ride it. With mounting horror, he saw Nicholas White, the seaman clinging to the jib-boom end, disappear into the face of the wave a good fathom under, as the little brig tried desperately to climb its featureless slope. All on deck stood frozen with fear. The two men clinging to the staysail netting were next to disappear, as the wave swallowed the *Beagle*'s entire bow. But she was still rising, her deck sloping further and further back, until it seemed she must be catapulted vertically into the raging sky. Then, at last, she breasted the wave, and FitzRoy felt his stomach plummet with the ship as she surfed crazily down the other side. There was White, still alive, gasping on the jib-boom; there were the sailors on the staysail netting, spluttering and choking but indubitably alive.

Any relief FitzRoy might have felt was short-lived. Another towering, monstrous wave was racing in on the heels of the first, only this time the *Beagle*'s momentum had been checked, her way deadened. She sat motionless in the water, waiting for the impact. There was nothing anybody could do but pray, and hold on tight.

The wave crashed front-on into the bow with a sickening shudder. The ship trembled from end to end at the shock. A pulverizing mass of green smashed across the deck, driving the air from the sailors' gasping lungs. Darwin, who had been shivering in his hammock, too sick to sense the danger outside, suddenly found himself submerged, as a wall of freezing seawater blasted the library door from its hinges and engulfed him. Again the *Beagle* tried to rise up the face of the wave, but this time she was only partially successful. She slewed wildly to port before tipping crazily over the crest and careening sideways down the backslope. Not only was her momentum checked now, but she was sitting beam-on, dead at the helm and thrown off the wind. If a third wave came, she was a sitting duck.

All eyes squinted fearfully into the driving sleet, trying to separate the scudding black clouds from the maddened, frothing water. Then they saw it: a third wave, taller than a townhouse, towering over the *Beagle*, bearing down upon them. The ship lolled, helplessly, like a beaten drunk trying to stand up and throw a last punch. *We're going to drown. What is it like to drown?* was all that anybody aboard the *Beagle* could think.

Like a broadside of cannon from a mighty frigate, the wave smacked hard into the ship's side, its whole immense crushing weight pounding on to her deck. The world simply turned black. Men floundered and struggled and fought, not to keep their balance or their bearings but to live, just to live. Then the world cleared, but it had been turned on its side. The *Beagle* was on her beam-ends, her lee bulwark three feet under, and she was struggling unsuccessfully to rise again. The lee-quarter boat, a brand-new reinforced whaleboat constructed by Messrs William Johns of Plymouth on the diagonal principle, and mounted several feet higher than the whaleboats of the previous voyage, had filled with water and disintegrated as surely as if it had been made from pasteboard; but its new improved davits clung stubbornly to the *Beagle*, refusing to let go, the wreckage of the whaleboat threatening to drag its mother ship down into the lightless depths.

The port side of the deck was trapped several feet under, labouring under a colossal weight of water that could not escape, Sulivan realized, because of the sealed gunports. Through a faceful of blinding spray he saw FitzRoy, Bennet and a terrified Hamond at the lee quarter, helped by three ratings, hacking at the tangled whaleboat davits with hatchets; but at the bulwark there was only Carpenter May, up to his waist in water, struggling vainly with his handspike to free one of the secured gunports beneath the surface. Sulivan splashed frantically across the deck to May, seized the handspike, plunged into the frozen darkness, located the gunport, and with one burly heave, burst it wide open. Immediately, water surged out through the newly opened escape route, and slowly, very slowly, the *Beagle* began to right herself.

A fourth wave now, all of them knew, and they were dead men. Now, with the gunport open and the wreckage of the whaleboat cut adrift, all eyes looked to windward, screwed up against the blinding sleet, searching for the fourth and final instalment, the wave that would bring about their end. But it did not come. For twenty, thirty, forty seconds they waited, as the *Beagle* rose agonizingly back towards an even keel, staring into the maelstrom. But the fourth wave did not come.

'What would Captain Beaufort have called that, then? A force fifteen?' Sulivan was breezy and light-headed with relief. Driven almost back to Cape Horn by the storm, they had run in behind False Cape Horn and sought refuge in the Goree Roads. There they had dropped anchor in forty-seven fathoms, friendly sparks flashing from the windlass as the chain hurtled round it, to rest and lick their wounds.

'I made a terrible mistake. You saved all our lives. After all the modifications I made to the *Beagle*, I thought . . . Well, the simple fact is, I was too proud.'

'Hang it, sir, that's tosh and you know it. You cannot blame yourself every time we run through a bad blow. It was the modifications that saved us. The old *Beagle* would have been crushed to matchwood. Yet not a spar was lost, nor a single man for that matter.'

'I should never have ordered the gunports secured. You were right and I was wrong.'

'The man has not been born, sir, who never makes a mistake,' responded Sulivan. 'All of us make mistakes, all the time. It is how one reacts to one's mistakes that is the measure of a man.'

'Put like that, Mr Sulivan, I suppose it does sound better,' conceded FitzRoy.

'That's more like it, sir. Now, shouldn't you be sitting here with charts and diagrams, trying to discover the measure of that storm?'

'There is no need. I have its measure already. You forget, I have had twenty-four days to think upon it.'

'And?'

'And the globe spins eastward. So does water, at a greater velocity – although with many a back-eddy. The atmosphere, which is almost free of obstacles, spins yet faster still. It too has back-eddies of wind, which articulate storm-breeding counter-spirals near the poles – together with a steady-flowing undertow at the equator – that's the trade winds. All the elements are pluming forward to the east, all of them by-products of the pull that affects the earth. You see? The weather may appear unpredictable, Mr Sulivan, but it is not. Its effects are complicated, but its core principle, as laid down by God, is blindingly simple. And if we understand the mechanical principle behind it, there is no reason to doubt that, one day, we shall be able to foretell the weather.'

FitzRoy had become increasingly animated as he warmed to his pet enthusiasm, the cares of leadership slipping visibly from his shoulders; Sulivan regretted that Darwin chose that very moment to march in and interrupt the captain's monologue.

'Good morning, Philos. I trust this lovely calm morning finds you well?'

Darwin stood and stared at FitzRoy as if he were quite mad to ask such a question, after all that they had endured. But having held the pose for a moment he relaxed suddenly, and shook his head in bemused wonderment.

'It's my own fault, I suppose, for agreeing to spend several years cooped up in your little cock-boat. All my papers and specimens are ruined – *all* of them – and not a few of my books. Luckily volume two of Lyell is unscathed, for I have not yet commenced it, as is my copy of *Persuasion*, for all that it is worth.'

FitzRoy roared with laughter. 'All of those unique specimens lost, and the means to interpret them, but you still have your Jane Austen! Why, we will turn you into a gossiping fishwife yet! Pray tell, Philos, why on earth you have such frivolities in your possession.'

'My sister Caroline packed it for me. It seems my family think you to be quite the Captain Wentworth, for some reason. And I suppose, after yesterday, that they are right.'

'Oh, but we have Mr Sulivan to thank for yesterday's heroics.'

'Not a bit of it!' protested Sulivan. 'But see here, Philos – I have brought you a present.' He leaned down under the table and produced a carefully wrapped box. 'Something else that survived yesterday's tribulations.'

'What is it?'

'The start of your new collection.'

Darwin unwrapped the packing and levered off the lid to reveal a sweetly glowing nasturtium flower – except that it was twice the size of any nasturtium he had ever seen before.

'It is a *Tropaeolum*. I discovered it in the Brazils. A *Tropaeolum majus*, I suppose, if its Peruvian cousin were to become the *minus*.'

'But, Sulivan, this is your very own specimen – I cannot possibly accept it as a gift!'

'You can, Philos, and you will. Thy need is greater than mine.'

'It is remarkable – wonderful! My dear fellow!'

'Mind you keep the little chap warm, now. I wedge him behind the galley stove at night, and stand him beneath the skylight by day.'

'You are too kind. I am overwhelmed.'

There was a knock at the door.

'Bless me,' murmured FitzRoy. 'The place is become like Regent Circus this morning. Come!'

FitzRoy's steward opened the door, and the three men could see the burly figure of York Minster silhouetted behind him.

'Er . . . Mr Minster, sir,' said the steward, unsure exactly as to how one might introduce such a 'gentleman'.

'Do come in, York, if you can find room.'

The Fuegian moved forward, as impassive as ever, although FitzRoy thought he detected a shade of contempt at the sight of three grown men sitting round a flower.

'I am sorry that we have failed to reach your homeland, York,' FitzRoy went on. 'Perhaps it was a mistake to try the direct route. But rest assured, I will get you there, either via the Magellan Straits and the Cockburn Channel, or by following the Beagle Channel westward to the sea. Here, let me show you a map.'

'York wishes not to go home.'

'I beg your pardon?'

'York wishes not to go home. York and Fuegia will live at Woollya with Jemmy, and Mister Matthews.'

'But the Woollya people are not of your tribe, York. That might be extremely dangerous, both for you and for her.'

'York wishes not to go home. York and Fuegia will live at Woollya with Jemmy, and Mister Matthews.'

There was silence in the little cabin. FitzRoy stared at York. Was he afraid of any further sailing? Would Matthews's mission represent a link to the world he was leaving behind? Or did he have some deeper plan? The Fuegian's face gave nothing away.

'Very well, York,' he said. 'So be it.'

They found the eastern entrance to the Beagle Channel easily enough, to the north of the Goree Roads, concealed behind Picton Island. There were thirty-three in the party, divided between the remaining three whaleboats: FitzRoy, Darwin, Bennet, Hamond, Bynoe, the Reverend Mr Matthews, the three Fuegians, and twenty-four sailors and marines. Sulivan had been left in command of the *Beagle*. Towed behind them was the yawl, into which had been loaded all the tools and implements needed to build the mission, together with the fabulous assortment of goods donated by the Church Missionary Society.

The early reaches of the channel were not as arrow-straight as the central section where they had discovered Jemmy, nor were the forested sides as vertiginous. There were settlements along the shore, where the arrival of three boatloads of pale-skinned human beings caused nothing less than a seismic shock. As they tacked slowly up the channel into the prevailing westerlies – the yawl being so overloaded that only sailpower could drag it forward – they saw panic-stricken, gasping men running at speed along the shore to spread news of their arrival. The runners were naked, their hair matted with clay and their faces decorated with white spots, and they ran so fast that blood poured from their noses and foam gurgled from their panting mouths. Canoes began to follow their progress at a distance, each marked by its distinctive plume of blue smoke.

'How incredible,' breathed Darwin, 'to go where man has never yet been.'

York sat back in the lead whaleboat, laughing immoderately. 'They are big monkeys. Fools! Ha ha ha!'

'These people are not my friends,' said Jemmy, his face a mask of shame. 'My friends are different. My friends are very good and clean.'

Fuegia, by contrast, was terrified, and after her first glimpse of the running men would not look again.

She has seen what she truly is, reflected Darwin.

The little girl buried her face in York's lap, her eyes screwed shut – which was a problem, as she had now become so fat that the sailors ideally wanted to shift her position to windward with each tack.

'Big monkeys! Fools!' shouted York, his taunts filling the echoing sound.

FitzRoy stared at Matthews, sitting vacantly in the stern, the breeze ruffling the down on his upper lip. *In many ways he is the fulcrum of all this activity. Yet he shows no emotion. There is no reluctance, no hesitation, but also no enthusiasm, no energy of character.*

Was Matthews steeling himself with quiet stoicism, sitting there in blank-faced silence, or was he just an unqualified teenage catechist, quaking on the inside? FitzRoy attempted the usually unrewarding task of making conversation with him.

'Mr Matthews, how are you looking forward to such a great challenge, which may very well become your life's work?'

'I fully intend that the natives shall receive all instruction in the principles of Christianity, sir, and in the simpler acts of civilised life.'

Another platitude. Surely the Church Missionary Society could have found someone more dynamic for their great enterprise? As they drew closer to their destination, FitzRoy's confidence in the chances of Matthews's success dwindled with every passing mile.

Darwin wiped a splash of seawater from his beard and stared at the youth. *He must be out of his mind*, he thought.

By the time the walls of the Beagle Channel narrowed, and it became recognizable as the ravine they had discovered almost three years previously, there were some thirty canoes in their wake, carrying at least three hundred Indians. Their pursuers stayed back, though – at night their fires were visible off to the east – preferring to shadow the little convoy at a distance. When the *Beagle*'s boats reached the turn-off to the Murray Narrows, the wind funnelling southward out of the channel suddenly filled their sails, and they surged ahead of their retinue. It meant, as they curved back round upon themselves into the bay at Woollya, that they would have a good few hours of peace in which to establish a camp.

For all apart from Jemmy, it was their first sight of Woollya, and the sun nudged aside the persistent grey clouds in celebration. There, in a sheltered cove, nestled an acre or so of rich, sloping pastureland, well watered by brooks and protected on three sides by low, wooded hills. The pretty little natural harbour was studded with islets, the water smooth and glassy, with low branches overhanging a rocky beach. It was so beautiful, so unexpected amid the wilds of Tierra del Fuego, that it possessed an almost dreamlike quality. It was the perfect place to build a mission.

'Jemmy, it's – it's idyllic,' said FitzRoy.

'I told you.' Jemmy beamed with pride. 'My land is good land.'

'The Lord is merciful,' said Matthews, with what sounded like relief.

FitzRoy gave the order to begin unloading the yawl. An area of pasture was staked out for the mission buildings, boundary markers were put up and sentries placed at each corner. There were wigwams over to the north side of the cove, but they were deserted. Darwin investigated a tall green cone on the shoreline, prodding it gingerly with a stick.

'It's a midden. An old shell-midden,' explained FitzRoy.

'Good grief,' said Darwin, withdrawing the stick. 'A nine-inch-thick coating of pure mould. Look – there are seasonal layers. One might be able to date this, like the rings of a tree.'

Something, some primitive instinct, told both men suddenly that they were being watched. They stood stock still, eyes fixed on the treeline. FitzRoy gestured the sailors to quieten their unloading. Each man held his position, tensed, motionless, silent. And then, at last, there was a rustling in the trees, and an extremely old man, painted white from head to toe, emerged into plain view.

'He's as white as a miller,' whispered Darwin.

The old man walked slowly and deliberately in a straight line towards Jemmy Button. The three Fuegians had been standing watching the unloading, Jemmy in his smart scarlet dress-coat and fashionably tight stockings. The white-painted man, ignoring York and Fuegia, took up a position a foot away from Jemmy and defiantly began to harangue him.

FitzRoy and Darwin came cautiously across. Presently the old man finished his tirade.

'What does he say, Jemmy?'

Jemmy stumbled, red-faced with confusion.

'I – I do not know. I do not understand him.'

'But that is your language, is it not?'

'English is my language now. I forget this language.'

'You have *forgotten* your own language?'

'I was young boy when I came with you. For many years I do not need it.' Jemmy turned to the old man. 'I do not understand you. *No sabe.* I do not understand you.' He seemed almost panic-stricken.

'I think he's telling the truth,' said Darwin.

There was another volley from the old man, who gestured angrily to FitzRoy and his companion, followed by an inadvertent guffaw from York Minster.

'Do you understand him, York?' asked FitzRoy sharply. 'Do *you* speak Yamana?'

'Yes.'

'You never told us you could speak Jemmy's language. Not once in three years.'

'You never ask me.'

FitzRoy could have strangled him, in theory at least. 'What does the old man say?'

'He says you are dirty men. You have hairs on your face. That is very dirty.'

'Capp'en Fitz'oy?' said Jemmy nervously.

'Yes, Jemmy?'

'I am afraid to stay here.'

With the Church Missionary Society's collection of soup tureens, tea-trays, beaver hats and fine linen forming another incongruous cone in the centre of the marked-off area, a party of sailors set to chopping the beech-logs, which, with the planking carried in the yawl, would go to construct the three mission cottages. Another group began turning over the topsoil for the vegetable garden, where they would sow carrots, turnips, beans, peas, leeks and cabbages. It was late in the year for planting – the various unforeseen delays on their journey south had seen to that – but many of the sailors had been farm-labourers in more prosperous times, and were sure that the tubers and seedlings would survive. The profusion of wildflowers in the Woollya meadows – none of them known to European eyes – and the rich dark soil, which was softer and more fertile that the usual acidic peat of Tierra del Fuego, augured well.

By the end of the first day, the canoes of the pursuing Fuegians were arriving by the score. Tribesmen came by land too, sweating and exhausted, until eventually a crowd of several hundred had been disgorged on to the beach. What had been a pleasant, deserted Eden became a milling throng, a semi-permanent camp the size of a small town. The Indians sat in naked rows, staring intently at the strange pale men going about their mysterious business. Their principal fascination, however, was reserved for Jemmy Button, who was followed by a hundred pairs of eyes wherever he went: they could not take their eyes off his lurid tail-coats, his polished boots and his gleaming white gloves. Not without trepidation, he went among them handing out little presents, nails, buttons and the like, which were invariably received without a sound or any flicker of expression. The natives of Woollya were, of course, no different from those they had seen further east, and Jemmy felt as naked as they were in his shame.

'They are monkeys. Fools. Not men!' said York with derision. To the Yamana, York appeared as one of the white men, a foreigner by dint of his European clothes; but more than that, he carried an aura about him, a sense of innate power, and they gave him a wide berth.

By night, the Fuegians would steal. No matter how many sentries were posted, the sailors would wake up with items missing – knives, spades, hammers, even their clothes and shoes – for there was nothing the Indians would not take. Even by day, the bolder ones were capable of the most audacious thefts. One Fuegian almost succeeded in removing Hamond's axe from under his arm without his noticing. Just as the haft disappeared, Hamond felt the faintest disturbance and turned to challenge the thief.

'Hey! That's m-my axe!'

The man nodded in supplication and returned the implement gracefully.

FitzRoy tried to defend the Fuegians later that night, as the officers lay in their makeshift tents, mere sailcloths slung across crossed oars.

'Think what treasures such tools represent to these men! Imagine the *Beagle*'s crew, surrounded by untended piles of gold and jewels. What would be the result?'

'We're all going to d-die in our b-beds,' said Hamond gloomily.

On the third day, Jemmy became excited, and announced that his family were approaching. Asked how he knew such a thing, he said that he had heard his brother shouting from his canoe, about a mile and a half away. The Fuegians' powers of hearing, it seemed, was as astonishing as their powers of sight. Sure enough, a quarter-hour later, a canoe containing Jemmy's mother, brothers and sisters swung into the bay. They stared in wonder at his finery, and the little girls blushed and hid in the bottom of the boat. Jemmy's elder brother, who appeared to have been elected spokesman, circled Jemmy cautiously and addressed him at length.

'I do not understand. *No sabe. No sabe.* Why you no speak *English*? Why you *no sabe*?' hissed Jemmy, urgently, and all could see that he was humiliated by the state of his family.

'Fools! Beasts!' chortled York Minster.

Eventually, Jemmy recalled enough rudimentary Yamana to conduct a halting conversation with his brother, punctuated with bursts of English and the occasional Spanish or Portuguese word. He was most concerned to clothe his family as soon as possible, and managed to persuade his mother into a smock. His brother was induced to cover his nakedness with a Guernsey frock, breeches and a lady's tartan cap.

'What does your brother say, Jemmy?' asked FitzRoy, desperate to make sense of whatever he could.

'He says my father is dead. He is dead at the last moon.'

'I am sorry, Jemmy. I am very sorry.'

Incredible. It is just as Bynoe said.

'Me no help it. Me know this already. Also, he say my mother was very sad when I leave. She look for me many months, search every bay, search every island.'

Darwin, who did not believe this for a second, thought that two horses in a field could not have been less interested in each other than Jemmy and the members of his family. In fact, the sound they made when speaking to each other, he concluded, was exactly that made by a man trying to encourage a horse – a sort of clicking noise produced from the side of the mouth. For all this scepticism, however, Jemmy's family became familiar figures around the camp; the elder brother was nicknamed Tommy Button by the sailors, and the younger one Harry Button.

Bennet and Bynoe made earnest efforts to engage with the Fuegians: the coxswain cast embarrassment aside, and sang and danced for them, accompanied by the surgeon on a Jew's harp. The natives' ability to remember and mimic the words was extraordinary, but sadly their sense of rhythm was nonexistent; so much so that when they attempted to join in, despite being word perfect, they would frequently start singing several seconds in arrears.

After two weeks' hard labour the mission was finished, and the crew could look proudly upon three log cabins with thatched roofs and a substantial vegetable garden, the whole enclosed by an elegant white-painted picket fence. The central cottage was given to Matthews, who assiduously furnished it with the best that the charitable ladies of Walthamstow had to offer – lacework, linen and framed samplers embroidered with improving texts – until it looked from the inside like a respectable parlour in rural Essex. The Fuegians were not the only ones capable of nocturnal stealth: all those implements most valuable to the new mission – spades, axes, knives and so forth – had been secreted by night in a false ceiling built into Matthews's cottage, and in a cellar under the floorboards.

The cottage to Matthews's right was given to Jemmy Button, and the cottage to his left to York and Fuegia, who were married – Matthews officiating – in a short ceremony that bewildered most of the participants and nearly all of the onlookers. FitzRoy himself gave the bride away, unsure whether the ceremony represented an important bridge with civilization or a desperate attempt to prolong an unconvincing illusion. They sang a hymn together, and Bennet felt more self-conscious than he had done dancing a jig for the natives.

On the day after the wedding they were due to take their farewells. Darwin emerged bleary-eyed from their tent to a grey and pleasantly sticky morning, rubbed his eyes, and thought about heading down to the shore to begin the daily task of washing his pale flesh before a hundred pairs of bewildered eyes. FitzRoy, pushing the canvas flap aside, crawled out into the daylight and stood beside him.

'Not such a bad day,' ventured the Philosopher.

'I beg to differ,' said FitzRoy abruptly. 'The women and children are gone.'

'I beg your pardon?'

'I said, the women and children are gone. It must mean they are planning an attack. I can think of no other explanation.'

Darwin peered at the patient multitude drawn up in lines beyond the mission's boundary markers. FitzRoy was right. Every single woman and child had vanished, Jemmy's mother and sisters included. Innumerable ranks of seated men returned his gaze implacably. A cold shudder ran down his spine. 'Could we repel such an attack?'

'Repel it? We are outnumbered more than ten to one. Even with guns, I doubt we could repel it. No, my friend, I intend to forestall it.' And FitzRoy stalked off to the perimeter, to discover what, if anything, the sentries had noticed during the night.

Nobody, of course, had seen or heard a thing. But as FitzRoy made his rounds, the old white-painted man stood up and approached McCurdy, one of the foretopmen, who stood at the nearest sentry-post. Nervously, McCurdy planted his feet apart and indicated, as had been made clear many times to the Fuegians, that they should not pass the boundary fence. The old man stared at him.

'He's a regular quiz, this one, sir,' said the sentry edgily. Suddenly, the old man spat directly into his face.

'Do not retaliate!' called FitzRoy. 'Do you hear me, McCurdy? Do *not* retaliate.'

'Aye aye sir.'

'Continue to indicate with your body position that he must not cross the boundary fence.'

'Sir!'

The old man essayed an extremely realistic mime of how McCurdy would shortly be eaten, after he had been first killed and skinned.

'If you retaliate, there will be a massacre. Simply block his path, but try to smile.'

McCurdy managed a glassy grin. The old man produced an axe, one that had been stolen a few days earlier, and raised it threateningly above his head, as if daring the sentry to take it off him. FitzRoy strode across with a rifle and fired into the air. All the Fuegians recoiled at the report of the weapon, but afterwards simply looked confused; a few scratched the backs of their heads, inspecting themselves for damage.

'Obviously they have never encountered a firearm,' said FitzRoy. 'Wait here.'

He ducked into Matthews's cottage and reappeared, holding a cut-glass Walthamstow vase, tapping it to indicate its solidity. Then, with the missionary framed open-mouthed in silent protest between his doorposts, FitzRoy placed the vase at a distance and blew it to pieces with his rifle. The old man stood paralysed with amazement, the stolen axe frozen mid-whirl above his head. A ripple of consternation passed through the native ranks. FitzRoy put down the gun, walked back to the old man, and gently prised the weapon from his fingers, giving him a polite pat on the back as he did so, as if to apologize for the peremptory nature of his display.

'That's told 'em, sir,' muttered McCurdy, under his breath.

The rest of the day passed uneventfully, but there was no hiding the palpable air of tension that clung about both sides of the divide like a chill mist. FitzRoy doubled the guard on the camp that night but, as it turned out, there was no need. When dawn broke, it transpired that – without any of the sentries seeing anything – every single one of the Fuegians had simply melted away. The little cove was utterly deserted.

The sailors' departure was postponed for several days, but the great army of Fuegians did not come back. Were they merely biding their time, or had the display of firepower frightened them away for good? How FitzRoy fervently hoped that the latter was the case, that the little mission would be given a fair chance to take root.

One day in late January he gave the order for Bennet to head back to the *Beagle* with one of the whaleboats and the yawl, while he and the other officers explored and surveyed the western arm of the Beagle Channel. They would return to Woollya to check on the progress of the mission after a month. Lashing rain attended the day of their departure. Before leaving, he went to see Matthews in his snug little parlour, where he found him buried deep in the scriptures.

'I feel obliged to make clear, Mr Matthews, that whatever your heart may feel, if your head tells you to return to England aboard the *Beagle*, then you must grasp the opportunity at once. No shame would attach to you, were you to take that decision. No honest man would blame you for such a course of action.'

'Captain FitzRoy, whether or not I should be blamed is neither here nor there,' replied Matthews blandly. 'The Lord God has given me a task, which I intend to fulfil to the best of my ability.'

He is either extraordinarily brave or he has no real understanding of what he is about to undergo.

'You are certain?'

'Absolutely.'

'Then I wish you the very best of British luck, and may God protect and preserve you.'

'Thank you.'

Down at the little jetty they had constructed, they said their farewells to Jemmy, York and Fuegia.

'You don't have to stay, Jemmy, if you don't want to,' FitzRoy offered. 'You may return to England with us, if you prefer.'

Jemmy shivered damply in his favourite pink suit, a bright slash of incongruous colour against the glowering sky. He stared at his shoes, where teeming raindrops were attempting unsuccessfully to garner a foothold on the glossy leather.

'No, Capp'en Fitz'oy. This is my country. These are my people. These are my friends and my family. I must stay here at Woollya. And – Capp'en Fitz'oy?'

'Yes Jemmy?'

'Thank you, Capp'en Fitz'oy.'

'Thank *you*, Jemmy.'

'Goodbye, Jemmy, old son,' said Bennet.

'Goodbye, Mr Bennet.'

'Now you'll be able to build that city you always dreamed about,' added Bennet softly. 'That big white city, with wide avenues, and squares, and fountains, and coaches, and all the ladies and gentlemen parading about.'

'Maybe one day you will come back to see it, Mr Bennet?'

'Yes, Jemmy, yes, I will. I will come back to see it.' And Bennet felt himself crumple inside, and he hugged Jemmy tightly, as much to disguise the tears that were coursing down his cheeks as anything else.

'Goodbye, Jemmy,' said Bynoe.

'Goodbye, my *confidential* friend.'

A little round cannonball rushed at FitzRoy, almost knocking him over. 'Fuegia love Capp'en Fitz'oy. Fuegia *love* Capp'en Fitz'oy.'

'Captain FitzRoy loves Fuegia,' he whispered, and stroked her hair, and York did not object because he saw that the captain's eyes were wet with tears as well.

The four boats pulled away into the sound, until the waving figures on the jetty were enfolded by the gloom and lost in streaming rain. Eventually, the distant glow of the mission oil lamp was all that remained, a tiny spark in the great dark shadow of Tierra del Fuego.

Chapter Sixteen

The Beagle Channel, Tierra del Fuego, 6 February 1833

'It is amazing!' remarked Darwin.

'What is? The glacier?'

The surveying party were setting up their instruments on a level stretch of beach opposite the face of a sheer, over-hanging glacier, a frozen cascade of beryl not a mile distant across the channel. It was a gorgeous and unexpectedly sunny day, and the brilliant colours within the ice cliff seemed to oscillate as they watched, shifting from jade through to amethyst and back again.

'No! I mean – of course – that the glacier is beautiful, but I was referring to Lyell.' Darwin sat down on a rock, quite oblivious of its slimy coat of putrefying seaweed, so excited that the book shook in his hands. 'Lyell has rejected the Biblical flood!'

'What?' FitzRoy could not believe his ears. Lyell, the eminent geologist, who had personally asked FitzRoy to supply specimens from the voyage to provide proof of the Noachian deluge?

'Here – he rejects the idea of a sudden débâcle at any point in the earth's history. He claims that any changes have been "gradual, constant and unimaginably slow".'

FitzRoy felt the cold knife of betrayal slide between his ribs. 'Then how does he explain the disappearance of the great beasts that once roamed the earth?'

'He thinks they simply died out of their own accord. That all species have a natural lifespan.'

'But what of our Megatherium, with its modern-day shells above and below?'

'Ah – here – he has an answer to that very question. He believes that marine invertebrates, no, any cold-blooded species, have a longer lifespan than their warm-blooded equivalents.'

'Indeed? And how, pray, did a land animal drown fifteen feet above the sea?'

'Well . . . I suppose it would have to have fallen into a river, drowned, then the body would have to have floated out to sea, sunk, and then the land would have to have risen above sea level. Over many, many thousands of years.'

'Lyell has taken leave of his senses.'

Darwin thought that he had better divert the course of the conversation.

'By the bye – do you think that this channel will lead us to the sea?'

'I am certain of it.'

'Then the south side – the mountain range on either side of the Murray Narrows – is effectively broken into two huge islands.'

'Indeed.'

'The island to the east side of the narrows consisted of stratified alluvium, like the north side of the channel here. But the island to the west' – he indicated the glacier suspended implausibly over the opposite shore – 'is constructed from old crystalline rock. Look.'

'What of it?' said FitzRoy irritably.

'Well, Jemmy told me that the land on his side of the narrows teems with fox and guanaco. But the island across the narrows, just a few hundred yards away, has neither. It is why such animals are unknown in York's country. So the animals only exist on the newer, alluvial rock.'

'Go on.'

'Well, the conditions, the vegetation, the habitat of the western side are the same. But if the guanaco or the fox ever lived there, something wiped them out. Then, when the lands were repopulated, the animals were obviously unable to get back westward across the channel. If the species indeed has a "natural lifespan", it was not that which ended their existence on those shores opposite.'

'By Jove, Philos, I do believe you are right.' FitzRoy found himself immensely cheered all of a sudden. 'Hang Lyell – I think you have it!'

Darwin smiled, happy to bathe in the glow of his friend's approval. Inwardly, he remained unsure, his mind a whirl of questions and answers – Lyell's suggestion that the land could rise and fall posed many of them – but he was relieved at least to have restored FitzRoy's mood.

'Excuse me, sir.' It was Hamond. 'I thought you m-might like a m-mug of t-tea, sir.' Since the storm off Cape Horn, his stutter seemed to have got worse.

'Why, thank you, Mr Hamond. Another mug would certainly not go amiss.' Between them, the surveying party had worked their way through four gallons that day already.

'The theodolite is set up, sir, and the m-micrometer and b-board, and Mr B-Bynoe is waiting with the b-bearing book.'

'Excellent, Mr Hamond. I shall be there as soon as I have drained this tea.' FitzRoy bent down to pick up his sextant and chronometer.

'Sir!' Hamond almost shouted. 'L-l-l-l-'

'What is it, Mr Hamond?'

'L-l-l-l-*look*, sir!'

Their gaze followed the line of Hamond's jabbing finger. There, right before their very eyes, the glacier was in calf. A huge sliver of ice a thousand feet high had parted from the ice cliff, and was falling, silently and gracefully, away from the main body and into the sound, like a white lace handkerchief dropped from a marble balcony into a deep blue pool. A moment later, an earsplitting thunderclap reached their ears; the three men stood transfixed as sound and vision were reunited, rapturous at one of nature's most awesome sights. As they watched, the enormous ice-spear scythed into the depths of the channel, then re-emerged in glittering, shattered chunks. A creamy wash furled out from the impact, no more than a distant spreading line on the smooth surface of the water, and a moment later a reverberating crash echoed from one cliff to another.

'Incredible. Quite incredible.'

'M-m-magnificent.'

'Oh, my God,' said Darwin, horror-stricken. 'The boats!'

'What?'

But Darwin was already away, hurtling hell for leather, Mr Lyell's considered opinions scattered wildly across the pebbles, as he raced down the shore towards the two whale-boats. A second or two later, FitzRoy and Hamond realized what Darwin had been quick-witted enough to apprehend first: that the boats were drawn up untethered on the quiet shore, that the huge wave now racing across the channel would surely suck them out to sea in its undertow, and that they were many a mile from the relative safety of the Woollya mission. Some of the crew had realized the danger too, and were rushing pell-mell down the beach; but it was clear, as the surging barrier of foam arched into a curling ten-foot breaker, that Darwin was the only one with a chance of reaching the boats first. Indeed, as long as he did not stumble over his own bootlaces, he was their only chance. Gasping for breath, his lungs bursting with pain, his long legs devouring the shingle, he flung himself forward, hurling himself upon the adjacent boat-ropes just as the wave erupted in a convulsing maelstrom over his head.

It was, in fact, the second time in less than a month that

the philosopher had suddenly found himself on the end of a battering-ram of icy seawater. This time, as he swirled upside-down in the churning spume, he suffered the added discomfiture of being pelted with a thousand stones by the frothing, maddened undertow. His feet jammed in the shingle and he straightened his knees, doggedly fighting to hold on to the boats as they shot past him on the accelerating backwash. The first crewman got to him in four feet of cerulean water and crushed ice, on the point of being dragged out into the middle of the channel. They formed a human chain to reel the two whaleboats and their protector back to the shore.

'I n-never knew how d-devilish p-painful cold could be,' stuttered Darwin, in a passable imitation of Mr Hamond, as they pulled him out half frozen to death.

He was their hero that night, and they fêted him as such around their campfire under the stars. They exchanged his sodden morning-dress for spare sailors' ducks and an old coat, so that – with his winter beard – he looked more like an inmate of the parish workhouse than a gentleman naturalist. 'I feel like a bear in an overcoat, grizzled and rough,' he complained, with a big grin plastered over his face.

Everybody roared with laughter, and ladled extra rations of salt pork, venison and ship's biscuit into his bowl.

That night, as Bynoe, Hamond and the men slumbered softly in the firelight, FitzRoy and Darwin sat up late, wreathed in blankets on the bare shore, tendrils of warm smoke entwining themselves round the swirls of their condensing breath.

'I say, FitzRoy.'

'Yes?'

'Do you ever think about . . . women?'

'Women?'

'Yes.'

FitzRoy's mind darted back to the recurring image of a pool of hot wax, congealing against Mary O'Brien's white skin.

'No. That is, I try not to. It is a distraction.'

'I have been thinking about women. All my sisters' letters ask me if I shall settle down upon my return – if I shall have a little wife for my little parsonage.'

'And what have you decided?'

'I have been considering the claims of my cousin, Emma Wedgwood. In many ways she is an eminently suitable candidate.'

'Do you love her?'

'Of course not.' Darwin laughed. 'She is my cousin. I love her as such, I suppose. But she is personable and charming and kind, qualities that augur well. What qualities would you look for in a potential wife?'

'I fear I have given it no thought. I do not really have time for such matters. I do not even write home.'

'You do not write *home*?'

'Oh, I cannot defend myself – certain people have been very kind in writing to me, and I have been shamefully remiss in failing to reply. But this Service is too important to allow myself to become distracted by correspondence. And I do not like to think of the men in the packet ships, risking their lives to deliver anything but the most vital consignments – your geological samples, for instance.'

Darwin wore a guilty look.

'My dear Darwin, forgive me. I do not mean to upbraid you. Mine is an idiosyncratic view, not shared by many. Letters from home are essential, of course, for maintaining the morale of those on board. In my case, it is also true that – as I have told you – I regard the *Beagle* as my home.'

'A home without women.'

'That is a sacrifice that all of us in the Service must make. But, pray, tell me where your thoughts lead you in this matter.'

'Well, I have made a list' – Darwin produced a crumpled piece of paper from his pocket – 'detailing the arguments in favour of and against marriage.'

'I am keen to hear them.'

'Well, marriage would of course bring with it the demons of fatness, idleness, anxiety, responsibility, perhaps even quarrels. I should lose the freedom to go where I like, and the conversation of clever men at clubs. I should be forced to visit relatives, to bend in every trifle, and to have the expense and anxiety of children. There would be less money for books. There would be a terrible loss of time – how should I manage my business if I were obliged to go walking with my wife every day? I never should know French, or see the Continent, or go to America, or go up in a balloon. I should be a poor slave, FitzRoy, worse than a negro.'

'It sounds as if your mind is made up. Bachelorhood beckons!'

'But wait! One cannot live a solitary life, friendless, childless and cold, with groggy old age staring back into one's wrinkly face from the looking-glass! There is many a happy slave, after all.' He gave FitzRoy a sidelong look, and both men smiled at the memory of their quarrel. 'A clever wife would be quite ghastly and tiresome. Romance, of course, palls after a while. No, I have decided upon a nice, soft, quiet wife who can play the piano in the evenings. Certainly, such a wife would be better than a dog.'

FitzRoy succeeded – just – in suppressing the desire to burst out laughing. He composed his features into their most solemn look. 'My dear Philos. If you indulge in such visions as nice little wives by the fireside of your country parsonage, then you shall certainly make a bolt from the *Beagle*. I fear you must remain contented with Megatheriums and icebergs, and not surrender yourself to these animal desires.'

Darwin looked searchingly at FitzRoy, wondering for a moment if he was being teased, but his friend remained convincingly po-faced. 'Well, I shall have plenty of opportunity to make my mind up, seeing that I am more than nine thousand miles from home.'

'Ah, my friend, then you have an advantage over me. For I am barely ninety miles from my home, which means I have precious little time to worry about who shall play the piano to me in the evenings.'

The smile that FitzRoy had been fighting to keep hidden finally crept out, and lit up his face.

The sun continued to shine, remarkably, for several days more, so it was with pink and blistered faces that they made their next discovery: that the Beagle Channel split into two arms, each ravine as deep as its fellow. In either direction, countless snowcapped peaks, four thousand feet in height, plunged directly into the water to continue their descent almost the same distance below the surface. Each arm was so straight that, in the far distance, the water disappeared over the horizon between its framing mountain walls. They sailed up the northern arm, where a pod of hourglass dolphins took it upon themselves to entertain them, leaping and gambolling before the whaleboats' bows.

To the north, the range of mountains soared to a single immense peak, rising sheer out of the water to almost seven thousand feet, which was studded with gigantic glaciers laced with tints of sky-blue and sea-green. At first they thought it must be Mount Sarmiento, but they were too far to the southeast. It was, they realized, an even bigger mountain, almost certainly the highest in Tierra del Fuego. FitzRoy named it Mount Darwin, foremost peak of the Darwin range, in honour of his friend. At the end of the northern arm they came to a large sound, bleak, desolate and deserted, which connected with the southern arm. They were, FitzRoy calculated, in the further reaches of Cook Bay, which opened out into the Pacific not far from York Minster. He gave the flat sheen of water the title of Darwin Sound, 'after my dear messmate, who so willingly encountered the discomfort and risk of a long cruise in a small loaded boat'.

They headed back by the southern arm, to the indignant fury of various kelp geese, steamer ducks and magellanic oyster-catchers. FitzRoy and Darwin even hauled one of the

giant kelp strands out of the water on to a shingle strand, to
see how far the plant's tendrils delved beneath the surface.
The kelp was nearly four hundred feet long, and teemed with
life: thickly encrusted corallines, molluscs, fish, cuttlefish, sea-
eggs, starfish and, hiding in the monstrous entangled roots, a
battalion of crabs of every size and variety. An excellent supper
of kelp and baked crab followed.

As they approached the divide in the channel once more,
they saw flashes of colour in the distance: a daub of pink here,
a dash of scarlet there. FitzRoy reached for the spyglass. It
was a small flotilla of native canoes. Even distorted by the
spyglass lens, what he saw turned his stomach to ice. One man
wore a beaver hat. Another had an earthenware chamber pot
on his head. A laughing child brandished a soup ladle and a
piece of tartan rug. The flashes of colour were strips of cloth,
tied about wrists and foreheads, cloth which FitzRoy immediately recognized as having belonged to Jemmy's suits.

'Dear God,' he said, and passed across the spyglass.

'Savages,' growled Darwin. 'Damned *savages.*'

'Shall we apprehend them, sir?' asked Bynoe.

'There is no point. Let us make all speed to Woollya. We
have no other recourse. Oars and sails. Row as if your lives
depended on it!'

As they shot past the little flotilla, a Fuegian pulled a face
at them, and mockingly waved an elephant's foot umbrella
stand above his head.

As the two whaleboats determinedly rounded the headland
into Woollya Cove, every gun bristling, upwards of a hundred
Fuegian natives scattered simultaneously, like a shoal of fish
surprised by approaching sharks. Two removed their feet from
a round pink object as they fled, which revealed itself to be
the foetal, naked person of Mr Matthews. Thus released, the
missionary leaped to his feet and ran screaming towards the
boats, all pretence at passivity gone, yelling the Lord's Prayer
at the top of his voice. 'Our Father! Our Father who art in

heaven! Hallowed be thy name, O Jesus Christ, oh hallowed be thy *name*!'

Matthews splashed frantically into the shallows, oblivious to the icy cold, and leaped into the burly red-coated arms of Marine Burgess, bringing him down in a tangled, soaking heap. So hysterical was the missionary that he refused to release his protector; Bynoe and Hamond had to disconnect his desperate bear-hug limb by paralysed limb before they could haul him into their boat. The other marines moved to secure the now empty beach.

'Matthews! Are you all right! What were they doing to you?'

'Yes! Yes! I think so! Our Father who art in heaven, hallowed, hallowed, *hallowed* be thy name!'

'Matthews!' FitzRoy grabbed a freezing ear in each hand. 'What were they doing to you?'

'They were shaving me.'

'*Shaving* you?'

'They put their feet on my head, and plucked the hairs from my upper lip one by one with mussel shells! The savages! By God, FitzRoy, it hurt like the devil!'

'Where are your clothes, man?'

'They took them! They took everything! They took them and tore them into strips and distributed them among the other savages!'

'Where is Jemmy? Is Jemmy all right?'

'I think so. They took everything of his, all his clothes too.'

'And York and Fuegia?'

'Oh, York is *fine*. York is just *fine*.'

There was no time to find out what this last remark meant. The sailors fanned out to search the property. They found Jemmy, crouched, naked and mud-stained, in the trampled remains of the vegetable garden, his hands covering his genitals in shame. His bare feet were sore and bleeding, unprotected by the hard calluses that soled the other Fuegians' feet. Anger, misery and embarrassment curdled as one on his features.

'Jemmy, are you all right?'

'My people,' he spat bitterly, 'are fools. Damned *fools*.'

'They took everything?'

'*Everything*. They are all bad men, they no *sabe* nothing, nothing at all. They are all very great damned fools.'

'Did your family not try to help you? Your friends? Your brothers?'

'My brothers steal most things of all! What fashion do you call that? My *brothers*!'

'What about York? Did he not try to protect you?'

'You ask York,' said Jemmy savagely. 'You ask York why he no help me.'

As if on cue, York Minster opened the door of his cottage and strolled nonchalantly out. Unlike the homes of Matthews and Jemmy, which had been gutted of their contents, their doors left hanging limply from their hinges, a glimpse over York's shoulder revealed a picture of domestic contentment. A smiling Fuegia Basket – or was it Fuegia Minster now? – sat in a rocking chair by the hearth, swaying gently back and forth, her stockinged feet stretched out on a woollen rug, a rag doll cradled in her arms. Improving religious prints decorated the walls. A half-eaten pot of marmalade sat on an occasional table. Clearly, York and his belongings had survived the return of the natives utterly unscathed.

'York?' said FitzRoy, in disbelief. 'They took none of your property?'

The big Fuegian said nothing, but merely glanced back inside the hut, as if to say '*Is that not self-evident?*'

'Why did you not help Jemmy and Mr Matthews?'

York smiled one of his cruel, wolfish smiles. 'They are many men. York is only one man.' And he strolled back inside and took his place at the hearth alongside Fuegia.

'Jemmy is *rude*,' confided Fuegia to FitzRoy through the doorway. 'Jemmy has *no clothes*!' she giggled.

When Matthews had calmed down sufficiently, he was able to tell his story.

'For the first few days after you left, there was quiet. Then, on the third day, the savages came back. They sat there, like a pack of hounds waiting to be unleashed. The next morning at sunrise they all began to howl – a sort of lamentation. Then that old scoundrel made a great parade of threatening me with a rock. I had to give them presents – clothing, crockery and food. Then they made the most hideous faces at me, and held me down and tore off my clothes and pulled out some of my hair. They did the same to Jemmy – Tommy Button burst out crying to see it, then they shouted at him and he joined in! They destroyed the garden – Jemmy tried to tell them what it was for, but they destroyed it anyway. Of course that filthy swine York did nothing to help. Didn't lift a finger. They didn't dare touch *him*, oh no. And everything they stole, they distributed equally between all the savages. Everyone got a share.'

'How primitive,' said Darwin.

'Ah, but they did not find the really valuable things they wanted! They did not find the secret cellar with the tools, or the compartment in the roof. The stupid, filthy, godless *savages*.'

'I presume,' said FitzRoy gently, 'that you would prefer to leave off this place, and take up your berth on the *Beagle* once more.'

'Captain FitzRoy,' gasped Matthews, 'wild horses could not persuade me to remain for one second further in these detestable latitudes. I cannot return home – the disgrace would be too great. My brother is a missionary in New Zealand. I shall make my way there.'

This was a very different Matthews, naked in his candour, from the young man who had been so ready to clothe himself with truisms and platitudes.

Once the excitement of the rescue had subsided, it was a subdued FitzRoy who took stock of the situation. The prospects for the little settlement, he realized, were bleak indeed. The seeds of civilization had been sown, but it was too late in the season for them to come to maturity. Jemmy, at least, was determined to continue, determined to make something of the Woollya mission. Like Matthews, the attack by the locals seemed to have wrought a change in him, but change of a more positive kind: a kernel of resistance had been exposed, once the soft outer layers had been peeled away. FitzRoy did all that he could to help: Jemmy was clothed once more, the whereabouts of the mission tools were revealed to all three Fuegians — each of whom was sworn to secrecy — and it was impressed upon York, in no uncertain terms, that the three must stick together through all their tribulations. That, said FitzRoy, was the civilized, Christian way. He would visit them again, he promised, in a year's time, when the surveying expedition left Tierra del Fuego for the last time, on its way home to England.

'I do hope,' said FitzRoy to Darwin, 'that our motives in taking them to England will become understood and appreciated among their fellow natives over the coming year so that our next visit might find them more favourably disposed towards us.' It was, he knew, a near-forlorn hope. 'After all, our three Fuegians possess the sense to see the vast superiority of civilized over uncivilized habits.'

'Indeed so,' said Darwin with a tinge of regret. 'Yet I am afraid that it is to the latter they must return.' *Their visit to our country has been of no use to them*, he thought. *No use whatsoever.*

Once more there were farewell hugs and tears, and once more sleeting rain attended their departure. Only this time there was no oil-lamp glow to act as a parting beacon, for it had been smashed and stolen, the meaningless pieces shared out as far-flung booty. As the whaleboats glided out into the sound, the three little cottages were soon lost to view, swallowed by the primitive dark.

Chapter Seventeen

The Falkland Islands, 1 March 1833

As the *Beagle* weathered the northern opening of Falklands Sound, the lookout spied a sail nosing above the northern horizon. The pendant numbers were prepared for the call-and-response.

'From the cut of her topsails, she's British,' said FitzRoy, squinting into his spyglass, 'but in these waters it pays not to take chances.'

'Why? What chances are there to take in these waters?' enquired Darwin peevishly.

'Because our friends in Buenos Ayres are forever beating the drum about the islands belonging to them.'

'I would have thought that Buenos Ayres was welcome to them.' Darwin indicated the miles of low, dismal moorland and sodden peat bog rolling away to starboard. He pulled his benjamin tighter about him, as the raw wind sent another squall of hail clattering off his back.

'My eye, Philos!' objected Sulivan. 'Why, this is God's own country! There are fish in the sea and cattle on the land, and not a factory or coach road in sight. Here is nature in the raw! And where else, Philos, could you enjoy all four seasons in one day, except perhaps up a Welsh mountain?'

Darwin smiled. 'I think you make my point for me most admirably. But what business have we here anyway, grabbing an island hard by the back door of Buenos Ayres?'

'On the contrary, Philos,' said FitzRoy patiently, 'we did not "grab" the islands. John Davis discovered them in 1592, when they were quite empty. The French *thought* they had discovered them in the last century, and founded Port Louis, then sold the place to Spain. The British in Port Egmont only discovered the Spanish in Port Louis five years later. Not long after that the Spanish were kicked out. But they, and their heirs, the Buenos Ayreans, have been bleating about it ever since.'

'Well, I think it looks a squalid little place.'

Sulivan clapped Darwin on the back. 'That's as may be, Philos – Port Louis is also the only place to take in supplies within three hundred miles of jolly old Terra del, and we have no supply tender. So you had better learn to enjoy it!'

Hamond brought news of the other vessel. 'It's HMS *Challenger*, sir. One of our b-brigs. B-bound for Valparayso, Chili via P-Port Louis. C-Captain Seymour, sir.'

'Not Michael Seymour? He was a fellow pupil of mine at the Royal Naval College. So old Seymour has himself a brig! What splendid news.'

Within the quarter-hour, the *Challenger* had run the Union flag up her mizzen-mast, inviting the captain of the *Beagle* to come aboard. Side-ropes and a boat-rope were rigged to receive the visiting cutter, and FitzRoy soon found himself on the *Challenger*'s poop deck receiving an enthusiastic welcome from his old schoolfriend.

'FitzRoy, my dear chap. Thank God you are alive.'

'Should I not be?'

'We knew you to be surveying in the vicinity of Cape Horn – those terrible storms! At least five vessels are missing, presumed lost. You were able to find a safe anchorage?'

'A safe anchorage? Far from it! We were under way

throughout, for twenty-four days. We were lucky not to be taken by Old Davy.'

'By the deuce, you must have the best of sea-boats to have come through such a blow in one piece.'

'She's a good old girl. But, my dear Seymour, you have your own fine brig – my congratulations to you, old friend. These are splendid news indeed. What business have you in Port Louis?'

''Tis but a flying visit. The Falklands are to have a permanent garrison, and we are merely their transport. Allow me to introduce to your acquaintance Lieutenant Smith.'

Smith stood drinking at the scuttle-butt with four of his marines. He was young and rosy-cheeked, and his curly blond locks gave him the air of a mother's boy, but his bearing and handshake told FitzRoy otherwise.

'I'm delighted to make your acquaintance, Lieutenant. How many are to be in your garrison?'

'Just myself and the four men you see here, sir.'

'You are to garrison the Falkland Islands with *five* men?' FitzRoy could not hide his disbelief.

The young man coloured. 'I gather, sir, that our presence is to be symbolic. As I understand it, the belief in Whitehall is that Buenos Ayres would not dare attempt to occupy a territory defended by British troops for that would constitute an act of war.'

Or they might just consider such a small garrison to be evidence of a lack of will on London's part, thought FitzRoy.

'Well, Captain Seymour, the *Beagle* is bound for Port Louis so I can save you a journey. I should be delighted to ferry Lieutenant Smith and his men the rest of the way.'

'FitzRoy, old man, that would be capital! You oblige me by your kindness, you really do. By the bye, do you have a Mr Darwin in the *Beagle*?'

'He is our natural philosopher.'

'Excellent. I have a letter for him, which I was to have left in the store at Port Louis. It is from a Professor Henslow at

Cambridge University, marked "Most Urgent", so the port-admiral in Rio decided to forward it post-haste. Now you may pass it to him directly.'

Darwin stood clutching the letter in a lather of excitement.
'Well?'

'The Megatherium heads, FitzRoy, and the other fossils, have been displayed before the cream of the academic world, at the Cambridge meeting of the British Association for the Advancement of Science. They were announced by Buckland himself. *Buckland himself!* Listen to this: "The fossil Megatheriums were fabulously prized, revealing features never seen before. Darwin is the word on everybody's lips. Your name is likely to be immortalized." Did you hear that, FitzRoy? My name is likely to be immortalized!'

'Philos, this is the most wonderful intelligence! Let us hope that some of your escalating fame shall accrue also to those officers who have furnished you with specimens. Mr Sulivan, Mr Bynoe—'

'But, of course, my dear FitzRoy. You have my every assurance on that point.'

'I must say I am relieved that the packing-crates were consigned to England in one piece. I was not entirely convinced of Mr Lumb's reliability on that count.'

'Well, most of them were. Henslow says, "The majority of specimens arrived in good order, but what on earth was in packet 223? It looks like the remains of an electric explosion, a mere mass of soot!" Good Lord, I wonder what it can have been. I fear I do not have an adequate record, after our soaking off the Horn.'

'Excuse me sir,' piped up Edward Hellyer, from the corner, 'but I have a record of the contents of every packing-crate consigned by the *Beagle*, sir. I maintained my paperwork in waterproof bags, sir.'

'You did? Well *done*, young man! Capital news!' Darwin was so delighted he looked as if he might burst.

'Well done indeed, Mr Hellyer,' said FitzRoy with quiet pride.

'The future has become a brilliant prospect, FitzRoy. I must collect as many specimens here in the Falklands as I possibly can.'

'Indeed you must. A Falklands kelp goose is the thing, I am told. It is different from the Fuegian variety, and no specimen has yet been captured. Let us see who can bag one first, shall we? Although I fear my skills with a rifle are as naught compared to yours.'

'Nonsense, my dear FitzRoy. I am sure you are my absolute equal in that respect. But let us have ourselves a sporting contest: the Captain's Cabin versus the Library. The first to boast a Falklands kelp goose is the winner!'

They shook hands on the wager.

They were still sixty miles short of the mouth of Berkeley Sound, the long inlet that sheltered Port Louis, when a reception committee appeared to shepherd them into land: swarms of tiny prion birds fussed about the rigging, black-and-white Commerson's dolphins formed a guard of honour before them, and tiny penguins with extravagant orange eyebrows splashed perplexedly in their wake. There was even a new kind of dolphin that nobody had seen before, which Darwin insisted be logged for posterity as *Delphinus FitzRoyi*.

As they rounded Volunteer Point, they overtook another sail: the sealing-schooner *Unicorn*, labouring eastward, which vessel signalled the *Beagle* to heave to. She was low in the water and clearly overloaded, but not with seals; rather, she was full to the gunwales with people. The *Beagle* pulled alongside, and this time it was FitzRoy's turn to receive a visitor. The *Unicorn*'s master, a short bustling sealer with side-whiskers and the broken remnants of a Scottish accent, panted up the man-ropes and made himself known.

'William Low sir, sealer, of Port Louis. Thank goodness you're here, sir, thank goodness you're here.'

As FitzRoy identified himself, he realized that the name was familiar. Then he remembered why – three Patagonian Indians and a stuffed horse on the windswept beach at Dungeness Point, back in April of '29.

'Forgive me, Mr Low, but I believe I was once passed a missive of yours by some Horse Indians.'

'Ah yes sir, the letter, the letter. Always does to keep in wi' the natives in my line of business.' Low spoke quickly and restlessly, and described impatient circles as he talked. 'I say "my line of business", sir, but my business is as good as shot. I am nearly ruined, sir – confined at anchor for sixty-seven days by the gales around the Horn, like a pea on a drum we were, and nary a fur seal to be had. Then on top of all that, sir, I needs carry the survivors of two other sealers. The *Magellan*, she's a Frenchy, and the *Transport*, she's a big Yankee boat. Both of them shivered to smithereens off the Horn, see, but they limped as far as West Falkland before running aground in the shallows. I needs ye to take some of them off my hands, sir.'

'Your humanitarian instincts do you credit, Mr Low. I should be delighted to help. May I introduce you to our ship's philosopher, Mr Darwin?'

'You say you are a resident of Port Louis, Mr Low?'

'Aye, that's right, sir, since eight years.'

'I don't suppose you could tell me if there is a bank in Port Louis where it might be convenient for me to cash a banker's draft on my father's account? I appear to find myself somewhat short of ready currency.' Darwin concealed his embarrassment beneath a cloak of insouciance.

'A bank, sir? There are but five buildings in Port Louis. The population's but twenty-three, just now. There's a general store . . . The storekeeper Mr Dickson, he's a Pat – from Dublin, sir – he looks to the Union Jack and flies it on a Sunday, or when a ship's in port. He might give ye a few bob up front if ye make it worth his while, sir, that's if ye can get a word in edgewise. Then there's Mr Brisbane, the local agent, who stands me in accommodation for the winter. Then there's a Frenchy, a soldier, the Capitaz we call him, and a German gent—'

'Pray excuse me, sir,' Bos'n Sorrell bobbed up and interrupted, 'but would that be Mr Matthew Brisbane, formerly master of the *Saxe-Cobourg*?'

'Aye, it's Mr Matthew Brisbane right enough.'

'That's my former ship, sir! Mr Brisbane and I were rescued from the wreck of the *Saxe-Cobourg* by the *Beagle*, back when Captain Stokes was in charge. He's a gentleman, sir, is Mr Brisbane.'

'Aye, that he is, sir, that he is. He's sailed more sea miles than I've had pusser's peas, has Mr Brisbane. Reckon he'll be mighty cheered to see you, will Mr Brisbane.'

'Extraordinary,' murmured FitzRoy. 'There must be fewer than a hundred Britons in the whole of South America, yet we continue to exercise a happy knack of finding one another. Tell me, Mr Low, as Berkeley Sound is new to me, would you be kind enough to act as our pilot on the approach? I take it you know the bay well?'

'I ken these islands like the back of my hand, sir. No need to flurry yourself – Berkeley Sound's no more difficult than a shilling trip round the harbour. But if you needs help I'm your man.'

'Well, Mr Low, your expertise is preferable to navigation by guess and by God. Which is in part why we shall be here for the next few months: we are to survey the islands for a new Admiralty chart.'

'A few months?' Low scratched the wiry stubble which stuck out haphazardly from his chin like scythed cornstalks. 'D'ye ken there's over four hundred islands? And as many bays and inlets. Just now I'd say you're looking at a good year, at the very least.'

'Four hundred islands?' FitzRoy's heart sank. They were fifteen months into their voyage, and their task was beginning to look nothing short of impossible. To map the Falklands, the whole of the South American coast from Punta Alta downwards, and

to complete the survey of Tierra del Fuego, not to mention
the constellation of tiny islands that lay to the south of Chili,
in such a limited time? Had the Admiralty simply given him
enough rope with which to hang himself?

'Mr Low,' he ventured, 'I apprehend from your earlier
remarks that the sealing season is now at an end.'

'That's if it ever began, Captain FitzRoy.'

'Tell me, Mr Low. What might your answer be, were I to
suggest that I should like to buy your boat?'

With Low piloting, the *Beagle* taking the lead and the *Unicorn*
falling into line behind, the two vessels ran confidently into
Berkeley Sound the following morning. A straggle of hollow-
eyed, exhausted French and American sealers slumped lifelessly on the decks of both ships, shivering in their tattered
clothes. Gruel-coloured clouds scudded across the sound,
sweeping down from broad, peat-thick valleys, before buffeting
away across low ridges littered with grey quartz boulders. Not
a single tree or shrub broke the monotonous, sombre moorland; brackish pools of yellow-brown water, gleaming dully
here and there, furnished the only relief from the drab uniformity. Monstrous wild bulls bellowed at them as they passed,
like Cretan sculptures made flesh, their horns jabbing accusingly from the scurrying mists at those who would trespass
upon their domain.

'Look 'ee, sir – see them? They're descended from escaped
cattle, left behind by the Spanish sixty years ago,' related Low.
'We shoots the cows for food, so there's a good many more
bulls just now.'

'They are so grotesquely large,' observed Darwin. 'Why did
the Europeans stock the islands with such an enormous breed?'

'Och, but they was quite normal-sized to begin with.
They've grown bigger since. They've separated out too. See
these here brown bulls? South of Choiseul Sound they're white
with black heads and feet. And over west they're smaller, and
lead-coloured, and the cows calve a month earlier.'

'They have changed size and split into three varieties in sixty years? Mr Low, that's quite impossible.'

'I'm telling you straight, sir. The wild horses now, they've shrunk. They're two-thirds the size of a normal horse – and there was no horses, mind, before the Frenchies and the Spanish came.'

'I find this impossible to credit.'

'Even the foxes are different, sir. See, they're smaller and redder in West Falkland than in the east. And the Fuegian fox is smaller still. But they're all of them twice the size of a British fox.'

Darwin's imagination performed somersaults. Self-selecting breeds? Inter-island mutability? But Lyell's latest volume had been quite explicit on this point. Variations within species were separately created by God at localized 'centres of creation'. Creatures could not simply adapt themselves in this radical manner. This strange, mad, half-Scottish sealer must be wrong.

Low was staring at him, reading every nuance of his scepticism.

'Here's Port Louis now, sir. Ye can ask the old 'uns there about it.'

Five little white crofters' cottages had materialized at the head of the rainsoaked sound. The capital of the Falkland Islands looked no more substantial than a large moorland farm.

'Dickson'll have the flag up for ye, sir, just you wait and see,' Low informed FitzRoy.

But as they waited and watched, heaving to before Port Louis, the Irish storekeeper did not make his expected appearance. The little settlement sat silent in the early-morning drizzle.

'It's very q-quiet,' said Hamond.

'Where the devil is Dickson?' said Low. 'That feller needs told to stay off the hard stuff.'

'Never mind Dickson – where the devil are the rest of them?' demanded Darwin.

'Should there not be boats?' FitzRoy asked. 'I see no boats.'

Low nodded. 'There should be a jolly-boat before the store. There should be people. Bairns.'

'Well, if they will not come to us, then we must go to them.'

FitzRoy gave orders for the cutter to be put into the water. Sulivan, Hamond, Darwin, Bynoe, Mr Low and Lieutenant Smith accompanied him on the short pull across to the settlement. As they stepped on to the pebbly beach, the silence was tangible.

They found Dickson in his store, face down, his throat cut, his blood soaked dry into the bare boards. The place had been looted and wrecked.

'Murderers,' breathed Sulivan. 'Rotten filthy murderers.'

FitzRoy turned Dickson's body over. 'Mr Bynoe?' he asked calmly.

'The blood is still sticky in one or two places. Given the damp conditions, sir, I'd say this was done yesterday.'

'So the assailants cannot have gone far. Mr Sulivan, take Mr Low and Mr Hamond and see if you can find Mr Brisbane. Here – take this.' He offered one of his pistols to Low, who accepted it gingerly, looking almost as nervous as Hamond beside him.

Sulivan's party found the next-door house, where Low lodged with Mr Brisbane, quite empty. There was no sign of the agent, but his half-eaten breakfast lay abandoned on the table. Whatever had occurred, Brisbane had obviously been taken unawares. FitzRoy, Bynoe and Lieutenant Smith, meanwhile, pushed carefully at the door of Jean Simon, the Frenchman: creaking, it swung carelessly open to the touch. They discovered the 'Capitaz' in his front parlour. He had obviously put up a terrific struggle. There were knife-slashes to his jacket and forearms, and blood was spattered on the walls. He had been dispatched by a gunshot, and lay against the far wall, his arms raised in useless protest, a look of astonishment fixed for ever on his face. A similar scene of horror presented itself in the adjoining houses. The entire population of Port Louis had either been done to death, had fled or had been led away.

'It would seem, Mr Smith, that your posting is to be anything but symbolic,' remarked FitzRoy grimly.

The young lieutenant breathed hard and tightened his grip on his rifle.

Reinforcements were hurried across from the *Beagle*, and the surrounding area was searched. FitzRoy discovered Mr Brisbane himself, or rather Mr Brisbane's feet, protruding from a hastily piled mound of rocks. The agent had been executed by a shot to the back of his head, presumably while kneeling, some two hundred yards behind his house. The corpse had subsequently been disturbed and chewed by dogs. The discovery brought a tear to the corner of the boatswain's eye. 'The filthy swine! Who would do such a thing to a gentleman like Mr Brisbane? He was a gent and a plain man, was Mr Brisbane.'

'I promise you, Mr Sorrell, we shall apprehend the villains who perpetrated this horror. You have my word on it.'

Finally, in the murky interior of a distant outhouse, they found the remaining inhabitants of Port Louis: two children, three women and a handful of older men, quaking with fear but alive and unharmed.

'Mr Channon! This is Mr Channon, sir!' Low identified the individual nearest to the door, who was blinking back the daylight that had suddenly flooded the little shed.

'Dear God! Have they gone? Please God, have they gone?'

'My name is Captain FitzRoy. You are quite safe. But who are "they"?'

'The Buenos Ayreans. They said they would take the islands back for Buenos Ayres. They took us prisoner!'

'How many Buenos Ayreans?'

'Ten. I think it was ten. Under a Captain Rivero. They have murdered Mr Brisbane in cold blood – and Mr Dickson. Lord preserve us!'

'We know. We have found them both. Do you know where these Buenos Ayreans have gone?'

'They planned to wait for the *Unicorn*, to murder Mr Low and steal his boat. But when they saw the naval vessel flying the Union flag make its way up the sound, they took fright and fled. They headed west, by the path to Port Salvador. They told us to stay here or they would come back and kill us. But they have taken all the horses.'

'This is Lieutenant Smith, of His Majesty's Royal Marines. You have my word – and his – that we will catch these murderers and bring them to justice. Now, let us get you all out from this damp shed, and before a warm fire.'

'The whole matter is so sordid,' Darwin concluded angrily. 'Our country, dog-in-a-manger fashion, seizes an island and leaves to protect it a Union Jack. The possessor has, of course, been murdered, and now they send a lieutenant, with four sailors, without any instructions, to deal with any eventuality! It is a paltry little police action unworthy of the Crown. And here are we, supposed to be going about the business of surveying and specimen-collecting, and instead we find ourselves embroiled in a contemptible little colonial war, in which an army of ten has attacked a town of twenty-three inhabitants!'

'We really have no choice in the matter,' said FitzRoy wearily.

'You know as well as I do, FitzRoy, that Buenos Ayres will paint this across South America as a just revolt, of their poor subjects groaning under the tyranny of England.'

'And you know as well as I do that what occurred was cold-blooded murder.'

'I fail to see why we cannot just give back the islands.'

'Back to whom? The penguins?'

'If necessary, yes. This is a miserable little seat of discord. The only thing these islands are worthy of is the contemptible scene that has been acted upon them.'

'You seem to forget that one of my duties as captain of one of His Majesty's vessels is to protect British subjects under any circumstances. That is a duty I do not intend to neglect – under any circumstances.'

'Without horses, it will be damn-near impossible to run them to ground,' said Lieutenant Smith. 'Any assault would be visible a mile off across these moors.'

'How about a night attack?' suggested Sulivan.

'It would only work if we could completely surround them in pitch darkness,' FitzRoy pointed out. 'They will not sleep far from their mounts, and will not be so foolish as to give away their position by camping around an unextinguished fire.'

'Have we the men to surround them?'

'We are nine marines on the *Beagle*, sir,' said Serjeant Baxter, 'plus however many matlows the captain can spare.'

'It is not enough,' said FitzRoy. 'Even if we could take up position in the dark, they are as likely to escape during the confusion of a night attack as during the day. No, gentlemen. We have two advantages. First, these are adventurers, not regular troops. Mr Channon tells us they wear no uniforms. So they will be cold and damp and tired, and will have to warm their bones by day. So they should assist us by giving their position away. Any column of smoke will be visible for miles. Second, the mobility they are relying upon will make them over-confident. They will be expecting an attack by sea from the east, and will be prepared at any time to flee further west. If we can anticipate their flight, indeed if we can precipitate it, our men could be lying in wait for them as they flee. Let them ride to us on their horses.'

Sulivan scanned the sparsely detailed Spanish chart they had come to improve.

'To be lying in wait to the west, sir ... well, that would entail our men marching fifty miles across open country from San Carlos Water, through soaking peat bogs and knee-deep swamps, with heavy packs.'

'Exactly. Not only will they not expect anyone to arrive from that quarter, they will certainly not be expecting it in three days' time.'

'Three *days*?'

'The *Beagle* can reach San Carlos Water betimes in the morning. After that, it is up to the Royal Marines. Lieutenant Smith? Serjeant Baxter? Can you and your men manage twenty-five miles a day across such terrain?'

'No question, sir,' said Smith confidently.

Serjeant Baxter's jaw hardened. 'We'll do it sir.'

'Observe,' said FitzRoy. 'To the west of Port Salvador there is only high ground – but it is split in two by a single valley here: the Arroyo Mato. If we can induce our quarry to head into that valley, they will fall into our trap. Mr Smith?'

'It sounds good, sir.'

'I think that on this occasion you had best dispense with your scarlet jackets, gentlemen. You will need to blend in with your surrounds rather better than you are accustomed to. And you and I, Mr Sulivan, shall also dispense with our uniforms. We shall approach from the east at first light in the *Unicorn*, disguised as sealers.'

'As sealers?'

'It is an obvious subterfuge to mask our approach. When this Captain Rivero sees us coming, he will see through it at once, and think it the best shot in our locker. With any luck he and his men will canter off up the valley, too busy mocking our efforts at concealment to be on their guard.'

'Will Mr Low consent to your using his boat in such a manner?'

'As of tomorrow, Mr Sulivan, the *Unicorn* will not be Mr Low's boat. It will be my boat.'

'*Your* boat?'

'My boat.' FitzRoy stood up to indicate that the discussion was over. 'Good luck, gentlemen. It's neck or nothing.'

'Good luck, sir.'

As Smith and Baxter made their exits, Sulivan hung behind, his face taut with concern.

'Yes, Mr Sulivan?'

'Sir, the *Unicorn*, I . . .'

'Mr May has looked her over. She is oak-built in a British yard, copper-fastened throughout, a hundred and seventy tons burthen, a first-rate sea-boat in very good keep, wanting only one or two sheets of copper and an outfit of canvas and rope. She will be ideal for our purpose.'

'But the cost, sir—'

'Six thousand paper dollars, that's about thirteen hundred pounds, for immediate possession, plus the services of Mr Low as pilot for a year. We can salvage the extra canvas and rope from the two wrecked sealers. She shall be renamed the *Adventure*, in order to keep up old associations, and we shall hire the American sealers to crew her. Mr Chaffers shall be her skipper, assisted by Mr Bennet and Midshipman Mellersh, until such time as Mr Wickham can pass over from Punta Alta. I shall send Mr Usborne to take his place.'

'American sealers? But—'

'I have memorialized the Admiralty requesting twenty supernumerary sailors for the longer term, and for the cost of her purchase to be defrayed. You do realize, Mr Sulivan, that the *Beagle* is the only survey vessel in operation today with no support tender? On our last voyage we were three ships, surveying only Tierra del Fuego. Now we are but one vessel, given a much wider area. The only way for us to complete our allotted task is if the *Adventure* surveys the Falklands for us, and is then adapted to carry our forward provisions. We shall get on faster, and much more securely, with a consort.'

'You know what I am saying to you!' burst out Sulivan. 'What if the Admiralty will not defray the cost? You have yet to hear about the *Paz* and the *Liebre*!'

'What if they will not?' asked FitzRoy lightly. *What if they will not indeed?* He thought of the letter he had just penned to Beaufort. '*I beg you, sir, pray fight my battle*,' he had written.

'What is most clearly expected of a gentleman,' he told Sulivan, 'is public service. Given voluntarily, and if necessary at his own expense. My conscience, Mr Sulivan, goads me to do all I can for the sake of what is *right*, without seeking for credit, or being cast down if everyone does not see things in the same light. I do not think there will be any more surveys of this area. Anything left undone by ourselves will remain neglected, to the detriment – very possibly the fatal detriment – of mariners to come. Further, the credit of the British as surveyors will be injured. I am not prepared for either of those eventualities to happen.'

'I know, sir, but *thirteen hundred pounds*?'

'Come, Mr Sulivan.' FitzRoy placed a hand upon his lieutenant's shoulder. 'What if our forthcoming action is a disaster? What if, by some mischance, the *Unicorn* is lost or taken? I have no other recourse – without you would prefer me to risk Mr Low's boat at no cost to myself?'

'No sir, but—'

'I may not proceed very quickly at my work, being only a beagle. But, at the end, a beagle is an animal with other worthwhile characteristics, I believe. Now, I think we have more important business at hand, do we not?'

'Yes sir, but . . .'

Sulivan gave up. Overwhelmed with concern as he was, he knew that nothing would divert FitzRoy from his course, once his mind was set. He could only pray that his friend had not just brought about his own financial ruin. The *Beagle*'s contingent of officers had now been reduced to a mere skeleton – the two of them apart, there were only the bos'n, the purser, Mr Bynoe, Mr Hamond and little Mr Hellyer remaining. Somehow, they would just have to make do.

Dense forests of entangled foliage writhed and coiled about each other, the swaying verdure teeming with life. Broad streams rolled and tumbled down side valleys before rushing to join the main torrent that parted the sodden moorland of the valley floor. But these teeming forests lay below the surface, on the kelp-choked coast of the islands, and the rivers and streams did not move, for they were rivers of barren, lifeless rock: great boulders and tiny pebbles of quartz, seemingly frozen in the act of flowing down the shallow valleys. How typical of this wretched place, thought Darwin, that everything should be so topsy-turvy. But from what peak had these numberless rocks been torn? There were no mountaintops here. Had they been brought from somewhere else by the deluge? How had Lyell's 'gradual change' turned parts of these drab, flat islands into what resembled the aftermath of a huge explosion?

The *Unicorn* slipped cautiously into Port Salvador, rain lashing her decks, the grey dawn slanting its uncertain light between the lowering clouds and rolling moors. It rained persistently in the Falklands, of course, but this was relentless. *Let us hope the marines have managed to keep their powder dry*, thought FitzRoy. Scouts had located Rivero's band the previous evening, exactly where he wanted them, grilling beef on the shore in the eastern reaches of the inlet, at the base of the Arroyo Mato. *Let us hope they have not had the wit to move position by night. Let us hope they are sufficiently unimaginative to head straight up the valley when they are disturbed. Let us hope that Smith and his men have located them too, and are in position.* What had seemed such a simple plan three days previously now seemed riddled with imponderables.

As FitzRoy intended, the *Unicorn*'s masts came into plain view long before the vessel itself, so that by the time they caught sight of Rivero's camp, it had become a scene of frenetic activity. Men were unravelling themselves from saddlecloth blankets and fumbling for guns and knives; others were on their feet already, untethering the horses. There were hasty confabulations on the shore.

Come on, come on, thought FitzRoy. *Make a run for it.*

He became aware of a set of white knuckles, gripping the rail to his right. It was Hamond. 'W-will we engage them, sir?'

'No, Mr Hamond, not if everything goes according to the plan. That side of things is up to Lieutenant Smith.'

'I h-hope everything goes according to the p-plan, sir.'

FitzRoy took pity on his old shipmate. 'If we find that we must engage them on shore, Mr Hamond, I should like you to stay aboard, and take charge of the *Unicorn*. Is that understood?'

'Y-yes sir. Th-thank you sir.'

But there was to be no shore engagement. The Buenos Ayreans were mounting their horses and trotting west up the valley, following the course of a muddy stream that tilted up between the boulders. It was all going according to plan. So far. FitzRoy raised his spyglass.

'They are putting the horses along.'

Come on, Smith. Where are you?

Rivero and his men had ridden a hundred yards up the valley now, their riderless mounts roped obediently behind, but there was still no sign of the marines. Perhaps the forced march had proved an impossible task? Perhaps they were trapped in a bog somewhere, up to their knees in stinking, cloying mud?

Suddenly a shot rang out, and the lead rider tumbled from his horse. A volley of firing followed, as Smith's marines stepped out from their concealing boulders on either side of the valley. Four or five more horsemen toppled from their saddles. The riderless horses, panicking, careered off in all directions. One Buenos Ayrean was dragged away by his terrified mount, his foot caught by the stirrup, his arms desperately shielding his head from the rocks that threatened to batter him to pieces. Another horse and rider could be seen galloping away at full speed up the valley. Two or three men had their arms up in attitudes of surrender.

'One of them at least has made his escape,' said FitzRoy, 'but I think we have the majority.'

'Bravo!' said Sulivan.

'Yes! B-bravo!' echoed Hamond.

The survey party worked with a renewed will thereafter. With Captain Rivero held in irons in the *Beagle*'s hold, awaiting trial in Rio de Janeiro, and all but one of his men killed or captured – Lieutenant Smith and his men had ridden off in pursuit of the escapee – the sailors' spirits were high on victory. By day they sprayed their names, and those of their friends and family, about the islands: Port FitzRoy, Darwin Harbour, Mount Usborne, Mount Sulivan, Port King, the Wickham Heights, and – in honour of FitzRoy's sister – the Fanny Isles. By night they sat around wreckwood fires telling stories and singing comic songs, and the devil take the hail-showers. They were, as Sulivan put it, 'in high feather'. They had two months to fill while the newly fitted-out *Adventure* was born from the remains of the old *Unicorn*, and they used them to cover huge swathes of territory.

A blustery morning found them setting up their lead- and transect-lines in a nearly closed bay to the south of Berkeley Sound – which, being naturally sheltered against the worst gales, seemed a better site for a harbour than Port Louis. The sudden bustle of unusual activity had not gone unnoticed, however. As the officers began to take their initial measurements of time, latitude and true bearing, an interested pair of eyes kept watch from the tussock grass above the beach. Yet although he could not be seen from the shore, the watcher was himself vulnerable to being observed from the higher ground behind; and so it came about that Darwin, returning from collecting geological specimens, caught sight of the watcher without being spotted in return. As stealthily as he could, heart pumping with excitement, he withdrew his geological hammer from his bag, and crept forward. So intent was his victim upon the inexplicable activities of the surveyors, that he seemed oblivious of what was about to befall him. Darwin raised the hammer high above his head, and brought it down with all his might. His victim collapsed with a howl of agony. It was the last sound he would ever make, his skull smashed in two as if it had been a boiled egg. On the beach, every man in the surveying party stood rooted to the spot, chilled by the sudden cry of mortal pain.

'Mr D-Darwin!' said Hamond. 'G-Good God, what was that *sound*?'

Darwin stood there looking sheepish. 'I've just killed the most *enormous* fox,' he said.

'It's fascinating. Either its senses have been quite dulled by the absence of predators, or it was so tame that it did not care.'

Darwin wriggled closer to the embers of the fire in his sleeping-sack. At the invitation of Mr Low, four officers were spending the night in the comparative warmth of the late Mr Brisbane's front parlour. Mr Hamond lay curled on the table-top, Mr Sulivan across three aligned chairs, the captain in a sagging flock sofa a good foot shorter than he was, while Darwin had bagged the warmest spot: he lay in the fireplace, staring at the orange glimmer of the peat as it ebbed in the darkness.

'I got the notion to use my hammer from Pernety,' he went on. 'I read that when he came here in 1764, the birds were so tame they would sit on his finger and allow themselves to be killed with a blow to the head. Since then they have been shot for food, and are more wary. I do believe that some of the birds here are migratory, and in Europe their nestlings are afraid from birth. There are rooks in Britain that will flee at the mere sight of a raised gun. What I should like to know is, has this acquired knowledge become hereditary? Has learning transmuted, if you will forgive the expression, into instinct?'

'It is a fascinating argument,' said FitzRoy. 'There is no question that mutability takes place *within* species, in conse-quence of altered climate, or food, or habits. Look at the Falklands cattle. But by what mechanism could *knowledge* be passed on through heredity?'

'I r-remember three hairy sheep being b-brought to England from S-sierra Leone as a c-curiosity, sir,' chipped in Hamond. 'Within a year they b-became woolly!'

'Exactly,' said FitzRoy. 'They were changed by *external* factors. It would not surprise me, for instance, to discover that the Falklands fox and the Fuegian fox are one and the same. That the animal has migrated eastward on the Falklands current, perhaps carried on floating ice or driftwood, and has increased in size here. All those penguins are obviously highly nutritious.'

'I'm afraid that point of view puts you in direct opposition to Lyell, my friend,' said Darwin. 'His latest volume rules out that very thing. He would ascribe every variation of that kind to its own "centre of creation", and therefore to its own species.'

'I am beginning to be less impressed by Mr Lyell with every passing day. He extols the virtues of gradual geological change, yet rules it out in animal variation.'

'Is that the johnny who denied the Biblical flood?' asked Sulivan.

'Yes.'

'He should take an excursion to the South Atlantic by surveying-boat. The evidence would be right before his jolly old eyes.'

'Mr Lyell is a genius,' said Darwin sniffily. 'He believes that the differences between two species of the same animal in two different regions cannot be superinduced during a length of time on account of the immutability of species.'

'It all depends on how one defines a species,' suggested FitzRoy. 'Every animal varies more or less, in outward form and appearance, from its fellows that habit different surroundings. But to fancy that every kind of mouse which differs externally from the mouse of another country is a distinct species is to me as difficult to believe as that every variety of the human race is a distinct species. A mouse is a mouse. A human is a human, be he an Englishman or a Fuegian. A fox is a fox, whether it be a Falklands fox or one of the type that Philos spends his days hunting to extinction in Shropshire. But a mouse cannot transmute into a cat. A fox cannot transmute into a penguin. A monkey cannot transmute into a human.'

'Philos is making a damned good job of extinguishing the race of Falklands foxes too, if you ask me,' said Sulivan. 'Expect to see it classified with the dodo soon.'

A chuckle ran round the room, and the hot breath of Darwin's laughter momentarily flared the glowing peat in the grate. 'I intend to make a special study of the tameness of the animal population before we leave,' he said. 'To ascertain by experimentation how fast each species learns from danger – then, perhaps, to take specimens on board, and see if their offspring really can receive their parents' newly acquired knowledge at birth. That way, I hope to prove whether or not Mr Lyell – Eeeegh!' He let out a piercing yell of disgust.

'W-what is it?' said Hamond, quaking.

'A rat! A huge rat!' shouted Darwin. 'Two huge rats! Oh, my God, they are attempting to share my sleeping-sack! Aaaah!' He wriggled frantically in the hearth.

'Sounds like they have heard about your special study, Philos, and are putting themselves forward!'

A roar of laughter rolled about the room at table-top level, punctuated by the anguished squeals of the philosopher, twisting and squirming below.

The next morning after breakfast they retreated to the *Beagle* – the rats having become something of a handful during the night – still debating the issue of animal variation. It was with regret that FitzRoy told himself he must break off to catch up with the ship's log, and requested his steward to locate Mr Hellyer. But a few moments later the steward returned with the news that Mr Hellyer was not to be found.

FitzRoy strode out on deck. 'Mr Bos'n, have you seen Mr Hellyer this morning?'

Sorrell fidgeted uncomfortably. 'Mr Hellyer, sir? I ain't seen him since yesterday, sir. I thought he was with you, sir.'

Further searches revealed that Hellyer was not on the ship.

'I thought I gave express orders that no one was to go out of sight of the vessel by himself except in civilized parts,' fumed

FitzRoy. 'It is a standing order that every man who goes ashore must be accompanied by at least two others.'

'I'm sorry, sir,' stumbled Sorrell. 'I can't say I saw him leave the ship, sir.'

Eventually, it was discovered that one of the Frenchmen had spotted Mr Hellyer the previous afternoon, heading east along the shoreline, away from the *Beagle*. The whaleboats were launched, but it seemed to take an age to lower them into the water. FitzRoy and Bynoe and Sulivan ran along the beach instead, fanning out as they did so, calling Hellyer's name, panic inflecting their voices, fear energizing their efforts.

In a little creek, a mile from the ship, Bynoe found Hellyer's clothes, together with his watch, in a neat pile. Beside them lay his gun, which had been discharged. Hellyer himself looked almost angelic, calm-featured, eyes closed, mouth open, floating palely just below the surface; his ankles still entwined by the kelp fronds that had held him in their sinuous embrace as the tide rose over his head. Not a foot from his outstretched hand, its neck broken by the bullet's impact, floated the wave-tossed body of a Falklands kelp goose.

FitzRoy came in response to Bynoe's shouts; he said nothing, but drew his sword. Without removing his coat, he plunged into the water up to his chest, cutting back the kelp fronds. He raised Edward Hellyer's white, lifeless body up high, and lifted it out of the creek and on to the shore. There, he fell to his knees, wrapped the boy's pale form tightly in his arms, and he began to heave, uncontrollably, with great, shaking sobs. Tears coursed down his cheeks, running unchecked, until they mingled with the seawater that streamed from his uniform into the cold Atlantic.

Chapter Eighteen

Patagones, Patagonia, 6 August 1833

———————

The tiny settlement of Patagones, defended by nothing but a wooden palisade, huddled against the crumbling bank of the Rio Negro. Only the fortified stone church stood out and beyond the defences, atop the bank, as if daring the godless Indians to do their worst. Just a few years back, there had been no white settlement this far south, but the fort at Argentina had held, and now more and more settlers were pouring across the Rio Colorado, fired by greed and bravado, ready to risk all they possessed to join the great land grab. But Patagones felt alone and exposed. Every whisper, every waving grass-stalk in the plains to the north, west or south occasioned a twitch of fear from its inhabitants. The east, where the blue Atlantic formed an implacable bulwark, was the only direction upon which they could safely turn their backs. The Horse Indians never attacked across water. They did not care for water. So the arrival of the *Paz* on this August morning was an unremarked event. The little village lay hushed in its inconspicuous hollow as James Harris, Charles Darwin and his new servant Syms Covington rode the tide in through the estuary.

In truth, Darwin was glad to be off the *Beagle*. Since

Hellyer's death, a vexation of the spirit had seemed to settle upon her company. FitzRoy's agony had been almost unbearable to watch. Unable to deal with his own helplessness in the matter, he had surrendered to the foulest of tempers instead. The officers had a code for it: 'How hot is the coffee this morning?' they would ask each other. The crew had learned to be more unstinting in their efforts than before, more exact in their work, to avoid their master's terrible displeasure. FitzRoy had wrestled with his faith, trying to come to terms with the act of God that had robbed an innocent, well-meaning boy of his life. The more he tried to convince himself that the tragedy had been part of some greater plan, the more uneasy Darwin had become. The moral certainty of Christianity was starting to exasperate him. He was a Christian, of course, but he was not *certain* of anything.

The only joy of the preceding few months had been the universal hilarity with which the crew had acclaimed the return of Lieutenant Wickham. Wreathed in a huge beard, every part of his face so bronzed and blistered by sun and salt that he could barely speak, Wickham had stepped aboard with the air of a crazed Byzantine hermit rescued from his pillar. He had been too bemused to see the joke at first, for his fellow officers on the two small boats looked little different, but Sulivan had clapped him on the back and made a fuss of him, and soon Wickham had found himself laughing with the rest. Despite conditions that had caused even the most experienced of them to feel continuously seasick, he and his men had completed their task ahead of schedule, even discovering a new river – the Chubut, the Indians called it – in the process. They would now transfer to the *Adventure*. That vessel was currently floating alongside the *Beagle*, before being warped to her, heaved 'keel out' and coppered below, to protect her from the shipworms of the Pacific. It promised to be a dull, claustrophobic August. For Darwin, the wildlife and geology of the pampas loomed large as an interesting, exciting alternative.

Harris, who was still contracted to the *Beagle* for another six weeks, had offered to accompany Darwin on an overland expedition from the Rio Negro all the way up to Buenos Ayres, a distance of more than five hundred miles. As for the servant, well – why not? FitzRoy had a steward. The officers had a steward. Why shouldn't he, Darwin, have a servant too, to do the messy tasks like skinning animals, carrying heavy fossils or retrieving shot ducks from wet kelp? The only slight difficulties had been in actually locating a servant and paying for him. FitzRoy had relented and donated Covington, the ship's fiddler, on the basis that he was by far the most promising student in his Sunday reading and writing classes, and that, as a horse-butcher's son, he knew something of animal anatomy. Darwin could not say he cared unduly for his new helper: although reasonably handsome of face, he was big-boned, mulish and ginger, and had nothing to say for himself. There was an odd, almost accusing look in the boy's eye. He was expensive too: as to the six-hundred-pounds-a-year cost, Darwin had decided that his father – in due course – would undoubtedly see the wisdom of his decision, and would forward him the money. In the meantime, he had secured another loan from Mr Rowlett, the purser. He was aware that his increasing requests for funds were causing him to resemble the midshipman in *Persuasion*, but there was no doubting that the addition to his status served him well. Covington had even packed his master's equipment for the trip: clasp knife, preserving spirit, specimen jars and corks, pencils and notebooks, guns and ammunition, compass and geological hammer, a spare pair of stockings and – a little touch of civilization – his cotton nightcap and a selection of silk handkerchiefs.

Harris, who was evidently a familiar face in Patagones, had managed to hire an armed escort in the shape of five gauchos. They were tall, leathery, swaggering men, with luxuriant moustaches and long black hair that snaked down their backs. They were reverentially, grinningly polite from the start to Don

Carlos, their *naturalista*, although their extravagant manners were clearly no more than a patina with which to coat a life lived at the edge of extreme violence. Each was badly disfigured by knife-cuts, a testament to the gaucho habit of settling even the pettiest disagreements with slashes to the nose or eyes. They looked, thought Darwin, as if they would cut your throat and make a bow at the same time. They wore white-striped ponchos and white boots, they rode white horses, they even smoked strange little cigars wrapped in white paper, which they called *cigaretos*. Before they knew that Darwin had learned Spanish, he listened to them conversing with a sixth gaucho, newly arrived in Patagones: was Don Carlos a *gallego*, the man wanted to know – was he worth robbing and murdering? No, they replied. This one is rich. This one is worth protecting. The rewards will be better.

The intelligence brought by the new arrival was encouraging for their prospects of a safe passage. General Rosas had been appointed by the government in Buenos Ayres to launch a war of extermination against the Indians, and to cleanse the countryside between the Rio de la Plata and the Rio Negro of their presence. To this end he was encamped eighty miles to the north, on the Rio Colorado, and had established a line of *postas*, or sentry-posts, between there and the capital. This would be the safest trail for Don Carlos to follow. Without further ado, that very afternoon, the party set out for the Rio Colorado, the gauchos in line ahead, their robes flowing, their spurs and swords clanking. They did not need supplies: they would eat on the hoof.

The countryside beyond Patagones was baked, lifeless, as bare and bristly as pigskin. What few grass-stalks eked out an existence here were brown and withered, the solitary bushes stunted and spiny. Bright splashes of colour, though, were provided by flamingos, poking about for worms in the *salinas*, great beds of salt five inches thick and many a league long. The gravel around these salt-flats was scattered with marine shells. The sea had been here, all right. But a single flood, of forty days and forty nights? Could it have left such thick salt deposits? Darwin knew in his heart that Lyell was correct on this point at least, that the ground hereabouts had been uplifted from the seabed.

Some twenty-five miles into the journey a lone tree appeared on the horizon, the solitary, neighbourless inhabitant of the arid plain.

'*Walleechu*,' said Esteban, the gaucho leader.

'I beg your pardon?' said Darwin.

'*Walleechu* – the god of the Indians.'

'The local Indians worship this tree,' explained Harris. 'It is the only one they have ever seen.'

As they drew closer, Darwin could see that, although bare of leaves on account of the season, the tree was festooned with offerings: cigars, bread, meat, strips of cloth, flasks of precious water and other offerings hung from its branches by lengths of coloured thread. About its base were strewn bleached horse-bones, the remnants of religious sacrifices.

'The Indians call it god. We call it dinner.' Esteban grinned as he unhooked the food and drink from the tree and placed it in his saddlebag for later consumption.

'Um ... should we really be doing that?' asked Darwin guiltily.

'It makes them happy.' Esteban shrugged his shoulders. 'They think God has paid them a visit.'

The gauchos spurred their horses northwards once more, their robes rippling. The Englishmen headed off in pursuit, Darwin with a degree of *élan* gleaned from years of experience, Harris's horse straining under the immense weight of its rider, Covington bringing up the rear, mute and ungainly on his long-suffering mount, saddlesore but uncomplaining.

That night they lay out under the stars in the boundless stillness of the plain, the Milky Way wheeling gloriously above them, its myriad uncountable pinpricks blurring into a soft arch of light that Darwin wished he could reach out and touch.

'It is the most beautiful thing I have ever seen,' he thought, then realized he had spoken aloud.

Harris, who had guzzled most of the food from the tree and was labouring at his night's rest, adjusted his bulk for a better look.

'The Indians believe that the stars are old warriors. That the sky is the field where they hunt ostriches. All those milky clouds of stars are the feathers of the ostriches they kill.'

How blissful, Darwin reflected, to be able to believe such a thing.

'Don Carlos?'

'Yes, Esteban?'

'May I ask you a question?'

'Of course.'

'Is it true that if you made a hole in the ground, if you dug far enough, you would come to a country where there was six months of day, and six months of night, and where the people walk upside-down?'

'One question with about twenty answers,' murmured Harris.

So Darwin discoursed at length about the rotation of the earth's axis in relation to the sun's light, about the earth's gravitational field, and about the broad make-up of the planet's various peoples. Harris came to his rescue whenever his Spanish faltered, until finally Esteban seemed satisfied.

'Don Carlos?'

'Yes?'

'May I ask you another question?'

'Of course.' Darwin wondered what great scientific or theological principle he would have to translate into pidgin Spanish next.

'You have travelled to many lands. Is it not true that the ladies of Buenos Ayres are the handsomest in the world?'

'Charmingly so,' Darwin reassured him, as solemnly as he could.

'Do ladies in any other part of the world wear such large combs?'

'No, they do not.'

'Look there!' said Esteban to his fellows. 'A man who has seen half the world says it is the case. We always thought it so, but now we know it!'

'Now may I ask *you* a question, Esteban?'

'Of course, Don Carlos.'

'Do you and your friends believe in God?'

Esteban laughed.

'In God, Don Carlos? There is no God. As you saw yourself – if you give your most precious thing to God, you might as well throw it away.'

The next day they passed the ruins of *estancias* – once-substantial farms, built by courageous but foolhardy settlers who had pushed just a few miles too far into unsecured territory. The buildings were blackened ruins, their corrals smashed down, the remains of their vegetable gardens parched and lifeless.

'The Indians always fire the farms,' explained Esteban, 'so that they cannot be reoccupied.'

'What happened to the farmers?' asked Darwin.

'What always happens to farmers. The young girls are taken as slaves. The rest – the men, old women and children – are tortured to death. They have their faces cut off and their throats slit.'

Darwin shivered. 'Are there any Indians here now?'

'Do you see any?'

Darwin scanned the empty horizon. 'No.'

Esteban laughed. 'Don Carlos, even if there were Indians here, you would not see them. They are too clever. But do not worry – we are not farmers, waiting like stupid fat ostriches to be put to the slaughter. We have fast horses, and guns, and knives, and we know how to use them. And you will see, Don Carlos, before the year is out, General Rosas will have destroyed every single Indian between the Plata and the Negro.'

'Have you and your men ever been attacked by Indians?'

'Of course. One time at Punta Alta there were four of us. We were surprised by Araucanians – raiders from across the mountains, to the south of Chili. They are the most dangerous. They use *chuzos* – long lances. I was the only survivor. I had the fastest horse.'

Darwin scanned the horizon once more, his stomach fluttering.

'Tell me, Don Carlos, do you like beef?'

'Do I like beef? Yes. Why?'

Esteban indicated a solitary Friesian cow, wandering the umber plains against a sky of the palest blue. 'Dinner for tonight,' he replied, and gave one of his fellow gauchos the nod to run it down. The man pulled his *bolas* out of his belt and set off after the animal, the three stone balls blurring into a perfect circle above his head as he thundered in pursuit. The cow gave a great moo and turned to flee, but the *bolas* whizzed with deadly accuracy from its assailant's hand: the speeding arc of the stones intersected with the graceful, rhythmic parabola of the animal's gallop, each bringing the other to an abrupt, chaotic stop. The cow lay pinned in the dust by the thongs, thrashing helplessly. Its distress cries were cut short in an instant, as the hunter dismounted in one swift move, drew his knife from his belt and slit the animal's throat. Then, before its death throes were even complete, the dust around it a red slick, its bulging white eyeballs staring up in terror, the gaucho sliced into its rump, cut out a block of steak sufficient for eight men, and wrapped it in his saddlecloth.

'Sharp work,' murmured Covington admiringly, opening his mouth at last. The *Beagle*'s voyage was the first time he had journeyed beyond the confines of rural Bedfordshire; it drew him closer to home to witness some skill or accomplishment that would have garnered a reassuring nod back in Ampthill.

'Are we going to just . . . *leave* the rest of it?' Darwin indicated the body of the cow, which had finally given up its struggle for life.

'There are many cows. You will see. They once belonged to the *estancias*. The Estancia del Rey had a hundred thousand head of cattle. There are still many left, running wild.' He indicated another cow on the northern horizon. 'Tell me, Don Carlos, do you use the *bolas* to catch cattle in your country?'

'Er, no, no, we don't.'

'Ah, so you use the *lazo* instead. Would any of you like to try the *bolas*?'

Harris declined, perhaps wisely in view of the fact that he appeared to weigh almost as much as his horse. Covington shook his head politely, out of deference to his master. Darwin, however, was enthusiastic: he took the *bolas* that had been unwound from the dead cow and whirred them above his head. It seemed easy enough.

He set off at a gallop, the others in pursuit. This time the cow, an Ayrshire, had considerable advance warning of his intentions, and began its flight at once, but Darwin's big white stallion soon overhauled it. Before long the two beasts were galloping alongside each other across the level ground. The philosopher unhooked the *bolas* from his saddle and rotated them at high speed about his upraised wrist; he took aim; and then he let fly. The *bolas* flashed from his arm and wrapped themselves neatly about the animal's fetlocks, bringing it crashing to the ground.

Unfortunately, it was the wrong animal. Darwin's horse, which had been *bola*'d many times as part of its training, knew exactly what to do: let the legs go limp, go into a roll, being careful not to crush one's mount. As horse and rider went flying, it even managed to deposit Darwin with some precision into a passing thornbush.

The gauchos arrived, almost sick with laughter. 'We have seen every sort of animal caught, Don Carlos, but we have never before seen a man caught by himself!'

Darwin's morning-coat was ripped almost beyond repair, but he did not care. Let them laugh – he would soon be in the way of it. He felt free, and wild, as if he was living the life of his dreams. If there was danger, then it gave the trip a relish, like salt to meat. That night, as they lay out under the stars, when he was absolutely sure that nobody was looking, he surreptitiously pulled off his nightcap and threw it away.

General Rosas' camp lay on the far bank of the Rio Colorado, a square of covered waggons a quarter-mile across that fenced in an entire army division and all its artillery pieces. After two and a half days without encountering a living soul, all of a sudden the empty landscape swarmed with soldiers: soldiers marching, soldiers riding, soldiers cleaning their weapons, soldiers lazing about, soldiers eating, drinking, gambling or picking fights with each other. The river itself, thick and muddy and bordered by reed-beds, cut and twisted through the baking plain; an immense troop of mares was being driven across it, on their way to provide food for the divisions fighting in the interior. Hundreds upon hundreds of horses' heads all pointing the same way protruded from the turbid current, ears alert and nostrils distended with effort, turning this way and that like a flotilla of fish, as if guided by a single collective intelligence.

'The gauchos love Rosas,' Harris explained to Darwin in English. 'They think he is one of them. He even dresses like them when he is among them. Anything they can do – horse-breaking, bareback-riding, whatever you care to name – he can do just as well. And he is a mortal strict disciplinarian. When he makes rules, he sticks by them. At his *estancia* once, he banned the carrying of knives on a Sunday. Then his steward pointed out that the general himself was carrying one. So he had himself put into the stocks for the day. When the steward took pity and released him, he had the man put in there instead, for violating the law. If he is not in charge of this country within a year or two, I'll eat my hat.'

'I should very much like to meet this General Rosas.'
Darwin turned to Esteban. 'How do we get across?'

'How do we get across, Don Carlos? We do what the horses
do. We swim.'

So saying, the gaucho stripped naked, rolled his clothes and
belongings into a bundle, and strapped them to the top of the
bewildered horse's head with his belt. Then he drove the animal
down the riverbank with a hefty smack, plunged into the water
after it, and held on to its tail while it pulled him across.
Whenever the horse tried to turn, or dislodge him, or alter its
course, he splashed water in its face to keep it on track. Pulling
powerfully against the flow, it was not long before the animal
had breasted the current, and horse and rider stood dripping
on the opposite bank.

Darwin was next to go, and made the crossing with
surprising ease. He was able to enjoy the luxury of donning
his battered morning-coat once more, while simultaneously
enjoying Harris and Covington's floundering progress through
the Rio Colorado's glutinous brown soup. How preposterous
Covington looked – he even swam gracelessly – while Harris
resembled a vast pink sea creature, his glistening flesh
porpoising unpleasantly through the turgid waters.

Once dressed and reconstituted on the far side, the party
reported to Rosas' sentries. They were escorting the famous
English *naturalista* Don Carlos, Esteban explained, who had
travelled many thousands of leagues in the hope of an audience with the mighty General Rosas. After an hour or so's
delay, they were informed that the general had indeed granted
an audience to his distinguished visitor, but that he would not
be at liberty to meet him until the following day. So, for the
next twenty-four hours, they had no option but to kick their
heels around Rosas' camp. There were a good many gauchos
in Rosas' ranks, men exactly like those of Darwin's escort, but
the vast majority of the uniformed foot-soldiers milling about
were either black – former slaves, presumably – or of mixed
race. Darwin thought he could detect some Indian blood

present as well. 'I know not the reason,' he remarked to Harris, 'but men of such origin seldom have a good expression of countenance.'

'They are a bunch of cut-throats, if you wish my opinion,' said Harris. 'We should stay close to the cut-throats we have hired.'

After an uneasy night spent huddled within the perimeter of the campfire glow, Rosas' sentries came for Darwin at first light. It was time to meet the general.

'I am indeed honoured that the famous English *naturalista* Don Carlos has come all this way to my humble camp. Please, I beg you to suffer my tardiness.'

In truth, Darwin had only been waiting five minutes in Rosas' tent, but from the gravity of the general's apology one would think it had been an hour.

'Please, say no more of it. And I am – I am not really very famous in my own country.'

'Don Carlos, I am not a man of science. But His Majesty's Navy would not appoint a *naturalista* for a voyage of such importance were he not of some standing. Is it not so?' Rosas smiled, displaying a set of perfect teeth. His was a dazzling, expensive smile, almost bereft of humour but awash with charm. His English was near-perfect, the language of an educated man, with only the faintest trace of an accent.

'I suppose so,' conceded Darwin immodestly.

'I knew it to be the case.'

Darwin could not believe how youthful the general seemed: he was forty years old, perhaps, but he possessed the athleticism and energy of a much younger man. Rosas' manner was warm and charismatic. His face was handsome and open, with a proud jawline and a strong, aquiline nose, the whole framed by neatly clipped sideburns. Only the defiant gleam of his dark, hooded eyes did not match the conventional picture of the romantic hero. He was not attired in his gaucho's costume today, but was immaculately kitted out in full dress uniform, with a red sash, a high, stiff collar and lashings of gold braid.

'You must excuse the formality,' said Rosas, catching Darwin's gaze island-hopping down his brightly polished brass buttons. 'Even in the midst of a war, one must conduct formal parades. But between you and me, Don Carlos, I am at my happiest out of uniform, dressed informally, out riding with my cattle, or playing with my children. I have an *estancia* – did you know that? – with three hundred thousand head of cattle. I am a simple man at heart, a family man. I loathe and despise war. But when our children are threatened, when our farms are threatened, when Christianity itself is threatened, what can we do but take up arms?'

'What indeed?' said Darwin, eager to agree with his charming host. 'Is the war going well?'

'As the gauchos always say, Don Carlos, "*¿Quien sabe?*" – but I am optimistic. You see, my friend, we are facing a new kind of war here today – not a conventional war but a war of sudden terror. We have all been reared on battles between great warriors, between great nations, between powerful forces and political ideologies that dominated entire continents. And these were struggles for conquest, for land, or money, and the wars were fought by massed armies. But a new and deadly disease has arisen – that is the only word for it – a desire among our enemies to inflict destruction unconstrained by human feeling on our women, on our children, on our civilian population. Our new world rests on order. The danger is disorder, and it is spreading like contagion.'

'I have seen the burnt-out *estancias*.'

'Then you will know exactly what I mean. We are so much more powerful in all conventional ways than those who would spread terror in our midst. The Indians do not have large armies or precision weapons. They do not need them. Their weapon is chaos. Even in all our might, we are taught humility. But in the end, Don Carlos, it is not our power alone that will defeat this evil. Our ultimate weapon is not our guns but our beliefs. Ours are not European values – they are the universal values of the human spirit. The spread of freedom is the best security for the free. It is our last line of defence and our first line of attack. Just as our enemy seeks to divide in hate, so we have to unify around an idea. That idea is liberty.'

'I suppose . . . the Indians would say it is their land to do what they wish thereupon.'

'Of course, Don Carlos, of course. When I speak of liberty, I speak of liberty for all. But they must accept liberty before they can enjoy its benefits. And what benefits, Don Carlos! At present, the land is unused, unexploited. What potential there is for farming, for mining, for shipping. What potential there is for jobs for all Indians, on the farms, on the mines, at the ports! Instead their chiefs and their priests insist upon preserving a medieval way of life. They deny progress. They deny civilization. They deny liberty itself. Their leaders are self-appointed – they even deny the will of their own people. Many of the followers of these leaders are fanatics, willing to die for their cause. My troops have just returned from an engagement in the *cordillera*. They killed a hundred and thirteen of these extremists, including forty-eight men, and recovered many stolen horses. My troops tell me that one dying Indian seized with his teeth the thumb of his adversary, and allowed his own eye to be forced out sooner than relinquish his hold. Another, who was wounded, feigned death, keeping a knife ready to strike one more fatal blow. I tell you, they are quite fanatical.'

'Forty-eight men dead!' Darwin did a little high-speed mental arithmetic. 'So . . . sixty-five of the dead were not men?'

'Sadly, Don Carlos, however surgical one attempts to be when one strikes at the heart of terror, there are always civilian casualties. These are to be regretted. Besides, the Indians do breed so. But my men are always careful to spare the lives of children caught in these encounters – they are given the chance to build new lives as servants in the great houses of our most powerful families. Don Carlos, I would be the first to admit that troops in this war, or any war, can occasionally let their enthusiasm run away with them. But to rein our troops in, to force them to fight with one hand tied behind their backs, could be fatally damaging to our cause. If we do not act strongly now, we will be guilty of hesitating in the face of this menace, when we should have given leadership. That is something history will not forgive. But before those history books are written, we will hunt down our adversaries, and we will continue to do so for as long as it takes to bring them to the justice that they deserve. This is not the time to falter – I will not be party to such a course. We must show that we have the courage to do the right thing.'

It was a powerful speech, and Darwin felt fairly blown away by the sheer persuasiveness of it. Rosas appeared to him as a Christian knight, standing defiant, boldly protecting the vulnerable and the innocent.

'They tell me, General, that this is a war with no prisoners taken.'

'On the Indian side, perhaps. They murder, they torture and they mutilate. We, of course, take our enemies prisoner in the conventional way. But I must stress that this is not a conventional war. So they are not *prisoners of war*. They are criminals, and liable to the due process of Christian justice as would any criminal be. And, as I am sure you aware, the penalty for murder, or for helping to plan or carry out murder, is death.'

'Of course.'

'Tell me, Don Carlos, are you disturbed by the sight of blood?'

'Not at all. I am a keen sportsman. Why, only yesterday, one of my gauchos slit the throat of a cow! I assure you, such things do not bother me.'

'Good. Then what you are about to witness will not seem very different. Come with me.'

He led Darwin out of the tent and across the makeshift parade ground, through a blizzard of salutes. They arrived at a large, fenced-off compound, where Indian prisoners knelt in chains, their eyes blindfolded and their mouths tightly gagged. Rosas spoke to the adjutant, who had three prisoners separated from the others and brought into an adjoining tent. Three loaded pistols were placed on the table opposite.

'These men,' Rosas explained to Darwin, 'were captured at the recent battle in the *cordillera*. We know from our spies that they were on their way to a general council of the Indians to plan a new wave of atrocities. They have already been condemned to death by due process of law. I am now prepared to offer them an amnesty – to show mercy – if they will only tell me where the council is taking place.'

Darwin looked at the three, who stood blinking and panting, their gags and blindfolds having been removed. They were superb physical specimens, in their mid-twenties perhaps, tall and muscular, each between six and seven feet tall, with long, wild, jet-black hair and coppery skin. Rosas nodded to the adjutant, who picked up the first pistol and placed it between the eyes of the first Indian.

'*¿Donde sera la reunion?*' demanded Rosas. Where will the council take place?

'*No sé*,' replied the Indian blankly. Rosas gave another nod, and the adjutant shot the prisoner through the head. Darwin almost jumped out of his skin. His ears rang from the deafening report of the gun. Blood pooled at the far wall of the tent, where the impact of the ball had flung the Indian's body. Darwin found himself gagging for breath.

The adjutant placed the second gun against the forehead of the second Indian. A cloud of blue smoke hung in the air from the first shot, making the general's point as eloquently as ever he could have done himself.

'*¿Donde sera la reunion?*' demanded Rosas, more forcefully this time.

'*No sé*,' replied the second Indian, bluntly, defiantly.

Again, Rosas nodded. Again, the adjutant shot the man

clean through the head. This time Darwin was prepared, but that did nothing to lessen the shock. He had seen public hangings outside the Old Bailey, of course, but this was a different sort of execution. Somehow the baying crowds, the food stalls, the ribald remarks, the sheer distance involved when the unfortunates of Newgate met their fate, all combined to lend the proceedings an air of bleak levity. This was altogether starker, more brutal. The second Indian jack-knifed backwards and slumped to the ground, his chains clanking once before falling silent. The adjutant placed the gun at the third Indian's temple, smiling this time. Rosas spoke once more. '*¿Donde sera la reunion?*'

'*Adelante. Dispara. Yo soy un hombre. Sé como morir.*' Go ahead. Fire. I am a man. I know how to die.

Rosas looked at him. '*Tu deseo ha sido concedido.*' Your wish has been granted.

Darwin stared hard at his feet. The noise of the third gunshot assaulted his eardrums. When he looked up, the third Indian was dead.

'Do you see what I mean?' asked Rosas. 'They are fanatics.'

'I can tell that what you have witnessed has disturbed you.'

Rosas' voice was full of concern. They sat in his quarters once more, a plate of fresh meat interposed between them on the table, but Darwin did not feel like eating.

'Allow me to apologize for your distress. But when you have seen what I have seen, Don Carlos – dead children, mutilated women – I must take the tough decisions that are necessary to modernize our society. Patagonia and the pampas must be opened up to free and fair settlement, and these criminals must be wiped out as part of our programme of national consolidation. Ours is a passion allied to reason, Don Carlos, an alliance of strength and justice for the many, and not the few, for the future, and not the past. We must develop a strong, united society, which gives each citizen the chance to develop their potential to the full.'

Sincerity shone from Rosas' every pore; Darwin felt the warmth of the general's conviction, and his doubts began to recede once more.

'I have heard tell, General,' he ventured, 'that you are the only man capable of bringing together Buenos Ayres, and Mendoza, and the United Provinces, and all the countries of this region.'

'Please, Don Carlos, I do not seek power for myself. I only want what is best for Buenos Ayres. But I tell you that if the countries that depend upon the silver trade were to form a federation – the federation of *Argentina*, let us say – with a single currency, a single defence policy, a single economic policy and a single law, then the benefits of such co-operation would be immeasurable. I do not speak of amalgamation into a single, huge nation, of course – nothing could be further from my mind – but to be left out of such a union would be a catastrophe, whether or not I were to lead it. It is better, is it not, to be a leading partner, helping to shape such a federation from the inside, than to be isolated on the outside?'

'Absolutely,' agreed Darwin. Rosas' logic was unanswerable.

The general indicated the plate between them. 'Please. Have something to eat. You must recruit yourself, and settle your stomach.'

Darwin took a reluctant bite. 'What is it? Veal?'

'Puma. Our puma-extermination programme has been a tremendous success. Already we have killed over a hundred pumas in three months. The benefits to agriculture are incalculable. I tell you, Don Carlos, the power of progress, allied to our essential values and beliefs, will prove unstoppable.'

Every syllable the general uttered seemed to be filled with integrity and scrupulous candour. Whatever the atrocities committed by either side in this nasty little Latin American war, here, Darwin felt, was a man with at least the potential to lead his people to some sort of salvation.

'Don Carlos, I am afraid that my time is running short. But before you return to your own country, let me make you two presents. First' – the general drew a piece of paper from the table drawer, scribbled a few lines thereon and sealed it with red wax melted in the candle flame – 'let me give you a passport. If ever you should meet any problems with officialdom, this paper should see you safely through. It is valid for all the territories under army control. Woe betide the man who dares harm any traveller carrying such a passport!

'Second, Don Carlos, I hope you will forgive my presumption, but I notice that your morning coat has become ripped. While I cannot hope to replace the costume of an English gentleman here on the Rio Colorado, I am told that you like to ride with the gauchos' – Rosas snapped his fingers, and a servant appeared at the tent flap – 'and that you are fast becoming an expert with the *bolas*.'

The servant marched across and presented Darwin with a complete gaucho costume – spurs, boots, striped white poncho, voluminous scarlet drawers – and his very own set of *bolas*.

'General Rosas! What a wonderful present! I couldn't possibly—'

'We will make of you *un gran galopeador* yet, Don Carlos!'

'I am indebted. Thank you so very, very much.'

'And remember.' Rosas reached across and clasped Darwin by the wrist. 'When you return to England, tell them that we are fighting the most just of all wars, because it is a war against barbarians.'

He is man of quite extraordinary character, thought Darwin. *I know that he will use his influence to the prosperity and advancement of his country.*

He walked from Rosas' tent in a daze.

'How was it?' asked Harris.

'Amazing,' replied Darwin. 'Quite amazing. He is an incredible man.'

Alongside a row of tents, a figure in bright clown's makeup was performing a slapstick act before a row of cross-legged troops.

'Who in God's name is *that*?' asked Darwin.

'Oh . . . the general likes to surround himself with the latest comedians and entertainers.'

'He did not strike me as a humorous individual.'

'Indeed not. But I dare say it makes him popular among the troops.'

Harris had woken that morning with a stomach complaint, having eaten none too wisely the previous evening, and announced to Darwin that he would travel with the next convoy of soldiers instead, in the hope of catching him up at some point. So it was that a column of six gauchos took the road north out of camp that day, a proud Don Carlos among their number, the solitary, lumbering figure of Syms Covington bringing up the rear in his naval ducks.

I really must get him a servant's uniform, thought Darwin. *He's making me look absurd.*

There were seventeen *postas* strung between the Rio Colorado and Buenos Ayres, a total of seventeen days' ride across the stark emptiness of the pampas. Throughout their journey, the evidence stacked up against FitzRoy and his Biblical flood. On the first day they crossed an eight-mile-wide belt of sand dunes, almost certainly the former estuary of the Rio Colorado at the point where it had entered the sea. On the second day, they came upon gigantic heaps of half-buried animal bones – the result, Esteban told him, of the *gran seco* drought of 1827–30, when a million cattle had perished for want of water.

What would be the opinion of a future geologist viewing such an enormous collection of bones? wondered Darwin. *The bones of all kinds of animals, embedded in one thick earthy mass? Would he not attribute it to a flood having swept over the surface of the land, rather than to the common order of things?*

He learned to catch partridge in a different way, by riding round them in ever-decreasing circles until the birds were sufficiently confused to submit uncomplainingly to their fate. He tried to catch armadillo, but they buried themselves in the sandy soil so quickly that he could not grab them fast enough. Esteban showed him how to fall from his horse directly on to one before it could disappear. The beast curled into an armoured ball in the gaucho's arms, like a giant woodlouse.

'It seems almost a pity to kill such nice little animals – they are so quiet,' said Esteban with a jaunty grin, sharpening his knife on the armadillo's hide before sliding it ruthlessly between two of its armoured plates. 'Dinner for this evening, my friends,' he announced.

At the *posta* that night, little more than an open shed with stabling for the horses and a fire of thistle-stalks, Darwin sat playing cards with the gauchos, drinking *maté* tea and smoking their little paper *cigaretos*. He lost money, of course, but that was as nothing to the joy of his companionship with these wild men. Covington, like Banquo's ghost, was a pale, sullen presence somewhere behind him, but he did his best to forget about Covington during the evenings. He had spent much of the day teaching the boy how to shoot birds with a rifle, using mustard-shot and dust-shot so as not to damage the all-important skins; by evening, Covington's principal duty was to melt into the background. Somehow, the servant's relentless indifference impinged upon the masculine solidarity that bonded him to these marvellous warriors, who were so fearless, so alert, so attuned to their surroundings. A faint cry in the distance, a call from the pampas so slight that Darwin had barely noticed it, froze the card-game in an instant. Every head inclined. One of the gauchos went to the door, knife drawn, and placed his ear to the ground. Then he stood up and laughed. 'Only a pteru-pteru, boys,' he said. 'Only a pteru-pteru.'

On the fourth day, Darwin galloped after a rhea, a South American ostrich, which scooted along the brow of a hill and opened its wings to catch the wind, like a ship-of-the-line making all sail. Proudly, he brought it down with his *bolas*, and the gauchos cut its throat. Covington skinned it, which left the boy crimson to the elbows; they kept the meat for dinner and the skin to be packed up and sent back to Henslow. Then they found its nest, packed with some twenty huge eggs, and rifled that too.

'If you are a *naturalista*, Don Carlos, then you should seek the *Avestruz Petise*,' said Esteban, as they loaded armfuls of eggs into their saddlebags.

'An *Avestruz Petise* — what's that?'

'It is a *ñandu* — an ostrich. But it is smaller, and more beautiful, with feathers down to its claws. Its white feathers are tipped with black, and its black feathers likewise are tipped with white. It is very rare indeed. I have only seen one in my whole life.'

'Esteban, I should very much like to capture an *Avestruz Petise*.'

They roasted Darwin's rhea at the *posta* that night, the best-kept sentry-post they had yet visited. The *posta*-keeper, an old black lieutenant, had been a slave in the West Indies and spoke English. Clearly, he took pride in his command and had worked painstakingly to improve the rudimentary little lodge. He had built a special room for visitors, decorated with cruci-fixes and engravings cut from the scriptures; there was a small corral for the horses, beautifully constructed from sticks and reeds; there were even little flower-beds planted around the building, which the lieutenant watered assiduously. It might have been a pretty freeman's cottage on Jamaica, but for the defensive ditch, and the line of straggly, beady-eyed vultures waiting hungrily for the next Indian attack.

'By your leave, sir,' said the lieutenant respectfully, 'but I believe you are the famous *naturalista* from England? I am very proud, sir, to have you as guest at my *posta*, sir, very proud indeed.'

'Thank you,' said Darwin graciously. 'Pray tell me, what is your name?'

'My name is Michael, sir. I have no other name. I have the honour five years ago to be released from my servitude to Mr Henry Morgan, sir, of Kingston, and to be made a free man. But there are not many opportunity for a free man in Kingston, sir, so I coming south, sir, to Buenos Ayres, where I am conscripted to the army, sir.'

'Conscripted? That cannot have pleased you, after all those years as a slave.'

'Oh, sir, I tell you, General Rosas is a great man, sir. He has give me this *posta*, sir, to command all by myself. Now the general, sir, he has make my dream come true, sir. He is an uncommon great man, sir.'

'Will you not join us, Michael? Will you not come and play at cards with us?'

'Oh no sir. Michael is a black man, sir. I cannot sit at cards with white men, sir, that would not be right, it would be disrespectful, sir.'

Embarrassment and confusion mingled in Darwin's expression. 'Really. I should be quite honoured.'

'No sir. You are most kind to Michael, sir, but that would not be the right thing, sir, not the right thing at all.'

He headed off to fuss over the night's bedding. The gauchos cackled quietly among themselves.

'I don't know why he bothers with his flowers and crucifixes so,' said Esteban, 'when all he has to look forward to is a knife in his back.'

'What do you mean?' asked Darwin sharply.

'*Posta*-keeper is the shortest job in the world, Don Carlos. The Indians will come. Maybe not tonight or tomorrow night. Maybe next month. But they will come one night, when he is alone. And they will kill him and burn his *posta*. To be a *posta*-keeper, my friend, is a one-way ticket to hell!'

'I thought you did not believe in God.'

'I do not believe in God. But I never said I do not believe in hell. We are all of us going to hell, Don Carlos!' Esteban laughed, cheerfully and throatily.

Michael reappeared with a fresh pot of *maté* and a solicitous look. 'I bring you some fresh hot tea, sir. I think maybe your old tea was gotten a little cold, sir.'

'Michael . . . ?'

'Yes sir?'

'Do you not worry that perhaps, one night, the Indians will come?'

'Oh, they will come right enough, sir, they will come, I

know that for sure. And when they come, Michael will sell his life dearly, sir, I know that for sure as well.'

'But aren't you . . . aren't you *scared*?'

'Michael has live a long time, sir, long enough for any man. And the general, sir, he has give me my dream, a little house of my own, sir, and make me a happy man. So when the Indians come to take it back sir, well, then Michael won't have nothing to live for no more, sir. So Michael will sell his life dearly, sir, when they come.'

He smiled at the simplicity of the equation, and moved away once more.

After the fifth *posta*, a black peaty plain opened out before them, with meadows of long grass and silvery patches of surface water. Ducks and cranes congregated on the mirror-smooth pools, and flocks of ibis flapped overhead. It was, Darwin told a phlegmatically unimpressed Covington, exactly like Cottenham Fen. They saw herds of wild deer, and clusters of ostrich, cattle and wild horses cropping the increasingly lush grass. That night giant hailstones as big as apples fell upon the *posta*, leaving the ground all about strewn with dead animals, and badly cutting the face of a gaucho who put his head outside to take a look.

'One more cut won't make a difference to *that* face,' remarked one of his fellows.

When the meat from the animals pounded to death by the hailstones ran out, one of the gauchos killed a deer, by the simple expedient of walking up to it and slitting its throat.

'They are afraid of men on horseback. Not of men on foot,' he explained.

The complete opposite of the reactions of a British deer, thought Darwin. *Yet the responses of a British deer are established from birth. Proof – absolute proof – that knowledge can transmute from generation to generation.*

Late on the eleventh day, as they trotted across a gently undulating plain of emerald grass, the breeze gusting in their faces, the gauchos stopped dead as one, as if someone had flicked an invisible switch. A deer stood silhouetted on the crest of a rise ahead, itself stock still, ears pricked. Esteban motioned urgently for silence.

'What is the matter?' hissed Darwin.

'That deer. Something has alarmed it. Something upwind. Something out of sight.'

He gave the order to dismount, and to keep as low as possible. One of the gauchos darted forward, his knife clamped between his teeth, and as he approached the brow of the rise, slithered forward on his belly. Peering over the ridge, he made hand signals back to the rest of the party.

'Three horsemen. They don't ride like Christians,' said Esteban.

'Are they Indians?' hissed Darwin, shocked.

'*¿Quien sabe?* If they are no more than three, it does not signify.'

'What if there are more than three? Maybe there are hundreds of them nearby!'

'*¿Quien sabe?* But load your pistol, and be ready to ride.'

Darwin's heart pounded in his chest. Indians, here, so close to Buenos Ayres!

A few minutes ticked by, excruciatingly slowly, but nobody moved an inch. Darwin's stomach felt impossibly heavy, like a pound of lead. The watcher on the hill lay stock still on his stomach, staring intently ahead. Then, finally, he moved. He stood up with a hearty belly laugh, and began to wave his arms manically back at them.

'*¡Mujeres!*' the man shouted across the meadow.

'They are women!' said Esteban with relief. 'That is why they don't ride like Christians – they are women!'

'*Women?*' said Darwin, incredulously. 'Women from *where*?'

The mystery was solved a mere league further on: a new *estancia* spread itself confidently before them, clean white lines at right-angles to the shining turf. The added presence of an entire troop of cavalry, heading south from Buenos Ayres, had obviously emboldened the womenfolk sufficiently for them to go out exploring for ostrich eggs.

Darwin's party approached the *estancia*'s main gate in scrupulous observation of the correct etiquette. There they waited, without dismounting, until the proprietor Don Juan Fuentes was fetched.

'*Ave Maria*,' said Esteban, saluting him.

'*Sin pecado concebida*,' replied Don Juan. Conceived without sin.

After that they were permitted to dismount, and their horses were taken away to be stabled. Following a passage of stiltedly formal conversation concerning conditions on the trail, a request was made – and granted as a matter of course – for overnight accommodation within the *estancia* walls. Furthermore, the celebrated *naturalista* Don Carlos was invited, as Don Juan's guest of honour that night, to a grand supper in the main house.

The sun blessed the *estancia* with its last few precious rays, then withdrew for the night. Safe inside the compound, Darwin decided to go for a stroll around this isolated outpost of civilization. The troops had lit their campfires, and were busy slaughtering a mare for their evening's feast. The hideous squeals of the victim gave the flickering firelight a primitive aspect: a bucket had been fetched to collect the animal's blood for drinking, and the thick crimson liquid pooled in the rusty vessel as if some Aztec ritual were being prosecuted. Liquor bottles were busily uncorked, and many a *cigareto* was ignited in the fire. The troops were at ease, confident. They knew that they were on the winning side, that Rosas would lead them to victory. Darwin retreated inside before the knife quarrels began.

Don Juan Fuentes' guests assembled in their finery for supper at ten, far later than they would have done in Europe: there were cavalry officers in full dress uniform, and ladies of the house in figure-hugging gowns that flared from the hip.

There were knives and forks and bowls too, the first cutlery Darwin had seen for some weeks, but the bowls held nothing but vast mounds of mare's flesh, exactly like those the troops were busy wolfing outside. The rough-hewn tables and chairs, the jugs of water and the beaten-earth floor put him in mind of a monastic refectory. There was no glass in any of the windows, and mosquitoes clouded the wavering candlelight like motes of soot. The talk was of General Rosas, and war, and the inevitability of final victory; such was the cultural and technological superiority of the white Christian race. Only when Darwin lit a *cigareto* with a Promethean – the new kind, which could be struck dry against any surface – did the talk of war cease. All talk, in fact, ceased. The table was paralysed, spellbound. Darwin struck another Promethean against his teeth. A rich landowner from Cordoba offered him a whole dollar for one of these magic sticks. The ladies' interest in the English *naturalista* suddenly blossomed. Then Darwin went one better: he produced his pocket compass. Unbounded astonishment followed, as the stranger proved himself capable of pointing out the approximate direction of Buenos Ayres, Cordoba and Mendoza, all by reference to a tiny machine kept in his pocket.

The lady to Darwin's left, a slender beauty with raven hair piled up in a jewelled comb, levelled her deep, dark eyes with his and told him that she had not been feeling well all evening: would he care to come to her room later that night, to effect a cure for any lingering traces of her ailment, using his little magic device? How on earth to react to such a brazen request? Thank heaven that Covington was elsewhere, making a fool of himself with the gauchos, no doubt, and not here to drink in his master's rich embarrassment. What perverse, sullen pleasures would he have taken from such an exchange? Darwin dithered. Really, he did not know how to behave in such circumstances. Was this *señorita* really a *lady*? Were there any real *ladies* in this part of the world? The question hung, pregnantly unanswered, between them. Then, the *señorita* settled the issue: she leaned forward, elegantly, seductively, and offered Darwin a morsel of roasted mare's flesh from the end of her own fork. He recoiled in astonishment. What manner of etiquette was this? Really, he had chanced among barbarians.

Making his excuses as hastily as possible, he drew back his chair, stumbled to his feet and took his *cigaretos* and Prometheans out into the night air. The cooling breezes of August took the edge off his anxiety, and soothed the sweat from his brow. He felt his pulse rate diminish. A silhouette staggered towards him out of the firelight, losing itself momentarily in the intervening blackness, before lurching finally into the oil-lamp glow at the door: a grinning soldier, quite profoundly drunk.

'Good evening,' said Darwin, politely, in Spanish.

The man bared all his teeth in a wolfish smile. Then he vomited, suddenly and violently, and a stream of regurgitated mare's blood splashed red across Darwin's new white boots.

They stayed three more days at the *estancia*, and towards the evening of the second day Harris caught them up. He was attached to a small troop of horsemen heading swiftly northwards, and was sweating profusely. To Darwin, the sight of a half-educated Englishman, even one with large damp patches spreading south from each armpit, was an improvement on the local sophistication level that could hardly have been bettered had King William himself shown up.

'Terrible business at *posta* four,' said Harris matter-of-factly.

A sinking feeling settled upon Darwin's gut.

'The place was burnt to the ground when we got there. Indian attack. Of course the *posta*-keeper had been murdered, poor devil. Elderly negro fellow. He had eighteen *chuzo* wounds. They cut him to pieces.'

'Did he sell his life dearly?' asked Darwin, his voice barely audible.

'I beg your pardon?'

'Nothing . . . it is nothing.'

'Did he sell himself dearly, did you say? I've really no idea.'

Darwin was keen to be away after that, to get back on the trail with his gauchos, to recapture the heady sense of freedom that had characterized the earlier part of the trip. They left the weary Harris behind again, a little miffed perhaps, but the sealer's spirits were soon raised once more by the enticing prospect of a feast of roasted mare's flesh. The party travelled north, across rich green plains thick with milling herds of cattle, horses and sheep, interspersed with beds of giant thistles that towered high above their heads. Finally, on the twentieth day, they came to the outskirts of Buenos Ayres. But all did not seem well. Plumes of smoke drifted upwards from the city centre. There was precious little traffic on the road.

'This is not good,' said Esteban, checking and rechecking the smoothness of his dagger's slide into and out of its scabbard. 'Don Carlos, you must push on to the city?'

'Yes . . . I mean, I have to rendezvous with the *Beagle*.'

'Very well. Then we shall proceed. But slowly.'

They pressed on watchfully, the outlying barns and cowsheds of the city gradually falling behind. Presently, they came to a roadblock, manned by a heavily armed gang of cutthroats. Rifles jutted at them from both sides of the road. The dangers of putting a foot wrong were emphasized by the swaying corpses of three or four fellow travellers, which dangled unpleasantly from the surrounding branches.

'What is happening in the city, my friends?' asked Esteban, loudly and confidently.

'What is happening, *friend*, is that we have taken control of the city for Rosas,' said the leader of the cut-throats, clearly enjoying his new-found status. 'No more will government officials plunder the state. No more will judges be bribed. No more will the head of the post office sell forged government notes. Either you are for Rosas or you are with our friends here.' He motioned to the corpses swinging waxen in the trees.

'We come from General Rosas' camp on the Rio Colorado,' avowed Esteban. 'We are his men.'

'What about *them*?' The cut-throat gestured to Darwin and Covington.

'This is the famous British *naturalista* Don Carlos and his servant. They are guests of General Rosas.'

'What is in these bags?'

'Specimens. Don Carlos is a *naturalista*.'

'What is a *naturalista*?'

'One who collects specimens.'

'The revolutionary government cannot permit foreign agents to enter Buenos Ayres. The British have seized the Islas Malvinas, our sovereign territory as determined by God.'

'These are not foreign agents. These are the guests of the general.'

The cut-throat leader jammed his rifle under Darwin's chin and motioned for him and Covington to dismount. Darwin, shaking, climbed down from his horse. Covington did likewise, mutely obedient. *We might be about to face our deaths, and he steps down like a misbehaved dog*, thought Darwin disgustedly.

'All foreigners have the potential to act as foreign agents. You gauchos may proceed. These two we will have to execute.'

'No! Wait! Wait one minute! Please!' Darwin, his words tumbling over one another in agitation, fumbled in his saddlebag, and finally – after a prolonged agony of searching that could not have lasted more than a second or two – produced General Rosas' 'passport'. The sentinels unfolded it with exaggerated gravity, and scanned it for several long minutes.

They cannot read, realized Darwin eventually. *They cannot damned well read.*

'This is General Rosas' seal. You may proceed. We are sorry to have held you up, sir.'

Relief sluiced through Darwin's mind, the lock-gates thrown open. His breathing came in short, deep gasps. *Thank you, Lord, oh, thank you, Lord.*

He touched his horse's flanks lightly with his big, burnished spurs and the beast began to walk slowly forward towards safety.

'Wait.'

What now? What now?

'This one.' The leader of the roadblock indicated Covington. 'Does he have a document?'

'No,' answered Darwin on Covington's behalf. 'He is my servant.' Thankfully, Covington did not understand Spanish.

'Then he must remain in custody until his credentials have been established. He must wait here with us.'

'Covington? They say you must wait here. With them. Until your . . . credentials have been established.'

'Sir.'

He doesn't even seem put out. The boy isn't even bothered. Does he not realize the danger he is in?

'I am sure you will be fine, Covington.'

'Sir.'

Grabbing his reins, Darwin urged his horse towards Buenos Ayres as quickly as dignity would permit, Esteban and his gauchos hard behind.

'"Until his credentials have been established"?' asked Darwin disbelievingly of Esteban, when they had rounded a bend in the road. 'How on earth can we "establish his credentials"?'

'How much money have you got?' asked Esteban.

'Philos! You are here, you are alive and well, and what is more you are become a gaucho!'

'I may thank kind Providence I am here with an entire throat.'

The lean, bronzed, powerful-looking stranger in gaucho rig who had thrown open the door of the captain's cabin of the *Beagle* bore only a passing resemblance to the pink, soft-cheeked young man dropped off at the Rio Negro six weeks previously. FitzRoy was extraordinarily glad to see him: as the ship had inched its way back up the coast, he had found himself frustratingly reminded at every turn of how solitary was the life of a naval captain. The slightest attempt to initiate a serious conversation with any of his officers, be it about geology, theology or zoology, had foundered on their continued respectful deference. He could have propounded any view, however nonsensical, and it would have met with polite acquiescence. He wanted to be *challenged*. He wanted to use his *mind*. Darwin, meanwhile, was solicitous.

'My dear FitzRoy, what news of the *Paz*, and the *Liebre*, and the *Adventure*? Will their lordships pay?'

'There is no decision yet. In truth, Philos, I am upon thorns to know the result. I must wait until Chili, it seems. But, my dear friend, tell me of your hair's breadth escapes and accidents! How many times did you flee from the Indians? How many precipices did you fall over? How many bogs did you fall into? How often were you carried away by floods? I am vexed to think how much sea practice you have lost, but I am *so* envious and jealous of all your peregrinations.'

'I'm sorry about the sea practice but, my dear FitzRoy, it is such a fine, healthful life on horseback all day – eating nothing but meat and sleeping in a bracing air! One awakes as fresh as a lark. Harris hired five gauchos. They were so spirited and bold, so modest respecting themselves and their country, so invariably obliging, so polite and so hospitable. I am sad to say, though, that they laugh at all religion.'

'So you have not passed your time among gentlemen?'

Darwin laughed. 'The complete and utter absence of gentlemen did strike me as something of a novelty.' He proceeded to describe his journey in detail, right up to and including the Buenos Ayres revolution that even now was

making itself heard: occasional distant gunshots ricocheted
within the walls of the city, before reverberating out into the
harbour. He did not, of course, mention that he had very
nearly returned to the *Beagle* minus one of her crew.
Amazingly, as luck would have it, he had found a bank open
and functioning amid all the looting and carnage, and had
managed to draw a bill for fifty pounds against his father's
account with Robarts, Curtis & Co. of Lombard Street. The
entire sum had been used to purchase Covington's freedom,
and not, he had sensed, before time: the servant's trigger-
happy jailers had quite clearly grown bored with their supine
hostage.

FitzRoy's eyes narrowed when he heard of the roadblock
and its cohort of armed thugs. 'This city is an absolute mess.
It is all the fault of that butcher Rosas.'

'Come, come, my dear chap, the general cannot have known
that this revolt was to take place in his name. This, doubtless,
was the act of the general's party, and not of the general
himself.'

'Philos, I doubt that anything very much happens in this
country without the general has intended it, or sanctioned it
at the least.'

'Personally, I found him to be a most charming and charismatic man. He is a strong commander, perhaps even a ruthless one, but are not all the most successful military men so?'

'Charming and charismatic he may be, but he is engaged
upon the most barbaric war of extermination against the
Indians.'

'I think you will find it is the Indians who are responsible
for the most barbaric of atrocities. Why, one of the *posta*-
keepers I met was brutally murdered not a few days afterwards.'

'He was not by any chance black, was he, this *posta*-keeper?'

'How did you know?'

'Were not the majority of the *posta*-keepers black?'

'Yes, but I fail to see . . . ?'

'Rosas makes officers of the blacks and he makes the *posta* a command. But the price of their promotion is death. It is the same with his armies. The front ranks, those who must take the most risks, are always black troops. Or they are "friendly" Indians, like the Tehuelches, to whom he has given the ultimatum, join the extermination or be exterminated.'

'I find your cynicism hard to credit. I tell you I have met the man − he is not some cold-eyed, calculating Tory minister. He is young, he is enthusiastic, and sincerity radiates from his every pore. As he told me himself, he is a liberal man.'

'A man should be judged by his actions, not by his own assessments of those actions.'

'Of course there are atrocities committed by both sides, FitzRoy. It is a brutal war against a godless enemy who is prepared to torture and kill without limit. Rosas has to meet fire with fire. But he does, at least, have the grace to spare the children of his enemies.'

'Spare them? He sells them as slaves!'

'They are sold as servants. There is a distinction. I believe that in their treatment there is little to complain of.'

'Well, the slavers' days are numbered. The news from London is that slavery has been banned throughout the empire. There are to be police ships hunting down the slavers. I am hopeful of a command myself in future.'

'This is excellent news. But we must not confuse the inhuman trade in human flesh with what is happening here in Latin America. What we are witnessing is the process of history. The inevitable eclipse of a weaker, primitive, heathen race by a stronger, more civilized Christian race. Be those races black or white is neither here nor there.'

'Is not one of the essential tenets of Christian civilization the *protection* of the weak, rather than their extirpation?'

'You are talking of mercy, of charity and of compassion − qualities that determine *how* a Christian should go about his business. But such qualities alone cannot prevent the victory of the strong over the weak. It is an unstoppable process. It is what happens throughout the animal kingdom every day, and humans are no different.'

'Perhaps they should strive to be so.'

'Perhaps, but Rosas is the stronger so he will win. It is clear to me that ultimately, he must be the absolute dictator of his country. It is the only way forward.'

'That is certainly the general's intention. Although whether the medieval dictatorship that will result constitutes progress, or will merely be a measure of how far man has fallen from his original state of innocence is open to debate.'

'You must forgive me, FitzRoy, but my appetite is getting the better of me – food supplies in the city were somewhat limited. I will take my supper in the gunroom, if they will have me – I believe that gunroom tea is at six – that is, if you don't mind?'

'No . . . of course not. As you will.'

Darwin swept out, his white gaucho robes rustling behind him. Suddenly, FitzRoy felt crestfallen. *Six weeks I have waited for someone to talk to,* he thought. *And now he is gone to gunroom tea, because I will not allow him his opinions without contradicting every single one.*

'Shall I be footman? Or, as in the household of a *Yorkshire* gentleman such as Mr Stokes, maid-of-all-work?'

A chuckle ran round the table. Gunroom tea that night was indeed a jolly affair, for Wickham, Stokes and the other officers had come across from the *Adventure* for a final meal together before heading south once more. It was Wickham who was ribbing Stokes now, passing around big hunks of roasted ostrich, the gunroom table being far too crowded for the steward to squeeze in and attend to his duties as he should.

'I'll have a leg, please,' replied Stokes, raising another laugh, for each of the bird's legs was bigger than his own brawny arm.

Darwin felt in his element. Here, embraced by the collective warmth of the gunroom, he felt able to recapture some of the camaraderie of the pampas, where he had enjoyed so many marvellous roast-meat suppers. And this evening there was snuff to follow. He proceeded to regale the company with tales of his *bolas*-lessons, the bringing down of his own horse and, finally, his successful capture of a rhea in full flight.

'Sounds a whole lot easier than shooting the blighters,' remarked Sulivan. 'This little fellow ran like the wind, scooting in and out of the bushes on his little furry feet. It took Martens three shots to bring him down.'

The little artist blushed in acknowledgement of his marksmanship.

Something jarred in Darwin's memory, but he could not work out what.

'How prime, though,' said Stokes through a mouthful of meat. 'Tastier than usual. It had odd feathers, didn't it?'

Sudden, hideous realization flooded through Darwin's mind.

'Oh, my God. Put that down!' he shouted, grabbing the bone from Stokes's hand just as the mate was about to take a bite, his teeth clamping shut on empty air.

'Philos? What's the flurry?'

'Stop eating! Stop eating! Give me the bones!' Darwin was positively frantic. He could quite clearly make out traces of feathers just above the claws of Stokes's ostrich leg.

'What is it?'

'It is the *Avestruz Petise*!'

'The have-a-what?'

'The *Avestruz Petise*! Where is the skin of this bird? The beak, the feathers?'

'In the galley, I suppose, but—'

'Nobody is to touch a morsel of this bird until I get back, do you hear? Not a morsel!'

Darwin tore out of the room, his striped poncho flapping behind him, leaving behind a bewildered silence.

'Whatever has got into old Philos?' wondered Sulivan at last.

'It's all those wide open spaces. One tends to lose one's sense of perspective, out on the plains,' suggested Conrad Martens, taking a discreet bite of *Avestruz Petise*.

Chapter Nineteen

Woollya Cove, Tierra del Fuego,
5 March 1834

———

The weather had deteriorated on their final approach to
Woollya, and with it a blanket of apprehension had been cast
across the spirits of the crew. All were afraid of what they
might find. It had been more than a year since their previous
visit: only the Reverend Richard Matthews, perhaps, secretly
wished ill on the fortunes of the settlement – if not those of
its inhabitants – for fear that he be cajoled into taking up his
place at the head of the mission once more.

'Terra del has recollected her old winning ways, I see,' said
Darwin bitterly. The deck heaved beneath his feet, as the ship
beat against a blue swell that was obstinately forcing its way
up the Beagle Channel. 'How I have missed her gentle breath.
What a charming country.'

Nobody spoke. Nobody felt like replying.

'If anyone catches me here again, I will give him leave to hang
me up as a scarecrow for future naturalists,' he continued,
addressing his remarks to no one in particular. As the old, familiar
waves of nausea wallowed up from his gut, he stomped off below
to 'take the horizontal for it' before it became too late.

The weather, in truth, had been unusually kind of late. They had enjoyed a fine Christmas at Port Desire in southern Patagonia: FitzRoy had determined that the crew of the *Beagle* should take on the crew of the *Adventure* in an athletic contest similar to the ancient Olympic Games. There had been running, leaping and wrestling matches, although the brutal favourite was undoubtedly the old sailor's game of Slinging the Monkey, in which some poor unfortunate was slung by his heels from a wooden tripod and swung from side to side, being beaten by all and sundry. The moment he managed to land a blow in return, he was permitted to swap places with the recipient. Darwin, as a landsman, had found it all rather barbaric, and had gone off shooting instead, procuring a two-hundred-pound guanaco for the Christmas roast. But he had to admit that FitzRoy's methods worked. All the officers and men were in a state of cheery perspiration when he returned, just as the captain (with the aid of a few dubious statistical calculations) declared the Olympic Games an honourable draw, and handed out prizes all round.

Just how well FitzRoy handled his crew was thrown into sharp relief at their next port of call, the Bay of St Julian. Both Drake and Magellan had been forced to execute mutineers here, variously beheading or hanging, drawing and quartering their victims. The surrounding place names – Execution Island, the Isle of True Justice, Tomb Point – bore witness to a very different era of seafaring. Darwin explored a few miles inland, coming across the fossil remains of a huge unknown mammal and, atop a hill, a desiccated wooden cross left by Magellan's expedition, shrivelled but intact after three centuries in the parched Patagonian air.

Thereafter the *Adventure* had turned east, Wickham and Co. gliding away to complete the Falklands survey under the expert tutelage of Low, the sealer; it was with considerable pride that FitzRoy had watched her go, her expensive transformation into lissom white swan now complete. By his side at the rail, breathing in his admiration of her sweeping, mellifluous passage, stood Coxswain Bennet. He had been earmarked as one of the *Adventure*'s contingent, but had begged his superior's permission to remain aboard the *Beagle*. The potential fate of Jemmy Button and his fellows gnawed away in a dark corner of his imagination just as furiously as it did in FitzRoy's own thoughts.

They had surveyed Wollaston Island and Cape Santa Inez on the way south, and the skipper had brought the suggestion of a tear to Hamond's eye by naming an inlet 'Thetis Bay'. They had scraped a submerged rock while working out of one uncharted harbour – a hair-raising moment, but fortunately the offending obstacle had not pierced the two inches of reinforced fir sheathing installed by FitzRoy at such enormous personal cost; the copper had been ripped from her false keel, but that was all.

Thereafter she had become the first full-sized ship to enter the Beagle Channel, squeezing in through the northern end of the Goree Roads behind Picton Island. The appearance of a brig in full sail had generated the same levels of native excitement as had their previous expedition in whaleboats: there were signal fires, frantic running men and a small flotilla of canoes trailing in their wake, smoke pluming behind them like so many tiny steamships. Some of the Indians waved their spears aggressively, but gestures that had felt threatening in an open boat seemed little more than pitiful when viewed from the heights of the *Beagle*'s heavily armed deck. Other natives sallied forth boldly to trade fresh fish and crabs in return for scraps of cloth.

'Where are you going?' was one shouted question that FitzRoy was able to decipher amid the chatter, from his rudimentary grasp of the Yamana language.

'Woollya,' he replied, pointing up the narrow channel between the cream-topped peaks.

'Much fighting at Woollya – many deaths – many bad things happen,' was the substance of the man's ominous reply.

'Tell me more,' he entreated this messenger, but to no avail.

Either his request was unintelligible, or there was no more to tell. The canoes peeled away before the *Beagle* got near Woollya, as if they could not bear to be present when she reached journey's end; as if they were ashamed to share the decisive moment when FitzRoy and his crew finally learned the truth.

The breeze shooed them through the Murray Narrows – familiar territory now – and then died away, leaving them in a calm, hushed world beyond. A demure veil of mist rose up from the water, through which small dark islets loomed one by one, counting down the yards to their goal. Even though they could see little, it was safe to take the ship through, for Woollya Cove and the whole of Ponsonby Sound had been surveyed during their last visit; so FitzRoy let the *Beagle* drift in as far as she could, her canvas gently flapping. There, as they hove to off Woollya, the mists finally parted, reluctantly, guiltily, to reveal the three mission cottages.

Each was a blackened, burnt-out ruin. The little white picket fence was thrown down. The neat lawn was weed-strewn and overgrown. This was not the mission but its skeleton, soundless, lifeless, picked clean of every scrap of re-useable material. Not a single teacup, not even a fragment of a teacup, remained. The place was utterly deserted. Not a living soul stirred. Only their own heartbeats could be heard.

In silence, they put the boats down, FitzRoy steeling himself as best he could. Nobody said a word. The splash of the oars, as they beat against the protesting waters, sounded a deafening tattoo within the misty confines of the bay. The scrunch of gravel as they ran into the beach was positively ear-splitting. As they stepped ashore it began to rain, great freezing dollops of it, lashing at their backs and spattering contemptuously against the splintered, carbonized planking of the three huts. There were, at least, no dead bodies. There was nothing. The secret cellar of Matthews's old cottage was thrown open, the black pit below an empty hole denuded of its former treasures. Silently, discreetly, the missionary mouthed a prayer of thanks for his own deliverance.

FitzRoy knelt in the vegetable garden, which had obviously been left entirely to its own devices since the previous year's trampling-down. There, nestling amid the disordered wet grass, lay a clutch of entirely healthy turnips and potatoes, which had pushed their way optimistically to the surface.

'You see?' he said, staring bleakly up at Sulivan and Bennet, the rain streaming off his face. 'It could have worked. It *would* have worked.'

Grief and defiance were mingled on his face. Bennet did not dare reply.

'You did everything you could. There was nothing more you could have done,' Sulivan reassured him.

'That's utter rubbish and you know it,' replied FitzRoy savagely. He looked back at the pathetically hopeful row of vegetables. 'Have these dug up and fed to the men. We might as well try to salvage something from this whole sorry mess.'

In the gloom of the afternoon, when the rain had washed away the mists, only to replace them with a wake of haggard, sorrowful clouds, FitzRoy sat alone in his cabin, running the events of the previous four years back and forth in his mind. What could he have done differently? What *should* he have done differently? Was there any point in crucifying himself? He looked across at the seat where Edward Hellyer had once sat, gazing up at him in awe and admiration. Yes, there was every point in doing so.

An urgent knock at the door interrupted his reverie. It was Bennet.

'Sir – a canoe. I'm sorry to interrupt, sir, but – there's a canoe.'

'Thank you, Mr Bennet. I shall be up presently.'

He tried not to let his heart thump. It was probably nothing – probably just a passing native family. *Compose yourself. You are in command, remember. It is time that you justified the Admiralty's faith in you, and that of your officers and men.*

He smoothed down his uniform and stepped on to the deck.

To the naked eye, the canoe was just a dark, approaching blot far out in the sound, distinguishable from the surrounding islets only by its gently rocking motion. He took the spyglass proffered by Sulivan. It was an unusual vessel, smaller than the average native canoe, remarkable both for the ragged flag flying from its prow, and for the absence of any sacred fire amidships. There were only two souls aboard. The first was a slender young woman paddling the craft, who – FitzRoy thought – conformed more to the Western ideal of beauty than to the burly, well-fed look that appealed to most Fuegian men. The other occupant was a man, naked and wretchedly thin, with long, disordered hair. FitzRoy felt that he did not recognize either individual, but it was hard to be sure, for as he raised the spyglass to his eye the man hurriedly concealed his face behind his hand in shame. For a moment he thought these two gestures unconnected, but then he remembered the Fuegians' extraordinary powers of eyesight. Even with the naked eye, the man could probably see the ship better than he could discern anything in the canoe through the blurry-edged lens of the 'bring-'em-near', as Jemmy had liked to refer to his spyglass. As FitzRoy continued to squint into the eyepiece, the Fuegian turned his back, apparently to avoid being recognized, and dipped his free hand over the side, before bringing it up to his face. *He's washing himself*, realized FitzRoy. *He's cleaning his face.* Finally, having completed his ablutions, the passenger brought his gaunt face slowly into view. He lifted one hand to his forehead, looked directly at FitzRoy, and touched the peak of an imaginary cap in naval salute. It was Jemmy Button.

Or, rather, it was Jemmy Button's shadow: a pale wisp of the sleek, well-fed, well-groomed boy they had left behind. As the canoe drew closer, FitzRoy finally had a proper view of the Fuegian's squalid condition. His hair was unkempt, greasy and matted, his eyes red-rimmed from the effects of woodsmoke, his modesty covered by a wretched scrap of

Walthamstow blanket slung about his hips. His skin was stretched taut across the concentric rungs of his ribs. So complete and grievous was the change that FitzRoy feared he might weep.

'My dear FitzRoy, you are crying,' said Darwin, who had materialized at his side, and he realized that in fact he had already let his emotions show. The philosopher put a consoling hand on his shoulder.

'Forgive me, Darwin . . . it seems I am disposed to play the woman's part today.'

'My dear man,' murmured his friend, 'poor Jemmy's appearance would be enough to move hardier souls than sailors.'

FitzRoy pulled himself together with an effort, and called for his steward. 'Fuller.'

'Sir.'

'Would you set the table for six, please? Mr Button is returned to the ship, and I should like to invite him and his companion to take supper with me. Would you also extend the invitation to Mr Bennet, Mr Bynoe, and to Mr Darwin, of course.'

'Aye aye sir.'

Jemmy's canoe was made fast alongside, and a peculiar little pantomime was enacted between the two Fuegians. Jemmy politely motioned for his companion to go ahead and scale the battens, saying to her in English, with a little bow, 'After you, Mrs Button.'

A scared look passed fleetingly across the woman's face as she responded, 'No, after *you*, Mr Button.'

'Please, Mrs Button, after *you*. Ladies first is proper.'

'Please, after *you*, Mr Button.' And then, after a frightened pause, 'Mrs Button no want go on ship.'

Jemmy put his arms tenderly about his wife and stroked her hair. 'Jemmy not be long. You wait here, Mrs Button.' Clutching a bundle wrapped with the remaining portion of blanket in the crook of one arm, he clambered aboard more nimbly than any of the crew had ever seen him move before.

'Jemmy, thank God you're alive.'

'Capp'en Fitz'oy. I knew you will come back. I say to Mrs Button, Capp'en Fitz'oy will not forget Jemmy, he will come back. She no believe you will come, Capp'en Fitz'oy, but I say to her, Capp'en Fitz'oy is English gen'leman, his word is his bond. He will come back for Jemmy Button.'

'You are married, Jemmy. My hearty congratulations.'

'Congratulations, Jemmy old son,' added a husky-voiced Bennet.

'Well done, Jemmy,' from Bynoe. 'She's a fine catch.'

'Thank you, my confidential friend. Jemmy is not proper married, like in church, but Jemmy remember words, say them again, so to be married in sight of God.'

'Your wife . . . she speaks English.'

'English Jemmy's language, not Yamana. English *good* language. Jemmy teach Mrs Button English. Capp'en Fitz'oy always say Jemmy is English gen'leman.'

As he uttered these last words, Jemmy's voice tailed off, and he looked down at his naked, emaciated frame. The others instinctively followed his gaze.

'Mr Bennet?' asked FitzRoy. 'Perhaps you would take Jemmy below and find him a suit of clothes. The best we have to offer.'

'It would be a pleasure, sir.'

Half an hour later, a fully clothed, scrubbed and shod Jemmy Button sat down to supper with FitzRoy, Darwin, Bennet and Bynoe, while Sulivan took command of the watch on deck. Despite being wooed with presents of handkerchiefs, blankets and a gold-laced cap that one kind crew member had purchased in Rio for his own wife, nothing would induce Mrs Button to leave her station in the bobbing canoe alongside. She sat alone and frightened as darkness fell; hers was an empty place at dinner. Fuller fetched plates of fish and crab-meat, followed by fresh-boiled turnips and potatoes. Jemmy held up his outer knife and fork and grinned at Bennet. 'With each course, you move in to the next two pieces of cutlery.' He repeated Bennet's own words back to him, even the inflections exact after four years.

'You remembered,' said Bennet. 'Sharp as a tack.'

Jemmy grinned again, this time with pride and pleasure at his accomplishment.

'So, Jemmy.' FitzRoy broached the obvious subject as gently as he could. 'If it's not too . . . painful, perhaps you could tell us what became of the mission.'

'The Oens-men came, Capp'en Fitz'oy, when the leafs turned red. Always when the leafs turn red there is no food, the Oens-men are hungry. So they come to my land. Yamana people always leave tents, run away. But Jemmy cannot leave mission. Have to stay with mission. Many Yamana people at mission, bad people, try to steal Jemmy's tools, Jemmy's clothes. Look for Jemmy's things, not look for Oens-men. God sends Oens-men to punish them. Oens-men come from the mountains behind Woollya, surprise Yamana people. Much fighting, many dead.'

'And York? Fuegia? Did they survive?'

Jemmy's face clouded with anger.

'York go to secret place under Mister Matthews's floor, take big spade. Says he will kill anyone who comes near. Pick up big stones. Oens-men afraid – not come near him. After Oensmen are gone, York says to Jemmy, it is not safe at Woollya. We must take tools, knives, axes, all precious things, go to York's land with Fuegia. Jemmy says yes, I will go with you. York makes big canoe. Before we leave, York sets fire to mission. Says bad people must not live there. We leave at dawn, travel west towards sunset. Sleep on island where channel goes two different ways. Jemmy wakes in night – hears noise. York is above him. York have moved quietly, like big cat. Jemmy tries to get free, but York have put his knife *here*, at Jemmy's throat. Makes Jemmy take off clothes. York takes *everything*, Capp'en Fitz'oy, *everything*. All Jemmy's clothes. Take shirt, breeches, gloves, nice shiny boots. All tools, *everything*. Leaves Jemmy to die on island. He say Jemmy foolish, he say white man foolish, he say Capp'en Fitz'oy foolish, all believe York lies. He say if Mister Matthews stayed he will kill him too. York say he too clever for white men, have clever plan from beginning. I say Capp'en Fitz'oy not foolish, I say Capp'en Fitz'oy English gen'leman. Keep his word. York laugh at Jemmy. Not see him again.'

Oh, but he was right, Jemmy – I have been so very, very foolish. York has outwitted us all. He meditated taking the best opportunity of possessing himself of everything right from the start. That is why he would not be left in his own country – for he would not have known where to look for poor Jemmy to plunder him. Such a betrayal – such a tragic course of events – and all for a box of tools. Everything undone for a box of tools.

'Then what happened, Jemmy? How did you get away from there?'

'I swim home, Capp'en Fitz'oy! York think is too far for Jemmy – many miles – thinks Jemmy will die. York say Jemmy go soft in Wal'amstow. But Jemmy good swimmer, like seal. Jemmy not soft. Jemmy swim all way back here. So York is big fool, not Jemmy.'

'And how are you now, Jemmy? Are you well, in yourself?'

'I am hearty, sir, never better. Jemmy eat plenty fruits, plenty birdies, ten guanaco in snow time. And too much fish,' he avowed, patting his stomach exaggeratedly. All present knew that he was lying.

'I am glad to hear it, Jemmy,' said FitzRoy limply, unable to think of any other response.

Jemmy put down his fork. 'Jemmy bring presents. Look.' He dragged his bundle from under the table and unwrapped the blanket. 'No money. No shops. Jemmy cannot buy presents. So he make them himself.'

With a flourish, he produced a handmade bow and arrows, and a quiver painstakingly sewn from guanaco-leather.

'For my old friend Schoolmaster Jenkins, of St Mary's Infants' School. Please to give to him.'

'I'll make sure he gets it, Jemmy, I promise,' said FitzRoy.

'These are for you, Mr Philosopher.' He handed to Darwin two immaculately carved spear-heads.

'Why, thank you, Jemmy. That's . . . that's most extraordinarily generous of you.'

'And for you too, my confidential friend.' There were two further spear-heads for Bynoe.

'Jemmy, I – I'm speechless.'

'For you, my great friend Mr Bennet, and for you, Capp'en Fitz'oy, I give you this.' Reverentially, he unrolled two otterskins, carefully cleaned and preserved. 'Better than guanacoskin. Better than sealskin. Very difficult to find. I catch them myself for my friends. My friends from Englan', who will never let me down as long as I shall live.' Jemmy's voice cracked as he reached the end of his speech.

'Thanks, Jemmy,' said Bennet, his voice so hoarse with emotion it could hardly be heard in the little cabin. A big fat tear rolled off the end of Jemmy's nose and fell with a splat on to the linen tablecloth.

'Jemmy, I . . .' FitzRoy tailed off in desperation. A low ululation of distress could be heard floating up from the canoe outside.

'Mister Button! Mister Button!' came Mrs Button's plaintive call.

'Jemmy,' said FitzRoy, taking the Fuegian's hands urgently in his own, 'do you want to come home with us? Home to England in the *Beagle*?'

'Mister Button! Mister Button!' came another moan from outside.

'Capp'en Fitz'oy, I . . .'

Jemmy's eyes were wet with misery. 'Jemmy must stay here with Mrs Button. She not want to come on the *Beagle*. Much scared of white people. Mrs Button is with child.'

'Congratulations, Jemmy . . . I – I didn't realize.'

'Jemmy's home is here. I am English gen'leman, Capp'en Fitz'oy, but Jemmy's home is here. Do you understand?'

'I understand. I understand, Jemmy, my dear, dear friend.' He clasped the Fuegian's hands so tightly that his knuckles blanched.

'But Capp'en Fitz'oy will come back? Will come back in the *Beagle* again to see Jemmy Button?'

'I . . . I'll do my best, Jemmy. It depends where the Admiralty sends me. But I promise I will do my level best to visit you in the future.'

'Thank you, my friend. I say to Mrs Button, Capp'en Fitz'oy will not forget Jemmy Button. He will come back. Capp'en Fitz'oy is English gen'leman.'

'Mister Button! Mister Button!' The call from outside was shot through with distress. FitzRoy relaxed his grip.

'You had better go, Jemmy. I should like to keep you with us, I should like that so very much, but I fear that you must leave.'

'Goodbye, my dearest friends. Jemmy will always remember you.'

'And we will remember you, Jemmy, I give you my word.'

'As an English gen'leman, Capp'en Fitz'oy.'

'As an English gentleman, Jemmy.'

The *Beagle* slipped her moorings at first light, and drifted serenely away from the shore on the morning tide. As she stood out of Ponsonby Sound, Jemmy and his wife crept wearily out from the clump of rushes where they had hidden for the night, their bodies curled protectively around a full blanket-load of presents. The Fuegian lit a signal fire to herald the ship's departure. FitzRoy and Darwin stood on the poop and watched the insubstantial column of smoke make its connection between the lonely meadows of Woollya and the passing clouds above. A gust of wind caught it and bent it like a reed, but it refused to break.

'Perhaps . . . perhaps some shipwrecked seaman will one day hereafter receive help and kind treatment from Jemmy Button's children. Perhaps they will be prompted by the traditions they will have heard, of men from other lands. Perhaps they will have an idea, however faint, of their duty to God as well as to their neighbour.'

Or perhaps, more likely, it has all been in vain. Literally, a vain scheme, conceived on too small a scale, with disastrous consequences for those poor souls involved against their will.

'My dear FitzRoy, I do not doubt for one second that he will be just as happy as if he had never left his country.'

'Do you really believe so?'

'I do.'

You are wrong, my friend, for I have given him a taste of a better life, then snatched it away. I have taken away his innocence, something I had no right to do. I wanted to bring him closer to God, but at the end it was I who played God, with the lives of other men.

The tiny figure by the signal fire was waving now, his hand describing wide, metronomic arcs as if he were copying the gesture from a handbook. Discreetly, Darwin left FitzRoy to his private agonies and wandered along the deck. He found Bennet grasping the rail with a hopeless ferocity, peering into the dawn light as if terrified of the moment when he might no longer be able to distinguish Jemmy from his surroundings.

'What really hurts, Philos,' said the coxswain, without averting his gaze even for a second, 'is that I know I'll never see him again.'

'I do not think any of us ever will.'

'It could all have been so different. If only we'd . . . if we'd . . . I don't know.'

'May I ask you a question, Mr Bennet?'

'By all means.'

'Do you believe in God?'

'Do I believe in God? Of course I believe in God, Philos. That is . . . on days like today . . . sometimes it's hard, Philos, sometimes it's hard. But do I believe in God? Yes. Yes I do. Leastways, I'm sure I do.'

Part Four

Chapter Twenty

Valparayso, Chili, 2 November 1834

———

'Raise tacks, sheets an' mains'l haul
We're bound for Vallaparayser round the Horn!
Me boots an' clothes are all in pawn
An' it's bleedin' draughty round the Horn!'

So sang the crew, with a surge of relief, as the *Beagle* and
the *Adventure* finally drew a line under the year's surveying
and headed for the sanctuary of Chili's warm, fruit-laden
valleys – except that, of course, there was no longer any need
to proceed via the Horn.

They had repaired the damage to the *Beagle*'s keel by running
her up to the Rio Santa Cruz in Patagonia and beaching her in
the estuary, where a forty-foot tide swept in and out. Laid up
on the sands amid a crowd of disgruntled sealions, the little ship
had assumed the proportions of a leviathan, her fat, glistening,
slimy belly towering above the crew, as if she might subside and
suffocate them were she to breathe out. While Carpenter May
and his team set to work, FitzRoy had mounted an expedition
upriver to try to reach the Andes from the east. Amid swarms
of persistent horseflies, they had man-hauled the whaleboats

against the icy current for three back-breaking weeks, using track ropes fastened to lanyards made from broad canvas strips. For two hundred and fifty miles they had pulled, up a lonely, twisting glen lined by black basalt cliffs. The countryside around, if one could call it that, was a featureless plain of volcanic lava, punishingly hot by day and freezing by night, its ebony sheen flat to the horizon. But the river had cut deep into the lava: the ravine up which they slogged was three hundred feet in depth and more than a mile across. Beady-eyed condors stood sentry on their basaltic battlements, but otherwise there were precious few living creatures to be seen. There were Indian tracks about their camp in the mornings, though, evidence that they had been thoroughly investigated during the night. Here, well south of the front line against General Rosas, it appeared that the white man constituted a mere curiosity and not an adversary to be feared. There were puma tracks, too, for the Indians were not the only lords desirous to know who had intruded into their land. As with the Indians, the men on watch had seen and heard nothing, not even a rustle in the reeds.

In silence the party trudged upriver, each man feeling the curious self-consciousness that comes from the knowledge of being watched. The Andes came in sight, and the river assumed the milky blue colour characteristic of glacial melt, but thereafter the mountains seemed to maintain a constant distance, refusing to come any closer. The men stood in their echoing glen and gazed at the distant snowy peaks, knowing that they had become the first Europeans to behold this view, but knowing also that they could go no further. It was, thought FitzRoy, a wild and lonely prospect, entirely fit for the breeding-place of lions.

Whether it was the isolation of their surroundings, or a sense of compromise brought on by the failure of the Woollya mission, FitzRoy and Darwin felt instinctively drawn to one another, not just emotionally but in their scientific analysis of the surroundings. Climbing the valley was like walking through a cutaway diagram of the different geological layers: with the precision of a well-set-out textbook, the scenery invited the two men to reconsider their arguments. Two weeks upriver they encountered a vast layer of marine detritus a hundred feet thick, containing smooth-rolled stones and the shattered remnants of delicate shallow-water sea-shells embedded in viscous mud. The shells, Darwin had to admit, had been smashed, crushed and mixed together as if by a great catastrophe. Whatever it was that had brought so many stones to one place must have been an event of terrifying force. Perhaps they had, after all, been torn down by the great tides of a flooded world. FitzRoy, too, felt in a mood to compromise. It had been so much easier to imagine the Biblical flood in the midst of Tierra del Fuego's lashing storms, but here in the desiccated plain his sense of certainty began to evaporate. Could such a vast layer of sea-detritus really have been effected by a forty-day flood? Surely it would have required an inundation of immense duration to roll these shingle-stones so smooth? How many millennia would the river have taken to cut a ravine through three hundred feet of solid lava? A sense of anxiety assailed him: the new science of geology promised to order God's universe, but here it also seemed to open the prospect that man might be more insignificant than he had ever realized. Was the world really aeons old, as Lyell was now suggesting? Was man really lost in time as well as in space?

'"The wilderness has a mysterious tongue, which teaches awful doubt,"' said Darwin, quietly, feeling Shelley's lines appropriate to the moment. FitzRoy felt bound to agree with him.

Conrad Martens sat down to paint the scene; then, with their food almost exhausted, FitzRoy gave the order to turn back. It took them just two days to shoot back downriver, to the rejuvenating sight of the *Beagle* standing at anchor, fresh-painted and jaunty as a frigate, and a cheerful, welcoming, 'Hello hello hello!' from Sulivan.

The *Beagle* had gone on to complete the survey of Tierra

del Fuego, while the *Adventure* had committed the last bays and headlands of the Falklands to paper. Finally, in late June, the two ships had battled through the western end of the Magellan Strait and stood out into the long swell of the Pacific, every inch of canvas straining. Here was a rugged granite coast pounded by angry seas and howling gales, splintered by the elements into a constellation of islands, the larger peaks stabbing out from the surf like the spires of inundated churches, the smaller shoals a clutter of headstones at their base. A Herculean surveying job lay before the two crews, far greater in scope than anything ever dreamed of in Whitehall. Safe anchorages were hard to come by: if there was space for only one vessel, then FitzRoy made sure, like a hen fussing over its chick, that the *Adventure* won the berth. One inky night the *Beagle* had nearly come to grief: peering into the blackness through driving rain, the lookout man had discerned a wall of rock looming off the starboard beam. Sulivan – who had charge of the middle watch – yelled an order, whereupon the watch scrambled to run the main-tack on board and haul off the main-sheet. The ship sprang forward like an arrow from a bow, the lee-clew of the mainsail scraping hideously along the black cliff face as it did so. A moment's indecision from any quarter would have been fatal, and once again all on board had reason to bless the rigour of FitzRoy's training.

Eight hundred miles of broken coastline were mapped and named: Mellersh, Forsyth, Stokes, FitzRoy and Rowlett lent their names to islands, as did the sadly departed *Paz* and *Liebre*. King and Chaffers gave title to a lonely channel each, while Bynoe was awarded a whole cape. Time and again the elements threatened to batter them to destruction. Even though the *Beagle* and the *Adventure* were working no further south than France lies to the north, giant icebergs barged each other aside in their efforts to get at the little ships and crush them to matchwood. Ceaseless rain and relentless waves saw to it that, month in, month out, nothing on the ships was allowed to dry out. The men's clothes literally rotted on their bodies.

Endless applications of salt rubbed their skin red raw. Their lips split and bled. The lack of fresh food in the southern winter took its toll: the purser, Mr Rowlett, lay in the sickbay of the *Beagle* doubled in agony with some unknown stomach complaint; even Stokes, the indefatigable Stokes, lay prostrate in the grip of a chronic chest infection, coughing up blood.

Finally, FitzRoy decided that his crew could stand it no longer, and ran north for Valparayso, praying all the way that the pair would pull through. At Cape Tres Montes, where a jutting peninsula forces the jostling battalion of islands to an abrupt halt, they beat out through relentless gales into the Golfo de Peñas – the aptly named Gulf of Pains – pursued by a derisive, shrieking pack of fulmars, shearwaters and diving petrels. Here they buried Rowlett at sea, sewn with due formality into his hammock, the final stitch through his nostrils, two roundshot at his feet to weigh him down. For Darwin, who had persuaded the amiable purser to advance him so much money during the voyage, the awful and solemn moment when the unforgiving waters covered his friend's body brought a vague, inexplicable thrill of guilt. FitzRoy's black despair was more focused, more ferocious in its intensity. He retreated into silent, furious thought. Rowlett, at thirty-eight, had been the oldest man aboard: he had, quite simply, not been strong enough to cope with the demands of the south. Stokes was younger, tougher, fitter, a teeth-gritted fighter. He would make it to Valparayso.

At last, after several hundred miles of impenetrable rain-soaked forest, the heavens cleared – as they always did at these latitudes – and Valparayso Bay opened out before them in the sunshine. The sky was clean and blue, the air was electric-dry, the sun was warm and forgiving: all nature here sparkled with life. The little town lay pillowed against rounded hills of warm red earth. Low, whitewashed houses with terracotta-tiled roofs curved around a crowded harbour embroidered with dainty sails. Higgledy-piggledy cottages, piled one on top of another, tumbled flower-strewn down the gentle slopes. Heady, aromatic vapours raced each other from the shore to be the first to greet the ships. And there, standing in an attitude of stern, avuncular protection behind the harbour's fringing hills, its sides a shifting palette of soft lilacs and violets in the delicate afternoon haze, was the snow-capped peak of Volcan Aconcagua, the highest point in the Americas.

There were rich English merchants aplenty in Valparayso – one of them, Richard Corfield, an old classmate of Darwin's from Shrewsbury. There would be parties here, and dinners, and good food, and female company too. The officers could shave their beards. They could dress decently. After the wintry beating they had taken, it felt as if they had suddenly fetched up in Paris or London on a perpetual summer's day. All, of course, were hungry for news from home. Was Lord Grey still the prime minister? No, he had resigned, but there was no word of a successor. Were the Whigs still in government? Yes, but they were calling themselves the Liberals now. Was the country now covered from end to end by railways? No, not yet, but it was only a matter of time. Darwin, who could not wait to get off the ship and sleep in a real bed once more, gathered his belongings and moved into Corfield's house. Most of the officers secured little cottages with flower-bedecked gardens where they could rest and recuperate, at least when they were not required to be on duty. FitzRoy, though, refused to leave the *Beagle*. He would neither abandon Stokes, who was best treated in the sanitized confines of the ship's sickbay, nor call a halt to the drafting of the Tierra del Fuego charts. Every evening he sat alone in his cabin, working late into the night, completing Stokes's task of converting their raw, soaking, hard-won observations into crisp, clean, dry maps. Wickham was deputized to attend the customary official functions and to carry out the normal shore duties of a visiting British naval captain. FitzRoy dared not be diverted, dared not slacken at his task, not even for a second. His determination was intense, his concentration furious. The voyage of the *Beagle* must be flawless in every respect.

Rowlett's death is upon my hands, he thought. *He put his trust in me, as so many have, and I failed to deliver him safely to his destination. At the very least, these charts will become his memorial. It is incumbent upon me to ensure that they are worthy of his memory.*

Twelve bloodshot eyes stared in disdainful response, as Darwin waved the packet provocatively back and forth before the weary scarlet eyelids. One of the condors hunched its shoulders with boredom. Another tested a manacled talon against its fetters for the hundredth time that day.

'Another glass of wine, old man?' asked Corfield.

'If you please,' said Darwin eagerly, feeling light-headed with pleasure after so long without tasting a drop. 'It is extraordinary. Look! They have absolutely no sense of smell.'

Again he waved the little packet in the air, to the supreme indifference of the assembled condors. Then he unwrapped it, and tossed the meat at the feet of the nearest of the gruesome creatures. Instantly, the whole garden went crazy, as the cackling recipient ripped and tore at his feast with beak and claws, while the other five thrashed violently at their manacles in an effort to steal it from him.

'You are a marvel, Darwin,' said Corfield over the din. 'I shall never forget you standing by the gas-light in our sixth-form bedroom, trying to divert the flame on to some magnesium with that little brass pipe of yours. It is a wonder you didn't blow up the whole school.'

'Why do you have condors in your garden, anyway?'

'Do you have any idea how difficult it is to buy peacocks in these parts?' joshed Corfield. 'I bought them for sixpence each from an Indian. Quite a number of landowners hereabouts have them. It is the fashion, I suppose. I wouldn't go too close – they are deucedly filthy creatures. That's why they are tethered.'

'I presumed it was to stop them flying away.'

'Oh, no, they cannot fly away very easily. They need a cliff and a prevailing wind to take off, especially after a feed. Rather like myself, old man. But they are absolutely riddled with lice. The one on the end is dying – look. All the lice crawl to the outside feathers when the bird is about to die.'

'Remarkable,' said Darwin, with genuine fascination.

'Remarkable, but disgusting. Actually, I think I shall get rid of them. The squawking gets on one's nerves after a while.'

Corfield's spacious garden, bisected by a clear rivulet of Andean water, stretched out languorously behind his attractive single-storey mansion in the wealthy suburb of Almendral. All the rooms opened directly on to a central quadrangle, and it was to this courtyard that he and Darwin repaired to escape the screeching and flapping of the merchant's pets. Corfield was short, balding, florid, dapper and confident.

'So – for what purpose may you have come to these parts?'

'My principal aim is to make an expedition into the high Andes. It is my dream to stand on an Andean pinnacle and look down on the plains of Patagonia below. I am a ship's naturalist now, you know.'

'You have come to admire the beauties of nature, eh? Well, I should be fain to have accompanied you, were you heading to St Jago. I myself enjoy admiring the beauties of nature, in the form of the rather fine *señoritas* there!'

'My intention is to prove Lyell correct,' Darwin pressed on, undaunted. 'Lyell is a geologist. He believes that geological change is an immensely slow process—'

Corfield cut him off: 'The cove who wrote *Principles of Geology*? I have all three volumes on my library shelves.'

'There is a third volume of Lyell?' Darwin could barely contain his excitement.

'Help yourself, old boy.'

'My God, Corfield. I cannot tell you how pleasant it is to meet with such a straightforward, thorough Englishman in these vile countries.'

Corfield laughed uproariously. 'Well, my dear man, I am a sufficiently thorough Englishman that I shall desist from accompanying you up the Andes! You are welcome to all those lice-ridden hovels in the mining districts. But if there is any material assistance I can offer in effecting your purpose, then I promise you of my service.'

'I say, Corfield, there is. Would you mind awfully cashing a bill for a hundred pounds for me? It is on my father's account. His money is as good as the bank.'

'I know. My father gets all his financial advice from yours. That would be no problem, old fellow.'

'This is most awfully generous of you.'

'Don't mention it. But I must say, Darwin, the last I heard you were bound for the parsonage! You're the last person I expected to see pitching up in Valparayso.'

'Oh, but I am a priest-in-waiting. The little wife and the little parsonage will follow in due course, have no doubt of that.'

But would they? Suddenly, Darwin was suffused with the certain knowledge that he had been putting off the parsonage because he no longer wanted it. He wanted to bestride the Andes. He wanted to uncover the mysteries of the scientific world. *He wanted to make a difference.* His father would be apoplectic with rage, of course. But then, his father was ten thousand miles away.

The supper party in Darwin's honour convened from nine o'clock in the long hall that spread itself along the southern side of the inner quadrangle. The *estrado*, a low, raised platform that ran the length of the inside wall, was scattered with carpets and velvet cushions for the women to sit upon, cross-legged like Moors. Leather armchairs were brought for the men. The first to arrive was Señora Campos, a tall, elderly, aristocratic Chilean lady with something of the condor in her demeanour. Her eye lit upon Corfield's atlas, which lay open on the piano, displaying a gaudy map of central Chili over which Darwin had pored enthusiastically that afternoon.

'¡Ah! Esta es contradança!' she announced. It is a country dance. '¡Qué bonita!'

Corfield whispered low in Darwin's ear: 'The standards of education in Chilean society may not be what you are used to, old man.'

Corfield's mulatto servants – or were they slaves? Darwin could not be sure – brought a huge gourd of *maté* on a silver salver, with sugar and orange juice mixed in, and a silver tube for sucking up the brew.

'It is considered rank bad manners to wipe the drinking tube after a lady has sucked it,' whispered Corfield, as Señora Campos lifted the tube to her parched lips.

Gradually, the other guests assembled: Major Sutcliffe, Mr Kennedy and Robert Alison, all merchants; Renous, a German trader; Señor Remedios, an elderly Chilean lawyer; and three young local *señoritas* who, it appeared to Darwin, had designs to become the *señora* of Corfield's household. Like the women of Buenos Ayres or Monte Video, they wore slender, figure-hugging garments, arranged nonchalantly to reveal their white silk stockings and pretty little feet. To his embarrassment, he could clearly see the embroidered garter visible beneath one girl's diaphanous petticoat. And, of course, the inevitable silk veils swirled up from their waists and over the backs of their extravagant hair-combs, before tumbling down over their faces, leaving one black, brilliant, inviting eye uncovered in each case. They took an unnecessarily long and lascivious time sucking at the drinking-tube. This was, he reflected, only an approximation to civilization.

'How wonderfully strange,' said Señora Campos over dinner, 'that I should have lived to dine in the same room with Englishmen. As a girl, I remember that at the mere cry of "*Los Ingleses*", every soul, carrying what valuables they could, took to the mountains.'

'Pirates,' explained Corfield helpfully. 'They used to loot the churches.'

'I assure you, madam, that most of my countrymen are the most devout Christians,' Darwin reassured her.

'But how is that so, Señor Darwin? Do not your padres,

your very bishops marry? It is a strange idea of Christianity.'

'It is a different sort of Christianity, madam, but it is Christianity all the same.'

'What surprises me,' said Major Sutcliffe huffily through a mouthful of ragoût, 'is that here we are in the modern age, and I cannot walk down the street without being followed by a gaggle of wretched children shouting *pirata* at me.'

'My servant,' offered Señor Remedios from beneath a pair of extravagant white eyebrows, 'saw your ships arrive in harbour. He said there was talk that your captain might be a pirate, or a smuggler.'

Darwin snorted. 'The person who could possibly mistake Captain FitzRoy for a smuggler would never perceive any difference between Lord Chesterfield and his valet!'

Renous the German, whose hair bristled spikily like a hedgehog poised to defend itself, posed a direct question of the lawyer: 'Tell me, Señor Remedios, what do you think of the King of England sending out a collector to your country to pick up lizards and beetles, and to break stones?'

'*Hay un gato encerrado aqui*,' replied the old man. There is a cat shut up here.

'What does he mean?' hissed Darwin to Corfield.

'It is a local expression,' Corfield hissed back. 'It means all is not well.'

'No man is so rich as to send out people to pick up rubbish,' concluded the lawyer. 'I do not like it.'

Renous gave Darwin a sympathetic look. 'I am something of a collector myself, Señor Darwin. I once left some caterpillars with a serving girl, giving her orders to feed them leaves so that they might turn into butterflies. The news was rumoured through the town, and the padres were consulted. The governor had me arrested on charges of sorcery. I suffered an unpleasant few days in the town lock-up before the mix-up was corrected.'

'So much for your modern age, Major Sutcliffe!' said Mr Kennedy, laughing.

'But are you not curious, Señora, concerning the works of nature?' persisted Darwin. 'Why a caterpillar turns into a butterfly? Why a volcano erupts? Why there are mountains here in Chili, but Patagonia to the east is as flat as a pancake?'

'All such enquiries are useless and impious,' replied Señora Campos with a sniff. 'It is quite sufficient that God has made the mountains thus.'

One of the sultry young women giggled.

There was a moment's awkward silence, before Corfield intervened, to steer the conversation discreetly on to other matters. Further dishes were brought, all of them of a fiery intensity, before the repast concluded with a very English jelly-pudding.

'Thought I'd make you feel at home, old man,' murmured Corfield, simultaneously managing a sly wink at the young lady to his right, as two scoops of jelly wobbled on to her plate.

Darwin waited for his own pudding to cease shimmying before he plunged in his spoon, but mysteriously, it refused to comply. Instead, the faintest of vibrations could be seen to agitate the translucent sheen of its surface. Inexplicably, the jelly seemed to tremble more, not less, the longer it sat on his plate.

One of the young women screamed. Señor Remedios hurled back his chair and jumped to his feet with an alacrity that belied his years. The servants were already running for the doorway, but it was a close contest between them and the guests. Even the English merchants had leaped up from their seats and were now hastening from the room. Darwin, dumb-founded, was left alone at the table. 'What is it?' he asked.

'An earthquake,' said Corfield, wiping his chin with his napkin and straightening his clothing as he, too, prepared to leave.

'Oh,' said Darwin stupidly.

'We have them every day or two in these parts. It is why we always leave the doors open, in case they jam shut. The vast majority amount to nothing – just a little rumbling sound.

But then again, the entire town of Copiapó was flattened a few years back. Are you coming?'

Darwin rose to his feet with as much dignity as he could muster. 'That was rather a case of the devil take the hindmost,' he said disdainfully.

'There is a want of habit in governing their fear in these parts. Unlike your Englishman, it is not a feeling they are ashamed of.'

'So I saw.' Darwin gave Corfield a nod of mutual superiority, then made for the door with noticeably more haste than would otherwise have been necessary.

'Come along – press it on! Lend a hand there, Covington!'

Darwin had set out for the Andes at dawn, on one of Corfield's horses, sitting astride Corfield's horsecloths, wearing Corfield's boots, spurs, stirrups and hat. His father, he assured himself, would settle his account with Corfield in due course. He had also hired two *guasos*, Mariano and Gonzales by name, in an attempt to re-create the atmosphere of his Patagonian expedition; but these Chilean gauchos, who had formerly been in the service of Lord Cochrane, were far too deferential. They refused, for instance, to take their meals with him, preferring to eat with Covington instead. Their dress, excepting a pair of absurd six-inch spurs, had none of the extravagance of their Patagonian counterparts; they wore plain ponchos and worsted leggings of a muted green. They knew nothing of the *bolas*. They never ate meat. They were, decided Darwin, men of the serving classes rather than true men of action. He felt secretly glad that, at the last minute, he had decided not to don his own gaucho costume.

He had also recruited an *arriero* – a muleteer in a felt top hat – who brought with him ten mules, led by their *madrina* or godmother, an old steady mare with a bell around her neck that the other beasts would follow anywhere, even over a precipice if necessary. This was a handy arrangement, as it was only necessary to recapture the *madrina* after a night's grazing, and the others would come obediently to heel. Each mule could carry a staggering three-hundred-pound load up the narrowest of defiles, which was why he had felt no compunction in bringing with him an entire bed, borrowed from Corfield's house. True, the frame was an unwieldy shape, but Covington had been deputized to walk behind the animal, on watch for any awkward shifts of balance. The bed would certainly provide a solution to the lice problem that Corfield had warned him about.

The party trudged upwards for hours through delightful sunshine, the scenery becoming increasingly verdant the higher they climbed. They passed shepherds' cottages, their shiny lawns smoothed out beside crystal-clear streams, and emerald fields studded with dairy cattle, all standing motionless like china figurines. There were groves of oranges and figs, and fluttering orchards of peach-blossom alive with humming-birds. Finally, a breathtaking view of Valparayso – Paradise Valley indeed – opened out far below, amid patchwork fields. It was, thought Darwin, joyfully, exactly like the colour-plates of the Swiss Alps one saw in annuals. He was not so carried away with enthusiasm, however, as to allow his sense of scientific enquiry to remain dulled. Where, he wondered, were all the wild animals? He had seen the occasional fieldmouse, and indeed had succeeded in catching one. In the still of the evening, he had heard the faint cry of the *bizcacha*, a burrowing rodent, and the unpleasant call of the goatsucker bird, which was said to be able to milk tethered goats with its beak. But that was all. Paradise Valley seemed a strangely depopulated Eden, as if the world was indeed brand new.

Of marine life, however, there was evidence aplenty. There were thick shell-beds arrayed in terraces up the mountain slopes, so vast they had been hacked into by local farmers as a source of lime. What on earth had caused these terraces to bank up there, covered as they were in sand and sea-rolled shingle? Many of the shells were embedded in a reddish-black mould, which under Darwin's portable microscope revealed itself to be marine mud, the minute, decomposed particles of organic bodies. He dug deeper, to find fragments of ancient pottery and the imprint of some plaited rush, long since rotted away. This made no sense. If, as Lyell insisted, shell-beds on mountainsides had been lifted gradually from the sea over limitless, timeless aeons, how could there be evidence of human habitation buried within? Perhaps FitzRoy was right after all. Perhaps the Old Testament was right. Perhaps this was the drowned detritus of the great flood.

Remember what Professor Sedgwick impressed upon you, he told himself. *One piece of evidence proves nothing to the geologist. Only an overwhelming mass of evidence can prove anything. Hold your tongue until you know the truth.*

'What are you looking for, Don Carlos?'

Mariano, tugged by curiosity, had wandered across from lighting the campfire.

'I am trying to establish what these sea-shells are doing here, halfway up a mountainside.'

'They are not sea-shells, Don Carlos. They are mountain-shells.'

Clearly, the *guasos* knew even less of the natural world than their gaucho cousins.

Darwin sat in silence until Mariano had wandered away, watching the valleys blacken and the snowy peaks of the Andes turn ruby in the setting sun. In the half-light, he perused Corfield's copy of Lyell's *Principles of Geology Volume 3* once again. Lyell was utterly unequivocal. The sea had been uplifted to the mountainsides. The process had occurred gradually, over countless millennia: like the formation of sedentary rock, it could never be witnessed by the naked eye. It was a process that was now completed, and indeed had been completed long before man had ever walked the face of the earth.

He gazed once more at the inexplicable staircase of shell-terraces below, marching down the mountain slopes to the sea. The evidence simply did not fit. Perturbed, he crossed the field in which they had made camp, changed into his nightclothes, jammed on a new nightcap, pulled back the sheets and climbed into bed.

In the clammy light of dawn, the view had all but disappeared. A fog bank had rolled in far below, curling into ravines, turning solitary hillocks into islets, and washing in slow-moving waves against the implacable black rocks. Shivering with cold, a warming cup of *maté* clasped between his hands, Darwin entertained the thought that the caves and bays of Tierra del Fuego must look like this from the air. Even as he shared the observation with himself, a gentle, rippling sea breeze caused the fog to eddy and break upon a shell-terrace far below, like a wave furling upon a beach.

Suddenly, his blood seemed to stand still in his veins. His heart felt as if it had stopped. His hands fell limp, and the cup of *maté* tumbled soundlessly to the grass at his feet. The answer – the answer to everything – had come to him so suddenly he almost believed for a moment that he had been shot. The shell-terraces were *beaches*. Each terrace was a beach. Each one had been wrenched into the air by an earthquake – a big earthquake, not the constant, minuscule tremors that plagued the inhabitants of Valparayso. The mountains were indeed rising from the sea. But they weren't doing it gradually. They were doing it in a series of violent lurches. They hadn't stopped rising – they were still doing it. Much of the uplift had occurred within the lifetime of man. That was why he had found pottery. It was why so few animals lived here – it was new country. Lyell was wrong. FitzRoy was wrong. The Bible was wrong. He – Charles Darwin – had the answer. How he burned with excitement, with pride, and with an overwhelming sense of *ownership* of this amazing, incredible idea.

'Is everything all right, sir?' Covington had spotted the teacup at his master's feet.

'Yes – no . . . That is, everything's fine.'

Dare he try to share his discovery with the mule-headed Covington? How he wished that FitzRoy were here. How he wished he could send a semaphore telegraph, right this minute, all the way to Henslow in Cambridge. *Dare* he try?

'Do you see these shell-terraces on the mountain slopes?' he began.

'Shell-terraces, sir?'

'Yes. Shell-terraces. Do you see how they rise, in steps?'

'Steps, sir?'

'Yes. Steps. They . . . Oh, never mind.'

'I'm sorry sir, I don't—'

'Go and . . . go and pack up my linen. I shall be there directly.'

'Aye aye sir.'

Still bewildered as to where he had gone wrong, Covington stomped off to see to his master's bedding.

'As for London – what is London? We can do anything in my country.'

This man should meet Lieutenant Sulivan, thought Darwin. His chest pulled taut and his head feeling light from the altitude, he sat upon a wrought-iron chair at the centre of a sunlit lawn, drinking chardonnay with Mr Dawlish, a mine-owner from Cornwall.

'You have never been to London, I take it?'

'Of course not,' said Dawlish. 'Whatever for would I wish to visit London? What is London?'

'What indeed?' said Darwin, for the avoidance of argument.

At the edge of the lawn, where ugly mounds of scarred earth formed primitive ramparts about an ink-dark mineshaft, a wiry, sweat-bathed Chilean miner in a leather apron emerged blinking into the light. He stood shaking on the rim of the shaft, ribs protruding, nostrils distended, muscles quivering, knees trembling with exertion. On his bare back, a two-hundred-pound load of copper ore strained against his shoulder-straps. He stared at the seated pair boldly from beneath his tight-fitting scarlet skullcap. Unsure how to respond, Darwin waved back limply, a gesture he regretted the moment he had made it.

'The shaft is four hundred and fifty feet deep,' explained Mr Dawlish, to account for the miner's shaking knees.

'There is a ladder?'

'No. But there are notched tree trunks, zigzagging up the inside. And I allow them to stop once for a rest, on the way up. They are fed upon boiled beans and bread twice a day – which is better than agricultural workers. They are also given two days off every three weeks.'

'That is generous,' agreed Darwin, comparing the arrangement favourably with conditions in his uncle's factories.

'I like to be generous. I was a miner myself, you see, back in Polzeath.'

'Really?'

'I came out here to make my fortune. I had heard that the Chilean mine-owners threw their copper pyrites away, thinking it useless. It was true. They knew nothing of the roasting process, which removes the sulphur prior to smelting. So for a few dollars I bought one of the richest veins in the country. And look about you now!'

Darwin looked about him. Mr Dawlish's property certainly did not *feel* as if it were at the heart of a mining-district. There were no clanking wheels, no roaring furnaces, smoke or hissing steam-engines. Just a series of holes in the ground. The mine was so primitive, in fact, that it had to be drained by men hauling leather bags of water up the shaft. All the ore, it transpired, had to be shipped to Swansea to be smelted.

'This mine is worth eight thousand pounds. I paid three pounds and eight shillings for it,' said Mr Dawlish expansively. 'As for London,' he repeated, 'what is London? We can do anything in my country.'

Idly, he picked a louse from his scalp, and flicked it away. Darwin felt relieved that he had brought his own bed.

'London *is* where the King lives,' he retorted, suddenly keen to ascribe at least one virtue to the British capital.

'I heard that George Rex had died,' said Mr Dawlish.

'He did. But there is a new king now.'

'Indeed? And how many more in the Rex family are yet alive?'

Darwin found himself lost for words.

They pressed ever upwards, past thundering mud-coloured torrents, to regions where the rocks lay freshly split and scattered by a thousand earthquakes. They hurried on past overhanging boulders that teetered implausibly above their heads, and precipices that fell away sheer to either side. The lush greenery of the lower slopes gave way to a matt-purple rock dotted with tiny alpine flowers, a landscape that was stark and majestic but never quite beautiful. They crossed rickety suspension bridges, mere bundles of sticks knotted together with thongs of animal hide, which swung precariously above rushing gorges. Led by their *madrina*, the mules never put a foot wrong. Only when they reached the snowline was Darwin's confidence shaken: here the near-vertical strata had been eroded into wild, crumbling pinnacles interspersed with columns of weathered ice. Atop one of the ice-towers, the melting snow had revealed the perfectly preserved body of a pack-mule, entombed upside down, all four legs in the air, frozen stiff where it had tumbled to its death from the path above.

Finally, with pounding heads and panting chests, they breasted the Peuquenes Ridge, the continental divide, at a height of thirteen thousand feet. Here, amid frost-shattered stones bathed silver by the moonlight, they made camp. A million stiletto stars pricked the night sky. So dry and still was the air that sparks flew from the saddle straps, and static electricity lifted the wool of Darwin's waistcoat. The *guasos* lit a fire, using little white flints that they gathered locally: Darwin was overjoyed to discover that these 'flints' were actually slivers of tropical sea-coral, baked rock-hard by volcanic action. But there was to be no hot food: the potatoes refused to cook, even though they sat boiling on the fire all evening.

'This cursed pot does not choose to boil the potatoes,' said Mariano, who had never made camp so high before.

'I told you we should have brought the old pot,' said Gonzales. 'This pot is cursed.' He, too, had never camped at such heights.

'It is the altitude,' Darwin tried to explain. 'There is less oxygen up here, so the water boils at a lower temperature. That is also why it is so difficult to breathe – why we are suffering from *puna*.'

'*Puna*, Don Carlos? *Puna* is caused by snow. Wherever there is snow, there is *puna*. Everybody knows that.'

The two *guasos* shook their heads at the Englishman's ignorance. Covington, unsure who to believe, stared dumbly at the ground. Darwin did not care. He was in heaven. He was the first geologist in all history to pass between the summits of the Andes. His cold supper of dried beef and palm-treacle tasted like manna from heaven.

I am alone here, he thought. In the electric silence of the mountaintops, he felt as if he could hear the chorus from Handel's *Messiah*, in full orchestra, trumpeting all its glory inside his head.

The next day they followed the path of an old watercourse, down into the dip that separates the Peuquenes Ridge from the higher Portillo Ridge to the east. To Darwin's astonishment and delight, the dry stream-bed levelled out, then began to wind its way uphill. This was incredible. Visible proof that the second ridge had uplifted since the first, that its rocks were younger. The Portillo Ridge appeared to be constructed of volcanic lava, which had solidified into porphyry, as if the lava had somehow been injected between the sandstone layers of the Andes. All along the *cordillera*, volcanic cones broke the jagged asymmetry of the mountain chain. What connection did these volcanoes have with the earthquakes that were jolting the Andes by stages into the air? Did the violence of the earth tremors release vents of lava that erupted at high pressure between the gasping rocks? Darwin's brain whirled, trying to encompass it all.

There were more frozen mules by the wayside now, and clusters of wooden crosses alongside the track. Condors wheeled in and out of the icy·clouds above. They were forced to stop every fifty yards for the mules to catch their breath. The lack of air produced the same sensation, Darwin noted, that he used to feel after a school run on a frosty day. The footprints of the mules crushed the snow crimson – not blood, as he first thought, but the tiny spores or eggs of some primitive organism, measuring less than a thousandth of an inch in diameter beneath the all-seeing scrutiny of his microscope. Finally the party arrived between the enclosing walls of the Portillo Pass, the 'little door' in the mountains, and gazed in awe upon the flat, featureless plains of the pampas below: a vast, sleeping expanse broken only by the rivers that ran away like silver threads in the rising sun, before losing themselves in the immensity of the distance. He had achieved his ambition.

They began their descent towards the border-post of the Republic of Mendoza. At their second halt Darwin laid animal-traps, and succeeded in catching another mouse.

'This mouse is different from the mice on the Chilean side.'

'Of course,' said Mariano, taking a cursory look. 'Chilean mice are different from Mendocino mice.'

'All the animals on the Chilean side are different from all the animals on the Mendoza side,' explained Gonzales, as if he were addressing an idiot.

'*All* of them? Are you sure?' He had to be careful here. Mariano and Gonzales had already failed to distinguish themselves on the natural philosophy front.

'Everybody knows this, Don Carlos. The condors, well, they can fly across from one side to the other. But the animals – they will not cross the passes. It is too cold. So the Chilean animals and the Mendocino animals, they are all quite different.'

Darwin reeled. This meant that the animals had come into being *after* the Andes had risen – and the Andes were still rising. So they could not, in fact, have been created by God on the sixth day. The two sets of animals were either new creatures, or – the terrifying enormity of the possibility raised the hairs aloft all the way down his spine – they had somehow transmuted, or metamorphosed, from original, common ancestors. At once, he felt puny and insignificant before the vast and scarcely comprehensible scale of such changes; one man alone, in the vastness of the *cordillera*. But at the same time he knew that the whole edifice of Christianity must heave and shake before the remorselessness of his logic, like an Andean pinnacle crumbling before the simple power of an earth tremor. *If I am right*, he thought, *if I am right – then my findings will be crucial to the theory of the formation of the world.*

'If you please sir – would you like me to kill and skin the mouse, sir?' enquired Covington, politely and resentfully.

How Darwin burned for a FitzRoy or a Henslow to be present.

The Mendoza customs and border-post proved to be a grubby hovel, staffed by two unshaven soldiers and a pure-bred Indian tracker, who was retained as a kind of human bloodhound in case any smugglers should attempt to give the post a wide berth. The three men were jumpy, and utterly bewildered by the concept of a *naturalista*. In an attempt to ease the administrative deadlock, Darwin produced his passport signed by General Rosas. One of the soldiers, a lieutenant who could read, perused the document and shot Darwin a look of disgust.

'If you are protected by the general, then you may proceed. The man who would deny passage to a servant of the general is not long for this world, as you are most probably aware.'

Darwin decided to let the accusation that he was anyone's 'servant' pass. 'The general has influence in Mendoza?'

'No, the general has no influence in our country. But it is only a matter of time. He has seized Buenos Ayres. He has taken control of most of the United Provinces. Many people have died. He is cleansing the country of Indians as far south as the Rio Negro. Now his armies are massing on the Mendoza border. We Mendocinos shall not be able to stop him. It is only a matter of time before we all become part of your general's empire.'

The last few words dripped from the officer's tongue like bad wine. Darwin remembered FitzRoy's caustic assessment of the general's motives, and reflected uneasily that perhaps his friend had been right, after all. He adopted his most soothing tones.

'I am not a personal acquaintance of the general. This passport was given to me as a representative of His Majesty King William IV of Great Britain.'

At this the other soldier perked up.

'Heh – Great Britain. That is near England, right?'

'After a fashion,' Darwin replied.

'You are a *pirata*?'

'No . . . no, I am not a pirate. As I told you, I am a *naturalista*. The two are really quite different.'

'*Naturalista . . . pirata . . .* Why do you *Ingleses* not keep to normal occupations?' the soldier grumbled to himself.

By nightfall, relations had improved sufficiently for Darwin's party to join the soldiers for supper around the rudimentary table of the border-post. His bed, which they had accepted without demur as part of a *naturalista*'s travelling accoutrements, had been installed in the back room. The border guards ate in silence, chewing slowly on hunks of boiled beef, while Mariano and Gonzales finally induced the recalcitrant potatoes to succumb to their fate. Halfway through the meal, a large black wingless bug fell from the thatched roof with a plop on to the table, where it sat, paralysed with confusion.

'What is that?' asked Darwin.

'It is a *benchuca* bug,' said the lieutenant. 'A bloodsucker.'

Experimentally, Darwin extended a fingertip towards the bewildered beast. Instantly, it seemed to come to its senses, seizing the digit between its forelegs and sinking its sucker into his flesh. Over the next few minutes it grew slowly fatter as it gorged itself with blood, until eventually it resembled a huge distended purple grape clamped to the end of his finger. Finally sated, it fell off, whereupon Darwin whipped out a little jar of preserving-spirits and swept the creature into it.

'Ha! You may have brought your own bed to avoid the lice, Don Carlos,' guffawed Mariano, 'but the *benchucas* live in the ceiling!'

That night, he discovered exactly what Mariano meant. As Covington, the soldiers, the muleteer and the two *guasos* slept swathed in blankets under the stars, he lay besieged between his crisp linen sheets. There seemed to be a whole army of *benchucas*. It was the most disgusting feeling to wake in the night, and sense their huge, soft, wingless bodies crawling all over him, sucking at his flesh. He lit a candle and burned several from his skin, but the supply seemed limitless. *A plague of benchucas*, he thought to himself. *How Biblical. Perhaps the Lord has visited them upon me, on account of my presumption.*

The next day they set off for the city of Mendoza, a two-day ride across baking, deserted plains. At one point a huge swarm of locusts flew overhead, heading northward in the direction of the city, a seeming harbinger of the destruction due to be unleashed by General Rosas. The swarm began as a ragged cloud of a dark reddish-brown colour, like smoke from some great plains fire, billowing several thousand feet into the air. Then a curious rushing noise made itself heard, like a strong breeze swishing through the rigging of a mighty ship-of-the-line, and countless millions of the insects whirred overhead. Occasionally, confused outriders crashed blindly into the slower-moving mule train below: more than one dazed locust hurtled into the yielding softness of Darwin's feather pillows, then marched testily up and down the bedlinen in search of food.

Mendoza's spires rose listlessly from the open plain ahead. They found the city forlorn and bereft of spirit, its inhabitants dazed like cattle, stupidly awaiting their fate. Robbed of all energy, one or two gauchos lounged drunkenly in the streets.

Mariano and Gonzales tipped their hats politely to a fat negress astride a donkey, her face disfigured by a huge goitre. Darwin bought an entire wheelbarrowload of peaches for threepence. They did not stay. Mendoza could await General Rosas without them.

They recrossed the Andes by a different route, taking the Uspallata Pass, a long, barren valley populated by innumerable wretched dwarf cacti. After a hard day's ascent through crumbled rocks, at a height of seven thousand feet, they came upon another marvel: an entire grove of petrified fir trees, jutting out from the mountainside at an acute angle. There were perhaps fifty marbled columns in this ghostly forest, as snow-white as Lot's wife, their trunks a stout five feet in circumference, their leaves and branches long since lost to history. They were perfectly crystallized: the tiniest details of the bark were visible, and the rings within the wood were as easy to count as those of a living tree. They projected from a sandstone escarpment, which meant that they must once have lain at the bottom of the sea. This eerie grove high in the freezing mountains, Darwin realized, had once waved to the breezes of the Atlantic shore. The trees must have become submerged and petrified *before* they were uplifted into the mountains. The land had sunk before it had risen. The surface of the earth must be in a state of continuous agitation, no more than a thin crust over a viscous layer, that heaved and buckled throughout countless millions of years. Once more his whole being thrilled to the enormity of his discoveries; once more he had to bite his lip in frustration that there was no one present to discuss them with, no one to sit back and whistle at the size of the fire he would light beneath orthodox opinion.

The pass itself was a chaos of huge mountains, criss-crossed haphazardly by profound ravines, a place so cold that the water froze solid in their bottles. The *guasos* called it Las Animas – the souls – in memory of all those who had slipped and plunged to their deaths. The mule train, piled high with bulging sacks of geological specimens, snaked the whole length of the treacherous pass and across the Bridge of the Incas, a flimsy arch dripping with icicles; a seemingly bottomless abyss yawned invitingly below. Darwin's bed sashayed at the back, its swinging motion caricaturing the gait of the animal that bore its weight; but the mule, like its companions, stayed surefooted throughout.

Shortly before they reached the top of the first ridge, they came upon low walls – the ancient ruins of a long-forgotten Indian village.

'Who lived here?' asked Darwin.

'Nobody lives here, Don Carlos,' explained Gonzales. 'Nobody can live here. It is too cold. There is *puna*. And there is no food, no water. Only snow, for the whole year.'

'I know that nobody lives here *now*, but obviously, somebody once did.'

'*¿Quien sabe*, Don Carlos?'

'How old are these ruins?'

'*¿Quien sabe*, Don Carlos?'

It was incredible. An entire mountain village, its walls thrown down by countless earthquakes no doubt, situated in a location where human life was completely unsustainable. There was only one possible conclusion: that the whole village had been jolted high above the snowline over thousands of years, by the monstrous, churning, grinding, heaving forces at work far below.

A golden dusk was settling on the lush green fields above Valparayso as Darwin marched down the valley, striding out in front of his mule train, bursting with energy, life and confidence for the future. The boughs hung heavy with glowing peaches, and the scent of drifting woodsmoke infused the air. A sweetly competing aroma of drying figs wafted down from the flat rooftops and out across the sunlit fields, where weary labourers could be seen walking home from their day's toil in the orchards. A church bell tolled lazily in the warm summer air. After the freezing, barren heights of the Andes and the stifling, deathly stillness of Mendoza, there was something welcoming, something . . . well, almost *English* about the scene. Perhaps a certain pensive English stillness was missing from the mood, but otherwise the similarities were unmistakable. As Darwin stood admiring the view, Covington, who was leading his master's horse, caught up.

'My water bottle, if you please, Covington.'

'Aye aye sir.'

I do wish he would leave off the nautical responses, thought Darwin irritably. *He's not on the ship now.*

Covington shuffled round to the horse's flank to retrieve the water bottle, placing his left hand clumsily on the animal's withers as he did so. Suddenly, with a strangled cry, he leaped back as if stung by a wasp.

'What *is* it?' snapped Darwin.

'There!' was Covington's garbled shout.

An indistinct black shape flapped unpleasantly between the animal's shoulder-blades.

'What on earth—?'

Mariano came up and shooed the creature away. It vanished into the dusk in a rustle of leathery wings, leaving two small bloody wounds where it had sat.

'Vampire bat, Don Carlos,' said the *guaso* matter-of-factly.

Darwin shuddered. No, this was not England. This was a very, very long way from England, a very long way indeed. And it was time, frankly, to be going home.

They attained the sanctuary of Corfield's mansion on the afternoon of the following day, to be greeted by the master of the house with his customary unflappable, immaculate style. White wine was brought, a great fuss was made of the explorer, and Darwin sat back in the garden to regale his host with tales of geological castles in the air: the beaches in the mountains, the river bed that flowed upward, the two sorts of mouse, the petrified forest, the deserted village in the clouds.

'Do you not see, Corfield?' he pressed home the point excitedly. 'There can be no reason for supposing that any great catastrophe has *ever* been visited upon the earth, in any former epoch! The Biblical flood is a myth!'

'I don't gainsay it, old man,' murmured Corfield soothingly.

As he spoke he blurred horizontally in the oddest fashion, before dividing into two Corfields, one on either side of Darwin's field of vision. All of a sudden, a huge wave of nausea welled up from below, far worse than anything Darwin had ever experienced on the *Beagle*.

'Corfield, old fellow?'

'Yes?'

'I think I'm going to be sick.'

A dark, fuzzy shape obscured the daylight that streamed in through the window. Somebody's silhouette. His sister Susan, perhaps, or Catty come to read to him from one of her Society for the Diffusion of Useful Knowledge publications. Except that this did not look like his bedroom at the Mount. Where the deuce was he? A noise burbled from the mouth of the silhouette – words, soothing words, like running water gurgling across pebbles. He tried to make sense of them. As his eyes adjusted to the light, the silhouette took on a familiar aspect. The features blurred into view. A nose, eyes, a mouth. He remembered that face from somewhere. The face was telling him that everything was going to be all right. The face was something to do with a sea voyage he had once been on. The *Beagle*. That was it. It was all coming back now. He was the ship's natural philosopher on HMS *Beagle*. He could hear waves – waves on the shore.

'Philos? Are you awake?'

Bynoe tried again, still softly, but with a little more urgency this time. Darwin was stirring. 'Philos? It's me, Bynoe.'

'Bynoe?'

'How are you feeling?'

'I . . . Where am I? How came I here?'

'You are at the house of Mr Alexander Caldcleugh.'

'Who?'

'Caldcleugh – he is a British mine-owner. You were taken ill at Mr Corfield's house, but he is from home. He had to visit St Jago on business last month. You were moved to Mr Caldcleugh's house because he resides closer to the shore – I estimated that the sea air might hasten your recovery.'

'Last month? How long have I been here?'

'Six weeks.'

'Six *weeks*? Then it is 1835! But what—?'

'You have had a high fever – possibly typhoid, I'm not sure. But you are much better now. Here, I have brought you some calomel. The Indian servants wanted to treat you using traditional herbs, all sorts of mumbo-jumbo, but I have been sure to keep you well supplied with modern medicine.'

'My dear Bynoe, how long have you attended upon me?'

Bynoe's vigil had stretched through every long day of the previous six weeks. 'Not long . . . just long enough to see you well again.'

'I had some wine – I think the wine was bad . . .'

'Perhaps it was the wine. *¿Quien sabe?* But you are on the mend now, Philos, and that is all that matters.'

A sudden stab of fear sliced through Darwin's brain, as the details of his Andean expedition came jolting back. 'My specimens! Where are my specimens?' He raised himself weakly on to one elbow.

'Do not trouble yourself, Philos. Your specimens are in good hands, you may be satisfied of it. Sulivan and I labelled them all up in your behalf, and had them packed into cases, with the help of your servant Covington. He is a most assiduous and intelligent fellow – I think you underestimate him.'

'But where are they?'

'Lieutenant Wickham said they were too many for the hold of the *Beagle*, especially as we are revictualling. But luckily for you the *Samarang* was in port, and Captain Paget agreed to take them on board. He will make sure they are delivered to your Professor Henslow, you can rely upon it.'

'Thank goodness for that.'

Darwin sank back into his pillow, relief washing over him. Then a further shaft of clarity pierced his delirium. 'Bynoe?'

'Yes?'

'Why is Lieutenant Wickham in the *Beagle*? He is the commander of the *Adventure*.'

A cloud passed across Bynoe's sunny countenance.

'Things have changed in the *Beagle*, Philos.' He sighed, turning his face to the window.

'What do you mean?'

'All is not well in our little vessel, my friend. I had hoped not to bring such matters to your attention, in your enfeebled state. But you have always been too sharp for me, Philos.'

'What has happened? What is the matter?'

'You will find out when you are recuperated. But I adjure you not to bother yourself now. You will be up and about soon, I am sure of it, but you need be in no hurry. The *Beagle* will wait for you. To be honest, Philos, there is not a great deal of activity aboard the *Beagle* at present. Everything has ground to a halt.'

Chapter Twenty-one

Valparayso Harbour, 11 January 1835

———

FitzRoy sat in his darkened cabin, staring at the charts of Tierra del Fuego that lapped meaninglessly across his table. He had put aside his pen several hours ago. It lay idle beside his mapping instruments, its nib dry and tired. The steward had brought dinner many hours previously, but FitzRoy had not acknowledged the knock at the door. Not a morsel of food had passed his lips all day. He was no longer hungry. It was as if all visible life in the cabin had slowed to a stop: the only movement remaining between the four walls was his pulse, beating quietly and desperately in his wrist.

His mind, though, was too filled with thoughts to be stilled, rushing, tumbling thoughts, each individual idea shining with clarity, but when mixed together, a dazzling incoherent whirl of insight that came too fast to be unravelled, marshalled or properly evaluated. Concentrating hard, he grabbed a passing gem from the torrent, and tried his damnedest to isolate it and appreciate its import. *The survey of Tierra del Fuego is not good enough*, the thought commanded him. *It needs to be done again. There are unnamed islets, imperfect depth-soundings, uncharted rocks. All of it must be done again, and done properly this time.*

He knew deep down that this was the only course. Sitting motionless in his seat, he experienced the same rising and falling sensation in his stomach that one endures when passing rapidly over the brow of a hill – a combination, he realized, of exhilaration at the chance to put right his mistakes, and fear at the thought that it might yet prove an impossible task. The solution to this dichotomy came to him in another brilliant revelation. This time he would not plot a course through the labyrinth. That had been his mistake. He would let the path choose itself. The pure light of heaven would shine forth in the darkness and illuminate their way.

As if on cue the door opened, flooding the little cabin with a dazzling light. The dust-motes went scurrying into the corners in a panic. Had the Lord sent a messenger? No. It was Darwin. He seemed excited. He was brandishing a piece of paper. Had he not been ill, been gone a long time?

'FitzRoy – my dear man – how are you? The most marvellous news! I have a letter from Henslow. The *Avestruz Petise* – the little ostrich, you remember? – it has arrived safely in Cambridge, and has been christened *Rhea darwinii*! And moreover – the specimen of that yellow tree fungus which the Fuegians eat has also been catalogued – it too is new to science and has been named *Cyttaria darwinii*! This is an auspicious day indeed!'

Darwin continued talking, but the words melded into an unbroken babble in FitzRoy's head. Something about a letter. How Darwin was a sensation in England. Then he remembered, grasping a hard concrete fact from the racing flow of his subconscious, that he, too, had received letters. Letters that Darwin ought to read. He pushed them across the table.

Stopped in his tracks, Darwin read the first missive with horror-stricken fascination. It was from the Admiralty.

Regarding the commission of the auxiliary surveying vessels *Paz* and *Liebre*. Their lordships do not approve of hiring vessels for the Service and therefore desire that they be discharged as soon as possible.

The second letter commenced with a severe reprimand for the time taken in completing the survey of Tierra del Fuego and the Falklands, before going on to address the hiring of the *Unicorn* and its rebirth as the *Adventure*:

Inform Captain FitzRoy that the lords highly disapprove of this proceeding, especially after the orders which he previously received on the subject.

'But this – this is a disgrace!' began Darwin indignantly. 'This is an entirely political manoeuvring. Much as it grieves me to say it, I fear that this has been effected by the Liberal administration solely because you are of a Tory family.'

'Headquarters have not thought it proper to give me any assistance. But assistance shall be provided from another quarter.'

Unsure what he meant, Darwin continued to vent his outrage: 'Whatever shall we do for room? I shall have trouble enough storing my collections! How shall I fit into the library with Stokes, King, Hamond *and* Martens?'

'Martens? Martens is gone.'

'Gone? Gone where?'

'There is no money for Martens. I sold the *Adventure* for seven thousand paper dollars – a loss of fifteen hundred dollars in all. Much of the money I received went to paying off her crew. It grieved me sadly to bring her to the hammer, but my friends here on board were seriously urgent on the matter. So the *Adventure* is gone.'

Suddenly, FitzRoy felt overwhelmed by a wave of sadness, at the loss of his beautiful white schooner, and also at the loss of an old comrade. 'The *Adventure* is gone. Skyring is gone.'

'Skyring? Who is Skyring?'

FitzRoy pushed another Admiralty missive across the table. Darwin read it aloud:

Regret to inform you of the death of Lieutenant William Skyring of HMS *Dryad*, formerly of HMS *Beagle* and

HMS *Adelaide*, murdered by natives on the coast of West Africa, May 1834.

'I took his command,' explained FitzRoy, mournfully. 'The *Beagle* was to have been his. Instead he has been murdered. At first I blamed myself. Then I realized that his death is part of God's plan. The good Lord has a task for all of us. My task is to return to Tierra del Fuego to begin the survey all over again.'

'What?' Darwin almost jumped out of his skin.

'My task,' FitzRoy reiterated patiently, 'is to return to Tierra del Fuego—'

'Have you taken leave of your senses?'

'The good Lord has commanded me—'

'Of this the good Lord deliver us!' Darwin protested. 'This is madness! You will have a mutiny on your hands! If you think for one minute that I would be prepared to risk my life by going back round the Horn – I signed on for this trip with the intention of visiting the coral islands of the Pacific, not to sit in a glorified skiff being battered by South Atlantic gales year in year out until her brittle perfectionist of a captain is finally satisfied with his labours!'

Of the competing emotions accelerating unchecked through FitzRoy's brain, anger came to the fore. He felt his gorge rising. 'My decision on the matter is final.'

Darwin could hardly believe his ears. He, too, began to flush angrily. His weeks at leisure in Chilean society had reminded him what it was to live an independent life, his every move no longer subject to the arbitrary whim of one man.

'Then I am afraid you must travel without a naturalist. I shall return to stay with Mr Corfield, or Mr Caldcleugh, at whose home I have been convalescing, and shall find a different passage.'

FitzRoy's eyes flashed. 'As always, you have taken so much, and have made no provision in return. I suppose we shall have to organize a party on board.'

'A party? What are you talking about?'

'A party to thank all those members of the British community here, whose favours you have so readily accepted.'

'There is no need for that! What ever do you mean by it?'

'I mean, sir, that you are the sort of man who would receive any favours and make no return!'

His face white with rage, Darwin stood up and stalked out of the cabin, slamming the door behind him. On the maindeck he ran into the shocked figure of Lieutenant Wickham, who tried to remonstrate with him: 'Confound it, Philosopher, I wish you would not quarrel with the skipper when he is overtired.'

'Overtired? His mind has become deranged! You may inform him of my resignation as natural philosopher of the *Beagle*. I shall not reside a moment longer in this ship of fools!'

Angrily, Darwin brushed Wickham aside and headed to his quarters to collect his belongings. Wickham, perturbed, knocked softly at the door of FitzRoy's cabin. There came no answer.

The landscape of the captain's cabin had turned cold, bleak and empty. In the grey, muddy light, the colours of the little room had receded to a flat, dull monotone, the few simple items of furniture assuming ghostly outlines and washed-out hues. The faint noises of the ship – the creaking of the rigging, the slap of water against the hull, the mutter of distant voices – had blended into a continuous note so muffled as to be unintelligible. None of this, however, mattered to Robert FitzRoy: he was no longer there, except physically. He was in another place.

That was the only way to describe his fear: another place. There was no logic to it, he knew that. He wanted to fight whatever it was that held him in the dark, that toyed with him, but there was no physical adversary present. There were not even any physical symptoms about his person. There was just a shapeless, nameless dread that had removed him to its lair, a place more terrifying than any nightmare he had ever endured. The harder he tried to escape, the more tightly he was confined there. Fright and hopelessness crowded his mind, his own personal prison guards in this other place.

His physical body lay curled in its cot, sobbing uncontrollably. How long had he been crying? Hours? Days? They were not tears of relief but tears that drowned him, tears with no beginning and no end, tears that welled up unchecked from somewhere deep inside. And when his tear ducts finally dried up, he continued to sob, heaving incoherently, his misery compounded by shame and self-loathing and lack of comprehension and anger at the pointlessness of it all. Sweat poured from his body. The letters from the Admiralty had prompted this change in his mental state, that much he knew. They had been the trigger, but no more. What had followed had been not just terrifying, but terrifyingly inexplicable. What in God's name was happening to him? He hugged his pillow for comfort, the only familiar point of reference in this alien environment. He wanted to turn over, but he could not remember how to do it – it seemed a colossal, unimaginable task, too frightening even to contemplate.

He had tried ordering himself out of his malaise. *Get up. Go over to the washstand. Call for water. Shave. Tasks you have completed easily, unthinkingly, a thousand and one times.* He had even got as far as putting his feet on the floor, but as soon as he had done so, a sudden wave of panic, an awful onrushing knowledge of impending doom, had broken over him, had driven the breath from his body. He had subsided back into the cot, palpitating, short of breath, every limb leaden with unaccountable fatigue.

He tried again. *Who are you?* Nobody. *What do you feel?* Nothing. *What can you do?* Nothing. *What do you know?* Nothing. *What do you understand?* Nothing. *I am nothing. There is nothing.* His entire being was reduced to a pure and simple manifestation of panic, an urgent physical discomfort with no prospect of relief, a sense of falling with no concluding impact to bring about merciful release.

Desperately, he fought to clear his mind. Even in the midst of the two great storms they had endured, at Maldonado and off Cape Horn, he had not been so overwhelmingly afraid. But he had to do something. *The more you manage to do, the less you will want to die.* Shaking, unable to stand, weak with lack of food, he succeeded with a supreme effort in surmounting the lip of the cot and collapsing to the floor. Slowly, very slowly, he pulled himself by his fingertips across the floorboards. At last, he reached up to the tabletop for pen and paper. *Please God, give me the strength to do what I have to do.*

He had the pen in his hand now, but he had forgotten how to write. There was no feeling in his arm, no feeling flowing through his hand, no feeling directing the nib.

Concentrate. You cannot escape this . . . creature. But you can free others from the consequences of its hold upon your spirit.

Laboriously, agonizingly, he began to write, each letter a station of the cross, until finally he was finished. There, on the floor between his enfeebled arms, wet and blotchy with his renewed tears, lay his written resignation as captain of the *Beagle*.

'Sir. I must ask you to reconsider. There is a universal and deeply felt grief on board at your decision.'

'Flattered as I am by the concern of the men, Lieutenant Wickham, I have no option but to resign my command. You saw for yourself that my mental state became quite suddenly maladjusted, so as to unfit me for the leadership of this or any vessel. It is quite clearly a hereditary predisposition.'

'Sir. Mr Bynoe says it is merely the effect of a want of bodily health, and of exhaustion following a period of onerous application to duty.'

'My dear friends.' FitzRoy reached across the table, placing five rake-thin digits across the back of Wickham's hand, and the remaining five across Sulivan's. 'That simply will not do. I must invalid, and appoint Mr Wickham to the command of the *Beagle*. My brains' – he permitted himself a wry smile – 'are even more confused than they used to be in London.'

'Sir – I will not accept it. I will not accept the promotion.'

'You have no option, Mr Wickham. I order you to assume command.'

Sulivan was almost in tears. 'Sir, look at the medical evidence. Any man would have been affected by the strain of being ordered to sell the *Adventure* – and at such a loss!'

'It is true, Mr Sulivan, that I am . . . involved in difficulties. My means have been severely taxed. This may even fix me out of England. And I grant you, it was a bitter disappointment to receive such orders. The mortification still preys deeply. But more distressing still – much more distressing – is that all my cherished hopes of completing the survey of South America must now utterly fail. The Admiralty has made it quite impossible for me to fulfil the whole of my instructions. But fail I have, and I must pay the price for it. My feelings and my health no longer respond to my commands, gentlemen. A mutiny has been effected. I must give way to someone better fitted for this command.'

FitzRoy felt exhausted but relieved: relieved that it was all over, relieved to be able to speak freely about his condition at last.

'But sir – what would be gained by your resignation? Absolutely nothing. The survey would not be completed. The orders in the event of a captain invaliding his command are most explicit.'

'Remind me.'

Wickham unfolded the Admiralty instruction sheet. '"The officer on whom the command of the vessel may in consequence devolve is hereby required and directed not to proceed to a new step in the voyage; as, for instance, if carrying on the coast survey on the western side of South America, he is not to cross the Pacific, but to return to England by Rio de Janeiro and the Atlantic."'

'It seems the author was almost prescient.'

'It means there can be no chain of measurements about the globe. The survey would go unfinished. The stigma of failure would attach not just to yourself but to the *Beagle* and all her officers. But were you to remain in command, there would still be time enough this summer to finish surveying the Chilean coast back down to Tres Montes, before heading home.'

'And what of northern Chili and Peru?'

Wickham offered a consoling smile. 'There shall be others after us, who shall survey the north. But our achievement to date – *your* achievement – shall accrue to the benefit of all those on board.'

'And what if I were to succumb to another attack of the blue devils – what then?'

'Then you have my word I should accept your invitation to assume command.'

'Please sir,' entreated Sulivan, 'you have been harassed and oppressed by troubles and difficulties of the most unexpected, the most unfortunate kind. It was undoubtedly these that caused you to fall ill for a brief period. But those troubles and difficulties are behind us – by which I do not mean to belittle the drain on your means, merely to say that the worst has now been thrown at you, and here you are, sir, in full command of your faculties, the finest leader and sailor that I, or any of us, have ever sailed under. The best man, the only man, to skipper the *Beagle*.'

FitzRoy looked from Wickham's round, honest, open, troubled face to Sulivan's dark imploring gaze. 'It seems, gentlemen, that the Admiralty has me between Scylla and Charybdis. Either the survey is to be abandoned at once, or it is to be left uncompleted. For the sake of those mariners who come after us, then, and only for their sake, we shall spend one more summer surveying the coast down to Tres Montes.'

Lit up with relief and delight, Wickham and Sulivan rose to shake his hand, but he cut them short with an upraised palm. 'But I also bear responsibilities to the officers and crew of the *Beagle*. Any sign whatsoever – *any* sign – that I am losing control of my wits once more, then you are to confine me in my cabin, by force if necessary. Is that understood?'

'Yes, sir − it is understood.'

The three men shook hands, and it was hard to say which of them prayed most fervently that the latest attack would prove to be FitzRoy's last.

'I thank the good Lord that you are back with us,' said Sulivan, pumping his captain's hand as if his life depended upon it.

FitzRoy felt himself bathed in the warmth and generosity of their love; but it was not enough to wash away the layers of shame and embarrassment that seemed to him to adhere to his immortal soul.

Chapter Twenty-two

Concepción, Chili, 20 February 1835

Darwin lay flat on his back in a sunlit apple-orchard, reading a letter from his sisters, their convivial words waving in and out of the dappled light. Fanny Owen had become the proud mother of a baby daughter. 'We look forward to visiting you and *your* little wife in *your* little parsonage' – yes, yes. Catherine had included a pamphlet from the Society for the Diffusion of Useful Knowledge: *Poor Laws and Paupers Illustrated*, by Harriet Martineau. Oh, yes – she was that dreadful fierce blue-stocking who tried to popularize Liberal policy by dressing it up in cheap romantic novellas. Ridiculous. What was this one about? A new theory devised by the recently deceased Reverend Thomas Malthus, an economist who had worked for the East India Company. Hmm.

Bereft of anything better to occupy his mind while his dinner chugged through his digestive system, Darwin began to read. Malthus's theory was pretty bleak. Apparently the population of Great Britain had doubled from twelve million to twenty-four million in just thirty years. Good grief. With the population rising faster than the food supply, struggle and starvation must inevitably result. Charity only aggravated the problem. Poor-relief hand-outs made paupers comfortable, and only encouraged them to breed. It was a vicious circle. The only answer was enshrined in a new Liberal Act of Parliament, the Poor Law Amendment Act, which established a national network of segregated workhouses. By making poor relief available only to new workhouses, pauper husbands and wives could be kept apart from each other and prevented from breeding. This would benefit the poor in the long run by making them self-reliant, and according dignity to their labours. It all made perfect sense. It certainly improved upon years of masterly Tory inactivity. The Tories had sat on their complacent aristocratic backsides for years, expecting the same little fields and allotments to produce sufficient food for ever-increasing hordes of starving, destitute peasants. The governments of Lord Liverpool and the Duke of Wellington had created a situation where the weakest went to the wall, and only the strongest survived. It was inhuman.

A faint rumbling interrupted Darwin's philosophizing, followed by a creak from the branches above, and a plump apple fell soundlessly on to his forehead. The moment, however unpleasant, served as a reminder that the problems of an over-crowded island were thousands of miles away, and of no immediate relevance to the greater concerns that currently occupied his mind. But no sooner had he filed the Reverend Thomas Malthus away in the further recesses of his brain than the ground was gripped by another low rumble – much louder this time, like the roaring of a bull in distant underground caverns – and a score of ripe apples plummeted from the trees above. The bombardment felt like being punched by several small boys at once. He noticed, as he attempted to compose himself following the assault, that his flagon of cider had glugged its contents wastefully on to the grass.

Darwin looked across to where Covington was attempting to untether Corfield's horse, but the manservant was fighting to keep his balance like a novice ice-skater. The solid earth of the orchard seemed to have lost all physical substance, as louder and louder bass rumbles shivered through the tree-roots.

Covington had grabbed the animal's bridle for support, but the frightened beast's legs had simply given way, splaying out in opposite directions as it neighed in terror. Darwin felt himself being rolled from side to side, a helpless sausage in a pan. He tried to stand, but it was no use: waves were rolling in from the east, and he felt as sick as he ever had aboard the *Beagle* in a heaving sea. He sat down again with a bump. The tree trunks were swaying, the lighter branches thrashing madly about, the ground undulating as if all the laws of physics had been suspended for the duration. It was absolutely fascinating. It was an earthquake all right. But not one of the inconsequential daily tremors that plagued Valparayso. This was a really, really big one.

'A large star on the horizon to starboard, sir.'

FitzRoy glanced at his watch. It was after midnight. A star on the horizon should not have been entirely unexpected. Had the watch taken up astronomy?

'Correction, sir. A large signal light on the horizon to starboard. A red signal light, sir.'

Again, it was not entirely unexpected that another ship should be ploughing the same furrow as the *Beagle*, hugging the Chilean coast rather than standing out into the Pacific. They were running north-west through the Chacao Narrows, which separated the mainland from Chiloé Island – a huge, wet, forested bulk that acted as a handy windbreak for Valparayso-bound merchantmen and packet-ships. The mainland was Araucanian territory, but in all their surveying operations they had seen hardly a sign of those redoubtable warriors, so feared on the Patagonian plains to the east. The Araucanians remained hidden in their hills, dim shadows in a veil of perpetual mist marking the western boundary of their proud, unconquered nation. Chiloé Island by contrast had been settled by the Spanish, but the settlers had merged with the native population to produce a desperately poor race of forgotten *mestizo* farmers, whose hand-pushed ploughs would have been considered primitive in medieval Europe. They used charcoal for money; pigs and potatoes were their only produce. With its endless rain-soaked bogs, woods and dank fields, Chiloé reminded FitzRoy uncomfortably of Ireland. The main town, Castro, was forlorn and deserted, with grass growing in its streets. At the big old church, built from shipwreck planks and iron, an elderly man rang the hour on the bell by guess-work, for there were no clocks or watches on the island. Travel was by *piragua*, a type of native canoe that – FitzRoy was excited to discover – exactly matched the *maseulah* canoes of south-east India. Had early man settled South America by ship from across the Pacific? No ships stopped at Castro now, that was for sure. Civilization seemed to have brought few benefits in its wake.

'Sorry, sir.' The lookout changed tack again. 'I don't think it is a signal light, sir. Leastways, I don't think it's another ship. It's uncommon bright, sir.'

All hands were crowded at the starboard rail now. The red pinpoint scintillated in the darkness, an impossibly sharp ruby glowing fiercely in a black velvet sky.

'It's b-beautiful, whatever it is,' said Hamond.

'It's like the star as what the three wise men followed to Bethlehem,' breathed a reverential Chadwick, one of the main-topmen.

'It's not a star,' concluded FitzRoy. 'There are no other stars in the sky, so I think we may safely assume high clouds. And it is not another vessel, for I can observe no sign of motion. It is on the land, it is prodigious far off, and I should guess it is several thousand feet up.'

As if on cue, the mysterious light chose to reveal its iden-tity. With a searing crimson flare and an ear-splitting explo-sion of rock, a column of light funnelled vertically upwards from the cone of the volcano. Torrents of lava spewed from splits in the mountain's nozzle, pouring in gorgeous, glowing rivulets down its slopes. Brilliant jets of flame lit up the night sky, bursting like the royal fireworks before scattering their abrupt reflections across the surface of the intervening sea. The silhouettes of vast boulders, each bigger than a house, were tossed effortlessly into the air by unseen forces lurking deep within the earth.

'It is Volcan Osorno!' said FitzRoy. 'Great God – this is incredible!'

While the crew stood transfixed by the light show, Stebbing fetched the captain's theodolite, and together they calculated the height of the eruption at 7550 feet.

'Look sir! To the north!'

Bennet was gesticulating at the prow. In the distance, beyond his outstretched finger, a further scarlet pinpoint had appeared in the dark; and beyond that, another, fainter spark.

'All the other volcanoes are erupting!'

'The whole of the Andes is going off tonight!'

'It's a regular knock-down!'

It was indeed an unbelievable sight.

The first shock hit the *Beagle* early the next morning, by which time the night's pyrotechnics had faded in the light of dawn, reduced to mere columns of smoke issuing sootily from the pristine file of snowy cones.

A shudder ran through the ship's timbers, juddering from one end of the deck to the other, turning her crew's knees instantly to india-rubber. It was not the sickening crunch that follows an encounter with a submerged rock; rather, a sudden, convulsing check to her momentum, as if she had collided with a whale.

'What the deuce was that?'

'Something in the water?'

'An earthquake!' said FitzRoy. 'By God, an earthquake! It is connected to the volcanic eruptions! It's not just a passing tremor – it is an absolutely *massive* earthquake!'

Just how massive an earthquake became apparent a few days later, as they neared the little town of Concepción, which lay concealed on a gentle slope behind the peninsular port of

Talcahuano. With a clatter, the *Beagle* ran through a shoal of seaborne timber: odd beams and planks at first, then huge joists and entire pieces of furniture, as if a thousand ships had been shattered in a gale. Eventually the master had to take evasive action, as whole chairs, tables, shelves, even an entire wooden cottage-roof shouldered their way through the jumble of flotsam. A whole file of bobbing church pews followed, and a seventy-strong congregation of dead cows, swept in a moment of bewilderment from some exposed headland. Then came the human corpses: white-faced, open-mouthed rag dolls, many of them incomplete, wallowing helplessly on the undulating sea, their arms thrown wide in various attitudes of supplication. FitzRoy slowed the *Beagle*'s speed, to minimize the risk of a serious collision. The sheer volume of debris had the effect of quietening the swell, so they glided gently forward, the funereal silence broken only by the dead and all the accoutrements of their former lives, knocking sightlessly at the hull as if in search of readmission to the land of the living. The crew's excitement at experiencing both a volcanic eruption and a full-scale earthquake had slowly subsided, to be replaced by a horror that escalated in leaps and bounds.

Ahead in the sea, they saw movement: a small child, pale as a sheet, sitting bolt upright in the prow of a skiff. The boy's hand tightly clasped that of an Indian woman, who lay face down in the bottom of the boat, her other arm thrown across the top of her head as if in self-protection. A few feet beyond this point of fervent union, both the woman and the skiff came to an abrupt end. Her body had been sheared off at the waist, along with the stern of the little craft, both sliced away in parallel as if by an enormous rough-edged scythe. Somehow the skiff remained afloat, the boy's weight shifting the centre of balance and raising the shattered edge clear of the water.

'Lower the dinghy, fast as you can!'

'Aye aye sir!'

A few short minutes later, the small boy's reluctant fingers had been prised from the hand of his dead guardian, and he stood wide-eyed at attention on the *Beagle*'s maindeck, swathed in a woollen blanket. FitzRoy knelt down and spoke to him, in the gentlest tones he knew. '*¿Cómo se llama?*'

'I'm sorry, sir, but I do not speak Spanish.'

'Well, well. You are an English boy. What is your name, young man?'

'Hodges, sir.'

'Well, Hodges, I think you have been a remarkably brave boy. My name is Captain FitzRoy. Do you live in Concepción?'

'In Talcahuano, sir.'

'And your mother and father? Do they live in Talcahuano with you?'

'My mother and father are dead, sir. The roof fell on them, sir. There was an earthquake.'

'I am very sorry, Hodges,' said FitzRoy, gravely, 'but let us thank God that you are alive. You have had a most remarkable escape. Where were you, when the roof fell in?'

'My governess Isabela took my hand and ran into the street when she heard the rumbling noise, sir.'

'Was that Isabela in the boat with you?'

'Yes sir. But my dog knew there was going to be an earthquake, sir. He ran away.'

'Your dog?'

'My dog Davy. All the dogs in town ran away before the earthquake, sir, into the hills. And all the birds flew away too, sir. Hundreds of them. Will Davy be all right, sir?'

'I should think so. Davy sounds like a very clever dog. I am sure he will have found a safe place to hide. But tell me, Hodges, how did you get into the boat?'

'After the earthquake Isabela said there would be a big wave, sir. A giant wave. She said we would be drowned if we stayed in Talcahuano with the Europeans. She said we had to take a boat into the bay. She said if boats are out far enough, they rise over the wave and it doesn't break on them, sir.'

'Is that what you did?'

'Yes sir, but all the water in the bay was gone, and all the fish were dead. There was no sea, sir. We had to run through the mud. Then we found a boat, and we started to row out, but then the first wave came sir.'

'The first wave?'

'There were three waves sir. They landed in the town, sir. Then the water came back with lots of tables and chairs and dead people in it. The first one landed on our heads. There was a big fishing-boat in the wave, sir, and the wave picked it up and it landed on Isabela.'

The little boy stiffened perceptibly at the memory, and FitzRoy reached out to place a comforting arm round his shoulders.

'I didn't let go of Isabela's hand, sir, because she told me not to. I did what Isabela said, sir. Nobody will be cross with me, will they, sir?'

'No, Hodges. You did the right thing, so you must not despond. You are a very brave boy.'

FitzRoy bit his lip. He simply could not find any adequate words. A clammy little hand gripped his, the tiny white fingers digging into his skin with astonishing intensity. His rosy flesh turned pale as death where the boy's grasp held him tight.

'Please sir, I don't want to be left alone again.'

'Don't worry, Hodges, I promise I shall not leave you alone. You are aboard a Royal Navy vessel, called the *Beagle*, and we have come to rescue whoever we can. We shall find Davy too, and rescue him. Should you like to help me captain the *Beagle*? You can show me where to go. We can captain the vessel together. Should you like that?'

'Yes sir. I should like that very much.'

FitzRoy hoisted Hodges on to his shoulders, and placed his peaked cap atop the boy's head.

'Now, Mr Hodges – I shall have to call you Mr Hodges, seeing that you're a ship's officer – the first order we need to give is to make all sail for Talcahuano. Do you think you can manage that? Then we shall go below and find you some food and water.'

'Yes sir.'

'Loud as you can.'

'Make all sail for Talcahuano,' said Hodges, in a tiny voice.

'Aye aye captain,' snapped the bos'n, and the men moved smartly to their stations as the order was relayed. Hodges clasped his arms around FitzRoy's neck and, finding warmth and life within his grasp, hung on for all he was worth.

They rounded the headland, to find that Talcahuano had simply been obliterated. Only a few bricks and remnants of wall remained: the rest had been sucked out to sea. Every living being in the little fishing-port had disappeared. Further up the hill, beyond the reach of the devouring waves, a ghostly pall of smoke still hung over the remains of Concepción, two whole days after the initial shock had destroyed the town. Even at this distance, they could see that not a building was left standing. The damage to Concepción was more picturesque than the surgical eradication of Talcahuano, but evidently it had been hardly any less deadly. FitzRoy, with the help of his new co-captain, gave the order to let go the anchors, stow the sails and hoist all the ship's boats into the water.

'Mr King.'

'Sir?'

The young midshipman who had once stood shivering, a frightened child, on watch all Christmas night at Barnet Pool, was now a strapping lad of nineteen, well capable of knocking down any surly mutineer.

'You are in charge of the *Beagle*. The forenoon watch shall be under your command. I want every scrap of food in the ship, and I mean every last canister, unloaded ashore at the double. Mr Sulivan, Mr Wickham, the rest of the ship's company shall make haste to Concepción, with every blanket, every spare scrap of clothing and every water bottle we can muster. Tell May to bring every tool he has in his possession.'

'Aye aye sir.'

King wore a bothered expression. '*All* our supplies, sir?'

'That is correct.'

'But what of our own requirements on the homeward journey, sir?'

'We shall sail back to Valparayso, Mr King, and I shall purchase further supplies. Now, look lively, all of you.'

'You heard the skipper!' barked Bos'n Sorrell. 'Get the lead out, all of you!'

Within the half-hour, a large party of officers and sailors splashed into the shallows at Talcahuano beach. FitzRoy, the tiny figure of Hodges astride his shoulders, marched determinedly out in front. Two fishing vessels, the *Paulina* and the *Orion*, lay crushed and broken on their sides halfway up the shore: amazingly, they were still anchored, but their anchor-chains were tightly wound about each other, in spiral testimony to their last whirling dance. Two hundred yards further up the hill sat a fat white schooner, upside down and mastless, broken open like a raw egg dropped from a height. Of Talcahuano's former existence there was absolutely no sign: just a few cold pools of salt water lay amid the ruins, glinting here and there with the body of a lifeless fish. The path up to Concepción felt slimy and rotten underfoot.

From a distance, Concepción put FitzRoy in mind of a romantic engraving of Tintern Abbey. The side walls of the cathedral were fractured but still standing, their arched windows devoutly intact; but the vast anchoring buttresses had been chopped away systematically as if by a chisel. In fact, all the walls that ran from north-east to south-west had survived; but those that ran at right angles had been utterly flattened. The cathedral's fortress-like front, which had been ten feet thick at the base, had subsided into an incoherent pile of masonry and beams. Huge stones had rolled out from the rubble and come to rest half-way across the plaza. Streets radiated from the square in a neat grid according to the conventional Latin American pattern, streets which had once been lined with smart low houses: now, ranks of heaped ruins and hillocks of brick had taken their place. The ground was fissured with crevasses, as if some invisible hand had grabbed the edges of the town like a laden tablecloth and yanked it tighter than its fabric could stand. Smoke-drifts rose from a score of small pyres where damp thatched roofs had collapsed on to smouldering housefires. Amid the rubble, the dazed survivors wandered aimlessly, or sat warming their hands before these sporadic blazes, a pale, bewildered, dust-covered host, weeping or calling helplessly for friends and relatives. It was the most awful spectacle that any of the *Beagle*'s crew had ever beheld.

FitzRoy split his men into four groups. 'Mr Hamond. Salvage what timber you can and have the carpenter's crew build temporary shelters in the centre of the plaza – away from the rubble, in case of aftershocks. Mr Bynoe. You will see to the wounded. Mr Sulivan. You and your men shall search through the rubble for survivors. Mr Wickham. See to it that everyone here receives food, clean water and at least one blanket. And try to keep them quiet – we shall not hear any tapping from beneath the rubble if there is a commotion.'

As the four officers moved smoothly to complete their appointed tasks, a shout rang out in English: 'Lord be praised! Young Hodges! You're alive!' A short, rotund gentleman emerged gasping into the plaza: the top hat on his head had been concertina'd almost flat, and his suit was coated from head to foot with white dust, as if he had come hot-foot from a scrap in a flour-mill.

'Who is that, Mr Hodges?' asked FitzRoy.

'That is Mr Rouse, sir,' answered Hodges, from beneath the comforting shadow of FitzRoy's peaked cap.

FitzRoy extended a hand as Rouse panted towards them. 'Captain FitzRoy of HMS *Beagle*, at your service.'

'You are Englishmen – thank God! How do? I am Rouse, the British consul.'

FitzRoy passed his water bottle to the consul, who took a healthy swig.

'Keep it – it's yours.'

'Most generous of you, sir. And I cannot tell you how mighty glad I am to see *you*, young Hodges!'

'Mr Hodges here has been a sound good fellow ever since we plucked him from the water.'

'Excellent! Sterling work, Hodges.' Rouse wiped his wet lips with the back of his hand, leaving a clown's pink smear bordering his mouth. 'And the, um . . . parents?' he mumbled, in the direction of his own floury feet.

FitzRoy shook his head wordlessly.

At that moment a low bass rumble echoed from the direction of the sea, and the ground seesawed gently beneath their feet. Hodges tightened his panicky grip.

'Aftershocks,' explained the consul. 'Nothing to worry about, young shaver. We've had several hundred in the last two days. But the tides have gone to the very d— . . . the tides have gone all over the place. They don't know when to come in and out. Everything is topsy-turvy.'

'It appears you have had an abominable time of it.'

'You can say that again. The whole town was flattened inside six seconds. I've lived here since a good few years, so I ran into the courtyard at the first rumble. I had just reached the middle when the wall behind me came thundering down, just where I had run from. I couldn't stand up for the shaking, so I crawled to the top of the pile, thinking that if I once got on top of that part which had already fallen, I would be safe. A moment later the opposite wall collapsed – a great big beam swept this close in front of my head! I could barely see a thing for dust. I managed to clamber over the rubble and out into the street. From there I could see Talcahuano and the bay – and then, Captain FitzRoy, I saw the damnedest thing. Forgive me, the most deuced thing. The sea was boiling!'

'Boiling?'

'It had turned quite black, and columns of sulphurous vapour were belching forth. There were explosions in the sea, like cannon-fire. All the water in the bay had receded, as if someone had pulled out a gigantic plug. Then I saw the first wave, many miles out to sea, racing in. When it reached the shore it tore up cottages and trees. At the head of the bay it broke into a fearful white breaker, at least thirty feet in height. It was a monstrous awful sight. And there were three waves in all, each more enormous than the last!'

FitzRoy, who had felt Hodges's little hands tighten like thumbscrews as the consul's account unfolded, attempted to indicate with his eyes that perhaps the subject was best saved for later. He was excused from having to explain himself verbally by a tremendous outbreak of yapping, as Coxswain Bennet marched into the plaza holding aloft a slab of tinned beef, pursued by an enormous pack of hungry dogs.

'Mr Bennet, what ever . . .'

'Forgive me absenting myself from duty for a few moments, sir,' apologized Bennet, poker-faced but for the hint of a grin, 'but I felt it important that we should find the absent Davy. It is my notion he shall be here somewhere.'

Sure enough, with a squeal of recognition, Hodges had located his errant pet. FitzRoy restored him gently to the ground, whereupon he charged headlong into the pack and flung his arms round a large black mongrel. FitzRoy recovered his cap from the dust, brushed it down and replaced it on his head. 'Mr Rouse, it is your business, I believe, to see to the welfare of British subjects on this coast.'

'Indeed, sir, but what—'

'If you would oblige me by seeing to the welfare of Mr Hodges here, I do believe I have some digging to do.'

FitzRoy removed the beef from Bennet's hand and transferred it to that of the consul. In an instant, Rouse was surrounded by the pack of yapping dogs. Propelling his coxswain forward with a friendly hand, FitzRoy took his leave of the helpless diplomat. 'I bid you good day, sir.'

Rouse attempted to return the greeting but his mouth simply gaped instead. The two men marched off in step to join in the rescue effort, leaving the consul a beleaguered island in a frothing canine sea.

Three days on, and the *Beagle*'s crew had succeeded in feeding, clothing and housing upwards of a hundred survivors. Innumerable broken bones had been splinted, and bruises treated with vinegar and brown paper. A further six people had been pulled alive from the rubble, including two members of a work gang who had been restoring the ceiling of the cathedral when it had collapsed upon them in an explosion of masonry. A further eight bodies had been found crushed in the wreckage of the building: the other seven members of the work gang, and an old man who had rashly tried to take refuge beneath the sculpted arch of the great door. FitzRoy had ordered a huge pit dug for the burial of the dead, and had done the best he could to approximate a Catholic service, although one old half-caste lady had wailed that a Christian burial was of no account, for the Christian God had proved Himself weaker than the volcano-god who had sent the earthquake.

Now the men of the *Beagle* lay exhausted, sprawled on their tarpaulins in the plaza, having done everything in their power to help. Only Wickham – who had been deputized to act as emergency ship's artist – was still hard at work, producing a highly polished line-drawing of the ravaged cathedral. A figure trotted into the plaza from the Talcahuano side: it was Rensfrey, one of the foretopmen.

'Begging your pardon, sir, but the compliments of Mr King. He says to tell you there's a schooner in the bay, sir. He believes it to be the philosopher, sir.'

'Mr Darwin?'

'Mr King says to say so, sir.'

FitzRoy grabbed his cap and sprang to his feet. 'Excellent news indeed! Thank you, Rensfrey, for your trouble.'

With the foretopman in tow, FitzRoy strode anxiously down to the shore, where he encountered Darwin stepping out of a dinghy, accompanied by a short, dapper man in an expensive hat. In the bay behind, a small but elegant private vessel of some thirty-five tons lay at anchor. Overwhelmed with delight and riven with guilt, the two friends embraced on the strand.

'Captain FitzRoy, may I have the honour of presenting to your acquaintance Mr Richard Corfield, merchant, of Valparayso?'

'How do, Captain FitzRoy?' said the swell.

'The honour is entirely mine, Mr Corfield. Forgive me, but I cannot help but admire your schooner, if indeed she is yours.'

'The *Constitución*? Oh, she's not a bad old girl. She's my boat after a fashion – that is to say, as of today she is yours.'

'Mine? Forgive me, but . . .'

'I am making you a present of her, old man, for as long as you require her.'

'I informed Corfield of your having to sell the *Adventure*,' Darwin chipped in. 'How you have insufficient boats to complete the South American survey.'

'Mr Corfield, I beg you will not do such a thing. Your generosity is too great – I cannot trespass upon your kind offices in this manner.'

'Nonsense, old boy,' said Corfield, jamming his hands in his coat pockets like a gleeful schoolboy. 'I never use her anyway. I'm always so monstrous busy. Make what you will of her.'

'Mr Corfield, I . . . I am speechless with gratitude . . .'

'Tish!' Corfield waved away FitzRoy's awestruck thanks.

'But my dear friend,' said Darwin, 'how marvellous to find you quite yourself again!'

'And as anxious to reach dear old England as you are.'

'But we have news for you, FitzRoy. A missive from Commodore Mason in Valparayso. Good news.' A grinning Corfield extracted the folded letter from an inside pocket. 'Forgive the intrusion into your privacy, old man, but the commodore made us sensible of the contents when he appointed us his messengers.'

FitzRoy broke the seal and unfolded the paper. After six years as a commander – an acting captain – he had finally been made post. He was a full captain at last. He should have been pleased as punch. Instead he felt strangely empty. He perused the rest of the letter. There remained only an order to report to Mason in Valparayso at his earliest convenience.

'Were there any news of further promotions – for Wickham or Stokes?'

'I do not believe so.'

'I had made representations ... I had hoped that their exertions might have obtained satisfactory notice at head-quarters ...'

'But are you not pleased?' asked Darwin, concerned. 'I apprehend that all goes by seniority from this point on – that this will like as not make you an admiral in due course.'

'That is so. Forgive me for seeming so ungrateful. I just wish that I could get one or two of my hard-working ship-mates promoted. That would have gratified me much more than my own advance, which has been too tardy to be much valued. Six years – some stay a commander for only a year. Plenty have gone over my head. I deserve it, of course, for having burned my fingers with politics.'

His star, he realized, which had once burned so brightly, had dimmed with time. To be given his own vessel at twenty-three – that had been special. Captain of a little brig at thirty, or nearly thirty – that was no great accolade. The promotion was no more than a poultice applied by Beaufort, or some other interested friend in high places, to cover the gaping sore of his recent run-in with their lordships. The true test would come when he returned to England, and received his next commission. Then he would discover whether or not he was still considered a high-flier. Perhaps a change of administration, from Liberal back to Tory once more, would make life easier for him and his crew.

'Are there any news yet of who holds sway in Parliament? Is there a successor to Grey?'

'My dear fellow, have you not heard?' blurted out Corfield. 'Parliament is no more. It has burned down!'

'Burned down! When?'

'Last October. The whole Palace of Westminster is gone – St Stephen's Chapel, the cloisters, the Painted Chamber, all of it. Only Westminster Hall has survived. Concepción is not the only place to have suffered a conflagration. Everything is in chaos.'

'*¿Quien sabe*, my friend?' said Darwin, clapping FitzRoy encouragingly on the back. 'Perhaps it is a bonfire that will instigate much-needed change.'

Let us hope so, thought FitzRoy.

The trio strolled uphill, to give Corfield and Darwin their first sight of the ruins of Concepción. All conversation ceased as the newcomers took in the scale of the devastation, the serried lines of silent debris where once people had lived, shopped and prayed.

'It is a bitter and humiliating thing to see,' said Darwin at last. 'Works that cost man so much time and labour, over-thrown in one minute. Such is the insignificance of man's boasted power. It is most wonderful to witness.'

'I say, steady on, old man,' said Corfield under his breath.

'Forgive me – I do not mean to forget my compassion – but from a scientific aspect this is absolutely fascinating.'

'Have you noticed how all the walls running north-west to south-east have been flattened,' said FitzRoy, 'but those running the other way have and large survived?'

'By God, you are absolutely right.'

'It is like a ship in a heavy sea. Lined up with the waves, she will ride the shocks, but bring her broadside-on, and she will be put over on her beam-ends. Proof that the shocks of an earthquake arrive by a kind of wave motion, flowing in a single direction.'

Both men were charged with excitement now. They were passing the ruins of a spacious merchant's house, when Darwin dived in suddenly, reappearing with a torn rug and a scattering of books extricated from the rubble. Swiftly, he laid the rug in the street and stood the books upon it spine uppermost, half of them aligned with the rug, the others at right-angles.

'Observe,' he commanded.

Kneeling at one end of the rug, he proceeded to tug it gently back and forth. At once, those books standing at right-angles to the direction of movement toppled over, but those aligned with it stayed upright.

'As I said, Darwin old man,' exclaimed Corfield, balling his hands deep into his pockets, 'you're a confounded marvel!'

Dusk found FitzRoy and Darwin many miles along the Pacific shore, kicking their heels on what remained of the outer wall of Penco Castle, a seventeenth-century Spanish sea-fort. The building had been devastated even before the recent earthquake; it now wore a battered, defeated aspect entirely in keeping with the imperial ambitions of its mother country. The tide was in, and dark magenta waves lapped at the old Spanish battlements, gradually teasing the ancient stones from their crumbling bed of mortar. As the sun had sunk towards the blue wall of the horizon, Darwin had breathlessly expounded his discoveries in the mountains, and the startling conclusions he had reached – all except one. He had withheld his disturbing ideas about the divergence of the wildlife on either side of the Andean *cordillera*: those deductions were of such devastating import that he would – he knew – have to choose his moment carefully. But his evidence for the intermittent and continuing uplift of the mountains seemed overwhelming.

'So you see,' he concluded, 'the uplift is not caused by the earthquakes. *The uplift is the cause of the earthquakes.*'

'From what you say I must do you justice,' conceded FitzRoy graciously. 'I shall write to Lyell confirming that it is so.'

'You oblige me by your understanding. But . . . does this new evidence not bring the story of the Biblical flood into question?'

'Not in the least. The one does not preclude the other. Earthquake and flood may exist side by side – indeed, the two may have occurred in tandem.'

'But surely all the evidence of land having been under water is caused by the earth's crust being in a continual state of change. Places now far above the sea were once beneath it. Districts may have been inundated in one quarter – but a universal deluge could never have happened!'

'My friend,' said FitzRoy gently, 'everything might not be as clear-cut as you think. You say the land has been rising regularly for thousands of years, and continues to do so?'

'Yes.'

'Then why is this two-hundred-year-old Spanish fort, built by the water's edge, *still* by the water's edge?'

Darwin looked about him. FitzRoy was right.

Why *had* Penco Castle not been uplifted from the water, preferring to crumble where it stood? He had no answer. It had all seemed so simple, up in the mountains, in his delight at finding what appeared to be a universal solution. It would take a lifetime of study, he realized, merely to chip away at a few of the lesser complexities of God's universe. He laughed out loud at the sheer size of the task, and how easily he had underestimated it.

'I am sure you are correct in your observations,' said a placatory FitzRoy, as the pair wound their way home, 'but I am afraid I cannot bring myself to question the written word of God. I am sure there is room in the scheme of things for both eventualities.'

As he spoke, a deep roar echoed from the unseen caverns of the underworld, and the earth shook as if a huge subterranean beast were rattling its cage. It was the biggest aftershock so far. FitzRoy and Darwin found themselves hurled to the ground, like two statues in the cathedrals of old Byzantium thrown down by the armies of the Saracens. Thus forcibly prostrated, both men spread their arms and legs wide to avoid being rolled over and over in the grass. A few seconds later, when the assault had finished, they raised their heads warily. There was something odd, something different about their surroundings. Darwin was first to his feet and first to realize what had happened, scrambling eagerly down the slope towards the shore.

'Look!' he said, literally hopping from one foot to the other with excitement. 'FitzRoy, look! Look at this!'

There, behind the frantic naturalist, a glistening mussel bed adhered to the rock. But the shellfish did not lie beneath the lapping water, as they had a few moments previously: they lay with rivulets of clear salt water streaming between them, several feet clear of the high-water mark.

Chapter Twenty-three

Valparayso, Chili, 16 June 1835

'Captain FitzRoy! Captain FitzRoy, sir!'

FitzRoy wheeled round. He had just stepped out of a dockside masthoop merchant's on to the cobbled main street of Valparayso. Perhaps fifty yards distant, on their way up from the wharf and standing out like a sore thumb among the respectable Chilean gentlefolk, were three filthy, emaciated Englishmen. Their hair was matted, their clothing ripped, and two of them wore what looked suspiciously like the remains of British naval officers' uniforms. Really, FitzRoy was not in the best of moods. He had brought the *Beagle* back to Valparayso to replenish her hold for the journey home, and to report to Commodore Mason as requested; but when he had rowed out to HMS *Blonde*, the commodore's flagship, her crew had been surly and diffident. The commodore was no longer in residence aboard, the lieutenant in charge had wearily explained. No, he did not know when, or indeed if, the commodore would be back. No, he could not be of any further help. The *Blonde*, FitzRoy knew, had once been the proud frigate of Admiral Byron himself. What on earth would the admiral have made of the state of the modern-day *Blonde*? Her unkempt decks and mildewed sails indicated a ship in decline, ill-disciplined and rudderless. Such neglect of a fine old vessel invariably roused his ire.

'It's Captain FitzRoy, isn't it, sir? Of the *Beagle*?' The three scarecrows had run all the way up the main street. Their leader introduced himself.

'Lieutenant Collins, sir, of the *Challenger*. This is Assistant Surgeon Lane, and this is Jagoe, ship's clerk.'

'The *Challenger*? Seymour's brig?'

'That's right, sir. You came aboard off Port Louis in the Falklands, sir. But the *Challenger* is lost, sir!'

'Lost? Lost where?' The blood ran cold through FitzRoy's veins.

'South of the river Leubu, sir. We were making eight knots an hour under treble-reefed topsails, courses and jib. By all fair calculations we should have been well out to sea – but something had happened to play merry hell with the tides and currents. Next thing we knew, sir, the officer of the watch noticed lines of foam in the water in the darkness. He ordered helm down and about ship, and Captain Seymour was fetched. The captain gave the order to haul the mainsail. The after-yards swung round, sir, but while we were bracing them up she struck. The rudder was destroyed, and the stern-post, the gunroom beams, the cabin-deck – all her timbers and planking were shivered to atomies, sir.'

'My God. Did she go down at once?'

'Not for a couple of hours, sir. The mate managed to get a line ashore in the jolly-boat. We cut the mizzen-mast down and made a raft, and got most of the supplies off. Just two men were lost in all, but the jolly-boat was the only one of the ship's boats to survive the impact. Captain Seymour ordered the three of us to sail her to Valparayso, to fetch assistance from the commodore, sir.'

'Thank God you have arrived safely. When did you get here?'

'Three weeks ago, sir.'

'Three *weeks*? What the deuce—'

'Commodore Mason, sir – he refused to send the *Blonde* south. He said it was too late in the season to land on a lee shore. And the Leubu river is Araucanian Indian territory, sir. He said it was too risky, sir. He didn't want to peril another ship. But we heard that the *Beagle* was due in port soon, so we waited—'

FitzRoy's jaw set hard. 'Then there is not another moment to lose.'

'Captain Seymour set up camp on high ground overlooking the river, sir. He had a ditch dug, and erected a defensive barricade from barrels and timbers that were thrown ashore. But there is only so much ammunition available, sir. Of course we couldn't get any of the cannon off the ship. We were hoping you might be able to use your influence to persuade the commodore to change his mind sir.'

'Oh, I shall make him change his mind, Lieutenant, I promise you of that,' said FitzRoy grimly. 'Where may I find this Commodore Mason?'

The three men from the *Challenger* led FitzRoy to a pretty gingerbreaded cottage in the suburbs. They held back at the end of the lane, while FitzRoy walked up and knocked smartly at the door. It swung open to the touch. Marching past a startled Chilean maid with no word of introduction, he found Mason slumbering in a cane chair on raised decking at the back of the house, under the shade of a canvas awning. The commodore looked as if he might once have been handsome: certainly, he sported the breeches and hairstyle of another era. But he was running to fat now, pink jowls inflating with each breath. His sandy hair had turned all but grey. The tracery of broken veins on his cheeks and nose, and the half-empty geneva bottle on the table, suggested even at this early hour that the commodore had been drinking.

'Captain FitzRoy, sir, of HMS *Beagle*, reporting as commanded,' said FitzRoy, doing his best to disguise his impatience. He was, at least, going to give the man a chance to explain himself.

'Is it your normal practice to enter the houses of superior officers without introduction, Captain?'

'The door was on the jar and unattended, sir.'

A harrumph from Mason. 'Well, I have been expecting you for some weeks. You have new orders. A pearl-oyster-fishing vessel, the *Truro*, has been plundered in one of the islands of Tahiti. The Admiralty is demanding compensation of two thousand eight hundred dollars on behalf of the owner. You are to make yourself known to Queen Pomare of those islands and extract the required sum of the Tahitians, using force if necessary. You are heading home via Tahiti, I take it?'

'In due course, sir. But in the meantime there is a more pressing matter. The crew of the *Challenger*, sir—'

'I know all about the *Challenger*, Captain.'

'Then may I take it you will be mounting a rescue effort without further ado, sir?'

'What you may take, Captain FitzRoy, is what you are given. Have I made myself clear?'

'Sir, the men of the *Challenger* have been encamped on an exposed and dangerous shore for some four weeks now—'

'The men of the *Challenger* will have to fend for themselves. Those are my orders. You have your own orders. The fate of the *Challenger* is none of your damned business.'

'Captain Seymour is an old friend of mine, sir.'

'Then you are allowing personal friendships to cloud your judgement, Mr FitzRoy. It would be foolhardy in the extreme to put more men on to that coast in the middle of winter. The Spanish have failed to defeat the Araucanians since three hundred years – I hardly see that one frigate's-worth of men will succeed where an entire nation has been found wanting.'

'There may be other means than military action, sir. Let me go, sir – I have only recently surveyed that very coastline.'

'Are you deaf, Captain?' Mason's tone was icy. 'I would remind you that you were only made post a few weeks since. You would do well to hold your tongue and go about your duty without further ado.'

'My duty, sir, is to go to the aid of my fellow officers and their men.'

'Your duty, Captain, is to do as you are commanded!'

'If you will not go to the aid of the *Challenger*, sir, then I shall have no option but to go myself.'

Mason's face turned puce as he levered himself from his chair. 'I will see you court-martialled if you do not get out of here this instant and do exactly what I tell you to do!'

'If you are too scared, sir—' began FitzRoy scornfully.

'Damn you for a scoundrel, sir! How dare you? You may be satisfied that you will pay for your impertinence!'

'On the contrary, sir,' said FitzRoy coolly, 'it is you who shall pay. I shall see to it on my return to England that you are court-martialled for cowardice.'

'By the devil!' spat Mason. 'If I was twenty years younger I would knock you down, you young puppy.'

FitzRoy's eyes gleamed. 'If you were twenty years younger you would not be standing now, you blackguard. That is, if I could bring myself to soil my hands upon a despicable coward – *sir*.' FitzRoy turned on his heel and stalked out of the house, leaving Mason speechless with rage.

He met the three ragged emissaries from the *Challenger* at the corner of the lane, their faces optimistic as puppies'.

'How was it, sir? Did the commodore change his mind?'

FitzRoy smiled grimly. 'Yes, Lieutenant. I found the commodore exactly of my opinion. He has ordered me to mount a full-scale rescue of the *Challenger*'s people. Follow me, if you please.'

The ship's company of the *Beagle*, mustered on the main-deck, waited expectantly for FitzRoy to speak. Something was up, they knew. Lieutenant Collins and his colleagues had been cleaned up and fed, and dispatched to wait on the wharf, safely out of earshot. FitzRoy was sure that he could trust each and every one of his own crew, but that was as far as it went. Poker-faced, he stepped up to the azimuth compass and gambled his entire career on a single eventuality.

'You will no doubt remember HMS *Challenger* from the Falkland Islands. I have grave news to impart. The *Challenger* is lost. Her crew are stranded three hundred miles south of here, in Araucanian Indian territory. To go to their aid would be a most dangerous venture. So dangerous, in fact, that the British officer commanding here in Valparayso, Commodore Mason, has refused to sanction any such rescue mission.'

A murmur of consternation rolled around the ship's company.

'I have decided to disobey that order.'

The murmur became an aftershock, a thunderstruck wave surging through the throng.

'It is my intention to commandeer HMS *Blonde*, the commodore's frigate. I am doing so in the contention that Commodore Mason is in serious dereliction of his duty. I am telling you this because I fear that the crew of the *Blonde* shall be almost no use as seamen. Were I to take a small contingent of men from the *Beagle* to lick them into shape, my task should be that much easier. So, in a moment, I shall call for volunteers. But I must warn you: our only hope of escaping the most serious repercussions, and it is a faint hope, will be to effect a successful rescue. I sustain myself with no flattering delusion otherwise. To be proved not only resolute and brave, but absolutely correct in taking authority into our own hands, will be the only possible defence of our actions. For all that I am aware, the men of the *Challenger* may already be dead. If our bid fails, I need not tell you of the consequences. Whoever volunteers risks not only their livelihood and their career, but also their neck. To be blunt, you might yet find yourself swinging at the end of a rope. But if nobody goes to their rescue, then the men of the *Challenger* will certainly die. Examine your consciences. I give you my absolute assurance, here and now, that there shall be no shame in failing to volunteer. No blame, no censure, shall attach to any man who prefers to leave this business to others. I am looking for fifteen men, and two officers. Think carefully before making your decision. Now – who is in for it?'

FitzRoy looked out across the mass of sailors and marines, and then behind him at the line of uniformed officers, their dark coats providing a neat and sombre backdrop to the raised stage of the poop deck. In front, a sea of hands had shot up, with not a dissenter among them. Behind, every single officer had taken a decisive step forward.

'Thank you, gentlemen. I am proud of each and every one of you. It seems I must choose among you. I shall inform you of my decision within a few minutes. You may return to your duties.'

As the milling crowd slowly dissipated, Darwin, who had observed proceedings from the rail of the companionway, gave FitzRoy a sympathetic smile.

'Whatever became of the officer who would follow any order given to him, however immoral, however illogical?'

FitzRoy grimaced. 'He grew up.'

John Biddlecombe, master of the *Blonde* and officer in charge of the afternoon watch, observed the *Beagle*'s packed cutter slice purposefully through the waters of Valparayso Bay with an inexplicable feeling of apprehension. Such was the determination etched into the approaching sailors' faces that, had they not been British tars, he would have said they wore the aspect of a boarding party. He recognized the captain, the highty-tighty sort who had been sniffing around that very morning, and had been sent away with a flea in his ear. His return, mob-handed, looked worryingly like some sort of retribution. *Let's hope he hasn't been stirring up trouble with the old man*, thought the master.

FitzRoy hauled himself aboard, followed by Coxswain Bennet, Bos'n Sorrell, Midshipman Hamond and fifteen hard-faced members of the *Beagle*'s company. He had deliberately opted, much to the bitter disappointment of Sulivan, Wickham and the others, to take with him his most junior officers: the higher up the tree his co-mutineers, the more they stood to lose. The only exception was Midshipman King. He dared not have looked the boy's father in the face, had he involved the younger King in an insurrection that had turned to catastrophe.

'Mr Biddlecombe, is it not?'

'Sir.'

'I have orders from the commodore to take command of the *Blonde*, and to proceed without delay to the mouth of the Leubu river where we are to effect the immediate rescue of the crew of HMS *Challenger*.'

'Orders from the commodore, sir?' Biddlecombe fairly goggled.

'As I said.'

'But where is the commodore, sir? Is he not to take command of the expedition himself?'

'The commodore is indisposed . . . He felt that his state of health was such that his presence would merely incommode our passage.'

That sounds like the cowardly old bustard, thought Biddlecombe.

'Tell me, is your bos'n aboard?'

'No sir, he is ashore. A number of the officers – Lieutenant Tait, Midshipman McKenna—'

'It matters not. I have brought sufficient matlows with me to cover any want of men. Mr Sorrell? The maindeck is yours. Let's have this ship ready for sea. The sooner we are under way the better.'

'You heard the officer,' growled Sorrell, advancing like a pugilist upon the *Blonde*'s startled crew. There was an air of confidence about the little Bristolian now: he seemed far removed from the nervous spinning-top of a man who had lashed out right and left with his rattan on FitzRoy's first day as captain. Today he did not use his rattan. He did not need to. He was imbued with purpose, and the afternoon watch could feel the force of his intent.

'Those topsail gaskets are slack! Those horses want mousing

– a man could fall from the yard if they're not tied properly! Where's the captain of the foretop?'

'Come on, look lively!' bellowed a furious Bennet. 'This is one of the King's frigates, not Almack's Assembly!'

The master's jaw, FitzRoy observed, had fallen slack.

'Let us see, Mr Biddlecombe, whether we cannot open the eyes of everyone, fore and aft, in this ship. Now, do you not have a course to plot?'

'Yes sir,' said the defeated Biddlecombe, and tottered off in search of his charts.

The country of Araucania, FitzRoy knew, was a beautiful, well-wooded land riven with steep, muddy ravines usually swelled to bursting with heavy rain. That, at least, was the theory. But embarrassingly, even with his newly drawn-up charts, he could not find the Leubu river for two days, so poor was the visibility. So thick were the wind and the rain, in fact, that he could scarcely discern the line of the surf, heavily as it beat upon the shore. The *Blonde* made sally after sally in towards the coast, the sea sucking at her hull as if to pull her on to the rocks, but, try as he might, he could find no sign of the missing crew. Finally, on the afternoon of the second day, Hamond caught sight of the *Challenger*'s flag through the spyglass, a faint rippling square on the distant heights, glimpsed for a scudding moment through rushing drifts of white. There was no way in for the big frigate, not on this coast, not in any weather. Her guns – which FitzRoy had hoped to have available as a bargaining tool – would be utterly useless in these conditions. He had no option but to haul off.

'Mr Bos'n!' he yelled, water sheeting from his oilskin. 'Hoist out the cutter!'

'Aye aye sir.'

'But – but you're mad, sir!' Biddlecombe protested. 'She'll be swamped by the waves. You'll never make it!'

'You have obviously never been surveying in Tierra del

Fuego, Mr Biddlecombe,' FitzRoy shouted into the master's ear.

Biddlecombe had proved a thorough liability on the voyage down; luckily Davis, the assistant master, had shown himself to be a capable sort. It was to both men that FitzRoy now gave the order for the *Blonde* to remain under way until he returned, making short tacks all night if necessary. With Bennet piloting the cutter, FitzRoy, Hamond and his fifteen handpicked sailors bounced crazily towards the shore through the drenching surf, searching in the gloom for the estuary opening.

'We're sh-shipping 'em green, sir,' said Hamond, as icy water creamed over their thighs for the hundredth time.

'When are we ever *not*, Mr Hamond?' said a smiling FitzRoy, who was bailing like a Trojan. He was doing good, he knew, simple, uncomplicated good; so he was, for the time being, a happy man. All the dangers, the risks to his career, were as nothing compared to the fact that here, with his men at his side, he felt that he *belonged*.

Finally, after two weary hours in the ocean's maw, they were regurgitated on to the sodden shore amid a network of mud-laced channels and boggy islands inhabited only by a few foul-smelling seals. They dragged the heavy cutter across the shoals, caked to the waist in thick, miry treacle, before flopping down in the wet grass of the river's southern flank. FitzRoy allowed them five minutes' rest and no more, then they ploughed on. Bennet was left on guard by the cutter, with a gun and a supply of ammunition; the others followed the course of the river-bank uphill through a cleft in the wooded slopes, peering through silhouetted trees and swirling mists for another glimpse of the *Challenger*'s elusive ensign. After a mile, the forest opened out once more, and they marched knee-deep, up a soaking, sloping meadow; but even as the woods parted, the clouds descended about them in a billowing curtain, leaving them alone and stranded in a ghostly world of green and white. FitzRoy began to realize, uncomfortably, that he had no idea where in this disorienting wilderness Seymour and his men might be holding out – assuming, that is, that they were still holding out. The only direction he could safely follow was up.

'Wh-what was that?' Hamond froze. There had been a clinking sound, faint but unmistakable, in the mists ahead.

'Quiet!'

There it was again. Nobody moved. Had it been dead ahead, or slightly to the side? Wherever it had emanated from, the sound had been borne away on the wind before it could be safely located. FitzRoy's finger tightened about the trigger of his pistol. As he watched, a ragged hole was blown in the mists ahead; and through it rode a horseman, astride a raven mount. He was tall and muscular, with bronzed skin and cheekbones like the shoulder-plates of Darwin's Megatherium. His long, lush black hair was parted in the centre and gathered by scarlet fillets. His countenance was grave, almost regal. He would have put FitzRoy in mind of Van Dyck's studies of Charles I, were it not for the striped poncho and the wicked-looking *chuzo*, his bamboo lance, which tapered to an iron-tipped point some twelve feet forward of his body.

Seaman MacCurdy began to raise his pistol, but FitzRoy gestured urgently for him to lower it again, for it was clear now that the horseman was not alone. The mists were scurrying away apprehensively, chasing one another hurriedly into the woods, to reveal that the wide clearing was no longer fringed with trees. Rather, a ring of horsemen surrounded the little party, upwards of three hundred in number. They had stumbled right into the Araucanian battle-lines.

'D-dear God,' said Hamond.

'Nobody is to fire a shot, or we shall be cut to pieces,' whispered FitzRoy. 'Place your weapons slowly and carefully on the ground.'

His men complied. Deliberately, FitzRoy stepped out in front of the group, towards the lead horseman, and laid his pistol before the horse's forelegs. The Araucanian raised his *chuzo*, handling it as deftly as a lancet despite its immense length, and placed the point under FitzRoy's heart. FitzRoy felt the iron tip gently pierce his uniform: a trickle of warm blood mingled with the icy rain running down the spearshaft, hot and cold pooling together against his undershirt.

'*Us'hae ihlca*,' FitzRoy said, in Alikhoolip. Put down your spear.

An amused ripple ran through the ranks of Araucanian warriors. A lieutenant trotted over and consulted briefly with his leader.

'Who are you, Spaniard, that you speak the language of the *Sapallios*?'

'I am not a Spaniard.'

'You look like a Spaniard.'

Desperately, FitzRoy fought to remember some of the entries in the Patagonian glossary he had compiled at Gregory Bay six years previously: unfortunately, it lay gathering dust somewhere in the British Museum, waiting to be catalogued, along with the other specimens from the first voyage.

'*Catiam comps español. Catiam* English. *Auros chuzo.*'

The horse-captain narrowed his eyes at this novelty. A Spanish officer who refused to fight and die like a man, but who insisted, in different languages, despite all evidence to the contrary, that he was not a Spaniard. His curiosity pricked, the warrior gestured for the other white men to remain where they were, and for FitzRoy to go ahead of him at spearpoint. The ranks of horsemen parted silently to let them through. FitzRoy walked uphill, his heart thumping in his chest; only the clanking of their spurs signalled that the Araucanian captain and his lieutenant were still behind.

Presently, they arrived at a rain-soaked encampment of smoke-shrouded tents. In the centre, rising above the others, was the dwelling of the *cacique*, or chief, guarded by a brace of fierce-looking warriors. The escort dismounted and, without further ado, prostrated themselves on the ground. FitzRoy was not quick enough following suit, and found himself hastened on his way by a heavy blow across the middle of his back. One of the guards placed a foot on his neck, pushing his face down into the mud. He could hear whispered consultations, all but drowned out by the spattering of the rain, which flicked off the mud into his eyes. Finally two feet, tightly clad in hand-stitched seal-fur riding-boots and surmounted by extravagant iron spurs cut in a sunburst design, made their elegant way out of the tent and stopped just before FitzRoy's nose.

He waited.

Surely these people possessed too much dignity, too much honour, to kill him here, now, in cold blood?

A commanding voice addressed him, in rough Spanish: 'I am the *cacique* of these people. These are my lands. Who are you, Spaniard, that you dare to enter my lands?'

'I am not Spanish, but English. I am a ship's captain. My name is Robert FitzRoy.'

'I am Lorenzo Colipí.'

FitzRoy craned his neck, and looked up at the chief in amazement. He found himself staring into the scarred, pitted and painted face of a fifty-year-old white man.

'You wish to know why I have white skin, like you.'

It was more of a statement than a question. His wrists bound, head hanging, FitzRoy knelt before Colipí in his tent. The Araucanian leader sat on a pile of skins, surrounded like a Turkish pasha by a flock of wives. The women were draped with beads and brass ornaments, their mantles secured by large, flat-headed ornamental pins. One was breast-feeding a boy who must have been all of ten years old. A guard stood with a sort of halberd pressed to the back of FitzRoy's neck, the cold iron blade pushing his head downwards at a suitably respectful angle.

'My mother was taken, when she was twelve, from an *estancia* on the other side of the mountains. My father's people drove the farmers from our lands and burned their farms. She was the only survivor – fortunate to be spared, and fortunate to be taken from her people. She was given to my father as one of his wives.

My father was Hueichao, who once had land in that place. Lorenzo was the name of her youngest brother, who was two when he died. She named me for him, and taught me the language of the enemy. You see, white man, among our people the leadership does not pass to the oldest son of the chief, for this has always made the Spanish weak. Our people choose the strongest man, the bravest man, to be their leader. They chose me. With my face, with my blood, I had no choice but to be the strongest and the bravest. It is my task now to lead my people to victory, to kill every Spaniard who sets foot in our country.'

'I apprehend that the Spanish are gone now, Great Chief. There are only the Chileans, and on the other side of the mountains, the Buenos Ayreans.'

'They are the same people. They have the same forefathers. Forefathers who agreed, three hundred years ago, that they would keep to the north of the Bío-Bío river. But again and again they have broken their forefathers' word. What kind of people are these, who do not respect the word of their ancestors? Their farmers take our land. Their soldiers kill our people. In the old days, their priests burned our people alive. Now there is a new butcher on the other side of the mountains, this Rosas, who sends the black-faced men to murder our families. He has big guns, which can kill many warriors with one shot. But he cannot drag his guns into the mountains. When he and his men try to take these mountains, they shall dig their own graves – you may be satisfied of it.'

'I am no friend to Rosas, Great Chief. One of his ships fired a cannon at my ship.'

'Then why do you trespass in my nation, like one of his spies? My men would have killed you, otherwise that you spoke in the language of the southern people. What is your business? Tell me why I should not have you put to death right here.'

'I make charts – maps of the ocean – so that other English ships will not be wrecked in the rough seas to the south. I have come to rescue the men in the camp on the hill.'

'Ah, the Spaniards in the little fort. They have guns, but they are in want of food and they are becoming sick. Their days are few.'

'They are not Spaniards. They are English, like me. They intended only to sail past your land. But the earthquake – when the ground shook – changed the currents, and their ship was wrecked upon your shore.'

'Ha, the shaking of the ground.' Colipí laughed bitterly, his greying topknot quivering with indignation. 'When we see the Spanish dig deep foundations for their buildings, we see them constructing their own sepulchres. They go in and pray to their God, then the building falls on their heads! He cannot protect them. Only the volcano-god can command the bulls below ground that cause the ground to shake. Always knowing this, at every full moon we sacrifice a bull to him so that he will protect us from the great bulls in their tunnels.'

It is exactly like ancient Crete, FitzRoy realized. *They share almost the same beliefs.*

'How many gods do the Araucanians have, Great Chief?' he ventured.

'We are not Araucanians,' spat Lorenzo Colipí angrily. 'That is the Spanish word. We are Mapuche. We have resisted the Spanish for three hundred years, and before them we resisted the great Inca. That is because the most powerful of all Gods, the God of Gods, El Chaltén, the God of Smoke, is our protector.'

'Where does El Chaltén live, O Chief?'

'Where does he live? *He* is a mountain, far to the south of here. A great mountain, which cannot be climbed. No white man has ever seen El Chaltén, and no white man ever shall. He is tall, and he reaches in pain to the sky itself, with two smaller pinnacles, one to each side.'

Like Jesus on the cross, thought FitzRoy.

'He has protected my people for thousands of years, since we came to these lands from the west.'

'Your people came across the sea from the west?' Excitement

speared through FitzRoy. 'I knew it. I have seen the *piragua* canoes. They have exactly the same canoes in the lands to the west.'

'Once we lived in the land of the setting sun. Our fore-fathers had red hair and blue eyes. Then the gods sent a great flood to punish the world, a flood that covered the land. The great ancestor, Chem, built a boat, which came to rest on the mountain of Theghin. The volcano-god signalled to him with spark and fire to come to the mountaintop, for it protruded safely from the waters. Then he sent Chem far to the east, to live here, in these lands. But every time a *cacique* dies, his spirit follows the setting sun west, back to the mountains of his ancestors. One day my spirit will make that journey.'

FitzRoy's mind reeled. *The flood. Shem, Noah's son. The ark on the mountaintop. The story is the same.*

'Is this what your father told you, Great Chief, or your mother?'

'It has been known to my people for thousands of years, for this is how the world was begun. You know it to be true, white man, for you have seen the boats of the west.'

It was incredible. *Proof, surely, that early man had spread over the earth after the deluge, that all men had shared a common ancestor not once, but twice. Proof of the universality of the deluge.* He had to get out of here alive, if only to tell this remarkable tale.

'And now, white man, you have come with fifteen warriors to rescue your friends. Fifteen warriors to throw down the Mapuche, who could not be thrown down by the Spanish or by the Inca? You are very brave, or very foolish, or both.'

'It was not my wish to throw down the Mapuche. Quite the reverse. I have given aid to the men of the south. I wished only to find my friends and leave your lands as soon as possible. I adjure you to show mercy.'

Colipí smiled. 'Your bravery as a warrior has come in aid of your cause. Because I believe that you are no Spaniard, you and your friends shall have until sunset tomorrow to leave our lands. Anyone remaining after that will be killed. Tell your friends in the land of the English that anyone who comes here to take our land will also be killed.'

'You are most merciful, Great Chief.'

The watching small boy detached himself from his mother's breast, and gazed at the Englishman with undisguised contempt.

Breathing hard, FitzRoy was led to the edge of the encampment, where his bonds were cut and he was pushed down the slope. A winter's dusk was settling upon the sombre, silent woods. Squelching downhill as fast as he could in the gloom, he located the meadow where they had been surrounded, but there was no sign of anyone from the *Beagle*, or of any tribesmen. It was almost dark now, and his options were few. He chose to gamble once more, and plunged into the impenetrable blackness of the fringing forest, heading upwards in a southerly direction. Even if he could not locate Seymour's hilltop position, he might at least find some vantage-point from which to view the surrounding country when it became light again. Time was short, but he had to move with caution, for he could see nothing at all. Again and again he stumbled over tree-roots, slipped into streams or crashed into low branches, until he was transformed into a terrible ogre of the forest, his body caked from head to foot in mud, his uniform ripped and flapping behind him. At long last, after several hours of patient struggle, he saw a solitary pinpoint of light flicker briefly between the trees. He called out, at the top of his voice, 'Challengers ahoy!'

A faint answering shout of 'Hallo!' came back from the pinnacle above, and a more welcome sound he had never heard. Blazing torches appeared at the walls of the British encampment, and within a few minutes, the muddy apparition that had emerged blinking like some stone-age tribesman from the forest was being hauled to safety over the makeshift barricades.

'Our tried friend Captain FitzRoy!' exulted a voice. It was

Michael Seymour, a great beaming smile on his face, missing a stone in weight and with several weeks' growth of beard clinging to his face. A huge cheer arose from the defenders, and Seymour embraced FitzRoy so tightly that when he finally withdrew the two were almost as muddy as each other.

'Mr Hamond has told us all about your efforts in our behalf.'

'Hamond is here?'

'They are all here.'

FitzRoy breathed a sigh of relief. 'The Araucanians have given us safe passage until nightfall tomorrow.'

'Thank the Lord. God bless you, FitzRoy – some food, here, for the captain!'

A plum-dough was brought out, which Seymour had been saving for the event of their rescue, and the lion's share was forced on an embarrassed FitzRoy. The massed ranks of Araucanians – wherever they were in the maze of trees – would no doubt have been bewildered, later that night, to hear an outbreak of spontaneous singing, comic songs and shanties overlapping, spilling over the little palisade and out into the night.

Daybreak found FitzRoy and Seymour still deep in conversation, laughing and joking about what they would say at each other's court-martials. The camp was abandoned soon after, with the mixture of relief and nostalgia that attends the end of any shared difficulty successfully overcome. Only the essentials were carried down to the cutter: it would take at least four trips to get the *Challenger*'s company off the beach. They found Bennet blue-nosed with cold, but otherwise hale and hearty, and immensely cheered to see his fellows again. Seymour, it was decided, would be the last man off; FitzRoy and Hamond would command the first run, and take charge of the wounded and the sick. The elements were still squally and tetchy, but in nothing so terrible a mood as they had been the previous day. They could see the *Blonde* clearly across a mile of broken grey water. FitzRoy had been concerned that Biddlecombe's short tacks might have taken her ever further from the coast, but the stern figure of Bos'n Sorrell, arms folded behind the wheel, had obviously attended to that difficulty. It was a rough crossing: the cutter was tossed about, her head turned this way and that by waves slugging at her from the opposite direction, and all aboard had to endure repeated facefuls of spray. A quarter-mile out from the beach, Hamond knelt over the side and, with what looked curiously like gratitude, voided the contents of his stomach into the sea.

'Lost your sea-legs, Mr Hamond?' enquired FitzRoy cheerfully.

'It's not s-seasickness, sir,' admitted Hamond, looking fleetingly guilty. 'It's sheer relief at g-getting away from there alive.'

FitzRoy had thought about not taking Hamond on the expedition but the man had volunteered, after all. In fact, Hamond had been as brave as any of them, in his way, and FitzRoy had appreciated a quiet, intelligent voice amid all the bravura aggression.

'I-I'm not sure I can t-take any more of this, sir.'

'Not long to go now, Mr Hamond. Another twenty minutes and we shall be in the *Blonde*.'

'Th-that's not what I m-meant, sir.'

FitzRoy looked into Hamond's eyes, two saucers in a pallid face, and at his hands, which were literally shaking with released tension. The young midshipman's nerves, he realized, were completely shot to pieces.

'I m-meant, sir, that I c-can't go on serving in the Navy. I just c-can't go on. I'm too f-frightened, sir.'

'I have come to report the successful rescue of the crew of HMS *Challenger*, sir, with no further casualties.'

Once again, FitzRoy found himself before Commodore Mason in the well-manicured setting of that officer's rented garden. The open geneva bottle stood to attention on the table.

Mason grunted. 'Do not think for one second that you have saved your skin, FitzRoy. I shall make damned sure you are court-martialled as a mutineer.'

'An accusation of the kind you describe could hardly fail to be damaging,' conceded FitzRoy expressionlessly, 'as, indeed, would a counter-accusation of cowardice in the face of the enemy and dereliction of duty. In fact, it is hard to see any benefit accruing to either of us from this sorry affair. But I should say, sir, that I have already composed a . . . rough draft of my report of the expedition.'

'To the devil with you and your report.'

'It is not a very detailed report, sir. It merely credits the successful rescue of the *Challenger* to the bravery of the officers and men of HMS *Blonde*, and by implication to her commanding officer, sir. No names are mentioned in this rough draft of what would – under normal circumstances – be regarded by the Admiralty as a most heroic action, sir.'

FitzRoy paused, to let this sink in. He could see the light dawning, gradually sweeping the shadows from Mason's furrowed brow.

'No names?'

'No sir. Just a straightforward rescue.'

Mason considered further.

'You have important business in Tahiti, do you not?'

'I believe so.'

'Then you had better get on with it, had you not? And this time you will obey your orders to the very letter. Is that clear?'

'That is clear, sir.' Mason, it appeared, had accepted FitzRoy's face-saving proposal.

'One further thing, sir.'

'Don't push your luck, Mr FitzRoy.'

'I have reluctantly agreed to terminate the commission of one of my officers. Mr Hamond is to leave the *Beagle* forthwith. I should like, with permission, to take Mr Davis from the *Blonde*, sir.'

'Who?'

'Your assistant master, sir. I should like him to remain behind and skipper the *Constitución*, a surveying schooner I have borrowed, on an expedition to northern Chili and Peru.'

'Should you indeed? Very well. If you say so,' acquiesced Mason gruffly. 'What's the matter with this Hamond fellow?'

'He is too frightened to continue in the Service, sir.'

'Cowardice, eh?'

'No sir. Mr Hamond is very far from being a coward. He appears to be suffering from a sort of extended shock. I think him an immensely brave man to admit to it, and to face up to it, sir.' FitzRoy touched the peak of his cap insouciantly and, without waiting to be dismissed, took his leave of the commodore. Only upon reaching the safety of the street did he allow himself a smile of relief.

Chapter Twenty-four

Chatham Island, Galapagos,
16 September 1835

'It is indisputable evidence!'

'My dear FitzRoy, one piece of evidence can rarely be said to be indisputable.'

'"Chem" is clearly Shem. "Mount Theghin" is indisputably Mount Ararat. The legends of the Araucanians testify to the global nature of the deluge. My dear Philos, what more proof could you desire?'

'But the story could have been introduced into the Araucanian tradition at any point – by the *conquistadors* perhaps – or even earlier, by a lone Christian travelling across the Pacific. Without a weight of evidence to back them up, the tales of this chief of yours – half a Spaniard, by his own admission – would scarcely hold up as scientific evidence.'

'But the word of God is not a matter of scientific conjecture! Even if there were not a huge weight of evidence for the flood, God's word is absolute!'

'You will allow me to observe, I hope, that there is also direct evidence *against* the flood.'

'Direct evidence against the flood? What evidence?'

'Evidence I have witnessed with my own eyes.' There was no other way forward now. His enthusiasm for argument heated under the broiling, oppressive, leaden Galapagos skies, Darwin blurted out the most controversial of his conclusions. 'I did not wish to say this before, FitzRoy, for fear of offending you, but the natural life that I witnessed on the Patagonian side of the Andes was entirely different from that on the Chilean side.'

'What of it?'

'The Andes are newly uplifted land, which means that the differing species on either side of the *cordillera* came into being *after* the mountains were created. Those species were not created on the sixth day. They have – they have—'

'Transmuted?' FitzRoy uttered the word calmly but grimly.

'Yes, damn it, they have *transmuted* into existence, in relatively recent geological times. You will find an entirely different species of mouse on either side of the *cordillera*. If God created mice at the beginning of time, then why do not identical mice swarm over the western and eastern slopes today?'

'What you speak of is adaptation. Variation within a species. Species themselves are immutable.'

'I tell you they were different species of mouse.'

'Come, Philos, if transmutation between species is possible, then show me *your* direct evidence. The fossil record does not convincingly document a single transmutation from one species to another. Where are the countless fossils of intermediate species, embedded in the crust of the earth? If wings grew from forelegs, where are the half-winged animals, and how could they have half-flown? If lungs grew from gills, where are the half-lunged fish, and how could they have half-breathed? If giraffes grew from antelopes, where are the fossils of all the short-necked giraffes?'

'The fossil record is less than perfect, I grant you, but geology is a new science. In future ages, perhaps the fossil links you speak of will be discovered. Discontinuities in nature do not by themselves speak against transmutation, because these intermediate forms are now extinct, and may have become so very quickly. Did we ourselves not find the remains of an aquatic rodent the size of an elephant? Who knows what two orders of animals that creature might have bridged?'

'Are you suggesting that your Chilean mice transmuted from aquatic elephants, or vice versa?'

'No, of course I am not. I have simply come to realize that creation is far more fluid a business than our Church allows. How different are the fat little Fuegians from their lean, tall Araucanian neighbours? Yet all are supposedly descended from Noah and his wife. Where are the intermediate fossils there? And both species shall become extinct, I fear, when General Rosas has his way.'

'Both species? The Fuegians and the Araucanians are men – one species – equal before the Lord, who one hopes in His mercy will save them from the depredations of your friend the general.'

'You believe God will save those heathen savages from the Christian armies? From white men?'

FitzRoy reacted with anger.

'Those "heathen savages" are heathens because they have yet to receive the word of God, and savages because they have yet to receive the blessings of civilization that attend it. Your friend Rosas may profess Christianity, but he is little more than a tyrant and a murderer who takes God's name in vain.'

'Perhaps the Fuegians are not men as we are, created indivisibly by God. Perhaps they are a separate species of man, more akin to the higher apes. I do not know. *I do not know*, FitzRoy. But I do know that to believe in every word of the scriptures, the ark, the creation of all life in a matter of days, is to believe in the impossible and the unintelligible.'

'If what you say is true, then the stars of heaven, the showers and the dew, the mountains and the hills may no longer be called to exalt the Lord with us by praise.'

'No. I merely question the word of God *as it is written by man* in the scriptures.'

'This won't do, Philos. The scriptures themselves say, "If any man shall take away the words of the book of this prophecy, God shall take away his part out of the book of life and out of the holy city." You are risking damnation in the hereafter!'

'Hang it, FitzRoy, such threats are themselves a damnable doctrine. The Old Testament is a manifestly false history of the origin of the world, and I do not believe that the true story of the creation of life by God is to be found there.'

'But look what you seek to put in its place!' Both men were fairly screeching at one another now. 'What are the chances of species somehow transmuting out of nothingness in the first instance? Something as beautiful and complex as a flower cannot result from a random process! An earthquake destroys a cathedral – it does not construct one! The grain that man makes into bread, the cattle that provide his meat and milk, the dogs that aid him in his work – did all these transmute by some accident of nature? A spider's web? A beautiful butterfly? An electric eel? Did all these transmute by accident as well?'

FitzRoy pulled a book from the shelf above. 'Listen to Paley: "The marks of design are too strong to be gotten over. Design must have had a designer. That designer must have been a person. That person is God."'

'I do not deny that the Lord God has designed all living things! I just . . . I just . . .' Darwin faltered, his sails sagging as the initial blast of his enthusiasm began to subside. 'I just believe that once an animal has been divinely created, it is free to transmute itself gradually, by some unexplained mechanism, into another related species.'

'Tell me, Philos, on your expedition, were there ants to be found on either side of the Andes?'

'Of course.'

'Different species of ant?'

'I dare say – I do not recall.'

'And the sterile worker ants – how precisely had they transmuted gradually from one species into another when they cannot breed?'

'I do not know.'

'You do not know. There is no mechanism to explain it – that is why you do not know. I repeat, what you have witnessed is *variation*. An adaptation from one mouse to another mouse through the vagaries of climate, which has been presupposed by God as part of His divine plan. A secondary consequence of a primary act of creation. There is a moral aspect to nature as well as a material aspect, and it is the task of science to link the material to the moral. Any man who denies this is deep in the mire of folly.'

Darwin attempted one last throw. 'If there is no such thing as transmutation, then why do the most closely allied species occur in the same countries? Why did the Lord place many species of penguin towards the South Pole, but none towards the North Pole?'

'You have yet to visit Australia, Philos. When you get there, you will find a swan identical in every respect to its British counterpart – except that where the British swan is white with a yellow beak, the Australian version is jet-black with a scarlet beak. The two birds were created many thousands of miles apart, in perfect isolation. Why? As objects of beauty, and no more.' FitzRoy folded his arms with cold satisfaction and sat back.

Darwin looked down at his shabby, sweat-stained shirt. All his shirts and waistcoats were showing their age now, patched and repatched as they had been during the preceding five years. He wanted to wear clean, new clothes again. He wanted to relax in his favourite armchair at the Mount. He was fed up with quarrelling. He was fed up with this wretched little cabin. He was fed up with ceaselessly feeling seasick. He was fed up with the dyspepsia and constipation and piles that had pursued him here from Valparayso. He seriously doubted whether any schoolboy had ever longed for the holidays as much as he craved his home and his family. The day when the lookout hailed the Lizard lights ahead would be a momentous one indeed. He no longer had the strength or the inclination to argue.

*   *   *

A few days later, Darwin, Covington and Midshipman King were landed in high surf on the north-east coast of Chatham Island, with armfuls of collecting-boxes. The water was goosepimple-cold on account of the polar current – Stebbing had fetched up a bucketful, which had measured 58 degrees Fahrenheit – but the air, roasting slowly in the glare of a high, burnished sun, had registered closer to 90. Darwin jammed his thermometer into the black sand, whereupon the mercury promptly shot off the scale, meaning that the ground temperature exceeded 137 degrees Fahrenheit. Within seconds, the glimmering heat had dried out their clothes, then resoaked the trio once more in their own sweat.

Before them lay a buckled, rippling, jagged country, black as anthracite, except that it resembled sea more than land, a churning nocturnal sea that had been paralysed in an instant. Everywhere they looked in this tortured, twisted wasteland were volcanic craters: craters bursting like sores from other craters, little craters concealed within bigger craters, craters with solidified lava spilling over their rims like boiling pitch caught at the moment of tipping from a cauldron. Here and there were fumaroles, smoking vents and steaming fissures that ran in angular, contrary splits against the flow of the rock. It was, reflected Darwin, reminiscent of the iron-foundry country around Wolverhampton. The south side of each crater was the lower, he noticed, and in some cases it had been destroyed altogether. *These cones have been formed under water*, he realized. *The wind and the waves here arrive from the south. They have battered at these rocks while they lay in the sea, before they ever were raised out of the water.*

By rights, such a furnace should have supported little in the way of life. The pitiless vertical sun, the stifling climate and the rocks that glowed like a cast-iron stove should have been no more hospitable than the infernal regions of Pandemonium itself. But it was not so: every square foot of land was dotted with shuffling, scaly, primordial creatures, while the surf teemed with darting, flashing shapes. The sea creatures were, for the most part, those of the polar regions – penguins, sealions and the like – whereas the cacti and lizards ashore were similar to those of the arid lands near the equator. Huge, crimson-chested frigate birds sailed overhead, puffed up with self-importance, arrowing down towards the surface of the sea where they would deftly pluck out a fish without even getting their feet wet. Little mockingbirds ran up and pecked at the explorers' boots. Bright vermilion Sally Lightfoot crabs swarmed across the glossy ebony rocks of the shore, shuttling backwards and forwards with aimless determination. It was an extraordinary panorama, the like of which none of them had ever seen.

The most commonplace denizen of Chatham Island was a fat, sluggish, sooty-coloured iguana, some three feet in length, clumsy of movement, with a horny mane, long webbed claws and a slack pouch hanging beneath its slack mouth. These imps of darkness lined the beaches, basking in the infernal heat, yet never straying more than ten yards from the sea. Occasionally one would lumber into the water, where it would be transformed into a sleek obsidian dart, its normally splayed legs tucked out of sight, its tail propelling it deftly through the water like a miniature crocodile. In common with the other land creatures of the Galapagos, these reptiles were extraordinarily tame, and utterly receptive to being poked and prodded. By way of an experiment, Darwin grasped one of the beasts by the tail, whirled it about his head and flung it into a tidal pool.

'What larks!' shouted Midshipman King, while Covington stared at his master with what looked like disapproval.

Really, it was good to be romping about the country with King once more; he was not much use as a naturalist's assistant, it was true, but he was much jollier than the servant. Covington, to be fair, was fast making himself indispensable – the horse-butcher's son was learning so quickly, he had even started his own limited sub-collection – but he remained curiously unapproachable. He was not, after all, a gentleman. King was putting the fun back into collecting.

'Look, Philos, it's coming back.'

The iguana had indeed crawled laboriously back to its former spot at Darwin's feet. As it arrived, he picked it up by the tail once more, and flung it back into the pool. Again, the beast attained the shore, and again disdainfully marched back to its place. A third time it was returned to the water, and a third time, pompously, patiently, it regained its former situation.

'Hereditary instinct is telling it that the shore is a place of safety,' concluded Darwin. 'I could kill it in an instant, yet it does not fear me.'

'Not very bright, is it, Philos?' said King cheerily.

'Lizards in Europe know to fear man,' Darwin mused aloud. 'It is a knowledge they possess from birth. Yet reptiles do not rear their young – indeed, they may never encounter them. They cannot teach their young anything. The knowledge is inherited. Were these iguanas to learn to fear man, how would that knowledge pass to their descendants?'

'Well . . . I suppose it wouldn't,' said King, by now somewhat baffled.

'He's talking about transmutation,' jabbed Covington, catching Darwin's eye and holding it for a telling second.

'Transmutation . . . That's a load of Godless gammon, isn't it?' said King, unhappily aware that he was not party to some shared knowledge.

'Yes. Yes it is,' said Darwin bluntly, and moved purposefully away across the corrugated ground.

They ascended the island's central cone by way of a series of paths through the undergrowth that seemed to be converging on some unknown central point. The mystery of who or what had made these tracks was solved when they came upon two huge tortoises, each as high as a man's chest, snuffling up the hill in front of them. The latter beast had the numerals '1806' carved into its shell. As the collecting party marched up behind, the animals took no notice; but when Darwin moved into the eyeline of the rear tortoise, it hissed at him, sat down, and withdrew its head and legs into its carapace.

'It seems they are quite deaf,' he deduced.

King took a run at the lead tortoise and leaped aboard. Even with the weight of a sturdy youth on its back, the vast reptile seemed unaware that anyone was behind or even upon it. Darwin jumped aboard too, but still the animal did not slacken its pace, keeping to a speed that – he calculated with the aid of his pocket-watch – would amount to about four miles per day.

'Giddy up!' yelled King, and thrashed the animal's hind-quarters with a switch. 'What about a race? We could be at the summit by the end of the week!'

Both men laughed, while Covington brought up the rear in respectful and possibly reproachful silence.

They lunched soon afterwards, watched by a large hawk that perched upon a low branch. Darwin approached the bird with his gun, and placed the barrel squarely in the centre of its face. The hawk remaining entirely unmoved, he nudged the nozzle against its beak, before finally shoving the bird to the ground. With an indignant flap of its feathers, it dusted itself down and climbed back to its perch as before.

'Extraordinary,' he murmured.

Covington, he noticed, was writing something in a small notebook. 'What is that, Covington?'

'It is nothing, sir,' mumbled the manservant.

'What is it?'

'It is my journal.'

'You keep a *journal*?'

'Yes sir.'

'Give it here.'

Covington complied, slowly and reluctantly. Darwin flicked through the pages. In a large, rounded, deliberate hand were entries – some of exceeding brevity – going back to the start of the voyage. Capital letters and underlined words mingled freely with those in lower case; on occasion, Spanish happily cohabited with English. Darwin stopped at the entry detailing their expedition northwards from the Rio Negro, in the company of Esteban and his gauchos.

> In the camp or country there are lions, tigers, deer, cavys, ostriches both large and small. <u>Aperea</u> here has a much finer fur THAN ELSEWHERE. THERE ARE <u>armadillos</u>. Partridges ARE both large and small (the former has a tuft or crest on its head). C. D. Caminando por tierra, desde Rio Negro a Buenos Ayres.

Darwin shut the journal and handed it back to its owner. 'Upon my soul, Covington, I never had you down as an author.'

'No sir,' muttered the big youth.

'Just so long as you remember that you are my servant, and that all important observations are to be shared. I am, if you recall, to be the author of the official natural history of the voyage.'

'Aye aye sir. Shall I do well not to write any more, sir?'

'As you will. It is up to you. Just so long as you remember.'

'Aye aye sir.'

After lunch, they pushed on to the principal crater, the floor of which was taken up by a grand assembly of blue-footed boobies. These preposterously earnest birds, white-bodied, black-winged, with bright turquoise beaks and feet, seemed to treat the business of guarding their nests rather casually. Darwin lobbed a few experimental stones at the nesting females, which bounced off their backs harmlessly, the victims looking no more than confused. King walked up and broke one's neck with his hat. The other birds around merely stared up at him with expectant faces.

'I suppose we had better shoot one to take with us,' said Darwin, loading his rifle with the mustard shot which would make a cleaner job than King's hat-brim. He levelled the barrel at the nearest booby. It gazed back at him, curious and uncomprehending. He tensed his finger on the trigger, and paused.

'Everything all right, Philos?'

'Yes, everything's fine. Do you know, King – I'm not sure I can actually do this.'

'How do you mean?'

'I mean, I am all for the chase, but this – this is ridiculous.'

And what is a love of the chase but a relic of an instinctive passion? It is like the pleasure of living with the sky for a roof – it is no more than the pleasure of a savage returning to his wild and native habits.

The bird continued to gaze stupidly up at him.

He handed the gun to Covington.

'Covington, shoot this bird, would you?'

'Aye aye sir.'

Covington brought the gun up to his shoulder, took aim and fired. There was a deafening explosion, and he fell back with a scream, blood pouring from his shattered ear. The flame from the flash-pan had escaped into the magazine and detonated the loose powder within: one side of the weapon lay ripped open, where the explosion had torn the gunmetal apart from the inside.

'Covington? Are you all right, man?'

Darwin and King, their ears ringing, knelt on either side of the writhing manservant, who appeared not to hear their urgent entreaties.

'Covington! Are you all right?'

One hand pressed to the side of his head, fresh, bright blood streaming between his fingers, Covington rolled on to his back, his frightened eyes attempting to focus on his would-be rescuers.

'Are – you – all – right?'

'I cannot hear you,' he whimpered. 'Whatever it is you are saying, sirs, I cannot hear you.'

The drizzle having cleared, the party took their dinner out of doors, at a table set up on the governor's lawn.

'More turpin?' said Lawson. 'It is the breast meat – the most capital cut.' He indicated the bowl of fatty, primrose-coloured meat that occupied pride of place in the centre of the table. 'The rest of the animal is of indifferent flavour, except when employed in soup. The calipash is thrown away altogether.'

'This is a local tortoise, I presume?' asked FitzRoy, taking an elegant bite.

'Oh no – we have them brought across from James, or Hood, or Albemarle,' said the governor cheerfully. 'Here on Charles Island, they have been hunted to extinction.'

The discovery of Lawson's existence had been both a stroke of luck and a surprise, in that FitzRoy and his officers had been unaware that the Galapagos Islands – previously the province of buccaneers and whalers – even possessed a governor. Stopping at the postbox on Charles Island, they had come across Nicholas Lawson astride his horse, collecting his mail. Lawson was able to inform them that the islands had recently been annexed by the newly established Republic of the Equator, and that the Ecuadorians had not only constructed a prison for some three hundred black convicts on Charles Island, but had appointed him – as an Englishman of standing – their governor. The penal settlement was situated one thousand feet up and four and a half miles inland, where sodden, hanging clouds buffeted the highlands each year between June and November, creating a temperate zone of ferns, grasses and woodlands. There the prisoners cultivated plantain, banana, sugar cane, Indian corn and sweet potato, and hunted the pigs and goats that were permitted to run wild between the trees. Lawson had promised FitzRoy and the officers of his service, and had invited them to visit his domain later that day to enjoy, a dinner of succulent roast tortoise with home-grown vegetables.

'It would appear that there was once a prodigious number of tortoises here,' said FitzRoy, gesturing across Lawson's precisely manicured lawn. Arranged at geometric intervals around the neat green rectangle, upturned tortoise carapaces served as pots for a colourful assortment of woodland flowers.

'Ah, the flowerpots,' said Lawson, smoothing the angles of

his clipped, triangular beard. 'We live something of a Robinson Crusoe existence here, Captain FitzRoy: happily self-sufficient in our necessities, but absolutely devoid of the merest luxury, and therefore forced to improvise. In answer to your question, there were indeed a great many turpin here, not ten years back. Some of the bigger frigates were taking away seven hundred at a time, to consume while crossing the Pacific. I myself once saw two hundred loaded in a day. Those that were too big to lift had the date engraved upon their carapaces: 1786 is the oldest I have yet witnessed. We killed those larger beasts ourselves where they stood, and carried the meat here, until every turpin on the island was gone. The other islands' populations are headed the same way. During the dry months they are killed for the water reserves in their bladders. The species shall be extinct, I believe, in another twenty years. Now our turpin must be brought from a variety of different islands, in an attempt to preserve the supply for as long as possible. Once they are gone, I dare say we shall consume the sea turtles.'

'It is an uncommon pity to see one of the Lord's creatures made extinct in this fashion,' offered a troubled Sulivan.

'But did the Lord not place the turpin here for man's benefit in the first instance?' said Lawson, carefully adjusting his wire-rimmed spectacles. 'One might reasonably propose it, Lieutenant.'

'Indeed one might.' Sulivan smiled politely.

'Forgive me,' said FitzRoy, who had been casting a scientific eye at the upturned tortoise-shells, 'but are there not some considerable differences between these several carapaces? Did you not say they originated in different islands?'

'You are most observant, Captain FitzRoy. The turpin of each island do not assort with each other at all. Those from Hood Island have a thick ridge of shell in front, turned up in the manner of a Spanish saddle, like that one there. The one to the left is from James Island – do you see? It is rounder and blacker, and its meat is incidentally more flavoursome.' He held up his loaded fork and smiled. 'Generally, the turpin of the lower islands have longer necks, whereas those of the high country are dome-shaped with shorter necks. You will find such variations in all the wildlife hereabouts, safe enough.'

'I am very much interested about this. Do tell us more.'

'You have seen the marine iguanas? The *Amblyrhynchus cristatus*? They are not strictly iguanas, I should say, but of the genus *Amblyrhynchus*. Well, they are larger on Albemarle Island. And there is also a land *Amblyrhynchus*, a burrowing animal, terracotta in colour, to be found only on Albemarle, James, Barrington and Indefatigable.'

'I apprehend that you are something of a naturalist, Mr Lawson.'

Lawson straightened his starched but threadbare waistcoat with a hint of pride. 'One does one's best to peg away at the subject, Captain FitzRoy. When one is a Robinson Crusoe, there is little else to occupy one's time.'

'The *Beagle* has its own naturalist, in Mr Darwin here.'

Darwin, who had been miles away, reliving the flaming explosion of his gun into Covington's ear over and over again in his mind, came to with a start. 'What? I'm sorry . . . I do beg your pardon . . .'

'Mr Lawson here was telling us of the varieties by which the wildlife of each island may be distinguished, and of his Robinson Crusoe existence.'

'Ah, but you will be interested to hear, Mr Darwin, that these islands had their own Robinson Crusoe,' related Lawson, pressing on to spare his inattentive guest any further embarrassment. 'His name was Patrick Watkins, an Irishman who was shipwrecked here at the turn of the century. He built a hut, and planted some potatoes he retrieved from his ship, and made a healthy living of it. By the time a vessel arrived to rescue him, he had become a ragged muffin, with wild, matted red hair and a beard down to his knees, and was sufficiently content that he quite refused to leave. He even abducted a Negro from a passing whaler to serve as his Man Friday, but the fellow escaped.'

A chuckle rippled round the table.

'You say that you are a naturalist, Mr Darwin.'

'Indeed.'

'Then you will be aware that the islands are volcanic, and of comparatively recent origin?'

'One could hardly fail to notice it.'

'It is my belief that we are not the only Robinson Crusoes here, Mr Darwin. The animal population of these islands finds its echo on the South American mainland. The south-easterlies wash driftwood from the mainland against our shores, as well as bamboo, cane-stalks and palm-nuts. One can see them strewn across the beaches at low tide. I believe that the animals of these islands floated across the Pacific on these natural rafts, and adapted to their surroundings once they had arrived. It is why there are no frogs or toads here.'

'Of course!' said Darwin. 'Because such reptiles cannot abide salt water.'

'Then the Galapagos are not an original centre of creation, but have been colonized since from other lands,' said FitzRoy. 'How fascinating.'

The debate was interrupted by the arrival of Bynoe, on a borrowed horse.

'Ah, the good doctor,' said Lawson, gesturing for Bynoe to dismount and take a chair at the feast. 'How is your patient? Recovering from his most tragic accident, I trust?'

Darwin cast a faintly guilty look in Bynoe's direction.

The young surgeon looked grave. 'Covington will live, I am glad to say. He begins to amend. But I do not think he will ever hear again. I am afraid he is become quite deaf.'

'These finches are not the same.'

'I beg your pardon, sir?'

'These finches are not the same as those of Charles Island. Nor, for that matter, do they even resemble each other.'

FitzRoy put down his collecting-cage and seated himself on a rock to watch. Bynoe came over and sat alongside.

'The ones we took on Charles had short beaks, thick at the base like a bullfinch. They were using them to squeeze berries and break seeds. But these birds have fine beaks, like a warbler. Look – that one there is piercing the fibre of the tree, in search of moisture I suppose.'

The two men observed the finches' miniature endeavours in absorbed silence for a few minutes, before Bynoe spoke: 'My God, sir, look. That little fellow there is using a twig like a tool. He appears to be trying to extricate something from the crevice in the trunk – an insect, or a grub.'

'Is it not extraordinary, Mr Bynoe? It is one of those admirable provisions of infinite wisdom by which each created thing is adapted to the place for which it was intended. One single species has been taken by the Lord and modified into a number of different varieties, for a number of different ends.'

Bynoe agreed that it was indeed extraordinary.

The *Beagle* lay anchored off the north-west coast of James Island, her decks groaning following a full victualling with thirty live tortoises, several piglets, and twenty sackfuls of convict-grown pumpkins and potatoes purchased from Mr Lawson for the journey home. The piglets, Lieutenant Wickham had noted with wry amusement, had been fetched aboard two by two. Now, the officers' collecting party was making a final sweep through the lowland thickets of Buccaneer Cove, just behind the rocky shore: it was to be the last halt of their visit to the islands.

Darwin, feeling debilitated and irritable and curiously bereft without the ministrations of his servant, had marched ahead: he now found himself suddenly at the centre of a clandestine meeting of several rust-red, swishing-tailed *Amblyrhynchus*. As the beasts adjourned their furtive business and lumbered away across the black lava, he was struck by the primeval nature of the scene: the reptiles had been first to colonize this virgin land, ahead of the higher mammals who were now driving them to extinction, the same process as had occurred throughout the rest of the earth during an earlier epoch. These land lizards, presumably, had transmuted from the marine lizards that had swum out to the newborn territory, just as the land tortoises would have transmuted from the sea turtles that were still to be seen making their laborious circuits of the islands. What was the creative force behind this explosion of life? Was it all controlled by the good Lord Himself? Or was it out of His hands, a process set in motion at the beginning of time that had been allowed to run riot of its own volition? One conclusion seemed reasonably certain: any species that moved into a new territory was reshaped by its altered environment to an extraordinary degree. Quite how, he did not know. There were clues here, he was sure, to that mystery of mysteries, the first appearance of new beings on the face of the earth; clues that might help to undermine the very stability of species itself. But they felt frustratingly and elusively out of reach. Here was a bare, naked rock that had been clothed for the first time in the not-too-distant past; here should have been everything he needed to crack the mystery. But in the absence of shade, with no escape from the beating sun, his head aching, his boils chafing and his guts rumbling, his brain simply refused to apply itself. He hated these islands, he realized. It was hard to imagine a location so entirely useless to civilized man, or even to the larger mammals.

Bynoe pushed through the leafless brush, mopping the sweat from his brow.

'Presents for you, Philos. For your collection. I found them in a fissure in the rock.'

Darwin forced himself to remember his manners. 'That is extremely decent of you, Bynoe. You oblige me.'

The young surgeon held out a boxful of giant tortoise eggs, perfect white spheres some eight inches in diameter. In his other hand he brandished a wooden cage. 'There are some interesting finches, too, that the skipper thought you should take a look at.'

'That is very kind . . . but I already have a pair.'

Darwin held up his own collecting-cage in which a sooty-coloured male finch and its tobacco-coloured mate twittered with annoyance.

'I think these are different, Philos. For one thing, the female of this pair is black.'

'Did you see the nest?'

'It was roofed, with a clutch of pink-spotted eggs. I have collected a few of those too.'

'Then it is almost certainly the same species. I dare say the female plumage darkens with age. But please inform the captain that I am most indebted to him for the thought.'

'I will, Philos, I promise.'

Bynoe moved away again, and Darwin was left to his thoughts once more.

If men and their dogs were now bringing destruction to the tortoise population of the Galapagos, because the huge reptiles were utterly ill-equipped to deal with their new predators, then surely there was no more wonder in the extinction of an entire species than in that of an individual? Was this the explanation for the jumps in the fossil record? Darwin's mind positively ached with the effort. He felt close, so tantalizingly close, to comprehending the scheme of things – to knowing the Lord's mind on this most momentous of issues. So close, but still not there.

Chapter Twenty-five

Point Venus, Tahiti, 16 November 1835

———————

Razor-sharp spires of rock, jagged like the shards of a broken window, the glens between them hiding quietly from the light of day; luxuriant groves of coconut palms crowding at their base, interspersed with stands of glossy breadfruit trees and cheerful clusters of bananas; below them, a glassy lagoon whispering softly at the sides of its fringing reef; and beyond that, breaker after breaker of dazzling white foam, beating optimistically against sturdy walls of coral, built up across the centuries by the herculean efforts of myriad tiny sea creatures. It was a picture all of them had seen a hundred times in engravings and watercolours, and daubed upon the canvas of their imaginations; but flushed with the brilliant light of the Pacific sky, it took on a welcoming glow to melt the weariest heart.

'Otaheite,' intoned FitzRoy reverentially.

'I apprehend that we are now to call it Tahiti,' objected Darwin.

'Indeed we are,' said FitzRoy, 'but Cook called it Otaheite by mistake, and I have too much respect for the great man to call it by any other name.'

It had been a glorious crossing, the *Beagle* swept across the Pacific on the warm trade winds, her studding-sails set, eating up the miles at a rate of one hundred and forty a day. The maindeck was thick with tortoises, an array of domes to match St Mark's Basilica in Venice, all sadly destined for the cooking-pot – save one fortunate individual by the name of Harry, which had been earmarked by Darwin as a domestic pet. Quite how his father would react to the sight of a giant Galapagos tortoise ploughing through his flower-beds was a question he intended to address at a later date.

The depth-sounding was called out as ten fathoms, and with it came the news that the tallow at the end of the lead-line was no longer picking up dead coral and sand but impressions of the living reef. FitzRoy gave orders for the yards to be trimmed round, the anchor cables to be ranged and anchor buoy ropes to be made ready. As the *Beagle* swerved impeccably into Matavai Bay, her foretopsail was backed, the rest of the sails were furled, and the anchor was released into the turquoise water. This was the exact spot, he reflected, from which Cook and Banks had observed the transit of Venus in 1769, and the knowledge gave him a thrill of association. Point Venus was one of the key points in Beaufort's chain of meridian distances around the globe, so FitzRoy, too, had celestial observations to make; after which there remained the research into the formation of coral islands that the hydrographer had asked him to undertake, and the unpleasant business of extracting a fine from the Tahitians at the behest of Commodore Mason. Much as he disliked doing that gentleman's dirty work, he had sailed so close to the wind in the matter of the *Challenger* that he dared not rock the boat any further.

As the *Beagle* slowed to a stop, natives in canoes carved from hollowed-out trees swarmed into the water, laughing, chattering and calling out to the ship. 'Hey, *manua! Manua!*' they shouted, as their little vessels crowded about the *Beagle*, their outriggers clattering against each other and frequently becoming entangled, such was their enthusiasm.

'It means man-o'-war,' said Stokes, realizing. '*Manua* means man-o'-war.'

'It's a regular crush!' said King.

'I understood the Tahitians to have become a Christian people,' said Darwin. 'I cannot say much for their observance of the Sabbath.'

'My dear Philos, we have crossed the international date line,' pointed out FitzRoy. 'Yesterday was Saturday, and today is Monday – one less Sabbath for you to worry about, my friend.'

'That's a puzzle and a half,' said Sulivan. 'How to observe the Sabbath when there isn't one. "Verily, thou art a God that hidest thyself"!'

The Tahitians poured aboard without waiting for an invitation, gleefully brandishing items for sale: fresh fruit, live piglets, sea-shells, and old coins that had once belonged to Cook's men on the *Endeavour* or Bligh's crew aboard the *Bounty*. The Tahitian males were broad-shouldered, athletic and muscular; the females were smooth-skinned and seductive, with white or scarlet flowers worn as earrings or pinned into their hair, which they wore with a curious monastic tonsure shorn from the crown. Both sexes were heavily tattooed, wore garlands of coconut leaves about their foreheads, and were quite naked to the waist; a combination that lent them a bacchanalian aspect, as well as contributing to the sailors' keenness in welcoming the younger women aboard.

'The shape of their . . . heads is most attractive, phrenologically speaking,' said Darwin, a faint flush of embarrassment colouring his cheeks.

'Indeed – it would seem to indicate good humour, a tractable disposition, and other civilized characteristics,' agreed FitzRoy, as scientifically as possible.

'They are quite ridiculously naked, of course,' grumbled his friend. 'Really, they are in want of some becoming costume.'

'Absolutely,' said FitzRoy, averting his gaze from the display of flower-bedecked nudity. 'The absence of any decorous attire imports a certain gracelessness, would you not say? Or are my ideas unduly fastidious?'

At this moment a jolly-faced, grinning Tahitian ran up to present them with a pineapple, and both men gratefully seized the opportunity to change the subject. Such exotic fruit – luxurious greenhouse rarities in England – were being distributed freely all round the deck.

'Pineapples here are so abundant that the people eat them in the same wasteful manner as we would eat turnips,' marvelled FitzRoy.

Darwin sank his teeth into the fruit's soft flesh, and gave his verdict. 'Mmm – this is better even than those cultivated in England, which I believe is the highest compliment that can be paid to any fruit.'

In an effort to restore order to the deck, Lieutenant Wickham had called for tables and benches to be fetched, and for some semblance of an English-style market to be established, which was not at all easy, given the presence of a herd of giant tortoises in the midst of proceedings. The shells of the great beasts would, of course, have made excellent surfaces for the display of goods, were it not for their habit of lumbering away mid-sale. Unlike the natives of South America, the Tahitians knew the value of money, especially paper money, and were not to be fobbed off with cloth or spare buttons: anything, it seemed, could be purchased for one *dala*, as they liked to pronounce the word 'dollar'. After some negotiation, Darwin employed the services of two roasted-banana salesmen as guides, to lead him on an expedition up the island's peak the following day.

Once the clamour of the impromptu market had ebbed somewhat, FitzRoy and Darwin were rowed ashore, to be taken in hand by a host of giggling children, who led them along a cool, winding path through the palms. Native huts were dotted between the trees, light, elegant constructions thatched with leaves, elliptical in shape, with bamboo frames and little cane fences. Cloth screens hung in the doorways, affording occasional glimpses of stools and baskets and calabashes of fresh water. One householder sat before his domain reading the New Testament, while his wife cleared away the broad leaves that had served them as breakfast plates, and two gurgling children played contentedly in the grass. It seemed to FitzRoy a beautiful miniature of a nation emerging from heathen ignorance, and modestly setting forth its claim to be considered civilized and Christian.

'*Ia-orana!*' called a voice. The phrase was a traditional Tahitian salutation, but the accent was unmistakably that of Limehouse Reach. Coming up the path to meet them, flanked by a bevy of soberly dressed native junior deacons, was a missionary priest, his hand extended in greeting. 'Welcome to Tahiti, gents. May I take the liberty of introducing myself? Charlie Wilson, chief missionary here at Matavai.'

The newcomer was short and solid, with massive brawny forearms, furred like a chimpanzee's: quite literally, a muscular Christian. His manner was entirely respectful and generous, if lacking in the refinements of etiquette, and his smile was warmly deferential; but here was a man who could look after himself, thought FitzRoy, a man who exuded physical confidence. How very different from their own Mr Matthews, no more than a peripheral figure when he had been most needed in Tierra del Fuego, who had all but become a recluse in the months since. Matthews had vanished into the bowels of the ship in shame, reduced to a pale-faced wraith visible only at mealtimes.

The introductions seen to, Wilson led them to his immaculate little wooden church in the forest, painted all in white, a neat and simple one-roomed cottage adjoining. But for the palm trees and the sultry heat, they might have been in rural Shropshire. Not for the first time that day, FitzRoy thought bleakly of the failure of the Woollya mission, and of the whereabouts of Jemmy Button. Would he ever see Jemmy again, he wondered, that poor lost soul whom he had elevated to Christianity, then abandoned to his fate in the Godforsaken wilds of the south? The contrast between this idyllic setting and his own doomed attempts to create something similar could not have been sharper. Humbly, he congratulated Wilson on the condition of his flock. 'A more orderly, quiet, inoffensive community I have not seen in any other part of the world,' he said. Darwin nodded vigorously in agreement.

'Where, may I ask, did you train as a priest, Mr Wilson?'

'Oh, I didn't train, sir – I have no formal training. The London Missionary Society, sir, it's congregationalist – a knowledge of the Lord's works and a willing heart is all as what's required. I was a coal-whipper, sir, at the Port of London, unloading the big coal ships from the north-east into barges and lighters. Black as a Negro I was at the end of every working day. Then I found God, sir – I was born again, as they say – and I decided to devote my life to His works. I was sent here to assist Mr Henry Nott, and when that good gentleman retired these five years past, I took over the mission. I say "retired", but Mr Nott needed the time to complete his great work, sir.'

'His great work? What great work would that be?'

'Why, none other than the translation of the Old and New Testaments into Tahitian – a work worthy of the very fathers of our church, sir, which has taken up no fewer than forty years of his life. Utaame, fetch Mr Nott here directly, if you please.'

One of the junior deacons was thus dispatched, and quickly returned with an elderly, shrivelled gentleman, the last few wispy strands of whose hair spiralled about his liver-spotted pate as if attempting to ascend to heaven by themselves. Nott's handshake was firm, though, and his blue eyes unclouded.

'It would appear, Mr Nott, that we may credit you before all others for the changes that have overcome this place since Cook's day,' said FitzRoy.

'Oh, I will take none of the credit, for that is the Lord's doing and I merely His willing instrument, and others like me.'

'You were the first missionary here?' asked Darwin.

'That I was.'

'Then may I propose that you are become too modest? Was this not the most savage of lands when you arrived?'

'Oh, it was an uncommon savage land, all right, and an ignorant one. There were human sacrifices, bloody wars where the conquerors spared neither women nor children, the wanton destruction of the aged, infirm or sick, and, of course, an idolatrous priesthood. It is not twenty years since I saw the Tahitians with my own eyes flee in terror at the sight of a horse – a "man-carrying pig", they called it.' A little wheezy chuckle escaped from Nott's turkey throat.

'It is not sixty years since Cook himself could see no prospect of a change in these parts,' added Wilson, in tribute to his senior.

'But God's love was within these people, gentlemen. By His light we have freed that love from its former cloak of savagery, intemperance and licentiousness. In Cook's time, it was the custom of the Tahitians to practise fornication as a matter of routine.'

The four gentlemen tut-tutted at this, but before he could stop it, a sudden, momentary image of a blob of molten candlewax, cooling white against Maria O'Brien's skin, flashed into FitzRoy's mind. He hurriedly filed the image out of sight. He was the captain of a surveying-brig, here to do his duty.

'The natives will persist in going about semi-naked, in their shame,' said Wilson, a disapproving look scudding across his countenance too, 'but the younger generation what pass through the mission schools are learning the virtue of covering their modesty. Though you will have noticed that the women shave their heads, and decorate their skin with needles, and draw attention to themselves by placing flowers in their hair and other means.'

Nott grunted. 'Oh, we have tried to persuade the ladies of the need to change their sartorial habits, but it is the fashion, and that is answer enough at Tahiti as well as Paris.' The old man stood up. 'But here, Captain FitzRoy, let me make you a present, in honour of your visit.' So saying, he reached up to a shelf and, with surprising strength, heaved down a large leatherbound volume that lay there. 'It is the Good Book, as translated into Tahitian. One of the first copies.'

'You are too generous, Mr Nott. I was unaware that your great work had been printed.'

'Printed? This is the Pacific, Captain FitzRoy. There are no printing-works on Tahiti. Every copy is transcribed by hand.'

'By *hand*?'

Amazed, FitzRoy opened the cover. Sure enough, thousands of pages were filled with serried rows of neat and apparently flawless script. 'But, Mr Nott, I cannot possibly accept the fruits of this – this *immense* labour.'

'Nonsense. It gives the Tahitians something to do, and diverts them from their formerly licentious ways.'

After dinner of roasted breadfruit, wild plantain and coconut milk, with pipes and snuff to follow, FitzRoy and Darwin were taken on a tour of the Matavai mission school. In a simple white-painted schoolroom, a young, smiling Tahitian deacon had charge of a class of perfectly drilled juniors, who rose to attention wearing identical shapeless smocks. Once again, FitzRoy regretfully called to mind the infants' school at Walthamstow, where the brooding figure of York had lurked amid the children, mulling over his grand plan. Once again, he felt humbled by the industry and dedication of the men from the London Missionary Society. He and Darwin bade a formal greeting to the class.

'The captain wishes you happiness,' the deacon made clear to his beaming pupils.

'And we wish happiness to the captain,' responded a small boy in the front row, seemingly unbidden.

'Should the captain and Mr Darwin like to see the children perform for their benefit?' the deacon asked respectfully.

'Why, yes, that would be most agreeable. Perhaps a little Tahitian dance?'

A confused hush fell upon the class.

'I am sorry, sir,' chimed the boy at the front with a polite smile, 'but dancing is forbidden in Tahiti, along with all other frivolous entertainments. Anyone caught dancing is to be reported to the watchman, who will take them to the district governor to be punished *most* severely.'

The following day the *Beagle*'s cutter was hoisted out, and FitzRoy and his officers were rowed along a twisting seven-mile channel in the coral to Papiete, the capital, where they attended morning service at the English church. The building was an eyesore, a high, box-shaped structure resembling a Thames brewery, its ugly gabled roof dwarfing the elegant thatching of the surrounding huts. The service, conducted by a Mr Pritchard in both English and Tahitian, was an interminable affair that taxed the patience even of Sulivan. The congregation of some six hundred souls – although kept in order by a beadle with a white wand – began to shuffle and whisper long before the end. Many of the worshippers wore European clothes, sent from London and distributed apparently at random: big, burly Tahitian men had forced themselves into coats so small the seams had split, their arms protruding from their shoulders like the sails of a windmill; while small children sat marooned in enormous benjamins, their hands unable to reach their cuffs, thereby giving the impression that they had been chopped off.

When the service had finished and the congregation had filed out, FitzRoy sat alone in the front pew and waited, while his officers formed a guard of honour outside the main door; for it was here, in the English church following the service, that Queen Pomare had decreed that he might have his audience. He did not have long to wait. After some fifteen minutes spent in contemplation of the task Commodore Mason had given him, he heard the clack of the heavy iron latch lifting from its slot, and the creak of the door as it swung slowly open. The Queen of Tahiti entered, followed by a phalanx of her tribal chiefs, grey-haired but muscular, tattooed and stripped to the waist. FitzRoy rose.

Queen Pomare was a vast woman, almost spherical in shape, loosely dressed in a long, dark, simple gown, fastened at the throat like a priest's cassock. Her hair was divided into two simple braids. She held no regalia, and wore no crown. Nor, in fact, was she wearing anything at all upon her head, hands or feet, nor any kind of girdle or sash to confine her dress. No ceremony attended her arrival. She walked alone up the aisle to meet him, wistfully but gracefully, an air of melancholy pervading her expression. It was clear that her undoubted piety derived from the teachings of the missionaries, but FitzRoy could not help lamenting, for her sake, that her sense of ceremony appeared to have been discarded in the process. Almost embarrassed at finding himself alone with the monarch, he bowed low before her.

'Your Majesty. I am Captain FitzRoy, of His Majesty's brig *Beagle*. I come to you on official business, as a representative of His Majesty King William IV of Great Britain, and most humbly request an audience.'

'Come, Fitirai. Sit with me.'

So saying, the Queen wedged herself into an adjoining pew – not even one of the principal pews by the pulpit, but a rough-hewn public bench. Unable to sit behind or in front of her, for that would have entailed one of them having to twist in their seat, FitzRoy slid in alongside the ample monarch.

'Your Majesty, a British vessel, the *Truro*, was fishing for pearl oysters in the Low Islands, that you call the Paamotu Islands, and was plundered of her catch by the islanders. The government of His Majesty King William has set the compensation for the plunder at two thousand eight hundred dollars, to be paid by Your Majesty's government at once.'

'I know about this ship *Truro*, Fitirai. The islanders of Paamotu live by their pearls. Then the *Truro* came, a big ship, to take away all their pearl oysters. The chief was not asked. No money was given.'

FitzRoy coloured. Really, he had been given an abominable task. 'Unfortunately, Your Majesty, under our law one cannot own the sea, or the creatures that live therein. In law, the men of the *Truro* had every right to fish there.'

'If the men of Paamotu came to the shores of Britain in a big ship and took all the oysters from one place, would the government of King William give its blessing?'

FitzRoy did not reply. Both of them knew the answer perfectly well.

The Queen continued: 'The men of Paamotu are warlike, Fitirai. I cannot make them do my bidding. When my husband the King was alive, it was different. His word was law. But the men of Paamotu will not do the bidding of a woman. Pomare is my husband's family name. My name was once Aimatta. I took my husband's name when he died, but I am not strong like the true Pomare. If I command the men of Paamotu to pay, they will fight rather than obey me.'

'You understand, Your Majesty, what will happen if payment is not made? There will be many ships, big ships with cannon. A harsh punishment will be exacted. I wish it were not so but—'

'I can see that it is not your wish, Fitarai. I know the money must be paid. We have no choice. My people are but weak children. We often expect to see our island taken from us, and ourselves driven off.'

'Your Majesty . . . I assure you – Great Britain has an extent of territory far greater than is sufficient for her wishes. Conquest is not her object. I come here only in search of justice.' The word 'justice' tasted like ash on his tongue.

'We wish to do our duty, Fitarai. But I do not possess two thousand eight hundred dollars. This is a huge sum of money. Pray excuse me while I speak with my chiefs.'

FitzRoy withdrew, and a small deputation of the Queen's advisers was summoned from the back of the church. A period of hushed consultation followed, before he was called back.

'I have decided, Fitirai. You shall have all the money in the royal coffer. The people of Papiete shall pay the rest.'

FitzRoy was aghast.

'But Your Majesty, the innocent natives of Otaheite ought not to suffer for the misdeeds of the Low Islanders. This is not justice.'

One of the chiefs answered on her behalf. 'The honour of the Queen is our honour. We will share her difficulties. We have determined to unite in her cause, and pay the fine demanded by the *manua*.'

The Queen fixed her sad gaze upon FitzRoy. 'My name, Aimatta. In our language, it means "the eater of eyes". There was a time when my people ate the flesh of other people. The men of Great Britain have brought the word of God to these islands, and have replaced the old ways with God's law, which must be obeyed. The law of Great Britain, they tell me, is God's law. So if it is written in God's law that we must pay, then we must pay.'

'Your Majesty . . . I thank you profoundly, in the name of King William and all my countrymen, for your wisdom and generosity. I hope Your Majesty and all the chiefs of Tahiti will do me the great honour of visiting the *Beagle*, and allowing my officers and crew to entertain you before we go off to England.'

'Thank you, Fitirai. You are a kind man. I accept your invitation.'

The Queen smiled and inclined her head, and the various chiefs followed suit. FitzRoy felt only a burning sense of shame.

The following day a trestle table, knocked together quickly by May, was set up in the lee of the church, just by the main door, where the big square bastion of Anglicanism blocked out the light of the rising sun. A strongbox sat on the table-cloth in front of Lieutenant Sulivan, and a ledger lay before Lieutenant Wickham. An armed marine stood guard to either side, while FitzRoy paced about in an agitated frame of mind.

A line of Tahitians queued to make their contributions, male and female, young and old, some virtually naked, some in their ill-fitting European clothes. There were elderly, stooped men clutching clay pots containing their life savings. There were small children, single coins clasped sweatily in their palms. Many of the islanders who had sold livestock and historical artefacts at the impromptu market on the *Beagle*'s maindeck were present, returning the coins they had accumulated so assiduously that day.

'Dash it, sir, this is rotten,' said Sulivan bitterly. 'Absolutely rotten.'

'It's a confounded filthy matter,' Wickham agreed, his jaw set tight. 'I didn't join the Service to go about the world stripping good Christian nations bare in this pinchbeck manner.'

'You do not need to tell me, gentlemen,' said FitzRoy with a scowl. Anger and embarrassment fought to overwhelm his customary good manners. Savagely, he kicked a stone into the grass.

'I feel like one of the moneylenders in the temple,' complained Sulivan.

I was brought up to obey orders, FitzRoy told himself. *To do my duty. But increasingly I am being given orders that do not tally with natural justice – with God's justice. Orders that I cannot in all conscience accord with. These people should be helped to found a decent, God-fearing society – not plundered, as if the Royal Navy were little better than pirates. Little better, even, than General Rosas.*

After four hours' march, the width of the ravine scarcely exceeded that of the bed of the stream, and near-vertical walls of volcanic lava a thousand feet high hemmed in the party on either side. Yet in the soft, porous rock, splashed by innumerable waterfalls and warmed by the steaming, humid climate, ferns, small trees, wild bananas and trailing plants sprang from every ledge or crevice. Using dead tree trunks as ladders, clambering up rock chimneys and knife-edge ridges, and employing ropes where necessary, they inched their way up the gorge. Darwin had scaled mightier mountains than this, but none so precarious or precipitous. Finally, after several hours of sweat-drenched effort, they hauled themselves out on to a cool, windswept plateau at the head of a waterfall. The view was spectacular.

'Good Lord, Covington – what I would forfeit for a cold beer!' he gasped, forgetting for the hundredth time that his remarks were falling literally upon deaf ears; not, he mused, that the response would have been very different in former days.

'Beer, very good!' giggled Hitote, one of the Tahitian guides. 'But no tell missionary!' He put one finger to his lips.

It was hard to see, up here, what they would do for food or shelter. The Tahitians had been insistent about the futility of lugging supplies up to the heights, particularly with regard to the delicately mooted suggestion of bringing an entire bed. Surely, now, they would have to furnish a miracle?

Furnish a miracle they did, however – constructing an entire house in a matter of minutes from bamboo-stems and banana-leaves, bound together with strips of bamboo-bark. Then, producing a small net from his loincloth, Hitote dived into the stream above the waterfall, flashing back and forth through the water like an otter, before emerging with a wriggling netful of tiny fish and freshwater prawns. A wild lily-root, sweet as treacle, would serve as pudding. A fire was lit, the dinner was cooked, grace was said, and finally the party fell upon their feast.

Shading the banks of the stream were the dark, knotted stems of a plant Darwin had not seen before, each leaf a sultry green ace of spades. 'What is that plant, Hitote?'

The Tahitian grinned conspiratorially. '*Ava*. Very good. Chew *ava*, see many strange things, feel good. When missionaries find *ava*, they burn it. Missionaries say is devil's plant. *Ava* only left now in mountains. You want try?'

Purely in the spirit of scientific enquiry, Darwin accepted

a slice after dinner. He found it acrid and unpleasant on the tongue, but before long a sense of well-being crept over him. He and Hitote sat out on the grass before the cliff-edge, gazing down upon the lavish sweep of the landscape, watching the play and interplay of colour, outline and shape as the sun's slanting rays and the gentle mountain breezes set the leaves dancing with each other, not just seeing but *feeling* the radiance of God's universe as its beauty swept over them. Darwin's eyes followed the course of the stream down the valley to Point Venus: there, opposite the stream's outflow, was a break in the encircling reef, where the *Beagle* lay at anchor, her officers no doubt carrying out depth-sounding experiments on the coral. Tiny men on a tiny boat, lost in a vista that he alone could see in its entirety, that he alone had the vision to encompass.

For years, men had thought that coral reefs grew up thousands of feet from the sea bed. Then Lyell, not unreasonably pointing out that coral cannot live below ten fathoms, had postulated that it grew instead from the rims of submerged volcanoes that were themselves rising from the seabed. His was the very latest theory on coral atolls. Lyell, however, had no answer to the reefs that fringed the Pacific's tropical coasts. Why was there a line of coral along the shore, then a further wall of it, half a mile off the beach? Lyell did not know. None of them knew. For Darwin, floating high above them all, the pieces of the universe suddenly seemed to fit together, as if part of a gigantic jigsaw. For if there was dead coral below the ten-fathom mark, then it must once have grown in the light zone nearer the surface. The coral was not *rising*, or it would have been pushed clean out of the water, like the sea beaches he had seen high in the Andes. The coral was *falling*. As it fell below ten fathoms each little creature died, while its fellows above struggled to grow back towards the surface. Coral atolls were the rims of volcanoes that had *sunk* below the surface. The fringing reef? Why, the fringing reef marked the line of an old beach, thrust suddenly below the surface – that was why there was a break in it, opposite the mouth of the stream, and opposite every stream, because the freshwater torrent would have cut through it in the days when it lined the shore. Coral was a shore creature. The coral out on the reef had suddenly found itself marooned in open water following the descent of the land, the Pacific falling as the Andes rose into the clouds.

Darwin lay back in the grass, a sense of profound relaxation stealing over him, while his mind floated away, high above their little eyrie, high above the limpid shallows of the lagoon and the dark, heaving waters of the ocean beyond.

'I have to hand it to you, Philos – you're a deuced marvel! You really do take the palm for deduction.'

'Well, I must confess, I did have a little . . . help.'

FitzRoy and Darwin had squeezed into the latter's cabin, the library shelves crammed not just with books these days, but with snakes and insects in jars, armadillo shells, stuffed birds and lizards, all the accoutrements of a natural-history museum in miniature. Darwin, who had outlined his theory of reef formation to FitzRoy, sat at the chart table, examining a section of live coral beneath his microscope.

'I could not swear to it,' he pronounced, 'but it appears to reproduce – asexually. There are similar creatures by the shore at Edinburgh. I used to wade through the shallows of Leith harbour with Professor Grant. "Zoophytes", he called them, plants that reproduce by releasing free-swimming eggs.'

'If it released an egg, how could it be a plant?'

'Well, like the coral, it is a creature so close to both categories that one could happily place it in either. They are animals *arranged* as plants.'

Both men sensed where the conversation might be headed. Professor Grant, scourge of the late unlamented McCormick, was a follower of Lamarck. Tiny sea creatures arranged as plants afforded perhaps the only real ammunition for the transmutationists as to the origins of animal life.

'It is a fine evening. Shall we take a stroll upon the deck?'

Darwin readily agreed to FitzRoy's diversion, and folded away his microscope. The pair walked out on to the main-deck, sidestepping a huddle of giant tortoises conspiratorially mulching a mound of green leaves, and headed for the starboard rail, where they stood in silence and drank in the view. The coconut palms lining the shore cut jet-black silhouettes into the purple evening sky. A loose-limbed youth was shinning with no apparent difficulty up one of the featureless tree trunks. Along the beach, a line of little cooking-fires blazed, putting FitzRoy in mind of the bonfires of Tierra del Fuego. Was it only a year and a half since they had braved the thundering seas and lashing rain of South America's wild tip, and gained admittance to that isolated, mysterious world, primitive man's last true kingdom on earth? It seemed like a lifetime ago. There the dogs had barked, the drums had beaten out their primal tattoo, and the surf had curled unchecked against the rocky shore. Here, the flames were reflected in the mirror of the lagoon, glittering like gems, and in their glow little children played, or sat in companionable circles singing sweet-voiced hymns, melodious and clear.

'What an opportunity for writing love-letters,' mused Darwin. 'Oh, that I had a sweet Virginia to send an inspired epistle to!'

The next evening, every one of the ship's boats was hoisted out and dispatched, under the reliable command of Mr Stokes, to ferry Queen Pomare and her retinue to the *Beagle*. May had rigged up a jury-cradle, so that Her gracious but undeniably weighty Majesty could be lifted aboard with all due dignity. A salute could not be fired, of course, for fear of disturbing the chronometers, but the ship was dressed with flags, and the crew sent into the yards to stand to attention and give Her Majesty a rousing three cheers as she rose slowly from the cutter. The poop deck had been cleared of tortoises, and a long table had been laid with linen, silverware and candles. So many years into the voyage, the fare was of necessity extremely simple, and

FitzRoy thought it no meal to put before a queen; he was conscious throughout of trying his damnedest to compensate for the shabby way in which she had been treated. But there were fireworks after the meal: every rocket, blue light and false-fire to be found on the ship was lit. All were received rapturously by the royal party, as well as prompting a chorus of ooohs from the Tahitians lining the bay. There were presents for each guest, followed by the entertainment: chairs were drawn up, and the best singers and musicians among the crew brought out to perform before the assembled dignitaries.

'I should like to present Harper, our sailmaker, singing "Rule Britannia",' announced Coxswain Bennet, to commence the concert.

'Peace be with you and your King William,' replied the Queen, smiling at him.

Harper's mellifluous baritone having been well received, Bennet stepped up once again to introduce Wills, the armourer, accompanied by Billet, the gunroom boy, performing 'Three Jolly Postboys'. It was a jaunty number, and the watching crew began to tap their feet and clap along. It soon became apparent, however, that something was wrong. The Tahitians were whispering and muttering among themselves in worried tones, and Queen Pomare's customary expression of placid melancholy had been replaced by one of genuine distress. FitzRoy waved the two performers to a halt. 'Pray forgive me, Your Majesty, but is something the matter?'

'This is not a hymn, Fitirai?' asked Pomare in dismay.

'No, Your Majesty. This is a . . . a sea song, not a hymn.'

'But, Fitirai – the singing of songs is forbidden in Tahiti, except hymns. Singing is one of the illicit pleasures, forbidden by God's law. We have followed God's commands, as told to us by your British missionaries. This is God's way. It is the British way. What is going on? I do not understand.'

Chapter Twenty-six

The Bay of Islands, New Zealand, 21 December 1835

Viewed through the spyglass, the little village of Kororareka seemed quiet enough, a drab and undistinguished huddle beneath a range of low, drizzly hills. Three whaling ships sprawled lazily at anchor, and the occasional solitary canoe could be seen pottering across the bay, but there was no boisterous welcome like the one that had greeted the *Beagle* in Tahiti. New Zealand's only English settlement presented a tidy, reticent aspect to the sea, as if its back were turned. Any closer inspection would have to wait, for the ship lay becalmed at the entrance of the Bay of Islands. Darwin, who had been feeling seasick for a week, used the respite to pace the poop deck irritably.

'Another wretched island. There is nothing I so much long for, as to see *any* spot or object which I have seen before, or *any* which I am likely to see again! To think this will be our *fifth* Christmas away from home!'

'We are all of us homesick, Philos,' muttered FitzRoy, as Darwin stalked past.

'I feel sure that the scenery of England is ten times more

beautiful than anywhere else we have seen on our travels. What reasonable person can wish for great ill-proportioned mountains, two and three miles high? Give me the Brythen, or some such compact little hill!'

Wickham and Stokes exchanged the faintest of grins.

'As for your boundless plains and impenetrable forests, who would compare them with the green fields and oak woods of England? People are pleased to talk of the ever-smiling sky of the tropics – what precious nonsense! Who admires a lady's face who is always smiling? England is not one of your insipid beauties. She can cry, and frown, and smile, all by turns.'

'Actually, when I went to Shropshire it looked rather like this,' offered King, helpfully. 'Imagine that those ferns behind the shore are meadows, and you will see the similarity at once . . .'

The young midshipman tailed off, as Darwin glared at him.

'Come on, Philos,' put in Sulivan cheerily. 'Let's not growl. What is five years around the world, compared to the soldiers' and sailors' lives in India?'

'I did not sign up to be a sailor! Not for five years, at least. And I am convinced that it is a most ridiculous thing to go round the world. Stay at home quietly, and the world will go round with you.'

With that, he stomped off to his cabin.

A light breeze picked up after dinner and gently ballooned the *Beagle*'s sails, enabling them to reach anchorage by early afternoon. FitzRoy, Sulivan and Bennet went ashore in the cutter. When they arrived at the main thoroughfare of Kororareka, they discovered that appearances had indeed been deceptive. The place was a pit.

A mucous coating of mud and faeces lined the main street, splattered by passing footsteps up the rough wooden walls of the adjoining buildings. Every second dwelling was either a spirit-shop, a musket-seller's or a public house. It seemed that the entire population – to judge from the evidence of those on view – was blind drunk. Two men were fighting at the end of the village. A whore, crawling on all fours, was retching up a thin stream of vomit, consoled by a scarcely less sober companion. A man with a Newcastle accent shouted meaningless obscenities at anyone who would listen. Everyone, worryingly, appeared to be armed. A heavily tattooed native, pasted with filth and wrapped in a grubby blanket, lurched towards them shouting angrily. 'You English captain! You help me!'

FitzRoy halted – he had little option, as the man had blocked his path – while Bennet moved protectively to the front in case the skipper needed rescuing.

'I am Captain FitzRoy. How may I help?'

'Englishman steal my wife! Take on whale-ship! You get my wife back!'

'Then you must call out the watch. The authorities.'

The man's face was a mask of furious incomprehension.

'Who is in charge here? Who is boss?' asked FitzRoy firmly.

'You English captain! You boss!'

Another native, long-haired and raw-boned, as well built and ferocious as the first, his face a whorl of angry black tattoo-cuts, bore down upon them. 'You help me!' he shouted. 'I work on whale-ship one year. Promise me big money. Leave ship, no money! White man steal my money!'

A drunken white woman cackled at them from a puddle of her own urine.

'Gentlemen – please!' FitzRoy managed briefly to silence the furious complainants. 'Who is the chief here?'

'No chief. This is white-man town!'

'Who is the British chief? The British resident?'

The second native jabbed a finger accusingly towards the far end of the street, whereupon the two supplicants fell to arguing with each other.

'Is it not mystifying?' pondered a troubled Sulivan, as the trio picked their way through the clinging mud. 'In a pleasant climate, surrounded by beautiful countryside, can one account for human nature degrading itself so much as to live in such a den?'

Bennet, who remembered his excursion into the rookeries behind Oxford Street with the three Fuegians, kept his thoughts to himself.

The main thoroughfare petered out at the foot of a small hill, atop which two flags fluttered gracefully from a white pole: the Union Jack, and another they did not recognize, a red cross on a blue background. The cottage of Bushby, the British resident, was the last house in the street. After they had pounded upon the front door for some minutes, a metal hatch was finally opened, and two frightened eyes peered out from behind a pair of cracked spectacles. Seeing their naval uniforms, the resident drew back a platoon of bolts and let them in, casting a furtive glance up and down the street before rebolting the door behind them. He beckoned them to follow him down a little corridor, scuttling ahead like a pursued mole, into a dark and shuttered parlour. Mr Bushby's left arm, they noticed, hung uselessly in a sling.

'Are you wounded, sir?' enquired Sulivan solicitously, once the introductions had been made.

'I was shot,' explained Bushby bluntly, 'during the course of a robbery upon this very house. The swine would have murdered me, but I escaped through the back door. Barely a day goes by, gentlemen, without another murder being added to the charge-sheet of villainy that shames this settlement.'

'Can you not take action against the miscreants?' asked FitzRoy. 'In a place this size, surely it must be possible to identify them?'

The resident laughed sardonically, a high-pitched little bark that escaped from his throat in a rush, his hands pawing nervously at his side-whiskers. 'I am a resident, gentlemen. I reside here. That is my sole occupation. I am not granted even the power of a magistrate. I am here to observe. There are no laws, no police and no judges to prevent the vicious, worthless inhabitants of this vile hole practising whatever excesses they wish – be it drunkenness, adultery or murder. They are escaped convicts, for the most part, from New South Wales

– although the whalers are no better. They are the very dregs
of the earth, all of them – a fact which, had I been apprised
of it in London, would have militated against my taking the
position.' Bushby shuddered at the full realization of what he
had got himself into.

'But what of the New Zealanders themselves – the natives?'
asked Sulivan. 'Do they posses no authority?'

'None in Kororareka, to be sure,' said Bushby bitterly. 'The
chiefs only stopped fighting each other long enough to declare
New Zealand a sovereign nation seven weeks ago. That is the
new flag up on the hill. But this is a nation in name only. It
is the New Zealanders themselves who require protection from
the abuses of the worst of our citizenry. I tell you, gentlemen,
these islands are gone to the very devil.' The resident drew his
coat about him and quivered with silent outrage.

'Pray excuse my asking, but what do you actually do here,
given that you are denied the opportunity to exercise
authority?' enquired FitzRoy.

'I grow vines. In my garden. Prior to taking up this position, I journeyed through France and Spain, solely for the
purpose of collecting vines to grow in my adopted country.
The climate here is most admirable for the production of wine.
You shall see, gentlemen – at a future day not only the citizens of New Zealand but of Australia, too, will have cause to
thank me, and to acknowledge my foresight.'

'I do not doubt it,' said FitzRoy hurriedly, for a fervent
gleam of enthusiasm had appeared in Bushby's eyes. 'And what
of the missionaries? We seek a clergyman by the name of
Matthews.'

Bushby's own missionary glow faded as quickly as it had
ignited. 'Matthews? Matthews is at Waimate. Would that I
were at Waimate, and not stationed here at the pointless behest
of His Majesty.'

'Waimate? Is it far?'

'It is but fifteen miles' walk. I shall take you there.'

*   *   *

The following day, augmented by Darwin and the *Beagle*'s own Reverend Mr Matthews, the party set out for Waimate, along a well-worn path cut through tall, waving ferns. At intervals they passed mean clusters of native houses, flea-ridden, smoky, windowless ovens in Bushby's derisive estimation. At one point they encountered a funeral ceremony, if that was indeed the correct word: the deceased, a woman, had been shaved, painted bright scarlet and staked out upright, flanked by two canoes driven vertically into the soil and surrounded by a ring of little wooden idols. As her macabre, rotting face looked on, her relatives beat themselves and tore at their own flesh until they were covered with clotted blood, in a communal howl of grief.

'By all that's holy,' said a shivering Matthews, who wondered if he had not merely exchanged the frying-pan for the fire.

'When Cook first discovered the island,' said Bushby, 'the New Zealanders threw stones at his ship and shouted, "Come ashore and we shall eat you all."'

'Phrenologically speaking, these are people of the most savage kind,' said Darwin.

They pressed on quickly.

Presently they came to a small creek, which had to be forded. Bushby kept a skiff tied up in the reeds, and as he untethered it a fiercely tattooed old chief, wreathed in a stinking blanket, appeared through the undergrowth and stepped into the boat, muttering a cursory word or two in his own language.

'They like to ride in the skiff. Sort of a pleasure cruise,' explained Bushby, as the chief took a seat unbidden opposite the Englishmen.

'I don't think I have ever seen a more horrid and ferocious expression,' whispered Darwin. 'It reminds me of one of the characters in Retzsch's outlines to Schiller's "Ballad of Fridolin".'

'It is not an expression,' said Bushby. 'The tattoo incisions destroy the play of the superficial muscles, giving an air of permanent aggression. The designs are actually heraldic ornaments.'

'Fascinating,' said FitzRoy. 'So all those cuts and whorls are the armorial bearings of a knightly warrior.'

'He can speak English, by the bye,' said Bushby.

'Good morning to you sir,' said Sulivan politely. The old chief bestowed a look upon him, which could have been anything from a friendly smile to a glare of demonic rage.

Matthews shuddered.

As they stepped out of the skiff at the end of their short trip up the creek, the New Zealander spoke. 'Do not you stay long. I shall be tired of waiting here,' he commanded Bushby, who ignored him.

'Good day sir,' said Sulivan.

'The hoary old villain,' muttered Darwin, when they were safely out of earshot.

Matthews, who had found it difficult since Tierra del Fuego even to say good morning to the captain without feeling guilty, remained silent, lost in his own thoughts and fears. But he need not have worried: after three hours' further walk through the ferns, the most extraordinary vista opened before them.

'Waimate, gentlemen,' said Bushby, with a wave of the hand.

There, placed as if by an enchanter's wand, was a fragment of old England. A church set amid golden cornfields; thatched cottages clustered around a stream, with a waterwheel to drive a little flour mill; orchards, groaning with every kind of ripe fruit; pigs and poultry running about, squealing and clucking; a barn, for threshing and winnowing, and a blacksmith's forge. To cap it all, a game of cricket was taking place on an adjoining meadow, the shouts of the white-clad players mingling with the thrum of insects carried past on the summer breeze.

'By the Lord Harry!' exclaimed Darwin.

The others stood open-mouthed; Matthews looked as if he would weep with relief.

'All of it constructed within these past ten years,' said Bushby.

'It certainly inspires high hopes for the future progress of this fine island,' marvelled FitzRoy.

A native miller came to the door of the mill, and waved a

polite good-day. His face was powdered white with flour.

'How very admirable,' said Darwin.

'Yours is the most extraordinary achievement, and we salute you for it,' said FitzRoy. 'Following our experiences of Kororareka, your mission was the very last thing we expected to see on these benighted shores.'

'Kororareka is known as "the Pacific Hell" for good reason, Captain,' replied the Reverend Clarke, earnest and long-nosed. 'Satan maintains his dominion there without molestation.'

'Sad to say, in nearly all the affrays there, it is the white man who is the aggressor,' said the older, graver Reverend Davies alongside him. 'Ignorance of the local language, customs or taboo marks has not caused so many quarrels as have deliberate insult, deceit or intoxication. As a nation we have cause to be ashamed.'

Four reverend missionaries sat around the farmhouse table: Messrs Clarke, Davies, Williams and Matthews. The elder Matthews, married to Davies's daughter, was an altogether more confident and inspiring character than his younger brother, whom he had not seen since the latter was a small boy. His delight at being reunited so unexpectedly with his sibling was genuinely affecting. The younger Matthews, for his part, had recovered some of the unctuous self-possession that had characterized his arrival aboard the *Beagle*, and was now basking vicariously in the glow of his brother's achievements. Together, the missionaries exuded a pious eagerness and generosity of spirit, undercut by that slight air of anxiety common to all pioneers in potentially hostile lands. The final member of the welcoming party, though, was an interesting exception: an elderly New Zealander, tall and spindly as a church steeple, attired in a shabby, long-tailed coat and threadbare pantaloons, his heavily tattooed face surmounted by a battered top hat. The old gentleman sat grinning and sipping tea from a cracked china cup, saying nothing but seeming thoroughly to relish the occasion.

'We are fighting a war,' said the elder Matthews, fist clenched, a flame in his youthful eyes. 'A war against ignorance and savagery, not just among the native population, where God's blessings have yet to percolate, but among those of our own kind who have relapsed from the state of grace that our civilization affords them.'

'My own feelings exactly,' said the younger Matthews, drawing confidence from his brother's stout piety. 'When the ranks of savages attacked the mission at Woollya, with their spears and their stones, I felt myself to be God's warrior, at war with the sins of ignorance and covetousness. I fought as bravely as I could, of course – had I a real army at my back I could have achieved something that day – but, being alone, my efforts were doomed to failure, and I was overwhelmed.'

Those who had been present when the drenched and beardless Matthews, gibbering with fear, had hurtled yelling into the lead whaleboat at Woollya, immediately formed a mental image somewhat at odds with the picture painted by the missionary; but for his fellows, his words seemed as hot coals upon the fire of their enthusiasm.

'Your efforts in Tierra del Fuego do *not* constitute a failure, gentlemen,' said the pale, whippet-like Mr Clarke. 'They are a most promising first step. You have lit a spark in that country, which, by God's grace, will never go out. Why, your experiences sound similar to our own first steps in this country. We too failed at first, but by God's blessing upon our exertions, we have at last succeeded far beyond our expectations.'

FitzRoy felt himself encouraged, consoled and strangely touched by their optimistic concern.

'When we first came here,' said Mr Williams, a stout, jovial Welshman with the air of a medieval archer, 'the New Zealanders' warlike tendencies had to be seen to be believed. One tribe went to war, I remember, because they possessed a barrel of gunpowder that would have gone to waste were it not used up!' He gurgled with laughter at the memory. 'Such attitudes can take a long time to change, is that not so, Chief Waripoaka?'

The old man at the end of the table continued to grin silently, but his steady gaze gleamed briefly at the mention of his name.

'Chief Waripoaka here was once a cannibal. But he was the first chief to be converted to God's word, and it was by his personal intervention, back in 1814, that our erstwhile colleagues King and Kendal were saved from being killed and eaten.'

At last, the wrinkled old fellow spoke, intoning his words like the tolling of a bell: 'Wonderful white men! Fire, water, earth and air are made to work for them by their wisdom, while we New Zealanders can only command the labour of our own bodies.'

'Now the chief drinks tea, instead of . . .' Williams paused, and opted to change tack rather than complete the sentence. 'We will not hear of your calling the Woollya mission a failure.'

'Jemmy is a spark all right, he's a bright spark,' said Sulivan, 'but he's a tiny spark in an almighty darkness.'

'We will send word to London,' said Williams. 'We in the Church Missionary Society have the whole organization of the Anglican Church at our backs. We do not operate independently of authority and of each other, like the London Missionary Society. We are no catechists, plucked untrained from ordinary life. We are professional men, trained in holy orders, a veritable army of God. We will have London send missionaries to Tierra del Fuego – a host of missionaries – to make contact with this Jemmy Button of yours, and kindle your spark into a blazing fire.'

Was it possible? Was it too much to hope for? A properly organized and equipped missionary effort, sent to the relief of Jemmy Button? FitzRoy could only dare to believe.

Mr Davies, apparently the *de facto* leader of the group, spread his hands in a gesture of restraint. 'I should stress that we are normally constrained to act only within a diocese of the Anglican Church. New Zealand falls within the diocese of New South Wales. But given that Tierra del Fuego is virgin territory, under no formal ecclesiastical control, I see no reason why Lambeth Palace might not be persuaded to make an exception. Be assured that we will do everything in our power to assist you, Captain FitzRoy.' The creases about Davies's eyes tightened imperceptibly. 'But we, too, should be most grateful were you to lend your reputation in assisting us.'

'How may I help you, gentlemen? You have only to ask.'

'A book has been published – a most regrettable book – which is gaining some notoriety but which paints an entirely false picture of the work we do here. You and your colleagues, as men of repute, can testify upon your return to England that this volume does not speak the truth, before any more damage can be done.'

'What is this book?'

Davies produced a slim, leatherbound volume: *Narrative of a Nine Months' Residence in New Zealand*, by Augustus Earle.

'Earle,' said FitzRoy, his eyes wide.

'By the Lord Harry!'

Sulivan, beside him, and Bennet, respectfully standing guard by the door, were instantly alert.

'You know him?'

'He was briefly our ship's artist,' confessed FitzRoy. 'But I had no knowledge . . .'

'Your former colleague was our guest here in 1827. Now he damns us for foisting Christianity upon a people "ill-adapted" to receive God's word. He claims that our "narrow outlook" has killed the "innocent gaiety" of the New Zealanders. I quote: "Any man of common sense must agree with me that a savage can receive but little benefit from having the abstruse points of the Gospel preached to him, if his mind is not prepared to receive them." I can see no logic to his reasoning. For how can any human mind not be ready to receive the word of God?'

'The man lived openly in sin – fornicated, no less – with a native woman,' huffed Mr Williams, all trace of his former jollity gone. 'If he had an interest about the "innocent gaiety" of the New Zealanders, it was with a view to plundering it for the benefit of his openly licentious habits!'

'Mr Williams is criticized by name in Mr Earle's volume,' said the elder Matthews, quietly. 'He is openly accused of lacking hospitality. Yet I know that my colleague here always treated Mr Earle with far more civility than his open licentiousness could have given reason to expect. Perhaps Mr Earle was disappointed at not finding the field of licentiousness here in New Zealand quite as formerly, on account of our efforts.'

'You see, it is our mission here not just to spread the word of God,' said Mr Clarke, his fingers enmeshed, 'but to suppress licentious habits and ardent spirits. To teach the virtue of covering naked flesh. To help the natives to understand that there is a state of future punishment awaiting those who do not follow the path laid out for them by the Church of England. Some of their customs are most barbarous: for instance, did you know that when a New Zealander falls ill, or meets some calamity, the other members of his tribe – even his family and friends – descend like locusts and rob him of all his belongings? Thus do the strong survive and the weak go to the wall. What kind of Godless system is that, for Earle or any other to advocate?'

'It is disgraceful,' said Darwin.

'You have my word, gentlemen,' vowed FitzRoy, a guilty pink flush about his cheeks. 'I shall use my every and utmost endeavour, upon returning to England, to promote your efforts to civilize the people of New Zealand and to counter Mr Earle's propaganda.'

'Wonderful white men!' intoned the chief.

'More tea, Chief Waripoaka?' said Davies, keen to present a little tableau of civilization.

'Good sweet tea,' said the chief, ladling spoonful after spoonful of sugar into his cup. 'Englishman meat taste too salty. Not taste sweet, like New Zealander. I eat a Captain Boyd once. Whaling captain. Too salty. Now Chief Waripoaka good Christian – no eat human meat. Drink sweet tea instead!'

The old man grinned conspiratorially, and took a big wet slurp from his teacup.

FitzRoy spent the next few days completing tests upon an ocean thermometer he had devised to detect and trace currents in the water. Darwin kept to the library, magnifying-glass fastened to his forehead by an elastic garter, microscope unfolded upon the table. Nobody went ashore: even the crew, it seemed, had little inclination to risk the dangerous flesh-pots of Kororareka. New Zealand, it appeared to FitzRoy, was at a crossroads. The settlements of Kororareka and Waimate offered two alternative visions of its future. British interven-tion was surely now essential, to rein in the excesses of his countrymen and to steer the fledgling nation down the Christian path. A British governor was required, backed up by a considerable force of troops, to restore order and to protect the native population. He would do his utmost, upon returning to England, to press for such a policy to be imposed.

He decided to weigh anchor and head home for England following Christmas dinner. As this could hardly be taken ashore, a small, uninhabited island out in the bay was selected, and Mr Stokes charged with organizing the day's festivities. With preparations well under way, FitzRoy, Bynoe, and King were rowed ashore to see Christmas taking shape. A large area of flat ground had been cleared, and planted with chairs and tables festooned with decorations. A Galapagos turtle was turning slowly on a large spit. At one end of the clearing they found a beaten-down circular area, with the remains of a cooking fire at its centre.

'It was still warm when we got here, although the island is deserted now,' related Stokes. 'Looks like somebody else had their Christmas dinner here before us.'

'Those are mighty big bones,' remarked FitzRoy. 'What are they? Beef? Lamb?'

Bynoe knelt down to have a look.

'Neither, I'm afraid. This is a human femur.'

There was a long silence. Eventually King spoke.

'The deuced filthy black savages.'

FitzRoy looked at him.

'And what makes you so sure, Mr King, that this was not the act of deuced filthy *white* savages?'

Chapter Twenty-seven

The English Channel, 1 October 1836

It took the *Beagle* just over nine months to arrive at that
glorious morning when, defying the swell, the crew could
clamber as one into the yards – not just the deck watch, but
the idlers and the off-duty men as well – each hopeful of
being the first to see a low, dirty blemish break the distant
line of the horizon. Every man aboard had 'Channel fever', as
they called it, a desperate, yearning desire to gaze upon the
undistinguished blue-grey hills of England's south-western tip.
For Charles Darwin, the sea had become a heaving desert, and
the previous nine months just so much existence obliterated
from the page of his life.

'I loathe, I abhor the sea, and all the ships which sail on
it,' he muttered to himself, as his stomach surged and his gorge
rose for the thousandth time that week. A blustery autumn
gale was driving the *Beagle* up through the western approaches
with close-reefed topsails set, the wind at her back, her progress
rapid but not rapid enough for her reluctant passenger.

It seemed like an age since they had sailed beneath the
revolving red beacon of the lighthouse in Sydney Cove, there to
discover not – as expected – a grubby, scratchy little settlement

akin to Kororareka, but a glorious gilded boomtown of wind-mills and white stone mansions shimmering in the heat. The liveried servants standing to attention on the coaches that clattered through the cobbled streets may have been ex-convicts; there may have been precious few gentlewomen in evidence; there may have been no sign of theatres, bookshops, galleries or any other outward manifestation of intellectual life; but there was no denying the incredible vibrancy of Australia's youthful capital. Captain Phillip Parker King was there to meet them, having retired from England to an estate on the Bathurst Road, and keen to reclaim his son. FitzRoy generously consented to Midshipman King's discharge from the Service, and there followed many an anguished farewell, Darwin's parting from his boisterous young friend being one of the saddest. They found Conrad Martens, too, in Sydney, the little Austrian's path having preceded their own footsteps across the Pacific: this was quite a stroke of luck, as it transpired that he had painted many of the locations subsequently visited by the *Beagle*, canvases that FitzRoy and Darwin were able to purchase from their creator at three guineas apiece. Darwin had felt himself obliged to draw a further hundred pounds on his father's account, complaining of Sydney's 'villainously dear' prices.

They had gone on to Hobart, where Darwin had with-drawn a further fifty pounds, and then to King George's Sound in south-western Australia, where they had witnessed an aboriginal *corrobery*: a meet of several hundred painted warriors drawn from two tribes, gathered to dance in contest against each other. The two battle-lines of performers had thrown themselves enthusiastically into terpsichorean imitations of emus and kangaroos, gleaming with sweat in the firelight, to be rewarded for their efforts with a mass handout of rice pudding doled up by the *Beagle*'s crew. Darwin, armed with a ladle, had been the principal server, and had assumed the gracious air of a nanny feeding her charges; although he professed the aboriginal warriors, whose nobility of bearing had been much admired by FitzRoy, to be among the very lowest of barbarians. The following day they had encountered real emus and kangaroos, bizarre strains of animal life so utterly different from any to be found elsewhere that Darwin had seriously begun to wonder whether there might not be two Creators.

May had seen the *Beagle* dock at Cape Town, where FitzRoy and Darwin had dined with the celebrated astronomer Sir John Herschel, who had travelled to southern Africa to witness the passage of Halley's comet. A shy, diffident, highly intelligent man with soil-rimmed fingernails, Sir John had listened with interest to their stories of Augustus Earle, and the missionaries of Waimate. He had subsequently put them in touch with the editor of the *South African Christian Recorder*, who had commissioned a piece – authored jointly by FitzRoy and Darwin – in praise of the missionaries' efforts in the South Pacific. Sir John had also given Darwin his newly published copy of *Volume 4* of Lyell, which promised to rid the voyage home of its threatened *ennui*: Darwin told himself he would eke out each and every one of its precious pages.

Cape Town brought further good news in the shape of letters from home, the first they had encountered in fifteen months. It was new mail: all the intervening correspondence seemed to have vanished into the ether, the sadly probable cause being that a mail packet, perhaps even two, had been lost at sea. There were a couple of letters for FitzRoy, one for Lieutenant Sulivan from Miss Young and, most thrilling of all, a brace of letters for Darwin from his sisters Catherine and Susan. Catherine reported that Professor Henslow had edited a number of Darwin's letters together, to form a paper on the link between earthquakes and the uplift of the Andes, which he had read to the Cambridge Philosophical Society in November: it had, by all accounts, caused a sensation. Public demand had seen the paper printed as a booklet, and Darwin was the name on everyone's tongue in polite society. Dr Darwin had been so proud that he had purchased a huge stack of copies, to be given away to friends and family. Although horrified at the thought of his dashed-off, misspelt prose being published without revision, the doctor's son could hardly fail to be delighted at the news.

Susan reported, meanwhile, that further extracts from his letters had been published in the *Entomological Magazine* at the instigation of Professor Sedgwick, who had given a lecture to the Geological Society of London on the subject of Darwin's findings in South America. No less a figure than Lyell himself had been in the chair, and had apparently been heard to remark: 'How I long for the return of Darwin.' Sedgwick had predicted that his former student would take a place among the leading scientific men should he return safely, while Samuel Butler had forecast that Darwin would surely have a great name among the naturalists of Europe. Darwin had read the letter with shaking hands. 'Papa and we often cogitate over the fire what you will do when you return,' his sister had written, 'as I fear there are but small hopes of your still going into the Church – I think you must turn Professor at Cambridge. We are fond of reading your exploits aloud to Papa. He enjoys it extremely, except when the dangers you run make him shudder.' Emboldened by the extraordinary vision of his father beaming with paternal pride, he had drawn a further thirty pounds on the doctor's account, and had given his pet tortoise Harry an unusually huge meal by way of celebration.

Cape Town should have been the *Beagle's* last stop, but FitzRoy had infuriated his impatient, ambitious young charge by recrossing the Atlantic, to recheck his longitudinal observations off the Brazilian coast. The diversion had at least afforded Darwin the chance of one final walk in the rainforest: it was a sentimental affair, as he knew in his heart that he would never – could never – leave Britain's shores again. Each of the brilliant and luxuriant sights that swam now before his sated eyes would fade, he knew, like a tale heard in childhood, the living flesh falling from his memories until only the skeleton of bald scientific fact remained, all those morsels of vibrant beauty reduced to a cold, inexorable agglomeration of statistics with which he would build a career. Ultimately, it was not something he regretted, for his career promised to be the most beautiful creation of all. And, as he reminded himself, his first glimpse of home would surely be better than the united kingdoms of all the glorious tropics.

The undulating months that passed, slow and tiresome, on the rising and falling Atlantic, were spent ordering and organizing the fruits of the voyage. Darwin discovered that he possessed no fewer than 1529 specimens preserved in spirits, and 3907 labelled skins, bones and other dried specimens. Covington was put to cataloguing each one by class, in his large, round, painstaking hand. The other officers had their collections to organize too, even though all had generously donated their most impressive specimens to the philosopher. Then there were the live animals on board: a Brazilian coatimundi, several Patagonian wild dogs, a Falklands fox and, of course, Darwin's giant tortoise. FitzRoy was tied up with the main business of the voyage, the editing and production of charts and sailing directions. He had dispatched more than a hundred maps to the Admiralty already: by the time he finished the men of the *Beagle* would have produced a staggering 202 charts and plans, a task that would require a minimum of two years' hard toil in London for him to complete.

There remained, of course, the matter of the book that FitzRoy and Darwin were due to write. The two men had been getting on extremely well of late, persuaded by their labours away from confrontation and into their private corners, but both knew that a deal had to be struck regarding the more contentious areas of the exercise. What would it say about the flood? What would it say about the creation and the extinction of species? About the very origins of life itself? By unspoken consent, they left the discussion until the last possible moment. Finally, on the day of their projected arrival, FitzRoy approached the subject over dinner, via a circuitous route. 'I fear I have been too busy to look at Lyell. Is there anything in his new volume that I should be aware of?'

'He is most interesting concerning the origins of life. He feels that life itself – its boundaries, its rules if you like – are all enshrined in natural laws laid down by God, laws which God Himself is bound to observe.'

'God might *feel* bound to observe His own laws, but He could hardly be *required* to do so. It sounds as if our friend Lyell is fudging the distinction between the laws of nature and the laws of God.'

'Is there a distinction?'

'I should think so. The laws of God, as laid down in the scriptures, are commands – rules composed by the divine legislator, which man disregards at his peril. The laws of nature, like the laws of physics, are not strictly laws. They are unwavering natural occurrences observed by man.'

'Whether they are true laws or not, the laws of nature are nonetheless immutable – for instance, the law of gravity cannot be altered.'

'Indeed. They are observations of fact that cannot be obeyed or disobeyed or altered by those subject to them. In my book, however, a law is a rule, which we as rational beings have the choice to obey or to disobey. It is the God-given power of rational thought that makes all the difference, that makes our relationship to God in His heaven superior to our relationship with nature's earthly power.'

'But, FitzRoy, is it truly logical to suggest that the universe is subject to the laws of nature, whereas mankind alone is subject to the higher law of God? Is thought, which in biological terms is a physical function of the organ of the brain, truly more wonderful than gravity, which is a physical property of matter?'

'Of course it is. It is the very property by which God distinguishes us from the animal kingdom.'

'But animals can think.'

'Not rationally. That is why I take such issue with transmutation and its propagandists. It is a damnable reduction of beauty and intelligence, of strength and purpose, of honour and aspiration. It reduces mankind to a casual aggregation of inert matter. Furthermore, I do not believe such a process can exist, for it is surely impossible, by virtue of those immutable laws of nature you speak about.'

'And yet you believe that men can transmute into angels.' Both men smiled at this.

'Here, my dear Philos, you have gone beyond the boundaries of nature and into God's heavenly realm. The legislator need hardly legislate in His own kingdom.'

'But, FitzRoy, is it not possible that some kind of transmutation can exist *within* God's law, and *within* the laws of nature? Does the idea of transmutation not frighten you merely becuase it would seem on the face of it to remove the need for God – when in fact that need not be a condition of its existence?'

'I am not frightened by transmutation – I am intellectually, morally and aesthetically repelled by it. Nature is not a progression. No creature is any more or less perfect than its fellows in the eyes of the Lord. Every creature is adapted to the condition and locality for which it is designed. You saw that in the Galapagos. If there has indeed been progress in nature for countless aeons, as you suggest, explain then the persistence of supposedly lower organisms, the primitive, the immobile, the microscopic creatures, all of which have remained completely unchanged since the dawn of time. Furthermore, why are fossilized sharks, crocodiles, tortoises, snakes, bats, frogs and so forth identical to their living brethren? Why have *they* not progressed?'

'If every species has a fixed lifespan, like an individual, then perhaps a transmuted species is the offspring of another, the Lord's way of giving birth to a new family of living creatures?'

'You still believe that entire species vanished from the globe by commonly expiring all at once? That there was no catastrophe? No flood?'

'The geological record, FitzRoy . . . I mean, where did all that water come *from*?'

'Perhaps the ice at the poles melted and the sea level rose? Who is to say that the earth's temperature has always been constant? Or perhaps there were immense tidal waves? Who is to say that the movement of heavenly bodies has always been constant?'

'But the science of geology now calls the Old Testament story into question. The earth is hundreds of millions of years old, not merely a few thousand!'

'Geology is a young branch of science, which has yet to undergo the trial of experience. I am convinced that in due course it will contribute its share of nourishment and vigour to that tree which springs from an immortal root. If the earth is indeed several hundred million years old, tell me, where has all the excess sodium chloride gone?'

'I beg your pardon?'

'Every year salts pour into the ocean. Yet apparently they have been doing so for hundreds of millions of years without altering its salinity. By now the sea should be a saturated solution, all life within it choked. Yet the fish in the ocean, and the fossil fish that once thrived within it, are identical.'

'I do not know about the salt, but the sea creatures uplifted high into the Andes did not get there in six thousand years, I assure you. The geological record is unequivocal.'

'Every major geologist believes in the flood. Buckland, Conybeare, Silliman in the United States—'

'They are all clergymen. Of course they believe in the flood.'

'So are you. Or, at least, a clergyman in training.'

'Not any more. I shall be a geologist, perhaps, or a naturalist, or both. But I cannot take up holy orders, FitzRoy. I cannot do it.'

'I am saddened to hear so. Why ever not?'

'I simply can no longer believe in the miracles of the scriptures. No sane man could believe in miracles! The more I know of the fixed laws of nature that pertain on this earth, the more incredible do such miracles become.'

'And the miracle of creation?'

'I believe God created all things – but I do not know how. Maybe some random principle applies . . .'

'Consider a butterfly, Philos. It grows from a caterpillar via an amorphous soup, a mere liquid that fills its chrysalis. The organizing principle of that transformation is external to the material substances involved. Do you not see? There is a pattern to the universe, an order. It is the same with the weather: weather patterns are not random, although they appear so to the untrained eye. We should be trying to deduce the patterns of God's ordered universe, not attempting to decry their very existence!'

Both men sat perfectly still, facing each other, not saying a word. It was a grim silence at first, then their expressions melted into wry smiles. The moment had arrived.

'And now, my friend,' said FitzRoy, 'I must prepare to have the disposal and arranging of your journal, to mingle it with my own, without offending you.'

'I am perfectly willing, of course,' replied Darwin carefully, 'but my conclusions must remain my own.'

'Of course. If you wish discreetly to dispute the flood, then you must do so, even if I should find it regrettable. You would not be the first. The same goes for the age of the earth, the extinction of species and other such matters. And I believe that your work on the subject of geological uplift, and the formation of coral atolls, constitutes a major contribution to our nation's scientific knowledge.'

'You are most kind.'

'Not at all, my dear friend. But as I am sure you are aware, to espouse transmutation is to risk everything. Social ostracism, ridicule, even hatred must follow, as your own grandfather regrettably experienced. It is, effectively, to abandon Christianity – and to abandon Christianity is to turn one's back on society. This book is to be the official journal of the voyage, sanctioned by the Admiralty. You are aware, I hope, that this voyage, and this volume, cannot be sullied by any suggestion of a transmutationist argument.'

'I am well aware of it.'

'My dear Philos, I must ask for your word as a gentleman that you will keep any such thoughts to yourself, to be aired only in private discussions such as these. That you will never make public your more . . . controversial conclusions. You are, it seems, to be for ever fixed in the public mind as the naturalist of the *Beagle*.'

'Of course. I understand completely, for I am well aware of the possible consequences of any such action. You have no cause for concern – I give you my word, FitzRoy.'

'Thank you, my friend. Thank you for your invaluable contribution to this voyage, for your insights and for your companionship, which I am sure has saved me personally from the most melancholy of fates. I am personally proud to have sailed with you.'

'On the contrary, FitzRoy, it is I who should thank you. You have given me a unique opportunity – an extraordinary opportunity – the like of which, I think, has been given formerly to very few naturalists, and certainly to no geologists. I shall remain eternally in your debt.'

The two men stood up and shook hands.

'And now, Philos, I have a surprise for you. At least, I hope it shall be a surprise.'

'I am agog.'

'My dear friend – I am to be married.'

'*Married*?'

Darwin was too stunned to offer his congratulations. He simply reeled. 'Married? But . . . to whom?'

'To Miss Mary Henrietta O'Brien, the daughter of Major General Edward O'Brien. I asked her father for her hand five years ago, before we sailed from Devonport.'

Darwin felt as if he had been shot. Five years confined in a tiny cabin with this man, all the confidences he had shared, and all the while . . . ! Objections and queries fought each other in his mind, competing to get to the front of a very long queue. 'But, FitzRoy, you do not write letters home,' he offered weakly, and sat down, his mental confusion apparently sapping his physical strength. 'You have not *written* to her.'

'My first and absolute duty on board is always to my men. I told her that it would be so. Of course, there was a risk that she might not wish to wait for me – a risk I had no option but to take into account. I am a serving naval officer. But Miss O'Brien wrote to Cape Town to confirm the arrangement. So you see, Philos, I am a very happy man.'

'But you never mentioned her! Not once. I told you everything. About Fanny Owen's betrothal. About Fanny Wedgwood's death. About my feelings for Emma Wedgwood. I confided my most private thoughts on the subject of marriage. And you – all the while, you concealed this most enormous of secrets from me – from everybody.' Darwin's stare was openly hostile and accusing now.

'My friend, forgive me, but that is simply the way I preferred it.'

FitzRoy looked him directly in the eye. *Why should I share my innermost confidences with you, or with anyone? My command of the* Beagle *is a matter for public record – but my emotions, my most private feelings and fears? They are a matter for myself and my God alone, and not for your prying ears. I cannot and will not share such confidences.*

Darwin stood up again, as FitzRoy sat down. 'You have my congratulations,' he finally managed to say, and walked stiffly and silently from the cabin.

Barrelling before the south-westerly blow, the *Beagle* sighted land, to cheers and hugs, on the first day of October. She made Plymouth dockyard on the second, in softly falling autumn rain. FitzRoy put on his dress uniform, and composed himself before his looking-glass. He was rake-thin, he knew, his skin a weatherbeaten copper, a pale, wiry exhausted shadow of the handsome young man who had put to sea five years previously. He was thirty-one. In all, he had spent nearly a quarter of his life aboard the *Beagle*. It was the same for the philosopher, he reflected, who had spent five of his twenty-seven years folded into his tiny quarters. Darwin, a once-burly six-footer, was no more than eleven stone in weight now, his prematurely thinning hair and thickening eyebrows combining with his long arms to lend him even more of a simian aspect than before. But whereas Darwin was champing at the bit to get off the ship, FitzRoy realized with a pang that this would be one of the most painful partings of his life. This ship was his body, its men his lifeblood. His relationship to the little vessel felt organic, indivisible and well-nigh impossible to break.

A surprisingly large crowd was gathering on the quay as they approached, augmented all the time by dark, running figures heading from the town. A small brass band had assembled in the drizzle, and had started to play a popular song apparently entitled 'Railways Now Are All The Go, Steam, Steam, Steam'.

'Is there a man-of-war due?' asked Wickham, glancing round worriedly as if the *Beagle* were about to be run down.

'I think it's all for us,' said Sulivan at last.

'For *us*? Whatever for?'

The crew were crowded at the rail or clinging to the rigging, desperate for a glimpse of their loved ones; but most of those on the dockside appeared to be strangers.

'Who the deuce are they all?' asked Wickham, with furrowed brow.

'My dear Wickham – you must excuse me! Oh, my God!'

With this most uncharacteristic exclamation, Sulivan tore himself away and threw himself excitedly at the rail. For there, hurtling down the white, marble-chipped avenue from the dockyard gates, her skirt flying, her bonnet-ribbons streaming behind her, her companion lagging breathless in her wake, all pretence of dignity thrown to the winds, was the overjoyed figure of Sophia Young.

The accommodation-ladder was put down, and the result was pandemonium, with as many people trying to get on to the ship as off. FitzRoy came forward to try to make some sense of the chaos. A press of aggressively ill-mannered men made a rush forward, all shouting at once.

'George Dance, *Morning Post*. I believe you have the celebrated Mr Darwin on board?'

'Where is Mr Darwin?'

'Arthur Hodgson, *Hampshire Telegraph*. May I speak to Mr Darwin?'

'Gentlemen, I beg you, order, please. I am Captain FitzRoy. I would kindly request that you speak one at a time.'

'You are the captain of the *Beagle*, sir? What was it like sailing with the world-famous Mr Darwin?'

'James Burling, *Times*. Could you describe Mr Darwin to us, sir?'

'May we speak to the great man?'

'Would you say it was an honour, sir, to have sailed with Mr Darwin?'

'What does Mr Darwin eat for his breakfast?'

'Is there a Mrs Darwin, sir?'

On the quayside, two young girls had unfurled a homemade banner reading WELCOME HOME MR DARWIN. FitzRoy wished he had been man enough to feel no wound to his vanity, for he considered the sin of pride one of his more regrettable weaknesses, but on this occasion he had no option but to concede defeat. He retreated, and left the maindeck to the stentorian tones of Lieutenant Wickham. Marine sentries were posted at the bottom of the accommodation-ladder, with orders to admit only respectable-looking persons aboard. The crowd continued to gather, meanwhile, as sightseers came down to view the *Beagle*, to lay a hand on her well-travelled hull, perhaps even to catch a glimpse of the celebrated Mr Darwin.

After a few minutes, FitzRoy was astonished to witness the elegant bonnet of a stylishly dressed woman appear at the rail, before the bonnet's owner somehow clambered up the battens and over the gunwale. Her rather more plainly dressed husband followed, and introduced himself to the bemused FitzRoy as George Airy, the newly appointed Astronomer-Royal.

'I'm afraid the sentry at the accommodation-ladder would not permit . . .'

'My dear sir, my dear madam, I am most terribly sorry. Please accept my most profound apologies – this is inexcusable. I shall speak to the miscreant most severely. I am afraid that this press of people has created confusion among my crew – it seems that half the country has taken up occupation as a journalist!'

'You can thank the steam-press for that,' smiled Airy. 'As the editor of the *Athenaeum* said, "It takes four men to make a pin, and two to describe it in a book for the working classes."'

Stokes was quickly deputized to show the dignitaries below, while an irritable FitzRoy took issue with the marine sentry.

'Damn it, Burgess, I have just had the Astronomer-Royal and his wife, no less, hauling themselves up the manropes because *you* would not admit them aboard!'

'I'm sorry, sir,' stammered Burgess, colouring. 'Mr Wickham said respectable, sir, and the gentleman did *not* look respectable. It's all these reporters, sir, as want to speak to Mr Darwin.'

'Where the devil is the philosopher, anyway?' FitzRoy caught sight of his steward crossing the deck. 'Fuller! Have you seen Mr Darwin?'

'He's gone, sir.'

'*Gone?*'

'Yes sir.'

'You mean, he has left the ship?'

'Yes sir.' Fuller looked unhappy.

'Gone without saying goodbye?'

'Yes sir. He, er—'

'Yes, Fuller?'

'He took Covington with him, sir.'

Chapter Twenty-eight

31 Chester Street, London,
8 October 1837

The FitzRoys travelled the short distance to Sunday service by barouche, partly because Mrs FitzRoy was six months pregnant, and partly because – even in such a well-to-do district as Belgravia – Sunday morning was not the best time to be out on the streets. Eleven in the morning was 'chucking-out time', when the bars and gin-palaces finally disgorged the drunken revellers of the night before, and it was not uncommon for churchgoers to have to negotiate brawling prostitutes, quarrelling labourers and any number of helpless or unconscious devotees of that other great spirit. FitzRoy liked to worship at the vast, Romanesque, pale-brick edifice of St Peter's, Eaton Square, for its ceiling caught the light from its great window and flung it down upon the congregation from high above, an important consideration for one who had spent the previous five years in the middle of the vaulting ocean. With its massive portico and six Ionic columns of honey-coloured stone the church resembled a temple of Ancient Rome, but he did not subscribe to the current and censorious school of thought that decried such architecture as pagan.

He liked to watch his wife at prayer, for the serenity of her devotions always reminded him of the night they'd met, and the calm, almost beatific manner in which she had seemed to float across the dance-floor. They had married at the end of December, Sulivan acting as groomsman just a couple of weeks before his own wedding to Miss Young, the *Beagle's* officers reunited joyfully twice in a fortnight. FitzRoy had barely known his bride, of course – they were only just getting to know each other even now – but right from the first her wisdom, her confidence and her sheer certainty that theirs was a union made in heaven had banished any doubts he might have felt. Their wedding night had been, quite simply, a revelation. There, in the dark, holding her in his arms for the first time, he had experienced feelings of happiness so profound and so unexpected that he could not have believed such an experience possible. He had fallen in love with his wife, utterly and without reservation, from that moment. It was, he felt, as if God had touched them both at the same instant.

They had taken the house in Chester Street while he laboured six days a week at the Admiralty, often late into the night, upon his charts and sailing directions, and upon the story of the voyage. They had holidayed just once – a visit to his sister's family at Bromham, near Bedford – but he had found the enforced lay-off frustrating. The compulsory rest day of the Sabbath was, of course, a weekly hindrance, but he was aware, too, of the benefits that such a respite afforded his physical, mental and spiritual health; and, of course, he wished to spend as much time with his new wife as possible before he returned to sea. After church they would join the traditional promenade of the great and good through Hyde Park and Kensington Gardens, and around Shrewsbury Clock. Despite her condition, Mary FitzRoy always insisted that a little light walk along the banks of the Serpentine river would do her good. On this particular Sunday, however, the crowds were thin: it was not just the hunting season that was taking its toll but the first of the winter smogs, a thin, yellow, insinuating, vinegary mist that dampened their clothing and caused their lungs to ache. He suggested that they cut short their constitutional, but she would not hear of it; indeed, she insisted on walking as far as the Uxbridge Road, which bordered the north side of the park.

There, outside the railings, a different world stared in, like spectators at the zoo. Drunken vagrants and starving agricultural labourers up from the countryside jostled for space with gaunt Irishmen.

'Spare a penny for a poor Johnny-raw, sir,' yelled a voice, but whose voice amid the forest of hands it was impossible to tell.

The high price of corn, the doctrines of the Reverend Thomas Malthus and the terrifying new spectre of the workhouse had turned even more people out on to the streets during the *Beagle*'s absence, swelling the army of the hungry and dispossessed. As if to taunt them, Sunday was the principal day for the city to suck in and chew up its livestock supplies: great droves of oxen, sheep and pigs, cart- and waggon-trains full of struggling calves, goaded and propelled forward by crowds of graziers, cattle-jobbers, pig-fatteners and calf-crammers, a squealing, bleating, lowing, shouting mêlée, surged up the Uxbridge Road towards the holding pound at Paddington. A knacker's drag jogged through the crowd of unheeding animals, laden with the obscenely mangled carcasses of dead and used-up horses, their torn-out bowels dangling over the side. Rabble-rousers moved among the mud and blood-spattered multitude distributing pamphlets and protest sheets, keen to provoke the dispossessed to anger; others sold Bible tracts, popular journals and Sunday scandal-sheets. No day, it seemed, was quite as boisterous, quite as hungry and desperate, quite as starkly bloody as the Lord's day. Mary FitzRoy momentarily detached her gloved hand from her husband's, went to the railing and shared the contents of her purse among the reaching hands.

'Take care, my dear,' murmured FitzRoy, his hand gripping his cane more tightly, but she moved among the beseeching supplicants like a yacht upon the sea, her donations a mere shining drop or two swallowed up by the hungry ocean.

Darwin trotted down the front steps of number thirty-six Great Marlborough Street to find his jobbed cabriolet the only one unattended, all the others at the little stand tenanted by loafing teenage drivers with hats and pipes at the most rakish angles their owners could affect. 'Have any of you fellows seen my devil?' he asked peevishly.

'Yer honour, he's just gorn a little way round of the corner for summat short. Why, here he comes, sir, right as a trivet. Jump up, sir.'

A small, gin-stunted coach-boy in frock-coat and top-boots took his place at the reins. Darwin settled in under the hood. 'Thirty-one Chester Street. And take care, if you've been gilding your liver.'

Cheerfully ignoring the gibe, the boy swung the buggy round through Argyll Place and joined the traffic stream heading south along Regent Street. From there they bore west down Conduit Street, linking up with Piccadilly via Old Bond Street, until finally they found themselves clattering down Grosvenor Place, keeping the wall of the still unnamed royal palace to their left. It was a whole year since he had seen FitzRoy; they had corresponded about their co-authored book entirely by letter, even though they lived less than two miles apart. Nor had he any particular wish to set eyes upon him now. What had occurred that morning, however, had altered matters. Gould's letter had thrown him into a panic of excitement. Unfortunately, he would have to negotiate a boatload of tiresome courtesies before he could get down to business, but that could not be helped. It was five o'clock in the afternoon, rather late to go visiting, but he knew FitzRoy well enough for such informality.

Grand, multi-storeyed mansions in white stucco stacked

up along Grosvenor Place; Chester Street proved to be one
of the narrow thoroughfares linking it to the equally
grandiose terraces of Belgrave Place. It was a prosperous area,
reflected Darwin; trust FitzRoy to pitch up on the aristocratic side of Regent Street. So much for his former cabin-
mate's supposed shortage of cash. Obviously he was enjoying
the benefits of full pay while he prepared the charts from
the voyage.

A flight of white marble steps led up to a wide, stucco-
fronted ground floor divided by a trio of arched windows;
thereafter the house was a plain brick, its upper windows more
prosaically rectangular. He handed his card to the housemaid
and enquired if the FitzRoys were 'at home'. The reply came
back in the affirmative, although the matter was hardly in
doubt as the lamps had already been lit to fend off the gloom
of the afternoon. He was shown past a panelled dining room,
up a spiral staircase at the rear of the house – the building
was only one room deep, he noted, more imposing from the
front than inside – and into a bright, pleasant drawing room
on the first floor where the FitzRoys dwelt amid dark
mahogany furniture.

'My dear Darwin,' said FitzRoy, rising, but his manner was
cold, and Darwin knew immediately that something was
wrong. It did not matter: his business here was more important than whatever was bothering the inflexible old
curmudgeon today.

'Mrs FitzRoy, may I have the honour of presenting to your
acquaintance Mr Charles Darwin.'

'The honour is all mine, Mrs FitzRoy, believe me. And if
you will forgive so forward an observation, I see that congratulations are shortly to be in order.'

'I am delighted to meet you at last, Mr Darwin.' Mary
FitzRoy extended a hand. 'And, yes, it would appear that we
are to be blessed, as I believe Lieutenant Sulivan and his wife
have been earlier this week.'

'I pity the poor lady, then, for I apprehend that her husband has a new commission, which will snatch him away at what must be an inopportune moment.'

'Mr Sulivan has command of the *Pincher*, my dear, an anti-slaving schooner due to sail for West Africa,' FitzRoy explained.

'Then we must be happy on Mr Sulivan's behalf. No one who enters into marriage with a naval officer can fail to be aware of the separations involved.'

Don't patronize me, thought Darwin. *I am only here on sufferance.* Mrs FitzRoy was astonishingly beautiful, he decided, but he could not work out whether her solemn, direct manner betokened gracious piety or insufferable self-satisfaction. Certainly, she did not seem the sort of empty-headed woman to dote on the romantic heroines of Byron and Scott. There was something intimidating about her, something almost evangelical.

'But I understand that we must congratulate *you*, Mr Darwin,' said the object of his study, as the housemaid served tea. 'My husband tells me that you are to be made a fellow of the Royal Society, and secretary of the Geological Society.'

'Indeed so. The offers came about through the good offices of Mr Lyell. I often dine at his club, or he at mine – did I tell you that I had been elected to the Athenaeum, along with Mr Dickens, the novelist?'

'What elevated circles you do move in, Mr Darwin.'

Again, Darwin had the faintest sense that he was being patronized, but he refused to be ashamed of his achievements.

'Oh, I have made a good many interesting new friends of late. I am a frequent guest at Mr Babbage's *soirées*, along with Herbert Spencer, Mr Brown the botanist, Sydney Smith, Thomas and Jane Carlyle – he writes all the articles on German literature in the *French Quarterly* – and Miss Martineau, of course, who is a friend of my brother.' *All fascinating and influential people*, he thought, *not tuppenny-ha'penny aristocrats.* 'The company cannot be faulted – sadly, it is my own digestion that usually lets me down.'

'You continue to remain unwell? We are sorry to hear it.'

His ill-health was evident. Darwin was even thinner and more sickly than he had been at the end of the voyage, a condition that lent his overhanging brow an air of perpetually furious concentration. He could not have weighed more than ten and a half stone.

'Yes, I appear to be suffering some sort of chronic complaint, brought on no doubt by many years of constant seasickness.' He grinned humourlessly at FitzRoy. 'I have tried all sorts of physic, from calomel to quinine to arsenic – even Indian ale – but nothing seems to work.' *Damn it, this was like confessing to a Catholic priest.* 'I dare say that London's murky atmosphere does my constitution no help.'

'Then perhaps you would be well advised to spend more time with your family in Shropshire.'

And less time collecting influential friends like trophies, thought FitzRoy. *He is here because he wants something, that much is clear. He would not come for any other reason.*

'I was back home only last week, in fact – I travelled by train as far as Birmingham. I cannot say that I was much impressed. One has to pay for one's own candles to read, and one must hire a footwarmer to stave off the cold. It was tremendously fast, though – just five hours, once the locomotive had been pulled up to Camden by the winding-cables.'

'And what intelligence is there of your family, Mr Darwin?'

'Oh, we have cause for great celebration. My sister Caroline is married now, to my cousin Josiah Wedgwood – the eldest son of my uncle Jos – who has recently returned from travelling in Europe.'

'And what of yourself? Is it your intention to take a wife?'

Mary FitzRoy posed the question with disarming directness, but Darwin deflected it. Negotiations with Emma Wedgwood were at too delicate a stage to make the matter public.

'I fear I am too busy cataloguing the specimens from the voyage to consider capturing such a rare specimen as a wife.'

'It would appear that both you and my husband will spend

more years organizing your discoveries than you spent actually circumnavigating the world.'

'What with the book and the charts, I feel like an ass caught between two bundles of hay,' put in FitzRoy, who had barely spoken, and only did so now for his wife's benefit. 'Both hail me, and tell me they require my undivided attention to do them full justice.'

What's biting the old goose? thought Darwin, but he ploughed on nonetheless. 'I have been fortunate enough to enlist the most excellent help, FitzRoy. Lyell has introduced me to Richard Owen, the Hunterian professor at the Royal College of Surgeons. Do you know Owen? He is the man who first coined the term "dinosaur". My fossils from Punta Alta are entirely new to science. He has christened the giant aquatic rodent a *Toxodon*, the giant armadillo is to be called a *Scelidotherium*, there is a giant sloth called a *Glyptodon*, and a giant guanaco that he has named *Machrauchenia*. Owen says, and this is the remarkable thing, that all the South American fossils are related to the animals still living on the same continent – it is as if there is a continuous process of change. Do forgive me, Mrs FitzRoy. All this scientific talk must be rather dull for you.'

'Not in the least, Mr Darwin – I am fascinated. Indeed, I am intrigued to know what you make of the recent discoveries in Trafalgar Square. I apprehend that workmen laying the foundations for the column have found the bones of enormous elephants, rhinoceroses and sabre-toothed tigers.'

Touché, thought FitzRoy, with a glow of pride.

'A fascinating discovery indeed,' replied Darwin evasively. 'And there are now live elephants and rhinoceroses – or should one say rhinoceri? – at the Zoological Society, and a giraffe too. They are the most astonishing creatures. You really must go, when your condition permits it. I was there yesterday – the Society is opened privately to members at weekends – did I tell you that I had been elected a member of the Zoological Society? – and I saw a chimpanzee named Tommy, who had been dressed up in human clothing and allocated a human nurse. I assure you, you would find his antics most amusing. During my visit, the nurse showed him an apple but would not give it him, whereupon Tommy threw himself on his back, and kicked and cried precisely like a human child. He then looked very sulky, and after two or three fits of passion the nurse said, "Tommy, if you stop bawling and be a good boy, I will give you the apple." The ape certainly understood every word of this – and though, like a child, he had great work to stop whining, he at last succeeded and got the apple, jumped into an armchair and began eating it with the most contented countenance imaginable!'

'And is your own interest in Tommy the chimpanzee a scientific one, Mr Darwin, or purely a matter of entertainment?'

'Well, I was at the Zoological Society principally to see Mr John Gould, the taxonomist. Did I say? He has agreed to classify all the birds that I collected on the voyage. Waterhouse is attending to the insects, Bell the reptiles, and my friend Leonard Jenyns the fish. In fact, it is upon a matter of Mr Gould's classification that I am here to see Captain FitzRoy. I wonder, Mrs FitzRoy, if you would be so kind as to permit us a few moments in private? It is a technical discussion – most tiresome, I assure you.'

'Of course, Mr Darwin. That would be no trouble at all.'

'Then, if you have no objection, my dear, we can repair to my study, upstairs,' said FitzRoy. 'Mr Darwin might like to inspect the work in progress.'

'And may I venture to hope, dear lady, that your confinement proceeds in as smooth and untroubled a manner as possible, God willing.'

The preamble completed, FitzRoy led Darwin up the winding staircase, noticing as he did so that the philosopher pulled a silver snuffbox from his coat pocket and took a furtive pinch, before loping on after him. They went into FitzRoy's study, as neat and tidy a workplace as his cabin in the ship had been, and shut the door.

'It is opportune indeed that you have chosen today to pay your visit,' remarked FitzRoy icily, 'for there is an urgent matter I must discuss with you. But you indicated that you also have business with me.'

'It is Gould,' said Darwin, simply. 'He has been working on the Galapagos finches. He says there are no fewer than four sub-groups, and that one, *Geospiza*, contains no fewer than six species with insensibly graduated beaks. *Separate species*, FitzRoy. The variants have become *separate species*.'

'I find that hard to credit.'

'All three mockingbirds are different species, too, from three different islands! All of them are unknown to zoological science. And Bell says that each of the lizards from each of the different islands are different species as well. I tell you, FitzRoy, these are not variants but *species*! Would that I had paid more attention to Lawson's lecture about the differing tortoise carapaces.'

'How came you by several different types of finch? Bynoe told me that you refused my offer of a cage of finches on James Island.'

'My assistant – Covington.' Darwin looked shamefaced. 'It was he who collected the birds. I failed to observe any distinction at the time. I am convinced that Covington's birds differ from island to island, but I cannot be absolutely sure of the labelling. I fear I have mingled together the collections that he made at the different locations. I never dreamed that islands just fifty or sixty miles apart, most of them in sight of each other, formed of precisely the same rocks, under the same climate, rising to a nearly equal height, would be differently tenanted. That is why I have come to you, FitzRoy. You and Bynoe . . . I know that you both made properly labelled and differentiated collections. I need your permission for Gould to access the collections made by yourself and Bynoe in the British Museum. I need your help, FitzRoy.'

'You ask for *my* help to try to prove your transmutationist theories?'

'I merely ask for access to the specimens.'

'You and this ornithologist of yours – this Gould – you claim that they are different species of finch, but I still fail to see by what *mechanism* any creature can cross the barrier between species. They are all finches. Surely by definition they are variants?'

'But, FitzRoy, I have the mechanism now. *I have the mechanism.* I read Malthus's *Essay on the Principle of Population*, and it came to me, as clear as day. Why is the world not overrun with rabbits, or flies, when they can breed at such an incredible rate? Why is the world not overrun with poor people? Answer: the weakest die off. Death, disease, famine, all take their toll. Only the best-adapted survive. It is why the lower races, such as the Fuegians and the Araucanians, will be eliminated, and why the higher, civilized white races will vanquish their territory. It is why Christianity conquers heathenism, because Christianity better meets the demands of life. Death is a creative entity! It preserves the most useful adaptations in animals, and plants, and people, and weeds out the least useful ones. So the favourable adaptations become fixed. That is how a species adapts.'

'All this does not explain how one species could possibly transmute into another.'

'Suppose six puppies are born. Two have longer legs, and can run faster. They are the only two of the litter that survive. The next generation – their children – shall *all* have longer legs. Species adapt by throwing up random variants – a process of trial and error – which persist if they are advantageous. They are selected, if you like, by nature herself, into winners and losers!'

'You are assuming that nature acts but externally on every creature. Yet the two are indivisible. Do not creatures define their own environment just as it defines them? Does not mankind, for instance, cut down the forests?'

'But this is where Malthus, God bless him, has given me so much! Mankind works *against* nature! We civilized men do our utmost to check the natural process of elimination. We build asylums for the imbecile, we treat the sick, we institute poor laws. Vaccination has preserved thousands who would formerly have succumbed to smallpox. Thus the weak members of civilized societies propagate their kind. What we are doing is highly injurious to the race of man!'

'You speak of Christian mercy as if it were somehow reprehensible. Malthus saw the expanding numbers of mankind as symptomatic of man's fall, not his rise through some brutal competition! He saw such a competition as one that must be halted, not celebrated!'

'But do you not see, FitzRoy? *Every single* organic being is in competition, striving to the utmost to increase in numbers! The birds that sing around us live on insects, or seeds, and are thus constantly destroying life. They in turn, and their eggs, are constantly destroyed by beasts of prey. Nature is not the creation of a benevolent God! The only order in God's universe is a coincidental side-product of the struggle among organisms for reproductive success.'

'What of co-operation in nature? Beetles that feed on dung? Birds that live on the backs of hippopotamuses?'

'Mere parasites.'

'What of beauty? What of the origin of life itself? What of something as beautiful and complicated as the human eye, which can adjust itself a million times faster than any spyglass? How did such a mechanism come into being through accidental modification? Only the Creator Himself could have designed such a thing.'

'Maybe the eye developed gradually, as man gradually designed the spyglass.'

'The gradual design of the spyglass was the product of God-given reason.'

'Must a contrivance have a contriver?'

'Yes, by definition! I cannot believe I am hearing you speak in this blasphemous fashion!'

'Come, FitzRoy, the design of a man is far from perfect.

We must rest for eight hours a day. We must feed ourselves three times a day. We eat and we breathe through the same orifice. We fall prey to every illness. We are not so wonderfully designed.'

'Tell me, then, about consciousness. How do your longlegged puppies account for the creation of consciousness? How is it that we are even having this conversation, are even aware of our own existence, if God has not given us the power of rational thought? How does your all-embracing theory explain generosity, kindness to strangers, self-sacrifice – qualities that I shall admit you seem to possess in short supply – unless man is created by God in His own image?'

Darwin, effervescing, sidestepped the insult. 'Man is arrogant indeed to think himself created by God in His image. Our image of God is merely human egotism made flesh. Whoever or whatever God is, He is more than merely mankind writ large. Humility leads me to the inescapable conclusion that we are merely animals.'

'Humility? You?' FitzRoy could barely splutter out the words. '"Shall the clay say to him that fashioneth it, what makest thou?"'

'Think about it – human and animal consciousness are not so dissimilar. Is our smile not our snarl? Are we so far from Tommy the chimpanzee? Is the black man, whose reasoning powers are only partly developed, not closer to the higher apes than the white man? Black and brown children look less like human beings than I could have fancied any degradation might have produced. Charles White has postulated an intermediate but taxonomically separate sub-group of dark-skinned people. Your Fuegians are living proof that Christian civilization is ephemeral, a mere gloss on the biologic facts – see how quickly they reverted to savagery! I tell you, FitzRoy, our Christian society is no more than an arm of nature – a Malthusian struggle for existence. Hobbes's *bellum omnium contra omnes*. We are riding a wave of chaos!'

'I will not have this – this *nonsense* in my house! The

civilized universe is fashioned by divine wisdom. It is a machine, and God is the mechanic!'

'If the universe is a machine, then life exploits only its stutters.'

'But this theory of yours, this *perversion* of Malthus, is a mathematical absurdity. Any single variation in any creature would be blended back into the species through breeding, being halved and halved again in successive generations until it disappeared. A marooned white sailor on an African shore could never blanch a nation of negroes!'

'Oh come, FitzRoy, it is patently obvious that there is much inherited variation. Successful characteristics are somehow dominant, otherwise every generation would be more uniform than the previous one. And those characteristics are passed down to both sexes by inheritance. Man would be as superior in mental endowment to a woman as the peacock is in ornamental plumage to the peahen, if the beneficial characteristics of the male sex were not equally transmitted between both sexes at the point of conception. That, my friend, is how one species of finch arrived at the Galapagos Islands, and transmuted itself gradually into a number of entirely separate species. Not variations, but *separate species*.'

'It is ironic – is it not? – that you make so much of the absolute barriers between species being supposedly thus vaulted, yet by your own argument, one species gradually transmutes into another without any impediment or barrier whatsoever.'

'You must help me, FitzRoy. You must give permission for Mr Gould to access those specimens.'

'You gave me your word that you would not publish any transmutationist argument! Your manuscript is complete – do you intend to rewrite it?'

'No – of course not. I shall adhere to my word. But I have to know. I *must* know the truth.'

'Why then should I help you? Why should I help you when you have delivered *this* to my house and to the publisher?'

FitzRoy angrily lifted the proof sheets of Darwin's manuscript from his desk and brandished them in the air.

'Aha! Now we are getting to the nub!' shouted Darwin. 'I could tell by your very demeanour upon my entrance that you were harbouring some ridiculous grievance at my work.'

FitzRoy began to read quotes scornfully from his blotter. '"No possible action of any flood could thus have modelled the land." "Geologists formerly would have brought into play the violent action of some overwhelming débâcle, but in this case such a submission would have been quite inadmissible."'

'I tell you, FitzRoy, no reputable geologist believes in the flood any more! Buckland has disavowed it! Sedgwick has disavowed it! Lyell's new volume entirely discredits the idea that there has ever been a major catastrophe on this earth! Lyell's volume, incidentally, which laments the delay to *my* book on account of *your* tardiness. Mr Lyell agrees with me that some part of your brain wants mending, for nothing else will account for your manner of viewing things!' Darwin was purple-faced with rage now, and FitzRoy not much better. Their argument could be heard all round the house.

'How dare you discuss me in such terms, or any terms, with Mr Lyell? Have you told your *new friend* of your transmutationist theories? I doubt it! For I, too, have read his latest volume, which makes it abundantly clear that although varieties may change a great deal, they can *never deviate far enough to be called separate species.*'

'Of course I have not discussed such matters with Mr Lyell! I have discussed my most private thoughts with you and you alone, because I was confined in a cabin with you for five years, and because I trusted you as my companion and as a gentleman to keep such confidences to yourself! Although, God knows I regret those confidences now. You gave me your word *as a gentleman* that you would have no objection to my casting doubt upon the Biblical flood in my account of the voyage, although now it seems that you have reneged upon that understanding.'

'On the contrary. You are quite entitled to print whatever nonsense you wish concerning the flood, although I believe our understanding was that you should do so discreetly. My objection to this volume is of an entirely different nature, and concerns the disgraceful remarks, or lack of them, on the title page.'

'On the title page? Remarks? What are you talking about?'

'Your page of acknowledgements, or lack of them, in which you ascribe your place on the voyage to the *wish* of Captain FitzRoy, and to the *kindness* of Captain Beaufort.'

'What of it?'

'I am further astonished at the total omission of any notice of the ship's officers, either particular or general. What of Sulivan? What of Stokes? What of Bynoe? Officers who assisted you in the furtherance of your views, and who gave you preference in the collection of specimens. A plain acknowledgement, never mind a word of flattery or fulsome praise, would have been slight return due from you to those who held the ladder by which you mounted to your current position. Or were you not aware that the ship which carried *you* safely round the world was first employed in exploring and surveying, and that her officers were not ordered or obliged to collect anything for you at all? To their honour, they gave you the preference. To your dishonour, you make no mention of them.'

'I shall write to them.'

'It is not enough. This page must be altered at the publisher's. I do not trust you to write to them.'

'You have the most consummate skill in looking at everything and everybody in a perverted manner! All this is about a simple oversight! You would do better to concentrate your energies upon finishing your part of the manuscript – which I would remind you was due for publication at the end of this month – than upon such petty matters. What in God's name is taking you so long? This delay is holding up my efforts to prosecute a successful scientific career.'

'You forget that I have two volumes to contend with,' said

FitzRoy, coldly. 'My own and the editing of Captain King's. A total of more than half a million words—'

'Half a million words? I read some of King's journal on the *Beagle*. No pudding for schoolboys was ever so heavy. It abounds with natural history of the most trashy nature. I trust that your own volume will present an improvement. Half a million words! No wonder the three volumes are to cost two pounds eighteen shillings!'

'The publisher Mr Colburn tells me that the high price derives from a shortage of rags to make paper. And, of course, your friends in the Liberal government continue to tax paper at a penny-halfpenny a pound.'

'Henry Colburn is a villain of the worst sort! I have had to pay him no less than twenty-one pounds ten shillings – in advance – for the copies I intend to distribute to my friends and family. That is more than I am receiving for my contribution! I am writing this book at a considerable loss. You, on the other hand, are on a full surveyor's salary.'

'On the contrary. As I am able to dedicate only part of my time to the surveying work, I have written to Sir Francis Beaufort offering to return half of my salary. And if the work continues beyond the end of 1838, I shall complete it unpaid.'

'Unpaid? Return half your salary? When you have found yourself in financial difficulties? You are quite mad!'

'No – I am not mad. I simply have ideas of money, and ideas of duty, which are different from persons such as yourself. A gentleman should always place duty and public service ahead of all other things. I am sure that it is a gesture that Sir Francis will properly appreciate, as being undertaken from the best of motives.'

Darwin sneered across the study. 'A gesture that has precipitated such universal admiration that you have not been reappointed to command the *Beagle*'s next voyage.'

'What?'

FitzRoy's blood had turned to ice.

'What did you say?' he repeated.

'It is nothing . . . just a rumour . . . Beaufort . . .' Darwin realized, uncomfortably, that he had gone too far.

FitzRoy was pressing him, desperate to know more: 'What do you know of the *Beagle* sailing again? What do you mean, "Beaufort"? You have met him?'

'He is a frequent guest at Mr Babbage's *soirées*,' confessed Darwin, weakly. 'He has lately become a considerable friend of mine. He has read my manuscript and given it his unqualified approval. He mentioned that the *Beagle* was sailing again, under Wickham, to survey the coast of Australia. I supposed that you knew . . .'

FitzRoy's expression revealed that, without a shadow of doubt, he had not known of Wickham's appointment.

Darwin barged on into the ensuing silence: 'Sir Francis has arranged for me to receive a government grant of a thousand pounds to edit five large illustrated volumes on the zoology of the *Beagle*, to be authored by Owen, Waterhouse, Gould, Jenyns and Bell. They are to be published by Smith and Elder – a *reputable* scientific publisher.'

FitzRoy was stunned. 'You are to produce an official guide to the zoology of the *Beagle* – with no reference to myself?'

'It was my understanding that you had been informed.'

'I think that you had better leave.'

Darwin rose without a word. Both men knew that their friendship was finally and irrevocably at an end. *The weakest go to the wall*, thought Darwin, angrily. *Your kind shall be swept aside like the great beasts of old. Scientists, industrialists, enterprisers, inventors, businessmen, these are the ones who shall inherit the earth. Your species has reached the end of its natural lifespan.*

FitzRoy's carriage deposited him outside the imposing stone portico of Montagu House, home of the British Museum. He stepped down as deftly as ever, but anyone who knew him well, seeing him alight, would have noticed that something was missing, a certain spring, an optimism in his step. Still ramrod straight, however, he rustled through the meagre crowds that pushed, head down, along Great Russell Street, his sober black frock-coat cut high at the neck and drawn tightly about him to keep out the cloying yellow mist that streamed in his wake. His bearing wore the dignity of habit; inside he felt like an empty shell, more like the ghost of Captain FitzRoy than his living, breathing spirit.

He was made to wait for what seemed an eternity in a narrow corridor behind the vestibule. Eventually an adenoidal clerk appeared, and announced that Mr Butters would see him now. The curator of Natural History was finally revealed to be a short, round, irritable man of middle age, attired in a sober and shapeless suit of comparable vintage, although the cinched-in waist hinted that its owner had once fancied himself as something of a swell about town. Even if that had indeed been the case, there was nothing swell whatsoever about Mr Butters's present-day incarnation. He looked his uninvited guest up and down with barely concealed headmasterly annoyance.

'And to what, Captain Fitzwilliam, do we owe the pleasure of your visit?'

'I am — that is, I was — the captain of HMS *Beagle*, a surveying-brig, from 1828 until the present day. If you will be kind enough to suffer the imposition, I am here on the matter of some specimens gathered by myself and Mr Bynoe, our surgeon, at the Galapagos Islands.'

'And how may I assist you with regard to these specimens?'

'A Mr John Gould, a taxonomist of the Zoological Society, wishes to examine the specimens in question further. I am here to make it clear to you that I have no objections whatsoever to Mr Gould's work — unless, of course, it should conflict with the researches being carried out by your own experts.'

'The Zoological Society, you say?' Butters pronounced the name of that new-fangled institution with the kind of lofty disdain he might have reserved for a gang of Thames mudlarks. 'We are very busy here, Captain Fitzwilliam.'

'FitzRoy.'

'I do beg your pardon, Captain FitzRoy. Do the officers of the Zoological Society not have sufficient animals of their own to experiment upon, without interrupting our own most industrious endeavours? They have a chimpanzee, I gather, dressed in a morning-coat for the entertainment of the public.'

If the museum was indeed the site of any industrious endeavours, then those labours were certainly not making their presence felt. The building was utterly silent, and the motes of dust that had risen politely at FitzRoy's entrance were now settling drowsily once more upon the aged books and charts that slept on Butters's desk. FitzRoy felt as if he had stepped back into the last century.

'These particular specimens – they are finches, of various types – are the subject of some considerable scientific controversy. Although I cannot say I agree with Mr Gould's diagnosis, I felt it only fair to give him the chance to examine the birds properly and at his leisure.'

'No good ever came of scientific controversy, no good at all. If you will take my advice, Captain FitzRoy, you will advise this Mr Gould to stick to dressing up chimpanzees.'

'Be that as it may, sir, I fear I must impose upon your kindness. It has become a matter of honour, sir.'

'Has it, by Jove?' Butters winced in disapproval. 'Well, we have a great many specimens here at the museum. Yours may not be easy to locate. They may not yet have been examined or catalogued. When did you say you returned?'

'One year ago. The twenty-sixth of October 1836.'

Butters burrowed into the teetering piles of books that cluttered the corner of his office, before emerging with a dust-coated ledger. 'HMS *Adventure* ... HMS *Agamemnon* ... HMS *Arethusa* ... Here we are, HMS *Beagle*. FitzRoy and – who was it?'

'Bynoe. Benjamin Bynoe.'

'Ah, yes. Specimens collected by Robert FitzRoy, Benjamin Bynoe, John Lort Stokes, Phillip Parker King ... not catalogued yet, I'm afraid. The cases haven't even been opened.'

'After a whole *year*?'

'As I believe I mentioned, Captain FitzRoy, ours is a busy department of a busy museum. We do not have the time to fling ourselves upon every crate or packing-case that every passing sailor chooses to deposit on our doorstep.'

'The collection of these specimens was not undertaken lightly, Mr Butters. Indeed, it was often undertaken at considerable personal risk to the officers involved. And for the record, your ledger is incorrect. Our midshipman's name was Philip Gidley King, not Phillip Parker King.'

'I very much doubt it, sir. We are not prone to such errors. Besides, Phillip Parker King is not a midshipman. According to the ledger, he was the expedition's commander.'

'Captain Phillip Parker King was the commander of the *first* expedition, which returned to these shores in October 1830. He has been retired these last seven years.'

'As I said. Not catalogued yet. The cases have not been opened.'

'The cases delivered here *in 1830* have not been opened?'

'As I believe I have made abundantly clear, Captain FitzRoy, ours is a busy department in a busy museum. No doubt they will be dealt with in due course. Now, if you will excuse me, I, too, am an extremely busy man. If your Mr Gould wishes to make himself known to me, I undertake to refer him to my clerical staff. I bid you good day, sir.'

FitzRoy crossed town, a prizefighter winded by blow after blow to the solar plexus who yet refused to buckle under. As he walked up the Admiralty steps, he realized that he had absolutely no memory of the journey he had just undertaken. He was a man in a daze. He scarcely had time to pull himself together before it was announced that the hydrographer would see him at once, even though he had taken the liberty of calling without an appointment.

At least Beaufort is being generous to me, he thought. *Which might yet be a good sign*. If it was true that he had lost the

Beagle, then – at best – it might mean a promotion. Alternatively, at worst, he might find himself relegated to a coastal guardship, and the relative ignominy of anti-smuggling patrols or fisheries protection. At least it would mean he could visit his wife more often. Whatever hand the good Lord and the Admiralty were about to deal him, it would surely be for the best, he reassured himself.

The door opened. Beaufort hobbled round his desk and limped across the turkey-carpet to pump his hand. FitzRoy's stomach knotted itself tightly into a ball. *Pull yourself together*, he told himself.

He smiled, and returned Beaufort's enthusiastic greeting. Was that sympathy or congratulation flickering in the Irishman's grizzled smile?

'Well, FitzRoy, I must congratulate you. Seymour has passed his court-martial with flying colours, no small thanks to you.'

It took FitzRoy a moment to realize what Beaufort was talking about.

'Your letter explaining that the ocean currents had been altered by the earthquake was entirely accepted by the tribunal. Seymour was completely exonerated of blame for the loss of the *Challenger*. Indeed, he was praised most highly for his subsequent conduct in protecting his men from the hostile Araucanian tribesmen. He has been honourably discharged, and given another brig.'

'Thank God. I am profoundly relieved to hear it, sir.'

'There was praise, too, for Commodore Mason, for the alacrity and bravery with which he came to Seymour's rescue.' Beaufort stared hard at FitzRoy, a glint in his eye. FitzRoy remained blank-faced. 'You don't have to tell me about it if you would prefer not to, FitzRoy,' he said, 'but there is precious little goes on in the Service that escapes my knowledge.'

'So I have heard, sir.'

Beaufort maintained his gaze for a moment or two more, after which his expression indicated that the matter had been dropped. 'Now. Your Lieutenant Sulivan – Commander

Sulivan, as we must now call him. What sort of a man is he?'

'He is as thorough a seaman, for his age, as I know. He is used to the smallest craft as well as to the largest ships. He is an excellent observer, calculator and surveyor. I may truly say that his abilities are better than those of any man who has served with me. Besides these advantages, he has the solid foundation of the highest principles and an honest, warm heart. Nothing on earth would induce Sulivan to swerve from his duty, even in the smallest degree.'

'Good. I was hoping you would say something of the sort. And I gather he has a soft spot for the Falkland Islands, is that not so?'

'He refers to them as God's own country.'

'The Admiralty has decided to appoint a naval officer to command the waters around the Falkland Islands, by way of a protection vessel. He shall also have responsibility for any isolated British communities on the South American coast.'

'I supposed that Sulivan was to have the *Pincher*, sir, on slaving duty.'

'Indeed so – he has already spent a fortune modifying her, I hear, according to the FitzRoy model.' Beaufort smiled. 'But this is a bigger job. A much bigger job. Not, mark you, that we should have any more trouble with the Buenos Ayreans. Government policy is to extend the hand of friendship to President Rosas, and to the new nation of Argentina.'

'And dare I say it, sir, we gave Rivero and his men a bloody nose at Port Louis.'

'Ah. I was coming to that.' Beaufort grimaced. 'The Argentines have made a complaint. Two complaints.'

'Two complaints, sir?'

'The first was that Captain Rivero's treatment – being manacled in your hold – infringed his rights as a citizen of the new Argentine Republic. The second was that, on a separate occasion, you insulted the commander of a Buenos Ayres guardship, and collectively abused the people of that city.'

FitzRoy could barely believe what he was hearing.

'But Rivero was a murderer, sir – a cold-blooded murderer. And their guardship attacked *us*. If I recall, I described its conduct as "rotten" and "uncivilized", sir.'

'I am sure your memory is exact, FitzRoy. Nevertheless, the government has decided to apologize to the Argentines, and has ordered Rivero and his men to be released without charge. The government are keen to have President Rosas on our side. Argentina could become a considerable trading market, especially for the sale of arms, what with their continuous wars in the south. I'm afraid you have to look at the wider political picture.'

'Indeed sir,' replied FitzRoy bleakly.

'And, of course, if friendly relations are maintained, then your friend Sulivan will be in no danger, sitting on his little rock in the South Atlantic. So let us hope for the best.'

'I am very glad for him, sir. Very glad indeed. But I came here, if you will forgive my boldness, to discuss my own situation. I heard from Mr Darwin that the *Beagle*—'

'Ah, yes. I owe you an apology for that. Mr Darwin should not have spoken out of turn as he did. It was an overheard remark – no more than a rumour at the time – but it has since become a matter of fact. The *Beagle* is to survey the coast of Australia, completing the task begun by King in the 'twenties. Captain Wickham is to have the command, with Lieutenant Stokes as his deputy. It will be a six-year voyage. You should not have found out in the way that you did, and for that you have my profound apologies.'

'I accept your apology unreservedly, sir.'

'But you have a family to consider now, FitzRoy. Would you have wished to be absent for six years?'

'I suppose not . . . but where does that leave me, sir? Am I to have an anti-slaving vessel?'

'Anti-slaving vessels are much sought after.'

'Or perhaps . . . They say there is to be a war against the Chinese. Perhaps a fighting commission, sir?'

'Well, of course, if there is war against the Chinese, then I am sure everything will change.'

With a terrible sense of foreboding, FitzRoy began to realize that whatever the news was, it was not good.

'There have been other complaints,' reported Beaufort, bluntly.

'Other complaints?'

'Surgeon McCormick, who left the *Beagle* at Rio de Janeiro. He presented an official complaint on the grounds that he had effectively been dismissed.'

'But that's—'

'Mr McCormick is not without influence. You are not the only man with friends in high places, FitzRoy. Except that your friends appear to be thinner on the ground than before. Ever since His Majesty died in the summer, the Liberals are keeping a velvet grip on the new Queen. There can be no help from that quarter. And the Tories, of course, seem quite incapable of winning an election. McCormick's complaints would have amounted to nothing much on their own, but these things add up, you know.'

'Evidently so.'

'Then, of course, there were those in the Admiralty who were not best pleased by your forcing their hand in the first place, and who were even less pleased by your decision to purchase no fewer than three supplementary schooners.'

'Three schooners without which I could never have accomplished my commission, sir – you know that. The chain of meridian distances . . .'

'I am grateful to you. But it was a commission of your own making – you know that.'

The two men faced each other across the desk in silence. Finally, FitzRoy spoke. 'So what am I to get, sir?'

'Damn it, FitzRoy, don't be obtuse. I am trying to be as clear as I can without rubbing it in.'

'I don't understand. I—'

'Yes, you do. There isn't going to be another boat.'

'There isn't going to *be* another boat?' FitzRoy fought for balance in his chair, as the room whirled round and round. 'For how long?'

'There isn't going to be another boat, ever again. Ever. It's over. I'm sorry, Robert. I did the best I could.'

FitzRoy shut his eyes, hung on to his chair arms and fought hard not to throw up.

Part Five

Chapter Twenty-nine

Durham, 13 April 1841

William Sheppard inspected himself in the looking-glass, and was forced to concede that there was much to admire there. The dazzling gold and crimson silk-and-velvet waistcoat, for instance, with its thunder-and-lightning buttons; the stylishly pinched boots in soft calves' leather; the fashionably chunky rings that raised a steely crenellation upon the line of his knuckles; the elegantly undersized watch at the end of its robustly plated guard-chain; and the extravagant, scented bandanna-handkerchief in maroon silk that he drew out now to complete the pose. No matter that his legs looked a little like pipe-cleaners in their buckskin tights. He was only in his mid-twenties, and his muscles would undoubtedly bulk out with age. No matter that his undeniably weak jawline appeared to have withdrawn its support for the flesh of his cheeks, causing an unsightly pink sausage to settle on either side of his rolling collar, one of a dozen that had been specially tailored for him in London. If he held his head high, the problem disappeared. It was a simple matter of remembering to maintain the correct posture at all times. And no matter that the hair on his head was already in full retreat, a disorganized ginger rabble on the run from an advancing regiment of pink freckles. A top hat, placed at a jaunty angle, created the convincing illusion that battle had not even been joined, let alone lost.

Sheppard's clothes became him. His home furnishings became him. The saloon of his brand-new villa had been decked out in the very latest India-patterned chintz and rose-coloured calico. There was an improved piano in the back drawing room, where a local music-teacher, hired for the duration, would perform Donizetti and Mendelssohn in the evenings. Afterwards, he would take supper at the fashionably late hour of ten o'clock, having dined at the equally modish hour of five. He ate fowl every day, with madeira and claret, and fresh fish from the coast at Whitby, where he kept a bathing-machine during the summer months. He took the London evening papers at breakfast, just a day and a half after their publication. He drove four-in-hand. He sat on the local bench and quarter-sessions, the Brewster sessions for licensing public houses, and the Poor Law Board of Guardians. He was the lord of all that he surveyed.

Now, at the age of twenty-six, he knew deep in his soul that he would soon outgrow County Durham. It was time to set his sights, and the tolerable fortune that his father had accrued from the coal-mining industry, on a bigger prize indeed: no less a jewel than a place in government. William Sheppard was to become a Parliament-man. He had been selected in the room of the present incumbent, the Honourable Arthur Trevor (who had gone to the Lords as Viscount Dungannon) to stand on the Conservative interest, as the party's candidate for Durham City. The general election could only be a month or two away now. Melbourne's administration was an utter shambles. Income tax was running at a staggering three per cent, half the country was up in arms through lack of food or lack of work, Chartist mobs preached violent revolution unchecked on every street corner, and the Liberal government seemed quite incapable of restoring order. A firm hand was needed. Sheppard's ringed finger closed over the top of his silver-topped cane like the gauntlet of a mailed knight. His time had come.

'Ram Das!'

His butler's starched white turban floated silently across the landing behind him, caught in the angle of the glass as its owner tried to pad unnoticed past the open doorway. As the man halted and deliberately retraced his steps, Sheppard fancied that he could discern a hint of insubordination in the set of the Indian's shoulders, and in the moment of hesitation that had preceded his about-turn. *By God*, he thought irritably, *I'll teach the fellow not to go skulking about the place like a common cracksman*! 'Ram Das. Fetch me a cheroot, and a brandy pawnee. And bring me the cellar book. I wish to inspect it. I am sure the rack punch has been diminishing faster than I have been drinking it.'

'A brandy pawnee. That's brandy-an'-water, sir?'

'Yes, Ram Das.'

'Very good, sir.'

The butler's face did not flicker, which irritated Sheppard all the more. Ignoring the insinuation of theft, the servant ghosted away across the landing as if pulled by invisible strings. It was all the rage to have Indian servants, of course, but Ram Das was not really an Indian. Not a full-blooded native, anyway. His real name was George Dawson, and he had been born in South Shields. His English mother had returned pregnant and disgraced from Cawnpore, where she had made the grotesque error, in Sheppard's eyes, of carrying on with a local minor official. Of course she had utterly sacrificed her station in the world as a result, and her half-caste son had grown up a ballast-man at the docks; but Miss Dawson, who had become a lonely spinster with nothing to do but dote on her sole offspring, had educated the boy at home – so, in spite of his colour, he was the only ballast-man in the north-east who could read and write. Sheppard had encountered him at the quarter-sessions, where he had proved a surprisingly articulate witness to an assault case; and, with a philanthropic gesture that had profoundly impressed himself if nobody else, he had stepped in to save the fellow from the short and brutal life of a dock labourer. There were times, however, when he had come to regret his generosity.

The butler returned, minus the requested brandy-and-water but bearing a visiting-card that cut a dun-coloured rectangle on its gleaming silver tray.

'Where the devil is my drink, Ram Das?' enquired Sheppard, peevishly.

'Beggin' your pardon, sir,' replied the servant, in his embarrassingly broad South Shields accent, 'but Lieutenant Colonel Taylor wishes to enquire whether or not you are "at home". He says it's urgent, sir.'

'For heaven's sake. Can't it wait 'til the morrow?'

'He says not, sir.'

Pringle Taylor was Sheppard's chief election agent. One of seven election agents, mind – Sheppard was not the sort to do this kind of thing by halves – but if the old man was barging in at this time of night then it probably was important.

'Very well then. Fetch him in.'

Sheppard was careful to let his servant know by his tone that his annoyance at the colonel's arrival would later be visited, with interest, upon the domestic staff. Ram Das departed, and returned with the unwanted caller in tow. Taylor was a lugubrious man with drooping moustaches, whose progress up the stairs resembled that of a melancholy Afghan hound lolloping after its master. Too young for Waterloo and now too old for the North West Frontier, the colonel had never seen action. Sheppard found it hard to imagine Taylor making any decisive contribution to the military fortunes of his country. The man was, however, a perfectly competent and diligent election agent, for which at least he could be thankful.

'How do, Taylor? I presume you haven't come here to partake of my brandy.'

'No, Mr Sheppard sir. There are news from London on the mail coach, sir – news you may find . . . incommoding.'

'Come on then man. Out with it.'

'Lord Londonderry, sir, being an influential man within the party hereabouts—'

'Yes, I'm well aware of who Lord Londonderry is, thank you, Colonel.'

'Lord Londonderry has selected a second candidate sir. For the seat sir.'

'By Jove! Has he indeed?'

Mentally, Sheppard cursed that old fool Londonderry, that old fool Taylor, and all the other old fools who made up the old-fashioned, disappearing aristocratic rump of the Tory Party. There were two seats in Durham City. At the last election the Tories and the Liberals had divided the spoils, one seat each. Unless there was to be an upheaval of seismic proportions, it meant that one of the Conservative candidates must lose out – and he was damned well going to make sure that the loser would not be himself.

'Do we yet know the name of Londonderry's man?'

'It is his nephew – a Captain FitzRoy.'

'His nephew. You surprise me. The name rings a bell, though.'

Sheppard pondered for a moment, then he had it. He crossed to the bookshelf, and took down the *Journal of Researches* by Charles Darwin. That was where he had heard the name before. FitzRoy was the sea-captain who had been privileged to ferry the famous scientist around the world. They'd authored a volume each, or something like that: Darwin's was a thriller, all about his adventures riding with the gauchos, and crossing the Andes single-handed; the sea-captain had written an interminable tract about the rights of negroes, all about their language and history and other such twaddle. Darwin's had become a best-seller, and had been reissued without its companion volumes – he checked the frontispiece of his own copy: published by John Murray, third edition – while everyone had ignored the mariner's dreary nonsense. And now the blighter had the gall to show up here, trying to snatch *his* parliamentary seat, just because he was a square-toed aristocrat with an important uncle. Well! – Sheppard's shellfish-pink lips clamped tight with determination – he would see about *that*.

Three days later he rode into the city, taking the closed carriage, naturally. As the horses' hoofs thundered assuredly down the rain-slicked cobblestones of Old Elvet, and the mighty silhouettes of castle and cathedral loomed through the blue-grey northern twilight ahead, Sheppard imagined himself a Christian knight, lance in hand, tilting at the fortress of some dark lord. The horses' momentum took the vehicle at a pace across Elvet Bridge and up the hill opposite; they pierced the dark lord's outer battlements of drab, slate-roofed houses with consummate ease. A sharp turn into the narrow confines of Saddler Street brought him to the very heart of the enemy's lair – the Queen's Head Hotel. As the postboys ran to take the ribands of his steaming chargers, he stepped down from the coach. He watched his boot-leather, soft as butter, settle confidently on the hard wet cobbles.

A sudden gust of cold air took him unawares. It may well have been springtime by the calendar, but there was a raw, sore chill in the air, and he wound his expensive cashmere comforter twice about his neck. That was the trouble with Durham – too deuced cold – but not for long, whatever this Captain FitzRoy had to say about it. He'd gone into FitzRoy's lineage – a real Park Lane aristocrat by the look of it, all race-balls and regatta gaieties and servants in shoulder knots. He probably passed his time hob-and-nobbing with the great and good. Well, his West End airs would cut no ice up here. *My father may have been a mine-owner*, thought Sheppard, *but he was a gentleman and he kept his carriage. I won't give you the pas, Captain Whatever-your-name-is.*

'Walk in, sir, walk in.'

The landlord, recognizing Sheppard for a gentleman, had scurried out to pay his respects, and to steer him away from any of his rowdier customers who might have chosen that moment to stagger out of the taproom. 'Do ye stop here, sir?' he enquired solicitously.

'No I do not,' replied Sheppard emphatically, annoyed the man had not realized that here was an individual of some stature within the County of Durham. All that would change very soon.

'We have a very fair room, sir, very fair. The bed's no' a large 'un but it's an out-and-outer to sleep in, sir, and there's a warm fire in the grate.'

'Thank you, but I do not require a room. I am here to visit one of your customers – a Captain FitzRoy.'

'Ah, the captain, sir, he arrived this afternoon. Follow me, sir, if you please.'

The landlord led the newcomer through the bar, not, as Sheppard expected, to the parlour but to a humble curtained booth in the travellers' room, containing only a lantern, a clock and the lone figure of FitzRoy, sitting before a supper of kippered salmon and finnan haddock.

'How do. I am William Sheppard.'

FitzRoy rose to his feet behind the rough little table and extended a hand. 'I give you good evening. Robert FitzRoy.'

'I'll take a chair if you'll allow me.'

'Please do. Shall I bespeak some more food?'

'No . . . thank you. I prefer not to eat 'til ten.'

'Pray forgive me – I am but three years out of the Service, and still take my meals according to the naval timetable.'

The potboy brought a jug of ale, and trimmed the lamp wick. Sheppard used the flurry of activity to scan his adversary for any physical signs of weakness. He had been expecting easy pickings – a pampered fat boy, no doubt – but the man sitting opposite was quite different from the FitzRoy of his imagination. His fellow candidate was slim, self-confident and well-mannered. There was a sadness about the eyes, which were dark and drawn, a softness to the cheeks, which were beginning to sag with age, and a hushed restraint to the speaking voice, which sat oddly upon a naval officer; but these were details, mere details. Sheppard immediately identified FitzRoy as a worthy opponent, and felt his own self-confidence slip as he did so. Not that he would give the fellow the satisfaction of seeing *that*. He proceeded with the due pleasantries.

'Pray tell – how was your journey?'

'Most satisfactory, thank you, although I dare say it will be easier still when the railway has reached Durham. I took the train from London to Peterborough, and from York to Darlington. I travelled the rest of the way by coach. I apprehend that the Newcastle and Darlington Junction Company is soon to complete the final stretch.'

'Indeed so. But as a naval man, I am surprised you did not take the steam-packet.'

'I . . . The timetable did not suit, I am afraid.'

He is lying, thought Sheppard, privately exulting to have scored such an early hit, albeit by accident. *He does not want to travel by sea. There is something of a history there, without a doubt.*

'So, Captain FitzRoy. It seems we have been chummed together.'

'Indeed so. I fear that I owe you an apology. When I accepted Lord Londonderry's offer of the candidateship I had no idea that there was to be another man standing on the Conservative interest.'

Sheppard smiled wolfishly. 'Let us say no more of it. Do you have a local agent?'

'A gentleman has been appointed to act on my behalf – a Major Chipchase.'

'Ah yes, Chipchase – a capital fellow,' observed Sheppard with mock-thoughtfulness, doing his best to indicate that he thought entirely the reverse. 'Lieutenant Colonel Taylor will be in the van of my team.' He put what he hoped was a subtle emphasis on the word 'team'. It would be an idea to dispirit this FitzRoy chap early on. 'Won't you take any ale?'

FitzRoy covered his mug with his hand. 'No, thank you. You are most kind, but water shall be quite sufficient.'

'I should be wary of the water hereabouts, if I were you.'

'I am obliged to you for your concern, Mr Sheppard, but I have drunk of the water in worse places than this delightful city, I assure you.'

'Then you must let me have the settlement of the ale at least.'

'I shan't hear of it. I must call the reckoning. You are my guest, and we are to work together closely over the coming weeks.'

'Even though we are to stand against each other in the poll itself,' remarked Sheppard pointedly.

'Even though we are to stand against each other in the poll itself,' smiled FitzRoy. 'I give you my parole, Mr Sheppard, that ours shall be a fair fight, and that I shall give you my every assistance in the weeks leading up to the election.'

'Unlike yourself, Captain FitzRoy, I make no fair pretence of family or blood. But it shall be a fair fight all right – I give you my parole to that.'

FitzRoy retreated to his little room high in the eaves of the Queen's Head, sat before the fire and took off his boots. His unopened trunk watched balefully from the corner, his personal possessions guarded like little prisoners by upright rolls of brightly curled paper: half-completed sea-charts and plans of South America and the Falklands, a task still unfinished after nearly five years, a task for which he had ceased receiving payment twenty-eight months previously, a task it seemed would never end, but which had still to be worked at most assiduously, for it was all he had left to cling to of his former existence. Suddenly he felt an immense wave of melancholy wash over him. He wished that he had not found Sheppard quite so obnoxious. He missed his wife and children, and he wondered what he was doing here, so far from home. He wished, too, that he had summoned up the courage to have travelled by coastal steamer – the courage, come to that, to step aboard any vessel at all. By way of consolation, he reached inside his coat for the only comforting object to hand: the letter he had received from Bartholomew Sulivan two days previously. It had filled him with joy, and it had broken his heart. It had been posted in Monte Video. 'My dear FitzRoy,' Sulivan had written, 'I hope your work goes on cheerily. We arrived here after a twelve days' passage and – would you believe it? – had not a breeze that we could call a gale of wind ...' A passage of nautical information ensued that plucked and tore at FitzRoy's sorrowful heartstrings, taking precedence, naturally, over the personal details that followed. Sophia Sulivan had gone with her husband, for the Sulivans had settled on a cattle-farm in West Falkland, where she had given birth to a son, James Young Falkland Sulivan, the first British subject ever to be born on the islands. When not patrolling his new domain aboard HMS *Philomel*, Captain Sulivan occupied his time collecting geological information on behalf of Darwin: the philosopher, it seemed, wanted him to research Agassiz's new theory, proposed before the Geological Society of London, that the earth had once been covered in great ice sheets: that the great rocks strewn across the Falklands valleys had been carried there not by a flood of water but by a flood of ice. In spite of the fact that he was a good Christian, and also of course because he was one, Sulivan had been only too happy to oblige the philosopher. Darwin, it transpired, was also married with child: he was living in Upper Gower Street with his wife Emma, his son William and his baby daughter Anne, Syms Covington and Harry the tortoise, who had been renamed Harriet, now that her gender had been properly diagnosed by Mr Bell.

Recently, however, the Sulivans' idyllic existence had been thrown over, for the *Philomel* had been temporarily transferred to Monte Video. Captain Beaufort's predictions for the region had not, it seemed, come true: General Rosas, having secured much of his southern frontier, had turned his attentions to his northern neighbour. Uruguay, the new president had declared, was historically the rightful possession of Buenos Ayres, and he had announced his intention to annex it by force. He had banned all British trade from the river Plate and its upper reaches, called the Parana, and was building shore batteries and gathering troops on the southern bank. The Admiralty had decided that the mere presence of Sulivan and the *Philomel* would be enough to deter the dictator. British families had been evacuated from Monte Video as a precaution, but surely, went official thinking, the general would not be foolhardy enough to fire upon a British ship? Sulivan himself evidently did not think so, for he had brought his own family with him to Uruguay for the duration: apparently he could not bear to be parted from the erstwhile Miss Young ever again. FitzRoy shivered to think of his friend, all alone in his little brig, standing between Rosas' forces and the barely defended Uruguayan capital; but if matters blew up, he reasoned, the *Philomel* could always put out to sea.

Astonishingly, upon arriving in Monte Video, Sulivan had run into no less a person than Midshipman Hamond, still adrift in South America, full of regret at his decision to leave the *Beagle*, and desperate to re-enlist. He had immediately appointed Hamond acting second lieutenant of the *Philomel*, and the two old shipmates were now planning the defence of Monte Video together. With a surge of pride and affection, FitzRoy recalled Hamond's stutter and his pale, wide-eyed features, and pictured him standing shoulder to shoulder with his tall, dark, intense, devout captain. He felt sure that the pair of them would not let him down.

Such were the details of Sulivan's life and career to date. His friend had reserved his real bombshell, however, for the end of the letter. How incredibly difficult must it have been for Sulivan to put pen to paper, to pass on such heart-rending news to his old skipper. Fuegia Basket had been found. It should have been a joyous piece of information, but the circumstances surrounding her discovery had ensured that it was anything but.

A sealer, recently returned from the western part of the straits of Magellan, told me that a native woman in her early twenties had come on board, who spoke English. She said: 'How do? I have been to Plymouth and London.' Without doubt it was Fuegia. She lived some days on board – I fear the term almost certainly bears a double interpretation – and was well rewarded for her troubles.

The young woman, it appeared, regarded herself as 'civilized', and would make her business only with the white sailors. Of York Minster, the sealer had not spoken.

FitzRoy folded the letter, replaced it in his coat pocket, and let the sadness overwhelm him utterly and completely. He surrendered outright to shame and defeat: it was a comprehensive realization of failure that the rapacious Sheppard had managed only to glimpse at the supper-table. He had failed Fuegia Basket. He had betrayed her. Worse than that, he had allowed her innocence to be taken away as surely as if he had taken it away himself.

'The committee will see you now, sir.'

The usher bowed and scraped as he made the announcement, demonstrating a level of deference normally reserved for the many peers of the realm who walked these corridors.

Edward Gibbon Wakefield had tipped him well enough to earn such fawning, but he prided himself that – when it came to earning the respect of the lower orders – his charisma was every bit the equal of his generosity. Wakefield simply oozed charisma. In his time he had charmed cab-drivers, serving-wenches, clergymen, society hostesses and, yes, peers of the realm. Even now, as his fortieth birthday receded into the distance and his fiftieth came ever closer, his square-jawed, handsome face and his brilliant white teeth glowed with youthful good health. His immaculately groomed silver hair and his finely tailored clothes spoke of a comfortable prosperity. His easy manner was at once likeable, reassuring and trustworthy. He bestowed an avuncular beam upon the grateful usher, stood up, straightened his coat, checked the watch in his waistcoat pocket, and strode into the committee room.

The business of Parliament was, of course, by necessity a little cramped these days: ever since the House of Commons had been razed by fire and its members had moved to temporary quarters, the committee business of both houses had been squeezed into a number of unsuitable little windowless rooms in the Lords. A thick, stifling atmosphere accosted Wakefield as he crossed the threshold, as if he had stepped fully clothed into a Turkish bath. The gaggle of clerks, witnesses, stenographers and dignitaries to his right were, for the most part, glistening, pink and uncomfortable; the committee members themselves, ranged in a semi-circle to his left, enjoyed a relative advantage in terms of space, but looked hardly any less ill-at-ease. In the middle, unoccupied, stood a solitary chair. This was his stage. He had remained cool in far stickier situations than this. Now was the time to be at his coolest.

'Mr Edward Gibbon Wakefield, your lordships, the founder and general manager of the New Zealand Company.'

Wakefield bowed deeply and impressively, and took the chair.

The House of Lords Select Committee on New Zealand had first convened in 1838, after promptings from FitzRoy and others that something needed to be done to address the lawlessness of that benighted nation. Thirteen New Zealand chiefs had even clubbed together and written to the British monarch, begging for protection against the depredations of her own subjects. But more importantly – far more importantly – the American flag had been raised at the Bay of Islands, while a French Catholic mission had suddenly appeared to the north of Kororareka. French naval squadrons had already invaded Tahiti, bombarding Papiete and forcing Queen Pomare to flee her kingdom, and now Paris was looking greedily to the west. Captain William Hobson had been dispatched hastily to the South Pacific to sign the treaty of

Waitangi with the thirteen chiefs, incorporating their nation into New South Wales, and to build a new capital city, to be named Auckland. The natives of New Zealand were to be given all the rights and privileges of British subjects. No white settlers could hold legal title to land unless the Crown had first purchased it from its native owners at a fair price. Only this month, the British government had gone even further, and had announced that New Zealand was to become an independent and protected colony of Great Britain. When he had heard that announcement, Edward Gibbon Wakefield had realized that, at last, his time had come.

'My lords,' he began, 'for too long, New Zealand has most selfishly and sordidly been used as a dumping-ground for the very worst of our people. The very dregs of our society. But are we a selfish and sordid people? I think not.'

An elderly peer in a bag-wig harrumphed his routine assent. Wakefield smiled a like-minded smile.

'Rather, this fine new nation should purposely be peopled with our very best men and women. Those gentlefolk who have found themselves thrown upon hardship and distress through no fault of their own, and who deserve to be granted a new beginning. My lords, our own island is become dangerously overcrowded. As you know, there is a want of corn to feed all our people. But were New Zealand to be cleared of her forests, were new cities to be constructed there, farms laid out and crops sown, harbours built and fishing fleets assembled, and, of course' – an expression of the deepest and most sincere piety moved across Wakefield's face – 'were great churches to be erected to the glory of God there, then in due course all Great Britain's problems might be solved. You might think all this an impossible dream, my lords, or at least a state of affairs that could not yet obtain for many a year. Then you must prepare to be amazed, my lords, when I tell you that *these great cities already exist.*'

There was a murmur of astonishment in the committee room.

'The New Zealand Company, my lords, is a philanthropic concern run by the Wakefield family with a view to encouraging the colonization of New Zealand by decent God-fearing folk. The first shiploads of settlers left these shores eighteen months ago, in vessels commanded by my brothers Arthur and William Wakefield, and my son Jerningham Wakefield. I have heard news – wonderful news, my lords – that this first party has founded no fewer than three new cities upon the Cook Strait, which divides the North and South Islands of New Zealand: the model and patriotically named cities of Wellington, Nelson and New Plymouth.'

'This is extraordinary, Mr Wakefield,' said the perspiring peer in the bag-wig. 'But what of the savages who formerly held title to those lands?'

'The New Zealanders are not savages, properly speaking,' said Wakefield, his tone one of gentle admonishment, 'but a people capable of civilization. A main object of the New Zealand Company will be to do all that can be done for inducing them to embrace the language, customs, religion and social ties of the superior race. Indeed, it is precisely this great work that I have come here today to address: for with your lordships' wisdom and assistance, I believe that the New Zealanders can be helped to realize their full potential, as partners in the building of a new and Christian nation. My son informs me that there is but one small stumbling-block: the regulation requiring all land sales to be carried out through the officers of the Crown. The governor's staff are but few in number, and are confined to Auckland, many hundreds of miles to the north. Inevitably, there have been considerable delays and confusions. Few land sales have taken place, and much fine arable farmland remains idle. What is needed, my lords, is not an administrative bottleneck through which all such land transfers must pass – a measure that could well see the progress of nation-building impeded for many a decade – but a general formula for land use, one that is fair and acceptable to all parties. I propose that the New Zealand Company settlers – those good

Christians who will, after all, provide the labour, the expertise and the funding required to build this new country – should be given a ninety per cent interest in all newly cultivated land; and that the New Zealanders themselves, who do not after all use their land, leaving it almost exclusively to Mother Nature's mercies, should retain a ten per cent stake. If, that is to say, the inferior race of New Zealanders can be preserved at all, in long-term contact with civilized man.'

There was a long pause while the committee digested Wakefield's remarks. Murmured conversations began to break out among their lordships, one sporing another like mushrooms. Wakefield could sense that his ideas were taking hold. He could almost taste the eagerness that his vision of a glimmering new nation had engendered. His manner, he knew, had been as engagingly plausible as his words. He had their lordships now. He had them right in the palm of his hand.

The chairman fanned his perspiring face with his papers, no doubt dreaming of gentle sea breezes rustling the cornfields of all those pretty, white-painted New Zealand farmsteads.

'Are there any questions for Mr Wakefield?'

None of the committee spoke. So far so good.

'If your lordship will permit me, I have two questions I should like to ask Mr Wakefield.'

The voice came from the back of the room. Wakefield swivelled round in his chair. There, amid the flustered pink clerks, was a grimly confident, dapper man in his mid-thirties. Wakefield immediately sensed that here was an adversary.

The usher identified the speaker. 'My lords, it is Captain FitzRoy, the prospective Conservative candidate for Durham City. If your lordships recall, Captain FitzRoy interrupted his campaigning in that constituency to travel down and give evidence to the committee yesterday morning.'

There was a brief flurry of conferring between the members, before the chairman reached a conclusion: 'Captain FitzRoy, the committee is prepared to entertain your questions. Pray proceed.'

'Your lordships oblige me greatly with your kindness. In

the first instance, I should like to ask Mr Wakefield: is it not the case that each of the prospective settlers taken by your company to New Zealand was made to pay a large sum of money for the purchase of land there – land that, when you accepted these sums of money, you had yet to acquire yourself, either legally or illegally?'

Wakefield smiled indulgently, like a priest accused by a small boy of hiding the fact that there is no God. 'Quite clearly, the gallant captain is labouring under a misapprehension. Each of our passengers was required to deposit a bond – no more – with the officials of the company, as a mark of the commitment they were prepared to make towards our enterprise. Our passengers, my lords, are the investors in this great enterprise, and what use is an enterprise without investors?'

There were murmurs of assent among the committee members.

FitzRoy returned to the attack: 'My second question is a rather simpler one. Is it not the case that both you and your brother Edward Wakefield served three years in prison for kidnapping a fifteen-year-old heiress and forcing her into marriage against her will, in a failed attempt to secure control of her family's inheritance?'

For perhaps the first time in his glib, confident career, Edward Gibbon Wakefield was stopped completely and utterly in his tracks. He sat there, silent, fuming, having not the slightest idea what to say, and knowing that whatever he decided, it would make not one whit of difference. All his patient hard work had been thrown away in an instant. He was left with just one simple fact at his disposal: the knowledge that someday, somewhere, somehow, he would finish this Captain FitzRoy for good. That much was certain.

'Thank you, Mr Wakefield. That will be all,' said the committee chairman.

The night before the election, FitzRoy walked the deserted gas-lit lanes alone, up Saddler Street and into the Bailey, following the ramparts that girded Durham's rocky peninsula. Above him, caught beneath a white moon, soared the medieval cathedral, 'Half church of God, half castle 'gainst the Scot'. Before him, the classical Georgian façades of the Bailey lined the city walls like lacy skirts. The houses were not much older than he was – he had been entertained and fêted in a good many of them over the preceding weeks – but here in the hissing, deserted half-light of the lamps, their spindly verticals and sagging horizontals seemed as lost in time as the unforgiving bastions above. Without the periwigs and bustles that had attended its birth, the Bailey wore a sad, ineffectual air, like a deserted ballroom after the guests have departed. Below the city walls, gardens and plantations reached down to the banks of the rushing Wear. Out in the black distance, amid the undulating hillsides and the torn-down forests, the nineteenth century was closing in on the old citadel with the pitiless inexorability of a modern-day Burnham Wood. Cast-metal foundries, iron-works, potteries, glass-houses, salt-works, brick- and lime-kilns, firestone and limestone quarries, all were marching slowly but implacably forward across the landscape. The vanguard of this irresistible host, the New Durham Gasworks, had already established a salient on the riverbank near Framwellgate Bridge. It was surely only a matter of time before the waters themselves were breached.

FitzRoy climbed up a side-lane to Palace Green, that lofty plateau where the election was to be held on the morrow, and gazed up at the crumbling battlements of the Norman keep: a tracery of wooden scaffolding already assailed its walls, where workmen prepared the castle for its new role as a university. The broken crenellations grimaced back helplessly, the last toothless frown of England's feudal power.

Election morning saw Palace Green dressed to the nines and giddy with high spirits, her jaunty mood and attire quite unrecognizable from the solemn seclusion of the night before. Blue flags and red flags rippled from their poles, blue banners and red banners swirled, blue bunting and red bunting fluttered, but wherever one looked the Tory red outweighed the Liberal blue, for Sheppard's squadron of agents had been conscientious in their work. There were 'Vote for Sheppard' placards by the score, a brass band with 'Vote for Sheppard' inscribed on the big drum, even horse-drawn carts with 'Vote for Sheppard' painted on their sides. The hustings, in the form of a two-storey wooden shed with a speaking platform protruding creakily above the heads of the crowd, had been erected before the Shire-Hall, wherein the Courts of Assize and Session had been closed for the day. Eleven hundred men were entitled to vote out of Durham's population of thirteen thousand, being the city's resident freemen and ten-shilling householders, and even now a team of harassed constables with staves was trying to ensure that they remained within the roped-off area, while the many hundred hangers-on who had come to jeer and laugh and join in the fun were kept outside. There were hot-pie men and puppet shows, youths selling muffins, men taking illegal bets, panicked horses both inside and outside the voting enclosure, rival musicians braying back and forth at each other in noisy competition, enterprising publicans carrying trays of drinks up from their beer-shops in the lower town, barracking party members, swearing drunks and catcalling small boys. Everyone, it seemed, wore a red or a blue favour. The candidates and their agents, arrayed upon the hustings, wore red or blue cockades upon their hats. Finally, the crier rang a bell and the mayor called for silence.

'Gentlemen, aldermen, freemen and brother electors of the City of Durham, we are met here today for the purpose of choosing two representatives in the room of William Harland, Liberal, and the Honourable Arthur Trevor, Conservative, to go forward from this city to the House of Commons.'

Granger, the Liberal candidate, smiled in triumph. Last time out, Harland had beaten him into third place by just two votes. This time, as the only Liberal candidate, his election was a certainty, and the blue-draped hordes yelled their delight when he stepped forward. His speech was short, and aimed squarely at the mercantile interest: Lord Melbourne's government was doing all it could for men of business, he said, but more time was needed for its austerity measures to work, and for an unruly populace to be brought under control. Loud cheers greeted his brief statement.

Cowper, the Radical candidate, was next. He wore no colours or favours, nor had he the slightest chance of victory, for his natural constituency stood disenfranchised beyond the ropes. His calls for universal suffrage and justice for the starving poor were met with forbearance by the electors, for the British have always sympathized with an underdog; but really, the good burghers of Durham were far too worried about being butchered in their beds by an unruly mob to consider granting them the power to go ahead and do it. Cowper retired, to isolated gibes and a hoarse cheer or two from the back. Lieutenant Colonel Pringle Taylor then stepped forward, and proposed William Sheppard as a fit and proper person to represent the electors of Durham on the Conservative interest. Raucous shouts of approval arose from that small section of the crowd gathered about Sheppard's brass band, where a phalanx of young men had been paid to provide raucous shouts of approval, but the rest of the multitude knew a pink-faced, moneyed youth when it saw one. A thumb in each waistcoat pocket, quivering like a sapling in a high wind, Sheppard stepped up in his new top-boots, and struck the jaunty pose he had practised so assiduously before his looking-glass.

'My brother electors,' he began, and then paused, for the voice that had issued from his throat was not his own but a strangulated parody of the same, 'allow me to state, with the utmost confidence, that nothing could be dearer to my heart than the trade and prosperity of all of you gathered here today, be you men of commerce or men of agriculture.'

'Ay, an' Headlam hens lays twice a day!' shouted a voice from the back, and there were cackles from that quarter.

'And why is your prosperity so dear to my heart? For unlike certain of the other candidates, who are not of this neighbourhead, I am a man of Durham. I was born and bred here.'

'Ef ye wor born an' bred heor, wey do 'ee crack so strange, like?' called another voice from beyond the ropes. It was true, Sheppard realized: in attempting to regain control of his wayward vocal cords, he had imposed a harsh, elocution-class formality upon them, with the result that his voice now resembled a comic impression of the local bishop.

'As many of you will know, I reside to the east of the borough of Elvet, not a mile and a half hence,' he continued huffily, making the fatal decision to engage with the crowd.

'An' what mayst thou be doin' heor, a' the way frae Elvet?' hooted his tormentor, this time to general laughter.

'And why, I ask you, is your prosperity so dear to my heart?' enquired Sheppard, who had lost his place.

'Aa wish ye'd stayed at hyem in Elvet wi' ye mammy!' yelled another voice, to widespread hilarity. Shouts and catcalls were coming thick and fast now. Why the devil were the constables not keeping order? Sheppard wondered despairingly. How was it that the great unsoaped were allowed to disrupt such an important occasion of state as this? He realized that he had not spoken for some seconds, and struggled to think what he might say next.

'Dost not knaa that blayte bairns git nowt?' gurgled another delighted voice. At last, the mayor attempted to call for silence, but it was too late. Pandemonium reigned. Red-faced with embarrassment, Sheppard took a step back in confusion. Mighty cheers greeted his apparent decision to concede defeat. Before he even knew it, Major Chipchase had moved forward to propose Captain Robert FitzRoy as a fit and proper person, and so on and so forth. Burning with shame, and sickened by the realization of impending defeat, Sheppard glared daggers of hatred at FitzRoy from the back of the platform.

The atmosphere was still rowdy, so FitzRoy simply took in his sails and waited for the storm to subside: he had addressed the men of the *Beagle* enough times to know a little of public speaking. Finally, he had quiet.

'There are seven thousand more people living in County Durham this year than last. Next year, there will be a further seven thousand. Seven thousand more mouths to feed. What shall we do, gentlemen? Shall we go on starving them, and forcing them into workhouses? And shall we go on building more workhouses every year, for every seven thousand more children that are born to the poor of this county? Until our county, and our country, is bursting at the seams, and the multitude of the poor and hungry rises up in fury against us? The Radical candidate, Mr Cowper, would give each and every one of them the vote, and let them decide their own future. He would let them follow the Chartist lead, and smash the machinery in our factories and mines and woollen-mills. He would have them loot the houses of gentlemen, 'til all prosperity is levelled to nothing, and every man made a pauper. One has only to look at the French example to see what happens when power is placed in the hands of the masses – terror, chaos, the destruction of wealth and property, the end of culture, the abandonment of religion, and the death of society itself.

'But the road that Lord Melbourne's government is following will take us there just as surely as if Mr Cowper were to lead us there himself. You may be satisfied of it. Already there has been one attempted revolution this year, in Newport. The factory system and the workhouses are not just breaking up families – they are literally starving our people to death. Are we not Christians, gentlemen? It would be an act of the most extreme injustice, I adjure you, if the wants of our population were not provided for. We must act, we must act humanely, and we must act now. This country must be governed in the interest of *all* its citizens, be they farmers or factory-men, rich men or poor. It must be governed by men of experience. Men who have been trained to lead from an early age, for the benefit of all. I have served this country as the captain of one of her naval brigs for eight years. Most humbly, gentlemen, I put myself forward and I promise you of my service.'

FitzRoy stepped back, to huge acclaim from the red fraternity, most of them farmers in from the countryside, who stamped, whistled and clapped with wild enthusiasm. The mayor called for a show of hands. Granger, the Liberal candidate, took the mercantile vote as expected, perhaps half the crowd packed into Palace Green. Cowper, to general laughter, polled seven votes. Sheppard, to another mighty cheer, carried perhaps twenty or thirty men with him − fewer, he reflected bitterly, than were even on his campaign payroll. FitzRoy took the other half of the electorate, some six hundred or so voters, to more ringing cheers and applause all round.

'Should you like to request a poll, Mr Sheppard?' asked the mayor, as if the result had been in any doubt.

'No, I should not,' hissed Sheppard, scarlet-eared, whereupon the mayor raised his voice and declared to the general populace that Thomas Granger and Captain Robert FitzRoy had been returned unopposed as Members of Parliament for Durham City. A vote of thanks was proposed to the mayor, the city aldermen and all the constables, and the crowd gradually dispersed to seek further merriment down in the town.

'I am extremely sorry,' offered FitzRoy to Sheppard, 'that today has not gone as you would have hoped.'

'It was a plant,' spat Sheppard.

'I beg your pardon?'

'You heard me. All your voters were Londonderry's men. All those farmers were his tenants. They were instructed to vote for you. The entire poll was hocussed from start to finish.'

'I am sorry, Mr Sheppard, but that is nonsense and you know it.'

'It is the truth, and you know it. And what is more, the whole world shall know it − I give you my parole to *that*, Captain FitzRoy.'

*   *   *

'A Bill to require and regulate the examination of all persons who wish to become masters or chief mates of merchant vessels – the honourable and gallant member for Durham City proposing.'

FitzRoy rose from the government benches. The temporary chamber of the Commons was perhaps a third full. High above, the featureless white-painted ceiling and the broad crescent-shaped windows immediately beneath were doing their best to brighten matters, but there was no countering the claustrophobic feel induced by the lack of light and the lack of width at ground level. Here only four rows of seating lined the walls, hemmed in by an overhanging gallery and an acreage of sombre walnut panelling. FitzRoy found himself staring through just a few feet of frowzy air at the faces of the Liberal MPs opposite. Even though it was the middle of the afternoon, the pendulous gas chandeliers, swaying gently on their immense chains, lent the lower part of the chamber an intimate, almost nocturnal feel, more suited to a gaming-house than a debating-chamber. Certainly, that was how a great many of the members appeared to view it: there were MPs in frockcoats and muddy riding-boots, MPs with their waistcoats and cravats loosened, an astonishing number of MPs wearing their hats, MPs reading newspapers, MPs fast asleep, even one member who had stretched out horizontally along a nearby bench, his hat shielding his slumbering eyelids from the gasglow. If anything, FitzRoy noted with distaste, a majority of the offenders were to be found on the Tory side of the house; many, he felt, seemed extremely young to be charged with the responsibility of representing a constituency. It was considered normal, he had discovered, for MPs to pay little or no attention to the proceedings of the House – as long as the stenographers got it all down, that was sufficient – and normal for MPs to show utter contempt for every convention of polite society. As he prepared to speak, his disciplined sea-captain's eye took in much that was to his distaste.

'Gentlemen, the British mercantile marine is now immense.

There are upwards of twenty thousand vessels of fifty tons burthen or more. Many of them carry fee-paying passengers.'

'I say, Fitz, hold that noise down. We were keeping it up pretty tolerably at the stump last night,' murmured a young buck nearby, his feet crossed on the back of the bench in front, his hands reclining behind his head, a meerschaum pipe jutting from his teeth. His friends guffawed in sympathy.

'And yet there is no examination of any kind with respect to the qualification of the officers. There are too many instances in which the indignation of Englishmen has been roused at the conduct of those who are entrusted with the command of these vessels.'

'It was a regular knock-down,' enthused another of the young bucks.

'You should join us tonight, Fitz,' said a second. 'A play and oysters, swallow off a few bumpers of claret, then off to a finish in Waterloo Road for champagne-and-madeira and the most beautiful women in London.'

'Best hundred guineas you'll ever spend,' sniggered a third.

FitzRoy cleared his throat. This was tougher than Durham.

'I once met a ship in the Pacific Ocean, which was no fewer than six and a half degrees out of her longitude. Upon my asking her captain how this was, he replied, "Why, sir, we do not come here to navigate, we come here to fish"!'

'We'll procure you a finer fish in the Waterloo Road than you'll ever catch in the Pacific, Fitz,' muttered one of the young blades, and all of them hooted with laughter.

These coxy young blackguards have supposedly been trained to lead their country from an early age, thought FitzRoy disgustedly. *That is, if you believe the electoral promises of the member for Durham City.*

'This Bill proposes that examining boards be set up in all our principal ports, to issue certificates to masters and chief mates of merchant vessels. Only a regulating system of this kind can avoid untrained officers obtaining command of these vessels by corrupt means.'

'And would those corrupt means,' boomed a blotchy-faced old Radical from beneath a wide-brimmed hat on the cross-benches, 'include the many instances of corruption detailed in *this* document?'

There was a cheer from those on the opposition benches who had been paying attention as he produced a pamphlet and waved it above his head. FitzRoy knew the document all too well: it was entitled *The Conduct of Captain Robert FitzRoy R. N. in reference to the Electors of Durham and the Laws of Honour, exposed by William Sheppard Esq*. The same thing happened every time he tried to speak. Sheppard's men had been as efficient as ever, and had flooded Westminster with copies.

'If anyone should get up in this House,' he snapped, 'and state that I have obtained my seat by corrupt practices, I will tell him that it is a foul lie and a calumny!'

'Go it, Fitz!' chortled one of the Tory bucks merrily, amid warm government applause.

'Do you deny, sir, that according to a member of *your own party*, you have lost your station as a gentleman?' shouted the blotchy Radical, to rival cheers. The House had woken up now, and both sides of the chamber were becoming interested in the spat.

'Tell us about how you can predict the weather again!' hooted an opposition MP, to howls of merriment.

'Order, order!'

The speaker intervened at last, and called upon Mr Chapman to second FitzRoy's Bill, and William Gladstone, president of the Board of Trade, to welcome the measure on behalf of the government. The brief flurry of activity over, the House settled back to its slumbers.

At the close of business, FitzRoy left the chamber and strolled up to the United Services Club in the Mall along with a few other ex-military MPs, escaping – as was their wont – the noxious vapours that wafted up from the river marshes on damp summer days. The Mall was leafier and cleaner than

Westminster, and he always felt that a few lungfuls of fresh grass-scented air helped to blow away the fetid vulgarity of Parliament.

As they mounted the steps to the USC, the air was split by a terrific crack, the report beating against FitzRoy's eardrums like tiny fists. He turned, as did his fellows. An extravagantly dressed figure stood in the street behind them, a long riding-whip gripped tightly in one hand, scarlet with anger to his ear-lobes and visibly shaking with nerves. It was Sheppard. The black leather thong snaked through the air, as if it were about to stripe FitzRoy's skin; but then, apparently, its owner thought better of the idea.

'Captain FitzRoy!' he shouted, with a strangled, high-pitched cry. 'I will not strike you. But consider yourself horse-whipped!'

Still trembling, Sheppard continued to swirl the whip in a slow loop about his head, the tip swishing provocatively close to FitzRoy's eyes with every circuit. FitzRoy raised his umbrella, caught the whip with a snap and jerked it harmlessly out of his would-be assailant's palm. 'Mr Sheppard. You are presumptuously impertinent,' he said grimly.

'And you, sir, are a liar and a coward!' shouted Sheppard, his voice struggling to force its way from his fear-constricted throat.

With an inarticulate cry of despair he hurled himself at his enemy, both fists whirling blindly. FitzRoy hit him once, cleanly and powerfully and not without a certain satisfaction. The young man went down as if he had been battered with a blacksmith's hammer, and lay groaning in the road. FitzRoy kept his fists raised.

'Captain FitzRoy, do not strike him again now he's down!' came a voice.

'There is no need,' breathed FitzRoy, his eyes blazing. 'I would not soil my hands upon the rascal.'

'Do you call yourself a gentleman, sir?' cried the agonized Sheppard, from the ground.

'Never mind, sir,' spat FitzRoy, contemptuously.

'I say you are a cowardly knave, sir!'

'Never mind, sir.'

'The question must be brought to the issue! I will have satisfaction, sir! Captain FitzRoy – I challenge you to a duel!'

A rictus of astonishment seized the little crowd.

A duel? This was the nineteenth century! He was the Conservative MP for Durham City! A duel? Had this stupid, idiotic youth gone out of his mind?

'Are you afraid to accept, Captain FitzRoy? Or will you have your reputation vilipended still further?'

'I am not afraid of you, you cur.'

'Then you had best find a second prepared to stand up in your behalf!'

FitzRoy's office in the temporary House of Commons was small to say the least, but it certainly did not seem large enough to hold Allen Gardiner. Although lacking in size, the man exuded the enthusiasm of an Alsatian dog. Talking to him was like being licked.

'Like yourself, sir, I am a former naval officer!' Gardiner's speaking voice came complete with exclamation marks, and the accompaniment of waving arms. 'Like yourself, sir, I believe that only the word of God can save the savage from eternal damnation! During my years in Zululand, it was I who converted none other than King Dingaan himself to Christianity!'

This was not necessarily a feather in Gardiner's cap, even if he seemed to think so. The 'Christian' King Dingaan had recently put to death 283 Boer settlers, men, women and children alike, and had torn out the heart and liver of their leader Piet Retief for use in ceremonial witchcraft.

'I apprehend from your expression that you have read in the newspapers of King Dingaan's, ah, aberration. It did make mortal bloodthirsty reading, I grant you, and I was ultimately obliged to leave Zululand in some haste. But many are the complicated circumstances in savage lands that make uneasy reading in cold British newsprint! One should not always take the newspapers at face value! I myself, sir, hold no brief for the slanders and slurs of our Liberal press regarding the Durham election!'

FitzRoy sighed. Sheppard had been writing to *The Times* again.

'You oblige me with your concern, Mr Gardiner. Forgive me, but did you say that you were a representative of the Church Missionary Society, or the London Missionary Society?'

'Neither, sir! I am a representative of the Patagonian Missionary Society, a new body founded by myself and the Reverend George Packenham Despard, with the object of bringing our Christian civilization to the Godless peoples of Tierra del Fuego! Mr Despard has been in contact with the Reverend Joseph Wigram, of the National Society for Providing the Education of the Poor in the Principles of the Established Church, who has informed us of three savages educated, on account of your far-sightedness, sir, at St Mary's school in Walthamstow. I have heard tell from the Church Missionary Society, sir, of your brave attempts to found a Christian mission in Tierra del Fuego. I apprehend that there is a savage yet alive, by God's grace, who is familiar with the teachings of Our Lord Jesus Christ – am I not right? A savage by the name of Jeremy Button? We of the Patagonian Missionary Society intend to establish contact with this Jeremy Button, and to found a new mission with all haste, with the object of spreading God's word among his people! We intend to do so, sir, before the perverse and corrupting influence of the Church of Rome can beat us to the mark! Are we to have your blessing, sir?'

Gardiner's arms had been revolving like the sails of a wind-mill during this last speech. Now he sat back as if waiting for a biscuit. Simply being in the man's company made FitzRoy feel weary.

'Undoubtedly, Mr Gardiner, the heathen peoples of Tierra

del Fuego could only benefit from the civilizing influence of
a Christian mission, properly ordered and managed in their
interest. But you are made aware, I trust, that this would be
a considerable task. I hope that your enthusiasm to gain some
advantage over the Roman Church will not induce you to act
precipitately. The construction of any building on Patagonian
soil is immediately attended by enormous interest among the
natives, who cannot but seem to hinder the measures taken
on their behalf.'

Gardiner removed his spectacles and grinned at FitzRoy
from beneath a mantle of close-cropped iron-grey hair.

'A floating mission, Captain FitzRoy! A *floating* mission!
That is my plan. You see, I have heard of the destruction of
your mission at the hands of ignorant natives. Any land-based
mission would inevitably be vulnerable to such an attack. But
a floating mission! Suitably armed, it would be invulnerable!
These months past, Mr Despard and I have collected funds
and recruited men appropriate to the fitting-out of no fewer
than two vessels suitable for this purpose – the *Speedwell* and
the *Pioneer*, two stout schooners. Is it not the most uncommonly ingenious idea?'

FitzRoy remained sceptical. 'I value your enthusiasm, Mr
Gardiner, and I am sensible of your seafaring experience. But
have you ever sailed in the vicinity of Cape Horn?'

'No, sir, I have not.'

Gardiner did, at least, have honesty on his side.

'Powerful westerly gales and the heaviest seas are its almost
universal attendants. It is a hard job for a fully crewed and
full-sized brig to stay afloat down there, never mind a schooner.
Why, even two hundred-and-twenty-ton schooners would
have their work cut out, coping with such elements.'

'Well, I should confess, Captain FitzRoy, that the
Speedwell and the *Pioneer* are of less than a hundred and
twenty tons burthen. Sadly, we were unable to raise more
than one thousand pounds to fund their purchase. They are
more launches than schooners: to be precise, they are the

pair of them twenty-six feet in length. But they shall be stoutly crewed – I have six good men and true! Pearce, Badcock and Bryant, who were Cornish fishermen, Erwin, our carpenter, Dr Williams, our surgeon, and Mr Maidment, who was a Sunday-school teacher.'

FitzRoy was appalled. Clearly, the man had not the faintest idea what he was letting himself in for.

'Mr Gardiner, I must urge you to reconsider. It is my sincere belief that your resources are as yet quite insufficient for the task. You should do well to take a little more time, and to raise a little more money.'

Gardiner grinned his disarming grin once again. 'I think you are forgetting something, Captain FitzRoy – something important. We have the protection of the good Lord. And with the Lord's protection coming powerfully in our aid, I feel sure that we shall surmount any obstacle!'

'Rum shrub?'

'No, thank you very much.'

'Please, please, take a chair.'

FitzRoy did as bidden.

'It seems that I owe you an apology, Robert. I never calculated about this fellow Sheppard proving to be so tiresome. I am fain to say that he will not be standing on the Conservative interest again, but I imagine that will be of little consolation.'

Lord Londonderry poured himself a large drink and plumped his ample frame into an equally ample sprung chair; the greasy oil-cloud on the crocheted antimacassar indicated that this was a favourite spot. There was something so, well, *avuncular* about his uncle that FitzRoy found it easy to forget he was in the presence of one of the most important men in the Tory Party, if not the whole country. The chubby smile, the softly arched eyebrows and the confiding manner all sat at odds with his reputation as a fiery-tempered and ruthless political operator. With his round face and sharp, curved nose, he looked like a friendly owl.

'He has challenged me to a duel. In the street.'

Londonderry chuckled softly. 'So I heard. How very melo-dramatic. Although you are aware, I trust, that my elder brother, your uncle Robert, fought two duels. He shot Canning in the left buttock!' He laughed uproariously.

FitzRoy's answering smile was, inevitably, somewhat muted. Viscount Castlereagh had suffered from the blue devils, just like himself. He had been forced into a duel, just like himself. He had gone on to commit suicide. It was not a comparison he relished.

'You cannot possibly fight the fellow. Imagine if you killed him! They would throw you in prison. The damage to the party would be irreparable.'

'Unfortunately, he is extremely hard to avoid. He is like a wasp.'

'I do not for one minute surmise he will go through with it. I am sure he is no more than a posturing hobbadehoy, letting off his steam. But even so, it is not a risk the party can take. I am afraid that young Mr Sheppard's behaviour might seriously jeopardy the both of you.'

'Otherwise than Mr Sheppard, I suppose that my contri-bution has been satisfactory? I have tried to serve the party in Parliament to the very best of my ability.'

'Your contribution to the Parliamentary party cannot be faulted, Robert – I do you justice on that. Regrettably, one's performance in the Commons is often less important than the perceptions of the voting public, however misguided those perceptions might be. Oh, I do not for one moment suggest that any scandal attaches to your reputation as a result of his antics – far from it. Rather, it is the antics themselves that are become an embarrassment. The party continues to be reported in the newspapers for all the wrong reasons, which cannot be to the good of any of us. I am sorry that it has not worked out for you, Robert. I entirely blame myself.'

FitzRoy began to experience the awful sinking sensation that had attended his last interview with Beaufort.

Londonderry leaned forward in his best confidential manner, and FitzRoy felt like a mouse beneath the owlish gaze.

'I shall be frank with you. A position has come up – a plum position – that may solve our little problem. You are aware, I take it, that the government has declared New Zealand an independent colony?'

FitzRoy nodded.

'Well, a colony needs a governor. A few years in New Zealand, and all these allegations of Sheppard's will be forgotten, as will this whole business of a duel.'

'What about Hobson, who negotiated the treaty? I surmised that the job was his.'

'I am afraid news came through yesterday afternoon that Captain Hobson has died of some beastly tropical illness. It was rather a drawn-out affair, by all accounts. Poor fellow, his death is the better for everyone.'

'I am sorry to hear it.'

'Funny thing is, the Church Missionary Society has already begun to lobby on your behalf. Cove by the name of Dandeson Coates, the secretary, wrote to the Colonial Office to say he'd received representations from a bunch of missionaries at a place called Waimate, demanding that you get the job. According to them, you're the only man to look after the welfare of the native race, in the largest sense of the word. In fact I was talking to Stanley, the secretary of state for the colonies, only this morning. It appears you are also the only man of any official stature in the whole country to have actually visited the place. So – what say you?'

FitzRoy recalled the gin-sodden, muddy hell of Kororareka; and the look of pure hatred that Edward Gibbon Wakefield had shot in his direction that day in the select committee room. Was New Zealand really a place he could take his wife and children?

'I would anticipate no great difficult with the New Zealanders themselves – but I foresee abundant trouble with the whites.'

'The potential benefits to your career in the long run would be considerable.' Londonderry was making it as clear as he could that a negative response was not an option.

By now, FitzRoy was past caring about the benefits or otherwise to his career in the long run. Was this the right course of action to take before God? That was the only question occupying his mind. *To do right, at whatever cost to myself, must be the governing principle of my conduct*, he reminded himself.

'Very well,' he said reluctantly. 'Should the job be offered to me, I shall accept it – subject, I must make very clear, to the agreement of my wife.'

The first cab at the stand was a gleaming new hansom, a racy two-wheeler with the driver perched way up at the back. A more sedate old four-wheeler sat behind it with a fatter horse, and FitzRoy found himself wondering whether it would be a breach of etiquette to displace the natural order of the queue; and whether, indeed, it was a sign of advancing old age to prefer a more traditional mode of transport. Perhaps it was indeed time to leave behind the chaotic buzz of London; time to exchange his life as it was for the chance to be in at the start of something big, to help build a brand new nation from scratch, to be a genuine force for good in this world. Perhaps the Almighty was giving him a chance to contribute to the well-being of mankind.

His reverie was interrupted by the tinny horn blasts and bawled headlines of a nearby news-vendor selling the *Evening Standard*.

'Battle on the river Plate! Argentine batteries engage British vessel! HMS *Philomel* hopelessly outnumbered and outgunned! A story o' heroism and tragedy!'

A hideous tidal wave of fear suddenly welled up inside FitzRoy, who felt as if he was drowning, right there in the street. He pushed through the little crowd at the news-stand. 'Give me a paper, if you please.'

'That will be threepence, sir.'

There were no stray coins adrift in his purse, or gathering fluff in the pockets of his surtout. 'I'm afraid I have no change. I only—'

'Werry sorry, sir, but three pennies buys a *Standard*. If you ain't got three pennies—'

Just give me a paper.'

FitzRoy almost threw a ten-shilling note at the news-vendor, leaving him speechless with astonishment, and snatched the paper from his hand. The headline read 'Naval Battle at Obligado'. As fast as he could, he devoured the story, his heart a pounding drum stretched taut with panic.

A chain had been placed by President Rosas' forces across the river Parana, guarded by an Argentinian frigate and two gunboats. Trapped and pinned down by withering enemy fire 'like large cricket balls', the *Philomel* and her companion vessels had suffered tremendous damage to their sails and masts. Three thousand men rained fire upon the British ships, either from the shore batteries or using field-pieces. Lieutenant Doyle on the quarter-deck had been beheaded by a cannonball. The situation had looked utterly desperate; but the smoothness of the river-water had at least enabled the *Philomel* to stay afloat, despite being holed in several places just above the waterline, and Captain Sulivan had coolly brought her guns to bear on the enemy. The ship's company, on account of their exemplary training and discipline, had never wavered in the face of over-whelming odds. Eventually, all of the shore batteries had been knocked out by ingeniously lobbing fire over their protective earthworks, with the exception of the number two battery.

Demonstrating extraordinary pluck and an utter disregard for his own safety, Captain Sulivan had left the *Philomel* in the command of Lieutenant Hamond, and had single-handedly launched an attack on number two battery in one of the boats. Under the cover of heavy musket fire, he had killed the gunnery crew in hand-to-hand combat and had spiked the Argentine heavy guns entirely by himself. The enemy frigate had been set ablaze and sent to the bottom, and the blockading chain had been cut by driving a merchant steam-vessel through it. Finally, Captain Sulivan had assembled a landing party of marines, at which point the enemy forces – mostly black conscripts – had fled in disarray. British losses had amounted to twenty-four men killed and seventy-two wounded. Enemy losses were estimated at eight hundred killed or wounded. Captain Sulivan was to be recommended for a decoration on account of his remarkable gallantry.

FitzRoy skim-read the whole story once more to be sure that he had missed nothing; then, he folded the paper and sank back against the wall, his knees weak, his body shaking, his heart still thumping, but thumping now with pride and happiness and sheer relief.

The news-vendor, disgruntled, appeared with hands cupped, a vast mound of dark pennies piled therein.

'Your change, sir. Nine shillings and ninepence.'

Chapter Thirty

Auckland, New Zealand,
23 December 1843

The *Bangalore* drifted through the darkened bay like a ghost, her sails glowing intermittently in the flickering torchlight from the town. Her skipper, Captain Cable, had misjudged her approach through Waitemata harbour and had missed the daylight altogether – as, indeed, he had misjudged so much during the journey. The captain had even gone to sleep one night in a secluded, smooth-water harbour in the Straits of Magellan, with all his yards and masts still aloft, and his lightest anchor run out on its shortest scope of chain. He did not possess a barometer, whereas FitzRoy had packed two in his luggage, and both were plummeting fast, down to twenty-eight inches. After a fierce, hissed argument, FitzRoy had persuaded the mate to let go a second, heavier anchor, its cable veered. At two a.m. there had been a roar to the west, followed by a dense cloud of driven water as high as the lower yards, and within seconds the *Bangalore* was very nearly over on her beam-ends, her passengers' screams almost inaudible over the terrifying shriek of the gale and the plaintive mewing of her straining anchor-chains. The first chain had snapped clean in two; but the second had held. FitzRoy had saved their lives. It was the low point of a journey that had been little short of agony for him, six whole months confined as a mere passenger on a Torbay merchantman whose skipper could not sail, could not navigate and could not read the weather conditions.

Little Robert, his son, pressed his nose to the porthole, staring at the blazing torches that glimmered on the Auckland shore. 'Father, are the torches for us?'

'Yes, Robert. Everybody is pleased to see us.'

'Everybody is pleased to see their new *governor*,' said Mary FitzRoy.

'It's my birthday on Thursday,' Emily reminded them all.

'Yes, dear. You shall be six.'

FitzRoy strode on deck to try to ascertain the real reason for all the torches. There was an agitation to their movements that appeared worryingly characteristic of a lynch mob. Auckland, he knew, was not safe at night, although the new capital was undoubtedly an improvement on Kororareka. There were no gas-lights and no hard footpaths. Everybody kept to their houses after sundown. Something was wrong.

A small boat was being rowed out energetically from the dock. In the stern, a pudgy, whey-faced youth in a lieutenant's uniform was gesticulating inarticulately. 'Are you the *Bangalore*?'

'Yes,' shouted one of her officers.

'Is the new governor on board?'

'I am here. Captain Robert FitzRoy, at your service.'

'Thank God,' cried the youth, and made ready to climb aboard. Gasping, he struggled up the manropes and flopped on to the deck, where he removed his hat, revealing a cranium shaped like a potato. 'Lieutenant Willoughby Shortland, sir, police magistrate and acting governor.'

'You are the acting governor of Auckland?' asked FitzRoy, with surprise.

'No sir,' said the youth. 'I am the acting governor of New Zealand, these few years past.'

Good grief, thought FitzRoy. 'Well, Mr Shortland, perhaps you can tell us what is afoot.'

'There are the most terrible news, sir!' gurgled Shortland. 'Arthur Wakefield is dead, sir, and thirty-five others, butchered by the savages. Butchered in cold blood, sir, on the banks of the Wairau river in Cloudy Bay, while going about the pursuance of their legal business! The townspeople are demanding action, sir. They are demanding revenge!'

FitzRoy opted to spend one more night on the *Bangalore* for his family's sake, and the following morning made what passed for a formal procession of arrival into Auckland. A hogshead of porter had diluted the previous night's collective anger, replacing it with an air of dissolute celebration. Barrels of pitch had been rolled out by the townspeople to furnish a huge bonfire. A ragged guard of honour had formed up, headed by an officer of the native department carrying a pole surmounted with a crown of flax, from which the new flag of New Zealand hung limply. Two drummer boys and a fifer struck up 'The King Of The Cannibal Islands'. There were perhaps fifty spectators – all white, for the New Zealanders had understandably made themselves scarce – and a detachment of the 80th Regiment from the new barracks at Point Britomart. The little procession marched from the dock up to Government House: FitzRoy and Shortland walked in front, Mrs FitzRoy held the hands of her two eldest children, and a small retinue of servants brought up the rear, pushing a cartload of luggage and the baby-carriage containing little Fanny. A table had been erected before the house, where documents setting out the proclamation and the various oaths awaited. As they passed the bonfire, a limp effigy was hurled into the flames, to the sound of drunken cheers.

'Look, Pappa,' said Emily. 'Guy Faux!'

'I do not think it is Guy Faux, my dear,' said FitzRoy. 'It is not November the Fifth.'

'Actually,' said Shortland with a grimace, 'I do believe it is meant to be me.'

Government House, even though it had been constructed by Captain Hobson but three years previously, was already falling apart. The walls were mildewed, the paintwork was peeling, the roof leaked and the room where Hobson had died still exuded the faint scents of calomel and death. FitzRoy might reasonably have expected his wife to appear crestfallen at such surroundings, but Mary FitzRoy stayed as determinedly serene as ever, simply applying herself without a word to making the place habitable for her children. All official formalities completed, FitzRoy surveyed his domain for the first time, gazing down across ragged green lawns to the wide sweep of the harbour: scruffy cottages had taken root here and there, like weeds that refused to be eradicated. The harbour was a good one, with four square miles of secure anchorage; but the bay was exposed to wind and rain, and – he noted with fore-boding – would be almost impossible to defend against attack. There was nothing he could do to change matters now. It was Hobson's choice indeed.

Half an hour later, he had his first official visitor: Mr Samuel Martin, the editor of the *New Zealand Gazette*. It was nine o'clock in the morning, and Mr Martin was already drunk. A burly, florid, red-faced man, he glared at the world from beneath eyebrows that resembled a pair of ferocious caterpil-lars; it took FitzRoy a while to realize that his apparently enraged expression was actually one of joviality.

'There's joy at your arrival, sir,' announced the editor. 'The rule of ignorance and stupidity has been terminated. Your governorship possesses the confidence of the entire European population.' He belched. 'That is, sir, on the presumption that a wise and rigorous policy is to be pursued with regard to the savages. That is what my readers expect.'

He threw down a copy of the *New Zealand Gazette*. It was quite unlike any newspaper that FitzRoy had seen before. It was half the size of a normal paper, and most of the front page appeared to consist of a giant, hysterical headline attacking Lieutenant Shortland. The acting governor was, according to the few brief paragraphs of newsprint left stranded at the bottom of the page, 'the acknowledged plague-spot of New Zealand'.

'What do you reckon, sir?' asked Martin proudly. 'It is a newspaper upon the new Australian model. One that speaks not just to but *for* the people.'

FitzRoy picked it up. Inside the cover was a large article by Jerningham Wakefield, demanding the extermination of the native population. 'The Saxon blood of the settlers will not long forbear under its grievances,' the son of Edward Gibbon Wakefield had written, 'for final victory must soon be ours. The time is not far distant when the rising generation of Anglo-Saxons will want neither the nerve nor the skill to hold their own against the savage, and will take ample and just vengeance for the opposition we are now encountering. The savages shall be crushed like wasps in the iron gauntlet of armed civilization.'

'Powerful stuff, ain't it?' grinned Martin, exhaling a ferocious cocktail of porter fumes and cheap tobacco smoke. 'The people want action, Captain FitzRoy. Thirty-five men murdered in cold blood. They want the perpetrators brought to justice.'

'You have my word I shall fully investigate the massacre at Wairau, Mr Martin.'

'An investigation be hanged, Captain FitzRoy. The people don't want an investigation – they want war.'

'War, Mr Martin? Do you know how many New Zealanders there are on these islands?'

Martin looked bamboozled. The porter was taking its toll.

'Upwards of a hundred thousand, as opposed to two thousand whites. There are a total of seventy-eight regular troops at my disposal – that's one company of the 80th Regiment – armed with just fifty muskets and a few fowling pieces. There are no fortifications here, no defensible positions, no place of shelter for the women and children, and no ship of war. The wooden houses of Auckland, and all the other isolated white settlements, would burn like dry grass. For war read suicide. One thing I shall not be doing, Mr Martin, is starting a war.'

Martin struggled to focus. His newspaper's point of view was not, it seemed to him, being taken very seriously. 'The choice is yours, Mr Governor. Just remember – if you cross the *New Zealand Gazette*, you cross the people of this country. And I'll tell you another thing – my proprietor ain't going to like it.'

'And who, pray, is the proprietor of the *New Zealand Gazette*?' asked FitzRoy, with ill-disguised distaste.

'Why, sir, Mr Edward Gibbon Wakefield, the owner of the New Zealand Company.'

To the further astonishment of Mr Samuel Martin and the *New Zealand Gazette*, not to mention the majority of Auckland's white settlers, Mr and Mrs FitzRoy invited the principal native chiefs of the entire Northland to dinner at Government House within the week, along with the senior missionaries of Waimate. They came not with the pomp and circumstance that would have attended a gathering of European rulers but, rather, they wandered in singly from the rain, each one uniformed in a stinking, second-hand European blanket wrapped tight about his body. They were large, powerful men, their luxuriant black hair oiled, and every inch of their faces minutely tattooed. In their physical strength their authority resided, for they had to prove their birthright on the field of battle. They were chiefs for life; only when they were too old to fight would they be replaced as rulers, but they would retain their status until death.

There was a seat for each chief around a long mahogany table covered with an immense white tablecloth, upon which were arrayed napkins, candlesticks, wine-glasses, silver knives and forks, bottles of Harvey sauce and cayenne pepper-shakers.

In the centre of the table were bowls of mutton-chops, boiled beef, ham, tongue, veal patties, pigs' trotters and potatoes, each dish topped rather prettily with snowflakes of plaster from the crumbling ceiling. Unlike the Fuegians, the New Zealanders did not attempt to eat the candles, but FitzRoy noted that their teeth were similar to those of their South American cousins, each tooth identical to its neighbours like those of a ruminant animal, quite unlike the wolfish selection that filled a white man's mouth.

'Friend Governor, salutations. This is our speech to you,' announced Chief Te Wherowhero. 'Let you not be a boy' – everyone present unavoidably glanced at Shortland – 'or a man puffed up. Let you be a good man.'

'I shall endeavour to live up to your expectations, Chief Te Wherowhero.'

'My husband is a very good man,' promised Mary FitzRoy, 'and he will treat all Europeans and New Zealanders exactly the same.'

'Captain Hobson said that every man would be treated the same,' retorted Hone Heke, an aggressive young chief with small, restless, deep-sunk black eyes, 'but we are becoming suitors to the white man. The settlers come to our land and put up fences where all men should be able to pass freely. They say we are Queen Victoria's slaves. They threaten us with English laws. They build prisons in the south, where our people are taken and beaten, even murdered. Is this the British justice we were promised?'

'Hone Heke speaks rashly.' An older chief, Waka Nene, his face daubed with red ochre, raised a hand in conciliation. 'It is not British justice that is at fault, but those who administer it. This evil is increasing in the south, at Wellington and Nelson. The love of the New Zealander for the white man is growing cold.'

'At Waitangi we gave the British only the right to control their own people – not the New Zealander,' retorted Hone Heke, jabbing the air with his table knife. 'Hobson promised us we would retain the rule of our chieftainship over our own people.'

'I have a copy of the treaty of Waitangi,' said FitzRoy, mystified. 'The chiefs quite clearly cede absolute control of New Zealand to the British government.'

'I fear that Captain Hobson may have been a little disingenuous,' explained the Reverend Mr Davies, shamefacedly. 'The New Zealand translation of the text given to the chiefs was not entirely the same as the English version sent to London.'

So, thought FitzRoy, *they were duped out of their country*. He felt mortified; but he could not fail to admire Hone Heke's fierce pride, his articulacy and intelligence. He could see in his wife's expression that she, too, felt his grievances as a good Christian should.

'My husband is a man of God, like the missionaries,' she said. 'Have the missionaries ever been less than honest with you?'

The chiefs had to admit that this was indeed not the case.

'Then you know that my husband will also be fair and truthful with you.'

'It is essential to the well-being of this colony that confidence and good feeling should exist between the two races of its inhabitants,' FitzRoy made clear. 'That is my goal. That is why the massacre at Wairau is such a tragedy.'

'I think you will find, Captain FitzRoy, that the massacre at Wairau is not the simple matter portrayed in the *New Zealand Gazette*,' muttered the Reverend Mr Williams, in an undertone that sounded at odds with his burly frame. 'The blame of the whole affair rests on our own countrymen, who began with much indiscretion and gave much provocation to the natives.'

Chief Waka Nene took up the story. 'The man called Arthur Wakefield arrived on the land belonging to Chief Te Rauparaha and Chief Rangihaeata. He built a hut to survey the land, to steal it for a white man's farm. The chiefs came to him and ordered him to leave, and burned the hut upon their land. Arthur Wakefield went to Nelson, to the police magistrate, and got a warrant for to arrest Te Rauparaha and Rangihaeata, for the crime of burning his property.'

'One of your police magistrates issued such a warrant, Shortland?' asked a disbelieving FitzRoy. 'I find that hard to credit.'

'Not one of my magistrates,' replied the youth, defensively. 'The Nelson Police Department belongs to the company, and all its magistrates are appointed by them. It's a company town.'

'Arthur Wakefield came back with thirty-five men,' resumed Waka Nene, 'armed with muskets, bayonets, pistols, swords, cutlasses and many rounds of ball-cartridge. He said the men were special constables. He had two pairs of handcuffs. He tried to arrest Te Rauparaha and Rangihaeata, but the chiefs would not go. So the white men opened fire, and killed many of our people. Chief Rangihaeata's wife and daughter were killed.'

'But that is disgraceful!' said Mary FitzRoy.

'The New Zealand people fired back, and there was a big battle. Many men died. When twelve of the white men lay dead, the rest of them surrendered, including this Arthur Wakefield. They waved a white flag. Rangihaeata was very angry about his wife and child. He had every prisoner beheaded. When our people fight, this is normal for us.'

There was a tight, anxious silence at the dinner-table.

It was broken by Hone Heke. 'You see? You white men talk to us about Christianity, and the gospel of peace, but your countrymen come among us with seven-barrelled guns!' Hone Heke's table manners, FitzRoy could not help noticing, were curiously elegant.

'The white men who came to Wairau were not Christian men,' insisted the elder Matthews passionately. 'God shall be their judge, may He have mercy on their souls. If they have done wrong then they shall go to hell. The same goes for those who ordered the execution of the prisoners.'

'Hell is for white men only,' Hone Heke corrected him, 'for there are no men half wicked enough in New Zealand to be sent to such a place. If Atua had intended our people to go to hell, he would have sent us word about it, long before he sent the white man into our country. Our people, when they die, go to an island off the North Cape, to live there in happiness for ever. We will have nothing to do with a God who delights in such cruelties.'

'Atua is the pagan deity of the New Zealanders,' whispered Davies to the FitzRoys.

'Listen, chiefs, and I shall tell you my verdict,' said FitzRoy. 'When I first heard of the Wairau massacre, I was exceedingly angry, and my heart was dark. My first thought was to avenge the deaths of the Europeans who had been killed, and for that purpose to bring many ships of war, sailing vessels, and vessels moved by fire, with many soldiers, and had I done so, you would have been sacrificed, and your villages destroyed.'

He hoped that this bluff was not too blatantly obvious: it had been made clear to him at the outset that there were to be no further troops under any circumstances. Seventy-eight was the absolute limit. Some of the chiefs seemed impressed, at least.

'The soldiers in red jackets practise every day with their weapons,' related one wide-eyed New Zealander to his neighbour. 'They will attack anyone their chief orders them to attack, no matter whether there is any just cause or not, and they will fight furiously until the last man is killed. Nothing can make them run away!'

Hone Heke, FitzRoy noted, was among those unperturbed by the supposed bravery of British troops. He resumed his verdict: 'But now that I have considered, I see that the white men were, in the first instance, very much to blame. They had no right to survey the land, or to build the hut as they did. Therefore I will not avenge their deaths. But I have to tell you that Chief Rangihaeata committed a horrible crime, in murdering men who had surrendered themselves in reliance on his honour as a chief. White men never kill their prisoners. So, for the future, let us live peaceably and amicably, whites and natives side by side, and let there be no further bloodshed.'

'The governor has spoken wisely,' said Waka Nene. 'Let all men heed his words.'

Hone Heke's small dark eyes flashed at FitzRoy for a moment, like a hawk sizing up its prey.

Mary FitzRoy placed a hand tenderly upon her husband's shoulder. It was after midnight, and he had been working at the colony's books since five in the morning; it had been the same story for three days past now, three days in which he had not felt able to spare his children even the briefest minute of his time. His wife had even taken on the task of writing letters home to his sister, to reassure her that they had arrived safely.

'You will strain your vision, Mr FitzRoy,' she said, a futile protest, for she knew that he would drive himself onwards at any task until it was completed. He turned to look at her but said nothing, and she saw the bleakness that bit deep into his features.

'You did say that the accounts were chaotic,' she prompted him.

'They are worse than chaotic, Mrs FitzRoy. If I have read them correctly, the annual income of the colony is approximately twenty thousand pounds a year. The annual expenditure is forty-nine thousand. Public works are at a standstill. There are thirty-three thousand pounds in unpaid salaries. New Zealand is bankrupt.'

'Can you not raise a loan?'

'London has strictly prohibited me from drawing on the British Treasury, or raising a loan of any kind. Besides, there is a letter here from the Union Bank refusing any further loans: there is already fifteen per cent per annum accruing on the unauthorized loans taken out by Hobson.'

'Can you not sell any government property, any government land?'

'Hobson sold all there was to sell for fifty thousand pounds.'

'What happened to the money?'

'By the looks of it, he drew it all out of the Treasury via a system of unauthorized bills, in order to meet his "expenses".'

'Captain Hobson was stealing from the Treasury?'

'Perhaps not just Captain Hobson. There are some extremely curious warrants for payment here to a Mr R. A. Fitzgerald, all of them issued by Shortland.'

'By *Shortland*?'

'I shall speak to him about it on the morrow.'

'If the colony is bankrupt, what does that mean in practice?'

'It means that all those poor wretches being disgorged from the company's boats will starve. Unless—'

'Unless what?'

'Unless, my dearest, they are given the native land for which they have paid the Wakefields so handsomely. Or unless I can feed and house them with my own money.'

'How much land shall they need?'

FitzRoy laughed bitterly, and gestured to the books banked up like earthworks on the desk. 'The total acreage of land sold by the New Zealand Company to its would-be colonists exceeds the total land area of New Zealand itself.'

Mary FitzRoy wanted to enfold her husband in her arms, as if he were a little boy; but he was the governor of New Zealand, and that would not, of course, have been entirely appropriate behaviour.

Shortland wrung his pudgy hands. A bead of sweat appeared at his temple, and made a furtive break for his collar. Goosepimpled with nerves, his skin assumed the consistency of a refrigerated chicken.

'I shall ask you again, Mr Shortland. Who is R. A. Fitzgerald?'

'He is a planter, sir, late of the West Indies.'

'What is your relationship to him?'

'Well, of course I know the man, sir, and I see him not infrequently.'

'What is your relationship to him?'

'I do not see how that is germane, sir, to—'

'What is your relationship to R. A. Fitzgerald?'

'He – he is my father-in-law, sir.'

'Your *father-in-law?*'

'Yes, sir.'

'How the devil did you get away with it? Were the accounts not audited?'

'All the colony's accounts have been audited, sir. All the payments therein have been officially authorized, sir.'

'By whom?'

'By the auditor, sir.'

'Obviously they have been audited by the auditor. I mean, what is the name of the auditor?'

Shortland rather shamefacedly looked at his boots.

'I shall ask you again, Mr Shortland. What is the name of the auditor?'

'I . . .'

'Well?'

'R. A. Fitzgerald, sir.'

'R. A. Fitzgerald is the *auditor?*'

'Yes, sir.'

'I shall expect your resignation within the hour.'

'But – my career will be finished, sir!' Shortland burst out.

'You should have thought of that when you issued the payments. Think yourself lucky I do not have you clapped in irons.'

'"Clapped in irons"?' sneered Shortland derisively. 'You are not on a brig now, *sir.* I was left here, on my own, with no money and no authority, for two years. Do you think Hobson did not have his hand in the till? It is the way things are done down here. You think you can just walk in and act the sea-captain – do this, do that? You shall not last five minutes here.

The company will crush you like an *ant*! Like they crushed
Hobson! You have been here but a few days, and already the
matter is quite obvious to everyone but you!' Shortland's whey
face had turned puce with indignation. 'You shall repent of
the way you have treated me!'

'Get out,' rapped FitzRoy. 'Get out of here and never come
back.'

'You're done for, FitzRoy,' spat Shortland, 'you and your
nigger friends!'

He marched out, slamming the door so hard that another
shower of white flakes spiralled seasonally down from the ceiling.

FitzRoy took the brig *North Star* to Wellington, a trip of ten
days, to confront the company in its southern heartlands. The
ship stank, for it had recently regurgitated another boatload
of diseased, wretched, stumbling immigrants on to the quay:
England's poverty-stricken underclass, who had given their
every last penny to the Wakefields in return for a future that
did not exist. With the help of the Waimate missionaries
FitzRoy had organized poor relief, paid for by himself and
administered by his wife. Tents were put up, and Mrs FitzRoy
moved among the would-be settlers distributing bread and
soup. It could only be a short-term solution. Desperate measures were called for.

A ferocious wind squeezing itself brutishly down the Cook
Strait made for an uncomfortable approach to Wellington.
Viewing the little town through a buffeting crowd of seagulls,
FitzRoy could not believe that the company had chosen such
an insane site for their headquarters. Hemmed in by high,
forested hills, Wellington could boast no level, cultivable land.
As a seaport, it was a disaster: the entrance to Port Nicholson
was long, narrow and studded with threatening black rocks,
making it almost a blind harbour. There was no shelter from
the relentless winds, and no prospect of defending the exposed,
straggling settlement from any native attack. Whoever had
selected Wellington's location was a fool. On closer inspec-

tion, the town reminded him of Kororareka: a shabby muddle of grog-shops and gun-dealers, populated by drunken, desperate men.

The arrival of the *North Star* at Lambton Quay and the news that the governor had come to town caused an immediate sensation. Even before FitzRoy's party had reached the town centre, filthy, bedraggled settlers were running to keep up. A copy of the *Nelson Examiner* was thrust into his hand, and one glimpse at its cover was enough for him to register that it was the sister paper to the *New Zealand Gazette*. Jerningham Wakefield had been busy with his pen once more. 'Our whole community,' it screamed, 'upbraids the governor with one accord. He has hounded a troop of excited savages upon a peaceable and scattered population. His policies risk the extermination of the Anglo-Saxon race in New Zealand.' White-lipped with anger at this excuse for measured journalism, FitzRoy pressed on to Barrett's Hotel, where a table was fetched and placed in the street, from which lofty heights he could address the populace. A noisy and excitable crowd had gathered, calling for the perpetrators of the Wairau massacre to be apprehended and hanged.

'I have investigated the massacre at the Wairau river,' FitzRoy began, silencing the crowd, 'and whether I try the proceedings of Mr Arthur Wakefield and his followers by general principles or by the laws of England, I am compelled to adopt the same conclusion: that their unhappy deaths were the result of their own actions. So manifestly illegal, unjust and unwise were the martial array and the command to advance that I fear the authors of that order must be held responsible for all that followed in sequence upon it. I shall therefore take no action against the native population.'

A score of angry voices burst out, and copies of the *New Zealand Gazette* and the *Nelson Examiner* were waved in outrage.

'The rebellion must be crushed!' shouted one man, who could be heard above the others.

'There has been no rebellion,' countered FitzRoy. 'These were British subjects defending their own property. The execution of the prisoners was a terrible crime by our standards, but normal by theirs. Yet it would not have happened had they not been attacked first. It must never happen again. Mistake me not, my friends, when I tell you that not an acre, not an inch of land belonging to the natives shall be touched without their consent. None of their villages, cultivated grounds or sacred burial places shall be taken from them while I have the honour of representing the Queen in this country. All parties, and I mean *all* parties, shall receive nothing but justice at my hands. There are many British persons who look on the natives of New Zealand as impediments to the prosperity of the settlers. To such persons I would say, the best customers of the settlers in New Zealand are the natives themselves. They are the purchasers of blankets, clothing, hardware, tobacco, soap, paper, arms, ammunition, boats, canvas and other articles, for which they pay in ready money, in food, in land and in their own labour. In future I expect the settlers to do all in their power to befriend and conciliate the natives, to forgive them and to make allowances to them, because they are the natives of this place, even if they *are* sometimes in the wrong. The only hope for the future of this nation is that we should extend the hand of friendship to our neighbours.

'Many of you will have come here believing that you purchased native land back in England. It is with regret that I must tell you that no illegal land deals shall be honoured, but I promise that each and every transaction will at least be fairly scrutinized. Meanwhile, in order to ease any hardship among those settlers not in possession of land, I shall issue notes as legal tender, to be used for poor relief. These shall not be banknotes as such, for they shall be valid but two years, but they shall be honoured by my administration.'

FitzRoy raised his newspaper aloft.

'One final point, gentlemen. The feelings displayed towards the natives in this newspaper are condemned by myself in the strongest terms. This . . . *publication* contains the most pernicious statements against the New Zealanders. Clearly, they are the work of a young, foolish and indiscreet man. I trust that, as its author has years before him, he will yet learn experience. That is all, gentlemen.'

FitzRoy stepped down from the table and entered Barrett's Hotel. The bustling outrage that had greeted his initial remarks had receded, to be replaced by an insidious, creeping sense of hatred.

It was not a couple of minutes before he was confronted in his room by a raging Jerningham Wakefield. The young man, who could hardly have missed the references to himself at the end of FitzRoy's speech, was scarlet with fury, his prominent Adam's apple rocketing up and down his sapling neck. Although he towered over FitzRoy, he looked in every danger of being blown off his feet by the next gust coming in off the Cook Strait.

'You *scoundrel*!' blurted Wakefield. 'My uncle lies murdered and you side with his killers? You have not applied even the simplest principles of justice! You have not yet listened to the white side of the story because you were determined, even before your enquiry, to decide entirely in favour of the savages!'

'I have *read* the white side of the story,' said FitzRoy, coldly, 'in this sorry rag you refer to as a newspaper.'

'A newspaper that reflects the public feeling of this colony!' shouted Wakefield.

'I know my duty and I will do it, without caring for public feeling. I come here to govern, not to be governed.'

'Do not speak to *me* as if I were a little middie on board your ship whom you can bully as you like. You treat our complaints as so much waste paper! I demand, on behalf of the New Zealand Company, that you take military action to apprehend my uncle's murderers.'

'Do you have absolutely *no* conception of how militarily helpless we are? I have but seventy-eight troops to put up against an entire nation. If we attacked the New Zealanders, they would retreat into their fastnesses, where no regular troops could follow. Thousands of warriors would join them. Hostilities against the settlers would then commence, and our ruin would inevitably follow. We should risk a sacrifice of life too horrible to contemplate. Wellington would be annihilated, and yourself and the company with it.'

'You damned fool! You think they will respect you for not punishing them? That they are now your friends? You do not know the New Zealanders – they will take your unwillingness to fight back on behalf of your fellow man as a sign of your own weakness! All you are doing is planning your own downfall! Ever since Wairau, the savages have been different – thieving, plundering, impudent, trying to frighten people, firing off muskets, practising their stupid war dances, buying a deal of gunpowder, making tomahawks, telling white people that they are cowards and that their queen is but a girl. That is because *you* have given them confidence. If we are murdered in our beds, it will be because you have as good as given them permission to do it!'

'And how much weaker would I seem, were I to launch a military attack that failed? Answer me that, Mr Wakefield. All I have done is to take the novel step of applying British law equally and fairly to both parties. If that scuppers some of your illegal land deals, then so be it.'

'You risk the ruin of the company and the entire settlement with your folly!'

'*I* risk the ruin of the company? It is not I who has flooded Wellington and Auckland with boatloads of angry settlers needing to be fed.'

'Then give them the land that is rightfully theirs – instead of issuing to them your worthless paper money! You possess no currency reserves. Your notes will be worth nothing, and shall only cause disastrous inflation.'

'I am well aware of the risks. I believe the risk that your settlers shall die of starvation to be the greater.'

Wakefield snorted. 'Governor's instructions forbid you to

establish a paper currency without special permission of the Crown first given. Only the Union Bank of Australia is allowed to issue notes.'

'You know nothing of the governor's instructions.'

'Don't I? Who do you think is the major shareholder in the *New Zealand Gazette* and the *Nelson Examiner* besides the New Zealand Company? The Union Bank of Australia, that is who. The same Union Bank that part-owns the company itself. And your governorship is in debt to the Union Bank to the tune of many thousands of pounds, thanks to that fool Hobson. They – we – shall want our money back immediately, Captain FitzRoy, and in genuine notes, not your worthless scraps of paper.'

'Do not try to blackmail me, you cur.'

'I have had about enough of your arrogance, and your dictatorial quarter-deck manner. You take advantage of your high station to lay aside all the feeling and demeanour of a gentleman. You think your governorship makes you powerful? You do not realize who you are dealing with. The company has many an influential shareholder in Parliament, on both sides of both houses. At least forty MPs own a stake. Even Lord Howick is a shareholder.'

'If the Queen herself were a shareholder it would not make one whit of difference.'

'We are shortly to begin publishing the *New Zealand Journal*, a British edition of the *Gazette*. Then all in Britain will be able to read of your folly. Who do you think owns Barrett's Hotel? I could have you turned out of your room at once, if I so chose, and I doubt you would find anyone else in Wellington to take you in.'

'There will be no need for that, Mr Wakefield. I shall not deign to remain in your company's settlement one day longer.'

'My father warned me about you, Captain FitzRoy. He was right, as always. And together we will finish you. We will finish you right off.'

FitzRoy and his little retinue of paid clerks walked back to

the *North Star* unattended and in silence. Nobody took off
their hat or bowed. There was none of the frantic excitement
that had accompanied their arrival. As luck would have it, a
bitter gust of wind plucked the governor's hat from his head
and hurled it into the harbour. As he went aboard his brig,
its crewmen busily trying to fish it out of the water, he could
hear the sound of raucous laughter breaking like waves at his
back.

Chapter Thirty-one

Auckland, New Zealand,
11 January 1845

'Pappa, that looks like you.'

'Yes Emily. It is a drawing of me.'

'But, Pappa, the drawing is of a black man. You are not a black man.'

Emily had caught him red-handed, leafing through his latest batch of bad notices in the press. There were many more titles to choose from, these days: the *New Zealand Herald*, the *New Zealand Spectator*, the *Auckland Gazette*, all of them company titles, spreading the Wakefields' pernicious gospel like missionary tracts penned by the Lord of the Flies himself. It was incredible that an immigrant population of just three thousand whites could sustain so many newspapers, but most of the settlers had nothing to do but read – or, in the case of the illiterate, have read to them – a rousing articulation of their burgeoning grievances. The object of their hatred, the governor who stood between them and the lands they believed to be rightfully theirs, had been caricatured as 'The High and Mighty Prince FitzGig the First, One of the Kings of the Cannibal Islands'.

'It is a funny drawing, Emily dearest. The artist wanted to make people laugh.'

'Did you laugh at it, Pappa?'

'Of course I did, when I first saw it. Now, my dear, forgive me, but Pappa is busy. Why don't you go and play in the sunshine with Robert and Fanny?'

His daughter headed off obligingly, and his protective gaze shepherded her out on to the sunlit lawn. Little Fanny was waddling about in her long clothes, a huge, beaming smile on her face; Robert was wheeling in circles around her, a toy sailing-boat fashioned from coral in his outstretched hand. Behind them, the coarse meadows that swept down to the harbour had been plentifully seeded with mean thickets of wooden dwellings. Their numbers were increasing: in places they had clustered into discernible streets, as if huddled together, whispering and plotting. To the north and west of the town, dark, brooding clouds were gathering. On the wooded, volcanic hills that formed a natural amphitheatre on Auckland's rim, long lines of native huts had appeared, each tribe allocated its own ridge. Ostensibly they were there to trade with the white man, but there was no doubting that there was a new ostentation, a new confidence in their behaviour: Wairau had unquestionably altered the psychological balance. An opposing army, thought FitzRoy, could hardly have encamped more skilfully or with a greater appearance of regularity.

Of course he had written to Stanley, the colonial secretary, requesting more money and more troops. Without money he could not build a school, or a church, or a hospital, or even any defences. The process of justice had been frozen, for there was no money to pay lawyers. Even legitimate land sales had stopped, for his administration had no funds with which to purchase land from the natives. He even had to keep a tight rein on his own currency issue, for fear of sending inflation spiralling out of control. Just a limited sum of money, he had told Stanley, would enable him to pay small salaries to friendly chiefs, to purchase their allegiance; as it was, the love of Christ instilled in some of the tribes by the Waimate missionaries was the only leash holding back the New Zealanders. The country was in a state of paralysis: all he could do was to keep the two sides at arm's length for as long as possible.

It had taken ten months for Stanley's reply to come back. No money and no troops would be forthcoming. The company had assured the government that New Zealand should be entirely self-supporting, which, of course, it could be, were its native population to be conveniently wiped out. Instead of troops, Stanley had commanded him to raise a defensive militia by arming the white settlers, an order so provocative and fool-hardy that he had felt obliged to disobey it. The natives under-stood, at least, that the red-jacketed soldiers were there to defend the law and the status quo, that they were a neutral force. Arming the mob of settlers would lead only to a blood-bath that would put Wairau to shame. News of his disobedi-ence, he knew, would soon reach London. The *New Zealand Journal* had without doubt arrived there long previously.

Wearily, he scanned the newspapers once more. 'Remove our curse – the native curse – and replace it by a blessing: a rational governor!' yelled one headline. He read on. 'The policy adopted by Governor FitzRoy towards the natives has produced the effect which all who know the savages' charac-ter foresaw and predicted – the same namely which is observed in spoiled and petted children, whom injudicious fondness renders presumptuous and impertinent – a pest to all around them.' He picked up the *Herald*. It made the point that 'the admission of the natives' absolute right to their land raises innumerable obstacles to beneficial colonization. It creates in the breasts of the natives an insatiable cupidity, which condemns them to listless inactivity and a continuance in barbarous habits.' Jerningham Wakefield, of course, expressed the strongest sentiments of all. Writing in the *Gazette*, he insisted that Governor FitzRoy had brought with him to New Zealand an illness that had infected the entire colony: 'It is disgusting to remark the purulent and contagious nature of the disease. It appears as though the moral plague of aversion to the settlers is spread by the mere breath and odour of authority.'

'Why do you bother to read them?'

His wife stood in the doorway, leaning with one hand upon the jamb to ease the weight of their fourth child, which was slung low in her belly, just a few short weeks from making an entrance into the world. Somehow she managed to maintain her regal bearing, even when braced against the plain wood of the doorframe. He remained in awe of her, just as he remained in awe of the continuing miracle of childbirth. Her piety was so simple, so reassuring, he had come to see it as a beacon that might yet lead him to safety. She was almost worshipped, too, by the colonists. When she moved among them dispensing food, water and blankets, they saw only an angel in white, floating in their midst. There were, of course, none of the whispered insults, guffaws and threats that attended FitzRoy's own progress about the town.

He put down the *New Zealand Gazette*. 'Why do I read them? Because London will read them. Because the chiefs will read them. Because the settlers will read them. And they will believe what is written therein about myself and about this colony.'

'Anyone who knows you will not believe them. Anyone who knows you and loves you, as I do, will know that these journals are written with not the slightest regard for the truth.'

'The settlers would appear to believe every word.'

'My dearest, the settlers have no choice but to believe, for without the fantasy that the natives' land belongs to them, what do they have? They are penniless and frightened and many thousands of miles from home.'

'What is important, Mrs FitzRoy, is what London believes. Therein shall lie our salvation, or our damnation.'

'London will choose to believe what it suits London to believe. I pray that God has granted Lord Stanley the wisdom to see the truth; but if that proves not to be the case, as indeed it may not, then you must be strong, my dearest, and endure, for the truth must always emerge in the end. Do not despond. We must both of us trust in a superintending Providence, in the knowledge that He must ultimately carry the day. Therein shall lie our salvation, and not our damnation.'

'You are right as always, my dear. But I am failing in a husband's duty, in leaving my beloved wife standing when she is with child! What has become of me?' He took his wife's arm and ushered her to a seat. 'Please forgive me my self-absorption. My manners are become utterly remiss.'

'Really, Mr FitzRoy,' she smiled, 'you do fuss overmuch.'

A polite cough from the doorway interrupted them. 'If you please, sir.'

It was Andrew Sinclair, FitzRoy's colonial secretary. The young Scot was actually a naval surgeon, who had headed south on a convict vessel the year before and had decided to stay on. Unable to trust any European in the colony besides the missionaries, FitzRoy had seized the opportunity of employing a Navy man in a much-needed position of responsibility.

'There are news from Kororareka sir. Chief Hone Heke and a band of men have cut down the flagstaff, two days ago, and have burned the British and New Zealand flags.'

FitzRoy remembered the lonely flagpole on the hill above the resident's house, which was empty now, Bushby long since fled.

'Was there a reason for this act?'

'One of his servants, a girl named Kotiro, has run off and married a white man of that town.'

'It is but a pretext. Hone Heke has a hundred servants. It is a calculated gesture against the symbol of British authority. He is probing, pushing, trying to provoke us to collision.'

'What shall we do?'

'Certainly, we cannot ignore it, but we must not be intemperate. Send orders for another flagstaff to be erected, and new flags to be flown. And send a message to Hone Heke that I am willing to meet with him personally, regarding his grievances.'

'Yes, sir.'

Sinclair performed a naval about-turn and exited the room, leaving FitzRoy alone with his wife. Concerned, she placed her hand upon his. 'Will it be the first shot of the war?'

'I most devoutly hope not, Mrs FitzRoy. For the sake of all our lives.'

A Navy brig that had docked at Auckland, HMS *Hazard*, ferried FitzRoy north to Kororareka some eight weeks later, together with fifty men of the 80th Regiment, the bulk of his troop strength, under Captain Maynard. News had come through that Hone Heke had cut down the flagstaff for a second time, and had refused FitzRoy's request for a meeting. The governor had ordered the pole to be re-erected yet again, this time with iron cladding about its base, and had issued a warrant for Hone Heke's arrest, on a charge of damaging crown property. There was now a price on the chief's head, which FitzRoy could ill afford, of one hundred pounds. It was, he knew, little more than a symbolic gesture.

On arrival at Kororareka, a council of war was called, to be held in the Christ Church, the only building in the grubby little town that even remotely deserved to be called salubrious. The Christian chief Waka Nene had been invited, as had Mr Williams, representing the Waimate missionaries, Andrew Sinclair, Captain Maynard and his two lieutenants, and the captain and ship's officers of HMS *Hazard*. The news was not good. Hone Heke's men had raided most of the outlying farms, robbing the occupants and burning the buildings to the ground. They had stolen a good many horses, which meant that their band was now mobile and fast. The formerly bois- terous, drunken occupants of Kororareka had become nervous and fearful, and were keeping to their homes. The crunch, FitzRoy sensed, had come. One mistake, one wrong decision by him, and scores of people could die. *I hold all these people's lives in my hands, not to mention the lives of my own family. Lord, give me the strength to act wisely and for the good of all.*

'Hone Heke sends you a message,' said Chief Waka Nene gravely, the intense black whorls that spiralled furiously about his face giving no clue to his expression. He handed across a piece of paper.

FitzRoy unfolded it and read it out:

> Am I a pig that I am thus to be bought and sold? I now offer a reward of one hundred pounds for YOUR arrest. I hereby give all white men two days to leave the town of Kororareka. Any whites remaining after two days will be killed.

'Damned cheek,' said Maynard, who had a ruddy-faced, confident air. 'The man is a self-important thief, who will run at the first sign of opposition.'

'Tell me, Captain Maynard,' asked FitzRoy, 'what battle experience do you and your men possess?'

'Well, sir . . . none of us has actually seen active service yet,' said Maynard, colouring even further, 'but we train every day. Believe me, sir, the New Zealander is not a man who can be talked to with any sort of hesitation. He must be talked to with a fixed bayonet, and we are the men to talk to him.'

FitzRoy's glance flicked across to Waka Nene, to see if Maynard's generalizations were having any effect, but the chief sat in impassive silence.

'We're fully able to give Heke and his followers a good chastisement, sir,' offered Lieutenant Randall, Maynard's immediate junior, an enthusiastic youth of some nineteen years.

You are just a boy, thought FitzRoy. *How typical of the Army to make lieutenants of barely trained younkers.*

'Your courage does you credit, Lieutenant Randall. But do not forget that there are no fewer than twelve thousand New Zealanders living in the vicinity of Kororareka.'

'A war would be disastrous for us all!' blared Williams, in his Cardiff baritone. 'Catastrophe! Especially a war over a flag on a stick! Can we not simply take the flag into safe-keeping until there can be no doubt as to its protection?'

FitzRoy shook his head. 'I am afraid, Mr Williams, that the flag symbolizes my authority, and that of Her Majesty, over this colony. It must stay up.'

'Hone Heke sees the flagstaff as a *rahui*.' Waka Nene broke his silence. 'A sign – a magic sign – to keep intruders away. If he cuts it down, it will weaken the white man's magic. Hone Heke is not a Christian.'

'What a lot of superstitious mumbo-jumbo,' scoffed Captain Maynard. 'Claptrap and balderdash.'

'If the flagstaff is cut down again, we will fight for it,' promised Waka Nene. 'We Christians are one tribe, and we will fight for the staff and for our governor.'

'I thank you, Chief Waka Nene, for your friendship and loyalty,' said FitzRoy, gravely.

'The trouble is,' Williams went on, 'that many of the young men have come to see the British as occupiers. They are flocking to Hone Heke's side. They see him as a leader beyond the reproach of the British.'

'I am afraid, gentlemen, that we must countenance the possibility that Kororareka will be attacked,' cautioned FitzRoy. 'Here is what we will do. Send messages to the remaining outsettlers that they cannot be protected unless they remove themselves to Kororareka. Mr Sinclair, if you would send urgently to Sir George Gipps, the governor of New South Wales: "Recent acts of open rebellion demand not only immediate help but permanent resistance. I cannot hope to prevent a desperately calamitous state of affairs unless supported immediately. A local militia, as I have repeatedly and plainly stated, cannot be trusted. Please send reinforcements urgently." Send also to Chief Hone Heke: "The flagstaff will be defended, and severe loss of life will certainly be the consequence of any further attack." Captain Maynard, you and your men will garrison the town. I suggest that the *Hazard*'s marines should cover the jetty, in case the town needs to be evacuated at short notice.'

'I'm sure that course will not be necessary, sir,' said Maynard.

'You can rely on us, sir!' added Lieutenant Randall brightly.

Exhilaration about the upcoming skirmish clashed with self-accusation in FitzRoy's head, as the knowledge that he might be about to risk men's lives in combat encroached at speed. He felt strange – as if a story was unfolding that was controlled not by him but by destiny.

'Thank you, Mr Maynard, Mr Randall,' was all he could manage.

With Waka Nene gone to rally the loyal tribes, FitzRoy sat alone the cabin allocated to him in HMS *Hazard*. His mind pulsed with activity, the various options open to him dividing, subdividing and rejoining each other once more like a river delta in flood. Andrew Sinclair brought the news that while Maynard's men had been gathering material to build their defensive structures, one of Hone Heke's raiding parties had cut down the flagstaff for a third time, iron cladding and all. The die, it appeared, was cast. FitzRoy, thought Sinclair, had a feverish appearance.

'Give the order that the flagstaff is to be erected once more.'

'For a fourth time, sir?'

'For a fourth time, Mr Sinclair.'

The young surgeon looked puzzled. 'Surely it is academic now, sir? Should not the men concentrate upon building up their defences?'

There are patterns to be followed, realized FitzRoy, *rituals to be observed. Sinclair cannot see this.* He shut his eyes, and suddenly he could see everything more clearly still. 'Give the order, Mr Sinclair. The flagstaff must stand. For it points our way to heaven.'

Sinclair gave him an odd look, and left the cabin.

FitzRoy settled back in his cot, if not contentedly then sure, at least, that he was doing the right thing. A wonderful conviction was growing inside him, that their mission here was somehow aligned with the universe and with God's will, that all these things shared the same grain. There was no point in resisting the natural course of events, as laid down by the Lord. It was a simple matter of following His purpose, and any kinks, any bends in their path would surely straighten themselves out. The forthcoming battle, all their destinies, even the very bedrock of New Zealand itself, all would reshape themselves in His image, smoothing their way forward. His way, it seemed, was clear.

It is, of course, well-nigh impossible to defend a town with fifty men, even a town of no more than a few hundred souls. For all his inexperience, Captain Maynard knew this; he concentrated his efforts upon fortifying the stockade that doubled as Kororareka's powder magazine, which he had placed under his own command, and upon building a musket-proof blockhouse on Flagstaff Hill, to be commanded by Lieutenant Randall. Captain Hazlewood and the small marine detachment of HMS *Hazard* would hold the jetty, as FitzRoy had determined, backed up by their brig's sparse and ancient muster of cannon. The hope was that this fortified triangle, each of its points within musket-range of the other, would deter the enemy from making an attack on the centre of the town. Mere lip service was paid to FitzRoy's bizarre order to waste their time rebuilding the flagstaff: it was hoisted to the vertical and clumsily roped to its own stump in an operation lasting no more than five minutes. Hone Heke was their priority now and it was the intention of the 80th Regiment, were he to launch an attack, to give him a bloody nose.

The New Zealanders, of course, waited until nightfall. In the dusk, the defenders could see rustlings and scurryings in the deep ferns at the edge of town. They did not fire their muskets: they had orders not to waste their ammunition. Nor were the natives likely to fire back yet. They were heavily armed, of course, for the Europeans had been eager to sell them munitions aplenty at inflated prices, but they had a more potent weapon at their disposal: fire. Kororareka was an entirely wooden town. When darkness fell, the *pakeha* would be burned out of their settlement.

The first flames appeared on the eastern side of town at about nine o'clock, licking at the rough boards of the settlers' hovels and quickly gathering pace, until towers of orange flame and fountains of sparks soared like fireworks into the night sky. Some of the attackers were visible now, their streaming hair caught in momentary silhouette against the conflagration. The terrified occupants were fleeing into the street, but the natives were not cutting them down with their muskets, which would have been the easiest of tasks. Instead, incredibly, they appeared to be dancing: drawn up in formation, yelling and chanting in rehearsed unison, their guns and tomahawks raised above their heads, their squat muscular limbs bound with red scarves and gleaming threateningly in the firelight. Their dance was not, in itself, worrying, but the sheer numbers involved were. Hone Heke had obviously garnered more native support than had been realized. The battle for the hearts and minds of the local population had clearly been lost. There were literally hundreds of attackers.

From his vantage-point among the marines guarding the jetty, FitzRoy could see the inhabitants streaming out of their houses in increasing numbers, abandoning their possessions, rushing pell-mell towards the strand. Besides the *Hazard*, there were two other ships in the bay that might provide refuge – the *St Louis*, an American corvette, and the *Matilda*, a whaler – and a flotilla of small boats could be seen putting to sea, their gasping occupants rowing for their lives as they strove towards safety. The flames were taking hold of main street now, devouring the buildings, columns of smoke winding powerfully about each other in their eagerness to choke the life out of anything that moved. Kororareka was proving to be little more than a tinderbox. Flagstaff Hill and the stockade might theoretically have been in line of sight of the jetty, but there was nothing to be glimpsed now beyond jumping flames, frantic sparks and swirling smoke-funnels. Any hope of further communication between the three redoubts was a forlorn one. Then the shooting started: fervent, intense shooting, from the base of Flagstaff Hill and from the buildings around the stockade, coming in short, impassioned bursts. The men of the 80th were blazing away into the darkness. All the marines from the *Hazard* could do was to sit tight and pray.

Entranced by the sheer extravagance of it all, FitzRoy had the exhilarating sensation that he was falling, the ground rushing up to meet him, except that it never arrived. Suspended there, he felt suddenly moved by the beauty of the spectacle, and filled with gratitude that God had chosen him to be at the heart of it. The others around him, he knew, saw only chaos and pandemonium, but he could discern a pattern, a kind of divine geometry. The resplendent illuminations and thunderous reverberations had built into a concerto in his head, his every sense crackling in wonderment and delight. The Lord had put Handel to shame.

The busy detonations of musket fire from over on Flagstaff Hill were receding now, a grand percussive movement coming to an end. Before long only individual reports could be heard, an isolated shot here and there, until the guns in that direction were finally stilled. Dimly, through the onrushing barrage of stimuli that whirled and danced past his senses, FitzRoy realized that young Lieutenant Randall and his men must be dead, that the Lord had carried them forward to a better place, to the wondrous fulfilment of His majestic purpose. But the firing from the stockade was still thick and angry, the rough staccato bark of the guns like dogs fighting in the night, and FitzRoy's heightened attentions were at once diverted.

Captain Maynard and the soldiers of the 80th were putting up a terrifically brave fight for men who had never seen action before. But they were defending a wooden stockade, in the midst of a wooden settlement that was succumbing at speed to ravenous flames and, to make matters worse, they were literally sitting atop Kororareka's rather substantial powder magazine. The gunfire from that quarter never once abated, to their credit; but then, with a mighty whoosh of light, and an earsplitting eruption of sound that could be heard across the entire Northland, God took Captain Maynard to His bosom as well, and all his men, and many of the native attackers with them. The blast illuminated the ships in the bay, lighting them a lurid orange like a Regent's Park diorama of the Great War, and almost blew Captain Hazlewood and his marines off their feet. FitzRoy wondered for a moment whether the Day of Judgement had finally arrived, and whether there would be trumpets. All around him were expressions of unadulterated horror, but he knew, if the frightened marines did not, that theirs was the chosen path, the one true way forward.

Dark shapes were appearing from the town now, running forward in waves, crouching and emptying their muskets. The marines at the jetty were returning fire. Captain Hazlewood shouted to the *Hazard* for boats, to commence a general evacuation; but as he got to his feet to signal to his men on the brig's deck, a ball hit him in the throat, and he subsided at FitzRoy's feet with a confused gurgle. Mr Williams, who was crouched next to FitzRoy, was grabbing at his sleeve, trying to impress upon him the precarious nature of their position, and their urgent need to get to the boats. This was puzzling: surely he, as a man of God, should have been capable of some deeper understanding? The *Hazard*'s guns had opened up, their sporadic *basso profondo* providing a counterpoint to the staccato crack of the marines' muskets, and the rattle of answering fire from the town. Whatever it was that Williams was saying now, his words were becoming lost, each one slipping soundlessly from his open mouth and flitting off to join the whirling symphony of noise. The man seemed to be in a state of entirely unmerited panic. The *Hazard*'s cutter had managed to row within yelling distance of the jetty, but most of the men at the oars had been shot, and it was bobbing stupidly in the water, about thirty yards out. Some of the marines on the jetty were ditching their muskets, their powder horns, their wad-cutters, rammers and all the other paraphernalia of the modern infantryman, and were making a swim for it.

'Captain FitzRoy! We must leave!' screamed Williams into his face, from just a few inches away.

Really, the man seemed to be incredibly agitated about something. There seemed to be some sort of problem. Where was Sinclair? Sinclair would know what to do. Perhaps it was time, at last, for all of them to take their places at the Lord's side. Or perhaps the Lord would come to them. Yes, that was it. The Lord would come to them.

As if on cue, there was a blinding white flash, and an obliterating roar that seemed to come from far out to sea. An instant later, a mighty crash rent Kororareka, shaking the ground and throwing up huge explosions of sparks and flame. A second colossal thunderclap followed, and after that, further dazzling pyrotechnics from what little remained of the town. FitzRoy thought that the heavens had literally parted, but then, in the light from the scorching flames sweeping through the blazing settlement, all of them managed to locate the source of the sound. There, out in the bay, as stately and disdainful as a swan, stood a mighty British ship-of-the-line, her huge guns effortlessly pulverizing the town and its new masters alike; what looked like a thousand red-jacketed troops were crowded at her rail, ready to disembark. Williams was on his knees now, shuddering and shaking with relief, giving repeated and strident thanks to God for their deliverance. How curious, thought FitzRoy, that he uses the medium of speech to address the Lord, that he cannot simply *feel* His presence.

The War of the Flagstaff had ended almost as suddenly as it had begun. The remaining New Zealanders, who had no answer to the overwhelming firepower of the British naval barrage, were fleeing into the hills in disarray. Within a quarter-hour, boatloads of uniformed troops had swarmed over the beach and taken control of the blackened ruins of Kororareka. As smoke drifted like incense across the placid obsidian waters, a graceful white whaleboat was seen to detach itself from the side of the mother ship and make pale, elegant progress to the jutting tip of the Kororareka jetty. A young officer stepped out, emerging through the ivory haze as if from the billowing clouds of heaven. He walked slowly towards them, quiet assurance and confidence informing his every step. FitzRoy realized then that he was staring into a looking-glass: that this figure was none other than himself, aged about thirty. This other FitzRoy even wore an identical governor's uniform. The Lord had reached back in time, had summoned a younger FitzRoy from the past – or an alternative FitzRoy, perhaps, whose life had taken different twists and turns – and had fetched him here, to deliver them all from evil. Truly, God's ways defied rational explanation. Lost in awe and wonder, he rose to his feet, and the two FitzRoys walked towards each other along the little wooden jetty, before halting, no more than a foot apart, at its centre. Only then did he realize that this other FitzRoy was not himself at all, but was somebody else, somebody entirely different.

'You are the reinforcements? From New South Wales?' gasped Williams. His cassock was covered with blood and pieces of torn flesh – not his own but the unfortunate Captain Hazlewood's – and he was trying frantically to wipe it off as he spoke.

'New South Wales? No. We come directly from Britain. Captain Grey, at your service. We arrived at Auckland just after you left. We were apprised of your situation and made our way straight here. We have arrived with not a moment to spare, it would appear.'

'Lord be praised,' groaned Williams, who was sweating profusely with relief. 'You have saved all our lives. I am the Reverend William Williams. This is Governor FitzRoy.'

'You are FitzRoy?' The newcomer turned his cool, detached gaze on the man at Williams's side. Captain Grey's every movement, his every word, was crafted with elegant precision, his manner reassuringly languid. He ran a swift, professional eye over FitzRoy's scuffed, blood-splattered uniform. 'It is with the greatest regret, sir, that I must inform you that you are to be relieved as governor of New Zealand forthwith, and replaced by myself, by order of Her Majesty Queen Victoria, and Lord Stanley, secretary of state for colonial affairs. I'm sorry, FitzRoy.'

'Replaced? But what . . . ?'

The words were not FitzRoy's, but Williams's. If the Lord had sent an emissary to assume command, thought FitzRoy, he could give no complaint. Captain Grey held forth an official-looking letter.

Williams took it and read it out, for he sensed that FitzRoy was in no state to do so. Most of it consisted of platitudinous tributes to the outgoing governor. '"Public spirit and disinterestedness . . . arduous duty . . . personal sacrifices so liberally made . . . most implicit reliance on your character . . . zeal for the Queen's service . . ."'

Williams looked up in bewilderment. Captain Grey gestured to the official documents attached to the letter. 'There was a House of Commons Select Committee on New Zealand, chaired by Lord Howick.'

'Lord Howick? But he's . . .'

'It received numerous submissions from the New Zealand Company regarding Governor FitzRoy's supposed "deficiencies". It was felt by the committee that the strength and persistence of press criticism would not have been such without some basis in truth. Furthermore, the dismissal of a loyal and hardworking public servant in Lieutenant Willoughby Shortland, the failure to apprehend the perpetrators of the Wairau massacre, the failure to raise a local militia and the issuing of paper money without prior permission were all factors that could not be overlooked. I fear that Lord Stanley was left with no choice. The summary of the committee's report is attached.'

With shaking hands, Williams read the committee's conclusions by the flickering firelight. '"Governor FitzRoy's zeal, however laudable, for the welfare of the aborigines, has rather outrun discretion ... The uncivilized inhabitants of any country have but a qualified dominion over it ... The acknowledgement by the Governor of a right of property on behalf of the Natives was not essential to the true construction of the Treaty of Waitangi, and was an error which has been productive of very injurious consequences ... The New Zealand Company has a right to expect to be put in possession by the Government, with the least possible delay, of the number of acres awarded to it ... The principles in which the New Zealand Company has acted in making reserves for the Natives, with a view to their ultimate as well as present welfare, and in making suitable provision for spiritual and educational purposes, are sound and judicious, tending to the benefit of all classes ..."'

Williams lowered the paper in outrage. 'But what shall happen to the New Zealanders?' he demanded, although he already knew the answer.

'I have over a thousand marines at my disposal, with more to follow. The New Zealanders are to be removed from the land. Any who resist, including the perpetrators of the massacre at Wairau, are to be arrested as criminals and hanged. I am afraid, gentlemen, that the due process of law must be followed. It is the mark of a civilized nation. Now, if you will excuse me, I have a country to take charge of.'

Grey walked on up the jetty, and FitzRoy wondered at the mellifluous simplicity of his movements. Truly, he thought, the Lord's emissary wore all the wisdom and majesty of God's kingdom, wrapped about him like a heavenly cloak.

Chapter Thirty-two

Down House, Downe, Kent,
27 February 1851

'Pappy! Pappy! Please can we go bug-hunting? I want to go bug-hunting *ever so*!'

George Darwin crashed the study door open so hard, it nearly jumped off its hinges. Behind his impish grin his elder sister Annie stood reproving in the doorway, her earnest round face and podgy cheeks full of precocious concern for her father.

'Leave him *alone*, Georgie. Pappy is working.'

Ever since the Darwins' eldest child, Willy, had been packed off to board with a private tutor as a precursor to his schooling, Annie had taken the lead among her siblings.

'Don't worry, Annie,' her father reassured her. 'It's almost midday.'

The children had been forbidden to enter the study before twelve, although with the racket they made in the hallway outside, it was a somewhat pointless stipulation.

'It's *almost* midday, but it's not *actually* midday, and Georgie is old enough to know the difference. I think he does it on purpose.'

She crossed the study, climbed on to her father's lap and

kissed him. 'Are you feeling better today, Pappy?'

'Yes, thank you, my dear,' he lied. He had counted no fewer than seven nasty boils on his rear that very morning. He had also to contend with dyspepsia and constipation, headaches, constant high temperatures and ceaseless vomiting. This plague had been visited upon him daily for some sixteen years now. On bad days, even his vision and hearing were impaired; on good days, he felt almost normal. Today was somewhere in between.

'Please—can—we—go—bug-hunting?' demanded George, although the end of the question became a surprised squeal as Etty, who was two years older than he, suddenly lifted him up and dumped him unceremoniously on to the 'microscope chair', the small black wheeled stool their father used when peering at his specimens. It was already battered and scuffed from all the times it had been kidnapped and removed to the drawing room, where it would be punted up and down with one or more tiny riders on board. Etty propelled George head first into the old green sofa: many small children would have seized such an excellent opportunity for a good yell, but George was more or less indestructible.

'Yes, we can go bug-hunting,' conceded their father. 'If – and only if – all of you leave my study at *once*. Coats on, and meet by the mulberry tree outside the nursery window in five minutes.'

With excited shouts the children charged out to locate their coats and comforters, scooping up little moon-faced Bessy, who had wandered confusedly through the doorway at that moment. Darwin put down his pen, and replaced the cap on the inkpot: he would finish his letter to Huxley later. He was preparing the ground for the publication of his forthcoming work on barnacles, writing to the likes of Hooker and Huxley to ensure that his book would receive good reviews from his friends and associates.

A bored-looking donkey was pulling an elderly mowing machine across the lawn as the children assembled, breath condensing with excitement, and set off eagerly through the yew trees. George made 'bug-hunting' sound far more thrilling than it was: in fact, they took the same walk every day at midday, down through the greenhouses and allotments to the little wood at the far end of the Darwins' eighteen acres. There ran the 'sand walk', a little circuit that they followed again and again, their father knocking over a stone with his iron-shod stick to count each revolution. The ritual never seemed to lose its fascination for the younger Darwins, however many times they followed it. They marched joyously down the cinder path, trailing smaller siblings (who never lasted the course), curious ponies, pet dogs, and – clutching baby Leonard – Miss Thorley, the children's governess, whose job it was to round up any stragglers and see them home safely.

Annie went ahead, pirouetting in front of her father. 'Look at me, Pappy!'

'A most beautiful dance, my dear.'

'Huh!' snorted George, derisively. 'Look at *me*, Pappy!' So saying, he dived head first into a gap in the shrubbery, quickly burrowing out of sight.

'Well hidden, Georgie! Most impressive.'

That is behaviourally analogous to young pigs hiding themselves, thought Darwin, and made a mental note to investigate the subject further. *It surely represents the hereditary remains of our savage state.*

The children charged this way and that, running ahead and doubling back, collecting 'specimens' for him from his own garden, which he had to pretend to find deeply impressive. Physically, he struggled to keep up. His forty-second birthday was not long past, but it might as well have been his seventieth, for all the strength he could bring to bear on a simple walk. He hobbled painfully through the greenhouses, leaning heavily on his walking-stick with every step.

'Pappy, Annie's brought you a present!' confessed Etty, no longer able to bear the burden of confidentiality.

'That was supposed to be a *secret*!' said Annie, indignantly. 'You've *spoiled* it now.'

'Well, I have no idea what the present is,' soothed Darwin, 'so I don't think the secret is spoiled at all. Am I allowed to know it?'

'I brought you out some snuff,' confessed Annie. 'From the silver box in the hall.'

Darwin was slightly taken aback.

'I know you like to sniff it every five minutes. But you can't have any when you're out walking, so I brought some with me.' She carefully unwrapped a little paper package.

'Every five minutes? Surely not!' he protested, embarrassed for himself if no one else.

'I listen out for you when we are in the nursery,' his daughter confided. 'I can hear the clink of the lid, so I always know when you are there.'

'Well, that is extremely kind and considerate of you, my dear,' he said, taking an extravagant sniff for her benefit.

There was a loud yell, indicating that George had accidentally run over little Frank. Miss Thorley, blunt-faced and carrying an air of worry like an old suitcase, scurried to console the child.

'*I*'ve brought you a present too,' said George defiantly, holding up the mangled remains of a small beetle.

Annie held her father's hand all the way round the sand walk.

The gong in the hall summoned Darwin and his wife to the dining room at one o'clock. They took dinner so late now – at six, according to the current fashion – that it was necessary for them to take luncheon in the middle of the day to avoid going hungry. Two liveried manservants served their food, the whole operation masterminded by Parslow, the butler.

'I see the kids has been gettin' theyselves dirty again, sir,' grumbled Parslow. 'Twenty pairs of little shoes there were to clean yesterday.'

'I'm sure you'll manage,' said Darwin absently. He regarded Parslow as even more hopeless than Covington, who had emigrated to Australia with Harriet the tortoise some years back; but the butler was at least prepared to lose to his master at billiards, on those rare occasions when the billiard-table was not covered in bird and rabbit skulls.

'Did you have a good morning's work, Mr Darwin?' enquired his wife, politely.

She was a good-natured soul to take an interest, he thought; the gold-rimmed spectacles perched on the end of her nose even imparted an academic air, although he knew he would have to keep his remarks general, were she to have any hope of understanding them.

'Yes, thank you, Mrs Darwin. I have been revising the chapter on semi-hermaphroditic barnacles. They are the most remarkable creatures. There is a tiny male inside the same shell as the female; a clue, perhaps, to the origin of the separate sexes.'

'I hope, Mr Darwin, that your scientific habit of believing nothing until it is proved shall not influence your mind to distrust those things which *cannot* be proved, and are above our comprehension.'

He smiled. 'I do believe, my dear, that you are accusing me of casting off God's gifts!'

'Of course not, my dear. But I am aware that you have honest and conscientious doubts, which cannot in themselves be a sin. Yet I cannot help thinking that if you were only to stop questioning, you might find yourself able to believe.'

'It is only through questioning that I know what to believe and what not to believe.'

'As long as you do not reject the prospect of salvation, for that might cause the most terrible consequences on the Day of Judgement. It is the day when I know I shall see my dear sister Fanny once more. I should be most unhappy if I thought that we should be parted on the same day. I so want us to belong to each other for ever.'

His wife's earnest expression, full of concern, the long nut-brown hair looped around the perfect oval of her face, her quiet but steadfast devotion, all these put him comfortingly in mind of his three sisters. He attempted to share this feeling of reassurance with her. 'My dearest, whatever it takes to spend eternity with you, be assured that I shall do it.'

'I *am* glad. I would not want the Lord to leave behind a soul so full of virtues.'

'The origin of life may be a mystery to me, my dear, but I know that it is one of the Lord's mysteries. I seek no more than to interpret His wisdom.'

'The origin of life is not *entirely* a mystery, Mr Darwin,' she said flirtatiously, patting the lilac muslin that stretched over her bulging belly. She was pregnant again, and eight months gone.

'More egg, sir?' said Parslow, gloomily.

After luncheon Darwin retired to the dark womb of his study, to take a cup of tea from his little pewter teapot and resume his correspondence. There were only five daily postal deliveries in Downe – nothing like the twelve in central London – but they brought sufficient letters to keep him occupied for several hours a day. Each letter brought facts and observations from a variety of correspondents, each fact a grain of sand in the mighty edifice he was slowly constructing. Gradually, his theory of natural selection was taking shape.

As was usual, he could only work at his desk for the first twenty minutes or so after luncheon. Then, in keeping with his daily ritual, he hobbled over to the curtained-off privy that occupied one corner of the room, dropped his trousers and sat down. The terrible, odious flatulence that followed every meal invariably began to make itself known around this time, peaking in a cacophony of burps and rumbles after an hour or so. Then, as the stabbing pains built to a crescendo, he would sink to his knees and the vomiting would begin. Clutching the rim of his little hip-bath for support, he would void his stomach just as he had once done on the *Beagle*, the sickly acid taste that flooded his mouth seemingly more revolting by the day. He hoped and pretended that his family could not hear him, but he knew in his heart that they surely could.

When the relentless waves of attacks had finally receded, he made himself presentable and left the study. Annie was waiting for him in the corridor, concerned incomprehension in her big, confused eyes. She moved towards him, put her girlish arms about his waist and held him tight.

Somewhere down in Charles Darwin's soul, a little voice offered a ludicrous but frightening suggestion: one that, for all the regularity with which he dismissed it, still persisted in returning. *Could this illness*, he wondered, *possibly – just possibly – be a punishment for my presumption from the Almighty?*

Darwin was wakened at five in the morning by Parslow, already dressed in his livery, ready with the towels and the bucket of iced water. At first his brain was befuddled by the strange surroundings: this was not his bedroom. Then he remembered. He was not at Down House. He was at Malvern, with Parslow. He could be allowed no further time to grapple with the question of his whereabouts. Speed was of the essence. He climbed out of bed and stripped naked, his mottled white body shaking in the winter cold. Parslow set to work with what seemed like undue relish, flaying his master with the soaking towels until his flesh resembled a lobster's. Then, when the servant had completed his assault, he lit the spirit lamp, and scorched his master's skin until it streamed with perspiration. After Darwin had drunk the tumbler of iced water provided, the compress of soaked and freezing linen was placed in his underwear, his mackintosh was buttoned over the top, and he and Parslow set out for their pre-dawn route march. At least, he felt that he was the one doing the marching: Parslow seemed to trail lugubriously at his side without ever slipping behind, a suspiciously impassive expression masking the man's feelings. Was that pleasure he saw lurking there for a moment?

Breakfast was the same every day: fresh meat on toast, with beef tea. No vegetables, bacon, butter, sugar, milk or spices of any kind were to soil the purity of his diet. Only meat could ensure the inner cleanliness that Dr Gully demanded of his patients. Gully it was who had invented the water cure, and a host of prestigious clients had testified to its effectiveness. The Carlyles had recommended it to Darwin personally; Tennyson, Dickens and Wilkie Collins were among those who had made the pilgrimage to Malvern.

Dr Gully, who rose considerably later than his patients, came to see Darwin after breakfast, just as his charge was undergoing the agonizing ritual of having his feet immersed in a tub of iced water seasoned with a little mustard powder. The doctor cut a mightily impressive figure, bespectacled, portly and confident, with a lion's mane of bronzed hair poised rigid but windswept above the upper slopes of his huge brow. He made Darwin, who was a big man, feel rather small.

'And how are we today?' enquired Gully, grandly.

'Improving, I feel,' ventured Darwin. 'Certainly the piles and skin eruptions have lessened, although I still have occasional tremblings and feelings of faintness. But my stomach actually seems to have improved since I stopped taking the blue pills.'

'That is hardly surprising. One can have too much mercurous oxide.'

'Dr Holland said I should take a purgative every day. He said that my stomach was being affected by toxicity of the blood – a kind of suppressed gout.'

'Far be it from me to question the expertise of your Dr Holland,' tutted Gully with a smile of pity, 'but here at Malvern we follow the most advanced regimens known to medical science. What you are suffering from, my dear fellow, is nervous dyspepsia, caused by badly balanced digestive organs irritating the brain and spinal cord. The effect upon the stomach is purely secondary, the result of a congestion of blood in the ganglionic nerves which surround it. My water cure will provide a counteraction – an external friction to counter the internal friction, thereby balancing the inner and outer pressures upon your body. We shall have you cured in no time.'

In the years since returning to England Darwin had tried arsenic, amyl nitrite, bismuth, electric chains, spinal anaesthesis, morphia pills, quinine and tartar emetic ointment in an effort to cure his persistent ailments. Dr Gully's water cure was just the latest in a long list but, somehow, he had a feeling in his gut that the swaggering doctor might finally be the man to crack the mystery.

'Time for the ice-water douche,' boomed Gully, and even as the words issued from his lips, Parslow was half-way up the waiting stepladder, eagerly clutching the bucket of iced water that he would soon upend over his master's cranium.

Annie had been sitting by the fireside, threading ribbons and sewing clothes for her dolls – her 'treasures', as she liked to call them – when she had quite suddenly keeled over. At first her parents had thought her to be play-acting, but there was no mistaking the clammy sheen of sweat upon their daughter's brow. She had been put to bed, and Dr Holland had been called. He had diagnosed bilious fever, of a typhoid character, and had prescribed an ordinary physic of camphor and ammonia. But Darwin no longer trusted Dr Holland: before the night was out, he and his wife had decided that, whatever the risks of the journey, Annie must be fetched to Malvern, and given over to the care of Dr Gully.

The following morning Darwin had set out at dawn, together with Brodie (the children's nurse), Miss Thorley the governess, Annie all wrapped in blankets, and little Etty, to keep her sister company. They took the Great Western Coach, for there was no train to Malvern, an exhausting, clattering journey through rolling meadows. Spring budded the fields, which would have made them feel optimistic, had not Annie cried all the way. Upon arrival, they installed themselves in lodgings at Montreal House, and Dr Gully was duly summoned. His diagnosis was simple but reassuring: just like her father, Annie's blood had become congested. Only a water cure would show improvement.

So began the familiar, alternating routine of icy beatings and showerings, followed by scorchings from the spirit lamp, the exhausted and bewildered child made to stand naked and shivering while an equally bewildered Brodie tipped buckets of near-freezing water over her head. What use was it, Darwin asked himself, trying to explain the workings of science to a servant or a little child? Annie's diet was to be even more restricted than his own: only brandy and gruel were to pass her lips. Somehow, though, the treatment that had so heartened her father, the treatment he was very nearly absolutely sure had produced an improvement, lost its bracing allure when visited upon the defenceless child he so adored. He winced every time she winced, and shuddered every time she shuddered. What was worse, the treatment seemed to be having no beneficial effect – indeed, Annie seemed to be getting mysteriously weaker. Her temperature continued to rise; she regularly vomited up the brandy-and-gruel mixture; and, when that had been comprehensively regurgitated, she brought up the bright green contents of her gall bladder, in a series of shuddering spasms.

Please, God, Darwin prayed, *bring her back. Bring back my own dear Annie, with her dear affectionate radiant face.* But God did not seem to be listening. As the priory bells rang out for Easter Sunday, her bladder became paralysed, and a catheter had to be inserted. She struggled at first, but when it was done she graciously thanked the doctor in a tiny voice, and held her father's hand. She looked, he thought, like a dear wingless angel. Barely daring to turn his back on her for one instant, he composed a short letter to his wife.

I wish you could see her now. The perfection of gentleness, patience and gratitude – she is thankful 'til it is truly painful to hear her, the poor, dear little soul. God only knows what will become of her.

In the night she stopped vomiting, and flooded her little bed with diarrhoea, but she seemed more relaxed thereafter, and even tried to sing to her father. He kissed her and told her that he loved her, and inside he dared, just, to be optimistic; but Dr Gully came after breakfast and took him to one side, and admitted that her new-found relaxation probably meant only that she had given up the fight.

Gully was correct, at least in this respect. Violent bouts of repeated diarrhoea set in, Annie's strength weakening with every bowel movement. By afternoon she had lost consciousness, her pulse failing, her body wasted and unable even to empty itself any more. That night Darwin, Brodie and Miss Thorley kept a candlelit vigil, while Etty, who did not really understand what was happening, slept in the next room. Dawn broke unseasonably warm, with stormclouds brewing in the hills, and before long a series of momentous thunderclaps split the sky in two. It was Brodie who first realized that Annie was dead – Darwin probably knew, but refused to believe it – and went into hysterics, screaming like a wild creature, her primeval, lung-bursting yowls pouring forth as if they would never end. Miss Thorley fainted, and Etty appeared in the doorway, weeping with fear at the noise, while lightning bolts hurled themselves pitilessly down from the heavens. Darwin would normally have been quite cross to see the servants lose control of themselves in this manner; but he could not say anything, for he had been struck dumb with horror, and he wanted to die, there and then, just like his daughter, so that the unbearable, unimaginable pain would go away.

The Reverend George Packenham Despard picked up a hansom at the stand on Oxford Street and, after a wearisome queue for the Tyburn turnpike, took the Uxbridge Road heading westwards out of town. On his left, workmen had almost finished rebuilding the marble arch that had once stood opposite the King's Palace. On his right, opposite Kensington Palace and the gravel-pits, the new suburb of Bayswater, with its gleaming wrought-iron cathedral at Paddington Station, was half-way to completion. The houses were decent enough, elegant stucco-fronted terraces for gentlemen and their families, but everyone in London knew the stigma attached to living north of the park. What stigma, then, should be attached to living north of the park and a further two miles to the west? Bowling at speed down Notting Hill, he found Norland Square amid brick-kilns beside the main road, just a hundred yards short of the old plague-grave at Shepherds Bush. This FitzRoy fellow could not be doing very well for himself. All the ground-floor rooms around the square had semi-circular bay windows, which struck Despard as a rather *nouveau-riche* touch. He tugged the bell-pull, and presented his card to the housemaid. No butler, he noted. Presently, he was admitted to the drawing room.

Captain Robert FitzRoy proved to be a slender character with thinning hair, sombrely dressed and of middling height. His nose was sharp, his ears were too large and the bags beneath his eyes were grey with fatigue. But although he looked tired and drawn, Despard thought he could detect a certain wiry grace within.

'My dear sir, you must forgive me,' explained FitzRoy. 'I am afraid that I had forgotten our appointment. My wife has not been well this last day or so. I proffer you my most sincere apologies.'

'Not at all, sir. I am extremely sorry to hear of your wife's malaise. May I be so impolite as to enquire the nature and progress of her ailment?'

'It was a most sudden affliction. At first we thought she was taken bad in the breath. But Dr Locock fears that it may be the cholera – she is feverish and cannot keep down any liquids. Yet she is young and strong – she is not yet forty – so we are all hopeful.'

'I shall pray for her myself.'

Even though he was merely a former schoolmaster, Despard felt that the taking of holy orders surely lent his prayers extra impetus, extra vigour and moral ascendancy when it came to catching the ear of the Lord.

'You oblige us both with your kindness.'

'Cholera is become the plague of our times. It is curious, is it not, that ever since the cesspits were closed over, and sewers fed directly into the river, measures taken to curb the influence of dangerous miasmas in our midst, the disease seems to have taken an even firmer hold than before?'

'Curious indeed.'

FitzRoy kept his responses to a minimum. Really, Despard's visit was quite dreadfully timed. He had asked the governess to take the children on a long day's outing, so as to leave him alone to tend his beloved Mary; then the housemaid had come to fetch him away from her sickbed. But as the man had an appointment, and had come all this way, there was really nothing FitzRoy could do but to honour his obligations. There was no doubting that Despard's Christian concern was genuine; but FitzRoy could discern something else there – an ill-concealed air of self-satisfaction regarding the progress of his own life and fortunes. Despard had a row of protruding upper teeth, which seemed to be attempting to smile delight-edly, while the lower set did its best to hold them back.

'You must forgive me, Mr Despard, but my time must be brief, of necessity. How may I help you?'

'Of course, of course. You are aware, I take it, of the fate of Mr Allen Gardiner?'

'I read in the newspapers that the bodies had been found. Mr Gardiner came to visit me when I was the Member of Parliament for Durham.'

'It is a tragic tale, Captain FitzRoy, but one to stir the heart of any God-fearing man. If you will permit me ... ?' With an air of sly showmanship, Despard produced a salt-stained, leatherbound notebook from within his coat.

'The journal of Allen Gardiner,' he breathed, reverentially opening the cover. 'They set sail on the *Ocean Queen*, bound from Liverpool to San Francisco, which landed the seven men and their two schooners in Banner Roads, Tierra del Fuego. Almost immediately, by the Lord's grace, they found near

Picton Island a snug and beautiful cove, smooth as a mirror, with green wooded slopes and copses of trees about its margin. Tragically, the fates were to prove unkind. A storm blew up and destroyed their schooners, which they had not thought to anchor. It was subsequently discovered that they had unfortunately left all the gunpowder for their muskets in the *Ocean Queen*, so they could not hunt for food. All their belongings were stolen by natives during the night. They built a little hermitage in a nearby cave, using the wreckwood from the schooners, and lit a fire to warm themselves; but tragically the walls of the hermitage itself were caught by the flames and burned to the ground. All setbacks, I am sure you will agree, that nobody could have foreseen.'

'Er ... quite.' FitzRoy could hardly believe what he was hearing.

'But here is the amazing part, Captain FitzRoy. The day after the fire they returned to the cave, to discover that a large rock had dislodged itself from the cavern roof and had crashed to the ground exactly where Mr Gardiner had intended to sleep. The fire was a miracle – a sign from the Lord! Of course, their regret was immediately exchanged for a humbling sense of the compassion of the Almighty, in so warning them from such danger.'

'I have no doubt of it,' said FitzRoy, drily.

'The next day they went fishing, but their net was torn to shreds by ice. Just listen to what Mr Gardiner wrote in his journal, and one cannot fail to be touched by his honest and simple piety: "Thus the Lord has seen fit to render another means abortive, and doubtless to make His power more apparent, and to show that all our help is to come immediately from Him."'

'What happened to them?' asked FitzRoy, as if the answer were not self-evident.

'They starved to death. But with all their hardships and privations, not one word of complaint appears to have been uttered. I am proud to say that they placed their full reliance on the mercies of Him whom they desired to serve. Listen to what Dr Williams had to say as he lay dying: "I am happy day and night . . . asleep or awake, hour by hour, I am happy beyond the poor compass of language to tell." And hear what Mr Gardiner himself wrote, upon his own deathbed: "The Lord in His providence has seen fit to bring us very low, but all is in infinite wisdom, mercy and love. The Lord is very pitiful and of tender compassion. When His set time is fully come, He will either remove us to His eternal Kingdom, or supply our languishing bodies with food convenient for us. Should it be His will that none of our mission should survive, would that He will raise up other labourers, who may convey the saving truths of the Gospel to the poor blind heathen around us."'

Despard shut the book. 'They have gone away,' he said simply, 'to regions of everlasting bliss.'

FitzRoy was stunned. He had known tough sealers, shipwrecked on the Fuegian coastline, survive for years on end by clubbing seals and penguins, catching fish, chewing tree-fungus or foraging for birds' eggs. Gardiner and his men appeared to have welcomed death with a passive and fanatical ecstasy, as if they were perversely determined to die. The man had quite clearly been insane.

Mr Despard smiled beatifically, his lower jaw having finally given up the ghost. 'Allen Gardiner has spoken to us all, and spoken for us all, in death. The Lord has heard his cry, and other labourers have come forward by the score to take his place. Since his death, the society's meetings and rallies have been packed. Well-wishers have donated thousands of pounds to build a new vessel, a full-sized vessel this time, to be named the *Allen Gardiner*. The Patagonian Missionary Society has hired a professional captain, one William Parker Snow –'

'I know Captain Snow. He is a good man.'

'– to sail the vessel on a return journey to Tierra del Fuego. This time we will make contact with the savage James Button, and ultimately we will build a Christian society, there in the harsh south, that will be the envy of the God-fearing world.

Imagine it, Captain FitzRoy! A place of gardens and farms and industrious villages, where the church-going bell may awaken the silent forests. Round its cheerful hearth and kind teachers, the Sunday school may assemble the now joyless children of Navarin Island. The mariner may run his battered ship into Lennox harbour, and leave her to the care of Fuegian caulkers and carpenters; and after rambling through the streets of a thriving seaport town, he may turn aside to read the papers in the Gardiner Institution, or may step into the week-evening service in the Richard Williams Chapel.'

Despard's face glowed with pious excitement. 'Have you seen our society's magazine, Captain FitzRoy? It is called the *Voice of Pity*.'

He handed FitzRoy a coloured pamphlet, already opened at a poem entitled 'Plea for Patagonia':

> *Weep! Weep for Patagonia!*
> *In darkness, oh! how deep,*
> *Her heathen children spend their days;*
> *Ah, who can choose but weep?*
> *The tidings of a saviour's love*
> *Are all unheeded there,*
> *And precious souls are perishing*
> *In blackness of despair.*

Underneath was the blunt appeal for hard cash:

> *We want £2300. We want it at once! Souls are in misery; sinners are dying; hell is filling; Satan triumphs! Give pounds if you can; give shillings if you cannot give pounds; give pence if you cannot give shillings; give a postage stamp if you cannot give pence!*

Despard took back the magazine. 'The Patagonian Missionary Society is on the march, Captain FitzRoy, and nothing can stop us. Even as we speak, good Christian ladies from Maidstone to Dundee are knitting dresses, to clothe the base nakedness of the savages.'

'What do you want from me?'

I have no money left to give, thought FitzRoy. *My wife's father pays for this house.* Instantly he regretted his self-centred thoughts.

'Only your blessing.' Despard smiled. 'I believe that you know a Captain Sulivan, the representative of Her Majesty's Navy in the Falkland Islands?'

'Of course. He was my friend and lieutenant.'

'Allen Gardiner wrote to Captain Sulivan prior to his departure, requesting that he sail across to Tierra del Fuego after a month or two to check on the progress of the mission. Regrettably, Captain Sulivan did not receive the letter until it was too late. HMS *Dido* had already found the bodies before the letter even reached the Falkland Islands. Captain Sulivan, I'm afraid, quite unnecessarily blames himself for the deaths of Allen Gardiner and his comrades.'

Quite unnecessarily indeed, thought FitzRoy.

'The captain has offered the Patagonian Missionary Society ten per cent of his salary in perpetuity – a most generous gift – and has agreed to become an honorary member of our committee. But all this is contingent on the society receiving your blessing for its intended plan of action.'

'And what, might I ask, is the society's intended plan of action?'

'It is none other, Captain FitzRoy, than your own plan of action!' Despard bared his teeth exultantly, like a large carnivorous rodent. 'Rather than attempt to build a mission in Tierra del Fuego from scratch, we shall begin by removing carefully selected savages – led, hopefully, by your old acquaintance James Button – to a mission station on the Falkland Islands. There we shall civilize them, and instruct them through benign guidance in the ways of the Lord. Only then shall we return them to Tierra del Fuego, to plant the seeds of civilization and to found the city of Gardineropolis!'

There was silence in the fusty drawing room.

'Well? Do we have your blessing, Captain FitzRoy?'

FitzRoy hesitated. He had no enthusiasm for Despard's fantasy. When he was younger, perhaps, untouched by bitter wisdom, he might have embraced the sheer ambition of the idea. New Zealand had changed all that: perhaps it was truly impossible to attempt to civilize the heathen without bringing about his destruction in the process. That process was something he no longer wished to be part of. He saw now, in a flash, that Despard's grand scheme was to be planned and executed not so much to the greater glory of God as to the greater glory of the Reverend George Packenham Despard. And yet – how could he possibly refuse Sulivan? Even if Sulivan was wrong to blame himself for Gardiner's fate, what right had he to block the path his old shipmate had taken towards redemption? Reluctantly, he felt that he had no choice but to acquiesce.

'Very well, Mr Despard. It appears to me that your present plan offers a fairer prospect of success than many other missionary enterprises at their commencement, and that it would be difficult to suggest one less objectionable in the circumstances. I give you my assent.'

Despard stood up and pumped his hand delightedly, and as he did so, a terrible foreboding seized hold of all FitzRoy's senses, and caused the hairs on the back of his neck to stand on end.

'You won't regret this, Captain FitzRoy,' gushed Despard.

Mary FitzRoy died that night, towards three o'clock in the morning.

Her husband sat alone with her, his eyes rimmed with wet light, watching her life ebb to nothing, his children and servants scattered throughout the house, sleeping their undisturbed sleep of blissful ignorance.

Death came so quickly, he thought, *so cruelly*.

Even in the final ravages of cholera, his wife had lost none of the serenity that had marked her out in life: her pale, waxy beauty seemed to suit her in death as much as it had when living. Unable to speak, she had opened her dark eyes in her final moments, had fixed them upon his, and had fiercely grasped his hand. *I love you*, she had been trying to tell him.

And now she was gone, her soul uplifted to heaven.

How he wished that Despard had not chosen that day to turn up and steal some of his precious final moments alone with his wife; had not chosen that day to tell him the story of Allen Gardiner's futile, idiotic self-sacrifice. Was Gardiner in heaven? He supposed so. Had there been a purpose to Gardiner's death? It was hard to see it, unless that purpose was merely to galvanize others.

Now the Lord had taken his darling Mary from him. For what reason, he could not fathom; but there had to be a reason, he was sure of it. For without a reason, what point was there to her life, to his life, to anyone's life? He owed it to her own piety to believe. He owed it to her memory to defend the Holy Spirit against those who would deny the message of the Gospels, that man was created by God in His image and would find salvation in heaven. By defending the path to heaven, he would defend her place there, and would keep the route open for himself to rejoin her one day. He would fight for her, would protect and love and cherish her, every single day that remained of his life. That was the promise he made her, there and then by her deathbed.

'I love you too, Mary,' he told her silent, unheeding form, the tears streaming down his face. He had never addressed her as Mary before.

Then the tears turned to sobs, until his whole body was racked with them, his chest heaving until he thought it would burst. And he remembered her whirling beneath a golden chandelier, a blob of molten wax congealing against her white skin.

With summer gone, the Darwin family phaeton waited patiently at Sydenham station for the Croydon train, originating at London Bridge. Theirs was not the fastest of carriages, and its slow, elderly horses, chivvied on by their slow, elderly coachman, frequently took longer to cover the few miles back to Downe than the train had taken to steam down from London. It did not matter. FitzRoy was in no hurry. Another few minutes would make no difference. The phaeton jogged its way across bare, chalky fields, and trotted gently down damp, winding lanes, where dew-beaded spiders' webs clung to passing hedgerows, until it came at last to a rambling, ivy-covered parsonage concealed by trees. The walls were criss-crossed by trellises, as if the building were trying to cover its own modesty. A newly constructed earth bank hid the front of the house from the road. The phaeton crawled to a halt, and FitzRoy alighted. A gloomy butler came to the door. The man's hair, he noticed, was far too long. Nor did any of the maids seem to be wearing mob-caps. The philosopher, it seemed, was as sloppy as ever.

Darwin had watched FitzRoy arrive, in the mirror he had erected by his study window, which pointed up the drive so that he might screen unwelcome visitors. Now he stood up and hobbled out to greet his former friend. At close quarters, though, he halted again, shocked by what he saw. This was not the FitzRoy he had once known. Of course, there were the expected sartorial changes – the shapeless black clothes and sprouting side-whiskers that had become the benchmark of civilized men everywhere – but, far more dismayingly, FitzRoy looked crushed by his loss. This was a beaten FitzRoy, his face a sagging picture of defeat, barely recognizable as the dashing, tireless young captain who could once have endured any ordeal, however taxing, without showing the slightest sign of fatigue.

For his part, FitzRoy was equally surprised to see that the philosopher's beetling brows had now become mere foothills beneath a gleaming dome-shaped summit, as if his thick triangular side-whiskers had yanked down the roots of all the hair above; and surprised, too, to see the philosopher's once huge and athletic frame reduced prematurely to a shambling wreck, bent for support over a carved walking-stick.

They embraced wordlessly.

'My friend,' said FitzRoy, at last. 'I am sorry for your loss.'

'And I for yours,' said Darwin.

'I must thank you, too, for proposing me as a fellow of the Royal Society. I consider it to be the greatest of honours.'

'It was not merely I who proposed you – Beaufort was instrumental as well – but it was thoroughly well merited.'

'I cannot deny that it is a welcome relief, at last, to receive some recognition for one's efforts.'

'It was the least we could do.'

Darwin put a friendly hand low on FitzRoy's back. 'Come, come. You must meet Mrs Darwin and all our children.'

As if on cue, an apple-box to which four wheels had been attached came hurtling into the corridor, propelled by one of the younger Darwins, with two even younger Darwins inside, both gleeful with excitement. They did not slow down, and FitzRoy had to leap out of the way to avoid being run over.

'Three o'clock from London Bridge coming through!' shouted the seven-year-old driver of the contraption as it passed. FitzRoy was mildly surprised that there were no words of admonition for the miscreants from their father.

They went into the drawing room, FitzRoy still clutching his top hat – for no one had taken it from him – where Mrs Darwin sat working at a piece of worsted with baby Leonard and Horace, her newborn, propped awkwardly on her lap. Like her husband, she was robed in black. She and FitzRoy were introduced, and for a while made polite conversation.

'Have you yet visited the Great Exhibition in Hyde Park, Captain FitzRoy?'

'Indeed. It is a quite remarkable testament to our nation's ingenuity. Clothes made by machines – who would have thought it?'

'Not just our nation's ingenuity, but our nation's enterprise,' said Darwin proudly. 'My wife's family mounted a stand at the exhibition.'

'We spent a whole week in London during the summer,' explained Emma. 'We visited the Crystal Palace every day. We saw the Great Globe in Leicester Square as well.'

'And your father?' said FitzRoy. 'Is he still . . . ?'

She shook her head, and her husband answered for her: 'I'm afraid not. Uncle Jos died of a stroke while you were in New Zealand.'

'I am so sorry to hear it. What of your own father, if I might dare ask?'

'He, too, has been taken from us, some four years past.'

The doctor had died slowly and agonizingly, his immense frame no longer able to lever itself from its bed, his breath coming in purple gasps.

'We must give thanks that two such very great friends were taken by the Lord to His bosom at such a short interval,' said Emma.

'Quite so,' agreed FitzRoy.

Darwin said nothing.

With an awkward pause brewing, he suggested that FitzRoy accompany him on the sand walk before luncheon, the children being instructed on this occasion to stay out of their way. The two men put on their coats and headed down through the allotments, FitzRoy having to reduce his pace to match his companion's painful hobble.

'So why did you leave Gower Street?' he asked his host.

'For the sake of my family's safety, principally. The Chartist mobs are getting bigger. London is getting bigger. Did you know there are now a million more Londoners than when we set sail on the *Beagle*? The rebellion can only be a matter of time.'

'It will not succeed.'

'It will not succeed, but how many innocents will die in the crushing of it? Or what if there is a general strike? Gentlemen and their families might well starve in their houses. Then there is the filth. Coal dust on the washing, horse dung in the streets, and the fog getting worse every winter.'

'You do not miss the Athenaeum Club? The Royal Geographical Society?'

'Sadly, my health does not permit me to keep up my duties at the RGS, or at the Geological Society.' Darwin ran mournfully through the list of his afflictions. 'But the penny post enables me to carry out most of my researches via correspondence.'

'And the play? Concerts? You do not miss those?'

'Oh, I was never one for the theatre. My own dear womankind plays Rossini and Beethoven to me on the piano of an evening, and reads me endless foolish novels.' Darwin smiled. 'I have all that I might want to entertain me right here at Down House. It may not be the most attractive dwelling in the district, but with a few modifications it has suited my needs ideally.'

'Oh yes? What modifications have you made?'

'Back stairs, so that we do not have to see the servants unless strictly necessary. A bedroom for my wife, for her use during pregnancy and accouchement.'

That must be very nearly all the time, thought FitzRoy.

'And the earth bank before the house, so that we are not disturbed by the general public. I do have a certain notoriety, you know.'

'I know.'

'And yourself, FitzRoy? Do you have a situation at present?'

'Not presently, no. I did not finish the South American charts and sailing plans until I returned from New Zealand. It was such a mammoth task, I confess I felt rather bereft when it was finished. Then, for a little while, I assisted the Admiralty in testing HMS *Arrogant*, a warship driven by a small screw propeller at the stern. It is the invention of a Swede, named Ericsson. But the design has been scrapped. The Admiralty came to the conclusion that it could never work and, indeed, that steam could never supplant sailpower.'

'And were those your own conclusions?'

'No ... no, my conclusions were entirely the opposite. I resigned from the project in somewhat awkward circumstances.'

Typical FitzRoy, thought Darwin. *Always inflexible. Never prepared to bend a little before the prevailing winds.*

'Since then, I have been trying without success to get the government to listen to my ideas regarding the feasibility of weather prediction. What about yourself? What researches have you undertaken of late?'

'I? I have been studying barnacles.'

I will not ask why, thought FitzRoy, *for it shall undoubtedly prove something to do with transmutation, and I do not wish to argue with him. Not today.*

Darwin, who was thinking along similar lines, went no further, but he found himself wanting to confide in FitzRoy, wanting to tell him all about the incredible variations he had discovered, all the proofs he had found that variation was a continuous process and not just the result of fixed geological events. He wanted this one person above all others, this stubborn mule, to assimilate the sheer weight of his arguments and concede defeat. He jabbed out a question: 'Have you read *The Vestiges?*'

'Hasn't everybody?'

The Vestiges of the Natural History of Creation was a popular transmutationist tract, trashily written by an anonymous author, that had dumbfounded the scientific world by selling forty thousand copies. British society, it seemed, was ready for a carefully reasoned argument postulating man's descent from the higher apes; but *The Vestiges*, unfortunately, wasn't it. The book's author had failed to come up with any sort of convincing mechanism for transmutation.

'I thought the zoology and geology were hopelessly amateur,' huffed Darwin. 'It was so bad, it could almost have been written by a woman.'

The Vestiges had shaken Darwin. At first, he'd feared that he had been beaten to the punch; then, when he'd realized he had not, he had been frightened at the sheer vitriol poured upon the author's head by the scientific community. Sedgwick, for instance, had called the transmutationist argument 'a filthy abortion, full of inner deformity and foulness'. No wonder the man – or woman – had remained anonymous.

'An extraordinary book. It claimed, if I remember, that cheese mites could be spontaneously generated by electricity,' said FitzRoy, wonderingly.

'There is no accounting for public taste,' said Darwin. He held himself back. How he wanted to present FitzRoy with a *real* transmutationist argument, convincingly thought through and backed up with detailed research. How he wanted to admit FitzRoy to the dark burrow of his study, reveal to him the semi-hermaphroditic barnacle beneath the microscope and shout: *'There! There is the origin of the male and female sexes! Adam's rib does not even enter into it!'*

FitzRoy could not help but reflect bitterly on the tide of condemnation that had greeted the publication of *The Vestiges* in polite society, as compared to the praise heaped upon Darwin's own books. *If people only knew the truth of his views, he would be a pariah; but instead it was my book that was slaughtered in print, by his friends in the liberal scientific establishment, and his that received all their good notices.*

A harsh crow-croak came from the chalk-fields beyond the sand walk thickets, heralding the approach of winter.

'Shall we go in for luncheon?' suggested Darwin. 'It is getting cold.'

They lunched in the old-fashioned Regency dining room, overlooked by eighteenth-century portraits of long-dead Darwins. The miserable, long-haired butler served the meal with an indifference bordering on dissent, dishing up inelegant servings of boiled mutton on a dainty Wedgwood dinner service decorated with a waterlily motif. Gazing at the dough-faced Darwin ancestors that lined the walls, it occurred suddenly to FitzRoy that his host was always looking backwards, always unhappy with the past, always trying to unravel it; whereas he, by contrast, quite secure in his knowledge of how mankind had arrived at this point, was always looking forward, always trying to better the future.

Two daguerreotypes stared balefully at them from the sideboard at the end of the room. The larger one showed a curiously dark-eyed, sad and thoughtful Darwin, a young boy in long clothes perched upon his lap. *That must be William*, thought FitzRoy, *the eldest son*. The other showed a sullen, fat-chinned girl, splayed awkwardly on a sofa in a chequered frock, her hair scraped into corn-dolly plaits about her ears. *That must be Anne, the child that died.* Emma Darwin followed FitzRoy's gaze, and caught him in mid-inspection. 'She is beautiful,' he told her quickly.

'We have lost the joy of the household and the solace of our old age, Captain FitzRoy,' said Emma. 'I always thought that, come what might, we should have had one loving soul whom nothing could have changed.'

'My daughter was generous, handsome and unsuspicious in all her conduct,' added her husband, 'free from envy and jealousy, good-tempered and never passionate. I only hope that she knew how much we loved her.'

'I hope that she does know how deeply, how tenderly we do still,' returned Emma, 'and how we shall ever love her dear, joyous face. May God's blessings be upon her.'

'May the Holy Spirit bless your endeavour to honour the Redeemer's name,' offered FitzRoy, who could see the excruciating pain of the Darwins' loss cut into their faces as if by a lancet.

'My lady is served, sir,' interjected Parslow, piling an inopportune mound of potatoes on to his mistress's plate.

'What of your own children, Captain FitzRoy? What is to become of them? They cannot remain in your household without a woman present.'

'No. My son, Robert, is joining the Service. He is old

enough now, at twelve, and I have secured him a berth. Thereafter, I hope he will attend the Royal Naval College. My sister Fanny and Lady Londonderry have kindly consented to look after the three girls. I will still visit them, of course, but it will be the most tremendous wrench. Emily is the very image of her mother.'

'You poor man,' said Emma. 'I know exactly how you feel. I miss my own dear Annie so. She was so popular in the whole household, Captain FitzRoy. All the servants adored her. I wish you could have seen it.'

'After her death, her nurse, Brodie, became quite hysterical with grief,' Darwin recounted. 'In the end I decided it best that she leave the family service. The woman was quite inconsolable.'

'Have you yet composed Anne's memorial?'

'There is no memorial,' said Darwin bluntly.

'No memorial?' FitzRoy tried and failed to hide his surprise.

'No memorial, and no stone angels on her grave. Only a plain headstone in Malvern churchyard, inscribed, "A dear and good child".'

Emma Darwin looked unhappy.

'It must be a pity for you both that she is buried so far away. I find it a great consolation to visit my wife's grave every day. I talk to her, and give thanks to God for her life, and give thanks that she is undoubtedly sitting at His right hand even now.'

'It is all right, FitzRoy, you may disapprove of me if you wish,' said Darwin. 'Heavens, I have known you long enough not to be offended by now. Say that you disapprove of my not providing my child with a memorial.'

'Of course I shall not say it. It is up to everyone to grieve for the loss of a loved one exactly as they wish.'

'It is just that, no matter how hard I look, I cannot see *any* divine purpose behind the loss of my daughter.'

'Nor can I see any divine purpose behind the loss of my beloved wife. But there must be one, must there not? Or why should a kind and much-loved child be taken away from you?

Why should a kind and much-loved woman in her fortieth year be taken away from me? It occurred because it was the Lord's will, that is why, and the Lord's will is exercised only for good, even if we may not know all His reasoning. So you may be assured that your daughter is by His side.'

'Oh, I assure you, FitzRoy, I dearly want to believe in an afterlife for my daughter. I want it as much as you do. But what is belief? Belief is no more than instinct. What is belief in an afterlife? Nothing more than a primitive being – man – deflecting his terror and helplessness in the face of death.'

Darwin was looking to provoke FitzRoy now. FitzRoy's calm face, his damned piety, his absolute certainty that he *knew*, were provoking him, and he wanted to provoke the man back.

'It is a view that leaves no room for divinity or moral redemption,' replied FitzRoy, softly.

'She was ten years old. She died in agony, for God's sake. Why should I have anything to do with a God who delights in such cruelties? I am not a savage!'

'Mr Darwin, *please*!' breathed his wife. 'The servants!'

'I think you need to decide,' said FitzRoy, 'whether you actively blame God for what has happened, or whether you are merely finding it difficult to believe in Him.'

'Go to the devil!' Darwin burst out angrily. 'You just do not understand, do you? The pair of you!' He rounded on his wife. 'Our daughter is *dead*. She is rotting in the *ground*. She is not "sitting at God's right hand in heaven". Why? Because heaven does not exist, and because God does not exist. There – I have said it now. *God – does – not – exist*. He is just our pathetic fears made flesh. Are you happy now? Do you want me to say it again, and then maybe perhaps it will finally sink in? GOD DOES NOT DAMNED WELL EXIST!'

Emma Darwin, tears stumbling from her eyes, stood up and fled the room.

Parslow, who had been about to offer FitzRoy a second helping of cabbage, thought better of it.

Part Six

Chapter Thirty-three

Woollya Cove, Tierra del Fuego, 9 November 1855

Captain William Parker Snow raised a hand, and let silence fall across the decks of the *Allen Gardiner*. His instincts, which had never yet let him down, were of the opinion that he was being watched. By whom, or what, he could not tell. Not a living thing stirred outside the ship. They had left the crowds of Fuegians that had chased them up the Beagle Channel panting helplessly in their wake. It was a bountiful evening, the first they had enjoyed since leaving the tropics, the water was glass, and a warm sun illuminated a row of blue-grey serrated peaks that jutted up in the distance like whales' teeth. In fact, the entire landscape put him in mind of his whaling days in Greenland. The peaks, he knew from FitzRoy's maps, were the Codrington Mountains. He had to take off his hat to his predecessor: FitzRoy's charts and sailing directions had proved nothing short of amazing. They were exact in every detail. It was as if the old captain had taken him by the hand and led him down here in person, a guardian angel guiding him safely between the frowning cliffs and snarling rocks.

Suddenly, a little splash caught his attention, and he glanced across in time to see the head of a seal dart beneath the surface. At least, he thought it had been a seal's head: it had flashed black and shiny for a moment, caught in the sunlight's slant. Certainly, no human being could survive in these freezing waters. A stark but momentary image, of two white eyes staring intently at him, was now imprinted upon his memory. He stroked the massive black beard that lay across his barrel chest like a slumbering bear, and pondered.

The silence was broken again, by a spontaneous outburst of hymn-singing from the prow, and for the thousandth time, Snow had reason to curse the missionaries and the crew they had recruited. The outbreak of war in the Crimea had meant that, for the first time in decades, it had been impossible to find experienced seamen in England's ports, but the Patagonian Missionary Society had compounded the problem by insisting that every crew member in the *Allen Gardiner* pass rigorous tests of Christian devotion. The result was a crew of fanatics, who couldn't sail, couldn't patch a leak, and who regarded his authority as secondary to that of Garland Phillips, the society's chief catechist on board. One of the men hailed from Stockholm, and could barely speak a word of English; two of them shared the same name, for heaven's sake, both being called John Johnstone; and the only one who wasn't an out-and-out zealot, Coles the cook, was a certified half-wit. The city of Bristol, apparently, had contained not a single Christian cook.

Phillips had decreed that there should be two services a day, even in the heaviest seas; when Snow had attempted to reduce the number to one, the ship's mates had simply refused to obey his orders. On one occasion in the South Atlantic, the crew had abandoned their stations and foregathered to pray, all dressed in their matching guernseys with 'Mission Yacht' sewn at the breast, in the midst of a howling gale: if the *Allen Gardiner* went down, ran the prevailing wisdom, then so be it, for that would be God's will. So helplessly had the ship yawed back and forth, that a passing French man-of-war had stopped to help, assuming her to have lost her rudder. In his entire professional career, Snow had never been so mortified.

'Mr Phillips!' he called, as much to put a stop to the hymn-singing as to attract the catechist's attention. Garland Phillips stalked up the maindeck, his tailcoat and long black hair flapping, a look of irritation replacing the self-confident sneer that served as his customary expression. *How very much I detest this man,* growled the captain to himself.

'Yes? What is it, Snow?' demanded Phillips.

'This is it. Woollya Cove. Journey's end.'

Phillips's eyes gleamed with excitement. Cupping his hands to his face, he began to call out, *'Oo-ee! Oo-ee!'*

The mountains caught his yodel and tossed it nonchalantly between themselves, but answer came there none. If they were indeed being watched, then the watchers remained cautious. Whereupon, a bright idea occurred to Captain Snow.

'Johnstone!'

'Aye aye sir!'

Two voices had answered in unison.

'No, not you, Johnstone, I meant the other Johnstone.'

'Aye aye sir!'

'Run up the Union Jack.'

'Aye aye sir!'

A moment later, as the familiar red, white and blue jerked limply into the foretops, two packed canoes emerged cautiously from the tussock grass of a nearby island and began to paddle towards the *Allen Gardiner*.

'Jemmy Button? Jemmy Button?' bellowed Snow.

In the lead canoe, a portly, dishevelled, middle-aged man stood up, quite naked, and began to gesticulate wildly at the ship. 'Yes! Yes!' he shouted. 'Jemmy Button! Me Jemmy Button!'

'God be praised!' said Garland Phillips.

An incredulous Snow called for sail to be shortened, and

all hands on deck. Before long, the entire crew stood transfixed at the rail.

'Capp'en Fitz'oy? Capp'en Fitz'oy come back for Jemmy?'
called the pot-bellied figure in the canoe.

'Captain FitzRoy is not here. I am Captain Snow.'

An air of panic suddenly pervaded the two canoes. The
little Fuegian was gesturing to the rowers to stop. Garland
Phillips seized Snow's arm.

'Captain FitzRoy has sent us,' he called out. 'He has sent
us to bring you to him.'

Astonished, Snow turned to stare at Phillips. The catechist
hissed at him, 'FitzRoy has given the expedition his blessing.
It is the same thing. Look to concentrate upon sailing the
ship, and let me deal with the natives.'

The Fuegians had resumed their rowing.

'If you please, where is the ladder?' called out Jemmy.

'Well, I'm blowed!' said Coles the cook. 'This beats me out
and out. What a queer thing! There's that blear-eyed, dirty-
looking, naked savage, speaking as clear to the skipper as one
of us, and I be hanged, too, if he isn't as polite as if he'd been
brought up in a parlour instead of born in this outlandish
place!'

'I can't make it out,' agreed one of the John Johnstones.
'Lots of wild barbarians civil to us, and now one of 'em talking
as plain a'most as ourselves! It knocks me down quite.'

'Be silent!' hissed Phillips. 'Throw him down a rope.'

A rope was tossed down, whereupon Jemmy Button and a
twelve-year-old child, possibly his son, stood up in the canoe
and enacted what now appeared to be a familiar ritual.

'After you, Wammestriggins.'

'No, no. After you, Jemmy Button.'

'No, no. Me insist. After you.'

'No, no. After you.'

Eventually, Jemmy grasped the rope and hauled himself up
with difficulty, followed by the rather more agile youth.

'Pank you,' said Wammestriggins, as helping hands leaned

down to pull him aboard. Both Fuegians wiped their feet politely.

'Me *know* Capp'en Fitz'oy come back,' said Jemmy proudly. 'Me *tell* them. Where is Capp'en Fitz'oy?'

'He is ... close by,' said Phillips. 'My name is Garland Phillips. I am a missionary.'

'Like Reverend Mister Matthews? Mister Matthews is my frien'.'

'That's right, Jemmy. Like the Reverend Mr Matthews. I am a reverend also.'

'Me know you flag. Me say to family, "Capp'en Fitz'oy's flag."'

'Would you like to come below, Jemmy?' enquired Snow. 'My wife is resting below. I should very much like you to meet her.'

'English lady your wife? English lady very pretty – very good looks. Like Capp'en Sisser.'

Jemmy's enthusiasm was abruptly replaced by a look of embarrassed realization, as he placed his hands over his genitals.

'Jemmy want breeches, if you please. Want braces, thank you very much.'

Phillips, who clearly thought this a promising sign, called for shirts and two pairs of breeches, although it was a while before any could be found that would stretch across Jemmy's near-spherical belly. Then, while their fellows waited patiently in the boats, the two Fuegians were led below and introduced to Mrs Snow. The captain, meanwhile, hurried to his shelves and returned with a copy of FitzRoy's book, *Narratives of the Voyages of the* Beagle.

'Look, Jemmy. Two portraits of you.'

Jemmy laughed, at first. The left-hand portrait showed a wild, shaggy-haired native, while the right-hand effort depicted him as the starched, preening dandy he had once become. Then, as he traced the line of the high, elegant collar with the tip of his forefinger, his expression became downcast.

'Beautiful clothes,' he said wistfully. 'Beautiful clothes for Jemmy.'

'What do you remember of God, Jemmy?' demanded Garland Phillips.

'Me remember God. People say in my country, no God. Me go tell them people, yes, God is in my country. He made me and them. Made trees, moon.'

Phillips rubbed his hands together with excitement.

'And what do you remember of England, Jemmy?' asked Mrs Snow, an earnest, long-nosed woman, her face restrained by a lilac bonnet.

'Jemmy stayed at Wal'amstow with Schoolmaster Jenkins. There was a great church-house, two churchmen, one white gown, one black. An organ make music, much noise. Jemmy meet King. All good in English country. Jemmy make many frien's. Capp'en Fitz'oy. Mr Bennet. Mr Bynoe. Many frien's.' Jemmy looked up at Mrs Snow with big, sad eyes.

'Is this your son, Jemmy?' she prompted.

'Yes. This my son – Wammestriggins! My wife in canoe!'

'Peased to meet you, ma'am,' said Wammestriggins.

'This is incredible,' breathed Phillips. 'He's taught his entire family to speak English.'

'Would you like some food, Jemmy?' asked Snow.

'Yes, if you please, Capp'en,' Jemmy nodded. 'English food good.'

Coles was quickly put to work, and before long a presentable meal of fresh fish, boiled duck and double-shotted plum duff had been rustled up. Both Jemmy and Wammestriggins picked up their knives and forks as if eating with European cutlery was second nature to them.

'What immaculate table manners you have, Jemmy,' Mrs Snow congratulated him.

'Capp'en Fitz'oy, he teach Jemmy how to eat like English gen'leman. Jemmy teach all family. Not eat like savage – eat like gen'leman. You see? My son Wammestriggins – eat like gen'leman.'

Wammestriggins had begun to transfer dainty portions of fish into his mouth, but Jemmy could not bring himself to start.

'Is everything all right, Jemmy?' asked Phillips. 'Is the food not to your liking?'

'Capp'en Fitz'oy gone for long time,' said Jemmy, almost inaudibly. 'But Jemmy know he come back. Jemmy tell his family, "Capp'en Fitz'oy will come back. He is Jemmy's frien'. He will come back for Jemmy ..."' He tailed off.

'Are you all right, Jemmy?' asked Mrs Snow.

For the second time in his life, big wet dollops were running down Jemmy's nose and splashing on to the table beneath.

Following dinner, the canoes that had relentlessly pursued the *Allen Gardiner*'s trail began to arrive at last. Jemmy preferred not to spend the night on the ship, for his wife was starting to panic, but returned at dawn, his new clothes caked in red mud because he had slept in them. By morning there were perhaps a hundred canoes packed with excited natives buzzing round the ship, like wherry-boats swarming about a prestigious launch on the Thames. Presents were distributed, of blankets, knives and carpentry tools; then Snow lowered the dinghy, and he, Phillips and his fellow-catechist Charles Turpin went with Jemmy to inspect the scant remains of FitzRoy's mission buildings. A silent host of curious Fuegians shadowed their every footstep, intent on every English word.

'Here Jemmy's house ... Here York and Fuegia's house ... Here Mister Matthews's house ...' Jemmy marched them past three discoloured squares in the grass, a few splinters of rotting board the only tangible reminder of FitzRoy's great experiment. Remarkably, Snow found a potato in the debris of the garden. Then, Jemmy produced a twenty-year-old axe, its blade worn to a sliver but still as sharp as the day it had been made. 'Capp'en Fitz'oy give me this,' he announced proudly.

Garland Phillips seized the Fuegian by both arms. 'We can build it again, Jemmy,' he said.

'What you mean? Jemmy no understan'.'

'Yes you do. We can rebuild the mission. But first you must come with us on the *Allen Gardiner*. Not to Britain – that is too far. But we have built another mission on the Falkland Islands. Come with us – bring your family, bring your friends – learn the ways of mission life!'

'Is too far. Jemmy go long way to Englan'. Maybe someone else want go to mission. Maybe my brother Macooallan.'

'Jemmy, it is just a few days' sail.'

'Mrs Button no want Jemmy to go.'

'Then bring her, Jemmy – bring her with you. Bring your whole family!'

'Will Capp'en Fitz'oy be there? At Falk'and?'

'No. He won't.'

It was Snow who had cut in bluntly. Phillips glared daggers at the burly captain.

'No, he won't be there now, Jemmy, but he will be there soon. Captain FitzRoy will be there soon. And Captain Sulivan – he lives at the Falklands – he will be there too.' Phillips gave Snow a look of triumph.

'Mister Sulivan good man. Good frien'. Mister Sulivan is Capp'en Sulivan now?'

'Yes. He is Captain Sulivan now.' Phillips could tell that Jemmy was wavering. 'It is a beautiful mission, Jemmy, on Keppel Island. You will have your own house, made of brick, like the houses in London. Our mission is named Cranmer, after the greatest Christian martyr, Archbishop Thomas Cranmer.'

'If you please, what is martyr?'

'A martyr, Jemmy? Martyrdom is the greatest accolade that can be bestowed upon any Christian. To die for one's faith. To die for the love of God. That is a martyr. God wants you to come to Cranmer, Jemmy. It is God's wish.'

Jemmy hesitated, dreaming of a pink suit he once owned.

His son came to his side and took his hand affectionately.

'I can bring Wammestriggins?'

'You can bring Wammestriggins.'

Jemmy paused for a further second, then made his decision.

'Very well. Jemmy will come, for five moons. No longer.'

The former Port William, recently made capital of the Falkland Islands and renamed Stanley in honour of the previous colonial secretary, stretched in three lines of damp wooden huts along the shore of a cigar-shaped natural harbour. It was the site chosen by FitzRoy himself as an alternative to Port Louis, a three-mile strip of sedate water studded with jetties and linked to the ocean by a rumbustious narrow channel. Snow thought that he had never seen such a drab settlement. Maybe it was the institutional white paint that had been chosen to decorate every hut in a dismal attempt at collective gaiety, already peeling in protest at the pounding it was taking from the elements. Maybe it was the dispiriting, regimented rows in which Stanley had been laid out. Or maybe it was the listlessness of the inhabitants, pensioners and poverty-stricken Irishmen all, who had been induced to remove themselves here by the official promise of a hundred acres of farmland each, plus a cow and a pig. The hundred-acre plots, the settlers had soon discovered, were parcels of worthless bog many miles deep in the interior; the pigs and the cows were feral beasts, roaming the islands in wild herds that, frankly, were anyone's for the taking if they were brave enough. To make matters worse, the prices of ordinary household goods in Stanley – all of which had to be imported from Britain – were running at four times the normal.

The hut of the islands' governor, Thomas Moore, was no better or worse than any of the others. A vicious wind cut through the cheap planking, whirling his official paperwork about the top of his rudimentary desk. Snow and Phillips stood uncomfortably to attention on the governor's rough dirt floor. *This truly is the end of the world*, thought Snow.

'Do you not think it discourteous, gentlemen, even impudent, that the Patagonian Missionary Society should see fit to take possession of an island under my governorship, without any reference to myself?' Moore glared at the pair.

'I supposed, sir, that the Reverend George Packenham Despard, the president of the Patagonian Missionary Society, had written to you regarding the establishment of our mission,' replied Garland Phillips coolly.

'Oh, Mr Despard wrote to me indeed,' growled Moore, a stout and pugnacious former military man. 'He wrote demanding that I allow him land to build a mission, "away from the depraved, low and immoral colonists of Stanley". I can assure you that his opinion of the settlers has caused much offence here. I can also assure you that he has received no affirmative response from myself, and yet here you are, sirs, demanding retrospective permission for the construction of a mission on Keppel Island!'

Snow wished that the ground would swallow him up.

'And let me assure *you*, sir,' replied Phillips even more smoothly, 'that the Cranmer Mission is a project dear to God's heart. It has the support of no less a dignitary than Captain Bartholomew Sulivan, of these very shores. If you would only contact Captain Sulivan—'

'Don't you know there is a war in Europe?' barked Moore. 'Captain Sulivan is from home. He has been called to fight the Russians.'

'Nonetheless, sir, his support for the Reverend Mr Despard's project has been unwavering throughout. Mr Despard is a visionary, sir, one of the greatest men of our times, and it has been a privilege for me to serve the Lord through him. With his guidance, the savage Jemmy Button and his fellow natives—'

'Jemmy Button, who was once bought for a button? I would remind you both of the slavery laws.'

'Jemmy Button, who has now *volunteered* to bring his family to Cranmer,' stressed Phillips. 'With the Reverend Mr Despard's guidance—'

'How many natives are in the party?'

'About twelve, sir.'

'And you are aware, I trust, of the Alien Ordnance passed by the Falklands Legislative Council, which imposes a levy of twenty shillings per foreign worker?'

'These are not workers as such, sir. If you would—'

'I consider it my duty, gentlemen,' cut in Moore, who was fast losing patience not just with Phillips but with life in the Falklands in general, 'to make strict enquiry as to whether these miserable savages have come voluntarily and with lawful contracts, as far as can be intelligible to their limited intellects. Not,' he added witheringly, 'that I wish to pour cold water upon your romantic enterprise.'

'You may be satisfied, sir,' retorted Phillips, 'that no less a person than the Reverend Mr Despard himself is due in Stanley ere long on the *Hydaspes*, a Patagonian Missionary Society vessel bound from Plymouth. I have no doubt, sir, that he shall settle any of the minor difficulties you have raised to your complete and utter satisfaction.'

Moore grunted, only partly mollified.

It was indeed just a few days later that the *Hydaspes* stood into the next jetty along from the *Allen Gardiner*, whereupon gangs of eager sailors in matching guernseys could be seen unloading Despard's wife, children, pigs, sheep, goats, ducks, hens, books, furniture and grand piano. Despard himself swept among the matlows dispensing God's blessings with a munificent air; but his smile faded and his brow clouded when Snow and Phillips emerged from the *Allen Gardiner* to welcome him to Stanley and to organize the transfer of his goods to their vessel.

'Captain Snow,' he boomed, 'I have received a communication in Monte Video, a most disturbing communication, from my catechist here' – Phillips, impassive, did not bother

to look embarrassed – 'suggesting that you actively encouraged the savage Jemmy Button to remain at Woollya, and not
to make the passage to Keppel Island.'

'I did so, sir, because I had my doubts – genuine Christian
doubts – regarding the manner in which he was enticed to
make the passage.' Snow gave Phillips a filthy look.

'You are a paid employee of the society, Captain Snow, and
as such you are not one of God's elect. You are not qualified
to express such doubts.'

'Missionary work, Mr Despard, should be about good deeds,
poor relief and spreading knowledge and understanding. It
should not be about planting an idol in the heathens' hearts;
introducing them to mystic ideas which they can only understand as you may choose to make them understood; and doing
so by various methods which are neither straightforward nor
truthful.'

Despard looked as if he would like to lean forward and bite
the captain. 'I would advise you, sir, to know your place.'

Snow was getting hot under the collar now. 'My place,
sir, is the place of any good Christian, to question the
immoral removal of these uncomprehending natives many
hundreds of miles from their homeland. Evil must not be
done that good may perchance – and only perchance – come
out of it.'

'Your place, Captain Snow, is on the *Hydaspes*, as a paying
passenger,' trumpeted Despard haughtily. 'You are dismissed
– dismissed, do you hear? – from the society's employ. Captain
Fell of the *Hydaspes* – a decent, God-fearing sailor, sir – shall
take your place at the helm of the *Allen Gardiner*. When, and
only when, a new captain is appointed to the *Hydaspes*, you
shall be free to quit these islands. In the meantime, I bid you
good day, sir.'

'You are a charlatan, sir!'

'And you are a scoundrel, sir!'

Only then, as they finally gave full vent to their anger, did
the two men realize that all work on the jetty had come to a

halt and that the entire company of ship's matlows stood frozen with surprise, staring in their direction.

Jemmy Button rested a weary boot on his spade, as Mr and Mrs Despard picked their way carefully down from Sulivan House. As was so often the case at Cranmer, a cold, sleeting rain was whipping eastwards out of a glowering sky. Jemmy was bundled up in a south-wester, a red comforter, a pea-jacket and heavy boots, not for warmth or protection – he actually felt rather overheated in such an ensemble – but because it was the most elegant sartorial combination he could concoct. The fact that he resembled a Dutch lugger had passed him by, although it made the crewmen laugh. He really should have resumed digging when the Despards came into view, but they had almost certainly spotted his inactivity already, so there was little further point pretending: he contented himself instead with straightening his aching back in a vaguely respectful manner. They were passing the cattle corrals now, where a sudden 'moo' caused Mrs Despard to leap quickly to her left. Jemmy suppressed a grin.

'Good morning, James,' called Despard, his huge semicircle of upper teeth on confident display. The Despards invariably called him James.

'Good morning, sar.'

'You have ceased digging, James.'

'Jemmy's boots get muddy. Jemmy not like his boots get muddy.'

'God loves good men, James. Good men are not idle. God does not love idle men.'

'No sar.'

'The Queen's birthday is in three days' time, and by then I want to see all five flagstaffs erected. Would you have Her Majesty's birthday pass without the Royal Standard and the Union flag flying over her distant domains?'

'No,' replied Jemmy, sullenly.

'No what?'

'No sar.'

'No sir, and no ma'am. There is a lady present. Do you see the other diggers being idle?' He gestured across the landscape, which was dotted with stocky Fuegians at work. 'I think not. Do you see Jamesina being idle? I think not.' Jamesina was the name the Despards had given to Lassaweea, Jemmy's wife. 'Jamesina has learned to work at the needle, in her rough way. She washes and irons clothes, prepares food and performs all manner of household duties. I expect you to follow her example, James.'

'Yes sar. Yes ma'am.'

'That's better, James,' said Despard, and he and his wife continued on their way, the clergyman audibly lamenting the general state of his charges. 'What you must remember, my dear, is that the savages are as self-willed and capricious as grown spoiled children, and require great patience and firmness to manage them, as well as an undaunted spirit.'

'I see that, my dear, I see that all too well.'

'I have great hopes, however, for young Threeboys.' Threeboys was the name the Despards had devised for Wammestriggins. 'His diligence as regards cleanliness is remarkable. So ambitious is he to become white that he ablutes often, in the hope of washing the brown out of his complexion. It is a most promising sign – a most promising sign indeed.'

By now the pair had arrived at Button Villa, the name given to the ten-foot-square brick hut into which all the Fuegians had been crammed. Gingerly, Despard pulled aside the calico window-blind, and peered in. He could see Jamesina sitting with her eight-year-old daughter Fuegia, as they had renamed Passawullacuds, her baby Anthony, as Annasplonis had been christened, and Threeboys himself. She was polishing a tin cooking utensil. Despard pushed open the door.

'Good morning, Jamesina.'

The Fuegian gave a little curtsy.

'Good morning, sar. Good morning, ma'am.'

'This is very good, Jamesina,' said Despard, taking the

utensil from her. 'You have cleaned this very well.'

'I have brought you a gift, Jamesina,' said Mrs Despard, opening her bag. 'It is a woven shawl, knitted by Mrs Harvey of York.'

'It is a woven shawl, knitted by Mrs Harvey of York,' replied Mrs Button, who still clung to the traditional Fuegian practice of repeating anything said to her that she did not understand.

'Thank you, ma'am,' prompted Despard.

'Thank you, ma'am,' said Jamesina, uncertainly.

'And you, Threeboys. What are you about this morning?'

'I have written a letter, sar, to Queen Victoria.'

'Indeed, Threeboys? May I see it?'

Threeboys handed over a piece of paper, upon which he had written in a painstaking hand:

Dear Queen
I am glad to saw much; to plane much. By and bye I shall be a carpenter. I shall visit England; and you will give me a hatchet, a chisel, and a bradawl; and I shall say, thank you.
Threeboys (Wammestriggins).

'That is excellent, Threeboys. Very good indeed. I shall post it for you.'

Despard slid the letter into his pocket; he would consign it discreetly to the fire later.

'I pray to God for Jesus Christ's sake to make me a good boy,' said Threeboys.

'God shall hear your prayer, Threeboys, I am certain of it,' said the delighted clergyman.

Mrs Despard, meanwhile, had plucked the sleeping Anthony deftly from his cot, and now cradled the child lovingly in her arms. 'Look, dearest. Is he not the *sweetest* little boy?'

'The Lord has blessed you, Jamesina, with a most attractive baby. I am sure that he will grow into a strong and healthy Christian.'

Something stirred beneath Mrs Button's newly acquired veneer of faith, and she held out her hands for the return of her son.

Reluctantly, Mrs Despard complied. 'Dearest,' she said to her husband after they had left Button Villa, 'do you think it would be possible for us to keep Anthony? I mean, after the Fuegians are gone?'

'Keep him, Mrs Despard?'

'We could give the child a healthful and civilized upbringing – a far cry from the life of savage despair that awaits him. And is it not said that savage mothers do not feel the same attachment to their children as would be felt by mothers of a more advanced race?'

'That is indeed said, my dear. You have made an interesting proposal – a most interesting proposal indeed. Perhaps it is not impossible that – on this point at least – the savages shall be able to see reason.'

In a graceful, lazy arc, almost the same one that had measured its flight in life, the goose plummeted soundlessly to the grass. Impressed with himself and grinning with pleasure, Threeboys lowered the gun.

'Well done! Well done, Threeboys!' said Despard, and clapped the boy on the back.

Really, things could not have been going better for the Reverend George Packenham Despard. The Fuegians had been at Cranmer for six months now, and despite the odd grumble at the length of their stay and the regime of continuous hard labour, there was no doubt that the mission and its inhabitants were finding mutual benefit in the arrangement. Jemmy and his relatives spent their days digging peat for fuel, painting window-frames, carrying paving slabs, tending the vegetable gardens, building bridges across streams and foraging for wreckwood on the beaches; gradually, they were learning the virtues inherent in honest servitude and Christian prayer and, gradually, the mission was nearing completion. The business with Snow had been awkward – Mrs Snow had virtually succumbed to a hysterical breakdown on the jetty at Stanley – but the man had clearly been a trouble-maker from the start. Captain Fell was a vast improvement, quiet but firm, and studious in his devotions. With Garland Phillips as a more than able sergeant-major, Despard was confident that he had assembled the right team to commence the building of another mission on the mainland of Tierra del Fuego itself. That jumped-up foot-soldier Moore had sent men down from Stanley to sneak around, but the natives had been on their best behaviour, and the governor's hirelings had returned empty-handed: there would be no more trouble on that score.

Now the Lord had further rewarded his humble endeav-ours by guiding his footsteps to Threeboys. Jemmy Button's son really was a most remarkable lad, being intelligent, loyal and devout. He would much rather keep this child than the gurning, fat-faced brown baby his wife seemed so enamoured with. Perhaps it might be possible to retain both. Certainly, the boy was a far better marksman than any other at the mission. Why, that morning alone he had shot no fewer than five wild geese and five loggerhead ducks. Despard decided that he would keep the geese for the white men – the flesh tasted better – and allow the boy to take the ducks back for the more primitive palates of his father and the other Fuegians. Really, the boy's father was the only remaining cloud on the Keppel Island horizon. It was hard to see why FitzRoy and Sulivan had made such a fuss about him. He was one of the dullest of his race, miserable, lazy, preening and stupid. All he did, it seemed, was complain continuously, about FitzRoy's absence, about Sulivan's absence, and about the fact that he had not been allowed to go home after 'five moons', a length of time he had appar-ently stipulated with no reference to anyone else. How much easier would it have been for all concerned if he had never come to Cranmer?

Despard and Threeboys marched triumphantly down from the rainswept, misty hills, taking the footpath home across the Despard Plain, the young boy struggling manfully under the weight of the ten limp-necked birds. They were no more than a few hundred yards short of their goal when a distressed Mrs Despard emerged from Sulivan House, her skirts billowing, her bonnet flapping. 'Mr Despard! Mr Despard!' she cried.

'What is it, Mrs Despard?' replied her husband, hastening towards her.

'I cannot find my comb.'

'Your comb?'

'My jewelled comb. I put it on the dresser this morning. Then, when I came to pick it up, it was gone. Vanished! I can only presume that the natives have stolen it.'

'Have they indeed?' Despard's broad jaw set tight. He was not the sort of man to see his wife standing distressed in a wet field, the wind tugging stray locks from beneath her indoor bonnet. He would punish most severely whoever it was that had reduced her to this.

'Come, Threeboys!' he commanded, and set off towards the mission cottages to fetch Phillips and Turpin. A minute later, the party had arrived at Button Villa, where an angry Despard flung open the door. A roomful of startled Fuegian men looked round from their luncheon.

'Search the property,' ordered Despard.

'What is—' began Jemmy.

'Somebody has stolen a comb. A jewelled comb. I intend to discover the identity of the thief,' announced Despard grimly.

Phillips and Turpin moved in and began to toss aside clothing, bedding, animal skins, anything they could find.

'You say we are thieves?' snapped Jemmy, openly angry for the first time since arriving. He made a stumbling translation for the benefit of his fellows, one of whom, Schwaiamugunjiz, began to shout at the missionaries in Yamana.

'Keep your temper,' ordered Despard.

'We are innocent as the newborn Christ!' insisted Jemmy, his wife cowering behind him as Phillips ripped open a home-made cushion.

'Never, ever take the Lord's name in vain again!' said Despard, with a voice of steel. He resorted to a much-taught formula to keep order. 'Who made the world, James?'

'God,' said Jemmy sullenly.

'Who made the sun and the moon?'

'God.'

'Who made you, James?'

'English God,' said Jemmy, diverting from the prepared text.

'God,' corrected Despard.

'English God – I am English gen'leman.'

'English gentlemen do not steal. Only bad men steal.'

'*I did not steal.*'

'We not stay Kebbel Island,' spat Schwaiamugunjiz. 'We go away when schooner come.'

There was silence in the little hut.

'There's nothing, sir,' reported Phillips. 'Leastways, it's not hidden in here, sir.'

Despard breathed hard. 'Very well. But do not for one minute think I have forgotten this. The search will continue. Remember this, James – all of you – we are all of us sinners. Do you understand? *We are all of us sinners.* And Christ our Lord suffered on the cross for our sins.'

Jemmy touched his forelock resignedly. 'Yes, sar. I know Son of God came down to die,' he replied. 'He died for his God, sar.'

Just after eleven o'clock on the morning of 28 September, Captain Fell decided that the tide and winds were fair, and a scowling band of departing Fuegians were allowed to assemble at the mission jetty at last. The start of the wild-bird-egg season, they had insisted, was only a week away, and they were more anxious than ever to be off. Despard was reluctant to see them leave, but his broaching of the possibility that Threeboys or Anthony be left behind to be fostered by his own family had soured relations to a near-critical level. An unsteady truce now prevailed, fragile enough for Despard to keep an escort of heavily built sailors at hand. As the Fuegians deposited their cloth bundles in a slovenly heap ready for embarkation, he rapped out a command to his bodyguard: 'Search them!'

The sailors moved forward and began to untie the bundles.

'We no thiefs!' shouted Jemmy. The missing hair comb had been found in the mission yard. Nobody knew how it had got there.

'Search their packs,' repeated Despard.

'You say Capp'en Fitz'oy is here. You say Capp'en Sulivan is here,' spat Jemmy. 'You lie. You try take away Jemmy's childs!'

'Hold your tongue, James Button,' commanded Despard.

'No thief!' shouted Schwaiamugunjiz angrily.

The contents of the Fuegians' bundles spilled out across the jetty. Jemmy's brother Macooallan assumed a guilty look as two turnips and a hammer were revealed among his belongings.

'Ha!' said Despard triumphantly. 'It seems that we do indeed have a thief in our midst.'

'No thief,' said Macooallan defiantly. 'Macooallan grow turnips. Macooallan eat turnips.'

'No,' said Garland Phillips, stepping forward to take the vegetables back. 'They grew on mission soil. They are not yours to remove.'

'Who turnips belong?' said Jemmy accusingly. 'Belong God?'

'Yes,' pronounced Despard, his arms folded as if to settle the matter. 'They are God's vegetables. And this is God's hammer. Now. It is time for you to board the vessel.'

Heads down, the line of sullen Fuegians did as they were bidden.

* * *

Battered and bruised, the *Allen Gardiner* limped into Woollya Cove close to a year after her previous visit. It had been a tough passage, the ship tossed around on mountainous seas like a piece of flotsam. A storm in the Beagle Channel had cracked the topsail halyards and torn down the mainsail as if it were bunting. Even the crew had lost some of their Christian enthusiasm for the venture, but Garland Phillips, who had been placed in command of the voyage by Despard, had maintained his grip. When two sailors had attempted to wash their clothes on a Sunday, he had ripped into them. 'Not in this vessel,' he had roared. 'It has been built, launched and sailed in God's service, and His holy day is not to be profaned in it with impunity. If you wash it will be at your cost!' The two men had slunk away, chastened.

'Sailors are like children,' Phillips had later confided to Captain Fell. 'The better they are treated, the more they want.'

Phillips's orders were to build a mission station on the scale of Cranmer at Woollya Cove. 'Spend every day with the natives,' Despard had advised him. 'Try them much with singing. Have a Sabbath morning and evening service on shore, that the natives may attend and be aroused to enquiry.' Phillips, as a result, had decided that the mission church should be the first building erected, and had immediately put the crew of the *Allen Gardiner* to work. Captain Fell, staid and solemn, marshalled his men to dig foundations and cut down trees for timber. The Cranmer Fuegians proved more reluctant accomplices, until a daily wage of five biscuits was agreed for their labours. Gradually, the little wooden church took shape; and gradually, canoe after canoe of curious natives arrived, until several hundred sat cross-legged in the wet grass, fascinated by proceedings. At first they were content to remain spectators, but eventually they began to inch forward by degrees, nosy and demanding, asking questions repeatedly of their countrymen. More thefts were reported.

'Can't you make them go away?' grumbled Phillips to Jemmy.

'You go away now! What you call this, come here? We no want you here!' shouted Jemmy in English, to a sea of uncomprehending faces.

'I mean, in Yamana,' said Phillips despairingly.

'Me no speak Yamana,' replied Jemmy tartly. 'Jemmy is English *gen'leman*.'

Phillips abandoned the exercise.

In an effort to dissipate the air of menace that was slowly thickening about the camp, Captain Fell ordered the entire store of mission clothing to be broken into and distributed. Before long there was barely a Fuegian at Woollya Cove who was not attired in some item of European finery. Men wore girls' lacy pantalettes about their heads; women wore men's brocaded waistcoats as underwear; heads were forced through the straining armholes of woollen vests.

'You look a fine fellow,' said Captain Fell to one barrel-chested specimen, who had worked out more or less correctly how to put on his suit of clothes.

'You look a fine fellow,' repeated the man.

Fell produced a small looking-glass from his pocket, and showed the man his reflection. With a yell, the Fuegian fled screaming into the trees.

By 9 November, the actual anniversary, God's house was almost – but not quite – completed. No matter: it was the Sabbath. It was an auspicious date, Phillips decided, for the first ever church service to be held on the mainland of Tierra del Fuego. The natives would be dazzled, he calculated, by the simple grace of the ceremonial and by the harmonic beauty of the hymn-singing. The entire ship's company rose in a body at sunrise and went ashore in the cutter, leaving only Coles the cook to mind the *Allen Gardiner*.

He watched them bob across the dark waters, the surface flecked here and there with wan pinpoints of light from the pale dawn. The sun seemed to take flight, and retreated behind a dense bank of cloud almost as soon as it had been spotted. It took the cutter a full twenty minutes to reach the shore, its dark cluster of heads getting smaller and smaller as it shrank into the distance. Bored, Coles fetched the captain's spyglass; he knew where it was kept.

After mooring the boat, the missionaries and sailors formed up in their smart guernseys and marched up to the church in a platoon order. *That'll show the darkies how it's done*, thought Coles. Before long he could distinctly hear singing, muffled but sweet, wafting like incense across the waters of the cove. The hymn, he recognized, was 'His Praise Who Is Our God'. He even fancied for a moment that he could hear Garland Phillips's proud tenor rising above the rest, sending the word of the Lord echoing out of the church and swooping between the wild peaks and lonely channels. You had to hand it to old Phillips. He was a tartar, all right, but he knew what he was doing. The hymn-singing was certainly having an effect on the Fuegians. Some of them were on their feet now, listening intently. Others were creeping down to the water's edge. What were they up to? Coles squinted through the glass. Why, the thieving buggers were stealing the cutter's oars! And on a Sunday an' all! They'd steal the cutter itself next, like as not, and then the crew'd be in a pickle. He tried to identify the miscreants, but they were too far away. Was that Jemmy? Hard to say. He noticed that Phillips's musket, which he'd left propped against the church door, was also missing. It had been there a moment ago.

Suddenly, smoke began to envelop the rear of the church, followed quickly by ravenous licking flames. *What the devil?* Choking and spluttering, the sailors and missionaries began to emerge from the building, wiping their streaming eyes, dirty smoke-clouds billowing out after them. Captain Fell was first, carrying his hat under his arm – Coles recognized the uniform and the pale disc of his bald head, which stood out pink at first, then crimson when the first rock battered him to the ground. Then there were scores of rocks, yielded by hordes of Fuegians, all suddenly converging on the church door. One by one, the congregation were brutally beaten to death as they were driven by the blaze out into the daylight.

His bowels loosening, Coles watched both John Johnstones dragged out by their hair and pulverized, one after the other, before the simple wooden porch. The Swede, Petersen, made a run for it, but got no further than ten yards down the slope before a smartly aimed rock brought him down. Then the savages were on him like jackals, raining blows upon the helpless, doomed sailor. Wait! There was another runner! This one had got away. Coles fought to refocus the spyglass. For a split second he caught sight of a dark, blurred figure, coat-tails flapping in the circle of light, long black hair streaming, haring towards the shore. It was Mr Phillips! *Go it sir, go it! Not the cutter, sir, not the cutter. The buggers have taken the oars!* But Garland Phillips was smarter than that. He was making for an unattended native canoe. *That's it sir, that's it!* Coles managed at last to bring the glass into focus. He was fit and fast, was Mr Phillips, and he ran like a gazelle on those long legs of his. He was giving himself a chance.

Phillips was plunging through the icy shallows now, scattering the gelid, viscous seawater into glittering cascades as if it were the warm, sparkling waters of the tropics. *Come on sir, come on!* He had reached the canoe now, untied it, and was climbing in. The savages were chasing him hard, for they were powerful buggers too, but they hadn't thought to make for their own canoes yet. They were hurling rocks, but the rocks were falling short. He had a slim chance, had Mr Phillips, but it was a chance all right. The catechist levered himself up on two wiry arms and remained there, momentarily suspended on the lip on the canoe, held for an instant too long in the centre of the lens; then the top of his cranium disintegrated in a silent red puff, a delicate crimson cloud of vapour, and Garland Phillips subsided slowly into the water, quite dead, looking rather astonished, his black hair and coat-tails waving, like the dark fronds of beckoning seaweed that welcomed him down into the scarlet sea.

A second later, the musket report rolled out grandly across

the bay. Coles lifted the spyglass and refocused it, trying to identify the shooter. There he was: young Threeboys, a little smile of pride on his twelve-year-old face, accepting the accolades of his fellows for what really was a first-rate piece of marksmanship.

Chapter Thirty-four

140 Church Road, Upper Norwood, 13 December 1856

———

FitzRoy rose at six, dressed, breakfasted, and had bidden goodbye to his wife by seven. It did not come easily to think of his cousin Maria as his wife: he had hardly known her before their marriage, and she was still a stranger in many ways. Maria Smyth was kind, gentle, plump, maternal and had still been a spinster at the unthinkable age of thirty, so the family had seized an undoubtedly useful opportunity to tie up two rather awkward loose ends. He was grateful for her furious dedication to the pursuit of matrimonial bliss, and he was almost – but not quite – in love with her; but both of them knew that Mary FitzRoy had been his true wife, and would reclaim that title from her usurper on Judgement Day. Maria did her best to make him happy, but nothing could make him happy, for his daughter Emily, wilful, beautiful and sole inheritor of the earthly spirit of her mother, had died in August at the tender age of eighteen; taken by the good Lord for the fulfilment of a divine purpose that seemed increasingly arcane, increasingly arbitrary and increasingly baroque in its cruelty as the years went by. He blotted out his grief by driving himself furiously at his work, staying late at the office until well into the evening. As he waved his wife goodbye he knew, as she did, that they would not meet again until shortly before it was time to retire for the night. Such was the case six days a week; only on the Lord's day would he relent, and pause to beg his Creator to grant him comprehension.

FitzRoy walked up Church Road towards the relocated Crystal Palace, then fed eastwards into the stream of black-clad, black-booted, black-hatted men heading down Anerley Road to the station and the seven sixteen Pimlico service operated by the Crystal Palace and West End Railway. Black was the colour of the cast-iron locomotive that would ferry them to London, black the colour of the coal that filled its tender. Black were the buildings that would consume this army, dirtied by the soot from a million coal fires; black was the newsprint they would consume *en route*, the vehicle of information and authority in this modern world. Black was the colour of innovation and progress. Why, then, did FitzRoy feel like a worker ant? When he was young, he had returned from the first *Beagle* voyage to a stumbling, poverty-stricken, directionless Britain in which men had dressed like hummingbirds. Now technology had taken a hand, and prosperity and security were being smelted and forged in a thousand factories. But technology had not been a liberating force, as he had hoped; rather, it constrained, it imposed uniformity. Men's individual souls, God's most precious gift, were being corralled like cattle by industrialists and factory-owners in Mammon's cause. Even time had been standardized: men's watches told the same time in East London as they did in West, in Norwich as they did in Plymouth. FitzRoy felt a sudden urge to stop in the middle of the swarm, and perform an about-turn; to shout at his fellows, that there were other places in this world, other peoples, that most of them would never even become aware of, other sights and sounds that were every bit as vital a part of God's universe as they were. He wanted to tell them of sixty-foot waves, of crashing earthquakes and exploding volcanoes, of majestic Araucanian tribesmen with long, tapering lances, of wild-haired, white-painted Fuegians lighting fires on their lonely windswept shores at the far end of the world; marvels to be celebrated and studied by modern man, not eradicated or homogeneated in the pursuit of commercial or political gain. He wanted to stop and shout all these things, but he could not, for Emily was dead, like her mother before her, and conformity was his only escape, his only refuge. It did not do, in the end, to question God's purpose unduly. That was Darwin's weakness, and the philosopher was surely doomed. In the end, all FitzRoy could do was put his trust in God, and live in accordance with His teachings; that was the silent promise he had made to his dying wife, and nothing would induce him to stray from that path, wherever it took him. The sole remaining purpose of his life was to serve her memory to the best of his ambitions. That was the way it must be.

It was December, so progress had even clouded the atmosphere. As the train pulled into the steamer dock platform at Battersea, a veil of dense, dirty-yellow mist descended, as if the air itself had grown mouldy. A sickly gleam betrayed a surreptitious attempt by the sun's rays to cut an opening in the fog. Ghastly, pallid circles rimmed the wintry gas lamps that burned all day and all night at this time of year, their futile oily smears more part of the problem than part of the solution. The paddle-steamer nudged cautiously across the crowded grey river, fearful of collision. The great army of black-clad office-workers stood in silence on the deck, like mourners at a wake, listening to the chug of the engine and the dull, rhythmic slap of water against the paddles. FitzRoy half expected, half wanted to see a great wall of water bear down on them out of the fog, wanted to battle it, to pit his wits against wild nature and emerge victorious, his adversary bested but not destroyed, racing away into the mist once more to challenge him another day.

The steamer docked at Westminster Pier and disgorged its

contents on to the misted cobbles. He made his way west, the crowd thinning, past the half-built stump of the new clock tower, to his cramped office in Parliament Street, in an over-spill building for the Board of Trade. His two clerks, Pattrickson and Babington, who had much less far to come, had already pulled off their coats and were jabbing the fire in the tiny grate to life. He had appointed Pattrickson, the more able of the two, his deputy; Babington, who should have taken precedence by social rank, was a loyal and enthusiastic youth and did not seem to object. A third clerk, Simpkinson, a *protégé* of Lord Derby, had proved so vain and useless that FitzRoy had released him; pointedly, the boy had not been replaced. It mattered not. The three of them would manage. The weather statistics they collated, FitzRoy knew, were read by nobody: their office existed only to fulfil Britain's obligations under the Brussels Marine Meteorology Conference of 1853. But however perfunctory the assessment of their work, he was determined that the work itself would be of the highest order. He always sent his clerks home at five, and – generously – at lunchtime on Saturdays, but he himself sometimes laboured until midnight, perfecting and fine-tuning the British Meteorological Register. He had even invented the FitzRoy barometer, a slender, elegant, Gothic, glassed-in device that measured temperature, humidity and atmospheric pressure; it had been mass-produced and loaned to more than a thousand merchant and Royal Navy ships. A network of agents around the British Isles had been paid fifty shillings for every skipper persuaded to contribute information. The results were remark-ably comprehensive: within a month or so of any given weather pattern occurring, his office could produce an exact chart of its progress. The endlessly repeating weather patterns had not escaped his notice. As always, he had his eye on a bigger goal than merely recording the past. He had his eye on the future.

'The old dry stick wants to see you, sir,' announced Babington cheerily. 'The messenger came by just before you got here.'

FitzRoy halted in the act of throwing off his coat. The 'old dry stick', as the young clerks referred to him behind his back, was Admiral Beechey – Chief Naval Officer, head of the Marine Department and their immediate superior – who worked a couple of minutes away at the Board of Trade itself. Beechey was a stickler for instant obedience. It would not do to keep him waiting.

'Thank you, Babington. I shall pay my respects to the admiral forthwith.'

It was not a bad nickname, he reflected, as he plunged back into the yellowy soup. Beechey had served under Franklin in the Arctic, and had even been made president of the Royal Geographical Society, but he was no fur-booted adventurer. Rather, he seemed like a dead tree, rooted to the spot but devoid of all vitality, gnarled in his disapproval of the budding efforts of his subordinates, but producing little of substance himself.

Admiral Beechey made him stand like a junior officer. Only ten years FitzRoy's senior, he specialized in heavy-handed sarcasm.

'Ah, Captain FitzRoy, I am so glad you are here. I was rather hoping you might enlighten me. Your latest chart appears to have been overrun by spiders. What, pray, are these markings intended to be?' He gestured to a map of the British Isles that lay unrolled across his desktop, which was festooned with tiny hubbed wheels trailing spokes of uneven length.

'It is a synoptic chart, sir. The markings are wind stars, a diagrammatic system I have devised for recording weather observations.'

'Why the deuce can't you enter them into a log as you're supposed to?'

'Seen on a chart, sir, distinctive patterns emerge. Storms appear to be rotary in construction, and to move in a principally easterly direction at about five miles per hour. For instance, sir, the storm that wrecked the Allied supply fleet off Balaclava had travelled eastward all the way across Europe.

It occurred to me, sir, that if such storms could be tracked quickly enough, we could use the electric telegraph to send warning of their arrival. My plan is to set up barometers at coastal observing-stations, and lay telegraph cables directly from those stations to the Board of Trade. We could collate meteorological information almost instantly, sir.'

'Your job, Captain FitzRoy, is to collate meteorological information for statical purposes, not to feed some fantastical notion of foretelling the weather. I do not know if you have been informed of it, but you are employed as a statist, not a sorcerer.'

'But if we analyse the statical facts, sir, we can deduce a dynamical, observable pattern. Weather currents are as predictable as ocean currents – we are all of us living in an ocean of air. And when these currents oppose or pass each other, they cause eddies or whirls on an immense scale in the air, not only horizontal but inclined to the terrain or vertical. That is how storms occur, sir – I am certain of it. Especially where heated air from the tropics encounters cold air coming down from the polar regions.'

'I would remind you of your position, Captain FitzRoy,' said Beechey coldly. Two diamond eyes gleamed in his small, shrivelled face. 'You were appointed to the post of statist through the good graces of the Earl of Derby, no doubt on account of your misfortunes in New Zealand, misfortunes that I have heard were occasioned entirely by your own failings. Do you really think the best way to repay that gentleman's kindness is to abuse your position in this manner? You have already caused his lordship considerable embarrassment by dismissing Mr Simpkinson, whose father is a highly influential gentleman and a personal friend of his lordship.'

'Mr Simpkinson had no scientific knowledge whatsoever, sir. He was not up to the job.'

'You are in no position to be the judge of such matters. I have considerable doubts as to whether you are up to the job yourself.'

FitzRoy tried again: 'If you please, sir, I am merely attempting to investigate the import of our meteorologic research. The influence of the heavenly bodies, for instance: if you will allow me to show you my findings, I can produce convincing evidence that solar activity may be influencing the earth's weather. Sunspots, in particular—'

'*Enough*, FitzRoy,' ground out Admiral Beechey. 'You are becoming impertinent. There shall be no more "synoptic charts". No more "wind stars". No more arrogant nonsense about being able to "foretell the weather". Not while I am the head of the Marine Department. Is that completely clear?'

'Yes sir.'

FitzRoy turned smartly and left Beechey's office without a word. In former times he would have felt defiant, would have worked out a way round the problem. Now he merely felt defeated and despondent. Making progress at Whitehall was like wading through a Falklands peat bog.

FitzRoy bought a copy of the *Daily Telegraph* for a penny at the W.H. Smith news-stand at London Bridge, then settled back into his seat on the Sydenham train. A skull, apparently belonging to a primitive branch of the human species, had been unearthed in the Rhineland; Fuhrott, its discoverer, had named it *Homo neanderthalis*. The news brought an ironic smile to his face, in the light of his destination. He had no idea why Darwin had demanded to see him, but he guessed that it was not for friendship's sake, not now, not after five years. He sensed, rather, that a specific purpose lay behind the invitation. Once, perhaps, he would have objected to venturing forth in ignorance, or even to being summoned in such a manner at all. Now, he realized ruefully, his was a life of being led.

The old phaeton collected him at the station and ferried him at a snail's pace across the chalk-fields to Down House. A housemaid opened the door – the lugubrious butler was obviously off on some errand – and FitzRoy was immediately assailed by a revolting, sickly reek, the unmistakable stench of the charnel-house. While his senses reeled, he saw Darwin hobbling forth from his study to welcome his guest.

'Ah, FitzRoy. Please excuse the smell. It is the rather regrettable result of my experiments. Mrs Darwin will scarcely forgive me.'

'My dear Darwin, it is nothing,' lied FitzRoy. 'But what on earth . . . ?'

'Pigeons. Hanging in the cellar and the outside sheds, waiting to be defleshed. Parslow and I are falling somewhat behind. I have become a pigeon-breeder.'

'A *pigeon*-breeder?'

Pigeon-breeding was the preserve of lonely clerks with clay pipes, who gathered in smoky beer-halls in Spitalfields and the Borough to discuss the relative merits of the turbit and the trumpeter, not of respectable gentlemen scientists residing with their families in country parsonages.

'Yes indeed. Pigeons. Fascinating. Why, if they only knew the amazing amount of solace and pleasure to be derived from the Almond Tumbler, then scarce any noblemen or gentlemen would be without their aviaries. It is a majestic and noble pursuit.'

Downy white feathers, FitzRoy observed, had drifted like snowflakes, undusted, into the darker recesses of the mantelshelves and the more obscure corners of the staircase. Through the open doorway of Darwin's study he could see out on to the lawn – or, at least, what had once been the lawn: row after row of vertical wires filled the horizon, each row an elegant prison for a feathery inmate. These, it appeared, were condemned cells, for whereas most breeders cosseted their pigeons like newborn babies, Darwin was apparently engaged in wholesale slaughter. Anyone else would have presumed the philosopher to have taken leave of his senses, but FitzRoy knew his man. All these cages, he guessed, were merely further means to an extremely familiar end.

Parslow chose that moment to materialize at one end of

the corridor, carrying a still-smoking shotgun and a score of dead partridges slung over one shoulder.

'More partridges, sir.'

'Oh! Yes. Put them in the cellar, would you, Parslow, with the rest?'

Parslow assumed an expression of extreme forbearance and trudged away.

'Let me guess,' said FitzRoy. 'Wild birds – for the purposes of comparison?'

'Oh no no,' replied Darwin quickly. 'A quite different experiment. Seed propagation. My son Georgie counts the seeds in the mud that adheres to their feet. I am trying to estimate the spread of plant species through animal hosts. Where is Georgie, by the way? Georgie!'

There was an almighty crash from upstairs, and a snub-nosed eleven-year-old face poked through the banisters above.

'Georgie, what are you *doing*?'

'We're playing soldiers, Pappy. We've hung two trapezes from the ceiling so we can charge each other. I'm the British dragoons and Bessy is the Russians.'

'Are you sure Bessy wants to play this game? She is only nine.'

'She did want to play, Pappy, until she fell off the second time.'

'Well stop it at once and come downstairs.'

'Pappy, may we play cricket in the corridor?'

'*No*. Come downstairs at once. There are partridges.'

'Partridges? Huzza!'

George Darwin shot down the staircase on a tin tray, narrowly missing his five-year-old brother Horace, who had chosen that moment to wander past the bottom step.

'Pappy, you know the fireworks for winning the war?'

'Yes, Georgie?'

'Will there be any more?'

'No, Georgie. The war is finished.'

'Oh. All right then.'

Apparently unfazed by this news, Georgie vanished into the cellar, followed by Horace, leaving FitzRoy and Darwin alone in the corridor once more.

'My dear FitzRoy, you must excuse my atrocious manners. Where was I?'

'Pigeons.'

'Oh, yes – pigeons. I have joined two clubs. The members call me "Squire".' Darwin preened, ever so slightly.

'Might I ask why?'

'Only if we shall not argue about it.'

FitzRoy smiled. 'You have my word.'

'Very well. I shall tell you on the sand walk. Fetch your coat.'

It was only then that Darwin noticed FitzRoy was still wearing his coat: none of the servants had thought to take it from him.

They set off through a cacophony of squawking, barking, bleating, oinking and droning, which came not from the pigeon cages, but from a variety of pens further back, containing sheep, pigs, cats, dogs, poultry and peacocks. There were phalanxes of beehives, and glass tanks crowded with fancy goldfish. The droning came from Darwin's eight-year-old son Frankie, who was making a fearful noise with a bassoon in the bushes.

'An unusual place for bassoon practice,' remarked FitzRoy.

'Oh, he's not practising it. He's playing it to the leaves of that plant to see if it will respond to the vibrations of the music. All the children help me with my experiments when they are old enough. Etty dusts the bees with flour, to trace their movements, and Bessy germinates hazel and asparagus seeds that have been immersed in salt water for several days.'

'Let me hazard another guess. Seed propagation?'

'On the mark!' Darwin looked pleased.

'And the pigeons?'

'Oh, yes – the pigeons!'

A shabby-jacketed pair of gardeners marched past, uncut

hair straggling from beneath their battered bowler hats. Darwin waited diplomatically for them to salute and move on; then he leaned in towards FitzRoy and adopted a furtive tone: 'What I am doing is picking birds with a particular characteristic, then trying to exaggerate that characteristic by selective breeding.'

'But, my dear Darwin, is that not what all pigeon-breeders do?'

'Precisely.' Darwin looked rather impressed with himself. 'It is my intention, over several generations of selective breeding, to create a new species.'

Great heavens, thought FitzRoy. *He actually intends to usurp the role of the Creator.*

'It should not be too difficult,' Darwin continued. 'After all, Mr Bult has achieved considerable gains in size, simply by crossing his pouters with his runts. It is my belief that pigeon species derive from a common ancestor. That Mother Nature is no more than a breeder herself, albeit on a remarkable scale.'

'If a central intelligence has bred different types of pigeon in the wild, then surely the breeder is God Himself?'

'*Chance* is the breeder, my friend. For the crossbreeds are random, and the failed varieties die out. The successful crossbreeds go on to form the basis of new species.'

'But crossbreeds are not successful in the wild. Farm-bred animals simply die out when released into the wild, like hothoused flowers in a cold climate.'

'Only because human breeders are looking for decorative variations, whereas nature inadvertently breeds species that are better suited to changes in climate, geology and so forth. We saw it with the Galapagos finches.'

'Nature, or God, has crossbred a single type of finch into a variety of finches, I grant you, just as a pigeon-breeder can create a variety of pigeons. But human breeders have never once succeeded in altering a skeleton, or the organs of nutrition, of circulation, of respiration, of secretion or of generation. When man tries to crossbreed species – actual distinct species

– the results are sterile. Look at the common mule. And you claim that where man, with all his ingenuity, fails, nature somehow succeeds by accident? Have you yourself succeeded in altering any of your pigeons at these fundamental levels?'

'No. But how much more powerful are the mighty forces of nature than the mere hand of man – able, surely, to alter the whole machinery of life? Let me give you an example. In North America the black bear was witnessed by Hearne, swimming with an open mouth for hours on end, catching insects on the water's surface. I can see no difficulty in a race of bears being rendered, by natural selection, more and more aquatic in their structure and habits, with larger and larger mouths, until a creature is produced as monstrous as a whale.'

FitzRoy laughed almost delightedly. He was beginning to enjoy himself once again, to relish the intellectual cut and thrust of his younger days, in spite of the grotesque presumption of his old shipmate's arguments.

'You are seriously suggesting that a bear might transmute into a whale? Where, then, is your half-creature – your half-bear, half-whale?'

'You think there is no evidence of physical transmutation? What are the fins of a penguin but its former wings? What is a man's useless nipple but the remains of a former breast?'

'Even assuming you are correct in these observations, you are describing changes within the species of penguins, within the boundaries of the human race. You will find no half-men, half-penguins anywhere! By what means do you believe these variations descend, that the species boundary is so easily crossed?'

'I call it *pangenesis*. I believe that every animal produces microscopic "gemmules", which collect in its reproductive organs for transmission to the next generation. Without doubt, sexual reproduction is the key to adaptation. The different colours of the human race, for instance, must have been caused by sexual selection – although it seems at first sight a monstrous supposition that the jet blackness of the negro has been gained this way.'

FitzRoy was incredulous. 'Can the Ethiopian change his skin, or the leopard his spots? What of the origin of life itself? How do you account for that, if you are not prepared to acknowledge our Creator?'

'Life itself must have started by chance too – in a warm pond, perhaps, galvanized by a bolt of lightning that fused random molecules together.'

'Lightning on a warm *pond*? What of human consciousness? Was that born of lightning on a warm pond as well?'

'Even man's vertebral skull, which contains our brains, is a sign of our descent from molluscal creatures with vertebrae but no head. Plato says in *Phaedo* that our imaginary ideas derive from the pre-existence of the soul. For pre-existence of the soul, one may substitute monkeys. We have animal ancestors, FitzRoy.'

'I'm sorry,' laughed his guest, 'but I simply refuse to acknowledge that my most august ancestors, the dukes of Grafton, are descended from apes!'

'My dear FitzRoy, can you not see that the utilitarianism that is changing our very society operates in nature as well? Open your mind to the idea of change, the idea of progress. Do not be hidebound by aristocratic privilege!'

Under former circumstances this last sentiment would have been an aggressive sally indeed, guaranteed to cause offence, but here it was delivered with a smile, and was accepted with one too, for nostalgia had the upper hand. This was a debate entered into by both parties with relish. Then, with a sudden stab, as a cold December gust came slicing in from the stubbly fields beyond the sand walk, FitzRoy remembered that Darwin had not invited him here to discuss pigeon-breeding and all its attendant ramifications. There was, no doubt, a deeper, darker purpose on the agenda. Both men knew what the pause in their conversation heralded.

'I have received a letter,' said Darwin at last, 'from a man named Alfred Russel Wallace. He is a former schoolmaster, no more, who has become a professional collector of specimens for gentlemen naturalists. He is currently exploring the Malay archipelago. He has written to me from the island of Ternate, near New Guinea. He has written to me, FitzRoy, to propose my own theory – the theory of natural selection. Like me, he believes that all species form a branching tree. The plain truth is, we have thought alike and have come to similar conclusions. I never saw a more striking coincidence. I have been collecting facts for twenty-five years, and Wallace reached the same conclusions as myself after thinking about the matter for just three days!'

He pulled Wallace's letter from an inside pocket and read out the salient paragraph.

'"The answer is clearly that on the whole the best fitted live. From the effects of disease the most healthy escape; from enemies, the strongest, the swiftest, or the most cunning; from famine, the best hunters or those with the best digestion; and so on. Then it suddenly flashed upon me that this self-acting process would necessarily improve the race, because in every generation the inferior would inevitably be killed off and the superior remain – that is, the fittest would survive."'

Darwin folded the letter and replaced it portentously in his pocket.

'What do you want of me?' asked FitzRoy, who knew very well what Darwin wanted of him.

'I should like to be released from my bond. I should like to write a book outlining my theories. In fact, I have already begun to write it, on the advice of Lyell. He says that my research consists of ugly facts, but facts nonetheless, and that if I do not publish them, Wallace will go ahead and publish regardless when he returns to these shores.'

'Shall you credit Wallace?'

'Lyell and Hooker have suggested a joint paper, in both our names, to be read to the Linnaean Society.'

A small private club of your friends and colleagues, thought FitzRoy. *In theory, you will have published jointly. In practice, the name Wallace shall never escape the society's four walls.*

Darwin looked shamefaced. 'Let me be perfectly honest with you, FitzRoy. Writing this book feels like confessing to a murder. My wife and my family will be heartbroken. But I believe, I truly believe in my heart, that nature's works are blundering, low and horribly cruel, and that it is my duty to say so. The chief good any individual scientific man can do is to push his field forward, a few years in advance of his age. For me to reach conclusions, and not openly to avow those conclusions, is to retard my field. It is a matter of principle.'

He is desperate for recognition, realized FitzRoy, *yet he fears the consequences – and rightly so.*

He fixed his gaze upon Darwin. 'If your theories be true, then religion is a lie, human law is a mass of folly and a base injustice, morality is moonshine, our labours on behalf of the black people of the world are the works of madmen, and men and women are only better beasts. If you succeed, the Church shall be ruined and all moral safeguards shattered. You will give succour and credence to the Chartists who seek to overthrow our society. You will remove the very *need* for God.'

'Perhaps not. Perhaps the success of *The Vestiges* has opened the way for healthy intellectual debate. Some scientists are with me – Huxley and Hooker, to name two. Owen, I must tell you, will be agin me: he believes that animals progress from one form to another only within basic species archetypes, as decreed by the will of God.'

'Thank heavens for the good sense of Mr Owen.'

'So, FitzRoy, will you release me from my obligations? Do I have your permission to publish?'

'Were I to withhold my permission, would it make the slightest bit of difference?'

'Probably not.'

'Then why ask?'

'Because I respect you as a former shipmate and a friend; because I am about to walk a difficult road; and because I should like your blessing, at least by default, for my journey.'

FitzRoy saw that there was no stopping him. He thought, then, of Mary, and of his vow to uphold the word of the Lord in her name for the rest of his born days. *He that believeth in me, though he were dead, yet shall he live; and whosoever liveth and believeth in me shall never die.* And yet, he was not his brother's keeper. He pondered for a while, then made his decision.

'Very well, Darwin. I will no longer hold you to your word. Go ahead and publish. But know that as of now I will be your enemy, and that I will do everything in my power to hinder you, and to hinder the public acceptance of your arguments.'

On the train back from Sydenham, FitzRoy unfolded and reread a letter of his own that he had kept quiet from his former cabin-mate. It was from his son, Robert O'Brien FitzRoy, now a midshipman serving on the Far Eastern station. It was just aimless chatter, most of it, intended to reassure a concerned parent that his offspring was happy and healthy with the sun on his back. But reading between the lines, FitzRoy thought he could detect the same loneliness, the same yearning for approval, that had so profoundly informed his own days as a young middie. Had he been a good parent? he wondered. Had he given the boy every advantage in life? He had sent him away to sea at twelve, which he considered to be the optimum age to begin a successful naval career. He would never have let the lad run riot, fixing trapezes to the ceiling or descending the stairs on a tin tray. One day, he knew, his son would thank him for instilling the virtues of discipline and hard work. But had he been too disciplined with himself? Had he worked too hard to afford his son sufficient of his own time?

A feeble winter light struggled to penetrate the rain-flecked windows as the train rolled through the filthy railway suburbs of South London, which seemed to be spreading as rapidly as soot exploding from a burst sack.

I have never neglected my duty for a minute, he comforted himself; and even as the thought crossed his mind, he realized that devotion to duty had been only the half of it. *The more I employed myself, the more I forced occupation, the more easily I got through the day*, he confessed inwardly. *My worst times have always been when I was alone and unemployed. What a life this is – the pains are far greater than the pleasures. And yet people set such a value upon existence, as if they are always happy.*

As if to prove his point, London Bridge station in mid-afternoon was full of good-natured trippers, braving the winter chills. The end of the war had lifted everybody's spirits: the women paraded in blooming crinolines and vast hats, while their black-clad beaux, wealthy enough not to work, sported slick military moustaches. The swirling skirts put FitzRoy in mind of the grand ball held in his honour at the Teatro Solis in Monte Video, a celebration that appeared to him now as a distant dream. All those brightly coloured dresses that had opened out like flowers, all now withered and faded, pressed lifelessly in the book of his memories. There were times when his youth felt like someone else's story – or perhaps *this* was someone else's life, *this* was the illusion, and back there, back then, was where he truly belonged. Had he been happy then, in his innocence? He suspected so. But he had taken Darwin with him for company, and the philosopher had come home with seeds adhering unwittingly to his boots, the seeds of the tree of knowledge.

He rode a hansom cab to Parliament Street, and found Pattrickson and Babington warming their hands at the little grate, a high tide of unattended synoptic charts surging across the table. He was mystified: they were usually the most diligent and enthusiastic of men. He could not help but sound a little tart.

'Why are you not transferring the meteorologic data to the log, as Admiral Beechey instructed?'

'Have you not heard, sir?' asked Babington, his face a picture of shock and news-bearing excitement.

'Heard what?'

'Admiral Beechey is dead!'

'Dead? How?' The admiral had been, if not a picture of health, then very much alive when FitzRoy had last seen him.

'He died this very afternoon, sir, of heart failure.'

'I . . . I'm sorry.'

FitzRoy really did not know what to say.

'I must confess, gentlemen, that I am not entirely sure what this news shall mean for us.'

'What it shall mean, sir? Surely, it means that you will be promoted to the admiral's former position, as Chief Naval Officer. It means that our work may continue, sir.'

The two of them sat there on their stools, no longer able to contain their true feelings, grinning like a pair of monkeys.

'FitzRoy, my dear fellow, come in, come in!'

'Your lordship.'

'Oh, there is no need to stand on ceremony. We are old hands, you and I. I hope I see you well, sir.'

The fourteenth Earl of Derby beamed effusively, warmth and sincerity radiating from every pore. He had been very handsome and sought-after in his youth, although these days his striking aquiline features were half sunken in his spreading face, his extravagant ginger side-whiskers had turned to grey, and he was terribly assailed by gout; but he had lost none of the charisma that had propelled him to the summit of the Tory Party. The familiarity of the welcome immediately put FitzRoy on his guard: Derby was a consummate politician, and he was not to be trusted. He had been a Whig, then a Liberal, then a follower of Canning, then a full-blown Tory; he had espoused slavery, and had helped to abolish it; he had spoken for and against Irish emancipation; as Lord Stanley, prior to his father's death, he had appointed FitzRoy governor of New Zealand, and then had dismissed him. In the process, he had amassed a personal fortune well in excess of a million pounds. Behind the affable manners, he was a cold, pragmatic businessman. He had been appointed prime minister twice, but had been overthrown twice, once by the Peelites and once by the electorate. Palmerston was prime minister now, but Derby was biding his time. He would be back.

The earl relaxed into his armchair, beneath a patriotic painting depicting the advance of the 7th Madras Native Infantry into Rangoon.

'Dreadful news about Freddie Beechey.'

'Most regrettable, my lord.'

'And, of course, it will mean a shake-up at the Marine Department. A man of your experience will be absolutely vital in the coming weeks. I tell you, FitzRoy, I don't know where the country would be without your knowledge, your dedication and your grasp of meteorologic science. I hear golden opinions of the work you are doing over at the Statical Department.'

Derby's tones were mellifluous and soothing. Hearing them was like being lulled to sleep by a favourite nanny.

'Thank you, sir. I am glad that our work is appreciated. If I may be so bold, I came here on the strength of that work, to see if the party would press my claim to be allowed to succeed Admiral Beechey as chief naval officer.'

Derby was not just the leader of the Tory Party; his cousin was president of the Board of Trade.

'Well, of course, it is a job you could do in your sleep. And it carries with it the rank of rear-admiral. And, I dare say, the one thousand pounds a year would not go amiss either!' Derby chuckled sympathetically. 'Where is it you are living now? Upper Norwood? Bad business – bad business.' The last few words were mumbled, a mutual embarrassment to be hurried past as quickly as possible. Derby cleared his throat.

'Well, let me say first that I have been working *extremely* hard in your behalf – you may be satisfied of it. As I am sure you are aware, a position of this importance attracts the very best of candidates. And I have some good news for you – qualified good news, I should say, but good news nonetheless. I hear that your seniority has come through. You are to be made rear-admiral, effective immediately. Congratulations, Rear-Admiral FitzRoy.'

'Thank you, my lord.'

'As to the matter of your promotion within the Board of Trade, I am afraid that the news on that count is not quite as good. Despite the best efforts of the party, the government has decided by the narrowest of margins that the claims of another candidate should be preferred.'

'Another candidate?' croaked FitzRoy. The disappointment was crushing. He felt both angry and humiliated.

'Oh, he is a splendid candidate, I am sure you will agree. He has our every support, and I have no doubt that you will feel privileged to serve under him. He distinguished himself considerably during the war – I appreciate, FitzRoy, that you were unlucky enough not to secure a command yourself but, damn it, the man is a bona-fide war hero and we should not begrudge him that – distinguished himself, I should say, not just by innumerable acts of bravery, but by several technical innovations as well. It was he who came up with the idea of cladding wooden hulls with iron plates, and fixing ships' guns to the deck. Then when the Russians filled the sea with infernal machines that exploded on impact with our ships, he invented a creeper device to sweep them out of the water. And he also dreamed up the idea of bombarding fortified Russian positions aerially, instead of front-on: a sort of concentrated vertical fire. His vessel fired more than three thousand "mortar bombs" during the taking of Sweaborg. He is just about to be made Companion of the Bath and, between you and me, he would have had a knighthood were it not for the jealousy of one or two of the senior admirals. You might even know him. Your new superior's name is Captain Bartholomew Sulivan.'

'Bartholomew Sulivan?' gasped FitzRoy. It was almost

impossible to take in. If he had not been sitting down, his legs would no doubt have given way.

'That's the chap. You don't have any objections, I take it?'

FitzRoy paled. How could he?

'No . . . none whatsoever.'

Derby smiled, the winning smile of a master strategist.

'No . . . I thought you might not.'

Chapter Thirty-five

Stanley, Falkland Islands,
12 October 1857

'All rise for the governor, Mr Thomas Moore, and justices of the peace, Mr Arthur Bailey and Mr John Dean.'

Everyone in the shabby wooden courthouse rose to their feet as the only gentlemen of any official consequence on the islands swept in. Outside, the baying of the angry mob could still be heard: a small rip to Moore's coat and Bailey's disarranged hair bore testimony to the buffeting they had taken on their way in. There was an expression of grim defiance on Moore's face. He would be damned if lynch law were to prevail in his colony. 'Bring in the prisoner,' he commanded.

Two gaolers entered, flanking the pathetic, bewildered figure of Jemmy Button, clad in rough overalls and bearing a cut forehead where a brick had glanced off his cranium. He had only narrowly escaped with his life. As he shuffled forward to the dock, the manacles that bound his ankles together clinking at the limit of every step, twelve furious, hostile faces glared at him. The jury was an extension of the crowd outside: this savage had murdered an entire party of white men, and they wanted to see him swing.

'Please state your name,' said the clerk.

'Jemmy Button, sar.'

'Please state your nationality.'

Jemmy looked confused.

'To which country do you belong?' interpreted Moore.

'I am English gen'leman, sar.'

'Excuse me, m'lud, but I believe that to be incorrect,' whispered the clerk.

'Button, you are not an English gentleman,' said Moore testily. 'And do not call me "m'lud", Haskins. "Sir" will suffice.'

Jemmy looked aggrieved. 'Capp'en Fitz'oy say I am English gen'leman.'

'Excuse me, sir,' continued the clerk, 'but the area of Woollya Cove from which the defendant hails is claimed by the government in Buenos Ayres, a claim our own government has fully recognized. Therefore technically, under international law, the defendant is a citizen of Argentina. Indeed, it is with the permission of the Argentinian government that we are able to go forward with these proceedings, sir.'

'Very well. Let us proceed with the oath.'

A Bible was fetched, and Jemmy stumbled through the responses.

'James Button, you are hereby charged with the murder of Captain Robert Fell, the Reverend Mr Garland Phillips, Mr John Fell, Seaman John Johnstone, Seaman John Johnstone, Seaman Hugh McDowall, Seaman John Brown and Seaman August Petersen. How do you plead?'

Jemmy looked puzzled.

'Did you kill those men?' interpreted Moore once again.

'No, sar! Jemmy kill nobody, sar!'

'Enter a not guilty plea,' Moore instructed the clerk.

Jemmy being further charged with incitement to murder, and with being an accessory to murder, not-guilty pleas were entered on all charges. Then the first witness was called, Captain William Smyley, a rumbustious American sealer in his mid-sixties.

The prosecuting counsel, for want of a genuine counsel on the islands, was to be Mr J. R. Longden, the colonial secretary. Longden stood up nervously, sniffing from the after-effects of a cold.

'You are Captain William Smyley?'

'I am, sir, though everyone here knows me as Fat Jack of the Bonehouse.'

'You are the captain of a sealing-ship?'

'Skipper of the brigantine *Nancy*, out of Rhode Island, as you well know, Mr Longden, sir.'

'Would you care to tell the court how you came to visit Woollya Cove?'

'I stood in to Stanley for supplies, and I was hired by the reverend over there' – he indicated Despard, who was perched like a vulture at the far side of the courtroom – 'to go to Woollya to search for the *Allen Gardiner*. He said it was overdue. The reverend wanted me to skipper his boat, but I preferred to take my own with my own crew. They're true sailors and men, sir. Anyhow, it was a rough crossing. On our first day out, a living gale struck the ship about three points off the weather quarter, at the very moment that the helmsman was in the act of putting her away to run before it. In an instant she was knocked down, with her yards in the water. Well, she gradually came to the wind and righted—'

'If you would confine your remarks to the events at Woollya Cove, Captain Smyley,' grumbled Moore. Court cases in London, he knew, could be interminable. Not so in his colony.

'Sure . . . so, we made all speed to Woollya Cove. We found the *Allen Gardiner* – she was deserted. She was just a shell. All her ironwork was gone, her sails had been stripped and her instruments stolen. There were scorchmarks on deck where the savages had lit fires. She'd dragged her anchor and drifted, but luckily the chain had gotten trapped under a submerged boulder, shortening her leeway, so she'd avoided the rocks.'

'You say she was deserted, that her crew was missing,' sniffed Longden. 'Were any of the natives present?'

'Soon after we arrived, a whole stack of canoes turned up. There was a white man in one of them – Mr Coles over there. He was with the accused. So we threw down ropes, and the two of 'em came aboard. The savage said he was hungry and thirsty, so I sent him to the galley for some scoff. Then Coles told me his story – all about the murders – and I figured if things got serious, we wouldn't have the ghost of a show. It was time to get the hell out of there. Also, I reckoned by the sound of it we had the ringleader on board, so I cut the painter of his canoe. The ship was put away immediately, we ran down Ponsonby Sound and were into Nassau Bay before the savage even noticed. And that's how he got here.'

'Thank you, Captain Smyley. No further questions, sir.'

The defence was to be conducted by Lieutenant Lamb, the local marine commander, a tall, well-bred youth who had never attended a court case before. He shuffled a stack of papers in what he hoped was a convincing manner, and rose to his feet.

'Captain Smyley, you are saying you *abducted* the defendant?'

'I'd call it a citizen's arrest, Lieutenant.'

'And how would you describe the defendant's demeanour upon boarding the *Nancy*?'

'The defendant's what?'

'His conduct, his bearing.'

'Well, that was the damnedest thing. He was real friendly, like he thought he was one of us. And he spoke better English 'n half my crew.'

'He made no attempt to resist abduction?'

'No.'

'Did that not strike you as curious behaviour for a guilty man?'

'Stupid behaviour. He is a savage, after all.'

Murmurs of assent could be heard from the jury.

'Captain Smyley, is it not the case that three years ago you acted in support of an American corvette threatening to bombard Stanley during a trade dispute, an action which I myself witnessed?'

'Objection sir,' butted in Longden. 'Captain Smyley is not on trial here.'

'Objection sustained.'

Lamb faltered. 'No further questions.'

Smyley stepped down with a grimace at the young lieutenant, and was replaced in the witness stand by a startled-looking Alfred Coles, who had been shoehorned into a borrowed suit. The cook's face had been scrubbed red and his hair tackled by a barber for the first time in many years: it stood up vertically in the blacking-brush style, as if he had been connected to an electric current. Guided by Longden, he talked the court through the terrible events at Woollya Cove, leading up to the shooting of Garland Phillips.

'And who would you say was the ringleader of this murderous gang, Coles?'

'Well, I can't be all that sure, 'cause the savages look uncommon alike, but it looked to me like Jemmy, sir. It wasn't him as killed the Scandihoovian, or as shot Mr Phillips, that was Threeboys, but I'm sure I saw Jemmy in the thick of it, I think.'

'Jemmy kill *nobody*!' burst out the defendant.

'You will be silent, Button, until it is time for you to give evidence,' rapped the governor.

Longden blew his nose and resumed his prepared questions. 'You say you are sure Jemmy was at the head of the mob?'

'I – I reckon so, sir.'

'Now is not the time for imprecision, Coles. Either you are sure or you are not.'

'Yes, sir . . . I'm sure, sir.'

'Thank you, Coles. No further questions, sir.'

Lieutenant Lamb took over the inquisition. 'Would you

care to tell the court what happened, in your own words, immediately after Mr Phillips was shot?'

'Well, I took a short survey, like, and I sees them canoes coming towards the ship. So I says to myself, you'd best get on, Alfred, or there'll be trouble. So I goes to the gig hanging in the davits, cuts her free, picks up a paddle from the scuppers, and starts rowing for the far side of the cove. One of them sees me, and they starts rowing in my direction. I was mortal afraid, sir, 'cause they was faster 'n me, and was gaining on me, but I got to the shore first and ran into the woods. I climbed up a tree, so's they couldn't see me, but I could see them, looking for me. So I waits until dark and I'm sure they've gone, then I comes down, and I be hanged if the bugg— if the natives haven't stolen the gig, sir.'

'One moment, Coles. May I ask, was the defendant part of the mob that pursued you?'

'Not so far as I could make out, sir, no.'

'Carry on, Coles.'

'So I says to myself, what's-a-do, Alfred? So I starts walking east. Four days I walked, living off berries like, hiding up in the day and walking at night. After four days I comes to a big river, too deep to ford and too cold to swim – like as not I'd freeze to death, I thinks to myself. By this time I's getting mortal hungry and sick, like, so I hails a native canoe.'

'You actually hailed a native canoe?'

'Yes sir.'

'And where did they take you?'

'Right back to Woollya, sir.'

'They returned you to Woollya Cove?'

'Yes sir. And they's all there, sir, hundreds of 'em, sir. I sees one of 'em wearing the captain's coat, sir, and some of 'em in mission guernseys. They takes my clothes off me, and plucks my beard 'n' eyebrows out with sea-shells, one hair at a time. I thought I was a dead 'un, sir. Then there's these big rows goin' on, about what to do wi' me, I thinks. Then Jemmy, sir, he sticks up in my behalf.'

'The defendant actually interceded for your life? What did he say?'

'Well, I don't rightly know, sir, not speaking the lingo an' all, but he tells me later, he's told 'em English gentlemen don't kill their prisoners, sir. Leastways, they gives me over to him, and he finds me some stockings, my own hat and trousers, and the captain's boots, and he gives me some food, sir. Then later on he gives me Mr Phillips's musket, a nightcap full of powder, some shot and some percussion caps, so's I can hunt for myself, sir.'

'He actually *gave* you Mr Phillips's musket? And ammunition?'

'Yes, sir. He said it was the good Christian thing to do, sir. And he said he'd buried all the bodies, sir, given 'em all a Christian burial, like. He said it's what Captain FitzRoy would have done, sir. He kept goin' on about the captain. He was no end funny about him, sir. He used to go on board the *Allen Gardiner* and sleep all night in the captain's cabin. I reckon it made him feel closer to old Captain FitzRoy in a funny way, sir. Not that there was anything left on board, mind – they even ate the soap. I heard two of 'em died from doin' that. They even smashed up the ship's clock when it stopped 'cause they reckoned it was dead.'

'So the defendant looked after you and kept you safe, until Captain Smyley arrived in the *Nancy*?'

'Yes, sir. Then I passed over here, sir.'

'Let me take you back now, Coles, to conditions at the Cranmer Mission on Keppel Island. Would you say that the Fuegians were happy there?'

'No, I wouldn't, sir. They wasn't happy at all.'

'Why not?'

'Well, 'cause they was little more 'n slaveys, sir. Reckon as they didn't like that much. Then Mr Despard, sir, he kept orderin' they's stuff to be searched. There was a few scuffles, like. Things was gettin' out o' hand once or twice.'

Despard, from across the courtroom, fixed Coles with a

fiery glare that threatened to scorch him to a crisp.

'Were you ever involved in any of these "scuffles"?'

'No more than I never ought to,' replied Coles uncomfortably. 'That'd be Mr Phillips, in the main.'

'So you deny that you yourself, Coles, once pushed one of the Fuegians into the hold of the *Allen Gardiner*?'

'Does you intend to 'criminate me sir? 'Cause I won't be 'criminated, sir, 'cause I ain't done nothin' sir.'

'Objection sir,' sniffed Longden, haughtily.

'Objection sustained,' agreed Moore.

'Er, thank you, Coles,' said Lieutenant Lamb, retreating once again in disarray. 'There are no further questions, Your Honour. I mean, sir.'

The next witness was to be Jemmy himself. A buzz of genuine hostility circulated around the cramped courtroom, rising above the flapping and banging of a few badly fixed planks, which were being shoved and slapped by the relentless winds outside. The little Fuegian looked frightened, aware at last perhaps that he had got himself into a precarious situation.

'Tell me, Jemmy,' said Longden in a deceptively friendly manner, 'did you enjoy your stay at Keppel Island?'

'No sar. Jemmy don't like Keppel Island, don't want to stop there, don't like it. Too much work, no seals to eat. Always Jemmy has to work.'

'And Mr Phillips and Captain Fell – were they among those who ordered you to do too much work?'

'Yes sar, Mister Phillips, Captain Fell, Mister Despard, always say do too much work sar. Not let Jemmy go home, sar.'

'So all in all, you might think you had a reasonable grievance against those gentlemen – kept there longer than you wished, made to work hard?'

'Yes sar, yes,' agreed Jemmy enthusiastically, pleased that at last someone was prepared to entertain his point of view. 'Reasonable grievance sar, yes.'

'Tell me, Jemmy, did you witness the deaths of Captain Fell and the others?'

'Yes sar, I see Captain Fell killed, all men killed, I put them in ground.'

'But you say you did not kill anybody yourself.'

'No sar. Jemmy kill nobody.'

'The court has heard, Jemmy, that your son Threeboys shot Mr Phillips. Is this what you saw?'

'No sar. Threeboys a good boy sar. No kill anybody. Please sar, do not punish Threeboys sar. He is a good boy.'

'So if you did not kill anybody, Jemmy, and Threeboys did not kill anybody . . . who did?'

'Oens-men, sar.'

'"Oens-men"?'

'Yes sar. Oens-men. The same as Patagonia bow-and-arrow men. Big bad men sar, come to my country, kill many people. No *sabe* God sar. Yamana man run away, sar.'

'I see.' Longden raised an eyebrow. 'And did you sleep in Captain Fell's cabin after his death?'

'No sar.'

'No? Who did?'

'Oens-men, sar.'

'The Oens-men slept in Captain Fell's cabin?'

'Yes sar. And – and men from York's country sar,' added Jemmy, desperately.

'"Men from York's country".'

'Yes sar – York Minster's country sar. Very bad men – eat other men. No *sabe* God sar.'

'And you say that your own tribe, your own family, was entirely innocent in this matter?'

'Yes sar, yes sar,' agreed Jemmy, clinging with relief to the fact that this man was clearly on his side.

Longden smiled. 'No further questions, Your Honour.'

Lamb rose with an overwhelming feeling of futility. By apportioning the blame to every conceivable demon that he could dredge from his imagination, his 'client' had as good as tied the noose about his own neck.

'Jemmy, the court has heard that you saved the life of

Alfred Coles. Why did you do that?'

'Mr Coles is English gen'leman sar, like Jemmy.'

'And how long did you look after Coles, once you had saved his life?'

'Four moons sar. Then Capp'en Smyley come, sar.'

'Whereupon you personally escorted him on board the *Nancy* and out of harm's way.'

'Yes sar. Mr Coles is Jemmy's frien' sar. Capp'en Smyley is Jemmy's frien' sar.'

Lamb could think of nothing else. 'Thank you, Jemmy. No further questions, sir.'

Beaming optimistically at having been allowed to make his position clear, Jemmy was led back to his seat. The final witness, the Reverend George Packenham Despard, then took the stand; but before he could answer any questions, a rotund, black-gloved Irishman rose to his feet, his face a tracery of tiny broken veins, and made his presence known. 'I am Mr Lane, sir, a solicitor of this town,' he informed the governor.

'Yes, Mr Lane, I know perfectly well who you are,' replied Moore brusquely. Lane was the only professional solicitor in Stanley: a notorious drunk, he had been struck off in Dublin, and had headed south to make his fortune, somewhat unsuccessfully to date. 'What do you want?'

'My services have been retained, sir, by the Reverend Mr Despard.'

'You have been retained by Mr *Despard*?' said a puzzled Moore. 'Mr Despard is merely a witness. He is not on trial.'

'Nonetheless, sir, in view of the importance of this case to the future operations and reputation of the Patagonian Missionary Society, Mr Despard has retained me as his attorney.'

'Well, this is most irregular.' Moore did not press the matter. The entire proceedings, in a town devoid of judges and containing only one professional lawyer, were most irregular. 'Your witness, Mr Longden.'

Longden sniffed again, to Moore's considerable irritation.

'Mr Despard, would you say you are well acquainted with the defendant?'

'Most certainly. I came to know him extremely well after he *volunteered* to stay at Keppel Island.' Despard looked across at Lane for approval. Clearly, he had been coached to steer well clear of any possible accusations of slavery.

'And how would you describe the defendant's character? Was he well conducted?'

Despard drew himself up to his full height and assumed an expression of pious regret. 'I am afraid he was without doubt the most lazy and lackadaisical of the natives at Cranmer. I found him to be dishonest, untrustworthy and argumentative; and, what is more, I had strong reason to suspect him of being a persistent thief.'

'You *lie!*' exploded Jemmy Button.

'You will be silent,' commanded Moore, 'or I shall have you removed from this court.'

Longden continued: 'Were you surprised, Mr Despard, when you heard of the tragic events that had unfolded at Woollya?'

'My heart was heavy with sorrow but, no, I was not surprised. Such an act of treachery was not at all inconsistent with what I had come to know of the defendant's character. But while we must all lament the cruel treachery of a supposedly friendly people, should we not thereby recognize the even more urgent duty of making known to them the word of truth and righteousness? Is the faithfulness unto death of the men whose loss we now deplore a signal for us to forsake the work they loved? I think not, gentlemen!' Despard looked round questioningly, in full pulpit mode now, his upper teeth bristling.

'That such a barbaric act should take place on the Sabbath day must have been particularly upsetting for you.'

'Do you know, Mr Longden,' smiled Despard, 'that was my first thought. But then I reasoned that God Himself must have appointed this day for the commission of these terrible crimes, in order to communicate the fact that here was Satan, raging against His work.'

On the word 'Satan', Despard's gaze swivelled accusingly in the direction of Jemmy, who glowered back at him like a sullen nephew at a hated uncle.

It was Lamb's turn to question the president of the Patagonian Missionary Society.

'Mr Despard, do you feel that your treatment of the natives at Cranmer contributed in any way to a build-up of resentment among them that might have occasioned the fatal attack?'

'Objection!'

It was Lane, the solicitor.

'These proceedings are being carried out under Sections 432 and 433 of the Merchant Shipping Act, and may concern themselves only with the abandonment of the *Allen Gardiner* and the fate of its crew. Lieutenant Lamb's question falls outside that remit.'

'Sir,' said Lamb to the governor, 'I am merely endeavouring to ascertain the precise nature of the relationship between the accused and the murder victims, the better to understand what happened at Woollya Cove.'

'Objection overruled, Mr Lane,' said Moore, shortly. 'Mr Despard, you will answer the question.'

'I do not wish to,' pronounced Despard munificently, his arms spread.

'Do you *decline* answering?' asked the astonished Moore.

'I have a right of silence, I believe?'

There was an outbreak of conferring on the bench. Lamb tried again. 'Did you search the bags of the natives at Keppel?'

Lane butted in: 'Once again, sir, that question is outside the remit of these proceedings according to the Merchant Shipping Act.'

'This is my court, Mr Lane. Will you answer the question, Mr Despard?'

'I will not.'

'You will permit me to observe that your conduct can only redound on you, to your own discredit.'

'I answer first and foremost to the authority of the good Lord, Mr Moore,' pronounced Despard sanctimoniously. 'It is by His desiring that I do not submit myself to such an impertinent line of questioning.'

'Very well,' said Moore, bristling. 'You may stand down. You too, Lieutenant Lamb.'

The remaining witnesses had little to add, being for the most part mission workers who remained stubbornly loyal to Despard, or who – on occasion – echoed Coles's reservations about their master's treatment of the Fuegians. Moore kept proceedings moving: by the morning of the third day, the court was ready to hear the closing statements.

Longden was the first to close, reminding the jury of what Coles had seen, and of his apparent conviction that Jemmy had been at the heart of things, before summing up: 'It is not very long since we deplored the frightful slaughter in India of whole companies of Christians. Lucknow, Cawnpore and Delhi are names written in letters of anguish on the hearts of thousands of our countrymen. The blood of Englishmen – the blood of martyrs – was shed there, just as it has been shed here, because of the treachery of the native race and the trusting nature of Britons everywhere. The Reverend Mr Phillips trusted Jemmy Button. Captain Fell trusted Jemmy Button. Both of them, and many other good men and true, have paid the price for that trust with their lives. For was it not this man's own son who fired the fatal shot? What knowledge does a young boy have of firearms and ammunition, unless so directed by his father? The defendant asks us to believe that strange tribesmen arrived from other lands without warning, and perpetrated some of the most terrible crimes that ever were heard of. Come, come, this won't do with me, and it won't do with twelve honest citizens of these islands either. The defendant is a cheat, a liar and a murderer, and were it not for the bravery and ingenuity of Captain Smyley he would not be before this court; but Captain

Smyley's quick thinking was his loss and justice's gain. Gentlemen of the jury, death is the only fitting punishment for crimes of this magnitude. Order must be restored, just as it was so effectively restored in India. Shall we see our world descend into chaos? Or shall we see civilized values reign triumphant? The decision is yours.'

Lieutenant Lamb, aware that it would be difficult now to extricate Jemmy from the commission of the crime, began his reply by attacking Despard instead. 'This gentleman *claims* that he is in the business of converting savages to Christianity. But can he show us one single native that he can confidently point out as converted? He cannot. Indeed, he cannot even find the courage, the honesty, to answer one or two simple questions. Had he answered those questions, gentlemen, it would have been no difficult matter to establish that Mr Despard is in fact little more than a grazier, a cattle-breeder, who enticed or entrapped a number of Fuegians into becoming his unpaid servants, or, to put it in other words, his slaves. If those natives were indeed kidnapped, and then kept to forced labour, is it surprising that murder should follow? I think not.

'But of the many natives who had grounds to bear a grudge against their captors, can we even be sure that we have before us the right man? Let us look in detail at the evidence of Coles the cook. He "reckons" – reckons, mark you – that he witnessed the defendant among a mob of some three hundred aggrieved natives, from a distance of a quarter of a mile away. By his own admission, he finds it difficult to distinguish one native from another. By his own admission, he did not actually see the defendant shoot Mr Phillips, or hurl the rock at Seaman Petersen, or administer the fatal blow in any of the cases under consideration. That simply is not good enough, gentlemen. That is not sufficient evidence to justify taking away a man's life, even the life of a savage.

'If Jemmy was indeed responsible, why then did he inter-cede on Coles's behalf with his fellows? Why did he treat him with such care and compassion for nigh on half a year? Why did he feed him and clothe him? Why did he give him *a loaded gun*? He knew that there would most likely be reprisals – if he was indeed guilty, why then did he not simply kill Coles, hide the body, scuttle the *Allen Gardiner*, and claim that the missionaries had never even been there? Everyone would have assumed them lost in a storm! But no. When Captain Smyley arrived, the accused went on board the *Nancy* of his own volition. *Of his own volition*. Was this the act of a guilty man? I will tell you, gentlemen, what it was. It was the act of a Christian. For Jemmy Button learned to love God not at Keppel Island, where he laboured against his will, but in England, where he was taken to be educated by Captain FitzRoy of the Royal Navy many years ago. He has lived peacefully among our people. He has learned our language. He looked after one of our own when others wanted to kill him. And how have we repaid him? By abducting him, by throwing him in chains, and by putting him on trial for his life. Gentlemen of the jury, there is only one possible verdict open to you. If you call yourselves Christians, you must find this man innocent.'

Lamb sat down. He had rather enjoyed the experience of legal speechifying, and was beginning to think that he might have chosen the wrong career by going into the military. He was confident, even, that his arguments would absolve Jemmy of the main charge of carrying out the murders. The lesser charges of incitement and being an accessory, however, were a different matter; and all three charges carried the death penalty. The odds remained that Jemmy was currently enjoying, if that was the word for it, his penultimate day on earth.

Briskly, Governor Moore began his own summing-up.

'Before I move on to the charges at hand, I should like to say this. It is almost certain from the statements of the defendant, from the discontented and threatening language used by the natives who were taken to Keppel, and from the bloody revenge which they took upon their return to Tierra del Fuego, that their residence at Keppel Island was enforced and irksome. I believe that it was practically impossible for Mr Despard or his agents, only acquainted as they were with a few words of the language of one tribe, to have made a contract which could for a moment be considered equal or fair with the savages. I should have hoped that, instead of availing himself of technical objections to defeat the course of this inquiry, Mr Despard might have availed himself of the opportunity to clear himself in open court of such grave suspicions. As it is, those suspicions have been necessarily aggravated by his studied concealment. In place of establishing the truth, the door has been left open for conjecture of all kinds. I am bound to say, too, that I do not think Mr Despard's measure of searching the natives prior to their boarding the *Allen Gardiner* was in any way judicious; and I must note that those natives searched appear to have been foremost in the murders. But murders they were, however they were occasioned, and as such they cannot be left unpunished.

'Gentlemen of the jury, I must stress to you that none of the provocations listed above constitute a justifiable defence for the act of murder. Nor are acts of Christian mercy, such as those shown by the defendant to the survivor Coles, to be classed as mitigating circumstances when it comes to determining the guilt or otherwise of the accused. You must concern yourself only with the facts of the case – did he or did he not commit the crimes of which he is charged? There is to be no balance of probability. You must be absolutely certain of his guilt before you enter a guilty verdict on any of the charges. On the charge of murder, you must be completely satisfied that the defendant personally took the life of one or more of the missionary party. On the charge of incitement, you must be completely satisfied that the defendant was a moving force in the mob, one of the ringleaders, if you like. On the charge of being an accessory, you must be completely satisfied that the defendant was a willing participant in the mob, that he was complicit in the crime and did nothing to try to prevent it. All three offences carry a capital sentence. This should not concern you. All you have to decide is the guilt, or otherwise, of the accused. You may retire now to consider your verdicts. Betimes in the morning, the court will reconvene to hear your decision, if you have yet reached one. The court is adjourned. Take the prisoner to the cells.'

Moore stood up, accompanied by his two fellow judges, and rustled out. Jemmy was pulled to his feet, chains clinking.

'Please sir,' he asked Moore's departing back, 'can Jemmy go home now?'

A typical Falklands gale howled that night, tearing in off the South Atlantic across the low, sodden hills. Loose tiles were plucked from the half-finished roofs of ramshackle houses; untethered tarpaulins were ripped from window-frames and sent scurrying into the night. The inhabitants of Stanley battened down the hatches and clustered in taciturn groups around guttering tallow candles. Down in the harbour, the water was black and choppy, and the ships at anchor heaved and gasped. In the harbour channel there was pandemonium, and in the ocean outside the breakers furled unchecked, pounding against the rocky coast. It was not a night to be out at sea. But had anyone braved the lashing rain and wind that buffeted the harbour front just after ten o'clock that evening, they would have seen that there were, indeed, brave souls prepared to risk the fury of the elements on such a night: a ship was running the harbour channel. Her sail had been shortened, but not perhaps as closely as it might have been. Whoever her captain was, he was in a hurry, and he was prepared to take risks. He was also an expert sailor: he was running the channel on a close-reefed foretopsail, a treble-reefed main topsail and a fore staysail, the whole manoeuvre executed with the precision of a surgeon, though her masts swayed like marram grass. Within a half-hour she was safe and anchored, and her cutter had been hoisted out. An imposing figure in a dark boat-cloak climbed down into the bucking little craft, and was rowed ashore with the minimum of fuss.

As the cutter bit into the seaweed-choked foreshore, the accompanying crunch torn away and flung unheard into the South Atlantic, the cloaked figure stepped out into the storm's embrace. He strode unhesitating up the muddy lanes, with which he obviously shared long intimacy. The occasional swaying lantern cast bright lurching ovals upon the rain-slicked mud, but the stranger had no need of any navigation lights. Within a minute his unerring footsteps had led him to the courthouse door, upon which he began to pound, a low, relentless drumbeat underscoring the sibilant hiss of the rain. Grumbling, one of the gaolers was roused from his stupor and stumbled to the door, a volley of choice words ready for whoever was foolish enough to be abroad on a night such as this. But when he drew back the bolts, and saw the identity of the newcomer, his demeanour changed. Deference and humility took over: he ushered his visitor in and respectfully took his cloak.

'Am I too late?'

'Sir?'

'Am I too late? The court case – is it done?'

'The case is done, sir, but the verdict is not due 'til the morrow.'

'Then there may be time yet. Show me to him.'

'Sir?'

'Show me to the prisoner.'

The gaoler did not hesitate, or question the newcomer's right to be shown to the defendant's cell; such was the man's instinctively commanding presence. His lantern flaring in the wintry gusts that squeezed themselves between the badly nailed planks, he led the way down the dirt-floored passage. At the end was a door, fastened with two bolts and a single stout padlock. Hands shaking with cold, he unfastened the lock and drew back the bolts. The door creaked open. The small, frightened figure of Jemmy Button sat behind a rough deal table, alone save for a flickering rushlight. Jemmy looked up, gave a little yelp of astonishment, drew back his chair and jumped to his feet. The visitor moved forward to embrace him. They made a strange pair, clutching each other in the gloom of that soaking Falklands night: the one short, round, woeful, clad in the cheapest prison garb; the other more than a foot taller, stern of brow and bald as an eagle, immaculately suited in the uniform of a British naval officer.

'Capp'en Sulivan,' said Jemmy.

'You may leave us,' said Sulivan to the guard, who obeyed without question.

'Capp'en Fitz'oy has sent you to Jemmy?'

'He is Admiral FitzRoy now. We both are. It is a higher rank than captain.'

'A'miral Fitz'oy.' Jemmy rolled the new word round his tongue, tried it out for size. 'A'miral Fitz'oy has sent you to Jemmy?'

'Yes. That's right. Admiral FitzRoy has sent me to you.'

'Why he no come himself, A'miral Sulivan?'

'Although he is an admiral his position is . . . difficult. It is not as easy for him to take leave, to command a ship, as it is for me. So I came instead.'

'You came to save Jemmy.'

Sulivan looked serious. 'I do not know, Jemmy. That depends.'

'That depends?'

'I came to tell the truth, Jemmy. I came to tell the court that I know you – that I know you to be a good man. But I will not lie to the court for you, Jemmy. You must know that. Once I have sworn my oath upon the Bible, I will tell only the truth.'

Silence breathed between them.

Sulivan was the first to break it. 'Tell me, Jemmy. Tell me everything that happened. From the very beginning.'

And so Jemmy told him the entire story of Keppel Island,

from the arrival of the *Allen Gardiner* to his abduction by the *Nancy*.

When he had finished his tale, Sulivan took each of Jemmy's hands in his own. Their eyes locked. 'Before God, Jemmy, I need you to tell me the honest truth. If you tell the truth, then there is nothing to be afraid of, for God will take care of you. It is very important that you understand that. Do you understand that?'

'Yes, A'miral Sulivan.'

'Now – did you kill any of those men?'

'No, A'miral Sulivan.'

'Did you have anything whatsoever to do with the deaths of those men? Did you encourage the idea, or even agree with it?'

'No, A'miral Sulivan.'

'Do you swear by Almighty God that that is the whole, the unvarnished truth?'

'Yes, A'miral Sulivan.'

'You would not lie to me, Jemmy, would you?'

'No, A'miral Sulivan. Jemmy swear it.'

Sulivan gazed searchingly into Jemmy's soul, hunting for some clue, some tiny sign that would point him towards the truth of what had happened.

I simply do not know, he had to admit. *I simply do not know whether or not he is telling the truth.*

'Another witness, Lieutenant Lamb?' complained Moore testily. 'You have already delivered your closing statement. I have never heard of such a thing.'

'The gentleman is a material witness, sir – a character witness – whose testimony was unfortunately not available until today, sir.'

'It is quite ridiculous. While we may find ourselves many thousands of miles from the mother country, that in itself is no reason to abdicate all sense of procedural responsibility. I will not allow it.'

'It is Rear-Admiral Sulivan, sir.'

'Rear-Admiral Sulivan? Why the devil didn't you say so? Fetch him in.'

Sulivan was duly fetched in, and introduced to the jury, although there was little need of it: all there knew, or had heard tell, of the islands' most famous former inhabitant.

'Rear-Admiral Sulivan's record of service,' intoned Lamb, 'both in defence of these islands and of his country, is second to none. Although he has now withdrawn from active service to take up the position of chief naval officer at the Board of Trade in London, it is but thirty-six months since he took command of HMS *Lightning*, the first ever naval paddle steam vessel, and HMS *Merlin* thereafter, in our glorious victory against the Russians. He was the author of the attack on Sweaborg, for which heroic action he was made Companion of the Bath. Last year he was selected to lead the naval review of the Baltic Fleet by Her Gracious Majesty the Queen at Spithead. He is without question the most celebrated, valorous inhabitant of these islands, in all their brief history.'

Sulivan found himself bathed in the frank admiration of the jury.

'Rear-Admiral Sulivan, how long have you known the defendant?'

'I have known him, indeed I have been proud to call him my friend, for twenty-seven years.'

'Would you say that the defendant is possessed of a savage – even a murderous – disposition?'

'Far from it. The defendant is a gentle man and a devout Christian. The defendant may have been left to his own devices in his native country these last two dozen years – and I blame myself as much as anyone for that lamentable state of affairs – but Jemmy Button once resided in England, and moved in the very gentlest society. Indeed, he was on intimate terms with no less a person than the King of England.'

This caused a considerable stir in the courtroom.

'If the defendant has been brought low once more, has slipped from those exalted heights, it is not his fault, I assure you. It is the fault of those who call themselves good Christians – and I include myself among their number – who have neglected him, who have left him to fend for himself, who have given him no recourse but to revert to his former savage state, in body if not in mind.'

'In your opinion, is it at all possible that the defendant is guilty of any of the charges laid before this court?'

Sulivan hesitated, for the merest flicker of an instant.

'No. The very suggestion is laughable. He is no more capable of committing a murder, or of inciting or being accessory to murder, than any of the respectable gentlemen sitting in this court.'

'Thank you, Rear-Admiral Sulivan. I have no further questions.'

There being – wisely – no questions from Mr Longden, the jurors retired to further consider their verdicts. The wait was not a long one, but for Sulivan the delay was agonizing. Had he done enough? It was impossible to tell. Only Jemmy, of all those in the courtroom, seemed to exude a sense of profound calm. Sulivan, he seemed to believe, had been sent by God to his rescue; although precisely which God he believed he owed his deliverance to, Sulivan was not at all sure.

At last, the jurors filed back into court.

'Have you reached a verdict?' asked Moore.

'We have, sir.'

'On the charge of murder, do you find the defendant guilty or not guilty?'

'Not guilty.'

'On the charge of incitement to murder, do you find the defendant guilty or not guilty?'

'Not guilty.'

'On the charge of being an accessory to murder, do you find the defendant guilty or not guilty?'

'Not guilty.'

There was a surge of relief in the packed chamber, a gaggle of voices all talking at once. Lieutenant Lamb, quite forgetting himself, was punching the air; Governor Moore was smiling; Despard was locked in angry consultation with Lane; while Sulivan found himself exultantly hugging Jemmy, and then, almost immediately, questioning his maker.

Has justice been done? he wondered. *Tell me, Lord, has justice been done? Or have I done a terrible thing?*

Chapter Thirty-six

The University Museum, Oxford, 29 June 1860

The Prince Consort's glance caught FitzRoy's, and for an instant their eyes locked. His Royal Highness was seated in the front row of the lecture room, legs outstretched and crossed at the ankle, immediately beneath the podium. He was slimmer and less robust-looking than FitzRoy had imagined, more youthful-looking than his forty-one years, not quite the staid, inflexible statesman of his portraits. His was, by all accounts, a formidable intellect: his presidency of the British Association for the Advancement of Science was no formal reflection of his status, nor was his attendance at a lecture on the subject of 'British Storms'. FitzRoy gripped the sides of the lectern, as he had once gripped the sides of the *Beagle*'s azimuth compass. This speech was as vital to the preservation of men's lives as any he had given on the maindeck.

'Your Royal Highness, my lords, gentlemen. On the twenty-fifth of October last year, the *Royal Charter* sank off the coast of Anglesey. It was a disaster that plunged the entire nation into the most severe traumatism. A modern iron clipper, equipped not just with sail but with an auxiliary steam engine to help her out of difficulty, went down with all hands within sight of the British coast. Over four hundred men, women and children lost their lives, not fifty miles from their destination, after a journey from Melbourne lasting many months. That this should have happened to a steam-vessel of the latest modern design seemed an impossibility; that a disaster of such Biblical proportions should have intruded into our modern age seemed incredible; but even modern man, with all his ingenuity, all his mechanical contrivances, ignores the power of the elements at his peril.

'Today I should like to pose an important question: was the loss of the *Royal Charter* merely a random act of God, the cruel whim of a capricious Creator? Or does God's universe follow a comprehensible pattern, an order of events that, by careful observation, we might yet learn to monitor and even anticipate?

'The answer, I believe, is that the universe is indeed a system, mechanical but at the same time beautiful and marvellous in its complexity, that we are only just beginning to comprehend. From many years spent charting and studying the meteorology of these islands, I have come to the conclusion that our weather is an integral part of this observable system. I believe that our weather can be foretold. I speak not of prophecies or predictions, but of informed scientific opinions; weather fore*casting*, if you like. I believe not only that the loss of the *Royal Charter* could have been prevented, but that other, similar disasters might yet be prevented.'

There was a murmur in the hall. Prince Albert, however, did not flicker.

'It seems, of late, that many men have been gazing through their microscopes. Perhaps we should all spend more time gazing through our telescopes.'

There was a communal chuckle. The scientific community, at least, was aware of FitzRoy's involvement in the furore surrounding the publication of Darwin's *The Origin of Species*: he had sent furious letters defending Old Testament orthodoxy to *The Times* under the pen-name 'Senex', a pseudonym born of the Latin proverb *Nemo senex metuit Iouem* – 'An old man ought to be fearful of God.'

FitzRoy warmed to his theme. 'Let me tell you about the British weather. There is in our latitudes a continuous alternation of air currents, which travel circuitously about each other; but while these are passing and repassing among themselves, the whole body of atmosphere in which they operate is moving incessantly towards the east, at an average of five miles per hour geographical. Because each storm is rotary in construction, there will usually be northerly, westerly or southerly airflows within the storm. When the *Royal Charter* gale crossed England, the winds within it howling at between sixty and a hundred miles per hour, the storm itself travelled at just *five* miles per hour. In advance of the storm, barometric readings fell sharply, for the barometer is among our most useful tools in determining the approach of a gale. But once the storm was upon us, much of the worst damage was caused by bad weather curling back into the east coast. The barometer, having already fallen, could give no warning of this. But there were other indications. Thermometers on the east coast plummeted ahead of the storm's arrival. There were extraordinary disturbances of the currents along telegraphic wires. There were great electric or magnetic commotions in the atmosphere. Auroras were unusually prevalent. Without question, this increased solar activity was fundamentally connected to the scale of the disturbance. All of these indications were – and are – measurable.

'The plan that I propose is simple: a network of observing stations, not just on our own coasts, but in mainland Europe and in the United States of America, to make just these measurements, and to give advance warning by electric telegraph of approaching storms. Yes, the United States! Why not? The transatlantic electrical cable may have been severed, but it is surely only a matter of time before it is reconstituted. Already the Americans, under the direction of Lieutenant Maury of the US Navy's Depot of Charts and Instruments, have produced maps of the main wind-fields of the earth. These charts do not unfortunately show wind strength – only direction – unlike our own system of synoptic charts and wind stars. But if the Americans can be persuaded to provide us with more comprehensive information, then whenever a storm arises, we shall be in a position to send warnings to our fishing fleets *before* they are put at risk. That's right – warnings before the bad weather arrives. That loss of life and destruction of property, which are currently so frequent on our exposed and tempestuous shores, could be diminished almost to nothing!

'Already, the groundwork for this scheme has been laid. During the last few years, I have been distributing barometers of my own design to fisheries around our coasts. The Duke of Northumberland has graciously paid for fourteen of them to be placed on the north-east coast. I have also developed a system of coastal signals based on brightly coloured cones and drums – symmetrical shapes that are unaffected by wind direction – which could be hoisted at shore stations, and which would be visible to offshore fishing fleets, naval and merchant vessels.'

FitzRoy began to unveil a series of charts, to demonstrate how these gale warnings would work. Still, the Prince remained impassive. Was he gripped, or just bored? Much depended on His Royal Highness's reaction. Since taking over from Beechey, Sulivan had given his old skipper absolute freedom to interpret his role as he wished; indeed, he had made it a condition of his appointment that he 'should not be obliged to direct Rear-Admiral FitzRoy in a sagacious condition'. He had even written to the government making clear his 'infinite respect' for FitzRoy's abilities as a seaman, his courage as a man and his self-sacrifice as a public servant. But Sulivan had not the resources to fund a full-scale network of coastal warning stations, or the influence to persuade government that the idea was anything other than fantastical nonsense. Instead, he had given FitzRoy *carte blanche* to go in search of his own patrons and benefactors. Very few potential patrons, though, had the ear of government. The man sitting in the front row was one such.

His diagrammatical display at an end, FitzRoy concluded his speech.

'In short, Your Royal Highness, my lords, gentlemen, I propose that this country should have the world's first storm-warning system, and the world's first weather forecasts. Thank you.'

The lecture room was only half full, but the audience's enthusiasm made up for any shortfall in its size. The Prince led the applause, FitzRoy noted with relief, a lead that others were quick to follow. As the members of the association milled about and gradually dispersed, he was summoned by an equerry to be presented to His Royal Highness.

'A most fascinating speech, Rear-Admiral FitzRoy.' Albert's German accent was as rich as his English was immaculate, and did not diminish his air of donnish gravity.

'Your Royal Highness is too kind.'

'I believe that I am lunching with the prime minister on Monday. If the occasion arises, I shall venture to enquire Lord Palmerston's views on this most interesting of topics.'

FitzRoy wanted to whoop in triumph. Instead he gave a little bow. 'I am both flattered and privileged by Your Royal Highness's interest.'

'I believe, Rear-Admiral, that you once sailed around the world with Mr Darwin, is that not so?'

'That is indeed so, sir.'

'But you are not of the same mind as your former companion.'

'Indeed not, sir. I find his conclusions somewhat ... distressing.'

'You are evidently not alone in your reservations, Rear-Admiral.' There was a sympathetic glint in the Prince Consort's eye. Of course His Royal Highness was careful never to express a public opinion on any controversial subject, political or scientific, but he was adroit nonetheless at getting his point across.

'Will you be staying in Oxford to attend Mr Draper's speech?'

Draper was an American, due to lecture to the association's zoological section on 'The intellectual development of Europe considered with reference to the views of Mr Darwin and others'. It was rumoured that the Bishop of Oxford himself intended to use the meeting as a platform to launch a violent attack on Darwin and his followers.

'I shall, sir,' said FitzRoy.

'I am envious, Rear-Admiral. Unfortunately a busy timetable of engagements precludes my joining you. As a keen breeder of farm animals myself, I should have been *most* interested to hear Mr Darwin's views on that topic put to the challenge.' It was, of course, out of the question for the Prince to attend what promised to be an aggressive confrontation. 'Do you think that your former shipmate intends to be present to defend himself?'

'Not if I know the man, sir. He is not one for a fight. I suspect that his illness shall most likely flare up again, at the last minute. If I recall, on the day of publication he found himself in need of urgent medical treatment at a sanatorium on the Yorkshire moors. The same affliction struck on the dates of two subsequent public meetings.'

Prince Albert smiled. 'Such a pity that Mr Darwin's bouts of infirmity should have coincided with so many valuable opportunities to defend himself.'

'Indeed, sir – but I am sure that his two bulldogs shall be there to growl out a defence of his hypothesis.'

In the absence of a single public comment or appearance from Darwin since publication seven months previously, Hooker and Huxley had invariably been sent forth to do battle on their master's behalf. *He is like a cowardly officer who sends his men into the field but remains behind himself*, thought FitzRoy contemptuously. *The only brave thing he ever did was to publish that book. But now he is to be episcopally pounded, and neither Hooker nor Huxley will be able to save him.*

*   *   *

Saturday dawned soft and sunny, and the city wore a bucolic air. For FitzRoy, the sense of sudden summer settling on the medieval quads recalled the chimeric summers of his childhood, when it seemed as if the previous century was not yet laid to rest: a pre-war world of pastoral certainties, before man had awakened to the complexities of the world around him. Man should have been able to work in partnership with God, should have found himself blessed by that understanding. Instead, just as in Eden, he had seized upon his new-found comprehension to engineer his own destruction. There was a new cathedral amid the spires of Oxford now, but it was built of iron and glass, not Cotswold stone. The Oxford University Museum, for all its ecclesiastical airs and Gothic grandeur, was a cathedral to science. For FitzRoy, science and religion should have been one and the same, the former merely a means to interpret the full majesty of the latter; but Darwin had set science against religion, had even gone so far as to postulate a Godless world. He had made himself instead the false god of science. He had even grown a long white beard, by all accounts, as if to parody the very image of his maker.

The country had been in uproar since the publication, the previous November, of *The Origin of Species*. The expected tide of condemnation had duly swamped its author, led – among others – by Darwin's former mentor Professor Sedgwick and his former friend Richard Owen, who in his younger days had catalogued the *Beagle* fossils. But to FitzRoy's astonishment and distress, once that tide had reached its high-water mark, a ferocious undertow of adulation had begun to pull in the opposite direction, a force exerted in the main by a younger generation whose lives had been cushioned by the prosperity of their age: young men who would never be asked to risk their lives in a roaring sea at the uttermost ends of the earth, who would never come face to face with their God.

The initial print-run of 1250 copies of *The Origin* had sold out before lunchtime on the first day of publication; not all the purchasers, it turned out, had required a copy the better to organize their rebuttals. Copies were being sold as fast as they could be printed, to genuine admirers of Mr Darwin and his ideas. Young couples were naming their children after him. He had even been made into the hero of a romantic novel. As he skulked behind the defensive earthworks of Down House, fanatical supporters and idle tourists camped outside, hoping to catch sight of the great man. Alone among the major European nations, Britain had come through the depressions of the first half of the century without violent revolution; but there was a residual, unfulfilled feeling of iconoclasm in the air, and Darwin had captured it. It was through science, not pikes and muskets, that the old order would be swept away by the young, the confident and the mechanically minded.

Even allowing for the enthusiasm of these new disciples, FitzRoy was stunned by the size of the crowd queuing to get into the museum. The association's lectures were open to the public, but it was rare indeed for a member of the public to turn up. Today the mere mention of the name 'Darwin' in the title of Draper's lecture had tempted close on a thousand people to attend a dry academic talk. Before long an official emerged and announced that the lecture would be moved to the long West Room, the museum's as yet unfurnished library, to accommodate the unexpected masses. There was a considerable delay while the West Room was got ready, but the crowd seemed unfussed; indeed, an enjoyable air of expectation was building, as the news spread that Bishop Wilberforce had indeed chosen today to lead the Church's counter-attack against the new heresy. The bishop, too, was not without his supporters. There were knots of priests here and there amid the merry throng of beery students. There were even a number of women present, fanning themselves with their handkerchiefs and filling out the queue with their ample crinolines; it was the first time FitzRoy had seen women at a scientific event. Truly, the world was changing.

At last, the doors opened and the crowd filed into the West Room, until it was filled almost to suffocation. Instinctively,

the various tribes present separated out, as if to a predeter-
mined command: journalists at the front, cassocked clergymen
grouped at the centre, the rowdier students in one corner at
the back, the women lined against the windows of the western
wall, their white handkerchiefs fluttering like a flock of
disturbed doves. Then, to a round of applause, the speaker
emerged on to the dais, followed by the various interested
parties: Bishop Wilberforce on one side, flanked by Richard
Owen, with Huxley and Hooker taking the opposite corner.
There was, of course, no Alfred Russel Wallace: he was still
collecting beetles in the Far East, blissfully unaware of the
explosion of interest in what was supposedly a joint theory.
And there was, of course, no Darwin.

Professor John Henslow, by whose recommendation
Darwin had first been appointed to the *Beagle*, was to be in
the chair. He shuffled to the front of the dais.

The man who started it all off, thought FitzRoy. *How fitting*.

Henslow was very old now, a mass of snow-white hair
wreathing his drooping face, his sad eyes focused somewhere
on the middle distance. He fixed this notional spot with his
basset-hound gaze and welcomed it to the association.

'Regrettably, Mr Darwin himself is unable to be present
this afternoon as he is undergoing urgent hydropathic treatment to his stomach. Please will you welcome our speaker
today, Mr John W. Draper of the University of New York.'

Draper came forward, to more enthusiastic applause. A
hushed silence ensued.

'My lords, ladies and gentlemen. Philosophically
speaking, I believe that the development of classical Greek
civilization can be divided into five well-marked periods –
the first being closed by the opening of Egypt to the Ionians;
the second, including the Ionian, Pythagorean, and Eleatic
philosophies, was ended by the doubts of the Sophists; the
third, embracing the Socratic and Platonic philosophies, was
ended by the doubts of the Sceptics; the fourth, ushered in by
the Macedonian expedition and adorned by the achievements

of the Alexandrian school, degenerated into Neoplatonism . . .'

Draper was still speaking to a hushed room, but it was a hush of disbelief. This was, conceivably, the dreariest public speaker that anyone present had ever heard. His nasal monotone rolled and flattened his words into an arid, featureless desert, with no prospect of relief on the horizon. It rapidly became clear that his thesis only drew peripherally upon Darwin's ideas, in that he was postulating a vague notion of biological process as a contributory factor to the development of Western thought. This was not what the crowd had come to hear. Unfortunately, Draper seemed of the opinion that this was precisely what the crowd had come to hear: he wore a smile of insufferable self-satisfaction throughout. His talk lasted for just over an hour, but it felt like five. Finally he was done, and retired to his seat to the barest smattering of applause. The ladies fanned themselves with their hand-kerchiefs again: it was quite breathlessly hot in the packed room. Henslow called upon the Right Reverend Samuel Wilberforce, Bishop of Oxford, to make his contribution to the debate. A low murmur of anticipation surged through the crowd: this was it. The preamble was over. Now the sparks would fly.

Wilberforce stepped forward, majestically clad in full episcopal robes and gaiters, whorls of disapproval etched into his face like a New Zealander's tattoo. He clasped his hands together, wrung them and waited for silence. 'Soapy Sam', they called him, supposedly because he always wrung his hands as if washing when sermonizing; but maybe there was more to it than that, for there was indeed something slippery about his ostentatious air of moral cleanliness. He had once been chaplain to the Royal Family, which position had left behind a residue of permanent unctuousness. But he was an experienced orator, was Soapy Sam, with a plummy, booming voice that was well used to reaching the back row of Christ Church Cathedral.

'The good Lord is many things,' he fulminated. 'He is the

Father, the Son and the Holy Ghost, three indivisible parts of the Holy Trinity. But if Mr Darwin's book is to be believed, He is also the Supreme Pigeon-fancier.'

Soapy Sam's face cracked into a grim smile. The audience laughed. This was more like it.

'I am not a scientist, or a pigeon-fancier. But I do have some experience in the teachings of the Lord. That is my area of specialization, if you like. So, I was not unnaturally intrigued to find out whether this book' – he produced from his robes a green, clothbound copy of Darwin's work – 'might give me cause to doubt any parts of that other book which I have studied throughout my entire life. I think you know the one I mean. It has not perhaps sold quite as many copies as has Mr Darwin's during these past seven months but, then, it has been on sale for two thousand years, and no doubt it will still be on sale two thousand years hence, when Mr Darwin's volume will have been quite forgotten.

'So what, then, did I make of *The Origin of Species*? What conclusions did I draw? I am sure you are all agog to hear. Let me tell you, I was most impressed by the assiduousness of Mr Darwin's scholarship. His writing is unusually attractive. It is a most readable book – indeed, its language is so perspicuous that it sparkles. And it contains a remarkable scientific discovery: the existence of a self-acting power in nature, continuously working in all creation, that Mr Darwin has entitled the Law of Natural Selection. He has identified the principal effect of the struggle of all creatures for life – that the strong will continually tend to extirpate the weak. And he has discovered that this process will encourage positive variation by weeding out the slow and the infirm, much as does a pigeon-fancier by design. I congratulate Mr Darwin upon his discovery!

'Curiously, Mr Darwin does not regard this process as universally applicable. He is confused, for instance, as to why the young blackbird should be spotted, or the whelp of a lion striped.' Wilberforce opened the book. 'According to Mr

Darwin, "No one would suppose that these spots and stripes are of any use to these animals, or are related to the conditions to which they are exposed." Their very prevalence and lack of utility, Mr Darwin believes, are an indication of common descent! But, Mr Darwin, any *observant* field naturalist will tell you that the spotted features of a young blackbird are one of the greatest protections to the bird, imperfect in its flight, sitting unwarily in its bush through which the rays of sunshine dapple every bough to the colour of its own plumage! The Supreme Pigeon-fancier, Mr Darwin, moves in a mysterious way!'

The audience roared its approval. This was good. Although he did not approve of the bishop's sneering style, FitzRoy had to admire his skill. The scientific content of his speech was Owen's, of course. Time had not been kind to Owen: he sat at the side of the dais, his long legs folded beneath his chair, smiling his dreadful, red-faced, cadaverous smile, like a latter-day Richard III. Tiers of bags ran down from his eyes to his skeletal cheekbones, wispy white side-whiskers masked his ears, while his pursed mouth was all but concealed behind a large, hooked nose. He was the superintendent of Natural History at the British Museum now, and he knew his subject as well as anyone in the country; it was a pity, really, that he was such an unattractive public speaker that the bishop had to serve as his mouthpiece. Yet Wilberforce brought episcopal prestige to bear on the occasion, as well as oratorical skill. FitzRoy was more than content to see him as the standard-bearer of reason on this occasion.

'Mr Darwin,' the bishop was roaring, 'sees his Law of Natural Selection as proof of the non-existence of God! On the contrary, it is in this very law that we see a merciful provision against the deterioration, in a world apt to deteriorate, of the works of the Creator's hands! Natural selection *prevents* the deterioration of existing species – it does not effect new ones! Has any pigeon-breeder in the country, for all his efforts, created anything that is not a pigeon? Has any pigeon-breeder created anything that could even survive in the wild? If, as Mr Darwin claims, one animal group can transform itself into a totally separate animal group, then surely we should have discovered animals with shared characteristics, from the group of animals they are evolving from, and the group of animals towards which they are evolving. There should be fossils that link the major animal groups. If mammals evolved from reptiles, where is the beast that has the features of both a reptile and a mammal? Where are these missing links?'

A huge cheer went up from the audience. At the edge of the dais, Owen flexed his fingers together and smiled a ghastly smile.

'According to Mr Darwin, the fossil record is "incomplete". Oh, but this is no accident. No! The fossil record is "*necessarily* incomplete"! According to Mr Darwin, transitional forms, precisely because they are transitional, are less likely to leave a fossil record than stabilized species. Is that not clever? The theory itself brilliantly explains why there is no evidence whatsoever to support the theory! There is only one adjective suitable to describe such logic: *unsatisfactory*. Scientists have searched in vain' – Wilberforce glanced triumphantly across at Owen – 'for any shred of evidence, any shred of proof, that any one individual species might have varied, be it ever so little, into a different genus. One tiny variation that might validate the conclusion that such variability is progressive and unlimited, so as, in the course of generations, to change the species, the genus, the order and, eventually, the class. That proof has not been found – *and it never will be.*'

The audience was going wild for Wilberforce. FitzRoy quietly clenched his fist. He was excited now, and ideas were coursing through his mind. He wished he could be up on stage himself, leading the onslaught.

'Each organism which the Creator educed was stamped with an indelible specific character, which made it what it was and distinguished it from everything else. Such character has been, and is, indelible and immutable. The characters which distinguish species from species now were as definite at the first instant of their creation as now, and are as distinct now as they were then. A rock-pigeon is what a rock-pigeon has always been!' Wilberforce thumped the podium with his fist. 'A man is what a man has always been!' He brandished the green book again. 'This hypothesis is so flimsy, so fanciful, that it might be the frenzied inspiration of an inhaler of mephitic gas! When tried by the principles of inductive science, it breaks down completely! The line between man and the lower animals is distinct. There is no tendency on the part of the lower animals to become the self-conscious, intelligent being that is man; nor in man to degenerate and lose the high characteristics of mind and intelligence. Man even possesses a unique lobe of the brain, the hippocampus minor, and cerebral hemispheres so large that they cover the cerebellum. These you will not find in any of the higher apes. But will you find them in Mr Darwin's book? No! For Mr Darwin's conclusions are mere hypothesis, nothing more, raised most unphilosophically to the dignity of a causal theory! Is it really, truly credible that a turnip strives to become a man?'

Another cheer rocked the hall. Wilberforce gestured for calm, his upper body slowly rotating until his stare focused, as if through a magnifying glass, upon a point in the exact centre of Huxley's forehead. He was full of confidence now, perhaps too much so. Huxley glared back balefully, his deep, dark eyes swimming in his bulldog face. *You are nothing,* Wilberforce's look seemed to say. *You are other ranks, and no more. Know your place.*

'It appears that I must give way to Mr Huxley,' said the bishop, his tones smooth and serpentine, 'but before I do so, I should like to ask him one question. If you are willing, Mr Huxley, to trace your descent from an ape on your grandfather's side, are you similarly willing to trace that descent on your grandmother's side?'

There was uproar in the hall. Some of the students, and some of the more gin-soaked journalists, burst out laughing.

There was genuine shock in many quarters: a commotion rippled out from the place under one of the windows where Lady Brewster had fainted. FitzRoy was appalled. The bishop had gone too far. In bringing Huxley's grandmother into the equation, he had insulted a lady. He had entirely handed the moral advantage to the opposition, with one carelessly offensive remark. *He has forgotten to behave like a gentleman.*

Up on the dais, Huxley's pasty face, set in a furious pout, disentangled itself from the large black beard that nested beneath his chin. He had been patronized all his life, and this was just one more example. Why was it so much worse to be descended from a monkey than to have been fashioned from dust? He wanted to see the foot of science pressed firmly on the neck of religion, and he saw his chance. He turned to Hooker. 'The Lord hath delivered him into mine hands,' he said, with mock-Biblical satisfaction; whereupon he rose, and made his way to the podium.

Anyone paying attention would have seen a stocky young man step forward, dressed in a plain, cheap waistcoat and a tailcoat that barely fitted him, both permanently crumpled from lives spent inside a suitcase. He was wedged uncomfortably into a high-collared shirt, his jet-black hair trimly parted and plastered down with macassar-oil, a pair of lorgnettes his only 'learned' affectation. But nobody was paying attention. Wilberforce's *faux pas* had thrown the audience into confusion. Huxley was speaking now, but he was accustomed in the main to gatherings of twenty or thirty bemused colliers. His voice was too quiet to carry above the commotion, his phrasing too inexact, too mumbled.

'Mr Darwin abhors speculation as nature abhors a vacuum. All the principles he lays down have been brought to the test of observation and experiment. The path he bids us follow is no airy track, fabricated of cobwebs, but a solid and broad bridge of facts, which will carry us safely over many a chasm in our knowledge. The right reverend bishop and his type, by contrast, look at creation as a savage looks at a ship, as a bewildering thing so far beyond their comprehension that they do not dare attempt a rational explanation. My lord's address was so full of old and disproved contentions that it lacked any scientific credibility whatsoever – each of which, I assure you, I intend to address individually. Let us begin with the fossil record, which my lord is so keen to utilize to his advantage. Those, like the bishop, who believe in the absolute truth of the Old Testament would have us believe that the earth was created in 4004 BC. Yet the soil is bursting with fossils that have been geologically proved to be many millions of years old! How can this be? Has God written on the rocks one enormous and superfluous lie for all mankind?'

Huxley tailed off. It was no use – he had lost his audience. The bishop's ill-judged abdication of the most basic good manners had triggered an earthquake, and the aftershocks were still being felt. He had to get the crowd back. He raised his voice.

'A man has no reason to be ashamed of having an ape for a grandfather!'

A hundred animated discussions whirling round the room skittered to a sudden stop. He had them now.

'If the question were put to me: would I rather have a miserable ape for a grandfather, or a man highly endowed by nature, and possessed of great means of influence, and yet who employs those facilities and that influence for the mere purpose of introducing ridicule into a grave scientific discussion – then I unhesitatingly affirm my preference for the ape!'

A huge roar of approval, led by the boisterous knot of students at the back, shuddered through the room. Huxley was ahead now, without doubt.

'Mr Darwin—' Huxley began, but his voice was drowned out, not by cries of antagonism but by cries of support.

'Dar-*win*! Dar-*win*!'

The students were chanting Darwin's name, as if to summon him up from behind his iron-age fortress of earthen banks. FitzRoy was surrounded by primitive, drunken braying, as ignorant as the yells of any crowd of natives on a Fuegian shore. His frustration boiled over. The rush of arguments in his head became a landslide, an avalanche, each irrefutable fact tumbling incoherently over the others. The inability of natural selection to account for the origin of life itself. The unsatisfactory reduction of the aesthetic, the emotional and the spiritual to mere epiphenomena. The falsity of Darwin's fossil narrative, which had been constructed on foundations that were geologically poles apart. The failure of natural selection to explain the development of complex organs, such as the eye, and their co-ordination in bodily systems. The presence of advanced creatures in the earliest strata of fossils, and of the most primitive creatures alive today. He felt both excited and agitated, and aggrieved by this sudden inarticulacy. Before he knew what he was doing, he had grabbed a Bible from one of the priests in the audience, and was waving it above his head.

'I implore you all to believe in God, rather than man!' he heard a voice shouting, and realized that it was his own. A chorus of jeers drowned him out.

On the dais, Professor Henslow had recognized him, and was trying to accord his interruption some sort of official status.

'Please! Ladies and gentlemen! Captain FitzRoy wishes to contribute to the debate! Pray silence for Captain FitzRoy!'

Nobody paid any heed.

FitzRoy tried to tell them that he had been there with Darwin, that he had observed the same things, that *The Origin of Species* was not a logical arrangement of the facts that he had witnessed, but his throat was constricting in the most alarming way, and he found that he could not speak. He could only wave the borrowed Bible above his head. Bizarrely, he became aware that he could distinguish each individual voice that made up the surrounding clamour, could follow each and every line separately, as if they were the instruments of an orchestra. He looked at Hooker seated on the platform, handsome and fine-boned, his wire-rimmed pebble spectacles perched elegantly on the bridge of his long nose, an amused smile on his face, and he realized that he could make out the waxy quality of the man's skin as if it were but an inch away, could see each of its tiny, downy hairs. His sight had become as crystal clear as his other senses, each of them intensified to a strength that only God Himself could possibly know. He could even feel the warmth of the little gas-jets on the walls. Electrical sensations ran up and down his limbs, and played across the surface of his skin. So intense were all these feelings, so wonderful and terrifying, that he thought perhaps he should try to fend some of them off, to find order amid the chaos; but they would not be deflected. They just kept coming, kept overwhelming him. And all the while, this man, this Captain FitzRoy, who was him and yet who seemed to stand apart from him, stood paralysed and pedestrian, holding aloft a borrowed Bible, making incoherent noises.

Somewhere deep within himself, beneath the whirling, unpredictable hurricane of sensations, a tiny spark of self-preservation remained. It told him to get out, to leave now, before something unimaginably awful happened. Captain FitzRoy heard this inner voice, as if from a great distance, and, remarkably, he listened to it. He put his head down and bulldozed his way to the exit, shouts and laughter reverberating in his ears. Driving himself ever onward, he did not stop until he reached the station, where, he noticed, he was still tightly clutching the borrowed Bible.

Chapter Thirty-seven

140 Church Road, Upper Norwood, 26 March 1865

'Another slice of cake for the vice-admiral, if you please, Hetty.'

'Yes, ma'am.'

'No, really, Fan, I've had enough.'

'Nonsense, Bob. You need feeding up.'

Hetty hovered uncertainly between FitzRoy and his sister, but Lady Dynevor, as she was now entitled to call herself, was insistent. Really, her brother did look painfully thin.

'Is he not in need of feeding up, ladies?'

Fanny and Katherine FitzRoy, who had accompanied Lady Dynevor on this Sunday visit to their father's house, delicately chorused their assent. Both had inherited a fair slice of their mother's poise and beauty.

'You need feeding up, Pappa!' gurgled Laura FitzRoy, plain and round, his only daughter by his second marriage, who had recently celebrated her seventh birthday.

'I do *try* to keep Mr FitzRoy healthy and well-fed, I really do,' protested Maria FitzRoy, her fingers nervously intertwined. As always, she found the elegance and self-possession of her husband's sister somewhat intimidating.

'Must you all speak about me as if I were not present, ladies?' said FitzRoy, raising his hands in mock protest.

The FitzRoy family were seated in the first-floor drawing room of the house in Church Road, which was a riot of chenille table-cloths, wax fruit under glass domes, crocheted chair-coverings, brass chimney-guards, potted plants and cheap bentwood furniture. If his wife preferred to compensate for their straitened circumstances with an ostentatious display, so be it. The fault was his, for failing to provide for her properly. He would have preferred a plainer style of decoration, in keeping with the ships' cabins of his youth, but he had no right to cavil. If his daughters and his sister had any objections, they did not show it.

'And what is this you are reading?'

Fanny picked up the portentous volume in its stout gilt binding that lay on the teapoy by FitzRoy's chair: *The Pentateuch and Book of Joshua Critically Examined, volume 4* by Bishop John Colenso.

'Shall you ever give your mind a rest, Bob?'

'Is that not an appropriate volume for the Sabbath?'

'No, it is not. Your head is filled with wind speeds and baro-metric pressures from Monday to Saturday. The last thing it needs on a Sunday is weighty theological debate.'

'I would rather wear out than rust out, Fan. Besides, it is an important book. Colenso is the first bishop of the Anglican Church to come out openly against the flood.' There was a sad tinge to FitzRoy's voice.

'And – may I guess – you are all too busily laying the blame at your own door?'

'If I had not selected Mr Darwin as a travelling compan-ion—'

'I think you do not give the Almighty enough credit, Bob,' his sister told him affectionately. 'These challenges would have arisen without your assistance. You cannot fight every battle. If you had not selected Mr Darwin as a travelling companion, then somebody else would have.'

'It does seem an uncommonly complex book for the day of

rest, dearest,' fretted his wife, glad to be able to shelter her own anxieties behind the imperturbable vanguard of her sister-in-law's concern.

'As usual, I am outnumbered five to one,' grumbled FitzRoy.

Of course, it was only when he was outnumbered five to one and ordered to stop working that he got any rest. During the week, he often survived on as little as five hours' sleep a night, so he appreciated the luxury of being allowed to down tools with a clear conscience. Nonetheless, his grown-up daughters usually chose to ask him polite questions about weather forecasting, knowing that it would put him at his ease and assuage his restless guilt.

'Pappa,' said Katherine, 'if you do not issue weather forecasts on the Lord's day, what if a storm were to strike a fishing fleet upon that very day?'

'One would hope that all good Christian men would refrain from putting to sea on the Sabbath, of course,' replied FitzRoy, whose features then softened into a smile. 'And, of course, the storm warnings to shipping are two-day warnings, so the Saturday warning covers the period 'til Monday morning. It would not do in these Godless times to depend upon the piety of our fellow citizens.'

'But, Pappa, how do you *know* what the weather shall be in two days' time?'

'There are advance warning stations in Bermuda, in Halifax in Nova Scotia, in Lisbon, Bayonne and Brest . . . Wherever our weather comes from, we are connected to the local observing-post by electric telegraph. My job is to determine when the weather shall arrive, and its exact strength and direction, and to compose that information into a forecast. Then I issue it to the newspapers, to the Admiralty, the Horse Guards, Lloyds, the Board of Trade and the Humane Society. Except on a Sunday, of course, when anyone impious enough to put to sea must rely on Saturday's information!'

'Forgive me, but it is the doorbell, dear,' interrupted his wife.

'Is it?' As he approached his sixtieth birthday, FitzRoy was going deaf. 'Who on earth can that be? Are we expecting anyone on the Sabbath?'

Hetty was already on her way out into the hallway to answer the door, followed by the excitedly bobbing figure of Laura. The maid returned a moment later, looking flustered and discomposed. 'Excuse me, sir, but I think you had best come. There is a gentleman—'

FitzRoy raised himself from his chair and stepped into the hall, to find a messenger in old-fashioned livery standing nervously inside the open front door. Down the steps, in the street beyond the front garden, stood a brougham bearing the royal coat of arms, its sleek horses steaming.

'Vice-Admiral FitzRoy, sir?'

'That is I.'

'Begging your pardon to be disturbing you on the Sabbath, sir, but I come at the express request of Her Gracious Majesty Queen Victoria. Her Majesty wishes to make the sea-crossing to Osborne House on the Isle of Wight later this afternoon, sir, and enquires as to the likely state of the weather in the Solent.'

'When shall Her Majesty leave?'

'The Royal Train departs at one.'

'Then I have an hour at most. Hetty, will you kindly entertain our visitor in the pantry? If you will excuse me . . .'

'Of course, sir.'

FitzRoy returned to the morning room, made his apologies, and explained that the womenfolk would have to take their stroll around Beulah Gardens without him, for – yet again – he had work to do. His sister blessed him with a rueful smile of concern as they made their way out.

'The infernals were cone-shaped, and made of zinc, about two feet deep and fifteen inches wide. The Baltic was full of 'em. There was a small glass tube of ignitable stuff in each one, hanging on an iron slide with springs. Well, our lads fished one out of the water and brought it to Admiral Seymour. Some of the officers remarked on the danger of it going off, whereupon Seymour said, "Oh no, this is the way it would go off," and shoved the slide in with his finger. It instantly exploded, burned every item of clothing off the admiral, and propelled him straight down the companionway, completely unhurt! – which was extraordinary enough. Then, even more extraordinarily, Admiral Dundas and Admiral Pelham demanded one of the infernals be brought to them, to see what had injured Seymour. Caldwell explained that whatever happened, they should not push in the slide like Seymour had. Whereupon Dundas replied, "What? You mean like this?" and pushed in the slide. So the deuced thing went off and blew the three of them off their feet. We found out later from a prisoner-of-war that the infernals were only prototypes – the real ones contained thirty-five pounds of powder, and would have taken both flagships to the bottom!'

FitzRoy laughed more from the pleasure of Sulivan's companionship than at the story, which he had heard at least four times – Sulivan did have a weakness for retelling old stories. The relentless official untruths, incompetence and confusion, the needless sacrifice and helplessness in the face of disease that had characterized the Crimean War had affected Sulivan badly, he knew; indeed, his friend was one of the very few officers to have emerged from the conflict with any credit. Retelling the famous tale served not just to cheer FitzRoy up but to gloss over a dark period in Sulivan's own life.

It was lunchtime, and the two admirals were feeling their way through a bilious, jaundiced mist, across Parliament Square to the Abbey. The traffic was almost impenetrably thick. Less robust these days, they paid a crossing-sweeper to negotiate their way through a bedlam of sheep and cattle, part of a herd being driven across Westminster Bridge that had become entangled with a carriage and pair, a hansom cab, a costermonger's cart and one of Dr Tivoli's patent omnibuses, the top hats of its passengers lining up in silhouette like smoking factory chimneys on the fog-shrouded roof. The heady stink of summer was a few months off yet, but in the meantime the bleating, mooing, whinnying, cursing mêlée gave off a thick, cloying stench that offered an appropriate foretaste. The brand new clock tower housing Big Ben soared above the tumult, not yet soot-blackened like the other buildings round the square, but pale and stately: by common consent, the design of Britain's newest landmark harked back to her medieval Gothic past, as if to ward off the encircling filth that poured forth from her factories, tramped across her fields and pastures, and laid siege to the remnants of her chivalric tradition.

FitzRoy and Sulivan found sanctuary in the pitch-dark vault of Westminster Abbey, her stained-glass windows shaded with soot. FitzRoy normally worked through luncheon without a break and without food, just as he often did at dinnertime; but today was different. Today he had no choice but to absent himself from work, for they had come on an important pilgrimage. Today, they had come to say a prayer for their old friend John Wickham. Wickham's health had taken a beating on the *Beagle*'s surveying voyage around Australia, forcing him to invalid from the Service in Sydney and to hand over the captaincy of the vessel to Stokes. He had taken more sedentary employment in the colony's government instead, eventually rising to become the governor of Queensland; in which exalted post, while relaxing with his wife one evening, he had started up suddenly, with his hand to his head, before falling dead in an instant. He had suffered – it was subsequently discovered – a massive stroke.

The two men offered up their prayers in silence, then Sulivan whispered, '"All flesh is grass, and all the goodliness thereof is as the flower of the field: The grass withereth, the flower fadeth: because the spirit of the Lord bloweth upon it."' And then: 'God bless you, Johnny.'

'The first of us to go,' reflected FitzRoy, and he remembered Wickham's booming voice, his tireless good nature, his broad, powerful shoulders, seemingly capable of bearing any load, and the cheery smile for ever set in his round, rosy-cheeked face. Peering back with tired eyes across the undulating landscape of the last thirty years, every day spent on the *Beagle* now seemed to him a time of untempered bliss; and he found himself overwhelmed with that profound nostalgic sadness that attends the memory of happy days gone by.

Silently, they shared their memories of their old shipmate. Then they made their way back out into the murk of Parliament Square, through besieging hordes of beggars and street-traders selling lucifers, dog-collars, nutmeg-graters and all manner of useless articles.

'How is your boy Tom going on?' asked FitzRoy, ignoring the pressing crowds.

'Splendidly well, thank you. He is just returned from three years in the West Indies. He is paying off at Sheerness, and should be home in a few days. What of young Robert?'

'He is a lieutenant now, on the Far Eastern station. He wrote me a letter from the Great Wall of China.'

'I am glad for you. I am sad to say, though, that Philos has lost another son – Charles, his youngest – to scarlet fever. He was weak in the head from birth, by all accounts. It is the third child he and his poor wife have laid to rest.'

'I am sorry. No doubt he will tell the poor woman that the race is to the strong – that nature is up to her usual tricks of ruthlessly weeding out imperfection.'

'You must not hate him, FitzRoy, for he is a good soul, despite what he has done. If he is indeed being punished by the good Lord, then surely he has suffered enough. I have prayed to the Almighty to show mercy upon him.'

'Oh, I do not hate him, my dear friend, you need have no fear on that score. I feel only the most acute pain that he has gone astray. He put himself under my protection, and I failed him as surely as I failed young Hellyer and Musters.' Had they lived, he reflected, Hellyer and Musters would have been in their mid-forties now.

'You have failed nobody.'

'I should have failed poor Jemmy too, had you not journeyed to his rescue. What a mess I have made of things.'

'I will not hear it. How many lives have been saved by your system of storm warnings? Several hundred, I'll wager. Fatalities have plummeted since you began issuing forecasts. There are many in this country who owe you a great debt.'

'*The Times* does not seem to think so.'

Sulivan made a rueful face, as FitzRoy stopped to buy the afternoon edition from a news-vendor.

'*The Times* is full of the most awful gammon, FitzRoy, you know that. It always has been.'

'I do find it confusing, I must say, that they run the daily weather forecast on one page while attacking it on another.'

For weeks now, *The Times* had been mounting regular editorial assaults on the work of FitzRoy's department, ridiculing weather-forecasting as a preposterous pseudo-science with no more basis in truth than the astrological weather predictions issued every January. The culprits were not hard to identify: each time a flotilla of fishing boats or a collier fleet stayed in port because of one of FitzRoy's storm warnings, the owners lost money. The fleet-owners were rich and influential people, more than one of whom had the ear of the editor of *The Times*. FitzRoy turned to the editorial page. Sure enough, the jibes were still coming thick and fast:

Whatever may be the progress of the sciences, never will observers who are trustworthy and careful of their reputations venture to foretell the state of the weather; particularly not in that singularly uncouth and obscure dialect employed by Admiral FitzRoy in his explanations. What he professes, so far as we can divine the sense of his mysterious utterances, is to ascertain what is going on in the air some hundreds of miles from London, by a diagram of the currents circulating in the metropolis! While disclaiming all credit for the occasional success

of the Admiral's predictions, we must however demand
to be held free of any responsibility for the too common
failures which attend these prognostications.

FitzRoy folded up the paper in exasperation.
'I shall have to write to them again,' he said wearily.

'The Right Honourable Member for Truro.'

Augustus Smith, MP, rose to address the Commons,
although in truth there was not a great deal of difference
between Augustus Smith standing and Augustus Smith seated,
so limited was the honourable gentleman's stature. He did,
however, compensate in girth for what he lacked in height:
there was quite a lot of Augustus Smith, but most of it liked
to stay close to the floor. Augustus Smith, MP, was the owner
of a fleet of fishing-vessels.

'Mr Speaker, gentlemen. I propose to address the disturbing
fad for weather prophecies, as propagated by Vice-Admiral
FitzRoy's department of the Board of Trade. Last Tuesday
week, what did the board prophesy with regard to the weather?
"Wind south-east to south-south-west, fresh moderate." And
what was the fact? The wind did not blow from those quarters at all. In fact, a gale blew down from the north! These
"forecasts", gentlemen, are no more than a disgraceful hoax,
perpetrated on an unwitting public at their own expense. Why
on earth should the government spend our money on a system
that might encourage fishermen and coastal sailors, calculating
a mere possibility of storm, to stay at home idly by the fireside, when we ourselves are ready to struggle through the wind
and rain to our places of work? It appears that the Vice-
Admiral's telegraphic system has cost the country, altogether,
the sum of forty-five thousand pounds! Whereas the other
purveyor of this vulgar and fallacious practice, Moore's
Almanac, offers predictions of a similar nature for the princely
sum of one penny! I assure you, gentlemen, that the results
worked out by Vice-Admiral FitzRoy are yet more wonderful

than even the various professors of the black arts have ever offered us.'

A contented chortle rumbled through the House. Few MPs on either side had much sympathy with lazy fishermen or collier crews who were not, like themselves, prepared to put in a full day's work.

Colonel Sabine rose to reply on behalf of the government.

'I can inform the honourable gentleman that out of fifty-six shipmasters queried to the end of last month, forty-six were in favour of the system of storm warnings; and that out of a total of 2,288 warning signals issued, a total of 1,188 were subsequently justified by the state of the weather within forty-eight hours. As regards to the telegraphic costs, I am able to reassure the House that a special rate has been arranged between Vice-Admiral FitzRoy and the telegraphic companies, thereby keeping costs to a minimum.'

Augustus Smith, who had never actually been to sea himself, but who saw no reason for sailors to be mollycoddled, rose with a cunning smile extending from one chubby cheek to the other. He planted both his thumbs in the pockets of his well-filled waistcoat. 'The honourable gentlemen informs us that of just over two thousand warning signals issued, just over one thousand of them were subsequently justified: a success rate, if I am not mistaken, of about fifty per cent. In other words, for a total expenditure of forty-five thousand pounds, Her Majesty's government has produced a set of statical results that could just as easily have been obtained by tossing a coin!'

A roar of approving laughter besieged the helpless Colonel Sabine.

'Should it not perhaps have occurred to the government to employ a gentleman of high scientific attainments in such a post, rather than a mere armchair sailor? Vice-Admiral FitzRoy, I have heard, is not a man of means. The gentleman – if indeed he is a gentleman – has clearly assumed a higher station in life than he can afford to sustain!'

Enthusiastic cheers followed hard on the approving

laughter. Colonel Sabine glanced embarrassedly round at his colleagues on the government benches. It was debatable, in fact, whether they could afford to sustain this whole meteorologic business.

By ten o'clock, the busiest time of the morning, the telegrams were pouring into the little office in Parliament Street like storm-water through a burst dyke. Babington fought to stay abreast of the flow, logging each one and reducing it or correcting it for scale-errors, elevation or temperature as required. As soon as they had been adjusted they were passed to FitzRoy, to be entered on to that day's chart of the British Isles. They did not have much time: the first forecast of the day had to be ready by eleven, for the *Shipping Gazette* and the second edition of *The Times*. Nobody spoke, but three pairs of hands fairly raced across the paper in front of them. It was like this every day: the preceding years had seen their routine become extremely well practised. Sulivan knew this, which was why he delayed his visit until the initial morning rush had begun to wane, and the copyists had taken on the burden of replicating the forecast goodness knows how many times, for the benefit of goodness knows how many recipients.

'Good morning, gentlemen. May I speak with you?'

FitzRoy looked up, pleased to hear his friend's kindly voice, but one glance at Sulivan's face told him that all was not well. His superior addressed the room. 'You might as well all hear what I have to say.'

Three expectant faces stared at him, like seals waiting to be dispatched.

'The Board of Trade has announced on behalf of the government that, as of Monday, the practice of issuing storm warnings and daily weather forecasts is to be discontinued.'

'But . . . ?'

'What . . . ?'

FitzRoy and his two assistants looked at each other, bewildered, disbelieving, aghast.

'It seems that the government has recently commissioned a report into the efficacy of weather forecasting from Francis Galton, the secretary of the British Academy. I have it here.'

'Francis Galton? *Francis Galton?* But he is . . . he is . . .'

FitzRoy left the sentence unfinished. Francis Galton was Charles Darwin's cousin.

'His conclusions are as follows.' Sulivan's tone was funereal. '"That there is no scientific basis for weather forecasting, which is therefore of no value whatsoever. That the forecasts and storm warnings have not been shown to be generally correct, because of which there is no evidence of their practical utility. That the work of Vice-Admiral FitzRoy's department has been prejudicial to the advancement of science, and has led the public to confuse real knowledge with unfounded pretences, and, in the end, to despise the former because the latter have proved to be unfounded. Finally, that there is no good reason for a government to continue to undertake the responsibility of issuing weather forecasts, or gale warnings to shipping."' Sulivan put down the report. This was one of the most difficult tasks he had ever been made to undertake. 'I am sorry, gentlemen. In my opinion, the report is a scandal and a disgrace, and it is motivated, if not by sheer ignorance, then by political and commercial considerations. I have registered protests at every level, but to no avail. The decision has already been made. I am afraid there is nothing any of us can do.'

'But what about the daily forecasts in *The Times?*' FitzRoy blurted out. 'What about the—'

Sulivan interrupted him: '*The Times* had already indicated to the Board of Trade its intention to discontinue printing the daily forecast.'

A mixture of rage and panic welled up inside FitzRoy. 'They have no idea of the mechanical complexity involved in preparing these forecasts!' he shouted. 'We are just three men, devising an instant forecast for the whole nation! Our evidence is blowing in the wind – Darwin can pickle his evidence, and pin it to a board, and study it at his leisure, for months if necessary! If we make a mistake, the elements will furnish a correction the very next day! If Darwin makes a mistake, no one will ever know, for the only correction is to be found in the scriptures that he chooses to disregard so casually! I am a scientist too – I know how little any scientist knows – Francis Galton knows even less than we do!'

'I do not think it is about Darwin or Galton,' replied Sulivan, miserably. 'I think it is about money. Loss of revenue for the fishing-fleets, the costs of telegraphy—'

'So coasters and fishermen must die for the sake of pecuniary interest? Lest occasionally a day's demurrage should be caused unnecessarily, or a catch of fish missed for the London market? Damn them – damn them all to hell! I shall pay the telegraphy costs myself, from my own purse!'

'You cannot, my dear FitzRoy. You have given too much already.'

It had been an empty boast, FitzRoy knew. He had, in fact, given everything. He was severely in debt. Only the salary from his current situation was keeping his head financially above water: without it, even the house in Norwood would have to go. Grief, agitation, frustration and helplessness boiled inside him. It was all so desperately *unfair*. He wrenched open a nearby drawer, grabbed a handful of papers, and flung them on to the table.

'Look – positive testimonies!'

One by one, he picked them up and read them out, almost hysterically: 'Local Marine Board, Dundee: "Storm signals very generally appreciated." The Sunderland pilots: "Great importance and great practical value." The collector of Customs at West Hartlepool: "Much trusted and attended to by sea-faring men." Mr G. S. Flower, collector of Customs at Deal: "The means of saving life and property to an immense extent." The secretary of the Liverpool Marine Board: "Very valuable."'

He flung the rest of the pile furiously into the corner of the room.

'The secretary of the Liverpool Marine Board!' he shouted, then tailed off, because he was aware that he was beginning to sound ridiculous, and because he never wanted to shout at Sulivan, not ever.

'I know . . .' said Sulivan helplessly. 'I am on your side . . .'

He was shot through with guilt and sadness, not just for the end of FitzRoy's dream, and for all the sailors and fishermen who would lose their lives, but because he knew that for FitzRoy it was the end. His friend was fifty-nine. He would never work again.

The reception for Captain Maury, of the US Navy's Weather Forecasting Department, was to take place that very afternoon at the French embassy in Knightsbridge. Distraught as he was, FitzRoy realized that he could not in all conscience miss the event. He had been communicating with Maury by telegraph for years, exchanging ideas and information. Many of his suggestions on the compilation of synoptic charts and the analysis of meteorologic information had been incorporated by Maury into the work of his own department. Forward observing stations in America had provided vital information to statists in both London and Paris, at least until the outbreak of civil war in the United States had curtailed the flow, and the Canadians had stepped into the breach. Now Maury had travelled many thousands of miles to Europe. He was to be fêted by the French for his work, and awarded the Légion d'Honneur. It would be churlish in the extreme, thought FitzRoy, to put his own personal disappointment before his gentility; he must show a proper appreciation of his American counterpart.

He did not take a hansom cab to Knightsbridge. Rather, he dipped his head like a bull, not looking where he was going, and plunged blindly through the crowds, which parted as if by tacit agreement to let him pass. On the way it started to rain, as he had known it would, a fierce, lashing westerly stinging his skin, little spikes of rain hurtling down from lowering skies ahead. Dimly, he became aware that he was passing Hyde Park on his right. *It is where I used to walk with Mary on a Sunday morning*, he recalled, and he thought how much he loved her, and he wished that he could take her gloved hand in his once more.

Somehow, his footsteps took him of their own accord to number fifty-eight, a tall, cream-coloured block in the classical style with its entrance beside one of the park gates. He presented himself at the main door, a rather weary, bedraggled figure, the front of his dress uniform blotched wet. He handed his sodden frock-coat to a servant, and was shown into the reception room, which was already brimful of people. He refused the offer of a drink; nor had he any wish to make small-talk. Instead, he bleakly joined the queue of guests waiting to be presented to Captain Maury. After an interminable wait behind a large woman with a pince-nez, it was his turn. Maury proved to be a grizzled veteran of FitzRoy's own age, with a thick southern accent and a pronounced limp, the result not of any military heroics but of a coach crash in his early thirties. The American pumped him by the hand.

'Admiral FitzRoy, this is an honour indeed. I've long admired the accuracy and thoroughness of your work.'

'On the contrary, Captain Maury, the privilege is entirely mine. It is a pleasure to make your acquaintance after all these years.'

'And how goes the work of you and your men, Admiral?'

FitzRoy paused. 'Extremely well, thank you. Might I enquire after the prospects of your own department?' He simply could not bring himself to share his humiliation with a stranger.

'Well, as you know, everything has been in abeyance. Now the war is over I'm hoping to return to New York to pick up the pieces. That's if they'll have an old Confederate like me back. Still, if they won't, there's plenty of good men in my department ready to take up the reins.'

'Indeed? How many are there in your department?'

'Before the war, I guess there were about fifty men, but I shall be asking for more this time around. How many are there in yours?'

'Including myself – three.'

'*Three?*'

'That's correct.'

'And you issue a daily forecast for the whole of Great Britain?'

'Yes.'

'But – but that's impossible.'

FitzRoy grimaced in acknowledgement, but had no time to reply, for the start of the presentation was suddenly announced, and Maury was whisked away. The French ambassador, the Prince de la Tour d'Auvergne, a slight figure with an elegant spearpoint beard who resembled a sixteenth-century Spanish portrait, stepped on to a small dais at one end of the room. He welcomed his guests in fluent English, and spoke in praise of Captain Maury's achievements. The captain, he said, had introduced the world to an entirely new branch of science. Hundreds of lives on both sides of the Atlantic had been saved thanks to the captain's early-warning stations. Who would have dreamed it possible, he marvelled, even a decade previously, that one day man might be able to foretell the passage of the very elements. This was Captain Maury's gift to the world. It was only right and proper that the government of His Most Excellent Majesty the Emperor Napoleon III should recognize the captain's achievements by awarding him the Légion d'Honneur. Amid warm and grateful applause, Maury walked forward, bowed his head, and accepted his decoration.

The ambassador, it seemed, had not finished: 'Ladies and gentlemen, I must tell you that we have not one, but two distinguished meteorologists present this afternoon. We are fortunate enough to be joined also by Vice-Admiral FitzRoy, of the Statical Department of the Board of Trade here in London.'

FitzRoy started at the mention of his name. The prince's speech had passed over his head largely unnoticed, like the

clouds that had raced past him on his journey over from
Parliament Street.

'Admiral FitzRoy has made his own hugely significant
contribution to the advancement of science,' the ambassador
was saying, 'for it was none other than Admiral FitzRoy, the
very man who stands before you now, who captained HMS
Beagle, the ship that ferried the celebrated Mr Darwin around
the globe. Without the admiral's efforts, the great works of
Mr Darwin might never have been brought to the public attention, for which endeavour we must all be truly thankful. As a
mark of the considerable esteem in which Admiral FitzRoy
is held by the government and people of France, I am pleased
to invite him forward to receive this lasting token of our
regard.'

Still in a daze, FitzRoy stumbled forward. Everyone was
looking at him, applauding. The Prince de la Tour d'Auvergne
was beaming at him, and thrusting a little wooden box towards
him. He took it, and opened it. Inside, nestled on a meagre
bed of straw, lay a small, mass-produced, bedside travelling
clock.

It was dark by the time he got back to Parliament Street, and
the gas-jets were burning low in the office. His two deputies
were working late, no doubt, packing up their papers or
telegraphing the shore stations to tell them that the forecasting
service had been closed down. But no: his young helpers had
left for the day. It was, in fact, the downcast figure of Sulivan
that he found there, sitting alone behind the table in a pool
of sickly yellow light. The fire had gone out. Sulivan looked
exhausted, a picture of misery.

Sulivan, for his part, thought that FitzRoy looked broken
and thin.

'Jemmy is dead,' he said simply.

FitzRoy did not reply, but hung his head and stared at the
floor.

'How?' he said at last.

'Of disease. What with the murders at Woollya and Mr Despard's dismissal, the Patagonian Missionary Society has been finding it mortal hard to raise funds in this country, so it has concentrated on soliciting charitable donations for the Fuegians among the Christian people of South America. The missionaries collected surplus clothing in Buenos Ayres, some of which undoubtedly once belonged to those carried off by malignant diseases. They distributed it at Woollya. Somehow the infected miasma seems to have hung about the clothes, although I have been assured by the society that they were properly aired. There was an epidemic. More than half the Fuegians at Woollya are dead, most probably of the measles. Jemmy is among their number.'

'Did he have a Christian burial?' asked FitzRoy, almost inaudibly.

'No,' replied Sulivan, ashamed. 'That is the worst part. It seems the Fuegians dispose of their dead by cremation, like many primitive societies. But they would not burn Jemmy's body, for in his death-throes he had requested "to be buried like an English gentleman". So they left him for the missionaries instead. The sailors and the missionaries, however, continue to blame Jemmy for the deaths of Captain Fell, Mr Phillips and the others, so they would not touch him, especially as he was diseased. His body was left to rot on the beach.'

'Poor Jemmy,' said FitzRoy, and a tear rolled down his cheek. 'Would that he had never met me. "If I had not come and spoken unto them, they had not had sin. But now, they have no cloak for their sin."'

'It is just as Philos once said,' reflected Sulivan. 'Wherever the European has trod, death and disease seem to pursue the aboriginal.'

'We were the disease. Don't you see that, Sulivan? You, and I, and Darwin – *we were the disease.*'

FitzRoy caught the last paddle-steamer across the river, and the last train back to Crystal Palace. The oil-lit carriages rattled mournfully over the South London rooftops on their elevated causeway, a dark sea on either side. *Down there*, thought FitzRoy, *life teems amid the courts and alleys and slums, spreading like a virus, and it will not stop until the whole of creation has been infected.*

Thick black smoke pumping from its engine, its brake-men clinging to their posts on the carriage-tops, the locomotive thundered into the cut at Norwood and came hissing to a stop at Crystal Palace station. Crowds of clamorous drunks emptied out of the third-class carriages, one pausing to be sick on the platform. FitzRoy waited for the throng to clear, before hauling himself wearily up the interminable staircase that zigzagged its way to street level. There were no hansoms remaining beneath the station's wrought-iron portico, so he trudged back up Anerley Road, the mud piling up against his boots, and into the gloom of Church Road, until at last he reached the stolid, semi-detached house that had become his home. Maria was waiting up for him, a lantern in one hand – the gaslight from the chandelier was so feeble, it could barely penetrate the darkness – and her face revealed both relief and concern as she came to meet him in the hallway. 'Is everything all right, Mr FitzRoy? Did you have an eventful day at work?'

'Yes, thank you, Mrs FitzRoy. Everything is fine. I had a really quite uneventful day at work. There is little I can tell you about my day at all.'

He put the little travelling clock down on the hall table, and they went upstairs to bed.

Chapter Thirty-eight

140 Church Road, Upper Norwood, 30 April 1865

FitzRoy was woken the following morning by the sound of the grandfather clock downstairs striking six. As his eyes adjusted to the gloom and his mind struggled to order its surroundings, Maria too stirred.

'Is the maid not late in calling us?' he murmured.

'It is Sunday, dearest,' she replied, without opening her eyes. 'There is no hurry for breakfast today.'

She rolled over, and he shut his eyes once more. As he lay motionless in the funereal dark, the events of the previous day reminded him coldly of their existence. He should, perhaps, have felt agitation or even despair, but he did not; instead, he felt only calm. He may even have drifted in and out of consciousness, for it barely seemed a whole hour before the clock struck seven. Hetty called them about twenty minutes after that, and he propped himself up on one elbow.

'My dearest?'

'Mmm?' purred his wife drowsily, from somewhere beneath the covers.

'Since the day we married, you have been the most loyal,

devoted and thoughtful companion that any man could have wished for. I am eternally grateful to you for all the kindness that you have shown me. I am only sorry that I have not been as good a husband as you have deserved.'

'Mmm,' demurred Maria, her fingers stretching out to intertwine with his.

'Thank you, my dear, for everything.'

Gently extricating his hand, he rose and went into the little bedroom where Laura slept, undisturbed by chiming clocks and the calls of servants. He kissed his daughter's forehead once, then passed into his dressing room and locked the door. A basinful of water had been poured out; all was ready for his morning shave. A clean ewer had been placed atop the washing stand, and his razor lay neatly parallel to the marble splashboard. He removed it from its leather case, unfolded it and inspected the blade, as he did every morning, for sharpness. Then he plunged his hands into the ice-cold water, pausing only momentarily to observe how pallid his skin became, how deathly white viewed through the prism of clear liquid. He thought then of Edward Hellyer, his moonstone face so peaceful amid the drifting kelp. Did God, he wondered, punish those poor souls who had seen fit to disobey a higher authority, even if theirs was a sincere and considered deed? Was it an act of bravery to do the wrong thing for the right reasons, or an act of weakness? He brought up two freezing handfuls and splashed his face, trying to clear his mind. He wanted his thoughts to be as lucid as possible, his equilibrium utterly undisturbed.

He attempted to examine himself inwardly, scanning the cognitive landscape for signs of irregularity. Everything was fine, of course. He had learned long ago that the mere process of worrying about mental instability was in itself a sure guarantee that none was present. Only when he allowed himself to become complacent did his condition steal up unawares, and complacency turn to fatal, misdirected certainty. This morning, he realized, he was barely certain of anything any more.

He inspected himself in the looking-glass, embedded so solidly in its scrolled and crested mahogany frame above the splashboard. At the centre of the bevelled rectangle he could see a drawn, grey-haired man staring back at him, a few weeks short of his sixtieth birthday, a lifetime of punishing, vigorous, self-imposed toil written into his features. He had lived his life long enough, he realized, to begin feeling the disappointment wrought by change. *A common illusion, that softens the prick of death.* Old men, wearied at the end of their lives, often took comfort from this: how much easier to quit the world if you feel that you no longer quite belong to it? But was he in need of comfort? No. He was braver than that.

He had been born into another century, almost; a world of coaching inns and sailpower, in which it had taken days, not hours, to travel from London to the coast. Now man had become stupendously powerful, not individually but collectively, and had concertedly begun to assault the bastions of nature. The journey to the coast took just two hours by steam train. News from America reached London in a matter of minutes. Everything had been mechanized, from death itself to the production of undergarments. Man had begun to dismantle the wilderness, recording and cataloguing its constituent parts, eradicating his fear of the unknown, and in doing so had set himself against God. He, Robert FitzRoy, had connived in this process as much as anyone; but even though he had helped to create it, this was no longer his world.

Some things, at least, had not changed. The endless struggle of good against evil still raged. God's love was still pitted against greed, hatred and selfishness. A lifetime on, and Trafalgar Square was still not completed. For all the changes that advancing knowledge had wrought, man was still, at heart, the same creature he always had been, lazy, venal, cunning, thoughtless and self-seeking. Perhaps, then, it was not man that had changed, not society even, but FitzRoy himself. Yes, that was it. It was he, and not the world, that had changed. He no longer *believed*. Oh, he still believed in God, but he was no longer sure that there was any point in trying to hold back humanity's blind march towards the inextricably linked goals of self-advancement and self-destruction. He no longer believed that one man could make a difference. Was that what Captain Stokes had realized, all those years ago, on a freezing, pebbly beach at Port Famine? Or had the race been to the strong, and Stokes merely a weakling?

When I was young, thought FitzRoy, *I was a voyager, traversing unknown seas, the master of my own destiny. The wind and the waves may have dashed themselves against me, but I fought through to discover new shores and unknown worlds. Then I became part of a machine, a mere cog in a wheel. They took away my liberty, my independence. But at least my toil served to smooth the way for other travellers, who followed in my footsteps. Now, they have removed even that small comfort from me. The solution is clear. I must travel to where they cannot reach me. I must voyage once more, to the furthest shore. I must undertake the ultimate journey. A journey without maps.*

He had not been given permission to undertake such a journey, of course. Technically speaking, it would be a sin to go. Once he had taken his leave, there could be no turning back. Once he had arrived, his only chance of redemption would be to throw himself upon the retrospective mercy of a higher authority. Would Mary be waiting for him there, he wondered, wreathed in a golden light on that distant shore? Would Jemmy be there too, and Musters and Hellyer, and his father, and old Skyring, and dear Johnny Wickham? Or was Darwin right? Was he just another monkey, too highly developed for his own good? There was only one way to find out.

The razor felt cold against his throat.

Author's Postscript

Author's Postscript

Robert FitzRoy was buried at All Saints Church, Upper Norwood, on 6 May 1865. His suicide was reported in the newspapers, but was largely eclipsed as a news event by the assassination of Abraham Lincoln. The funeral was a quiet family affair. All the surviving officers of the *Beagle*, with whom (Sulivan excepted) he had long ago lost touch, had written to the Statical Department of the Board of Trade asking to attend but, sadly, as the office had been closed down, their letters remained unanswered. By coincidence, however, Sulivan and Babington went into the office on the day before the funeral to clear away their papers, just as Maria FitzRoy's brothers arrived to collect her husband's belongings. As a consequence, the pair received a last-minute invitation and travelled down to Norwood to attend the ceremony. Sulivan later sent Darwin a letter, relating how a grief-stricken Maria FitzRoy had collapsed at the graveside. All FitzRoy's former crew members were united in their sorrow; the regret expressed by Darwin, although undoubtedly sincere, was noticeably more muted.

Robert FitzRoy, it transpired, was utterly bankrupt. He had expended his entire fortune, over £6000 (equivalent to more than £400,000 in today's money), in subsidizing the public purse for the benefit of others. When this came to light, Sulivan inaugurated the Admiral FitzRoy Testimonial Fund, to save Maria and Laura from destitution, and succeeded in persuading the government to pay back £3000 of the money FitzRoy had laid out. Darwin contributed a further £100. Queen Victoria, perhaps in gratitude for all those private weather forecasts, gave Mrs FitzRoy the use of a grace and favour apartment at Hampton Court Palace. She died there, peacefully, in December 1889.

After FitzRoy's death, his storm warning and weather forecasting apparatus was broken up. His drums and cones were taken into storage, his electric telegraph lines ripped apart. Despite an anguished letter of protest from his wife, Augustus Smith MP more or less gloated over FitzRoy's death in the House of Commons. Just as other European countries and the United States took up weather forecasting in earnest, political pressure exerted by those who stood to benefit financially saw the science of meteorology damned in Britain, the country of its birth, as a nonsense. The fishing-fleet owners, however, had reckoned without the ordinary sailors and fishermen to whom FitzRoy had been a hero. Such was the outcry at the scrapping of his storm warnings that two years later, in 1867, his network was reinstated. Within ten years, daily weather forecasts had made a belated reappearance.

In meteorological terms, FitzRoy had been a man quite astonishingly ahead of his time. Even today, the connection he made between sunspots and weather patterns continues, by and large, to be pooh-poohed by the British Meteorological Office. Now, with all the satellite technology available to them, our official forecasters have achieved a 71 per cent accuracy rating for their twenty-four-hour rain forecast: but the private company Weather Action, owned by Piers Corbyn, which uses sunspot activity as a basis for its forecasts, achieves a long-range accuracy rating of 85 per cent.

Besides inventing the weather forecast, Robert FitzRoy's contribution to nautical history was considerable. His navigational charts of Patagonia, Chile, the Falklands and Tierra del Fuego were so exhaustively precise that they continued to be used until recently: only aerial photography has managed to improve upon his extraordinary accuracy. Undoubtedly he saved hundreds, if not thousands, of lives. He introduced the system of masters' certificates for ship's officers. He pioneered the use of the lightning conductor and the Beaufort Scale. He introduced the terms 'port' (as opposed to 'larboard') and 'dinghy' (as opposed to 'jolly-boat') into the Royal Navy. But perhaps FitzRoy's greatest accomplishment lay in the individual achievements of those who sailed with him in the *Beagle*. Never can such a concentration of talent have been collected in one place before or since; never can it have been brought to fruition so lovingly. David Stanbury has listed some of the notable positions later held by the officers of the *Beagle*, including FitzRoy and Darwin:

> No less than five of the *Beagle*'s officers were destined to reach the rank of admiral; two became captains of the *Beagle*, two, eventual Fellows of the Royal Society. They also included Governor Generals-to-be of New Zealand and Queensland; a Member of Parliament; future Heads of the Board of Trade and the Meteorological Office; two artists who achieved considerable renown in the country of their adoption; three doctors; the prospective Secretaries of the Geological Society and the Royal Geographical Society; an Inspector of Coastguards; an Australian property magnate; the founding father of the British colony of the Falkland Islands; six highly professional surveyors; four botanists of sufficient standing to correspond with the great Hooker at Kew; five active collectors whose specimens were to be eagerly described by the Zoological Society and the Natural History Museum; one of the founders of the science of meteorology; and the author of *The Origin of Species*.

It is an extraordinary list, all the more so because it was entirely achieved by the crew of one tiny surveying-brig.

The work of Charles Darwin aside, one is immediately

struck by the career of Bartholomew Sulivan, who not only distinguished himself in the field, invented iron cladding for ships, minesweeping, concentrated mortar fire (thereby anticipating aerial bombardment from aeroplanes) and the Royal Naval Volunteer Reserve, but who also – on a more peaceable note – brought back the common nasturtium (*Tropaeolum majus*) from South America. After FitzRoy's death he resigned his position, and retired to the south coast with his wife Sophia, where he spent most of his time sailing model ships with his grandchildren. He was knighted in 1869, and lived until 1890; although his retirement was marred by the death of his son Tom, who fatally contracted malaria at Monte Video in 1873. FitzRoy's son Robert was luckier. He enjoyed a glittering naval career, reaching the rank of rear-admiral in 1894, in which year he became commander of the Channel Squadron. He, too, was knighted.

The story of the *Beagle* and her crew following FitzRoy's enforced retirement is worth relating. The third voyage, commanded by John Wickham, was a gruelling expedition to survey those Australian coasts left uncharted by Phillip Parker King. After commemorating their old shipmates by naming Port Darwin and the FitzRoy river, the crew began to survey the Victoria river late in 1839. There a shore expedition was surprised by a war party of aborigines, one of whom ran Lieutenant Stokes through with his spear. He was rushed to the operating table where, in an emergency operation, Benjamin Bynoe saved his life. After Wickham (who had suffered repeated attacks of dysentery) left the ship in Sydney for a life in the colonial service, Stokes took over as captain, and brought the *Beagle* home. She never sailed again, but became a fixed coastguard watch vessel on the river Roach in Essex, renamed the *WV7*. In 1870, she was sold to Murray and Trainer, scrap merchants, for £525. Stokes came to say goodbye, and salvaged a small piece of timber, which he later had fashioned into a little round keepsake box; it was recently put on display at the National Maritime Museum. Early in 2004, a team of marine archaeologists, using ground-penetrating radar, located the remains of the *Beagle* under twelve feet of mud and marsh on the north bank of the Roach. She had been stripped of all her beautiful wooden trimmings, so lovingly installed at FitzRoy's expense: all that remains is her hull. There are now plans to excavate the wreck. Stokes himself completed a further survey of New Zealand in command of the paddle steamer *Acheron*, before becoming a rear-admiral in 1864, vice-admiral in 1871, and full admiral in 1877.

The careers of all the *Beagle*'s officers pale into insignificance, of course, beside the lasting, worldwide fame of her passenger, Charles Darwin. He completed eight further major works following *The Origin of Species*, including *The Descent of Man*. He was never honoured by the British government, although three of his sons were eventually knighted; but when he died in 1882 he was given a grand funeral at Westminster Abbey, with Wallace, Huxley and Hooker among the pall-bearers. The cause of his crippling illness has remained a mystery ever since. Some detractors regard it as entirely psychosomatic, but a more convincing theory is that he had been struck down by Chagas' disease, a debilitating condition spread by the *benchuca* bug, the unpleasant blood-sucking insect he had allowed to crawl over his skin in such numbers in the Andes. It would be an irony indeed if his life had ultimately been ended by an insect that had collectively learned, as a species, to use thatched roofs as a springboard from which to launch attacks on sleeping victims. As to FitzRoy's illness, his madness was almost certainly undiagnosed manic depression, undiagnosed because the condition had yet to be identified. Today it is treatable with lithium; in the early nineteenth century it was simply a terrifying and inexplicable companion for those – like FitzRoy – who were otherwise of sound mind.

Of the other participants in this story, Darwin's servant Syms Covington moved to Twofold Bay in New South Wales, from where he would often send specimens of the local fauna back to his former employer. After a time as a gold panner, he became the postmaster of Pambula and started an inn there, named the Retreat; it is still open, and its red tin roof and double chimneys still poke above the trees beside the Princes Highway. He died in 1861. Of the *Beagle*'s two artists, Augustus Earle returned to London, where he died in 1838; Conrad Martens opened a studio in Pitt Street, Sydney, and became a notable Australian painter. He died in 1878. His neighbour Philip Gidley King became something of an Australian celebrity in his later years, on account of his connection with Charles Darwin and the *Beagle*.

The preposterous surgeon Robert McCormick continued to blunder his well-connected way from expedition to expedition. He sailed with the great Sir James Ross to the Antarctic, and incensed his commander so greatly that Ross dedicated the rest of his life to blocking McCormick's further promotion. The surgeon subsequently wrote his autobiography, in which he refused to mention the names of FitzRoy or Darwin, or acknowledge that he had once served aboard the *Beagle*. He would admit only that for a brief period he had found himself 'in a false position, on board a small and very uncomfortable vessel'. Robert McCormick lived to an unjustly ripe old age, and died fêted and admired, every inch the famous explorer, in 1890.

The Reverend Richard Matthews suffered a far less respectable end: his days as a missionary in New Zealand came to a premature close when he was discovered to have misappropriated a large quantity of money from the mission at Wanganui. He departed life a destitute bankrupt, having lost the use of one eye. Bishop Wilberforce – 'Soapy Sam' – was another man of the cloth to meet an unfortunate fate. He died in 1873 from head injuries caused by a fall from his horse. 'For once,' remarked Thomas Huxley, 'reality and his brains came into contact, and the result was fatal.' The Reverend George Packenham Despard, forced by pressure from Sulivan to relinquish his tenure as head of the Patagonian Missionary Society, was unable because of the Woollya scandal to find himself an alternative position in the English Church. Harried through the courts for unfair dismissal by Captain Snow, he too eventually fled to Australia.

Following Despard's resignation, the new head of the society in Tierra del Fuego, the Reverend Waite Stirling, salvaged the *Allen Gardiner* and resolved to take a party of Fuegians to be educated in England, just as FitzRoy had done. He set sail in 1866, with four natives on board, including Threeboys. While in England they were introduced to the Reverend Joseph Wigram, the young man who had fixed up their forefathers' education in Walthamstow all those years before. He was now the Bishop of Rochester. Predictably, perhaps, Stirling's venture had tragic consequences. Two of the four passengers perished on the trip home. One, Uroopa, died of consumption: he was baptized as John Allen Gardiner shortly before his death, and lies buried in the graveyard at Stanley. Threeboys, by now a young man, died of Bright's disease, a European kidney complaint unknown in Tierra del Fuego; he, too, was baptized before his death, as George Button. Waite Stirling was rewarded with the bishopric of the Falkland Islands for his efforts.

The sudden removal of Despard and the departure of Stirling left the Fuegian mission in the hands of Despard's stepson, Thomas Bridges, who appears to have been made of sterner stuff than Despard himself. Bravely, in the light of what had happened to Phillips, Fell and the rest, he built up a one-man mission on the shores of the Beagle Channel. Against the odds, it flourished. His wife came out to join him, and he adopted Jemmy Button's two orphaned grandsons, with financial assistance from a number of sponsors back in England. The first child, who was sponsored by the Beckenham branch of the Patagonian Missionary Society, he named William Beckenham Button. The other was sponsored by Sulivan, Darwin, Hamond, Stokes and Usborne: he was christened Jemmy FitzRoy Button.

As part of his studies into the Fuegians' way of life, Bridges made a remarkable discovery: that their language, which Darwin had presumptuously assumed to consist of a few limited clicks and grunts, was astonishingly rich and poetic. The average working vocabulary of an adult Fuegian was around 32,000 words (compared to the 20,000 or so in the vocabulary of the average modern-day European). The word 'Yammerschooner', incidentally, which was common right across Tierra del Fuego, did not mean 'give to me', but 'please be kind to me'.

One day in 1873, an Alikhoolip canoe, foraging deep into Yamana territory, arrived at Bridges's mission. Paddled by two young men, it contained a vast, toothless old woman in a battered old bonnet. Bridges came out to meet the visitor, flanked by his own two infant children. 'Little boy, little gal,' said the old lady, stepping out of the boat. It was Fuegia Basket, who had heard tell of the lone white man living on the eastern shores of the channel and had demanded to be taken to him. They talked at length. Fuegia's memories of London were vivid, and her recollections of FitzRoy fond and detailed; bizarrely, however, she had forgotten how to sit on a chair. York Minster, she revealed, had been murdered, speared in the back by the brothers of a man he himself had killed. She had a new husband now, aged just eighteen. Ten years later, in 1883, Bridges returned the compliment and visited Fuegia at her home. She was in poor health, and he later heard that she had died soon afterwards.

Bridges's idyll could not last, of course. The genocidal wars set in train by General Rosas had inched their way southwards down the South American continent throughout the intervening years. The Araucanians (or Mapuche, or Oensmen) had fought a long, brave and desperate battle akin to that of the Native Americans of the USA, but their mounted cavalry could never be a match for heavy artillery, or the newly invented machine gun. Finally, by the 1880s, they were massacred and defeated, and Tierra del Fuego lay at the mercy of the whites. In September 1884, four warships of the

Argentinian Navy arrived at the mission, and informed Bridges that all his land was now military property. The mission was to become a penal colony. A garrison of twenty men was left behind, one of whom was suffering from measles. The resulting epidemic killed every single Fuegian in the area, including William Beckenham Button and Jemmy FitzRoy Button. Forced from the land, Bridges gave up missionary work and founded a ranch to the east of the Beagle Channel called Harberton, after his wife's home village in Devon. It is still there today.

The Argentinian government decided to open up the whole of Tierra del Fuego to sheep farming, and systematically wiped out the native guanaco population, which would otherwise have competed with the sheep for the limited amount of grass. The guanaco, of course, also sustained the local native population. Mass starvation followed, and the Fuegians became a 'problem' for the white settlers, especially if they tried to hunt the sheep instead. A few years later it was officially decided that the Fuegians themselves were 'vermin', and should be eradicated. A reward of a pound was paid for each decapitated Fuegian head. Packs of armed gauchos on horseback descended on Tierra del Fuego, eager for the kill; indeed, bloodthirsty bounty hunters arrived from all over the world. One Scotsman named McInch, who styled himself 'King of the Rio Grande', managed to shoot and behead fourteen Fuegians in a single day. In the weasel words so common to colonial genocide, the eradication of the starving Fuegians was described as a 'humanitarian' measure. By 1908, only 170 pure-bred natives remained in the whole of Tierra del Fuego. By 1947, their number had dwindled to forty-three. Today there are none. Bridges's mission has become the Argentinian town of Ushuaia.

The man who began the extermination progress, President Juan Manuel de Rosas, tore up the constitution of Argentina and made himself dictator for life. He imposed domestic 'law and order' through a network of spies and secret police, and by the disappearance of political opponents. His portrait was compulsorily displayed in public places and in churches. The frontispiece of this book bears the legend 'closely based upon real events', and indeed it is so; but this is a novel, not a history book, so I have felt free to fill in gaps and invent conversations where records are incomplete. No record exists of Rosas' speech that so impressed Charles Darwin; we know he was impressed, because we have his notebook, although he had learned enough of Rosas to revise his opinion by the time he came to write up the *Beagle* voyage. In inventing Rosas' self-justification, I have taken the liberty of drawing almost exclusively on the words of Tony Blair, and the various self-justifications he produced to defend his foreign policy adventures with George Bush in the Middle East and Central Asia. It is only an exercise, perhaps, but the words do seem to fit extraordinarily well. In fairness to Darwin, I should say that he did not directly witness the execution of the three prisoners; this 'privilege' was conferred upon another European traveller whom Darwin met there.

Rosas, like so many of his ilk, eventually pushed his military adventures a step too far. Eager to increase his territory, he attempted to invade both Brazil and Uruguay at the same time. It was a vicious and senseless war: at one point, he ordered the execution in cold blood of five hundred Uruguayan prisoners-of-war (of Indian extraction, naturally). But Rosas had bitten off more than he could chew, and his armies were eventually defeated at the battle of Caseros. Where did the fallen dictator go? Why, to England, of course, where this most brutal of mass-murderers was received by the British government with open arms. He was treated as a dignitary and given a luxurious retirement home at Swaythling, Hampshire, funded by the taxpayer, where he peacefully ended his days in 1884.

Britain's subsequent colonial involvement in the other territories that FitzRoy had tried to defend was equally inglorious. When the French brutally invaded Tahiti without provocation in 1843 (they still haven't given it back), the British offered their protection to Queen Pomare, and initially sheltered her aboard a Royal Navy warship. Although she was no warrior, she stoutly launched an armed revolt against the French occupiers, having secured a guarantee of British support. The government in Paris, however, came to an arrangement with the government in London: the British, behind Pomare's back, tore up their treaty and betrayed her to the French in return for a cash payment.

In New Zealand, with official backing (prompted by the New Zealand Company), the new governor launched yet another genocidal campaign to exterminate the native population. George Grey was granted all the benefits that FitzRoy had been denied: twice his predecessor's salary, triple his operating budget, a cash sum of £10,000 to fill the hole left by the company's dubious financial practices and, of course, a large force of troops. The treaty of Waitangi was unceremoniously ripped up as Grey plunged the entire country into war. Ironically, he hit upon the ingenious plan of attacking the Maori (as they now call themselves) on a Sunday, when many of those converted to Christianity would be at prayer. In the early battles, a substantial number of native chiefs fought on the British side, because they had been promised that their ancestral lands would not be touched if they did so. It was a lie. Eventually, Grey succeeded in appropriating all native land for the New Zealand Company, and in exterminating most of the native population. He was knighted for his efforts.

If I have been unkind to one person, it is to Thomas Moore, the Falklands governor. Although the islands are frequently and erroneously held up as a piece of British colonial thievery, there was in fact no native population to subdue: when the islands were discovered, they were deserted. They were certainly not stolen from Argentina, a country that did not even exist when John Davis first sailed by. Thomas Moore was always careful, though, to uphold the civil rights of any Fuegian natives brought to the islands. I doubt very much that he ever intended to put Jemmy on trial for his life. Although it is true that Jemmy was kidnapped by Smyley, nearly lynched by the mob and accused of murder by Coles, the court case was more in the way of a tribunal; if Moore intended to hammer anyone, it was Despard. The governor probably always intended to release Jemmy in the end. The deliberations of the jury and Sulivan's last-minute arrival are, I am afraid to say, the one piece of pure fiction in this book; although Fitzroy's genuine rescue of the *Challenger* owes much to the imagination, as the real truth was only ever hinted at in the official record.

Elsewhere, I have sometimes conflated events for reasons of simplification: Darwin made more than one trip with the gauchos, for instance, and more than one Andean expedition; the *Beagle* made two visits to the Falklands. Occasionally, I have conflated the timescale of events, and in the case of Jemmy's son, two characters: Threeboys is a composite of himself and Billy Button, another son, who confusingly replaced him at the Cranmer Mission midway through the Despards' tenure. Otherwise, the events in this book are as they happened. The language employed in the story, although remarkably ornate at times, is exactly as it would have sounded, and – where records have been kept – exactly as it was used. The one exception to this is the word 'ship', which the sailors of the *Beagle* would never have employed to describe their own tiny brig. They would have used the word 'boat' to describe both the *Beagle* and her cutters, whaleboats and so forth, which I felt might make some of their dialogue rather confusing, to us if not to them.

Today, intrepid travellers – or simply those interested in maps – will find reminders of Robert FitzRoy and Charles Darwin wherever the *Beagle* travelled. There are FitzRoys and Darwins in Australia, Tierra del Fuego and the Falklands. Although he would probably not have approved, El Chaltén, the god of smoke, the holy mountain of the Araucanians, was renamed Mount FitzRoy after the Patagonian tribes lost their fight for survival. In New Zealand, there are FitzRoy streets in Auckland and Wellington (although these were later additions), as well as streets named after Grey, Hobson, the ex-convict Edward Gibbon Wakefield, and even Lieutenant Shortland. In Upper Norwood, now part of London, a small street running off Church Road has been renamed FitzRoy Gardens. Perhaps most significantly of all, in February 2002, the shipping area previously known as Finisterre was renamed FitzRoy, to honour the man who had invented the shipping forecast. It is the only sea area named after a person, which would undoubtedly have delighted the hero of this book.

As for the surviving physical evidence of FitzRoy's story, there is no longer a great deal to see. The specimens he collected – not those assembled by Darwin – were eventually catalogued by the British Museum, and make up their '*Beagle* Collection'. FitzRoy's former residences are all now in private hands, although Down House, where Darwin lived, is open to the public. Outside Britain, the fort in Montevideo is as it was, and the Falkland Islands and the Galapagos Islands are more or less unchanged. A main road has been driven across the Uspallata pass from Mendoza to Santiago, and the remains of the petrified forest that Darwin discovered can still be seen by the roadside; only the bases remain, though, the rest having been carried away by over-enthusiastic souvenir hunters. The fossil beds of Punta Alta fared even less well, being destroyed by the Argentinian Navy during the construction of the Puerto Belgrano naval base. Further south, in 1981, a team from a Chilean survey vessel climbed Mount Skyring: under a cairn at the summit, they discovered the mementos left there by the men of the *Beagle* 150 years before, still – amazingly – in perfect condition. Perhaps most incredibly of all, at the time of writing, Darwin's tortoise Harriet is still alive and enjoying a well-deserved retirement in Australia.

FitzRoy's grave can be visited, of course, in the churchyard of All Saints, Upper Norwood; a Grade II listed monument, it was restored in 1997. Visitors to the Falklands should still be able to find poor Edward Hellyer's gravestone, on a lonely headland at Duclos Point, near Johnson's harbour. And should anyone feel especially adventurous, there is a rough track, down by the Straits of Magellan, that leads to a wild and lonely beach, where lies the grave of Captain Pringle Stokes of HMS *Beagle*, without whose suicide this whole extraordinary story would never have happened.

Acknowledgements

I should like to thank my father, Gordon Thompson, for his tireless and invaluable assistance, both in the researching and the plotting of this book; the indefatigable Pippa Brown, for coming to the rescue of an abysmal index-finger typist, and typing out the entire manuscript; Martin Fletcher and Bill Hamilton, for all their helpful suggestions, and the wonderful Lisa Whadcock for the benefit of her wisdom and insight; Peter Ackroyd, for pointing me in the direction of George Scharf; the staff of the London Library, for their assistance in locating long-forgotten electoral results and ancient guides to Durham; Robert and Faanya Rose, for graciously inviting me into FitzRoy's old home in Chester Street; the Norwood Historical Society, for its help in locating FitzRoy's latterday whereabouts; John Morrish, for allowing me access to his unpublished manuscript about living with manic depression; Tom Russell and Paul Daniels (no, not that one) for slogging up to the fort in Montevideo Bay with me; Patrick Watts (he won't remember, it was so long ago) for giving me a guided tour of Stanley harbour; the staff of the Fazenda Bananal Engenho de Murycana in Brazil, for showing me round their property; and the penguins of Dungeness Point in Patagonia, for taking care of me when I was the only human being for miles and miles around.

Bibliography

I am, of course, indebted to the various biographers of Robert FitzRoy: H. E. L. Mellersh (*FitzRoy of the Beagle*, Rupert Hart-Davis, 1968), Paul Moon (*FitzRoy, Governor in Crisis 1843–1845*, David Ling Publishing, Auckland, 2000), Peter Nichols (*Evolution's Captain*, Profile, 2003) and those exceptional scholars John and Mary Gribbin (*FitzRoy*, Review Books, 2003). These last two works were suddenly published in the middle of my writing this novel, and afforded me considerable assistance. There are, of course, Darwin biographies by the score, but it would be difficult to better Janet Browne's *Charles Darwin* (2 vols, Jonathan Cape, 1995), Adrian Desmond and James Moore's *Darwin* (Michael Joseph, 1991), Randal Keynes's *Annie's Box: Charles Darwin, His Daughter and Human Evolution* (Fourth Estate, 2001), Ronald W. Clark's *The Survival of Charles Darwin* (Random House, 1984), and covering this area alone, Richard Keynes' exceptional and infallible *Fossils, Finches and Fuegians* (HarperCollins, 2002). Keynes was also responsible for *The Beagle Record* (Cambridge University Press, 1979). From a pictorial point of view, Alan Moorehead's *Darwin and the Beagle* (Hamish Hamilton 1969) and John Chancellor's *Charles Darwin* (Weidenfeld & Nicolson 1973) were especially valuable.

Jemmy Button has been the subject of one excellent biography, Nick Hazlewood's *Savage* (Hodder & Stoughton, 2000), as indeed has the *Beagle* herself (*HMS Beagle*, Keith S. Thomson, W. W. Norton & Co., New York, 1995). Then, of course, there are FitzRoy and Darwin's own works. Darwin's *The Voyage of the Beagle* and *The Origin of Species* are available in many editions. By contrast, FitzRoy's *Weather Book, Remarks on New Zealand* and *Narrative of the Voyage of HMS Beagle* are hard to find outside the Bodleian (the library's copies of the latter volumes still had their pages uncut – nobody had bothered to read them in 165 years); extracts from his *Narrative* were, however, published by the Folio Society of London in 1977. Charles Darwin's correspondence has been edited for publication over many disparate volumes by his granddaughter Nora Barlow. Bartholomew Sulivan's letters were edited by his son, Henry Norton Sulivan (published by Murray, 1896), although they too are long out of print; as is Augustus Earle's *A Narrative of Nine Months' Residence in New Zealand*, which was published by Longman & Co. in 1832. *The Journal of Syms Covington* has only been published on the Internet, by the Australian Science Archives Project, on ASAPWeb, 23 August 1995. Among other contemporary documents, the report of the 1860 British Association meeting in Oxford was published in the *Athenaeum* magazine. The British Government Select Committee reports on New Zealand are also available for scrutiny, at the House of Lords Record Office, London.

For technical maritime information, I used the book that FitzRoy himself always recommended to his subordinates: *The Young Sea Officer's Sheet Anchor* by Darcy Lever (John Richardson, 1819, miraculously reprinted by Dover Maritime Books, Toronto, 1998). But I am also indebted to Christopher Lloyd (*The British Seaman 1200–1860*, Collins, 1968), Michael Lewis (*England's Sea-Officers*, Allen & Unwin, 1939), Henry Baynham (*Before the Mast*, Hutchinson & Co., 1971), Stan Hugill (*Shanties and Sailors' Songs*, Barrie & Jenkins, 1969), Lew Lind (*Sea Jargon*, Kangaroo Press, 1982), Nicholas Blake and Richard Lawrence (*The Illustrated Companion to Nelson's Navy*, Chatham Publishing, 2000), Peter Kemp (*The Oxford*

Companion to Ships and the Sea, Oxford University Press, 1976), Tristan Jones (*Yarns*, Adlard Coles Nautical, 1983), W. E. May (*The Boats of Men of War*, National Maritime Museum/ Chatham Publishing, 1974 and 1979), the long-deceased Captain Charles Chapman (*All About Ships*, Ward Lock, 1866), Frederick Wilkinson (*Antique Guns and Gun Collecting*, Hamlyn, 1974), and Colonel H. C. B. Rogers (*Weapons of the British Soldier*, Seeley, Service & Co., 1960); and, of course, I must not forget the contemporary works of Captain Marryat, Sir Francis Beaufort and Sir Home Popham, and the considerable later writings of C. S. Forester, Patrick O'Brian and Dudley Pope.

For help with the descriptions of London, I should like to thank Peter Ackroyd (*London – the Biography*, Chatto & Windus, 2000), Peter Jackson (*George Scharf's London 1820–50*, John Murray, 1987), Eric de Maré (*London 1851*, The Folio Society, 1972), and Felix Barker and Peter Jackson once more for *London* (Cassell, 1974). The parliamentary scenes came courtesy of *The Houses of Parliament – History, Art and Architecture* (ed. Christine and Jacqueline Ridley, Merrell, 2000) and *The London Journal of Flora Tristan* (first published in France, 1842; modern edition trans. Jean Hawkes, Virago, 1982). Another contemporary perspective came from George Cruikshank (*Sunday in London*, Effingham Wilson, 1833). More general historical information came courtesy of contemporary issues of *The Ladies' Magazine*, as well as Elizabeth Burton's *The Early Victorians at Home* (Longman, 1972), A. N. Wilson's *The Victorians* (Hutchinson, 2002), J. F. C. Harrison's *Early Victorian Britain* (Fontana, 1988), G. M. Trevelyan's *English Social History* (Longman, 1944), Christopher Hibbert's *Social History of Victorian Britain* (Illustrated London News, 1975), Leith McGrandle's *The Cost of Living in Britain* (Wayland, 1973), D. J. Smith's *Horse Drawn Carriages* (Shire Publications, 1974), Henny Harald Hansen's *Costume Cavalcade* (Eyre Methuen, 1972), and Daniel Pool's *What Jane Austen Ate and Charles Dickens Knew*

(Simon & Schuster Inc., USA, 1994). Dickens himself was shamelessly plundered for much of the vocabulary, as were Thackeray, Hughes and Captain Marryat.

For the Durham scenes, I consulted *A Historical, Topographical and Descriptive View of the County Palatine of Durham* by E. Mackenzie and M. Ross (Mackenzie & Dent, 1834), *The History & Antiquities of the County Palatine of Durham* by William Fordyce (Thomas Fordyce, 1855), *Cathedral City* by Thomas Sharp (The Architectural Press, 1945), *In and Around Durham* by Frank H. Rushford (Durham County Press, 1946) and *Durham* by Sir Timothy Eden (Robert Hale, 1952).

Among the various scientific books and articles consulted during the preparation of this novel, I should like to mention *Bones of Contention* by Paul Chambers (John Murray, 2003), *Return to the Wilberforce-Huxley Debate* by J. Vernon Jensen (British Journal for the History of Science, 21, pp. 161–79, 1988), *A Journey to a Birth – William Smith at the birth of Stratigraphy* by L.R. Cox (International Geological Congress, 1948), *The Pony Fish's Glow, and Other Clues to Plan and Purpose in Nature* by George C. Williams (Basic Books, 1997), *Darwinism – A Crumbling Theory and Evidence for Creation by Outside Intervention* by Lloyd Pye (Nexus Magazine, volume 10, number 1, December 2002–January 2003 and volume 9, number 4, June–July 2002), *FitzRoy's Foxes and Darwin's Finches* by W. R. P. Bourne (Archives of Natural History, 1992, 19 (1)), *Noah's Flood – the Genesis Story in Western Thought* by Norman Cohn (Yale University Press, 1996), *The Weather Prophets: Science and Reputation in Victorian Meteorology* by Katharine Anderson (*History of Science*, 37, June 1999), *Matthew Fontaine Maury – Scientist of the Sea* by Francis Leigh Williams (Rutgers University Press, New Brunswick, NJ, 1963), *From Wind Stars to Weather Forecasts: The Last Voyage of Admiral Robert FitzRoy* by Derek Barlow (Weather London, 1994, volume 49, number 4), *Not in our Genes* by Steven Rose, Leon J. Kamin and Richard C. Lewontin (Penguin, 1984),

The Biblical Flood – A Case Study of the Church's Response to Extrabiblical Evidence by Davis A. Young (Paternoster Press, 1995), and of course many, many fine articles by the inimitable Stephen Jay Gould. For their insights into the processes of manic depression, I am utterly indebted to the work of Andrew Solomon, Dr Irene Whitehill, Sally Brampton and John Morrish.

As to the geographical descriptions, the vast majority were obtained by personal visits to the actual locations. FitzRoy and Darwin themselves provided plenty of supplementary assistance, as did *A Journey in Brazil* by Louis Agassiz (1868, modern ed. by Praeger, Westport, CT, 1970), *Giants of Patagonia* by Captain Bourne (Ingram, Cooke & Co., 1853), and *The Narrative of the Honourable John Byron* (Baker & Leitch, 1778). John Campbell's *In Darwin's Wake* (Waterline, 1997) provided specific information regarding the *Beagle's* South American anchorages.

RONAN BENNETT

Havoc, in its Third Year

ENGLAND IN THE 1630s – A TIME OF CHANGE AND
TURMOIL, TEEMING WITH FEARFUL RUMOURS OF
INVASION AND CONSPIRACY.

On a winter's day, when rain and wind rage round his
lonely farmhouse, coroner John Brigge is called to
investigate an Irishwoman accused of murdering her baby.
The town's powerful Puritan faction insists on the woman's
guilt, but a vital witness has disappeared, and Brigge,
hugging a secret of his own, senses that something is being
kept hidden. With his wife pregnant, he wishes for nothing
more than to stay quietly with her on his farm. Yet listening
to the demands for a hanging without delay, Brigge can't
refuse to take his next step. Reluctantly, he sets out to search
for the missing witness.

Praise for HAVOC, IN ITS THIRD YEAR:

'A gripping novel . . . staggered with betrayal and intrigue
and suffused with the hot threat of violence. Bennett's prose
is economical, powerful, and often poetic' *The Times*

'Bennett's evocation of a corner of England on the edge of
apocalypse is wonderfully done' *Guardian*

'Compelling and ultimately bracing reading' *Irish
Independent*

'Deserves a significant place in the modern canon' *Observer*

'It is a thrillingly satisfying piece of work' *Sunday Telegraph*

'[Bennett] has a great deal to tell us, and he does it with
skill, beauty and human sympathy' *Financial Times*

0 7472 6034 6

review

JUDE MORGAN

Passion

In the turbulent years of the French Revolution and the Napoleonic Wars, three poets – Byron, Shelley, Keats – come to prominence. This electrifying novel explores their short, extraordinary lives through the eyes of the women who knew and loved them – intensely, scandalously and sometimes tragically.

Four women. From widely different backgrounds, they are linked by a sensational fate. Mary Shelley: the gifted daughter of gifted parents, for whom passion leads to exile, loss, and a unique fame. Lady Caroline Lamb: born to fabulous wealth and aristocratic position, who risks everything for the ultimate love affair. Fanny Brawne: her quiet, middle-class girlhood is transformed – and immortalised – by a disturbing encounter with genius. Augusta Leigh: the unassuming poor relation who finds herself flouting the greatest of all taboos.

Critical acclaim for *Passion*

'Wonderful – rich, authentic, beautifully written' Tracy Chevalier

'I loved Jude Morgan's *Passion*, which seems to me to achieve exactly what historical fiction is for, namely to illuminate the past to the present . . . Compellingly written, and stylish with it' Joanna Trollope

'Unputdownable. Stunningly well researched, its multi-stranded epic qualities can't fail to hook and seduce' *Guardian*

'An epic feat both of imagination and of research . . . Morgan takes us deep into the souls of these extraordinary women, filling us with admiration for their defiance of convention' *Marie Claire*

0 7553 0403 9

review

ANDREA LEVY

Small Island

It is 1948, and England is recovering from a war. But at 21 Nevern Street, London, the conflict has only just begun.

Queenie Bligh's neighbours do not approve when she agrees to take in Jamaican lodgers, but with her husband, Bernard, not back from the war, what else can she do?

Gilbert Joseph was one of the several thousand Jamaican men who joined the RAF to fight against Hitler. Returning to England as a civilian he finds himself treated very differently. Gilbert's wife Hortense, too, had longed to leave Jamaica and start a better life in England. But when she joins him she is shocked to find London shabby, decrepit, and far from the city of her dreams. Even Gilbert is not the man she thought he was.

Small Island explores a point in England's past when the country began to change. In this delicately wrought and profoundly moving novel, Andrea Levy handles the weighty themes of empire, prejudice, war and love, with a superb lightness of touch and generosity of spirit.

'Wonderful . . . seamless . . . a magnificent achievement' Linda Grant

'A great read . . . honest, skilful, thoughtful and important' *Guardian*

'A cracking good read' Margaret Forster

'Never less than finely written, delicately and often comically observed, and impressively rich in detail and little nuggets of stories' *Evening Standard*

'Is as full of warmth and jokes and humanity as you could wish' *Time Out*

'Gives us a new urgent take on our past' *Vogue*

0 7553 0750 X

review

You can buy any of these other **Review** titles from your bookshop or *direct from the publisher.*

FREE P&P AND UK DELIVERY
(Overseas and Ireland £3.50 per book)

Passion	Jude Morgan	£7.99
Havoc, in its Third Year	Ronan Bennett	£7.99
This is Not a Novel	Jennifer Johnston	£7.99
Only Human	Susie Boyt	£7.99
The Mysteries of Glass	Sue Gee	£7.99
American Gods	Neil Gaiman	£7.99
Despite the Falling Snow	Shamim Sarif	£6.99
Secrets of a Family Album	Isla Dewar	£6.99
The Distance Between Us	Maggie O'Farrell	£7.99
Green Grass	Raffaella Barker	£6.99
The Haven Home for Delinquent Girls	Louise Tondeur	£7.99
Ghost Music	Candida Clark	£7.99

TO ORDER SIMPLY CALL THIS NUMBER

01235 400 414

or visit our website: www.madaboutbooks.com

Prices and availability subject to change without notice.